'... this novel with its shape and its economy, told with humour, intelligence, and a generous and fairminded spirit, is a tribute and a triumph.'

Globe & Mail

'This novel, so vast and so amiably peopled, is a long, sweet, sleepless pilgrimage to life. ... Such writing reminds us that there are secrets beyond technique, beyond even style, which have to do with a quality of soul on the part of the writer, a giving of oneself. ... His novel deserves thousands of long marriages and suitable readers.'

JAMES WOOD *Guardian*

'A phenomenon, a prodigy, a marvel of 19th century-style storytelling in the language of today. ... It is hard to believe that Seth is only one man. ... This is quite a novel.'

PATRICK SKENE CATLING *Evening Standard*

'*A Suitable Boy* modulates unawkwardly from moments of delicate emotional and psychological accuracy to scenes of panoramic drama ... it lines up with its eminent 19th-century predecessors in combining depth of imagination with breadth of appeal.'

PETER KEMP *Sunday Times*

'No-one, surely, could wish this novel shorter. ... the greatness of the novel, its unassailable truthfulness, owes less to research than to imagination, an instinctive knowledge of the human heart.'

SALLY LAIRD *Observer*

'A big book in more than size. *A Suitable Boy* will win readers for decades to come.'

Macleans

'... vastly entertaining.'

Ottawa Citizen

ABOUT THE AUTHOR

Vikram Seth was born in 1952. He trained as an economist and has lived for several years each in the UK, California, China and India. He is the author of *The Golden Gate: A Novel in Verse*, described by Gore Vidal as 'The Great Californian Novel', *From Heaven Lake: Travels through Sinkiang and Tibet*, and four volumes of poetry.

BY THE SAME AUTHOR

Mappings (*poems*)
From Heaven Lake: Travels through Sinkiang and Tibet
The Humble Administrator's Garden (*poems*)
The Golden Gate: A Novel in Verse
All You Who Sleep Tonight (*poems*)
Three Chinese Poets (*translations*)
Beastly Tales From Here and There (*poems*)
Arion and the Dolphin (*libretto*)

A Suitable Boy
Volume Three

VIKRAM SETH

Little, Brown & Company (Canada) Limited
Boston   London   Toronto

Canadian Cataloguing in Publication Data

Seth, Vikram, 1952–
A suitable boy: a novel

ISBN 0–316–78151–7
I. Title

PR9499.3.S39S95   1993   823   C93–093137–8

Printed in England by Clays Ltd, St Ives plc

Little, Brown & Company (Canada) Limited
148 Yorkville Avenue, Toronto, Ontario, Canada

This Canadian edition dedicated to
Christine Cooke MacGregor
1950–1992
A very suitable girl

To
Papa and Mama
and
the memory of Amma

A WORD OF THANKS

To these I owe a debt past telling:
My several muses, harsh and kind;
My folks, who stood my sulks and yelling,
And (in the long run) did not mind;
Dead legislators, whose orations
I've filched to mix my own potations;
Indeed, all those whose brains I've pressed,
Unmerciful, because obsessed;
My own dumb soul, which on a pittance
Survived to weave this fictive spell;
And, gentle reader, you as well,
The fountainhead of all remittance.
Buy me before good sense insists
You'll strain your purse and sprain your wrists.

CONTENTS

ACKNOWLEDGEMENTS

The author and publishers would like to thank the following for permission to quote copyright material:

The Ministry of Human Resources Development, Govt. of India for extracts from *Letters to Chief Ministers*, Vol. 2, 1950–1952 by Jawaharlal Nehru, general editor G. Parthasarathi (Jawaharlal Nehru Memorial Fund, distributed by Oxford University Press, 1986)

HarperCollins Publishers Ltd. for extracts from *The Koran Interpreted* by A.J. Arberry (George Allen & Unwin Ltd.; and Oxford University Press, 1964)

Oxford University Press for an extract from *The Select Nonsense of Sukumar Ray* translated by Sukanta Chaudhuri (Oxford University Press, 1987)

Faber & Faber for an extract from the poem 'Law, Say the Gardeners' published in *W.H. Auden: Collected Poems* edited by Edward Mendelson (Faber & Faber)

Penguin Books Ltd. for extracts from *Selected Poems* by Rabindranath Tagore, translated by William Radice (Penguin Books, 1985)

Bantam Books Inc. for extracts from *The Bhagavad-Gita* translated by Barbara Stoler Miller (Bantam Books, 1986)

The Sahitya Akademi for extracts from *Mir Anis* by Ali Jawad Zaidi published in the series 'Makers of Indian Literature' (Sahitya Akademi, 1986)

The Gita Press, Gorakhpur for extracts from *Sri Ramacharitamanasa* translated into English (Gita Press, 1968)

While every effort has been made to trace copyright holders and obtain permission, this has not been possible in all cases; any omissions brought to our attention will be remedied in future editions.

MEHRAS

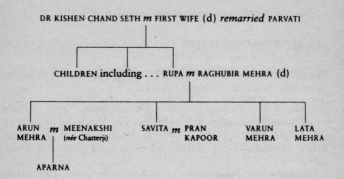

DR KISHEN CHAND SETH *m* FIRST WIFE (d) *remarried* PARVATI

CHILDREN including . . . RUPA *m* RAGHUBIR MEHRA (d)

ARUN MEHRA *m* MEENAKSHI (*née* Chatterji)   SAVITA *m* PRAN KAPOOR   VARUN MEHRA   LATA MEHRA

APARNA

KAPOORS

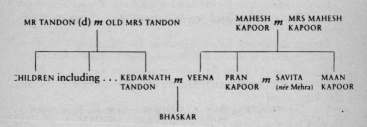

MR TANDON (d) *m* OLD MRS TANDON   MAHESH KAPOOR *m* MRS MAHESH KAPOOR

CHILDREN including . . . KEDARNATH TANDON *m* VEENA   PRAN KAPOOR *m* SAVITA (*née* Mehra)   MAAN KAPOOR

BHASKAR

KHANS

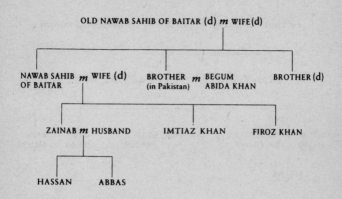

OLD NAWAB SAHIB OF BAITAR (d) *m* WIFE (d)

NAWAB SAHIB *m* WIFE (d)   BROTHER *m* BEGUM   BROTHER (d)
OF BAITAR   (in Pakistan) ABIDA KHAN

ZAINAB *m* HUSBAND   IMTIAZ KHAN   FIROZ KHAN

HASSAN   ABBAS

CHATTERJIS

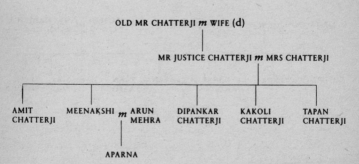

OLD MR CHATTERJI *m* WIFE (d)

MR JUSTICE CHATTERJI *m* MRS CHATTERJI

AMIT   MEENAKSHI *m* ARUN   DIPANKAR   KAKOLI   TAPAN
CHATTERJI   MEHRA   CHATTERJI CHATTERJI   CHATTERJI

APARNA

(d)=deceased

The superfluous, that very necessary thing . . .
VOLTAIRE

The secret of being a bore is to say everything.
VOLTAIRE

Part Fourteen

14.1

MAHESH KAPOOR left for his farm in Rudhia in early August in the company of Maan. Now that he was no longer a Minister, he had a little more free time for his own pursuits. Apart from supervising the work on the farm itself – the main activity at present was the transplantation of rice – he had two other purposes in leaving Brahmpur. The first was to see if Maan, who had proved himself uninterested and unsuccessful in working in Banaras, might possibly be happier and more effectively employed in running the farm. The second was to ascertain from where he could best fight a candidate from the Congress Party for an Assembly seat in the coming General Elections – now that he himself had left it and joined the newly formed Peasants' and Workers' Peoples' Party – the KMPP for short. The obvious rural choice was the constituency that contained his farm – which was in the Rudhia subdivision of Rudhia District. As he walked around his fields, his mind turned once more to Delhi and the great figures of the strife-ridden Congress Party vying with each other for power on the national stage.

Rafi Ahmad Kidwai, the wise, wily and playful politician from U.P. who had been responsible for a spate of resignations from the Congress, including Mahesh Kapoor's, was anathema to the Hindu-chauvinist right-wing of the party – partly because he was Muslim, partly because he had twice orchestrated opposition to the attempts of Purushottamdas Tandon to become President of the Congress Party. Tandon had been narrowly defeated in 1948, and had narrowly won in 1950 – in a dubiously fought battle made more bitter by the knowledge that whoever controlled the Congress Party machine in 1951 would have control over the selection of candidates for the forthcoming General Elections.

Tandon – a bare-footed, bearded, austere and rather intolerant man, seven years Nehru's senior and, like him, from Allahabad – now headed the organization of the Congress Party. He had chosen his Working Committee

3

largely from the party bosses of the individual states and their supporters, for in most of the states the party machinery was already in the control of the conservatives. Since Tandon had insisted that the Congress President's choice of his Working Committee should be unfettered, he did not include – and had indeed refused to include – either his defeated opponent Kripalani – or Kidwai, who had planned Kripalani's campaign. Prime Minister Nehru, already upset by Tandon's election, which he rightly interpreted as a victory not only for Tandon but for Sardar Patel, his own great conservative rival, had at first refused to join a Working Committee that excluded Kidwai. But in the interests of unity, because he saw the Congress as the only cohesive force in the localized and divided web of Indian politics, he swallowed his objections and joined it.

Nehru sought to protect his policies as Prime Minister from any possible onslaught by the activist Congress President by proposing party resolutions on each of his main policies, all of which had been overwhelmingly passed by the assembled party. But passing resolutions by acclamation was one thing, controlling the personnel of the party – and the selection of candidates – another. Nehru was left with the uneasy sense that the lip-service that was being paid to the policies of his government would change once the right-wing got its own slate of MLAs and MPs into parliament and the state legislatures. Nehru's vast popularity would be used to win the elections, and then he would be left stranded and impotent.

The death of Sardar Patel, a couple of months after Tandon was elected, had left the right wing without its greatest strategist. But Tandon proved to be a formidable opponent in his own right. In the name of discipline and unity he attempted to suppress dissenting groups within the party, such as the Democratic Front established by Kidwai and Kripalani (the so-called K-K Group), which were outspoken in their criticism of his leadership. Stay in the party and support the Working Committee, they were warned, or get out. Unlike his compliant predecessor in the job, Tandon also insisted that the party organization as represented by its President had every right to advise, and indeed control, the policies of the Congress Government headed by Nehru – down to the question of banning hydrogenated cooking oil. And on every important issue his views were diametrically opposed to those of Nehru or his supporters – men such as Kripalani and Kidwai or, closer to Brahmpur, Mahesh Kapoor.

Apart from economic differences, the Nehruites and the Tandonites saw the Muslim question in an entirely different light. Throughout the year there had been a great deal of mutual snarling by India and Pakistan across their borders. It had appeared several times that war might be imminent over the problem of Kashmir. While Nehru saw war as a disastrous possibility for the two poor countries, and attempted to come to some kind of understanding with the Pakistani Prime Minister Liaquat Ali Khan, many embittered members of his party were in favour of war with Pakistan. One member of his Cabinet had resigned, formed his own Hindu revivalist party, and was even talking of conquering Pakistan and reuniting it by force with India. What made things worse was the steady stream of refugees, mainly now from East Pakistan into Bengal, that put an unsupportable burden upon the state. They were fleeing because of ill-treatment and insecurity in Pakistan, and several hardliners in India suggested under a theory of reciprocity that for each Hindu migrant from Pakistan a Muslim should be expelled from India. They saw matters in terms of Hindus and Muslims, of collective guilt and collective revenge. So successfully indeed had the two-nation theory – the Muslim League's justification for Partition – taken root in their own minds that they saw Muslim citizens of India as Muslims first and Indians only incidentally; and were willing to visit upon their heads punishment for the actions of their co-religionists in the other country.

Such talk repelled Nehru. The thought of India as a Hindu state with its minorities treated as second-class citizens, sickened him. If Pakistan treated its minority citizens barbarically, that was no reason for India to do so. He had, after Partition, personally pleaded with a number of Muslim civil servants to remain in India. He had accepted, if not exactly welcomed, into the Congress fold, a number of leaders who had belonged to the Muslim League, which had virtually ceased to exist in India. He had attempted to reassure Muslims who, because of ill-treatment and a sense of insecurity, were still migrating to West Pakistan through Rajasthan and other border states. He had preached against communal enmity in every speech he had given – and Nehru was much given to speeches. He had refused to countenance any of the retaliatory actions urged on him by many of the dispossessed Hindu and Sikh refugees from Pakistan, by the right-wing parties, and by the right wing of his own party. He had tried to soften some of the more draconian decisions of the Custodian-General of Evacuee Property, who had often acted more in the interests of those who hankered after evacuee property than of the evacuees themselves. He had signed a pact with Liaquat Ali Khan which had reduced the likelihood of war with Pakistan. All these actions infuriated people who saw Nehru as a rootless, deracinated Indian, whose sentimental creed was a pro-Muslim secularism, and who was divorced from the majority of his own Hindu citizenry.

The only problem for his critics was that his citizenry loved him and would almost certainly vote for him, as it had done ever since his great tour in the 1930s, when he had travelled around the country, charming and stirring up vast audiences. Mahesh Kapoor knew this – as, indeed, did anyone with the faintest knowledge of the political scene.

While walking around his farm, discussing with his manager irrigation problems in a season when rainfall had been disappointing, Mahesh Kapoor's mind often turned to Delhi and to the momentous events that, he felt, had left him no choice but to leave the party to which he had given his allegiance for thirty years. He, like many others, had hoped that Nehru would come to see how futile were his efforts to maintain his policies in the face of Tandon's activities and would take some firm measure of control; but Nehru, though his own supporters were haemorrhaging away from his party as it drifted into its right-wing orbit, refused to leave the Congress or to take any positive action other than to plead, in meeting after meeting of the All-India Congress Committee, for unity and reconciliation. As he vacillated, his supporters floundered. Eventually, by late summer, a point of crisis had been reached.

In June a special convention of the Congress Party was held in Patna. There, at a parallel convention, the fledgling KMPP was established by several leaders, including Kripalani, who had recently resigned from the Congress, accusing it of 'corruption, nepotism and jobbery'. Kidwai, without actually resigning from the Congress, had been elected to the Executive Committee of the KMPP. This action brought down upon him the wrath of the right-wingers; for how (as one of them wrote to Tandon) could he continue to be a Central Minister of the Congress government and simultaneously belong to the executive of the party that was one of its most vociferous opponents – one which, indeed, hoped to supplant the Congress itself? Kripalani had tendered his resignation as a member of the Congress Party to Tandon, but Kidwai had not. Surely, argued his critics, he had better do so at once.

In early July the Working Committee and then the All-India Congress Committee met once again in Bangalore. Kidwai was asked to explain himself by the Working Committee. He hedged, claimed in his easygoing way that he had no immediate intention of resigning from the Congress, stated that he had tried to get the KMPP session postponed but had failed to do so, and expressed his hope that the Bangalore session of the Congress would make his anomalous position and the atmosphere in general much clearer.

The Bangalore session, however, did no such thing. Nehru, seeing at last that resolutions in his support were not enough, demanded something much more concrete: a complete reconstitution of the two most powerful committees of the Congress – the Working Committee and the Central Election Committee – so as to reduce their domination by the right wing. At this, Tandon offered to resign together with the whole of his Working Committee. Fearing a permanent split in the Congress, Nehru backed down. A few more conciliatory resolutions were passed. Some pulled in one direction, some in another. On the one hand the Congress disapproved of groups within its ranks; on the other, there would be an open door back to the party for those 'seceders' who agreed with the general aims of the Congress. But rather than rejoin the Congress, two hundred more Congressmen resigned and joined the KMPP at Bangalore. The atmosphere remained as murky as ever, and Rafi Ahmad Kidwai decided that the time for vacillation had passed. The battle had to be joined.

He returned to Delhi and wrote a letter to the Prime Minister, resigning both from the Cabinet as Minister of Communications and from the Congress Party. He made it clear that both he and his friend Ajit Prasad Jain, the Minister for Rehabilitation, had resigned because they could not stand Tandon or his policies or his undemocratic method of functioning. They emphasized that they had no quarrel with Nehru himself. Nehru pleaded with them to reconsider their decision, and this they did.

The next day they both announced that they had decided not to resign from the Cabinet after all. They also announced, however, that they would continue to work against the Congress, at any rate against the Congress President and his cohorts, whose views and strategies ran counter to every important resolution or declaration of the party. Their statement explaining their decision was a startling one, coming as it did from two Ministers of the Government:

> Is there a parallel in the world where the executive head, i.e. President of an organisation, is the very antithesis of everything that the organisation stands for? What is there in common between Shri Purushottamdas Tandon and the policies of the Congress – economic, communal, international and refugees? Even at this juncture when our ways parted, we wished and hoped that the working of the Congress would fall in line with its profession.

Tandon and the old guard, goaded by what they perceived as rank disloyalty and indiscipline, demanded that Nehru call his Ministers to heel. There was no way that the dissidents could be allowed to function as Ministers and attempt at the same time to do down their own party. Nehru was forced, sadly, to agree. Jain remained in the Cabinet, agreeing not to issue further provocative statements. Kidwai, unable to agree to such a constraint, offered once more to resign. This time Nehru realized that it would be fruitless to plead with his old colleague and friend, and accepted his resignation.

Nehru was now more isolated in his own party than ever. Together with all the crushing burdens of the Prime Ministership – the food problem, the war-mongering on both sides of the border, the Press Bill and the Hindu Code Bill and the endless legislation to be passed through Parliament, the relations between the Centre and the states (which had come to a boil with the declaration of direct Central rule in Punjab), the day-to-day running of the administration, the working out of the First Five-Year Plan, foreign affairs (an area that particularly exercised him), not to mention endless emergencies of one kind or another – Nehru was weighed down by the hard realization that his ideological opponents in his party had, in effect and at last, defeated him. They had elected Tandon, they had forced Nehru's supporters to leave the Congress in droves and form a new opposition party, they had taken over the District Congress Committees and Pradesh Congress Committees and the Working Committee and Central Election Committee, they had forced the resignation of the Minister who, more than any other, was sympathetic to his way of thinking, and they were poised to select their own conservative candidates for the impending General Election. Nehru's back was to the wall; and he may perhaps have reflected that it was his own indecisiveness that had helped put it there.

14.2

CERTAINLY, Mahesh Kapoor thought so. He was in the habit of unburdening himself to whoever was at hand, and it happened to be Maan with whom he was walking through the fields on a tour of inspection.

'Nehru has finished all of us – and himself in the process.'

Maan, who had been thinking about the wolf-hunt he had enjoyed when he was last in the area, was brought back to earth by the despair in his father's voice.

'Yes, Baoji,' he said, and wondered how to go on from there. After a pause he added, 'Well, I'm sure something will work out. Things have swung so far this way that they have to correct themselves.'

'You are a fool,' said his father shortly. He recalled how annoyed and disappointed S.S. Sharma had been when he and some of his colleagues had said they were resigning from the party. The Chief Minister liked to balance the Agarwal and Kapoor factions of his party against each other, so that he himself had maximum freedom of action; with one wing missing, his craft listed uncomfortably and his own decision-making abilities were necessarily more constrained.

Maan was silent. He began wondering how he could get away to pay a visit to his friend the Sub-Divisional Officer, who had organized the hunt a couple of months earlier.

'That things will swing back into order once they've been displaced is an optimistic and childish conceit,' said his father. 'The toy you should be thinking of is not the swing but the slide,' he continued after a pause. 'Now Nehru cannot control the Congress. And if he cannot control it, I cannot rejoin it – nor Rafi Sahib, nor any of the rest. It's as simple as that.'

'Yes, Baoji,' said Maan, taking a mild swipe at a tall weed with his walking-stick, and hoping that he was not going to be treated to a long lecture on the rights and wrongs of various party positions. He was in luck. A man came running across the fields to announce that the jeep of the Sub-Divisional Officer Sandeep Lahiri had been sighted heading towards the farm.

The ex-Minister growled: 'Tell him I'm taking a walk.'

But Sandeep Lahiri appeared a few minutes later, walking gingerly (and without his accompanying policemen) along the little ridges between the fields of emerald-coloured rice. On his head was his sola topi, and there was a nervous smile above his weak chin.

He greeted Mahesh Kapoor with a mere 'Good morning, Sir,' and Maan, whom he had not expected to see, with a hello.

Mahesh Kapoor, who was still used to being addressed by his erstwhile title, looked a little closely at Sandeep Lahiri.

'Yes?' he asked abruptly.

'Quite a pleasant day —'

'Have you simply come to pay your respects?' asked Mahesh Kapoor.

'Oh, no, Sir,' said Sandeep Lahiri, horrified by the thought.

'You have not come to pay your respects?' asked Mahesh Kapoor.

'Well, not not to — but, well, I've come for a little help and advice, Sir. I heard you had just arrived here, and so I thought —'

'Yes, yes —' Mahesh Kapoor was walking on, and Sandeep Lahiri was following him on the narrow divider, rather unsteadily.

Sandeep Lahiri sighed, and plunged into his question. 'It is like this, Sir. The government has authorized us — us SDOs, that is — to collect money from the public — voluntary donations — for a small celebration on Independence Day, which is — well — just a few days away now. Does the Congress Party traditionally have any particular hold on these funds?'

The words 'Congress Party' struck an angry chord in Mahesh Kapoor's breast. 'I have nothing to do with the Congress Party,' he said. 'You are well aware of the fact that I am no longer a Minister.'

'Yes, Sir,' said Sandeep Lahiri. 'But I thought —'

'You had better ask Jha, he virtually runs the District Congress Committee. He can speak for the Congress.'

Jha was the Chairman of the Legislative Council, an old

Congressman who had caused Sandeep Lahiri much trouble already, ever since the SDO had arrested his nephew for hooliganism and affray. Jha, whose ego required him to interfere in every decision of the administration, was the cause of half of Sandeep Lahiri's problems.

'But Mr Jha is –' began Sandeep Lahiri.

'Yes, yes, ask Jha. I have nothing to do with it.'

Sandeep Lahiri sighed again, then said:

'On another problem, Sir –'

'Yes?'

'I know that you are no longer Minister of Revenue, and that this is not a direct concern of yours, but, Sir, the increase in the number of evictions of tenants after the Zamindari Act was passed –'

'Who says it is not my concern?' asked Mahesh Kapoor, turning around and nearly bumping into Sandeep Lahiri. 'Tell me who says that?' If there was one subject that cut Mahesh Kapoor to the quick, it was this unspeakable side-effect of his pet legislation. Peasants were being evicted from their homes and lands all over the country, wherever Zamindari Abolition Bills were being or had been passed. In almost every case the intention of the zamindar was to show that the land was and always had been under his direct cultivation, and that no one other than him had any rights in it at all.

'But, Sir, you just said –'

'Never mind what I just said. What are you doing about the problem?'

Maan, who had been walking behind Sandeep Lahiri, had also stopped. At first he looked at his father and his friend, and enjoyed their mutual discomfiture. Then, looking upwards at the great cloudy sky that merged with the far horizon, he thought of Baitar and Debaria, and sobered up.

'Sir, the scale of the problem defeats the imagination. I cannot be everywhere at once.'

'Start an agitation,' said Mahesh Kapoor.

Sandeep Lahiri's weak chin dropped. That he, as a civil servant, should start any kind of agitation was unthinkable

– and it was amazing that an ex-Minister had suggested it. On the other hand, his sympathy with the evicted peasants, dispossessed and destitute as they were, had forced him to speak to Mahesh Kapoor, who was popularly seen as their champion. It had been his secret hope that Mahesh Kapoor himself might stir things up once he realized the scope of their distress.

'Have you talked to Jha?' asked Mahesh Kapoor.

'Yes, Sir.'

'And what does he say?'

'Sir, it is no secret that Mr Jha and I do not see eye to eye. What distresses me is likely for that very reason to delight him. And since he gets a large part of his funds from the landlords – '

'All right, all right,' said Mahesh Kapoor. 'I'll think about it. I have just arrived here. I have had hardly any time to ascertain things – to talk to my constituents – '

'Your constituents, Sir?' Sandeep Lahiri looked delighted that Mahesh Kapoor should be thinking of fighting from the Rudhia subdivision seat instead of from his regular urban constituency.

'Who can tell, who can tell?' said Mahesh Kapoor in sudden good humour. 'All this is very premature. Now that we are at the house, have some tea.'

Over tea, Sandeep and Maan got a chance to talk. Maan was disappointed to learn that there were no immediate prospects of a hunt. Sandeep had a distaste for hunting, and organized a hunt only when his duties demanded it. Luckily, from his point of view, they no longer did. With the rains, poor though they were proving to be this year, the natural food chain had revived and the wolf menace had subsided. Some villagers, however, attributed their greater security to the personal intercession of the SDO with the wolves. This, together with his clear goodwill towards the people under his care, his effective on-the-site methods of determining the facts of a case in the course of his judicial duties (even if it meant holding court under a village tree), his fairness in revenue matters, his refusal to countenance those illegal evictions that came to his notice, and his firm hold on law and order in his subdivision, had made Sandeep Lahiri a popular figure in the area. His sola topi was, however, still an object of mockery for some of the younger people.

After a while Sandeep took permission to leave. 'I have an appointment with Mr Jha, Sir, and he is not someone who cares to be kept waiting.'

'About the evictions,' continued the ex-Minister of Revenue, 'I would like to see a list for this area.'

'But, Sir –' began Sandeep Lahiri. He was thinking that he had no such list, and wondering whether he should, ethically speaking, part with it even if he had.

'However inadequate, however incomplete,' said Mahesh Kapoor, and got up to escort the young man to the door before he could mention some new scruple that had occurred to him.

14.3

SANDEEP LAHIRI'S visit to Jha's office was a fiasco.

Jha, as an important political figure, a friend of the Chief Minister, and the Chairman of the Upper House of the state legislature, was used to being consulted by the SDO on all important matters. Lahiri on the other hand saw no need to consult a party leader on matters of routine administration. He had not very long ago been at university, where he had drunk deeply of the general principles of constitutional law, the separation of the party and the state, and liberalism à la Laski. He tried to keep local politicians at arm's length.

A year in his post at Rudhia, however, had convinced him that there was no getting around direct summonses by senior political leaders. When Jha was foaming, he would have to go. He treated such visits as he would the outbreak of local pestilence: as something unforeseeable and unwelcome, but which necessitated his presence. If it was a drain on his time and his nerves, it was part of the penumbra of his job.

It would have been too much to expect the fifty-five-year-old Jha to come to the young man's office, though strictly speaking that was what the proprieties required. But out of a sense of what was due to age rather than to the Congress Party, the SDO went to visit him instead. Sandeep Lahiri was used to Jha's rudeness, so he had come prepared with a sort of silly-ass look that hid what he was really thinking. On one occasion, when Jha had not offered him a seat — apparently because of absent-mindedness, but more probably to impress his underlings of his superiority over the local representative of the state — Lahiri had, equally absent-mindedly, helped himself to one after a few minutes, smiling weakly and benevolently at Jha.

Jha, however, was in a genial mood today. He was smiling broadly, his white Congress cap askew on his huge head.

'You also sit, you also sit,' he told Sandeep. They were alone, and there was no one who needed to be impressed.

'Thank you, Sir,' said Sandeep, relieved.

'Have some tea.'

'Thank you, Sir, I normally would, but I have just had some.'

The conversation circled, then alit.

'I have seen the circular that has been distributed,' said Jha.

'Circular?'

'About the fund-raising for Independence Day.'

'Ah, yes,' said Sandeep Lahiri. 'I was wondering if I might ask for your help with that. If you, Sir, respected as you are, were to encourage people to contribute, it would have a considerable effect. We could collect a substantial amount, and put on a good show — distribute sweets, feed the poor, and so on. In fact, Sir, I am counting on your help.'

'And I am counting on your help,' said Jha, with a broad smile. 'That is why I have called you.'

'My help?' said Sandeep, smiling helplessly and warily.

'Yes, yes. You see, Congress also has plans for Independence Day, and we will take half the funds you collect, and use them for a separate display – a very good display to help the people and so on, you see. So that is what I expect. The other half you use as you like,' he added generously. 'Naturally, I will encourage people to contribute.'

This was precisely what Sandeep had feared. Though neither the older nor the younger man referred to it now, a couple of Jha's henchmen had made overtures of this kind to Sandeep a few days earlier; the proposal had gone entirely against his grain, and he had told them so. Now he continued to smile in a silly way. But his silence distressed the politician.

'So, then, I will expect half the funds. Good?' he said, a little anxiously. 'We will need the money soon, we will need a couple of days to organize things, and you have not yet begun your collection.'

'Well –' said Sandeep, and threw up his hands in a gesture that implied that if matters were in his discretion, he would have been delighted to give the entire sum he collected to Jha to do with as he pleased, but that, alas, the universe had been cruelly disposed to prevent him from receiving that pleasure.

Jha's face darkened.

'You see, Sir,' said Sandeep, moving his hands around freely in curves of helplessness, 'my hands are tied.'

Jha continued to stare, then exploded.

'What do you mean?' he almost shouted. 'No hands are tied. Congress says that no hands are tied. Congress will untie your hands.'

'Sir, it is like this –' began Sandeep Lahiri.

But Jha did not let him continue. 'You are a servant of the government,' said Jha fiercely, 'and the Congress Party runs the government. You will do as we tell you.' He adjusted the white cap on his head and hitched up his dhoti under the table.

'Mmm,' said Sandeep Lahiri in a noncommittal voice, donning a frown as perplexed and silly as his smile.

Realizing that he was making no headway, Jha decided

on a conciliatory and persuasive tack. 'Congress Party is the party of Independence,' he said. 'Without Congress there would be no Independence Day.'

'True, true, very true,' said the Sub-Divisional Officer, nodding his head in gratified agreement. 'The party of Gandhi,' he added.

This comment caused geniality to flood back into Jha's ample frame.

'So we understand each other?' he said, eagerly.

'I hope, Sir, that we always will – that no misunderstanding can ever make its way into our relations,' replied Sandeep Lahiri.

'We are two bullocks of one yoke,' said Jha dreamily, thinking of the Congress election symbol. 'Party and Government pulling together.'

'Mmm,' said Sandeep Lahiri, the dangerously silly smile appearing again on his face in order to mask his Laskian doubts.

Jha frowned. 'How much do you think you will collect?' he asked the young man.

'I don't know, Sir, I haven't done this sort of collecting before.'

'Let us say, five hundred rupees. So we will get two hundred and fifty, you will get two hundred and fifty – and everyone will be satisfied.'

'Sir, you see, I am in a difficult position,' said Sandeep Lahiri, biting the bullet.

This time Jha said nothing, simply staring at the presumptuous young fool.

'If I give you some of the money,' continued Sandeep Lahiri, 'the Socialist Party will want some, the KMPP –'

'Yes, yes, I know you have visited Mahesh Kapoor. Did he ask for money?'

'No, Sir –'

'Then what is the problem?'

'But, Sir, to be fair –'

'Fair!' Jha could not mask his contempt for the word.

'To be fair, Sir, we would have to give an equal amount to all these parties – to the Communist Party, to the

Bharatiya Jan Sangh, to the Ram Rajya Parishad, to the Hindu Mahasabha, to the Revolutionary Socialist Party –'

'What!' burst out Jha. 'What?' He swallowed. 'What? You are comparing us to the Socialist Party?' He hitched up his dhoti once again.

'Well, Sir –'

'To the Muslim League?'

'Certainly, Sir, why not? The Congress is just one of many parties. In this respect they are all the same.'

Jha, utterly outraged and nonplussed, the image of the Muslim League spinning like a Divali firework through his head, glared at Sandeep Lahiri.

'You equate us with the other parties?' he asked, his voice trembling with anger that was almost certainly unfeigned.

Sandeep Lahiri was silent.

'In that case,' continued Jha, 'I will show you. I will show you what the Congress means. I will make sure that you are not able to raise any funds. Not one paisa will you be able to get. You will see, you will see.'

Sandeep did not say anything.

'Now I have nothing to say,' continued Jha, his right hand gripping a light blue glass egg that acted as a paper-weight. 'But we will see, we will see.'

'Well, yes, Sir, we will see,' said Sandeep, getting up. Jha did not get up from his chair. Turning at the door Sandeep aimed his weak smile at the furious Congressman in a final attempt at goodwill. The Congressman did not smile back.

14.4

SANDEEP LAHIRI, deciding that there was not much time to spare, and fearing that Jha was quite likely right in his estimate of his fund-gathering abilities, went that afternoon to the marketplace in Rudhia dressed in his khaki shirt and shorts, and with his pith helmet on his head. A small crowd gathered around him because it was not obvious what he was doing there and because, in any case, the visit of the SDO was a notable event.

When a couple of shopkeepers asked him what they could do for him, Sandeep Lahiri said, 'I am collecting funds for the Independence Day celebration, and have been authorized to ask the public for contributions. Would you like to contribute something?'

The shopkeepers looked at each other, and simultaneously, as if by previous consultation, each took out a five-rupee note. Lahiri was known to be an honest man and had used no pressure of any kind, but it was probably best to contribute, they thought, when he asked them to, even if it was to be spent on a government sponsored event.

'Oh, but that's too much,' said the SDO. 'I think I should set a maximum of one rupee per person. I don't want people to contribute more than they can afford.'

Both shopkeepers, very pleased, pocketed their five-rupee notes and offered him one-rupee coins instead. The SDO looked at the coins, and then absent-mindedly put them in his pocket.

The news spread through the marketplace that the SDO himself was asking for money for Independence Day, that it was going to feed children and the poor, that there was no duress and that he had set a maximum of one rupee for each contribution. This news, together with his personal popularity, worked like magic. As he strolled casually through the lanes of Rudhia, Sandeep – who hated making speeches in his flawed Hindi and felt awkward about the whole business of asking for money – was besieged by smiling contributors, some of whom had heard that Jha was opposed to their SDO's fund-gathering campaign. Sandeep found himself reflecting that in these early years of Independence, local Congressmen had already – through their venality, self-importance and blatant influence-peddling – made themselves quite unpopular, and that the people's sympathy was entirely on his side in any struggle with the politicians. If he had stood for an election against Jha, he would probably, like most young SDOs in their fiefs, have won. Meanwhile, Jha's henchmen, who had come out quickly and in force to try to persuade people to give money for the Congress celebration and not for the government one, ran into a wave of popular resistance. Some people who had already deposited a rupee into Sandeep's kitty, decided to contribute once again, and Sandeep could do nothing to stop them.

'No, Sir, this is from my wife, and this is from my son,' said one triple contributor.

When his pockets were full of coins, Sandeep took off his famous sola topi, emptied his pockets into it, and used it as a bowl for further contributions. From time to time he mopped his forehead. Everyone was delighted. Money rained into his hat: some people gave him two annas, some four, some eight, some a rupee. All the urchins of the marketplace formed a processional tail behind him. Some shouted, 'SDO Sahib ki jai!' Others stared at the treasury that was building up in his hat – more coins than they had ever seen in one place – and took bets on how much he would gather.

It was a hot day, and Sandeep paused occasionally for breath on the ledge of a shop.

Maan, who had driven into town, saw the crowd and waded into it to see what the matter was.

'What are you up to?' he asked Sandeep.

Sandeep sighed. 'Enriching myself,' he said.

'I wish I found it so easy to make money,' said Maan. 'You look exhausted. Here, let me help you.' And he took the sola topi from him and started handing it around for contributions.

'I say, you'd better not do that. If Jha hears about it, he won't be pleased,' said Sandeep.

'Bugger Jha,' said Maan.

'No, no, no, here, dear fellow, give it back,' said Sandeep, and Maan gave him his hat back.

After half an hour, when his hat had filled up, and both his pockets were bulging again, Sandeep stopped in order to count the money.

He had gathered an unimaginable eight hundred rupees.

He decided to stop his collection at once, even though

there were plenty of people eagerly reaching forward with their coins. He had more than he needed to put on a really excellent show for Independence Day. He made a little speech thanking the people for their generosity and assuring them that the money would be well used; he masculinized a great many Hindi nouns in the process.

The news spread through the bazaar and reached Jha's ears, which grew red with anger.

'I will show him,' he said aloud, and turned back home. 'I will show him who is the boss in Rudhia.'

14.5

HE was still fuming when Mahesh Kapoor came to visit him.

'Oh, Kapoorji, Kapoorji, welcome, welcome to my poor house,' said Jha.

Mahesh Kapoor was short with him. 'Your friend Joshi has been evicting tenants from his land. Tell him to stop. I won't have it.'

Jha, his cap askew, looked shrewdly at Mahesh Kapoor and said, 'I haven't heard anything of the kind. Where has your information come from?'

'Don't worry about that, it's reliable. I don't want this sort of thing taking place on my doorstep. It gives the government a bad name.'

'Why do you care if the government gets a bad name?' said Jha with a broad smile. 'You are no longer part of it. Agarwal and Sharma were talking to me the other day. They were saying that you had joined Kidwai and Kripalani merely to make a K-K-K group.'

'Are you mocking me?' said Mahesh Kapoor angrily.

'No, no, no, no — how can you say that?'

'Because if you are, let me tell you that I am prepared to fight from this constituency if necessary to make sure that the farmers here are not maltreated by your friends.'

Jha's mouth opened slightly. He could not imagine Mahesh Kapoor fighting from a rural constituency, so closely associated was he in everyone's mind with Old Brahmpur. Mahesh Kapoor had rarely interfered much in the affairs of Rudhia, and Jha resented his new activist role.

'Is this why your son was making speeches in the market-place today?' Jha said in a surly tone.

'What speeches?' said Mahesh Kapoor.

'With that boy Lahiri, that IAS fellow.'

'What are you talking about?' said Mahesh Kapoor dismissively. 'I'm not interested in all that. All I can tell you is that you'd better get Joshi to lay off – or else I'll get a case registered against him. Whether I'm in the government or not, I don't want the Zamindari Act to become toothless, and if necessary I am prepared to become the local dentist.'

'I have a better suggestion, Maheshji,' said Jha, hitching up his dhoti aggressively. 'If you are so keen on a rural constituency, why not fight from Salimpur-cum-Baitar? Then you can make sure that your friend the Nawab Sahib doesn't evict his tenants, as I understand he is very skilled in doing.'

'Thank you, I will take note of your suggestion,' said Mahesh Kapoor.

'And do tell me when your party, the – what is it called? – it is so difficult to remember these alphabet parties that keep springing up – the KMPP – yes, KMPP – manages to get a hundred votes, Maheshji,' said Jha, who was delighted that he could parley thus with a man who had been so powerful just a few weeks earlier. 'But why have you left us Congress-wallahs bereft of your presence and wisdom? Why have you left the party of Nehru? Chacha Nehru, our great leader – how will he manage without people like you – people of enlightened views? And, more to the point, how will you manage without him? When he comes to ask the people to vote for Congress, do you think they will listen to him or to you?'

'You should be ashamed to take Nehru's name,' said Mahesh Kapoor heatedly. 'You believe in nothing he does, yet you will use him to catch your votes. Jha Sahib, if it were not for Nehru's name, you would be nothing.'

'If. If,' said Jha expansively.

'I have heard enough nonsense,' said Mahesh Kapoor. 'Tell Joshi that I have a list of the tenants he has turned out. How I have got it concerns neither him nor you. He had better reinstate them by Independence Day. That is all I have to say.'

Mahesh Kapoor got up to go. As he was about to leave the room, Joshi, the very man he had been talking about, entered. Joshi looked so worried that he hardly noticed Mahesh Kapoor until he bumped into him. He looked up – he was a small man with a neat white moustache – and said:

'Oh, Kapoor Sahib, Kapoor Sahib, such terrible news.'

'What terrible news?' said Mahesh Kapoor. 'Have your tenants bribed the police before you could get to them yourself?'

'Tenants?' said Joshi blankly.

'Kapoorji has been writing his own Ramayana,' said Jha.

'Ramayana?' said Joshi.

'Must you repeat everything?' said Jha, who was beginning to lose patience with his friend. 'What is this terrible news? I know that this Lahiri fellow has managed to extort a thousand rupees from the people. Is that what you came to tell me? Let me tell you that I will deal with him in my own way.'

'No, no –' Joshi found it difficult to speak, so momentous was the information he was carrying. 'It is just that Nehru –'

His face was wobbling with unhappiness and alarm.

'What?' said Jha.

'Is he dead?' asked Mahesh Kapoor, prepared for the worst.

'No, far worse – resigned – resigned –' gasped Joshi.

'As Prime Minister?' asked Mahesh Kapoor. 'From the Congress? What do you mean "resigned"?'

'From the Congress Working Committee – and from the

Central Election Committee,' cried Joshi miserably. 'They say that he is thinking of resigning from the Congress altogether – and joining another party. God knows what will happen. Chaos, chaos.'

Mahesh Kapoor realized immediately that he would have to go back to Brahmpur – and perhaps even to Delhi – for consultations. As he left the room he turned back for one last glance at Jha. Jha's mouth was open, and his hands were clutching the two sides of his white Congress cap. He was entirely incapable of concealing the powerful emotion that had seized him. He was in a state of violent shock.

14.6

MAAN had remained behind on the farm when his father had rushed off to Brahmpur in the wake of the news of Nehru's resignation from his party posts. There had been talk of a crisis in the Congress Party for over a year, but there was no doubt now that it was truly upon them. The Prime Minister of the country had virtually declared that he had no confidence in the elected leadership of the party whom he represented in Parliament. And he had chosen to make this declaration just a few days before Independence Day – the 15th of August – when he, as Prime Minister, would speak to the nation from the ramparts of the Red Fort in Delhi.

Sandeep Lahiri, meanwhile, briefly addressed the assembled population of Rudhia from a podium erected at the edge of the local maidan. He took charge of feeding the poor with the help of various women's organizations in the town. He distributed sweets to children with his own hands – a task he found pleasant but awkward. And he took the salute at the boy scouts' parade and the police parade and hoisted the national flag, which had been filled beforehand with marigold petals, a shower of which fell on him as he looked up in surprise.

Jha was not present. He and his supporters boycotted

the whole show. At the end of the ceremonies, after a local band had struck up the National Anthem, and Sandeep Lahiri had shouted 'Jai Hind!' to the cheers of a couple of thousand people, more sweets were distributed. Maan gave him a hand with this, and appeared to be enjoying it a great deal more than Sandeep. The children were finding it difficult not to break ranks and had to be restrained by their flustered teachers. While all this was going on, a postman came up to the SDO, and handed him a telegram. He was about to put it absently into his pocket, when it struck him that it might contain something of importance. But his hand was sticky with jalebis, and he asked Maan, who had managed to avoid that particular hazard, to open it for him and read it out to him.

Maan opened the envelope and read it out. At first the message did not quite register on Sandeep, but then he frowned, and it was not a silly-ass frown but an aggrieved one. Jha had moved fast, it appeared. The telegram had been sent by the Chief Secretary of Purva Pradesh. It informed Shri Sandeep Lahiri, IAS, of his transfer with immediate effect from the post of Sub-Divisional Officer of Rudhia subdivision to a post in the Department of Mines at Brahmpur. He was to relinquish charge as soon as the officer to replace him arrived, on the 16th of August, and to report at Brahmpur the same day.

14.7

ONE of Sandeep Lahiri's first acts upon arriving in Brahmpur was to request an interview with the Chief Secretary. A couple of months earlier, the Chief Secretary had dropped him a note to say that he had been doing an excellent job in his subdivision, and had especially commended his role in solving – by on-the-spot inquiries in the villages – a large number of land disputes that had appeared for some years to be intractable. He had assured Lahiri of his full support. And now, in effect, he had pulled the rug out from under his feet.

The Chief Secretary, busy though he was, granted him an interview at his house the same evening.

'Now I know what you are going to ask me, young man, and I will be quite frank with you. But I must tell you in advance that there is no question of this order being rescinded.'

'I see, Sir,' said Sandeep, who had grown very fond of Rudhia, and had expected to serve his full term there – or at least to be given the time to apprise his successor of the problems and pitfalls – as well as the pleasures – that he was likely to encounter, and the various schemes that he had set in train which he would be sorry to see fall into neglect.

'You see, orders in your case came directly from the Chief Minister.'

'Did Jha have anything to do with this?' asked Sandeep, frowning.

'Jha? Oh, I see – Jha, from Rudhia. I'm afraid I couldn't tell you. It's certainly possible. I'm beginning to think that anything's possible these days. Have you been treading on his toes?'

'I suppose I have, Sir – and he on mine.'

Sandeep filled the Chief Secretary in on the details of their conflict. The Chief Secretary's eyes drifted across his table.

'You do realize that this is a premature promotion, don't you?' he said at last. 'You shouldn't be displeased.'

'Yes, Sir,' said Sandeep. And indeed, the position of Under-Secretary in the Department of Mines, though lowly enough in the hierarchy of the Indian Administrative Service, ranked higher than the post of SDO, with all its freedom of action and its life in the open air. He would in the normal course of things have been transferred to a desk job in Brahmpur six months later.

'Well, then?'

'Did – well, Sir, if I might ask – did you say anything to dissuade the Chief Minister from getting rid of me?'

'Lahiri, I do wish you wouldn't see things in that light. No one has got rid of you, and no one wishes to. You have an excellent career ahead of you. I cannot go into details, but I will tell you that the first thing I did upon receiving the CM's instructions – which, incidentally, did surprise me – was to call for your file. You have an excellent record, with a number of good marks and only one bad mark against you. The only reason that I could think of that the CM wanted you out of Rudhia was that Mahatma Gandhi's birth anniversary is coming around in a couple of months. It appears that your decision in that troublesome matter last year rather annoyed him; I assumed that something had jogged his memory of late, and he thought that your presence in Rudhia might be a provocation. Anyway, it will be no bad thing for you to spend some time in Brahmpur early on in your career,' he continued in a genial tone. 'You'll be spending at least a third of your working life here, and you may as well see how things run in the labyrinths of the state capital. My only specific advice,' continued the Chief Secretary, now rather glumly, 'is that you should not be seen at the bar of the Subzipore Club too often. Sharma, being a true Gandhian, doesn't like people drinking; he makes rather a point of summoning me for some emergency work late in the evening whenever he hears I'm at the club.'

The incident that the Chief Secretary had referred to a little earlier involved the railway colony at Rudhia where the previous year a number of young Anglo-Indian men – the sons of railway employees – had smashed the glass in front of a notice-board that contained a poster of Mahatma Gandhi, which they had then proceeded to deface. There had been an uproar in response, and the offenders had been arrested, beaten up by the police, and hauled up before Sandeep Lahiri in his magisterial incarnation. Jha had screamed for their trial on the grounds of sedition, or at the very least of having grievously injured the religious sentiments of the population. Sandeep, however, had realized that these were hotheaded but not really ill-meaning young men, who had had no inkling of the possible consequences of their actions. He had waited for them to sober up, and then – after dressing them down and making them

27

apologize in public, had discharged them with a warning. His judgment with respect to the charges sought to be brought against them had been succinct:

> This is quite evidently not a case of sedition: Gandhiji, revere his memory though we do, is not the King-Emperor. Nor is he the head of a religion, so the charge of injuring people's religious sentiments does not hold either. As for the charge of mischief, the smashed glass and defaced portrait do not cost more than eight annas, and de minimis non curat lex. The defendants are discharged with a warning.

Sandeep had been itching for some time to use this Latin tag, and here was the ideal opportunity: the law did not concern itself with trifles, and here was a trifling matter, at least in monetary terms. But his linguistic pleasure was not without cost. The Chief Minister had not been amused, and had instructed the previous Chief Secretary to enter a black mark against him in his character roll. 'Government have considered Mr Lahiri's ill-judged decision in the case of the recent disorder in Rudhia. Government note with regret that he has chosen to make a display of his liberal instincts at the cost of his duty to maintain law and order.'

'Well, Sir,' said Sandeep to the Chief Secretary, 'what would you have done if you had been in my place? Under what provision of the Indian Penal Code could I have chopped off those silly young men's heads, even if I had wished to?'

'Well,' said the Chief Secretary, unwilling to criticize his predecessor. 'I really can't go into all that. Anyway, as you say, it is probably some recent contretemps with Jha that has got you transferred, not that earlier incident. I know what you're thinking: that I should have stood up for you. Well, I have. I made sure that your transfer was not a lateral one, that it involved a promotion. That was the best that I could do. I know when it is useful, and when it is not, to argue with the Chief Minister – who, to give him his due, is an excellent administrator and values good officers. One day, when you are in a position similar to mine – and I don't see why, given your potential, you shouldn't be – you will have to make similar, well, adjustments. Now, can I offer you a drink?'

Sandeep accepted a whisky. The Chief Secretary grew boringly expansive and reminiscent:

'The problem, you see, began in 1937 – once you got politicians running things at the provincial level. Sharma was elected Premier, as it was then called, of the Protected Provinces – as our state then was. It became fairly obvious to me early on that other considerations than merit would apply in promotions and transfers. When the lines of power ran from Viceroy to Governor to Commissioner to District Magistrate, things were clear enough. It was when the legislators crawled into every level except the very top that the rot started. Patronage, power-bases, agitations, politics, toadying to the elected representatives of the people: all that kind of stuff. One had to do one's own duty of course, but what one saw sometimes dismayed one. Some batsmen could now score a six even if the ball bounced within the boundary. And others were declared out even if they were caught outside the boundary. You see what I mean. Incidentally, Tandon – who's been trying to declare Nehru out by insisting on the rules by which the Congress plays the game – was a fine cricketer – did you know that? – when he was at Allahabad University. I believe he captained the Muir Central College team. Now he goes around bearded and barefoot like a rishi from the Mahabharata, but he was a cricketer once. Cricket has a lot to answer for. Another?'

'No, thanks.'

'There's also the fact that he was the Speaker of the U.P. Legislative Assembly during those years. Rules, rules, and very little flexibility. I always thought it was us bureaucrats who were the sticklers for rules. Well, the country's burning and the politicians are fiddling, not very tunefully at that. It is up to us to keep things going. The iron frame and all that: rusting and buckling, though, I'd have to say. Well, I'm almost at the end of my career, and I can't say I'm sorry. I hope you enjoy your new job, Lahiri – Mines, isn't it? Do let me know how you're getting along.'

'Thank you, Sir,' said Sandeep Lahiri, and got up with a serious expression on his face. He was beginning to understand all too well how things worked. Was this his own future self he had been talking to? He could not hide from himself his dismay and, yes, it would not be too much to say, his disgust, at this new and most unwelcome insight.

14.8

'SHARMAJI came here to meet you this morning,' said Mrs Mahesh Kapoor to her husband when he returned to Prem Nivas.

'He came himself?'

'Yes.'

'Did he say anything?'

'What would he say to me?' asked Mrs Mahesh Kapoor.

Her husband clicked his tongue in irritation. 'All right,' he said. 'I'll go and see him.' It was more than civil of the Chief Minister to have come in person to his house, and Mahesh Kapoor had a shrewd idea of what he wanted to discuss. The crisis in the Congress was the talk of the country now, not just of the party. Nehru's resignation from all his party offices had made certain of that.

Mahesh Kapoor called ahead, then visited Sharma at home. Though he had left the Congress, he continued to wear the white cap that had become a natural part of his attire. Sharma was sitting on a white cane chair in the garden, and stood up to greet him as he approached. He should have looked tired, but he did not. It was a warm day, and he had been fanning himself with a newspaper, the headlines of which spoke of the latest moves to conciliate Nehru. He offered his erstwhile colleague a chair and some tea.

'I needn't go around in circles, Kapoor Sahib,' said the Chief Minister. 'I want your help in trying to persuade Nehru to return to the Congress.'

'But he has never left it,' said Mahesh Kapoor with a smile, seeing that the Chief Minister was already thinking two steps ahead.

'I meant, to full participation in the Congress.'

'I sympathize, Sharmaji; these must be troubling times for the Congress Party. But what can I do? I am no longer a member of the party myself. Nor are many of my friends and colleagues.'

'The Congress is your true home,' said Sharma, a little sadly, his head beginning to shake. 'You have given everything for it, you have sacrificed the best years of your life for it. Even now you are sitting in the same position in the Legislative Assembly as before. If that wedge is now labelled the KMPP or something else, I still look upon it with affection. I still consider you my colleagues. There are more idealists there than in those who have remained with me.'

Sharma did not need to state that by this he was referring to the likes of Agarwal. Mahesh Kapoor stirred his tea. He felt great sympathy for the man whose Cabinet he had so recently resigned from. But he hoped that Nehru would leave the Congress and join the party that he himself had joined, and he could not see how Sharma could have imagined that he, of all people, would be keen to dissuade him from doing so. He leaned forward a little and said quietly: 'Sharmaji, I sacrificed those years for my country more than for any party. If the Congress has betrayed its ideals, and forced so many of its old supporters to leave —' He stopped. 'Anyway, I see no immediate danger of Panditji leaving the party.'

'Don't you?' said Sharma.

A couple of letters lay in front of him, and he now handed one of them, the longer one, to Mahesh Kapoor and tapped his finger on a couple of paragraphs at the end. Mahesh Kapoor read slowly, not looking up till he had finished. It was one of Nehru's regular fortnightly letters to his Chief Ministers and was dated August 1 – two days after his friend Kidwai, having withdrawn his resignation, had resigned again. The last part of the long letter, which ranged over the entire gamut of foreign and domestic developments, went as follows:

24. There has been frequent reference in the press recently to resignations from the Central Cabinet. I confess I have been greatly troubled over this matter, for the two persons concerned have been valuable colleagues who have fully justified their membership of Government. There was no question of a difference of opinion in regard to governmental policy. Difficulties arose about other matters relating to the National Congress. I do not propose to say anything about this subject here because you will probably soon see some statements in the press which will explain the present position. That position only indirectly affects the Government. Essentially it is a question of the future of the Congress. This is not only of interest to Congressmen but to everybody in India, because the role of the Congress has been great.

25. The next session of Parliament begins on Monday next, August 6th. This is the last session before the elections. It has heavy business before it, some of which is of importance and must be passed during the session. Probably this session will last for about two months.

Yours sincerely,
Jawaharlal Nehru

Mahesh Kapoor, reading the letter in the light of Nehru's resignation less than a week later from the Congress Working Committee and Central Election Committee, could see why Sharma – or anyone else – might think that these resignations were preliminary to Nehru's complete resignation from the Congress. 'Because the role of the Congress has been great' sounded ominously lukewarm.

Sharma had put down his cup and was looking at Mahesh Kapoor. Since the latter made no comment, he said, 'The U.P. Congressmen are going to try to persuade Nehru to withdraw his resignation – or at least to persuade Nehru and Tandon to come to some kind of compromise. I too feel we should send a group to speak to him. I am prepared to go to Delhi myself. But I want you to come with me.'

'I am sorry, Sharmaji,' said Mahesh Kapoor with some annoyance. Sharma might be the great conciliator, but he surely could not imagine that he could persuade him, who was now a member of the opposition, into such a self-defeating position. 'I cannot help you. Panditji respects you, and you will be as persuasive as anyone. For my part, I, like Kidwai and Kripalani and all the others who have left the Congress, hope that Nehru will join us soon. As you say, we have some elements of idealism. Perhaps it is time that politics was based on issues and ideals, and not on the control of party machines.'

Sharma's head began to nod slightly. A peon came out onto the lawn with a message, but he waved him away. For a while he rested his chin on his hands, then said, in his nasal but persuasive manner:

'Maheshji, you must be wondering about my motives, perhaps even about my logic. It may be that I have not made my visualization of the situation clear. I will put before you several pictures. First: Suppose Nehru leaves the Congress. Suppose further that I do not wish to fight him in the forthcoming elections, perhaps because of my respect for him, perhaps because I fear to lose, and – as an old man – care too much about my own self-respect. At any rate, I too resign from the Congress. Or if not from the Congress, from active participation in affairs of state – from the government, from the Chief Ministership. The state will require a new Chief Minister. In the present configuration, unless the ex-Minister of Revenue rejoins the party and persuades those who left with him to rejoin, there will be only one contender for the mantle.'

'You would not permit Agarwal to become Chief Minister,' said Mahesh Kapoor in a hard voice, making no attempt to conceal his resentment and shock. 'You would not deliver the state into his hands.'

Sharma cast an eye around the garden. A cow had got into the radish patch, but he ignored it.

'I am only drawing imaginary scenes,' he said. 'Let me

33

draw a second one. I go to Delhi. I try to talk to Nehru, to persuade him to withdraw his resignations. He, for his part, renews his standard assault on me. He wants me at the Centre, in the Cabinet – a Cabinet now already depleted by resignations. We both know Jawaharlal, we know how persuasive he can be. He will say that more important than the Congress Party is the good of India, the government of the country. He wants good administrators at the Centre, people of stature, people of proven competence. I am only repeating the kind words he has already repeated a score of times to me. So far I have always found some excuse for getting back from Delhi. People say I am ambitious, that I prefer to be King in Brahmpur rather than a baron in Delhi. They may be right. But this time Jawaharlal tells me: "You are asking me to act against my own inclinations for the good of the country, yet you refuse to do the same yourself." It is an unanswerable argument. I go to Delhi as a Cabinet Minister, and L.N. Agarwal takes over as Chief Minister of Purva Pradesh.'

Mahesh Kapoor remained silent. After a while, he said: 'If – if this were the case, and this – this man took over, it would only be for a few months. The people would throw him out in the coming elections.'

'I think you underestimate the Home Minister,' said S.S. Sharma with a smile. 'But now, suppose we leave this bugbear behind and think in broader terms: in terms of the country itself. Do you or I want the kind of battle that will ensue if Nehru leaves the Congress? If you recall the bitterness that was generated in the battle within the Congress Party when Tandon got elected – and it is no secret that I too voted for him rather than Kripalani – can you imagine the bitterness of the battle in the General Elections if Nehru fights on one side and the Congress on the other? Whom will the people turn to? Think how their hearts will be torn, their loyalties divided. The Congress, after all, is the party of Gandhiji, the party of Independence.'

Mahesh Kapoor forbore from remarking that it was the party of a good deal else besides: nepotism, corruption, inefficiency, complacency – and that Gandhiji himself had wanted it dissolved as a political force after Independence. He said: 'Well, if there has to be a battle, it should be fought during these elections. If the Congress uses Nehru to fight its election battles and then turns against him because its right wing has most of the MLAs and MPs in its pocket – that will be far worse. The sooner the matter is fought out, the better. I agree that the two of us should be fighting on the same side. I wish, Sharmaji, that I could persuade you to join my party – and then persuade you to persuade Nehru to do the same.'

The Chief Minister smiled at what he chose to interpret as an attempt at humour by Mahesh Kapoor. Then he picked up the second letter that he had in front of him and said:

'What I am showing you now is not one of Panditji's regular fortnightly letters, but a special letter to the Chief Ministers. It is supposed to be secret. It is dated a couple of days after he wrote to Tandonji submitting his resignation. If you read it you will see why I am so worried about the possibility of divisions in the country at this time.' He handed Mahesh Kapoor the letter, then said: 'I have not shown this to anyone yet, not even to anyone in my Cabinet, though I have told Agarwal to come around to read it because it concerns him as Home Minister. And I will naturally discuss it with the Chief Secretary. It would not be good if the contents of this letter got around.'

He then got up and walked over with the help of his cane to tell his gardener to chase the cow out of the vegetable garden, leaving Mahesh Kapoor to read the letter. Parts of it read as follows:

New Delhi
9 August, 1951

My dear Chief Minister,
    The Indo-Pakistan situation shows no signs of improvement. The most that can be said is that it has not grown any worse, but it is bad enough. On the Pakistan side, feverish preparations for war are taking place. . . .

Considering the question logically, I do not consider war likely. But logic does not explain everything and, in any event, we cannot base our activities on pure logic. Logic would not explain the spate of propaganda, full of hatred and falsehood, that issues from Pakistan. . . .

There was a sound of aggrieved if patient lowing from the far end of the garden. Mahesh Kapoor's eyes skimmed rapidly down the letter. Nehru was now talking about the Indian Muslims:

. . . Sometimes it is said that there might be bad elements among the Muslims who might give trouble. That is quite possible, but I think it highly unlikely that any major trouble will come from that direction. We should be careful of course in regard to strategic areas or vital spots.

I think it is much more likely that trouble may come from Hindu or Sikh communal elements. They would like to take advantage of the occasion to misbehave towards Muslims. If any such thing occurs, it will have very bad consequences and will weaken us. Therefore, this kind of thing must not be allowed to happen. This is of major importance and we must give full protection to our minorites. This means also that we must not permit any propaganda on the part of Hindu or Sikh communal organizations, which is on a par with Pakistan propaganda on the other side. There have been some recent incidents of this where, lacking originality, the Hindu Mahasabha people have tried to imitate the Pakistanis. They did not succeed to any extent. But it is quite possible that if we are unwary and some incidents happen, the communal elements might take advantage of them. I would, therefore, specially request you to keep this in mind. . . .

These are speculations which I am sharing with you. We have to be prepared for all emergencies and, in a military sense, we are so prepared from now onwards. I still hope and partly believe that there will be no war and I do not wish to do anything on our side which might perhaps tip the balance on the side of war.

Hence my earnest request to you that no public activity that savours of war preparation should be indulged in or encouraged in others, while at the same time our minds must keep prepared.

You will please keep this letter as top secret and not to be shared with others except, perhaps, a very few.

Yours sincerely,
Jawaharlal Nehru

14.9

WHEN Sharma returned from chasing the cow out of the further reaches of the garden, he found Mahesh Kapoor pacing up and down, restless and troubled. 'You see,' said Sharma, homing unerringly into his thoughts, 'you see why we cannot have any unnecessary divisions of opinion in the country at this time, of all times. And also why I am so keen to persuade you to return to the Congress. Agarwal's attitude to the Muslims is well known. As he is the Home Minister, well, I have to leave certain matters in his hands. And the calendar this year makes things worse than ever.'

This last sentence took Mahesh Kapoor by surprise. 'The calendar?' he asked, frowning at Sharma.

'Here – let me show you –' The Chief Minister took a small brown diary out of his kurta pocket. He pointed to the beginning of October. 'The ten days of Moharram and the ten days leading up to Dussehra almost coincide this year. And Gandhi Jayanti falls within the same period.' He closed the diary and laughed humourlessly. 'Rama, Muhammad, and Gandhiji may all have been apostles of peace – but in combination there could be nothing more explosive. And if in addition there is war with Pakistan, and the only cohesive party in India is bitterly divided within itself – I fear to think of what will happen throughout the country between the Hindus and the Muslims. It will be as bad as the Partition riots.'

Mahesh Kapoor did not reply. But he could not deny to himself that he had been deeply affected by the arguments of the Chief Minister. When offered more tea, he accepted, and sat down on a cane chair. After a few minutes he said to his former chief, 'I will think about what you have said.' He was still holding Nehru's letter in his hands. In fact, unconsciously, he had folded it lengthwise two or three times.

It was unfortunate that L.N. Agarwal should have chosen that very moment to visit the Chief Minister. As he walked across the lawn he noticed Mahesh Kapoor. Mahesh Kapoor nodded, but did not get up to greet him. He did not intend to be discourteous, but his thoughts were far away.

'About Panditji's letter –' began L.N. Agarwal.

Sharma reached out for the letter, and Mahesh Kapoor handed it over in an absent manner. Agarwal frowned, obviously displeased that the letter had been shared with Mahesh Kapoor: Sharma appeared to be treating him as if he were still a member of his Cabinet, instead of the renegade that he was.

Perhaps sensing his thoughts, S.S. Sharma began to explain, rather apologetically: 'I was just discussing with Kapoor Sahib the urgency of bringing Panditji back into full participation in the Congress. We cannot do without him, the country cannot do without him, and we must persuade him by any means we can. It is a time to close ranks. Don't you agree?'

A look of disdain slowly formed on L.N. Agarwal's face as he thought about this attitude: dependent, cringing, weak.

'No,' he said at last. 'I do not agree. Tandonji has been democratically elected. He has constituted his own Working Committee, and it has managed very well for several months. Nehru has participated in its meetings; he has no right to try to change its membership now. That is not his prerogative. He claims to be a democrat; let him prove it by doing the right thing. He claims to believe in party discipline; he should abide by it. He claims to believe in unity; let him stand by his beliefs.'

S.S. Sharma closed his eyes. 'That is all very well,' he murmured. 'But if Panditji —'

L.N. Agarwal almost exploded. 'Panditji — Panditji — why should everyone go whimpering and pleading for everything to Nehru? Yes, he is a great leader — but are there no other great leaders in Congress? Does Prasad not exist? Does Pant not exist? Did Patel not exist?' At the thought of Sardar Patel his voice almost choked with emotion. 'Let us see what happens if he leaves us. He doesn't have the least idea how to organize a campaign, how to gather funds, how to select candidates. And he will have no time, as Prime Minister, to storm the country — that is quite obvious. He has too much on his plate as it is, attempting to run it. Let him join Kidwai — he'll get the Muslim vote all right. But we will see what else he gets.'

Mahesh Kapoor got up, nodded curtly to the Chief Minister, and began to walk away. The Chief Minister, distressed and annoyed by Agarwal's explosion, made no attempt to stop him from going; Agarwal and Kapoor in one place did not form a happy combination.

It is like dealing with two refractory children, he thought. But he called out after Mahesh Kapoor:

'Kapoor Sahib, please think about what I have said. We will talk about this again soon. I will come over to Prem Nivas.'

Then he turned to Agarwal and said, with displeased nasality: 'An hour's good work destroyed in a minute. Why are you going out of your way to antagonize him?'

L.N. Agarwal shook his head. 'Everyone is afraid to speak his mind,' he said. He reflected that matters in Purva Pradesh had become much clearer now that the leftists and secularists in Congress did not have Mahesh Kapoor's fine kurta to cling to.

Instead of taking offence at the roughness of this last remark, S.S. Sharma said to him in a calmer voice: 'Here is the letter. Read it through and tell me what steps you think are appropriate. Of course, we are located nowhere near the borders of Pakistan. Still, some measures may be necessary to control the more excitable newspapers – in the case of panic, I mean. Or incitement.'

'Certain processions may need to be controlled as well,' said the Home Minister.

'Let us see, let us see,' said the Chief Minister.

14.10

THE uncertainties of the great world were complemented in Brahmpur by the smaller certainties of the calendar. Two days after the flag-hoistings and orations of Independence Day – the most unsettling of the five that India had so far celebrated – came the full moon of the month of Shravan, and the tenderest of all family festivals – when brothers and sisters affirm their bonds to each other.

Mrs Mahesh Kapoor, however, who was normally keen on festivals, did not approve of Rakhi or believe in it. For her it was a typically Punjabi festival. She traced her ancestry back to a part of U.P. where, according to her, at least among khatris, the festival on which brothers and sisters more truly affirmed their bonds was Bhai Duj – located two-and-a-half months from now among the little glut of smaller festivals clustering around the almost moonless skies of the great festival of Divali. But she was alone in this; neither of her samdhins agreed with her, certainly not old Mrs Tandon, who, having lived in Lahore in the heart of the undivided Punjab, had celebrated Rakhi all her life like all her neighbours, nor Mrs Rupa Mehra, who believed in sentiment at all costs and on every possible occasion. Mrs Rupa Mehra believed in Bhai Duj as well, and sent greetings on that day too to all her brothers – the term included her male cousins – as a sort of confirmatory affirmation.

Mrs Mahesh Kapoor had clear but undogmatic views on various subjects relating to fasts and festivals: she had her own views of the legends underlying the Pul Mela as well. For her daughter, however, living in Lahore with the Tandons had made no difference. Veena had celebrated

Rakhi ever since Pran was born. Mrs Mahesh Kapoor, whatever she thought of this festival, did not try to dampen her daughter's enthusiasm for coloured thread and shiny florets when she was a little girl. And when Pran and Maan used to come to their mother as children to show her what their sister had given them, her pleasure was never entirely feigned.

Veena went in the morning to Prem Nivas to tie a rakhi around Pran's wrist. She chose a simple rakhi, a small silver flower of tinsel on a red thread. She fed him a laddu and blessed him, and received in exchange his promise of protection, five rupees and a hug. Although, as Imtiaz had told him, his heart condition was a chronic one, she noticed that he was looking quite a bit better than before; the birth of his daughter, rather than adding to the strain of his life, appeared to have relieved it. Uma was a happy child; and Savita had not got overly or prolongedly depressed in the month following her birth, as her mother had warned her she might. The crisis of Pran's health had given her too much concern, and reading the law too much stimulation, for a lapse into the luxury of depression. Sometimes she felt passionately maternal and tearfully happy.

Veena had brought Bhaskar along.

'Where's my rakhi?' demanded Bhaskar of Savita.

'Your rakhi?'

'Yes. From the baby.'

'You're quite right,' said Savita, smiling and shaking her head at her own thoughtlessness. 'You're quite right. I'll go out and get one at once. Or better still, I'll make one. Ma must have enough material in her bag for a hundred rakhis. And you – I hope you've brought a present for her.'

'Oh, yes,' said Bhaskar, who had cut Uma a bright and multicoloured dodecahedron out of a single sheet of paper. It was to hang above her cot and she could follow it with her eyes as it twirled around. 'I coloured it myself. But I didn't try to use the minimum number of colours,' he added apologetically.

'Oh, that's fine,' said Savita. 'The more colours the

better.' And she gave Bhaskar a kiss. When the rakhi was made, she tied it over his right wrist while holding Uma's hand inside her own.

Veena also went to Baitar House, as she went every year, to tie a rakhi around Firoz's wrist, and Imtiaz's. Both were in, since they were expecting her.

'Where is your friend Maan?' she demanded of Firoz.

As he opened his mouth to speak, she popped a sweet in.

'You should know!' said Firoz, his eyes lighting up in a smile. 'He's your brother.'

'You needn't remind me,' said Veena, vexed. 'It's Rakhi, but he's not at home. He has no family feeling. If I'd known he would still be at the farm, I would have sent him the rakhi. He really is very inconsiderate. And now it's too late.'

Meanwhile the Mehra family had duly dispatched their rakhis to Calcutta, and they had arrived well in time. Arun had warned his sisters that anything more elaborate than a single silver thread would be impossible for him to conceal under the sleeve of his suit, and therefore entirely out of the question for him to wear to work at Bentsen Pryce. Varun, almost as if to flaunt a garish taste that could be guaranteed to exasperate his elder brother, always insisted on elaborate rakhis that reached halfway up his bare arm. Savita had not had the chance to meet her brothers this year, and wrote them long and loving letters, rebuking them for being absentee uncles. Lata, busy as she was with *Twelfth Night*, wrote them brief but tender notes. She had a rehearsal on the actual day of Rakhi. Several of the actors were wearing rakhis, and Lata could not help smiling in the course of a conversation between Olivia and Viola when it struck her that if the festival of Rakhi had existed in Elizabethan England, Shakespeare would certainly have made much of it, with Viola perhaps bewailing her ship-wrecked brother, imagining his lifeless, threadless, untin-selled arm lying outstretched beside his body on some Illyrian beach lit by the full August moon.

14.11

SHE also thought of Kabir, and of his remark at the concert — so long ago, it seemed — about having had a sister till last year. Lata still did not know for certain what he had meant by the remark, but every interpretation that came to her mind made her feel deeply sorry for him.

As it happened, Kabir was thinking of her that night as well, and talking about her with his younger brother. He had come back home exhausted after the rehearsal, and had hardly eaten any dinner, and Hashim was unhappy to see him look so spent.

Kabir was trying to describe the strangeness of the situation with Lata. They acted together, they spent hours in the same room during rehearsals, but they did not talk to each other. Lata seemed to have turned, thought Kabir, from passionate to ice-cold — he could not believe that this was the same girl who had been with him that morning in the boat — in the grey mist in a grey sweater, and with the light of love in her eyes.

No doubt the boat had been rowing against the current of society, upstream towards the Barsaat Mahal; but surely there was a solution. Should they row harder, or agree to drift downstream? Should they row in a different river or try to change the direction of the river they were in? Should they jump out of the boat and try to swim? Or get a motor or a sail? Or hire a boatman?

'Why don't you simply throw her overboard?' suggested Hashim.

'To the crocodiles?' said Kabir, laughing.

'Yes,' said Hashim. 'She must be a very stupid or unfeeling girl — why does she delight in making you miserable, Bhai-jaan? I don't think you should waste any time on her. It doesn't stand to reason.'

'I know it doesn't. But, as they say, you can't reason someone out of what they've never been reasoned into in the first place.'

'But why her?' said Hashim. 'There are plenty of girls who are crazy about you — Cubs the Cad.'

'I don't know,' said Kabir. 'It mystifies me. Perhaps it was just that first smile in the bookshop – and I'm still feeding on the meaningless memory of it. I don't even think it was me she was smiling at. I don't know. Why was it you whom Saeeda Bai latched onto on Holi evening? I heard all about that.'

Hashim blushed to the roots of his hair. He didn't suggest a solution.

'Or look at Abba and Ammi – was there ever a better-matched couple? And now –'

Hashim nodded. 'I'll come with you this Thursday. I, well, I couldn't come yesterday.'

'Well, good. But, you know, don't force yourself, Hashim. . . . I don't know if she notices your absence.'

'But you said she had a sense about – well, about Samia.'

'I think she senses it.'

'Abba pushed her over the edge. He gave her no time, no sympathy, no real companionship.'

'Well Abba is Abba, and it's pointless complaining about who he is.' He yawned. 'I suppose I am tired, after all.'

'Well, goodnight, Bhai-jaan.'

'Goodnight, Hashim.'

14.12

JUST over a week after Rakhi came Janamashtami, the day of Krishna's birth. Mrs Rupa Mehra did not celebrate it (she had mixed feelings about Krishna), but Mrs Mahesh Kapoor did. In the garden at Prem Nivas stood the undistinguished, rough-leafed harsingar tree, the tree that Krishna was reputed to have stolen from Indra's heaven for the sake of his wife Rukmini. It was not in bloom yet, and would not be for another two months, but Mrs Mahesh Kapoor stood before the tree for a minute just after dawn, imagining it covered with the fragrant, star-shaped, small white-and-orange flowers that lasted only a single night before falling to the lawn beneath. Then she went inside, and summoned Veena and Bhaskar. They were staying at Prem Nivas for a few days, as was old Mrs Tandon. Kedarnath was away in the south, soliciting the next season's orders at a time when, owing to the moisture in the air, the production of shoes in Brahmpur was slower than usual. Always away, always away, Veena complained to her mother.

Mrs Mahesh Kapoor had chosen a time of day when her husband would not be at home to mock her devotions. She now entered the small room, a mere alcove in the verandah separated by a curtain, that she had set aside for her puja. She placed two small wooden platforms on the floor, on one of which she sat, on one of which she placed a clay lamp, a candle in a low brass stand, a tray, a small bronze bell, a silver bowl half full of water, and a flatter bowl with a small heap of uncooked grains of white rice and some dark red powder. She sat facing a small ledge above a low cupboard. On this ledge stood a number of bronze statuettes of Shiva and other gods and a beautiful portrait of the infant Krishna playing the flute.

She moistened the red powder, then leaned forward intently and touched it with her finger to the foreheads of the gods, and then, leaning forward once again and closing her eyes, applied some to her own forehead. In a quiet voice she said:

'Veena, matches.'

'I'll get them, Nani,' said Bhaskar.

'You stay here,' said his grandmother, who planned to say a special prayer for him.

Veena came back from the kitchen with a huge box of matches. Her mother lit the lamp and the candle. Noisy people, the endless guests who stayed at Prem Nivas, were walking around talking on the verandah outside, but they did not distract her. She lit the lamp and candle, and placed these two lights on the tray. Ringing the bell with her left hand, she picked up the tray with her right, and described a motion in the air around the portrait of Krishna —not in the form of a circle but something much more irregular, as if she were circumscribing a presence that she saw before her eyes. Then she got up slowly and quite painfully from her confined posture, and did the same for the other gods in the statuettes and calendars scattered around the little room: the statue of Shiva; a picture of Lakshmi and Ganesh together, which included a small mouse nibbling at a laddu; a calendar from 'Paramhans and Co., Chemists and Druggists' of Rama, Sita, Lakshman and Hanuman with the sage Valmiki seated on the ground in front of them writing their story on a scroll; and several others.

She prayed to them, and she asked for comfort from them: nothing for herself, but health for her family, a long life for her husband, blessings on her two grandchildren, and ease to the souls of those no longer here. Her mouth worked silently as she prayed, unselfconscious of the presence of her daughter and her grandson. Throughout she kept the bell lightly ringing.

Finally, the puja was over, and she sat down after putting the things away in the cupboard.

She turned to Veena, and addressed her with the affectionate word for 'son':

'Bété, get Pran on the line, and tell him I want to go with him to the Radhakrishna Temple on the other side of the Ganga.'

This was shrewd. If she had phoned Pran directly, he would have tried to wriggle out of it. Veena, however, who knew he was well enough to go, told him quite firmly that he couldn't upset their mother on Janamashtami. So in a short while all of them – Pran, Veena, Bhaskar, old Mrs Tandon, and Mrs Mahesh Kapoor – were sitting in a boat that was making its way across the water.

'Really, Ammaji,' said Pran, who was not pleased to be dragged from his work, 'if you think of Krishna's character – flirt, adulterer, thief –'

His mother held up her hand. She was not annoyed so much as disturbed by her son's remarks.

'You should not be so proud, son,' she said, looking at him with concern. 'You should humble yourself before God.'

'I may as well humble myself before a stone,' suggested Pran. 'Or ... or a potato.'

His mother considered his words. After a few more splashes of the boatman's oars, she said in gentle rebuke: 'Don't you even believe in God?'

'No,' said Pran.

His mother was silent.

'But when we die —' she said, and was silent once more.

'Even if everyone I loved were to die,' said Pran, irked for no obvious reason, 'I would not believe.'

'I believe in God,' volunteered Bhaskar suddenly. 'Especially in Rama and Sita and Lakshman and Bharat and Shatrughan.' In his mind there was no clear distinction yet between gods and heroes, and he was hoping to get the part of one of the five swaroops in the Ramlila later this year. If not, he would at least be enrolled in the monkey army and get to fight and have a good time. 'What's that?' he said suddenly, pointing at the water.

The broad, grey-black back of something much larger than a fish had appeared momentarily from beneath the surface of the Ganga, and had sliced back in again.

'What's what?' asked Pran.

'There — that —' said Bhaskar, pointing again. But it had disappeared again.

'I didn't see anything,' said Pran.

'But it was there, it was there, I saw it,' said Bhaskar. 'It was black and shiny, and it had a long face.'

Upon the word, and as if by magic, three large river-dolphins with pointed snouts suddenly appeared to the right of the boat and started playing in the water. Bhaskar laughed with delight.

The boatman said, in his Brahmpuri accent: 'There are dolphins here, in this stretch of the water. They don't come out often, but they are here all right. That's what they are, dolphins. No one fishes them, the fishermen protect them and kill the crocodiles in this stretch. That is why there are no crocodiles until that far bend, there beyond the Barsaat Mahal. You are lucky to see them. Remember that at the end of the journey.'

Mrs Mahesh Kapoor smiled and passed him a coin. She remembered the time when the Minister Sahib had lived for a year in Delhi and she had gone on a pilgrimage to the region hallowed by Krishna. There, in the deep water of the Yamuna just below the temple at Gokul she and the other pilgrims had watched transfixed as the large black river turtles swam lazily to and fro. She thought of them, and of these dolphins, as good creatures, innocent and blessed. It was to protect the innocent, whether man or beast, to cure the recurring ills of the world, and to establish righteousness that Krishna had come down to earth. He had revealed his glory in the Bhagavad Gita on the battlefield of the Mahabharata. Pran's dismissive manner of speaking of him – as if God should be judged by human standards rather than trusted and adored – disturbed and hurt her. What, she asked herself, had happened in one generation that of her three children, only one continued to believe in what their forefathers had believed for hundreds, indeed thousands, of years?

14.13

ONE morning, a few weeks before Janamashtami, Pandit Jawaharlal Nehru, his mind ostensibly on his files, was thinking back to the time when he was very young, and was unable to keep awake, despite all his mother's blandishments and reproaches, until the midnight hour when Krishna was born in the prison cell. Now, of course, he rarely got to sleep before midnight.

Sleep! It was one of his best-loved words. In Almora Jail he had often been worried by the news he received of his wife Kamala's condition, and his helplessness upset him for a while, but somehow he still managed to sleep soundly in the hill air. On the verge of sleep he often thought what a wonderful and mysterious thing it was. Why should he awake from it? Suppose he did not wake up at all. When he had watched by his father's sickbed, he had mistaken his death for a deep sleep.

He sat at his desk now, his chin resting on his hand, and glanced for a second or two at the photograph of his wife before continuing with his dictation. Thousands of letters every day, a relay of stenographers, endless work in Parliament and in his offices in the South Block and in his office here at home, endless, endless, endless. It was a principle with him never to leave any paper undealt with, any letter unanswered when he went to sleep. And yet he could not help feeling that a sort of vacillation lay hidden in this dispatch. For though he kept up scrupulously with his paper-work, he was too self-analytical not to realize that he avoided coming to terms with less tractable matters – more muddled, more human, more full of bitterness and conflict – like the one that faced him in his own party. It was easier to be indecisive when busy.

He had always been busy except when he was in jail. No, even that was not true: it was in the many jails he had known that he had done most of his reading and almost all of his writing. All three of his books had been written there. Yet it was there too that he had for once had the time to notice what he now had no time to: the bare treetops day by day becoming greener above the high walls of Alipore Jail, the sparrows nesting in the huge barred barn that had housed him in Almora, the glimpse of fresh fields when the warders opened for a second or two the gate of his cell yard in Dehradun.

He got up from his desk and went to the window, from where he had an unimpeded view of the entire garden of Teen Murti House. This used to be the residence of the Commander-in-Chief under the Raj, and it was now his residence as Prime Minister. The garden was green with the monsoons. A little boy of four or five, the child of one of the servants perhaps, was jumping up and down beneath a mango tree, trying to pluck something from a low branch. But surely it was a little late for mangoes?

Kamala, now – he often felt that his imprisonment had been harder on her than on him. They had been married – married off to each other by their parents – very young, and he had only forced himself to make time for her when her illness was beyond cure. His autobiography had been dedicated to her – too late for her to have known. It was only when she was almost lost to him that he had realized how much he loved her. He recalled his own despairing words: 'Surely she was not going to leave me now when I needed her most? Why, we had just begun to know and understand each other really; our joint life was only now properly beginning. We relied so much on each other, we had so much to do together.'

Well – all that had been a long time ago. And if there had been pain and sacrifice and long absence when he had been detained as a guest of the King, at least the battle-lines had been clear. Now, everything was muddied. Old companions had turned political rivals. The purposes for which he had fought were being undermined and perhaps he himself was to blame for letting things slide so long. His supporters were leaving the Congress Party, and it had fallen into the hands of conservatives, many of whom saw India as a Hindu state where others would have to adapt or suffer the consequences.

There was no one to advise him. His father was dead. Gandhiji was dead. Kamala was dead. And the friend whom he might have unburdened himself to, with whom he had celebrated the midnight hour of Independence, was far away. She, so elegant herself, had often teased him about his fastidiousness in dress. He touched the red rose – in this season it came from Kashmir – in the buttonhole of his white cotton achkan, and smiled.

The naked child, having missed several times, had now got a few bricks from near a flowerbed, and was painstakingly building himself a little platform. He stood on it and reached out towards the branch, but again without success. Both he and the bricks came tumbling down.

Nehru's smile grew wider.

'Sir?' said the stenographer, his pencil still poised.

'Yes, yes, I'm thinking.'

Huge crowds and loneliness. Prison and Prime Minister-ship. Intense activity and a longing for nothingness. 'We too are tired.'

He would have to do something, though, and soon. After the elections it would be too late. In a sense this was a sadder battle than he had ever fought before.

A scene from Allahabad more than fifteen years earlier came before his eyes. He had been out of prison for five months or so, and expected any day to be re-arrested on some charge or other. He and Kamala had finished tea, Purushottamdas Tandon had just joined them, and they were standing together talking on the verandah. A car had driven up, a police officer had got out, and they had known immediately what it meant. Tandon had shaken his head and smiled wryly, and Nehru had greeted the apologetic policeman with the ironically hospitable comment: 'I have been expecting you for a long time.'

Out on the lawn now, the little boy had piled the bricks on top of each other in a different formation, and was tentatively climbing up again. In an all-or-nothing endeavour, instead of merely reaching out towards the branch, he jumped up to grasp the fruit. But he did not succeed. He fell, hurt himself on the bricks, sat down on the damp grass, and began to cry. Alerted by the sound, the mali emerged, and took in the scene in an instant. Conscious that the Prime Minister was watching from the window of his office, he ran towards the child, shouting angrily, and struck him hard across the face. The child burst into a renewed fit of weeping.

Pandit Nehru, scowling with anger, rushed into the garden, ran up to the mali, and slapped him several times, furious that he should have attacked the child.

'But, Panditji –' said the mali, so thunderstruck that he made no attempt to protect himself. He had only been teaching the trespasser a lesson.

Nehru, still furious, gathered the dirty and terrified little boy into his arms, and, after talking to him gently, put him down. He told the mali to pluck some fruit immediately for the child, and threatened to sack him on the spot.

'Barbarous,' he muttered to himself as he walked back across the lawn, frowning as he realized that his white achkan was now entirely smeared with mud.

Delhi, August 6, 1951

Dear Mr. President,

I beg to tender my resignation from membership of the Congress Working Committee and the Central Election Board. I shall be grateful if you will be good enough to accept these resignations.

Yours sincerely,
Jawaharlal Nehru

This formal letter of resignation to the President of the Congress Party, Mr Tandon, was accompanied by a letter beginning: 'My dear Purushottamdas,' and ending:

You will forgive me if by resigning I cause you embarrassment. But the embarrassment has been there anyhow for both of us and others and the best way to deal with it is to remove the cause.

Yours affectionately,
Jawaharlal Nehru

Mr Tandon replied as soon as he read the letter a couple of days later. In his reply he wrote:

You have yourself as the leader of the nation appealed to Congressmen and to the country to present a united front to the situation that is facing us both externally and internally. The step that you propose to take, namely, that of resigning from the Working Committee and the Parliamentary Board, goes directly against that appeal for solidarity and is likely to create a schism in the Congress which has greater potentiality for harm to the country than any that the Congress has yet had to face.

I beg of you not to precipitate a crisis at the present juncture and not to press your resignation. I cannot accept it. If you insist on it the only course left to me will be to place it before the Working Committee for consideration. I trust that, in any case, you will attend the meeting of the Working Committee on the 11th instant.

If, to keep you in the Working Committee, it is necessary or desirable that I should resign the president-ship of the Congress I am ready to do so with great pleasure and goodwill.

Yours affectionately,
Purushottamdas Tandon

Pandit Nehru replied the same day, making rather clearer than before what had been on his mind:

I have been long distressed at the attitude of some persons which indicated that they wished to drive out others from the Congress who did not fit in with their views or their general outlook. . . .

I feel that the Congress is rapidly drifting away from its moorings and more and more the wrong kind of people, or rather people who have the wrong kind of ideas, are gaining influence in it. The public appeal of the Congress is getting less and less. It may, and probably will, win elections. But, in the process, it may also lose its soul. . . .

I am fully conscious of the consequences of the step I am taking and even the risks involved. But I think these risks have to be taken, for there is no other way out. . . .

I am more conscious than anyone else can be of the critical situation which the country has to face today. I have to deal with it from day to day. . . .

There is no reason why you should resign the president-ship of the Congress. This is not a personal matter.

I do not think it would be proper for me to attend the meeting of the Working Committee. My presence will embarrass me as well as others. I think it is better that the questions that arise should be discussed in my absence.

*

Mr Tandon replied the next day, which was the day before the actual meeting of the Congress Working Committee. He agreed, 'It is no use winning the elections if, as you say, the Congress is "to lose its soul" in the process.' But it was clear from his letter that the two men had very different conceptions of the soul of the Congress. Tandon wrote that he would place Nehru's letter of resignation before the Working Committee the next day. 'But that need not prevent your taking part in some other matters. May I suggest that you come to the meeting though only for a short time and that the matters which concern you may not be discussed in your presence.'

*

Nehru attended the meeting of the Working Committee and explained his letter of resignation; he then withdrew so that the others could discuss it in his absence. The Working Committee, faced with the unimaginable loss of the Prime Minister, attempted to find some way of accommodating him. But all immediate attempts to mediate the conflict failed. One possible means was to reconstitute the Working Committee and appoint new general secretaries of the Congress so that Nehru would feel less 'out of tune' with them. But here Tandon put his foot down. He said he would rather resign than allow the office of the Congress President to become subservient to that of the Prime Minister. Appointing the Working Committee was part of the role of the former; it could not be tampered with at the will of the latter. The Working Committee passed a resolution calling upon Nehru and Tandon to confer to solve the crisis, but could do nothing further.

Two days later, on Independence Day, Maulana Azad resigned from the Congress Working Committee. Just as the resignation from the Congress of the popular Muslim leader Kidwai had stung Nehru into action, the resignation of the scholarly Maulana cemented it. Since it was largely these two leaders at the national level whom the Muslims looked to in their post-Partition uncertainty – Kidwai because of his own great popularity, not only among Muslims but among Hindus, and Azad because of the respect in which he was held and the fact that he had Nehru's ear – it now appeared that the Congress was in danger of losing its Muslim following entirely.

S.S. Sharma made every possible effort to dissuade Nehru from what looked increasingly like a collision course between him and Tandon. In this, Sharma was one of many, for leaders like Pant of U.P. and B.C. Roy of West Bengal had attempted to do the same. When they got to Delhi, however, they found Nehru as vaguely adamant as ever. But this time S.S. Sharma's ego was slightly hurt: Nehru did not suggest that he come to Delhi and join his Cabinet. Presumably he either knew that Sharma would beg off as usual – or he was not pleased with Sharma's attempts to paper over the cracks in the party – or else the invitation had been displaced by other matters of greater urgency that were on his mind.

One of these matters was a meeting of the Members of Parliament from the Congress Party, which he had called in order to explain the events that had led to the drastic rift and his resignation. He asked them for a vote of confidence. Whatever their political complexion (and there were, as Nehru was soon to discover when the bill to reform Hindu law was brought up before Parliament, many die-hard conservatives among them), most Congress MPs perceived the dispute largely in terms of a conflict between the mass party and the parliamentary party. They were not enamoured of the thought that the Congress President would try to dictate policy to them through resolutions of the Congress, as he had on several occasions stated that he had the right to do. Besides, they knew that without the national image of Nehru they would have a very difficult time getting themselves re-elected in a few months' time. Whether it was because of the fear that they would lose their soul or their power or the elections, they overwhelmingly passed a motion of confidence in his favour.

Since confidence in Nehru as such had never been at issue, Tandon's supporters resented this action, which smacked of the build-up to a showdown. They were also somewhat surprised by Nehru's most uncharacteristic unwillingness to back down, to understand their point of view, to postpone unpleasantness, to compromise. He was talking now of insisting on a 'change of outlook' and a 'clear-cut verdict'. And rumours had begun to float about of the possibility of Nehru taking on the Congress Presidency together with the Prime Ministership, an onerous – and, in some ways, ominous – combination that he had in the past declared himself against on principle. Indeed, in 1946, he had resigned the Congress Presidency to become the Prime Minister. But now that the main threat to his power came from within the Congress Party itself he had begun to hedge on the issue.

'I definitely think that it is a wrong thing practically and even otherwise, for the Prime Minister to be the Congress President,' he declared at the end of August, just a week before the decisive meeting of the All-India Congress Committee in Delhi. 'But that being the general rule, I cannot say what necessity might compel one to do in special circumstances when a hiatus is created or something like that.'

The typically floppy Nehruvian tail to that sentence could not entirely counter the surprising inflexibility of the body.

14.15

WITH every passing day, however, it became increasingly clear that the month-long deadlock could not be resolved except by some desperate expedient. Tandon refused to reconstitute the Working Committee at Nehru's dictation, and Nehru rejected anything less if he was to rejoin it.

On the 6th of September, the entire Working Committee dramatically submitted their resignations to Tandon, hoping thereby to retrieve what would otherwise have been, in an open conflict, an irretrievable position for both him and them. The idea was that the much larger body of the All-India Congress Committee (due to meet two days later) should now pass a resolution asking Nehru to withdraw his resignation, expressing confidence in Tandon, and requesting Tandon to reconstitute the Working Committee by election. Nehru and Tandon could then draw up a slate of candidates jointly. Tandon could remain President; he would not have surrendered any presidential prerogatives to the Prime Minister; he would merely have implemented, as he was bound to, a resolution of the AICC.

This should have been, the Working Committee thought, agreeable to both Nehru and Tandon. In fact it was agreeable to neither.

That evening Nehru told a public meeting that he wanted the All-India Congress Committee to make it entirely clear which way the Congress should go and who should hold its reins. He was in a fighting mood.

The next evening Tandon too, at a press conference, refused the face-saving formula proffered by his Working Committee. He said: 'If I am asked by the All-India Congress Committee to reconstitute the Working Committee in consultation with A, B, or C, I would beg the AICC not to press that request but to relieve me.'

He placed the responsibility for the crisis squarely on Nehru's shoulders. Nehru had tendered his resignation over the issue of the reconstitution of the Working Committee; and, by so doing, he had forced its members to tender their own.

Tandon stated that he could not accept these forced resignations. He repudiated any suggestion by Nehru that the Congress Working Committee had failed to implement Congress resolutions. He made a few references to Pandit Nehru as 'my old friend and brother' and added: 'Nehru is not an ordinary member of the Working Committee; he represents the nation more today than any other individual does.' But he reaffirmed the inflexibility of his own stand, which was one based on principle; and he announced that if no acceptable formula could be reached by mediators, he would resign from the Congress Presidency the next day.

And this was what, the next day, with good grace –

despite the many personal attacks against him in the press, despite what he saw as the impropriety of Nehru's tactics, and despite the bitterness and length of the battle – he did.

In a noble gesture, which did much to assuage any residual bitterness, he joined the Working Committee under the newly-elected Congress President, Jawaharlal Nehru.

It was in effect a coup; and Nehru had won.

Apparently.

14.16

THE jeep had hardly arrived at Baitar Fort than Maan and Firoz got horses saddled and rode off to hunt. The oily munshi was all smiles when he saw them, and brusquely ordered Waris to make the necessary preparations. Maan swallowed his gorge with difficulty.

'I'll go with them,' said Waris, who was looking even more rough-hewn than before, perhaps because he appeared not to have shaved for a few days.

'But have a bit of lunch before you disappear,' said the Nawab Sahib.

The two impatient young men refused.

'We've been eating all along the way,' said Firoz. 'We'll be back before dark.'

The Nawab Sahib turned to Mahesh Kapoor and shrugged.

The munshi showed Mahesh Kapoor to his rooms, almost frantic with solicitude. That the great Mahesh Kapoor, who by a stroke of the pen had wiped vast estates off the map of the future, was here in person was a matter of incalculable significance. Perhaps he would be in power again and might threaten to do worse. And the Nawab Sahib had not merely invited him here, but was behaving towards him with great cordiality. The munshi licked the edge of his walrus-like moustache and puffed up the three flights of steep stairs, murmuring platitudes of intense geniality. Mahesh Kapoor said nothing in reply.

'Now, Minister Sahib, I was given instructions that you

were to stay in the best suite in the Fort. As you see, it overlooks the mango orchard and then the jungle – there is no sign of disturbance, none of the hubbub of Baitar town, nothing to disturb your contemplation. And there, Minister Sahib, as you can see, are your son and the Nawabzada riding through the orchard. How well your son rides. I had the opportunity of making his acquaintance when he was last at the Fort. What an upright, decent young man. The moment I set eyes on him I knew that he must come from a remarkable family.'

'Who is the third?'

'That, Minister Sahib, is Waris,' said the munshi, who succeeded in conveying by his tone of voice, how very little he thought of that bumpkin.

Mahesh Kapoor paid the bumpkin no further attention.

'When is lunch?' he asked, looking at his watch.

'In an hour, Minister Sahib,' said the munshi. 'In an hour. And I will personally send someone up to inform you when it is time. Or perhaps you would care to walk around the grounds? The Nawab Sahib said that you wish to be disturbed as little as possible these next few days – that you wish to think in quiet surroundings. But the garden is very fresh and green in this season – perhaps a little overgrown, that's all – but nowadays, with the new financial stringency – as Huzoor is aware, this is not the most auspicious of times for estates such as ours – but we will make every effort, every effort to ensure that your stay is a happy one, a restful one, Minister Sahib. As Huzoor has no doubt been informed already, Ustad Majeed Khan will be arriving here later this afternoon by train, and will be singing for Huzoor's pleasure both today and tomorrow. The Nawab Sahib was most insistent that you were to be allowed time to yourself for rest and thought, rest and thought.'

Since his effusive prattle had elicited no response, the munshi continued:

'The Nawab Sahib himself is a great believer in rest and thought, Minister Sahib. He spends most of his time in the library when he is here. But if I might suggest to you one or two of the sights of the town that Huzoor would find interesting: the Lal Kothi and, of course, the Hospital, which was founded and expanded by former Nawabs, but which we continue to contribute to, for the betterment of the people. I have already arranged a tour –'

'Later,' said Mahesh Kapoor. He turned his back on the munshi and looked out of the window. The three horsemen appeared sporadically along a forest trail, then grew increasingly difficult to follow.

It was good, thought Mahesh Kapoor, to be here at the estate of his old friend, away from Prem Nivas and the bustle of the house, away from the mild pestering of his wife, the constant incursions of his relatives from Rudhia, the management of the Rudhia farm, away – most of all – from the confused politics of Brahmpur and Delhi. For he was, most atypically, sick of politics for the moment. No doubt he would be able to follow events via the radio or day-old editions of the newspapers, but he would be spared the direct personal turmoil of contact with fellow-politicians and bewildered or importunate constituents. He had no work in the Secretariat any more; he had taken leave from the Legislative Assembly for a few days; and he was not even attending meetings of his new party, one of which was to be held in Madras next week. He was no longer certain that he really belonged in that party even if he still, nominally, belonged to it. In the wake of Nehru's famous victory over the Tandonites in Delhi, Mahesh Kapoor felt the need to re-assess his attitude towards the Congress. Like many other secessionists, he was disappointed that Nehru had not split the party and joined him. On the other hand, the Congress no longer appeared to be such a hostile place for those of his views. He was especially interested in seeing what the mercurial Rafi Ahmad Kidwai would do if Nehru asked the seceders to return.

So far, however, Kidwai had acted his usual elusive self, keeping his options open with a series of contradictory statements. He had announced from Bombay that he was delighted by Nehru's victory, but that he saw little prospect of his own return to the Congress fold. 'Realizing now that their election prospects were not bright they have deserted Mr Tandon and sponsored Pandit Nehru's candidature. This is pure opportunism. The future of the country is dark if such opportunism is tolerated,' he said. However, the wily Mr Kidwai added that if certain 'undesirable elements' who were still entrenched in the executives of states such as Uttar Pradesh, Purva Pradesh, Madhya Pradesh, and Punjab were to be removed by Pandit Nehru, 'then everything would be all right'. As if to make matters murkier, he mentioned that the KMPP was thinking of an electoral alliance with the Socialist Party, and that then 'the chances of the party succeeding in most of the states are very bright'. (The Socialist Party, for its part, showed no enthusiasm to ally itself with anyone.) A couple of days later Kidwai suggested a purge of 'corrupt elements' in the Congress as a condition for winding up his own party and rejoining the Congress. Kripalani, however, who was the other half of the K-K combine, insisted that there was no question of his deserting the KMPP and rejoining the Congress, no matter what its internal rearrangements.

Kidwai was something of a river-dolphin. He enjoyed swimming in silty water and outwitting the crocodiles around him.

Meanwhile, all the other parties were commenting, with various degrees of heat, upon Nehru's reassertion of his power within the Congress. Of the socialist leaders, one denounced the combination of the Congress Presidency with the Prime Ministership as a sign of totalitarianism; one said that this was not a worrying possibility, as Nehru did not have the makings of a dictator; and one simply pointed out that, as a tactical move, the Congress had improved its chances in the General Elections.

On the right, the President of the Hindu Mahasabha inveighed against what he called 'the proclamation of dictatorship'. He added: 'Although this dictatorship has raised Pandit Nehru to the highest pinnacle of glory, it has also got within itself the germs of his fall.'

Mahesh Kapoor attempted to dismiss this confusion of opinion and information from his mind and tried to come to grips with three straightforward questions. Since he was feeling sick of politics, should he simply leave politics and retire? If not, which party was the best place for him – or should he fight as an Independent? And if he decided to remain and fight the next election, what was the best place for him to fight from? He walked up to the roof, where an owl, ensconced in a tower, was startled by his approach; he walked down to the rose-garden, where the flowerless bushes edged the fresh green lawn; and he wandered through some of the rooms of the Fort, including the huge Imambara downstairs. Sharma's words to him in another garden came back to haunt his mind. But by the time the anxious munshi had found him and announced that the Nawab Sahib was awaiting him at lunch, he was no nearer a solution.

14.17

THE NAWAB SAHIB had been sitting for the last hour in the huge, vaulted, dust-pervaded library with its green glass skylight, working on his edition of the poems of Mast, some of the documents and manuscripts for which were held here at the Fort. He was deeply saddened by the deterioration of this magnificent room and the poor condition of its holdings. He planned to move all the Mast materials to his library in Brahmpur at the end of this visit, together with some of the other more precious contents of the Baitar Fort library. Given his reduced means, the library at the Fort was becoming impossible for him to maintain – and the dust and confusion and infestation of silverfish grew worse month by month.

This was somewhat on his mind when he greeted his friend in the great, gloomy dining hall decorated with dark portraits of Queen Victoria, King Edward VII and the Nawab Sahib's own ancestors.

'I'll take you to the library after lunch,' said the Nawab Sahib.

'Good,' said Mahesh Kapoor. 'But the last time I entered

a library of yours I recall that it resulted in the destruction of one of your books.'

'Well,' said the Nawab Sahib thoughtfully, 'I don't know which is worse: the cerebral seizures of the Raja of Marh or the cancer of the silverfish.'

'You should keep your books in better order,' said Mahesh Kapoor. 'It's one of the finest private libraries in the country. It would be a tragedy if the books were to be damaged.'

'I suppose you might say it is a national treasure,' said the Nawab Sahib with a faint smile.

'Yes,' said Mahesh Kapoor.

'But I doubt that the national purse would open itself to help maintain it.'

'No.'

'And, thanks to plunderers like you, I certainly can't any longer.'

Mahesh Kapoor laughed. 'I was wondering what you were aiming at. Anyway, even if you lose your case in the Supreme Court you'll still be a few thousand times richer than me. And I work for my living, unlike you – you're just decorative.'

The Nawab Sahib helped himself to some biryani. 'You're a useless person,' he countered. 'What does a politician do, in fact, except make trouble for others?'

'Or counter the troubles that other people make,' said Mahesh Kapoor.

Neither he nor the Nawab Sahib needed to mention what he was referring to. Mahesh Kapoor had succeeded, while he was still with the Congress, in getting the Minister for Rehabilitation to bend the ear of the Prime Minister to get the government to grant the Nawab Sahib and Begum Abida Khan certificates entitling them to the permanent retention of their property in Brahmpur. This had been necessary in order to counter an order by the Custodian-General of Evacuee Property issued on the grounds that Begum Abida Khan's husband was a permanent evacuee. Their case was only one of several where similar action had needed to be taken at the governmental level.

'Well,' continued the ex-Minister of Revenue, 'where will you cut back when half your rents disappear? I really do hope that your library won't suffer.'

The Nawab Sahib frowned. 'Kapoor Sahib,' he said, 'I am less concerned about my own house than those who depend on me. The people of Baitar expect me to put on a proper show for our festivals, especially for Moharram. I will have to keep that up in some fashion. I have certain other expenses – the hospital and so on, the monuments, the stables, musicians like Ustad Majeed Khan who expect to be retained by me a couple of times a year, poets who depend on me, various endowments, pensions; God – and my munshi – knows what else. At least my sons don't make vast demands on me; they're educated, they have their own professions, they aren't wastrels, like the sons of others in my position –'

He stopped suddenly, thinking of Maan and Saeeda Bai.

'But tell me,' he continued after the briefest of pauses, 'what, for your part, are you going to do?'

'Me?' said Mahesh Kapoor.

'Why don't you run for the elections from here?'

'After what I've done to you – you want me to run from here?'

'No, really, Kapoor Sahib, you should.'

'That's what my grandson says.'

'Veena's boy?'

'Yes. He's worked out that this consituency is the most favourable for me – among the rural ones.'

The Nawab Sahib smiled at his friend and looked towards the portrait of his great-grandfather. Mahesh Kapoor's remark had made him think of his own grandsons, Hassan and Abbas – who had been named after the brothers of Hussain, the martyr of the festival of Moharram. He thought for a while of Zainab too, and the unhappiness of her marriage. And, fleetingly and regretfully, of his own wife, who lay buried in the cemetery just outside the Fort.

'But why do you think it is such a good idea?' Mahesh Kapoor was asking.

A servant offered the Nawab Sahib some fruit – including custard-apples, whose short season had just begun – but the Nawab Sahib refused them. Then he changed his mind, felt three or four sharifas and selected one. He broke the knobbly fruit in half and scooped out the delicious white pulp with a spoon, placing the black seeds (which he transferred from his mouth to the spoon) on the side of his plate. For a minute or two he said nothing. Mahesh Kapoor helped himself to a sharifa as well.

'It is like this, Kapoor Sahib,' said the Nawab Sahib, thoughtfully, putting together the two equal scooped-out halves of his sharifa and then separating them. 'If you look at the population in this constituency, it is about evenly divided between Muslims and Hindus. This is just the kind of place where Hindu communalist parties can whip people into an anti-Muslim panic. They have already begun to do so. And every day there are fresh reasons for Hindus and Muslims to learn to hate each other. If it isn't some idiocy in Pakistan – some threat to Kashmir, some plot, real or imagined, to divert the waters of the Sutlej or to capture Sheikh Abdullah or to impose a tax on Hindus – it is one of our own home-grown brilliances like the dispute over that mosque in Ayodhya which has suddenly flared up again recently after lying quiet for decades – or our own Brahmpur version, which is different – but not so vastly different. Bakr-Id is coming up in a few days; someone is certain to kill a cow somewhere instead of a goat, and there'll be fresh trouble. And, worst of all, Moharram and Dussehra will coincide this year.'

Mahesh Kapoor nodded, and the Nawab Sahib continued. 'I know that this house was one of the strongholds of the Muslim League. I have never held with my father's or my brother's views on the subject, but people do not discriminate in these matters. To men like Agarwal the very name of Baitar is like a red rag – or perhaps a green one – to a bull. Next week he will try to force his Hindi bill through the Legislative Assembly, and Urdu, my language, the language of Mast, the language of most of the Muslims of this province, will be made more useless than ever. Who can protect us and our culture? Only people like you, who know us as we are, who have friends among us, who do not prejudge us because you can judge us from experience.'

Mahesh Kapoor did not say anything, but he was moved by the trust reposed in him by the Nawab Sahib.

The Nawab Sahib frowned, divided his black sharifa pips into two separate piles with his spoon, and went on. 'Perhaps it is worse in this part of the country than elsewhere. This was the heartland of the struggle for Pakistan, this is where much of the bitterness was created, but those of us who have not been able to or have chosen not to leave our homeland are now a smaller minority in a predominantly Hindu territory. No matter what troubles rage around us, I will probably manage to keep my head above water; so will Firoz and Imtiaz and Zainab – those who have means always manage somehow. But most of the ordinary people I talk to are downcast and fearful; they feel beleaguered. They mistrust the majority, and they feel mistrusted by them. I wish you would fight from here, Kapoor Sahib. Quite apart from my support, I hear that your son has made himself popular in the Salimpur area.' The Nawab Sahib allowed himself a smile. 'What do you think?'

'Why don't you stand for election yourself?' asked Mahesh Kapoor.'Quite frankly, I would rather stand, if I have to, from my old urban constituency of Misri Mandi, re-drawn though it has been – or, if it has to be a rural one, from Rudhia West, where my farm is located. Salimpur-cum-Baitar is too unfamiliar. I have no personal standing here – and no personal scores to settle.' Mahesh Kapoor thought for a moment of Jha, then continued: 'It's you who should stand. You would win hands down.'

The Nawab Sahib nodded. 'I have thought about it,' he said slowly. 'But I am not a politician. I have my work – if nothing else, my literary work. I would not enjoy sitting in the Legislative Assembly. I have been there and I have heard the proceedings and, well, I am not suited for that kind of life. And I'm not sure I would win hands down.

For a start, the Hindu vote would be a problem for me. And, most importantly, I just couldn't go around Baitar and the villages asking people for votes – at least I could not do that for myself. I would not be able to bring myself to do that.'

He looked up again, rather wearily, at the sword-bearing portrait on the wall before continuing: 'But I am keen that a decent, a suitable man wins from here. Apart from the Hindu Mahasabha and that lot, there is someone here whom I have been good to and who hates me as a result. He plans to try to get the local Congress ticket, and if he becomes the local MLA, he can do me all kinds of harm. I have already decided to nominate a candidate of my own who will fight as an Independent in case this man does get the Congress nomination. But if you stand – whether from this KMPP or from the Congress, or as an Independent – I will make sure that you get my support. And that of my candidate.'

'He must be a very compliant candidate,' said Mahesh Kapoor, smiling. 'Or a self-abnegating one. A rare thing in politics.'

'You met him briefly when we got down from the jeep,' said the Nawab Sahib. 'It's that fellow Waris.'

'Waris!' Mahesh Kapoor laughed out loud. 'That servant of yours, that groom or whatever, the unshaven chap who went off hunting with Firoz and my son?'

'Yes,' said the Nawab Sahib.

'What kind of MLA do you think he would make?'

'Better than the one he'd displace.'

'You mean, better a fool than a knave.'

'Better a yokel, certainly.'

'You're not serious about Waris.'

'Don't underestimate him,' said the Nawab Sahib. 'He may be a bit crude, but he's capable and he's tough. He sees things in black and white, which is a great help when you're electioneering. He would enjoy campaigning, whether for himself or for you. He's popular around these parts. Women think he's dashing. He's absolutely loyal to me and the family, especially to Firoz. He would do anything for us. I really mean that – he keeps threatening to shoot people who have done us harm.' Mahesh Kapoor looked a little alarmed. 'Incidentally, he likes Maan; he took him around the estate when he was here. And the only reason he's unshaven is because he doesn't shave from the sighting of the new moon till Bakr-Id, ten days later. Not that he's all that religious,' added the Nawab Sahib, with a mixture of disapproval and indulgence. 'But if he doesn't have to shave for one reason or another, he feels that he may as well take advantage of the dispensation.'

'Hmm,' said Mahesh Kapoor.

'Think about it.'

'I will. I will think about it. But where I stand from is only one of three questions in my mind.'

'What are the other two?'

'Well – which party?'

'Congress,' said the Nawab Sahib, naming without hesitation the party which had done so much to dispossess him.

'Do you think so?' said Mahesh Kapoor. 'Do you think so?'

The Nawab Sahib nodded, looked at the debris on his plate, then rose. 'And your third question?'

'Whether I should continue in politics at all.'

The Nawab Sahib looked at his old friend in disbelief. 'It's something you ate this morning,' he said. 'Or else a piece of wax in my ear.'

14.18

WARIS, meanwhile, was having a fine time away from his standard duties in the Fort and the officious eye of the munshi. He galloped happily along; and although he took with him the gun that he had obtained a licence for, he did not use it, since the hunt was not his prerogative. Maan and Firoz enjoyed the ride as much as the hunting; and there was enough game for them to spot or follow even though they did not actively seek it out. The part of the estate through which they rode was a mixture of firm woodland, rocky soil, and what in this season was sporadic marsh. Early in the afternoon, Maan saw a herd of nilgai splashing through the edge of the marsh at a distance. He aimed, fired, missed, and cursed himself good-naturedly. Later, Firoz got a large spotted deer with magnificent antlers. Waris noted the spot, and when they passed a small hamlet not far away he told one of the local men to get it to the Fort on a cart by the evening.

Apart from deer and wild boar, which they spied only occasionally, there were a great number of monkeys, especially langurs, and a great variety of birds, including peacocks, scattered throughout the forest. They even saw a peacock dancing. Maan was transported with pleasure.

It was a warm day, but there was plenty of shade, and from time to time they rested. Waris noticed how delighted the two young men were in each other's company, and he joined in their banter whenever he felt like it. He had liked Maan from the first, and Firoz's friendship with him cemented his liking.

As for the two young masters, having been cooped up in Brahmpur for a while, they were happy to be out in the open. They were sitting in the shade of a large banyan tree and talking.

'Have you ever eaten peacock?' Waris asked Maan.

'No,' said Maan.

'It's excellent meat,' said Waris.

'Come on, Waris, the Nawab Sahib doesn't like people shooting peacocks on the estate,' said Firoz.

'No, no, by no means,' said Waris. 'But if you shoot one of them by mistake, you may as well eat the bastard. No point in leaving him to the jackals.'

'By mistake!' said Firoz.

'Yes, yes,' said Waris, making an effort at invention or recall. 'Once there was a sudden rustling in the bushes when I was sitting under a tree – just as we are sitting now, and I thought it was a wild boar – so I shot at it, and it was only a peacock. Poor thing. Delicious.'

Firoz frowned. Maan laughed.

'Shall I tell you the next time I do that?' asked Waris. 'You'll like it, Chhoté Sahib, let me tell you. My wife is an excellent cook.'

'Yes, I know,' said Firoz, who had several times eaten jungle-fowl cooked by her.

'Chhoté Sahib always believes in doing the right thing,' said Waris. 'That's why he is a lawyer.'

'I thought that was a disqualification,' said Maan.

'Soon, if they make him a judge, he will get the zamindari decisions reversed,' asserted Waris.

There was a sudden movement in the bushes not thirty feet away. A large wild boar, its tusks lowered, came charging in their direction, aiming either towards them or past them. Without thinking, Maan lifted his rifle and – hardly taking conscious aim – fired at it when it was just a dozen feet away.

The boar collapsed in its tracks. The three of them got to their feet – at first in fear – and then, standing around it at a safe distance, heard its grunts and squeals and watched it thrash about for a minute or so, while its blood soaked the leaves and mud around it.

'My God –' said Firoz, staring at the beast's huge tusks.

'Not a fucking peacock,' was Waris's comment.

Maan did a little dance. He was looking a little dazed and very pleased with himself.

'Well, what will we do with it?' said Firoz.

'Eat it, of course,' said Maan.

'Don't be an idiot – we can't eat it. We'll give it to – well, someone or other. Waris can tell us which of the servants won't object to eating it.'

They loaded the boar onto Waris's horse. By the time it was evening they were all tired. Maan was resting his rifle in the saddle, holding the reins in his left hand and practising polo strokes with his right. They had come within a few hundred yards of the mango orchard, and were looking forward to a rest before the evening meal. The deer would have preceded them; perhaps it was being prepared at this very moment. It was almost sunset. From the mosque at the Fort they could hear the sound of the evening azaan in the muezzin's fine voice. Firoz, who had been whistling, stopped.

They were almost at the border of the orchard when Maan, who was riding in front, saw a jungle cat on the path – a couple of feet long, lithe and long-legged, with fur that looked to him almost golden, and with sharp, greenish eyes that it turned upon him in an intent and narrow, almost cruel, gaze. The horse, who had not resented the weight of the boar or its scent of death, came to an immediate halt, and Maan again instinctively raised his rifle.

'No – no – don't –' cried Firoz.

The jungle cat bounded away into the tall grass to the right of the path.

Maan turned angrily on Firoz.

'What do you mean – don't? I would have had it.'

'It isn't a tiger or a panther – there's nothing heroic about shooting one. Anyway, my father doesn't like killing what we can't eat – unless, of course, it's an immediate threat.'

'Come on, Firoz, I know you've shot panther before,' said Maan.

'Well, I don't shoot jungle cats. They're too beautiful and harmless. I'm fond of them.'

'What an idiot you are,' said Maan regretfully.

'All of us like jungle cats,' explained Firoz, who didn't want his friend to remain annoyed. 'Once Imtiaz shot one, and Zainab didn't speak to him for days.'

Maan was still shaking his head. Firoz drew alongside him and put his arm around his shoulder. By the time they had crossed the orchard, Maan was mollified.

'Did a cart carrying a deer come this way?' asked Waris of an old man who was walking through the orchard with a stick.

'No, Sahib, I haven't seen any such thing,' said the old man. 'But I've only been here a little while.' He stared at the trussed-up boar, its huge-tusked head hanging across the haunch of Waris's horse.

Waris, pleased to have been called Sahib, grinned and

said optimistically: 'It's probably got to the kitchen by now. And we'll be late for the evening prayer. Too bad,' he grinned.

'I need a bath,' said Firoz. 'Have you had our things put in my room?' he asked Waris. 'Maan Sahib is sleeping in my room.'

'Yes, I gave orders just before we left. That's where he slept the last time too,' said Waris. 'But I doubt he'll be able to sleep tonight with that grim fellow gargling away till the early hours. Last time it was the owl.'

'Waris pretends to be thicker than he is,' said Firoz to Maan. 'Ustad Majeed Khan will be singing tonight after dinner.'

'Good,' said Maan.

'When I suggested getting your favourite singer over, my father got annoyed. Not that I was really serious.'

'Well, Veena studies music under Khan Sahib, so we're used to that sort of gargling,' said Maan.

'Here we are,' said Firoz, dismounting and stretching himself.

14.19

THE excellent dinner included a roasted haunch of venison. They ate not in the dark-panelled dining room but in the highest of the several open courtyards under a clear sky. Unlike at lunch, the Nawab Sahib was rather quiet throughout dinner; he was thinking about his munshi, who had annoyed him by complaining about the size of the fee that Ustad Majeed Khan now felt he should command. 'What? All this for a song?' was the munshi's view of the matter.

After dinner they adjourned to the Imambara to listen to Ustad Majeed Khan. Since Moharram was still a few weeks away, the Imambara continued to be used as a general meeting hall; indeed, the Nawab Sahib's father had used it as a durbar of sorts except during Moharram itself. Despite the fact that the Nawab Sahib was in general devout – there were, for example, no drinks served at dinner – a number of paintings depicting scenes from the martyrdom of Hussain decorated the walls of the Imambara. These, out of consideration for anyone who followed very strictly the injunctions against representational art, especially with respect to religious depiction, had been covered with white cloth. A few tazias – replicas in various materials of the tomb of Hussain – stood at the far end behind tall white pillars; some Moharram lances and standards stood in a corner.

Chandeliers glinted down in red and white from the ceiling, but the electric bulbs they contained had not been lit. So that the distant sound of the generator would not disturb them, the hall had been lit by candles instead. Ustad Majeed Khan was notoriously temperamental when it came to his art. It was true that he often practised at home in the midst of an appalling domestic racket, the result of his wife's excessive sociability. But when he performed, even the necessity of earning his living at least partly through the diminishing patronage of zamindars and princes would not allow him to compromise with the seriousness of attention he demanded – and the absolute lack of disturbance. If it was true, as it was said, that he sang for himself and God alone, it was equally true that this bond was strengthened by an appreciative audience and strained by a restless one. The Nawab Sahib had not invited any guests from the town of Baitar, largely because he had not found anyone there who appreciated good music. Apart from the musicians there was no one but himself, his friend, and their two sons.

Ustad Majeed Khan was accompanied by his own tabla player; and by Ishaq Khan as an accompanying vocalist, not as a sarangi player. The great musician was now at the stage where he treated Ishaq not as a student or even a nephew but as a son. Ishaq had all the musicality Ustad Majeed Khan could have wished for in a student; and he had, besides, that passionate reverence for his teachers – including his own late father – that had got him into trouble with his Ustad in the first place. Their subsequent reconciliation had astonished them both. The Ustad had

73

seen in it the hand of God. Ishaq did not know what to ascribe it to, but was deeply grateful. Since adaptation to the style of the main performer was instinctive to him as a sarangi player, Ishaq, who had a fine voice, quickly adapted himself to the style of his teacher; and since his teacher's style drew with it a certain bent of mind and a certain manner of creativity, within a few months of his first lessons with Ustad Majeed Khan he was singing with a confidence and ease that first alarmed, and then – despite his own considerable ego – pleased the Ustad. At last he had a disciple worthy of the name; and one, moreover, who more than compensated in the honour he did him for any fleeting dishonour he may have been guilty of in the past.

It was late when they settled down after dinner, and Ustad Majeed Khan immediately, and without tackling any lighter raga to warm up his voice, began to sing Raag Darbari. How appropriate, thought the Nawab Sahib, was the raag to the surroundings, and how his father, whose one sensual vice had been music, would have enjoyed it had he been alive. The regally slow unfolding of the alaap, the wide vibratos on the third and sixth degrees, the stately descents in alternating rises and falls, the richness of the Khan Sahib's voice accompanied from time to time by his young disciple, and the invariant, undazzling, solid beat of the tabla created a structure of majesty and perfection that hypnotized both musicians and audience. Very rarely did any of the listeners even say, 'wah! wah!' at some particular brilliance. It was more than two hours and late after midnight when he ended.

'See to the candles, they are guttering,' said the Nawab Sahib quietly to a servant. 'Tonight, Khan Sahib, you have outdone yourself.'

'Through His grace, and yours.'

'Will you rest a little?'

'No, there is life in me still. And the will to sing before this kind of an audience.'

'What will you give us now?'

'What will it be?' said Ustad Majeed Khan, turning to

Ishaq. 'It's far too early for Bhatiyar, but I'm in the mood for it, so God will forgive us.'

The Nawab Sahib, who had never heard the master sing with Ishaq before, and had certainly never seen – or even heard of – the Khan Sahib consulting anyone about what he should or should not sing, was astonished, and asked to be introduced to the young singer.

Maan suddenly recalled where he had seen Ishaq Khan.

'We've met before,' he said before he could give himself time to think. 'At Saeeda Begum's, wasn't it? I've been trying to work it out. You were her sarangi player, weren't you?'

There was a sudden and frigid silence. Everyone present except the tabla player looked at Maan with discomfiture or shock. It was as if no one wanted to be reminded at this magical moment of anything from that other world. Whether as patron or employee or lover or acquaintance or fellow-artist or rival, in one sense or another every one of them was tied to Saeeda Bai.

Ustad Majeed Khan got up, as he said, to relieve himself. The Nawab Sahib had bowed his head. Ishaq Khan had started talking in a low voice to the tabla player. Everyone seemed eager to exorcize this unwanted muse.

Ustad Majeed Khan returned and sang Raag Bhatiyar as beautifully as if nothing had happened. Now and then he paused to sip a glass of water. At three o'clock he got up and yawned. As if in response, so did everyone else.

14.20

LATER in their room, Maan and Firoz lay in bed, yawning and talking.

'I'm exhausted. What a day,' said Maan.

'It's good I didn't open my emergency bottle of Scotch before dinner, or we'd have been snoring through the Bhatiyar.'

There was a pause.

'What exactly was wrong about my mentioning Saeeda Bai?' asked Maan. 'Everyone froze. So did you.'

'Did I?' said Firoz, leaning on his arm and looking at his friend rather intently.

'Yes.' Firoz was wondering what, if anything, to say in reply, when Maan went on: 'I like that photograph, the one by the window of you and the family – you look just the same now as then.'

'Nonsense,' laughed Firoz. 'I'm five years old in that photograph. And I'm much better-looking now,' he added in a factual sort of way. 'Better-looking than you, in fact.'

Maan explained himself. 'What I meant was that you have the same kind of look, with your head tilted at an angle and that frown.'

'All that that tilt reminds me of is the Chief Justice,' said Firoz. After a while he said: 'Why are you leaving tomorrow? Stay for a few days more.'

Maan shrugged. 'I'd like to. I don't get much time to spend with you. And I really like your Fort. We could go hunting again. The trouble is that I promised some people I know in Debaria that I'd be back for Bakr-Id. And I thought I'd show Baoji the place as well. He's a politician in search of a constituency, so the more he sees of this one the better. Anyway, it's not Bakr-Id so much as Moharram that's important at Baitar, didn't you tell me?'

Firoz yawned again. 'Yes, yes, that's right. Well, but this year I won't be here. I'll be in Brahmpur.'

'Why?'

'Oh, Imtiaz and I take it by turns: Burré Sahib one year, Chhoté Sahib the next. The fact is, we haven't shared a Moharram since we've been eighteen. One of us has to be here, and the other in Brahmpur to take part in the processions there.'

'Don't tell me you beat your breast and flagellate yourself,' said Maan.

'No. But some people do. Some even walk on fire. Come and see it for yourself this year.'

'Perhaps I will,' said Maan. 'Goodnight. Isn't the light switch by your side of the bed?'

'Do you know that even Saeeda Bai closes shop during Moharram?' asked Firoz.

'What?' said Maan in a more wakeful voice. 'How do you know?'

'Everyone knows,' said Firoz. 'She's very devout. Of course, the Raja of Marh will be pretty annoyed. Usually he counts on having a good time around Dussehra.'

Maan's response was a grunt.

Firoz went on: 'But she won't sing for him, and she won't play with him. All she'll consent to sing is marsiyas, laments for the martyrs of the battle of Karbala. Not very titillating.'

'No,' agreed Maan.

'She won't even sing for you,' said Firoz.

'I suppose not,' said Maan, slightly crestfallen and wondering why Firoz was being so unkind.

'Nor for your friend.'

'My friend?' asked Maan.

'The Rajkumar of Marh.'

Maan laughed. 'Oh, him!' he said.

'Yes, him,' said Firoz.

There was something in Firoz's voice that reminded Maan of their younger days.

'Firoz!' laughed Maan, turning towards him. 'All that is over. We were just kids. Don't tell me you're jealous.'

'Well, as you once said, I never tell you anything.'

'Oh?' said Maan, rolling over on his side towards his friend, and taking him in his arms.

'I thought you were sleepy,' said Firoz, smiling to himself in the dark.

'So I am,' said Maan. 'But so what?'

Firoz began to laugh quietly. 'You'll think I've planned all this.'

'Well, perhaps you have,' said Maan. 'But I don't mind,' he added with a small sigh as he passed a hand through Firoz's hair.

MAHESH KAPOOR and Maan borrowed a jeep from the Nawab Sahib and drove off towards Debaria. So full of pits and pools was the dirt road that led off the main road to the village that it was normally impossible to get to it in the monsoon. But they managed somehow, partly because it had not rained too heavily in the past week.

Most of the people they met were very pleased to see Maan; and Mahesh Kapoor – in spite of what the Nawab Sahib had told him – was quite astonished at the popularity of his vagabond son. It struck him with amazement that of the two activities necessary for a politician – the ability to win votes, and the capacity to do something with your mandate after victory – Maan possessed the first in abundant measure, at least in this constituency. The people of Debaria had taken him to their hearts.

Rasheed, of course, was not there, since it was term-time, but his wife and daughters were staying with his father rather than hers for a few days. Meher and the village urchins and the shock-headed Moazzam were all delighted at Maan's arrival. He provided even more entertainment than the various black goats tied up to posts and trees around the village that were due to be sacrificed the next day. Moazzam, who had always been fascinated by Maan's watch, demanded to see it again. Even Mr Biscuit paused in his eating to yell out a triumphant if variant version of the azaan before Baba, furious at his impiety, dealt with him.

The orthodox Baba, who had told Maan to come back for Bakr-Id but had very much doubted that he would, did not actually smile – but it was very apparent that he was glad to see him. He praised him to his father.

'He is a good boy,' said Baba, nodding vigorously at Mahesh Kapoor.

'Yes?' said Mahesh Kapoor.

'Yes, indeed, he is very respectful of our ways. He has won our hearts by his simplicity.'

Simplicity? thought Mahesh Kapoor, but said nothing.

That Mahesh Kapoor, the architect of the Zamindari Abolition Act, had come to the village was a great event in itself, and it was also a matter of great consequence that he had arrived in the Nawab Sahib's jeep. Rasheed's father had no strong views on politics except if something impinged on his interests: any such view was communism. But Baba, who wielded considerable influence in the surrounding villages, respected Mahesh Kapoor for his resignation from the Congress at about the time that Kidwai had resigned. He also identified, as did many people, with the Nawab Sahib.

Now, however, he thought – and said as much to Mahesh Kapoor – that the best thing would be for all men of good will to rejoin the Congress. Nehru was firmly back in charge, he felt, and with Nehru, more than with anyone else, people of his community felt safe. When Maan mentioned that his father was considering the option of contesting from Salimpur-cum-Baitar, Baba was encouraging.

'But try to get the Congress ticket. The Muslims will vote for Nehru – and so will the chamars. As for the others, who knows: it will depend on events – and how you run your campaign. The situation is very fluid.'

That was a phrase that Mahesh Kapoor was to hear, read, and use a great deal in the days to come.

The brahmins and banias of the village came separately to see him as he sat on a charpoy under the neem tree outside Rasheed's father's house. The Football was particularly ingratiating. He told Mahesh Kapoor of Baba's methods of foiling the Zamindari Act by forced evictions (omitting his own attempts in the same direction), and offered to act as Mahesh Kapoor's lieutenant in the area should he choose to run from there. Mahesh Kapoor, however, was noncommittal in his response. He did not much care for the scheming Football; he realized that there were very few brahmin families in Debaria, none in the twin village of Sagal and not many in the villages around; and it was clear to him that the man who mattered most of all was the ancient and energetic Baba. He disliked what he heard about the evictions, but he tried not to dwell on the sufferings he knew they caused. It was difficult to be someone's guest and prosecutor simultaneously, more particularly if you were hoping to seek their help in the near future.

Baba asked him a number of questions over tea or sherbet.

'How long will you be conferring on us the honour of your presence?'

'I will have to leave this evening.'

'What? Aren't you going to stay for Bakr-Id?'

'I can't. I've promised to be in Salimpur. And if it rains, the jeep will be stuck here, perhaps for days. But Maan will be here for Bakr-Id.' Mahesh Kapoor did not need to mention that if he was sounding out a future fief the subdivisional town of Salimpur, with its concentrated knot of population, was an essential stop, and that his participation there in the Id celebrations would pay rich dividends in the future. Maan had told him that his secular stand was popular in the town.

The one person who had very mixed feelings about Mahesh Kapoor's visit was the young Netaji. When he heard that Mahesh Kapoor was in the village, he rushed back from Salimpur on his Harley Davidson. Netaji, who had recently been put up for election to the District Congress Committee, felt that this was an opportunity for contact-making that was too good to be true. Mahesh Kapoor had a name and a following, and, however thinly such silver was beaten into foil, he hoped that some of it might cover him as well. On the other hand, he was no longer the powerful Minister of Revenue but plain Shri Mahesh Kapoor, MLA, a member no longer of the Congress but of a party of uncertain prospects and unmemorable name that even now seemed riven with disagreement about whether to wind itself up. And the acrobatic Netaji, who had his ear to the ground and his finger to the wind, had concrete proof of Mahesh Kapoor's weakening might and clout. He had heard about Jha's power in Mahesh Kapoor's own tehsil of Rudhia, and had imbibed with particular satisfaction the news of the swift transfer of the arrogant English speaking SDO who had snubbed him so painfully on the platform of Salimpur Station.

Mahesh Kapoor took a walk around the village in the company of Maan and Baba – as well as Netaji, who forced himself upon them. Mahesh Kapoor appeared to be in an excellent mood; perhaps the respite from Prem Nivas had done him good – or the open air – or Majeed Khan's singing – or simply the fact that he could see political possibilities in this constituency. They were tailed by a motley gang of village children and a small, black, continually bleating goat that one of the children was driving along the muddy path – a glossy-headed goat, with pointed little horns, thick black eyebrows and mild, sceptical yellow eyes. Everywhere Maan was greeted with friendliness and Mahesh Kapoor with respect.

The great monsoon sky over the twin villages – indeed, over much of the Gangetic plain – was overcast, and people were worried that it might rain the next day, on Bakr-Id itself, and spoil the festivities. Mahesh Kapoor for the most part managed to avoid any political talk. All that sort of thing could be left to electioneering time. Now he simply made sure that he was recognized. He did namasté or adaab as was appropriate, drank tea, and made small talk.

'Should I go around Sagal as well?' he asked Baba.

Baba thought for a second. 'No, don't do that. Let the web of gossip do its work.'

Finally, having made his rounds, Mahesh Kapoor drove off, but not before thanking Baba and saying to Maan:

'Perhaps you and Bhaskar are right. At any rate, even if you didn't learn much Urdu, you weren't wasting your time.'

Maan could not remember the last time his father had praised him. He was extremely pleased, and more than a little surprised. A couple of tears came to his eyes!

Mahesh Kapoor pretended not to notice, nodded, looked at the sky, and waved in a general way to the gathered populace as the jeep squelched off.

MAAN slept in the verandah because of the possibility of rain. He woke up late, but did not find Baba louring angrily over him asking him why he hadn't been to morning prayer.

Instead, Baba said: 'So you've got up, I see. Will you be coming to the Idgah?'

'Yes,' said Maan. 'Why not?'

'Then you should get ready quickly,' he said, and patted a fat black goat that was browsing meditatively near the neem tree.

The others in the family had preceded them, and now Baba and Maan walked across the fields from Debaria to Sagal. The Idgah was located in Sagal; it was part of the school near the lake. The sky was still overcast, but there was also an undercast of light that added brilliance to the emerald colour of the transplanted rice. Ducks were swimming in a paddy field, scrabbling for worms and insects. Everything was fresh and refreshing.

All around them, approaching the Idgah from different directions, were men, women and children, all dressed in festive attire – new clothes, or – for those who could not afford them – clothes that were spotlessly clean and freshly pressed. They converged on the school from all the surrounding villages, not merely from Debaria and Sagal. The men were for the most part dressed in white kurta-pyjamas; but some wore lungis, and some allowed themselves coloured kurtas, though of a sober colour. Maan noticed that their headgear varied from white, close-fitting filigreed caps to black, glossy ones. The women and children wore brightly coloured clothes – red, green, yellow, pink, maroon, blue, indigo, purple. Even under the black or dark blue burqas worn by most of the women Maan could see the hems of their coloured saris or salwaars, and the attractive anklets and chappals on feet patterned with bright red henna and splashed with the inescapable mud of the monsoon.

It was while they were walking along the narrow paths

that a man, old, thin and hungry-looking, and dressed in nothing but a dirty dhoti, intercepted Baba and, with his hands folded, said in a desperate voice:

'Khan Sahib, what have I done that you should do this to me and to my family? How can we manage now?'

Baba looked at him, thought for a second, and said: 'Do you want your legs broken? I don't care what you say now. Did you think about this when you went to the kanungo to complain?'

He then kept walking towards Sagal. Maan, however, was so troubled by the man's look – half of hatred born of betrayal, half of supplication – that he stared at his deeply wrinkled face and tried to recall – as he had with the sarangi player – where he had seen him before.

'What's the story behind this, Baba?' he asked.

'Nothing,' said Baba. 'He wanted to get his grasping fingers on my land, that's all.' It was clear from his voice that he wished to dismiss the subject from his mind.

As they approached the school, the sounds of a loud-speaker could be heard repeating the praises of God or else telling the people to get ready for the Id prayers, and not to delay too long at the fair. 'And, ladies, please make yourselves proper; we are about to start; please hurry up, everyone.'

But it was difficult to get the holiday-making crowd to hurry up. Some people, certainly, were performing their ritual ablutions by the edge of the tank; but most of them were milling around the stalls and the improvised market that had formed just outside the school gates along the length of the earthen embankment. Trinkets, bangles, mirrors, balloons – and, best of all, food of all kinds from alu tikkis to chholé to jalebis extruded spluttering into hot tawas, barfis, laddus, flossy pink candy, paan, fruit – everything that Mr Biscuit could have dreamed of in his least constrained imaginings. Indeed, Mr Biscuit was loitering near a stand with half a barfi in his hand. Meher, who had been given some sweets by her grandfather, was sharing them with other children. Moazzam, on the other hand, was busy befriending various vulnerable children –

'for their money', as the shaven but mustachioed Netaji pointed out to Maan.

The women and girls disappeared into the school building, from where they would watch and participate in the proceedings, while the men and boys arranged themselves in rows on long rolls of cloth in the compound outside. There were more than a thousand men present. Maan saw among them several of the elders of Sagal who had given Rasheed so much trouble outside the mosque, but he did not see the sick old man whom Rasheed and he had gone to visit – not that in such a large gathering it was possible to be certain about who was not there. He was asked to sit on the edge of the verandah next to two bored policemen of the P.P. Police Constabulary, who lounged about in greenish khaki and surveyed the scene. They were there to see that order was maintained and to act as witnesses in case the Imam's sermon contained anything inflammatory, but their presence was resented, and their manner betrayed that they knew it.

The Imam began the prayers, and the people stood up and knelt down as required with the awesome unanimity of the Islamic service. In the middle of the two snatches of prayers, however, there was a sound of distant thunder. By the time the Imam had begun his sermon, the congregation appeared to be paying more attention to the sky than to his words.

It began to drizzle, and the people started getting restless. Eventually they settled down, but only after the Imam had interrupted his sermon to upbraid them:

'You! Don't you have any patience in the sight of God – on the day we have met to remember the sacrifice of Ibrahim and Ismail? You put up with rain in the fields, and yet on this day you act as if a few drops of water will dissolve you away. Don't you know how those who are doing the pilgrimage this year are suffering on the scorching sands in Arabia? Some of them have even died of heatstroke – and you are in terror of a few drops from the sky. Here I am talking about Ibrahim's willingness to sacrifice his son, and all you are thinking of is keeping dry – you will not even sacrifice a few minutes of your time. You are like the impatient ones who would not come to prayer because the merchants had arrived. In the Surah al-Baqa-rah, the very surah after which this festival is named, it says:

> Who therefore shrinks from the religion
> of Abraham, except he be foolish-minded?

And later it says:

> We will serve thy God and the God of thy fathers
> Abraham, Ishmael and Isaac, One God;
> to him we surrender.

Is this the quality of your surrender? Stop it, stop it, good people; be still, and do not fidget!

> Surely, Abraham was a nation
> obedient unto God, a man of pure faith
> and no idolater,
> showing thankfulness for His blessings;
> He chose him, and He guided him
> to a straight path.
> And We gave him in this world good,
> and in the world to come he shall be
> among the righteous.
> Then We revealed to thee: "Follow thou
> the creed of Abraham, a man of pure faith
> and no idolater."'

The Imam got quite carried away with his quotations in Arabic, but after a while he returned to his quieter discourse in Urdu. He talked about the greatness of God and his Prophet, and how everyone should be good and devout in the spirit of Abraham and the other prophets of God.

When it was over, everyone joined in asking for God's blessings, and, after a few minutes, dispersed to their villages, making sure they returned by a different route from the one they had taken to arrive.

'And tomorrow, being Friday, we'll get another sermon,' some of them grumbled. But others thought that the Imam had been at his best.

14.23

AS he walked back into the village, Maan bumped into the Football, who drew him aside.

'Where have you been?' asked the Football.

'To the Idgah.'

The Football looked unhappy. 'That is not a place for us,' he said.

'I suppose not,' said Maan indifferently. 'Still, no one made me feel unwelcome.'

'And now, you will watch all this cruel goat business?'

'If I see it, I'll see it,' said Maan, who thought that hunting, after all, was as bloody a business as sacrificing a goat. Besides, he didn't want to get into a false compact of solidarity with the Football, whom he did not greatly care for.

But when he saw the sacrifice, he did not enjoy it.

In some of the houses of Debaria, the master of the house himself performed the sacrifice of the goat or, occasionally, the sheep. (Cow sacrifice had been forbidden in P.P. since British times because of the danger of religious rioting.) But in other houses, a man specially trained as a butcher came around to sacrifice the animal that symbolized God's merciful replacement for Abraham's son. According to popular tradition this was Ishmael, not Isaac, though the Islamic authorities were divided on this matter. The goats of the village seemed to sense that their final hour was at hand, for they set up a fearful and pitiful bleating.

The children, who enjoyed the spectacle, followed the butcher as he made his rounds. Eventually he got to Rasheed's father's house. The plump black goat was made to face west. Baba said a prayer over it while Netaji and the butcher held it down. The butcher then put his foot on its chest, held its mouth, and slit its throat. The goat gurgled, and from the slash in its throat bright red blood and green, half-digested grass poured out.

Maan turned away, and noticed that Mr Biscuit, wearing a garland of marigolds that he must have somehow procured at the fair, was looking at the slaughter with a phlegmatic air.

But everything was proceeding briskly. The head was chopped off. The skin on the legs and underbelly was slit and the entire skin peeled off the fat. The hind legs were broken at the knee, then bound, and the goat was hung from a branch. The stomach was slit, and the entrails, with their blood and filth were pulled out. The liver and lungs and kidneys were removed, the front legs cut off. Now the goat, which only a few minutes ago had been bleating in alarm and gazing at Maan with its yellow eyes, was just a carcass, to be divided in thirds among the owners, their families, and the poor.

The children looked on, thrilled and enthralled. They especially enjoyed the sacrifice itself and later the spilling out of the grey-pink guts. Now they stared as the front quarters were set aside for the family, and the rest of the body chopped into sections across the ribs and placed on the scales on the verandah to be balanced. Rasheed's father was in charge of the distribution.

The poor children – who got to eat meat very rarely – crowded forward to get their share. Some clustered around the scales and grabbed at the chunks of meat, others tried to but were pushed back; most of the girls sat quietly in one place, and eventually got served. Some of the women, including the wives of the chamars, appeared to be very shy and could hardly bring themselves to come forward to accept the meat. Eventually they carried it off in their hands, or on bits of cloth or paper, praising and thanking the Khan Sahib for his generosity or complaining about their share as they walked to the next house to receive their portion of its sacrifice.

THE previous evening's meal had been hurried because of the preparations for Bakr-Id; but today's late afternoon meal was relaxed. The tastiest dish was one made from the liver, kidneys and tripe of the goat that had just been slaughtered. Then the charpoys were shifted under the neem tree beneath which the goat had earlier been quietly browsing.

Maan, Baba and his two sons, Qamar – the sarcastic schoolteacher from Salimpur – as well as Rasheed's uncle, the Bear, were all present for lunch. The talk turned naturally to Rasheed. The Bear asked Maan how he was doing.

'Actually, I haven't seen him since I returned to Brahmpur,' confessed Maan. 'He has been so busy with his tuitions, I suppose, and I myself with one thing and another –'

It was a feeble excuse, but Maan had not neglected his friend by intention. It was just the way things happened to be in his life.

'I did hear that he was involved in the student Socialist Party,' said Maan. 'With Rasheed, though, there's no fear that he'll neglect his studies.' Maan did not mention Saeeda Bai's remark about Rasheed.

Maan noticed that only the Bear seemed truly concerned about Rasheed. After a while, and long after the conversation had passed on to other matters, he said: 'Everything he does he does too seriously. His hair will be white before he's thirty unless someone teaches him to laugh.'

Everyone was constrained when talking about Rasheed. Maan felt this acutely; but since no one – not even Rasheed himself – had told him how he had disgraced himself, he could not understand it. When Rasheed had read Saeeda Bai's letter to him, Maan, being denied an early return to Brahmpur, had been seized with such restlessness that he had very shortly afterwards set out on a trek. Perhaps it was his own preoccupation that had blinded him to the tension in the family of his friend.

14.25

NETAJI planned to hold a party the next night – a feast of meat for which he had another goat handy – in honour of various people of importance in the subdivision: police and petty administration officials and so on. He was trying to persuade Qamar to get the headmaster of his school in Salimpur to come. Qamar not only flatly refused, but made no secret of his contempt for Netaji's transparent attempts to ingratiate himself with the worthy and the influential. Throughout the afternoon Qamar found some way or other of needling Netaji. At one point he turned to Maan with new-found friendliness and said, 'I suppose that when your father was here, he was unable to shake off our Netaji.'

'Well,' said Maan, resisting a smile, 'Baba and he very kindly showed my father around Debaria.'

'I thought it might be something like that,' said Qamar. 'He was having tea with me in Salimpur when he heard from a friend of mine, who had dropped in, that the great Mahesh Kapoor was visiting his own native village. Well, that was the end of tea with me. Netaji knows which cups of tea contain more sugar. He's as smart as the flies on Baba's sputum.'

Netaji, affecting to be above such crude taunts, and still hopeful that he might be able to bag the headmaster, refused to get outwardly annoyed, and Qamar retired, disappointed.

Not long after this late lunch Maan took a rickshaw to Salimpur in order to catch the train back to Baitar. He didn't want to arrive after Firoz had left. Although it was easier for Firoz, given his profession, to get away from Brahmpur than it was for Imtiaz, he might well turn out to have some date in court or some urgent call from a senior for a conference that would cut short his visit.

An attractive young woman with hennaed feet was singing a song to herself in the local accent as the rickshaw passed her. Maan caught just a few lines as he turned around to get a glimpse of her unveiled face:

'O, husband, you can go but get me something from the
   fair –
Vermilion to overfill the parting in my hair.
Bangles from Firozabad, jaggery to eat –
And sandals made by Praha for my henna-coloured feet.'

She gave Maan a glance that was at once amused and
angry as he gazed at her without embarrassment, and the
memory of her look kept him in good spirits all the way to
Salimpur Station.

14.26

NEHRU'S coup was not followed by wholesale subservience
to his desires.

In Delhi, in Parliament, opposition by MPs from all
sections of the House, including his own, forced him to
abandon his attempt to pass the Hindu Code Bill. This
legislation, very dear to the Prime Minister's heart – and to
that of his Law Minister, Dr Ambedkar – aimed to make
the laws of marriage, divorce, inheritance and guardianship
more rational and just, especially to women.

Nor were the more orthodox Hindu legislators by any
means on the defensive in the Legislative Assembly at
Brahmpur. L.N. Agarwal had sponsored a bill that would
make Hindi the state language from the beginning of the
new year, and the Muslim legislators were rising one by
one to appeal to him and to the Chief Minister and to the
House to protect the status of Urdu. Mahesh Kapoor, who
had returned to Brahmpur from the countryside, took no
active part in the debate, but Abdus Salaam, his former
Parliamentary Secretary, did make a couple of brief
interventions.

Begum Abida Khan, of course, was at her oratorical
best:

Begum Abida Khan: It is all very well for the honourable
Minister to take the name of Gandhiji when espousing the

cause of Hindi. I have nothing against Hindi, but why does he not agree to protect the status of Urdu, the second language of this province, and the mother-tongue of the Muslims? Does the honourable Minister imagine that the Father of the Nation, who was willing to give his life to protect the minority community, would countenance a bill like the present one which will cause our community and our culture and our very livelihood to die a lingering death? The sudden enforcement of Hindi in the Devanagari script has closed the doors of government service on the Muslims. They cannot compete with those whose language is Hindi. This has created a first-class economic crisis among the Muslims – many of whom depend on the services for their livelihood. All of a sudden they have to face the strange music of the P.P. Official Language Bill. It is a sin to take the name of Gandhiji in this context. I appeal to your humanity, you who have shot us and hunted us down in our houses, do not be the author of further miseries for us.

The Hon'ble the Minister for Home Affairs (Shri L.N. Agarwal): I will ignore, as I am sure the House would wish me to, this last remark, and simply thank the honourable member for her heart-felt advice. If it were equally brain-thought, there might have been grounds for accepting it. The fact of the matter is that duplication of all government work in two languages, two scripts, is utterly impracticable and unworkable. That is all there is to it.

Begum Abida Khan: I will not appeal to the chair against the expressions of the honourable Minister. He is telling the whole world that he thinks that Muslims have no rights and women have no brains. I am hoping to appeal to his better instincts, but what hope do I have? He has been the prime mover in this government policy of stifling Urdu, which has led to the disappearance of many Urdu publications. Why is Urdu receiving this step-motherly treatment at his hands? Why can the two brother languages not be adopted together? The elder brother has a duty to protect the younger brother, not to torment him.

The Hon'ble the Minister for Home Affairs (Shri L.N.

Agarwal): You are asking for a two-language theory now, you will be asking for a two-nation theory tomorrow.

Shri Jainendra Chandla (Socialist Party): I am pained at the twist given to the debate by the honourable Minister. While Begum Abida Khan, whose patriotism nobody can doubt, has only asked that Urdu should not be stifled, the honourable Minister is trying to import the two-nation theory into the debate. I too am dissatisfied with the progress of Hindi. All the work in offices is carried on in English still, despite the many resolutions and regulations. It is English that we should be working to displace, not each other's languages.

Shri Abdus Salaam (Congress): Some of my constituents have brought to my attention the fact that difficulties have been created in the syllabus for Urdu-reading students and that they have thus been deprived of the chance to study Urdu. If a small country like Switzerland can have four official languages, there can be no reason not to treat Urdu as at least a regional language in this state, which is several times as large. Facilities ought to be provided – and not only in name – for the teaching of Urdu in schools.

The Hon'ble the Minister for Home Affairs (Shri L.N. Agarwal): Our resources, unfortunately, are not unlimited. There are many madrasas and religious establishments all over the state where Urdu may be taught. As regards the official language of the state of Purva Pradesh, things must be made abundantly clear, so that there is no confusion, and people do not move on the wrong tracks from childhood, only to discover later that they are at a disadvantage.

Begum Abida Khan: The honourable Minister talks about how things must be made clear. But even the Constitution of India is not clear about the official language. It has stated that English will be replaced at the Centre after fifteen years. But even then it will not happen automatically. A commission will be appointed, which will go into the whole question and report to the government as to what progress Hindi has made and the question of replacing English completely will then be decided on a reasonable basis, not by fiat and prejudice. I wonder, if a foreign language like English can be tolerated in this way, why can Urdu not be tolerated? It is one of the glories of our province – it is the language of its finest poet, Mast. It is the language of Mir, of Ghalib, of Dagh, of Sauda, of Iqbal, of Hindu writers like Premchand and Firaq. Yet even though it has a richer tradition, Urdu does not claim equal status with Hindi. It can be treated like any other regional language. But it must not be dispossessed as is being done.

The Hon'ble the Minister for Home Affairs (Shri L.N. Agarwal): Urdu is not being dispossessed, as the honourable member supposes. Anyone who learns the Devanagari script will find no difficulty in coping.

Begum Abida Khan: Can the honourable Minister tell this House in all heart-felt honesty that there is no real difference between the two languages except one of script?

The Hon'ble the Minister for Home Affairs (Shri L.N. Agarwal): Heart-felt or otherwise, that is what Gandhiji planned: he aimed for Hindustani as the ideal, which would take both languages as its source.

Begum Abida Khan: I am not talking about ideals and about what Gandhiji planned. I am talking about facts and what is happening all around us. Listen to All India Radio and try to understand its news bulletins. Read the Hindi versions of our bills and acts – or if, like me and other Muslims and even many Hindus of this province, you cannot read them, then have them read out to you. You will not understand one word in three. It is all becoming stupidly and stiltedly Sanskritized. Obscure words are being dug out of old religious texts and being reburied in our modern language. It is a plot of the religious fundamentalists who hate anything to do with Islam, even Arabic or Persian words that the common people of Brahmpur have used for hundreds of years.

The Hon'ble the Minister for Home Affairs (Shri L.N. Agarwal): The honourable member has a gift for fantasy that excites my admiration. But she is, as usual, thinking from right to left.

Begum Abida Khan: How dare you speak like that? How dare you? I would like full-fledged Sanskrit to be made the official language of the state – then you too will see! One day it will be full-fledged Sanskrit that you will be forced to read and speak, and it will make you clutch at your hair even harder. Then you too will be made to feel a stranger in your own land. So it will be better if Sanskrit is made the official language. Then both Hindu and Muslim boys will have an equal start and be able to compete on an equal footing.

The debate proceeded in this manner, with importunate waves of protest washing over an adamant sea-wall. Finally, closure was moved by a member of the Congress Party and the House rose for the day.

14.27

JUST outside the chamber Mahesh Kapoor collared his old Parliamentary Secretary.

'So, you rogue, you're still with the Congress.'

Abdus Salaam turned around, pleased to hear the voice of his ex-Minister.

'We must talk about that,' he said, glancing a little to left and right.

'We haven't talked for a long time, it seems to me – ever since I've been in the opposition.'

'It isn't that, Minister Sahib –'

'Ah, at least you call me by my old title.'

'But of course. It's just that you've been away – in Baitar. Associating with zamindars, I hear,' Abdus Salaam couldn't help adding.

'Didn't you go back home for Id?'

'Yes, that's true. We've both been away, then. And before that I was in Delhi for the AICC meeting. But now we can talk. Let's go to the canteen.'

'And eat those fearful greasy samosas? You young people have stronger stomachs than us.' Mahesh Kapoor appeared, despite everything, to be in a good mood.

Abdus Salaam was in fact quite fond of the greasy samosas that the canteen provided as one of its snacks. 'But where else can we go, Minister Sahib? Your office, alas –' He smiled regretfully.

Mahesh Kapoor laughed. 'When I left the Cabinet, Sharma should have made you a Minister of State. Then you at least would have had an office of your own. What's the point of remaining a Parliamentary Secretary if there's no one to be secretary to?'

Abdus Salaam too started laughing in a gentle way. He was a scholarly rather than an ambitious man, and he often wondered how he had strayed into politics and why he had remained there. But he had discovered he had a sleepwalker's flair for it.

He thought about Mahesh Kapoor's last remark. 'If nothing else, there's a subject to handle,' he responded. 'The Chief Minister has left me free to manage that.'

'But until the Supreme Court decides the matter there's nothing you can do about it,' said Mahesh Kapoor. 'And even after they've decided whether the First Amendment is valid or not the zamindars' appeal against the High Court judgment about the act itself will have to be decided. And any action is bound to be stayed till then.'

'It's only a question of time; we'll win both cases,' said Abdus Salaam, looking into the vague middle distance as he sometimes did when thinking. 'And by then no doubt you will be Minister of Revenue again – if not something even better. Anything could happen. Sharma could be kicked upwards to the Cabinet in Delhi, and Agarwal could be murdered by one of Begum Abida Khan's glances. And since you would be back in the Congress you would be the obvious choice for Chief Minister.'

'Do you think so?' said Mahesh Kapoor, looking at his protégé piercingly. 'Do you think so? If you are doing nothing better, let's go home for a cup of tea. I like these dreams of yours.'

'Yes, I have been dreaming a lot – and sleeping a lot – these days,' said Abdus Salaam cryptically.

They continued to talk as they strolled along to Prem Nivas.

'Why did you not intervene in the discussion this afternoon, Minister Sahib?' asked Abdus Salaam.

'Why? You know the reason perfectly well. I can't read a word of Hindi, and I don't want attention drawn to the fact. I'm popular enough among the Muslims – it's the Hindu vote that will be my problem.'

'Even if you rejoin the Congress?'

'Even if I rejoin the Congress.'

'Do you plan to?'

'That is what I want to talk over with you.'

'I might be the wrong person to talk to.'

'Why?' asked Mahesh Kapoor. 'Surely you're not thinking of leaving it?'

'That's what I want to talk over with you.'

'Well,' said Mahesh Kapoor thoughtfully, 'this will require several cups of tea.'

Abdus Salaam did not know how to make small talk, so hardly had he sipped his tea than he plunged straight in with a question.

'Do you really think that Nehru is back in the saddle?'

'Do you really doubt it?' countered Mahesh Kapoor.

'In a way I do,' said Abdus Salaam. 'Look at this Hindu Code Bill. It was a great defeat for him.'

'Well,' said Mahesh Kapoor, 'not necessarily. Not if he wins the next election. Then he'll treat it as a mandate. In a way he's made certain of that, because it's now become an election issue.'

'You can't say he intended that. He simply wanted to pass the bill into law.'

'I don't disagree with that,' said Mahesh Kapoor, stirring his cup.

'And he couldn't hold his own MPs, let alone Parliament, together to pass it. Everyone knows what the President of India thinks of the bill. Even if Parliament had passed it, would he have signed it?'

'That is a separate issue,' said Mahesh Kapoor.

'You're right about that,' admitted Abdus Salaam. 'The

question in my mind, though, is one of grip and timing. Why place the bill before Parliament when there was so little time to argue it? A few discussions, a filibuster, and it was bound to die.'

Mahesh Kapoor nodded. He was thinking about something else too. It was the fortnight for the performance of shraadh, the rites to appease the spirits of one's dead. Mahesh Kapoor could never be prevailed upon to perform these rites, and this upset Mrs Mahesh Kapoor. And immediately after this fortnight came the nights of the Ramlila leading up to the fiery celebration of Dussehra. This was the great Hindu festive season, and it would continue till Divali. Nehru could not possibly have chosen a worse time, psychologically speaking, to introduce a bill that attempted to upset Hindu law and transform Hindu society.

Abdus Salaam, after waiting for Mahesh Kapoor to speak, continued: 'You saw what happened in the Assembly, you can see how the L.N. Agarwals of this world continue to operate. No matter what happens at the Centre, that is the shape of things to come in the states. At least, so I think. I do not see much changing. The people who have their hands on the party levers – people like Sharma and Agarwal – will not easily let Nehru prise them off. Look at how quickly they're rushing to form their election committees and to start their selection of candidates in the states. Poor Nehru – he is like a rich merchant, who, after crossing the seas, is drowned in a little stream.'

Mahesh Kapoor frowned: 'What on earth are you quoting from?' he asked.

'From a translation of your Mahabharata, Minister Sahib.'

'Well, I wish you wouldn't,' said Mahesh Kapoor, annoyed. 'I get enough of it at home without you – of all people – joining in.'

'I was only making the point, Minister Sahib, that it is the conservatives, and not our liberal Prime Minister, despite his great victory, who are still in control. Or so I think.'

Abdus Salaam did not sound unduly distressed by what doubtless must have distressed him a good deal. If anything, he sounded light-hearted, as if the pleasure of expounding the logic of his scenario sufficiently counterpoised the grimness of the scenario itself.

And, Mahesh Kapoor reflected, marvelling a little at the young man's attitude, things were, if looked at clearly, quite grim. Less than a week after Nehru had defeated Tandon – one of the two crucial resolutions for which had been sponsored by a party boss from West Bengal – the Congress Executive Committee and Election Committee from the state of West Bengal had with miraculous haste begun to deal with the applications for the nomination of candidates. Their purpose was clear: to forestall the effects of any change from the top, and to present the Centre with a fait accompli: a slate of candidates for the General Elections prepared and in place before any possible secessionists could return to the Congress fold and make a bid for candidature. The state Congress bosses had had to be restrained from carrying out their designs by the Calcutta High Court.

In Purva Pradesh too, the State Election Committee of the Congress had been elected with astonishing speed. Under the Congress constitution this had to consist of the President of the State Congress Committee and not more than eight nor less than four other members. If such haste had really been necessary in order to cope with urgent preliminary work, the entrenched powers could have contented themselves with electing a minimum of four members. But by electing all eight and not leaving a single spot vacant for anyone who might later return to the Congress, they had made it clear that, whatever they said in public in deference to Nehru's wishes, they were not serious about wishing the seceders to come back. For it was only through the activities of the Election Committee that Congressmen belonging to various groups could hope to get their due share of candidates – and through them their share of privilege and power.

Mahesh Kapoor could see all this, but he still had faith –

or perhaps hope would describe his feeling better – that Nehru would ensure that those who were ideologically close to him would not find themselves displaced and marginalized in the states. This was what he now suggested to Abdus Salaam. Since Nehru faced no one who could pose the least threat to himself in the party, he would surely ensure that the legislatures of the nation would not be filled for the next five years by those who paid no more than lip-service to his ideals.

14.28

ABDUS SALAAM stirred his tea, then murmured, 'Well, from what you have said I can see you are veering towards rejoining the Congress, Minister Sahib.'

Mahesh Kapoor shrugged his shoulders. 'Tell me,' he said, 'why are you so dubious about it? How can you be so sure he won't gain – or regain – a grip on things? He turned the whole party around and seized the reins when no one expected it of him. He may surprise us further.'

'I was at the All-India Congress Committee meeting in Delhi, as you know,' said Abdus Salaam casually, focusing on a spot in the middle distance. 'I saw him seizing the reins at close range. Well, it was quite a sight – do you want a first-hand account?'

'Yes.'

'Well, Minister Sahib, it was the second day. There we were, all of us, in the Constitution Club. Nehru had been elected President the previous day – but of course he had not actually accepted. He said he wanted to sleep over the matter. He asked us to sleep over the matter. Everyone slept over the matter, and the next afternoon we waited for him to speak. He had not accepted, of course, but he was in the chair. Tandon was among the leaders on the dais, but Nehru was in the chair. The previous day he had refused the chair, but today, well, today, perhaps he thought that such extreme delicacy might be misinterpreted. Or perhaps Tandon had put his foot down and refused to sit where he so clearly was not wanted.'

'Tandon,' admitted Mahesh Kapoor, 'was one of the few who refused to go along with the decision to divide the country when the Congress Party voted for Partition. No one says he's not a man of principle.'

'Well,' said Abdus Salaam in passing, 'Pakistan was a good thing.'

Seeing Mahesh Kapoor look shocked, he said: 'For one thing, with the Muslim League wielding so much power in an undivided India neither could you have got rid of princely states like Marh nor forced through the abolition of zamindari. Everyone knows this, yet no one says so. But all this is water under the bridge, history, spilt milk. So there we were, Minister Sahib, looking reverently upwards at the dais, expecting the conqueror to tell us that he would take no nonsense from anybody, that he would make sure that the party apparatus responded to his slightest touch, that the candidates for the elections would all be his men.'

'And women.'

'Yes. And women. Panditji is keen on female representation.'

'Go on, go on, Abdus Salaam, get to the point.'

'Well, instead of getting a commander's battlecry or even a pragmatist's plan, we got a speech about the Unity of the Heart. We should think above divisions, splits, cliques! We must pull along like a team, a family, a battalion. Dear Chacha Nehru, I felt like saying, this is India, Hindustan, Bharat, the country where faction was invented before the zero. If even the heart is divided into four parts can you expect us Indians to divide ourselves into less than four hundred?'

'But what did he say about candidates?' asked Mahesh Kapoor.

Abdus Salaam's answer was not reassuring.

'What would he say, being Jawaharlal? That he just did not know and did not care who belonged to which group. That he entirely agreed with Tandonji that the right way to choose a candidate was to choose a man who did not apply for the slot. Of course, he could see that this might not always be possible in practice. And when he said this, Agarwal, who was sitting near me, visibly relaxed – he relaxed and he smiled. I can tell you, Minister Sahib, I did not feel very reassured by the nature of that smile.'

Mahesh Kapoor nodded and said, 'And then Panditji agreed to accept the Presidency?'

'Not quite,' said Abdus Salaam. 'But he said he had thought about it. Luckily for us, he had been able to obtain some sleep that night. He confided in us that the previous day, when his name had been put up and accepted at once, he did not quite know what to do. Those were his words: "I did not quite know what to do." But now, having slept over it, he told us that he realized that it was not an easy matter for him to escape from this responsibility. Not an easy matter at all.'

'So all of you breathed a sigh of relief.'

'That, Minister Sahib, is correct. But we had breathed too early. A niggling doubt had struck him. A minor doubt, but one that niggled. He had slept, and made up his mind. Or almost, yes, almost made up his mind. But the question was: had we slept and made up our minds again – or at least not changed our minds? And if we had, how could we show him that we meant it? And how could we make him believe it?'

'Well, what did you do?' asked Mahesh Kapoor rather shortly. He found Abdus Salaam's mode of narration far too leisurely for his tastes.

'Well, what could we do? We raised our hands again. But that was not enough. Then some of us raised both our hands. But that would not do either. Panditji wanted no formal show, no re-voting with hands or feet. He wanted a demonstration of our "minds and hearts". Only then could he decide whether to accept our request or not.'

Abdus Salaam paused, awaiting a Socratic response, and Mahesh Kapoor, realizing that things would not move without it, supplied it.

'That must have put you in a quandary,' he said.

'It did indeed,' said Abdus Salaam. 'I kept thinking: seize the levers of power; select your candidates. He kept talking about minds and hearts. I noticed Pant and Tandon and Sharma looking at him in perplexity. And L.N. Agarwal kept smiling his twisted little smile to himself.'

'Go on, go on.'

'So then we clapped.'

'But that did not do either?'

'No, Minister Sahib, that did not do either. So then we decided to pass a resolution. But Pandit Nehru would have none of it. We would have shouted "Long live Pandit Nehru!" till we were hoarse, but everyone knew that that would have put him in a temper. He does not care for personality cults. He does not care for flattery – for patent or vociferous flattery. He is a democrat through and through.'

'How was the problem resolved, Salaam? Will you please tell your story, without waiting for me to ask you questions?'

'Well,' said Abdus Salaam, 'there was only one way to resolve it. Exhausted, and unwilling to sleep over anything again, we turned to Nehruji himself. We had racked our brains and thought ourselves thin, and none of our offerings had been acceptable to him. Perhaps he would grace us with a suggestion himself. What would satisfy him that our hearts and minds were with him? At this, our supreme leader looked perplexed. He did not know.'

'He did not know?' Mahesh Kapoor could not help exclaiming.

'He did not know.' Abdus Salaam's face took on one of Nehru's more melancholy expressions. 'But after a few minutes of thought he found his way out of the difficulty. We were all to join him in a patriotic shout of "Jai Hind!" That would show him that our hearts and minds were in the right place.'

'So that was what you did?' said Mahesh Kapoor with rather a rueful smile himself.

'That was what we did. But our first shout was not full-throated enough. Panditji looked unhappy, and we could see the Congress and the country collapsing before our eyes. So we raised another shout, a mighty cry of "Jai Hind!" such as almost caused the Constitution Club to collapse about our ears. And Jawaharlal smiled. He smiled. The sun came out and all was well.'

'And that was that?'

'And that was that.'

14.29

EVERY year at the time of shraadh, Mrs Rupa Mehra had a struggle with her eldest son, which she, after a fashion, won. Every year, Mrs Mahesh Kapoor had a struggle with her husband, which she lost. And Mrs Tandon had no struggle at all, except with her memories of her husband; for Kedarnath performed his father's rites in full accordance with his duty.

Raghubir Mehra's death had fallen on the second day of a lunar fortnight, and therefore, on the second day of the annual 'fortnight of the ancestors', pandits should have been called to the house of his eldest son to be feasted and given gifts. But the thought of plump, bare-chested, dhoti-clad pandits sitting around in his Sunny Park flat, chanting mantras and gobbling down rice and daal, puris and halwa, curds and kheer, was anathema to Arun. Every year Mrs Rupa Mehra tried to persuade him to perform the rites for his father's spirit. Every year Arun dismissed the whole farrago of superstitious nonsense. Mrs Rupa Mehra next worked upon Varun and sent him the necessary money for the expenses, and Varun agreed – partly because he knew it would bother his brother; partly because of love for his father (though he had a hard time believing, for instance, that the karhi, which was one of his father's favourite foods, and that he was therefore supposed to include in the pandits' feast, would eventually get to him); but mainly because he loved his mother and knew how badly she would suffer if he refused. She could not perform the

shraadh herself; it had to be done by a man. And if not by
the eldest son, then by the youngest – or, in this case, the
younger.

'I will have no such shenanigans in this house, let me tell
you that!' said Arun.

'It's for Daddy's spirit,' said Varun, with an attempt at
belligerence.

'Daddy's spirit! Utter rubbish. Next we'll have human
sacrifice to help you pass your IAS exams.'

'Don't talk like that about Daddy!' cried Varun, livid
and cowering. 'Can't you give Ma some mental
satisfaction?'

'Mental? Sentimental!' said Arun with a snort.

Varun didn't talk to his brother for days and slunk
around the house, glaring balefully; not even Aparna could
cheer him up. Every time the phone rang he jumped.
Eventually it got on Meenakshi's nerves, and at last even
Arun in his native-proof casing began to feel slightly
ashamed of himself.

Finally Varun was allowed to feed a single pandit in the
garden. He donated the rest of the money to a nearby
temple with instructions that it should be used to feed a
few poor children. And he wrote to Brahmpur to tell his
mother that everything had been performed properly.

Mrs Rupa Mehra read the letter to her samdhin, translat-
ing as she went along, with tears in her eyes.

Mrs Mahesh Kapoor listened sadly. Her annual battle
was fought not with her sons but with her husband. The
shraadh for her own parents was satisfactorily performed
each year by her late brother's eldest son. What she wanted
now was that the spirits of her father-in-law and mother-
in-law should be similarly propitiated. Their son, however,
would have nothing to do with it and rebuked her in his
usual manner:

'Oh, blessed one, you've been married to me for more
than three decades and you have become more ignorant
with each passing year.'

Mrs Mahesh Kapoor did not answer back. This encouraged her husband.

'How can you believe in such idiocy? In those grasping pandits and their mumbo-jumbo? "So much food I set aside for the cow. So much for the crow. So much for the dog. And the rest I will eat. More! More! More puris, more halwa." Then they belch and hold out their hands for alms: "Give according to your grace and your feelings for the departed one. What? Only five rupees? Is that the extent of your love for them?" I even know of someone who gave snuff to a pandit's wife because his own dead mother liked snuff! Well, I won't disturb my parents' souls with such mockery. All I can say is that I hope no one dares to perform shraadh for me.'

This stung Mrs Mahesh Kapoor into protest. She said: 'If Pran refuses to perform shraadh for you, he will be no son of mine.'

'Pran has too much good sense,' said Mahesh Kapoor. 'And I'm beginning to think that Maan is a sensible boy too. Don't talk just of me – they wouldn't even perform it for you.'

Whether Mahesh Kapoor took delight in baiting and hurting his wife or not, he certainly couldn't stop himself. Mrs Mahesh Kapoor, who could bear much, was almost in tears. Veena was visiting when this argument broke out, and her mother said to her:

'Bété.'

'Yes, Ammaji.'

'If such a thing happens, you will tell Bhaskar that he is to perform shraadh for me. Invest him with the sacred thread if necessary.'

'Sacred thread! Bhaskar will not wear a sacred thread,' said Mahesh Kapoor. 'He'll use it to fly a kite with. Or as Hanuman's tail.' He chuckled rather maliciously at the sacrilege.

'That is for his father to decide,' said Mrs Mahesh Kapoor quietly.

'He is too young anyway.'

'That also is for his father to decide,' said Mrs Mahesh Kapoor. 'Anyway, I'm not dying yet.'

'But you certainly sound determined to die,' said Mahesh

Kapoor. 'This time every year we go through the same stupid kind of talk.'

'Of course I am determined to die,' said Mrs Mahesh Kapoor. 'How else can I go through my rebirths and finally end them?' Looking down at her hands she said, 'Do you want to be immortal? I can imagine nothing worse than to be immortal, nothing worse.'

Part Fifteen

LESS than a week after her letter from her younger son, Mrs Rupa Mehra received a letter from her elder son. It was, as always, illegible – and illegible to the extent that it seemed almost to amount to contempt for any possible reader. The news it contained was important, however; and it did no good to Mrs Rupa Mehra's high blood pressure as she tried desperately to decipher bits of it through a forest of random curves and spikes.

The surprising news related mainly to the Chatterji children. Of the two women, Meenakshi and Kakoli, one had lost a foetus and the other had gained a fiancé. Dipankar had returned from the Pul Mela still uncertain, 'but at a higher level'. Young Tapan had written rather an unhappy but unspecific letter home – typical adolescent blues, according to Arun. And Amit had let it drop when he had called around one evening for a drink that he was rather fond of Lata, which, given his extreme reticence, could only mean that he was 'interested' in her. Making sense of the next few squiggles, Mrs Rupa Mehra was shocked to understand that Arun did not think this was such a bad idea. Certainly, according to him, it would take Lata out of the orbit of the entirely unsuitable Haresh. When the idea was put before Varun, he had frowned and said, 'I'm studying,' as if his sister's future mattered not at all to him. But then, Varun was becoming moodier and moodier since his IAS preparations had restrained his Shamshuing. He had behaved most oddly over Daddy's shraadh, attempting to turn the Sunny Park house into a restaurant for fat priests, and even asking them (Meenakshi had overheard him) if shraadh could be performed for a suicide.

With a few remarks about the impending General Elections in England ('At Bentsen Pryce we consider it Hobson's choice: Attlee is puerile and Churchill senile') but none about the Indian elections, with a casual admonition to Mrs Rupa Mehra to mind her blood sugar, and to give his love to his sisters, and to assure everyone that Meenakshi was fine and had suffered no lasting harm, Arun signed off.

Mrs Rupa Mehra sat stunned, her heart beating dangerously fast. She was used to re-reading her letters a dozen times, examining for days from every possible angle some remark that someone had made to someone else about something that someone had thought that someone had almost done. So much news – and all so sudden and substantial – was too much to absorb at once. Meenakshi's miscarriage, the Kakoli-Hans nexus, the threat of Amit, the non-mention of Haresh except in an unfavourable passing remark, the disturbing attitude of Varun – Mrs Rupa Mehra did not know whether to laugh or to weep, and immediately asked for a glass of nimbu pani.

And there was no news of her darling Aparna. Presumably she was all right. Mrs Rupa Mehra recalled a remark of hers, now family lore: 'If another baby comes into this house, I will throw it straight into the waste-paper basket.' Precocity appeared to be the fashion among children these days. She hoped that Uma would be as lovable as Aparna, but less trenchant.

Mrs Rupa Mehra was dying to show Savita her brother's letter, but then decided that it would be far better to break the various bits of news to her one by one. It would be less disturbing to Savita, and more informative for herself. Without knowing either Arun's strong opinions or Varun's apparent indifference, where would Savita's own judgment in the matter of Amit lie? So! thought Mrs Rupa Mehra grimly: this must have been behind his gift to Lata of his incomprehensible book of poems.

As for Lata – she had been taking an unnecessary interest in poetry these days, even attending an occasional meeting of the Brahmpur Literary Society. This did not bode well. It was true that she had also been writing to Haresh, but Mrs Rupa Mehra was not privy to the contents of those letters. Lata had become cruelly possessive of her privacy. 'Am I your mother or not?' Mrs Rupa Mehra had asked her once. 'Oh, Ma, please!' had been Lata's heartless reply.

And poor Meenakshi! thought Mrs Rupa Mehra. She must write to her at once. She felt that a creamy cambric was called for, and, her eyes moist with sympathy, she went to get the writing paper from her bag. Meenakshi the cold-hearted medal-melter was replaced for a while with the image of Meenakshi the vulnerable, tender, broken vehicle for Mrs Rupa Mehra's third grandchild, who she felt was bound to have been a boy.

If Mrs Rupa Mehra had known the truth about Meenakshi's pregnancy or her miscarriage, she would doubtless have been less than sympathetic. Meenakshi, terrified that her baby might not be Arun's – and, in milder counterpoint, concerned by what a second pregnancy would do to her figure and social life – had decided to take immediate action. After her doctor – the miracle-working Dr Evans – had refused to help her, she went for advice to her closest friends among the Shady Ladies, swearing them first to secrecy. She was certain that if Arun heard about her attempt to free herself from this unwanted child, he would be as unreasonably angry as he had been when she had liberated herself from one of his father's medals.

How unfortunate, she thought desperately, that neither the jewellery theft nor Khandelwal's dogs had shocked her foetus out of her.

Meenakshi had made herself quite sick with abortifacients, worry, conflicting advice and tortuous gymnastics when one afternoon, to her relief, she had the miscarriage of her dreams. She phoned Billy immediately, her voice unsteady on the line; when he asked anxiously if she was all right, she was able to reassure him. It had been sudden and painless, if alarming and, well, horribly messy. Billy sounded miserable for her sake.

And Arun, for his part, was so tender and protective of her for days afterwards that she began to feel that there might be at least something to be said for the whole sorry business.

15.2

HAD wishes been horses, Mrs Rupa Mehra would have been riding at this very moment on the Calcutta Mail, and would soon have been questioning everyone she knew in

Calcutta and Prahapore about all they had been doing or thinking or planning or professing. But, quite apart from the cost of the journey, there were compelling reasons for her to remain in Brahmpur. For one thing, baby Uma was still very little, and needed a grandmother's care. Whereas Meenakshi had been by turns possessive of Aparna and perfectly happy to ignore her (treating her mother-in-law as a kind of super-ayah while she traipsed about Calcutta, socializing), Savita shared Uma with Mrs Rupa Mehra (and with Mrs Mahesh Kapoor when she visited) in a natural, daughterly way.

Secondly – and as if there had not been drama enough in the letter she had received from Arun – this evening was the performance of *Twelfth Night*. It was to be held in the university auditorium immediately after the Annual Day ceremonies and tea, and her own Lata would be in it – as would Malati, who was just like a daughter to her. (Mrs Rupa Mehra was well-disposed towards Malati these days, seeing in her a chaperone rather than a conniver.) So would that boy K; but thank God, thought Mrs Rupa Mehra, there would be no more rehearsals. And with the university break for Dussehra in just a couple of days, there would be no great possibility of chance meetings on campus either. Mrs Rupa Mehra felt, however, that she must remain in Brahmpur just in case. Only when, for the short Christmas vacation, the whole family – Pran, Savita, Lata, Lady Baby and materfamilias – visited Calcutta would she desert her reconnaissance post.

The hall was packed with students, alumni, teachers, parents and relatives together with smatterings of Brahmpur society, including a few literary lawyers and judges. Mr and Mrs Nowrojee were there, as were the poet Makhijani and the booming Mrs Supriya Joshi. Hema's Taiji was there together with a knot of a dozen giggling girls, most of them her wards. Professor and Mrs Mishra were present. And of the family, Pran of course (since nothing could have kept him away, and he was indeed feeling much better), Savita (Uma had been left with her ayah for the evening), Maan, Bhaskar, Dr Kishen Chand Seth and Parvati.

Mrs Rupa Mehra was in a high state of excitement when the curtain went up to a sudden hush from the audience, and to the strains of a lute that sounded rather like a sitar, the Duke began: 'If music be the food of love, play on –'

She was soon entirely carried away by the magic of the play. And indeed, there was no major mischief, other than some incomprehensible bawdy and buffoonery, in the first half of the play. When Lata came on, Mrs Rupa Mehra could hardly believe that it was her daughter.

Pride swelled in her bosom and tears forced themselves into her eyes. How could Pran and Savita, seated on either side of her, be so indifferent to Lata's appearance?

'Lata! Look, Lata!' she whispered to them.

'Yes, Ma,' said Savita. Pran merely nodded.

When Olivia, in love with Viola, said:

'Fate, show thy force. Ourselves we do not owe:
What is decreed must be; and be this so!'

– Mrs Rupa Mehra nodded her head sadly as she thought philosophically of much that had happened in her own life. How true, she thought, conferring honorary Indian citizenship on Shakespeare.

Malati, meanwhile, had the audience charmed. At Sir Toby's line, 'Here comes the little villain – How now, my nettle of India?' everyone cheered, especially a claque of medical students. And there was another great round of applause at the interval (which Mr Barua had placed in the middle of Act III) for Maria and Sir Toby. Mrs Rupa Mehra had to be restrained from going backstage to congratulate Lata and Malati. Even Kabir-as-Malvolio had so far proven to be innocuous, and she had laughed with the rest of the audience at his gecking and gulling.

Kabir had donned the accent of the officious and unpopular Registrar of the university, and – whether this would prove beneficial for Mr Barua's future or not – it increased the present enjoyment of the students. Dr Kishen Chand Seth, in fact, was Malvolio's only supporter, insisting loudly in the interval that what was being done to him was indefensible.

'Lack of discipline, that is the trouble with the whole country,' he stated vehemently.

Bhaskar was bored with the play. It was nothing like as exciting as the Ramlila, in which he had obtained a role as one of Hanuman's monkeysoldiers. The only interesting part of this play so far had been Malvolio's interpretation of 'M, O, A, I'.

The second half began. Mrs Rupa Mehra nodded and smiled. But she nearly started from her chair when she heard her daughter say to Kabir: 'Wilt thou go to bed, Malvolio?' and she gasped at Malvolio's odious, brazen reply.

'Stop it – stop it at once!' she wanted to shout. 'Is this why I sent you to university? I should never have allowed you to act in this play. Never. If Daddy had seen this he would have been ashamed of you.'

'Ma!' whispered Savita. 'Are you all right?'

'No!' her mother wanted to shout. 'I am not all right. And how can you let your younger sister say such things? Shameless!' Shakespeare's Indian citizenship was immediately withdrawn.

But she said nothing.

Mrs Rupa Mehra's uneasy shufflings, however, were nothing compared to her father's activities in the second half. He and Parvati were seated a few rows away from the rest of the family. He started sobbing uncontrollably at the scene where the disowned sea-captain reproaches Viola, thinking her to be her brother:

> 'Will you deny me now?
> Is't possible that my deserts to you
> Can lack persuasion? Do not tempt my misery
> Lest that it make me so unsound a man
> As to upbraid you with those kindnesses
> That I have done for you.'

Loudly sobbed Dr Kishen Chand Seth. Astonished necks swivelled swiftly towards him – but to no effect.

> 'Let me speak a little. This youth that you see here
> I snatched one half out of the jaws of death,
> Relieved him with such sanctity of love, –
> And to his image, which methought did promise
> Most venerable worth, did I devotion.'

By now Dr Kishen Chand Seth was gasping almost asthmatically. He started pounding the floor with his stick to relieve his distress.

Parvati took it from him and said, rather sharply: 'Kishy! This isn't *Deedar*!' – and this brought him heavily back to earth.

But not much later, the distress of Malvolio – cooped up in an inner chamber and driven from bewilderment almost to madness – evoked further distress, and he began to weep to himself as if his heart would break. Several people around him stopped laughing and turned to look at him.

At this, Parvati handed him back his stick and said, 'Kishy, Let's go now. Now! At once!'

But Kishy would have none of it. He managed to control himself at last, and sat out the rest of the play, rapt and almost tearless. His daughter, who had no sympathy whatsoever with Malvolio, had grown increasingly reconciled to the play as he made more and more of a fool of himself and finally came to his undignified exit.

Since the play ended with three happy marriages (and even, Indian-movie-style, concluded with the last of four songs), it was a success in the eyes of Mrs Rupa Mehra who had, miraculously and conveniently, forgotten all about Malvolio and the bed. After the curtain-calls and the appearance of shy Mr Barua to calls of 'Producer! producer!' she rushed backstage and hugged Lata, and kissed her, make-up and all, saying:

'You are my darling daughter. I am so proud of you. And of Malati too. If only your –'

She stopped, and tears came to her eyes. Then she made

an effort to control herself, and said, 'Now get changed quickly, let's go home. It's late, and you must be tired after talking so much.'

She had noticed Malvolio hanging around. He had been chatting to a couple of other actors, but had now turned towards Lata and her mother. It seemed that he wanted to greet her, or at any rate to say something.

'Ma – I can't; I'll join you all later,' said Lata.

'No!' Mrs Rupa Mehra put her foot down. 'You are coming now. You can clean off your make-up at home. Savita and I will help you.'

But whether it was her own new-found thespian confidence or merely a continuation of Olivia's 'smooth, discreet, and stable bearing', Lata simply said, in a quiet voice:

'I am sorry, Ma, there is a party for the cast, and we are going to celebrate. Malati and I have worked on this play for months, and have made friends whom we won't see until after the Dussehra break. And please don't worry, Ma; Mr Barua will make sure I get home safely.'

Mrs Rupa Mehra could not believe her ears.

Now Kabir came up to her and said:

'Mrs Mehra?'

'Yes?' said Mrs Rupa Mehra belligerently, all the more so because Kabir was very obviously good-looking, despite his make-up and curious attire, and Mrs Rupa Mehra in general believed in good looks.

'Mrs Mehra, I thought I would introduce myself,' said Kabir. 'I am Kabir Durrani.'

'Yes, I know,' said Mrs Rupa Mehra rather sharply. 'I have heard about you. I have also met your father. Do you mind if my daughter does not attend the cast party?'

Kabir flushed. 'No, Mrs Mehra, I –'

'I want to attend,' said Lata, giving Kabir a sharp glance. 'This has nothing to do with anyone else.'

Mrs Rupa Mehra was suddenly tempted to give both of them two tight slaps. But instead she glared at Lata, and at Kabir, and even at Malati for good measure, then turned and left without another word.

'WELL, there are many possibilities for riots,' said Firoz: 'Shias with Shias, Shias with Sunnis, Hindus with Muslims –'

'And Hindus with Hindus,' added Maan.

'That's something new in Brahmpur,' said Firoz.

'Well, my sister says that the jatavs tried to force themselves onto the local Ramlila Committee this year. They said that at least one of the five swaroops should be selected from among scheduled caste boys. Naturally, no one listened to them at all. But it could spell trouble. I hope you aren't going to participate in too many events yourself. I don't want to have to worry about you.'

'Worry!' laughed Firoz. 'I can't imagine you worrying about me. But it's a nice thought.'

'Oh?' said Maan. 'But don't you have to put yourself in front of some Moharram procession or other – you one year, Imtiaz the next, I thought you said?'

'That's only on the last couple of days. For the most part I just lie low during Moharram. And this year I know where I will spend at least a couple of my evenings.' Firoz sounded deliberately mysterious.

'Where?'

'Somewhere where you, as an unbeliever, will not be admitted; though in the past you have performed your prostrations in that shrine.'

'But I thought she didn't –' began Maan. 'I thought she didn't even allow herself to sing during those ten days.'

'She doesn't,' said Firoz. 'But she has small gatherings at her house where she chants marsiyas and performs soz – it really is something. Not the marsiyas so much – but the soz, from what I hear, is really astonishing.'

Maan knew from his brief incursions into poetry with Rasheed that marsiyas were laments for the martyrs of the battle of Karbala: especially for Hussain, the grandson of the Prophet. But he had no idea what soz was.

'It's a sort of musical wailing,' said Firoz. 'I've only

heard it a few times, and never at Saeeda Bai's. It grips the heart.'

The thought of Saeeda Bai weeping and wailing passionately for someone who had died thirteen centuries before was both perplexing and strangely exciting for Maan. 'Why can't I go?' he asked. 'I'll sit quietly and watch – I mean, listen. I attended Bakr-Id, you know, at the village.'

'Because you're a kafir, you idiot. Even Sunnis aren't really welcome at these private gatherings, though they take part in some processions. Saeeda Bai tries to control her audience, from what I've heard, but some of them get carried away with grief and start cursing the first three caliphs because they usurped Ali's right to the caliphate, and this enrages the Sunnis, quite naturally. Sometimes the curses are very graphic.'

'And you'll be attending all this soz stuff. Since when have you become so religious?' asked Maan.

'I'm not,' said Firoz. 'In fact – and you'd better not tell anyone I said this – but I'm not a great fan of Hussain. And Muawiyah, who got him killed, wasn't as dreadful as we make him out to be. After all, the succession was quite a mess before that, with most of the caliphs getting assassinated. Once Muawiyah set things up dynastically, Islam was able to consolidate itself as an empire. If he hadn't, everything would have fallen back into petty tribes bickering with each other and there'd be no Islam to argue about. But if my father heard me say this he'd disown me. And Saeeda Bai would tear me apart with her own lovely soft hands.'

'So why are you going to Saeeda Bai's?' said Maan, somewhat piqued and suspicious. 'Didn't you say you weren't exactly made welcome there when you happened to visit?'

'How can she turn back a mourner during Moharram?'

'And why do you want to go there in the first place?'

'To drink at the fountain of Paradise.'

'Very funny.'

'I mean, to see the young Tasneem.'

'Well, give my love to the parakeet,' said Maan, frowning. He continued to frown when Firoz got up, stood behind his chair, and put his hands on Maan's shoulders.

15.4

'CAN you imagine,' said old Mrs Tandon: 'Rama or Bharat or Sita – a chamar!'

Veena looked uncomfortable at such an outright statement of the feelings of the neighbourhood.

'And the sweepers want the Ramlila to continue after Rama's return to Ayodhya and his meeting with Bharat and the coronation. They want all those shameful episodes about Sita put in.'

Maan asked why.

'Oh, you know, they style themselves Valmikis these days, and they say that Valmiki's Ramayana, which goes on and on about all these episodes, is the true text of the Ramayana,' said old Mrs Tandon. 'Just trouble-making.'

Veena said: 'No one disputes the Ramayana. And Sita did have a horrible life after she returned from Lanka. But the Ramlila has always been based on the Ramcharitmanas of Tulsidas, not Valmiki's Ramayana. The worst of all this is that Kedarnath has to do so much of the explaining on both sides and has to shoulder most of the trouble. Because of his contact with the scheduled castes,' she added.

'And I suppose,' said Maan, 'because of his sense of civic duty?'

Veena frowned and nodded, not sure if the irresponsible Maan was being sarcastic at her expense.

'I remember our days in Lahore – none of this could ever have happened,' said old Mrs Tandon with tender nostalgia and a look of shining faith in her eyes. 'The people contributed without being asked, even the Municipal Council provided free lighting, and the effigies we made for Ravana were so frightening that children would hide their faces in their mothers' laps. Our neighbourhood had the best Ramlila in the city. And all the swaroops were brahmin boys,' she added approvingly.

'But that would never do,' said Maan. 'Bhaskar would never have been eligible then.'

'No, he wouldn't,' said old Mrs Tandon thoughtfully. This was the first time she had considered the matter from this angle. 'That would not have been good. Just because we aren't brahmins! But people were old-fashioned then. Some things are changing for the better. Bhaskar must certainly get a part next year. He knows half of them by heart already.'

15.5

KEDARNATH had, in this matter of the actor-deities or swaroops, been surprised to find that one of the leaders of the untouchables was the jatav Jagat Ram from Ravidaspur. It was difficult for him to think of Jagat Ram as having anything to do with local agitation, for he was a fairly sober man who had concentrated, by and large, on his work and his large family; and had played no active role in the strike in Misri Mandi. But Jagat Ram had, by virtue of his relative prosperity – if it could be called that – and the fact that he was at least minimally literate, been pressured by his neighbours and fellow-workers into representing them. He did not want to accept; having accepted, though, he did what he could. However, he felt at a disadvantage in two respects. First, it was only by stretching a point that he could claim to have a stake in what went on in Misri Mandi. Secondly, since his livelihood depended on Kedarnath and other local figures, he knew that for the sake of his family he had to tread carefully.

Kedarnath for his part was not unsympathetic in a theoretical sense to the general question of opening up the field of actors. But the Ramlila in his eyes was not a competition or a political act but an enactment of faith by the community. Most of the boys who acted in it had known each other from childhood, and the scenes that were represented had the sanction of hundreds of years of tradition. The Ramlila of Misri Mandi was famous throughout the city. To tack on scenes after the coronation of Rama struck him as being pointlessly offensive – a political invasion of religion, a moralistic invasion of morality. As for some sort of quota system among the swaroops, that would only lead to political conflict and artistic disaster.

Jagat Ram argued that since the brahmin stranglehold over the parts of the heroes had been broken in favour of the other upper castes, it was a logical next step to allow the so-called lower castes and scheduled castes to participate. They contributed to the success of the Ramlila as spectators and even to a small extent as contributors; why not then as actors? Kedarnath responded that it was obviously too late to do anything this year. He would bring up the matter with the Ramlila Committee the following year. But he suggested that the people of Ravidaspur, which was largely a scheduled caste community – and from which the claim largely emanated – should perform a Ramlila of their own as well, so that the demand would not be seen as invasive and mischievous, merely a way of prolonging by other weapons the conflict that had had its first culmination in the disastrous strike earlier in the year.

Nothing was really resolved. Everything was left in uncertainty. And Jagat Ram was not really surprised. This was his first venture into politics, and he had not enjoyed it. His childhood hell in a village, his brutal adolescence in a factory, and the vicious world of competitors and middlemen, poverty and dirt in which he now found himself, had served to turn him into something of a philosopher. One did not argue with elephants in a jungle when they were on the rampage, one did not argue with the traffic in Chowk as it hurtled past in murderous confusion. One got out of the way and got one's family out of the way. If possible, one retained what dignity one could. The world was a place of brutality and cruelty and the exclusion of people like him from the rites of religion was almost the least of its barbarities.

The previous year one of the jatavs of his own village, who had spent a couple of years in Brahmpur, had gone back home during the harvest season. After the comparative freedom of the city, he had made the mistake of imagining that he had gained exemption from the generalized loathing of the upper-caste villagers. Perhaps also, being eighteen years old, he had the rashness of youth; at any rate, he cycled around the village singing film songs on a bicycle he had bought from his earnings. One day, feeling thirsty, he had had the brazenness to ask an upper-caste woman who was cooking outside her house for some water to drink. That night he had been set upon by a gang of men, tied to his bicycle, and forced to eat human excreta. His brain and his bicycle had then been smashed to bits. Everyone knew the men who were responsible, yet no one had dared to testify; and the details had been too horrendous for even the newspapers to print.

In the villages, the untouchables were virtually helpless; almost none of them owned that eventual guarantor of dignity and status, land. Few worked it as tenants, and of those tenants fewer still would be able to make use of the paper guarantees of the forthcoming land reforms. In the cities too they were the dregs of society. Even Gandhi, for all his reforming concern, for all his hatred of the concept that any human being was intrinsically so loathsome and polluting as to be untouchable, had believed that people should continue in their hereditarily ordained professions: a cobbler should remain a cobbler, a sweeper a sweeper. 'One born a scavenger must earn his livelihood by being a scavenger, and then do whatever else he likes. For a scavenger is as worthy of his hire as a lawyer or your President. That, according to me, is Hinduism.'

For Jagat Ram, though he would not have said this aloud, this was the most misleading condescension. He knew that there was nothing innately worthy about cleaning lavatories or standing in a foul-smelling tanning-pit – and being duty-bound to do so because your parents had. But this was what most Hindus believed, and if beliefs and laws were changing, a few more generations would continue to be crushed under the wheels of the great chariot before it finally ground to a bloodstained halt.

It was with only half a heart that Jagat Ram had argued

that the scheduled castes should be allowed to be swaroops in the Ramlila. Perhaps, after all, it was not a question of a logical next step so much as an emotional one. Perhaps, as Nehru's Law Minister Dr Ambedkar, the great, already almost mythical, leader of the untouchables, had asserted, Hinduism had nothing to offer those whom it had cast so pitilessly out of its fold. He had been born a Hindu, Dr Ambedkar had said, but he would not die a Hindu.

Nine months after the murder of Gandhi, the constitutional provision abolishing untouchability was passed by the Constituent Assembly, and its members broke out into loud cheers of 'Victory to Mahatma Gandhi'. However little the measure was to mean in practical as opposed to symbolic terms, Jagat Ram believed that the victory for its formulation lay less with Mahatma Gandhi, who rarely concerned himself with such legalisms, than with quite another – and equally courageous – man.

15.6

ON the 2nd of October, which happened to be Gandhiji's birthday, the Kapoor family met at Prem Nivas for lunch. A couple of other guests had dropped in and were invited to join them. One was Sandeep Lahiri, who had come to ask after Maan. The other was a politician from U.P., one of the secessionists from the Congress, who had rejoined, and was attempting to persuade Mahesh Kapoor to do the same.

Maan arrived late. It was a public holiday, and he had spent the morning at the Riding Club playing polo with his friend. He was getting to be quite good at it. He hoped to spend the evening with Saeeda Bai. After all, the Moharram moon had not yet been sighted.

The first thing he did when he saw everyone gathered together was to praise Lata's acting. Lata, feeling herself suddenly the centre of attention, blushed.

'Don't blush,' said Maan. 'No, blush away. I'm not flattering you. You were excellent. Bhaskar, of course, didn't enjoy the play, but that wasn't your fault. I thought it was wonderful. And Malati – she was brilliant too. And the Duke. And Malvolio. And Sir Toby of course.'

Maan had spread his praise too liberally by now for it to make Lata uncomfortable. She laughed and said:

'You've left out the third footman.'

'Quite right,' said Maan. 'And the fourth murderer.'

'Why haven't you come to the Ramlila, Maan Maama?' asked Bhaskar.

'Because it just began yesterday!' said Maan.

'But you've already missed Rama's youth and training,' said Bhaskar.

'Oh, oh, sorry,' said Maan.

'You must come tonight, or I'll be kutti with you.'

'You can't be kutti with your uncle,' said Maan.

'Yes, I can,' said Bhaskar. 'Today is the winning of Sita. The procession will go all the way from Khirkiwalan to Shahi Darvaza. And everyone will be out in the lanes celebrating.'

'Yes, Maan, do – we'll look forward to it,' said Kedarnath. 'And then have dinner with us afterwards.'

'Well, tonight, I –' Maan stopped, sensing that his father's eyes were upon him. 'I'll come when the monkeys first appear in the Ramlila,' he finished lamely, patting Bhaskar on the head. Bhaskar, he decided, was more monkey than frog.

'Let me hold Uma,' said Mrs Mahesh Kapoor, sensing that Savita was tired. She looked at the baby, trying to work out for the thousandth time which features belonged to her, which to her husband, which to Mrs Rupa Mehra and which to the photograph so often pulled out these days for reference, comparison or display from Mrs Rupa Mehra's bag.

Her own husband, meanwhile, was saying to Sandeep Lahiri: 'I understand you got into trouble this time last year over some pictures of Gandhiji?'

'Er, yes,' said Sandeep. 'One picture, actually. But, well, things have sorted themselves out.'

'Sorted themselves out? Hasn't Jha just managed to get rid of you?'

'Well, I've been promoted –'

'Yes, yes, that's what I meant,' said Mahesh Kapoor impatiently. 'But you're very popular with everyone in Rudhia. If you weren't in the IAS, I'd have made you my agent. I'd win the elections easily.'

'Are you thinking of standing from Rudhia?' asked Sandeep.

'I'm not thinking of anything at the moment,' said Mahesh Kapoor. 'Everyone else is doing my thinking for me. My son. And my grandson. And my friend the Nawab Sahib. And my Parliamentary Secretary. And Rafi Sahib. And the Chief Minister. And this most helpful gentleman,' he added, indicating the politician, a short, quiet man who had shared a cell with Mahesh Kapoor many years ago.

'I am only saying: We should all return to the party of Gandhiji,' said the politician. 'To change one's party is not necessarily to change one's principles – or to be unprincipled.'

'Ah, Gandhiji,' said Mahesh Kapoor, not willing to be drawn out. 'He would have been eighty-two today, and a miserable man. He would never have reiterated his wish to live to be a hundred and twenty-five. As for his spirit, we feed it with laddus for one day of the year, and once we've performed his shraadh we forget all about him.'

Suddenly he turned to his wife: 'Why is he taking so long making the phulkas? Must we sit here with our stomachs rumbling till four o'clock? Instead of dandling that baby and making it howl, why don't you get that halfwit cook to feed us?'

Veena said, 'I'll go,' to her mother and went towards the kitchen.

Mrs Mahesh Kapoor once more bowed her head over the baby. She believed that Gandhiji was a saint, more than a saint, a martyr – and she could not bear that anything should be said about him in bitterness. Even now she loved to sing – or to hear sung – the songs from the anthology used in his Ashram. She had just bought three postcards issued by the Posts and Telegraph Department in his memory: one showed him spinning, one showed him with his wife Kasturba, one showed him with a child.

But what her husband said was probably true. Thrust to the sidelines of power at the end of his active life, his message of generosity and reconciliation, it seemed, had been almost forgotten within four years of his death. She felt, however, that he would still have wanted to live. He had lived through times of desperate frustration before, and had borne it with patience. He was a good man, and a man without fear. Surely his fearlessness would have extended into the future.

After lunch, the women went for a walk in the garden. It had been a warmer year than most, but this particular day had been relieved by a little morning rain. The ground was still slightly moist, and the garden fragrant. The pink madhumalati creeper was in bloom near the swing. Mixed with the earth beneath the harsingar tree lay many small white-and-orange flowers that had fallen at dawn; they still held a trace of their fugitive scent. A few gardenias remained on one of two sporadically bearing trees. Mrs Rupa Mehra – who had been singularly quiet during lunch – now held and rocked the baby, who had fallen fast asleep. She sat down on a bench by the harsingar tree. In Uma's left ear was a most delicate vein that branched out into smaller and smaller ones in an exquisite pattern. Mrs Rupa Mehra looked at it for a while, then sighed.

'There is no tree like the harsingar,' she said to Mrs Mahesh Kapoor. 'I wish we had one in our garden.'

Mrs Mahesh Kapoor nodded. A modest, unhandsome tree by day, the harsingar became glorious at night, full of a delicate fragrance, surrounded by enchanted insects. The tiny, six-petalled flowers with their orange hearts wafted down at dawn. And tonight it would again be full, and the flowers would again float down as the sun rose. The tree flowered, but kept nothing for itself.

'No,' agreed Mrs Mahesh Kapoor with a grave smile. 'There is no tree like it at all.' After a pause she added: 'I will have Gajraj plant a seedling in the back garden at

Pran's house, next to the lime tree. Then it will always be as old as Uma. And it should flower in two or three years at the most.'

15.7

WHEN Bibbo saw the Nawabzada, she quickly thrust a letter into his hands.

'How in heaven's name did you know I would be coming here tonight? I wasn't invited.'

'No one can be uninvited tonight,' said Bibbo. 'I thought the Nawabzada might be alive to the opportunity.'

Firoz laughed. Bibbo loved intrigue, and it was good for him that she did, because it would have been impossible otherwise for him to communicate with Tasneem. He had seen her only twice, but she fascinated him; and he felt that she must surely feel something for him, for although her letters were gentle and discreet, the very fact that she wrote them without her sister's knowledge required courage.

'And does the Nawabzada have a letter in exchange?' asked Bibbo.

'Indeed, I do; and something else besides,' said Firoz, handing her a letter and a ten-rupee note.

'Oh, but this is unnecessary —'

'Yes, I know how unnecessary it is,' said Firoz. 'Who else is here?' he continued. He spoke in a low voice. He could hear the sound of a lament being chanted upstairs.

Bibbo reeled off a few names including that of Bilgrami Sahib. To Firoz's surprise there were several Sunnis among them.

'Sunnis too?'

'Why not?' said Bibbo. 'Saeeda Begum does not discriminate. Even certain pious women attend — the Nawabzada will admit that that is unusual. And she does not permit any of those mischievous imprecations that mar the atmosphere of most gatherings.'

'If that is the case I would have asked my friend Maan to come along,' said Firoz.

'No, no,' said Bibbo, startled. 'Dagh Sahib is a Hindu; that would never do. Id, yes, but Moharram – how would that be possible? It is a different matter altogether. Outdoor processions are open to everybody, but one must discriminate somewhat for a private gathering.'

'Anyway, he told me to give his love to the parakeet.'

'Oh, that miserable creature – I would like to wring its neck,' said Bibbo. Clearly some recent incident had reduced the bird's lovability in her eyes.

'And Maan – Dagh Sahib, I mean – also wondered – and I too am wondering – about this legend of Saeeda Begum quenching the thirst of travellers in the wilderness of Karbala with her own fair hands.'

'The Nawabzada will be gratified to know that it is not a legend,' said Bibbo, feeling a little annoyed that her mistress's piety was being questioned, but then suddenly giving Firoz a smile as she remembered the ten-rupee note. 'She stands at the corner of Khirkiwalan and Katra Mast on the day the tazias are brought out. Her mother, Mohsina Bai, used to do it, and she never fails to do it herself. Of course, you wouldn't know it was her; she wears a burqa, naturally. But even when she is not well she keeps that post; she is a very devout lady. Some people think one thing precludes another.'

'I do not doubt what you say,' said Firoz seriously. 'I did not mean to give offence.'

Bibbo, delighted with such courtesy from the Nawabzada, said:

'The Nawabzada is about to get a reward for his own religiosity.'

'And what is that?'

'He will see for himself.'

And so Firoz did. Unlike Maan, he did not pause to adjust his cap halfway up the stairs. No sooner had he entered the room where Saeeda Bai – in a dark blue sari with not a jewel on her face or hands – was holding her session than he saw – or, rather, beheld – Tasneem sitting at the back of the room. She was dressed in a fawn-coloured salwaar-kameez. She looked as beautiful, as delicate as the first time he had seen her. Her eyes were filled with tears. The moment she saw Firoz she lowered them.

Saeeda Bai did not lose a syllable of her marsiya as she saw Firoz enter, though her eyes flashed. Already the listeners were in a high state of excitement. Men and women alike were weeping; some of the women were beating their breasts and lamenting for Hussain. Saeeda Bai's own soul seemed to have entered the marsiya, but one part of it observed the congregation and noted the entrance of the Nawab of Baitar's son. She would have to deal with this trouble later; for the moment she had simply to bear it. But the agitation she felt communicated itself into the force of her indignation against the killer of Imam Hussain:

'And as that accursed mercenary pulled out the bloodied
                                                                              spear
The Prince of Martyrs bowed his head in gratitude to
                                                                              God.
The hell-bent, brutal Shamr unsheathed his dagger and
                                                                              advanced
The heavens shook, the earth quaked seeing such foul,
                                                                              odious acts.
How can I say how Shamr put the dagger to his throat –
It was as if he trampled on the Holy Book itself!'

'Toba! toba!' 'Ya Allah!' 'Ya Hussain! Ya Hussain!' cried the audience. Some were so choked with grief they could not speak at all, and when the next stanza revealed his sister Zainab's grief – her swooning away – her shock when she reopened her eyes and saw her brother's head, the head of the Holy Prince of Martyrs, raised upon a lance – there was a dreadful silence in the audience, a pause before renewed lamentation. Firoz glanced at Tasneem; her eyes were still cast down, but her lips moved to the famous words that her sister was reciting.

'Anis, thou canst not write of Zainab's lamentations
                                            more!
The body of Hussain lay there, unburied, in the sun;
Alas, the Prophet found no peace in his last resting place!
His holy progeny imprisoned and his house burnt down!
How many homes Hussain's death left all ruined,
                                            desolate!
The Prophet's progeny, thus never prospered after him.'

Here Saeeda Bai stopped, and looked around the room, her eyes resting for a moment on Firoz, then on Tasneem. After a while she said, casually, to Tasneem: 'Go and feed the parakeet, and tell Bibbo to come here. She likes to be present at the soz-khwani.' Tasneem left the room. Others in the audience began to recover, and talk among themselves.

Firoz's heart fell. His eyes followed Tasneem to the door. He was in a state of volatile distraction. He had never seen her look so beautiful as now, unadorned, her cheeks stained with tears. Lost in contemplation, he hardly noticed when Bilgrami Sahib greeted him.

But Bilgrami Sahib was now telling him about the time he had visited Baitar during the Moharram celebrations – and Firoz's mind was drawn back against his will to the Fort and the Imambara with its red-and-white chandelier and the paintings of Karbala on the wall and the marsiyas chanted under the hundreds of flickering lights.

The Nawab Sahib's great hero was Al-Hur, the officer who had been sent at first to seize Hussain; but who at the end had detached himself with thirty horsemen from the main force of the enemy and had joined the weaker side to face inevitable death. Firoz had tried to argue the point once or twice with his father; but had given it up. His father, whom Firoz suspected of being half in love with noble failure, felt too strongly about the matter.

Saeeda Bai now began singing a short marsiya particularly suited for soz. This contained no introduction, no elaboration of the physical beauty of the hero, no vaunting on the battlefield by the hero of his lineage and prowess and exploits, no long battle-scenes, no description of horse or sword, almost nothing but the most moving parts of the story: the scenes of leave-taking from his loved ones, his death, the lamentations of the women and children. At the lamentations Saeeda Bai's voice rose into the air in a strange sobbing wail, intensely musical, intensely beautiful.

Firoz had heard soz before, but it was nothing compared to this. He turned to the spot where Tasneem had been sitting, and noticed the frivolous Bibbo there instead. Her hair was undone, and she was crying her eyes out, beating her breast and leaning forward as if she were about to faint with sorrow. So were many of the women around her. Bilgrami Sahib was sobbing into his handkerchief, which his hands clutched in the gesture of prayer. Saeeda Bai's eyes were closed; even for this supremely controlled artist, her art had passed beyond her own restraint. Her body, like her voice, was shaking with grief and pain. And Firoz, though he did not realize it, was himself weeping uncontrollably.

15.8

'WHY did you miss last night?' demanded Bhaskar, who had been promoted tonight to be Angad, a monkey-prince, because the boy playing that part had fallen ill, probably from growling himself hoarse on previous evenings. Bhaskar knew Angad's lines, but unfortunately there was nothing to say today – it was all just running around and fighting.

'I was asleep,' said Maan.

'Asleep! You are like Kumbhkaran,' said Bhaskar. 'You missed the best part of the battle. You missed the building of the bridge to Lanka – it stretched across from the temple to the houses there – and you missed Hanuman going to get the magic herb – and you missed the burning of Lanka.'

'But I'm here now,' said Maan. 'Give your uncle some credit.'

'And this morning, when Daadi was worshipping the weapons and pens and books, where were you?'

'Well, I don't believe in all that,' said Maan, attempting a different tack. 'I don't believe in weapons and shooting and hunting and violence. Did she worship your kites as well?'

'Aré, Maan, shake hands with me,' said a familiar voice out of the crowd. Maan turned around. It was the Rajkumar of Marh, accompanied by the Vakil Sahib's younger brother. Maan was a bit surprised to see the Rajkumar here, at this neighbourhood Ramlila. He would have thought he would be at some great, soulless, official one, trailing his father around. Maan shook hands with him very cordially.

'Have some paan.'

'Thanks,' said Maan, took two, and almost choked. There was a powerful dose of tobacco in the paan. For a minute or two he was literally speechless. He had planned to ask the Rajkumar what he was doing these days without even his studies to occupy him; but by the time he had recovered, young Goyal, who appeared to be very proud to be sporting minor royalty around, had quickly dragged the Rajkumar away to introduce him to someone else.

Maan turned and stared at the effigies. Along the western edge of the square of Shahi Darvaza stood three huge figures – fierce and flammable – of wood, cane, and coloured paper, with red light-bulbs for their eyes. The ten-headed Ravana required twenty bulbs, which flickered more menacingly than those of his lieutenants. He was the embodiment of armed evil: each of his twenty hands carried a weapon: bows made of cane, maces made of silver paper, wooden swords and discuses, bamboo spears, even a mock-pistol. To one side of Ravana stood his vile brother Kumbhkaran, fat, vicious, idle and gluttonous; and to his other side stood Meghnad, his courageous and arrogant son who just the previous day had struck Laksh-man with a javelin in the breast and almost killed him. Everyone was comparing the effigies with those of earlier years, and excitedly anticipating their conflagration as the climax of the evening: the destruction of evil, the triumph of good.

But before that could happen, the actors playing the parts of these figures had to meet their fates in due order before the public eye.

At seven o'clock the loudspeakers overhead belched forth a sudden cacophony of drumbeats, and the little red-faced monkeys, made up to look fierce and martial with all that art, indigo and zinc oxide could contrive, swarmed out of the temple building in search of the enemy, whom they quickly found and noisily engaged with. Screams were heard, together with pious shouts of 'Jai Siyaram!' and demonic cries of 'Jai Shankar!' Even the vowels in the name of Lord Shiva, the great patron of Ravana, had been extended in a mocking and sinister manner, so that the sound that emerged was more like 'Jai Shenker!' This was followed each time by Ravana's bizarre and grisly laugh that chilled the blood of most of the spectators, even if it made the actor's friends laugh.

Two khaki policemen of the local constabulary wandered along here and there to ensure that the monkey and demon hordes kept to the agreed geographical limits, but since the monkeys and demons were far swifter than the forces of the law, they gave up after a while, stopped at a paan-shop, and demanded free paans instead. Round and round the policemen, in and out of the square, past their own parents who could barely recognize them, and through the lanes ran the monkeys and demons, past the small general store, the two temples, the small mosque, the bakery, the astrologer's house, the public urinal, the electrical junction, and the doorways of the houses; sometimes they were chased into the open courtyards of houses, and chased out again by the Ramlila organizers. Their swords and lances and arrows got stuck in the coloured streamers overhanging the lane, and ripped the overhead banner that read in Hindi: *The Ramlila Welfare Committee heartily welcomes you.* Finally, exhausted, the two armies gathered in the square and glared and growled at each other.

The army of monkeys (with a few bears thrown in) was

led by Rama, Lakshman and Hanuman. They had tried to hunt down Ravana, while the twelve-year-old boy playing the beautiful, abducted Sita watched from a balcony above with — so it appeared from his expression — supreme indifference. Ravana, pestered and harried by the monkeys and shot at by his arch-enemy Rama, was on the run and demanded to know where his brother Kumbhkaran had got to — why was he not defending Lanka? When he heard that Kumbhkaran was still sunk in a gluttonous stupor, he demanded that he be woken. The demons and imps did their best, passing food and sweets over the huge, supine form until the scent aroused him from his sleep. He roared, stretched, and gobbled up what was offered to him. Several demons polished off some of the sweets themselves. Then the battle began in earnest.

In the rhyming verse of Tulsidas, which could hardly be heard on the pandit's megaphone above the clamour:

'Having feasted on the buffaloes and drunk off the wine, Kumbhkaran roared like a crash of lightning.... The moment the mighty monkeys heard this, they rushed forth crying with joy. They plucked up trees and mountains and hurled them against Kumbhkaran, gnashing their teeth all the while. The bears and monkeys threw myriads of mountain-peaks at him each time. But neither did he feel daunted in spirit nor did he stir from his position in spite of the best efforts on the part of the monkeys to push him back, even like an elephant pelted with the fruits of the sun-plant. Thereupon Hanuman struck him with his fist and he fell to the earth, beating his head in great confusion. Rising again, he hit Hanuman back and the latter whirled round and immediately dropped to the ground.... The monkey host stampeded; in utter dismay none dared face him.'

Even Bhaskar, who was playing Angad, was knocked down by the mighty Kumbhkaran and lay groaning piteously underneath the pipal tree where he used to play cricket.

Despite the arrows of Rama, the wounded monster was

undeterred. 'He burst into a terrible roar and, seizing millions and millions of monkeys, dashed them to the ground like a huge elephant, swearing by his ten-headed brother.' The monkeys cried to Rama in distress; he drew his bow and fired yet more arrows at Kumbhkaran. 'Even as the arrows struck him, the demon rushed forth, burning with rage; the mountains staggered and the earth shook as he ran.' He tore up a rock; but Rama cut off the arm that bore it. He then rushed forward with the rock in his left hand; but the Lord struck off even that arm and it fell to the ground.... 'Uttering a most terrible shriek, he rushed on with wide open mouth. The saints and gods in the heavens cried out in their terror, "Alas! Alas!"'

Seeing the distress of the very gods, the All-merciful Rama finally cut off Kumbhkaran's head with another arrow, and let it fall to the ground in front of his horrified brother Ravana. The trunk still ran madly on, until it was cut down. It then fell to the ground, crushing beneath it monkeys, bears, and demons alike.

The crowd yelled and cheered and clapped. Maan cheered with them; Bhaskar stopped groaning, got up and shouted with joy. Even the subsequent deaths in battle of Meghnad and the arch-enemy himself could not match the delight everyone felt at the death of Kumbhkaran, who was a seasoned actor of many years' standing and had mastered the art of terrifying both antagonists and audience. Finally, when all the actor-demons lay dead in the dust, and 'Jai Shenker!' was heard no more, it was time for the pyromania.

A red carpet of about five thousand small firecrackers was laid out in front of the demon effigies, and lit with a long fuse. The racket was deafening, truly enough to make saints and gods cry out, 'Alas! Alas!' The fire, the sparks, the ash reached the balcony above and made Mrs Mahesh Kapoor wheeze and choke before the unbreathable acrid air was borne away by the wind. Rama fired an arrow at each of Kumbhkaran's arms and they dropped away, manipulated from behind by the prop-man. Again the audience gasped. But instead of striking off his head, the handsome blue figure in his leopard-skin now took a rocket out of his quiver, and aimed it at Kumbhkaran's armless body. The rocket hit the corpse; it lit up in flames, and was consumed in a series of thunderous explosions. Kumbhkaran had been stuffed with fireworks, which now whizzed about him; a green bomb on his nose went off in a fountain of coloured sparks. His huge frame collapsed, the organizers of the Ramlila beat the remnants down to ash, and the crowd cheered Rama on.

After Lakshman had dispatched the effigy of Meghnad, Rama finished off the evil Ravana for the second time in the evening. But to the alarm of the crowd the paper, straw and bamboo with which he had been stuffed refused to burn. There was a sense of alarm now, as if this did not augur well for the forces of good. It was only with the addition of a bit of kerosene that Ravana was finally done away with. And again, with a few strokes of the organizers' lathis and a thorough dousing with pots and pans of water poured down by cheering people from the balconies above, the once-malevolent ten-headed effigy was reduced to ash and charred cane.

Rama, Lakshman, and Hanuman had retired to one side of the square when a rather mocking voice in the crowd reminded them that they had forgotten to rescue Sita after all. Back they hurried over the black-ashed ground, across the scorched-paper residue of five thousand firecrackers. Sita, clad in a yellow sari, and still looking fairly bored with the proceedings, was handed down to them from her balcony without much ceremony and restored to her husband.

Now, with Rama, Lakshman, Sita and Hanuman all together at last, and the forces of evil finally vanquished, the crowd responded enthusiastically to the pandit's prompting:

'Raghupati Shri Ramchandra ji ki —'
'Jai!'
'Bol, Sita Maharani ki —'
'Jai!'
'Lakshman ji ki —'

'Jai!'

'Shri Bajrangbali ki –'

'Jai!'

'Kindly remember, good people,' continued the pandit, 'that the ceremony of Bharat Milaap will take place tomorrow at the time announced on the posters, in Rama's capital of Ayodhya, which for our purposes is the small square near the temple in Misri Mandi. That is where Rama and Lakshman will embrace their long separated brothers Bharat and Shatrughan – and fall at the feet of their mothers. Please don't forget. It will be a very moving performance and will bring tears to the eyes of all true devotees of Shri Rama. It is the true climax of the Ramlila, even more than the darshan you have had tonight. And please tell everyone who has not had the fortune to be present here to go to Misri Mandi tomorrow night. Now where is the photographer? Mela Ram ji, kindly step forward.'

Photographs were taken, arati was performed several times with lamps and sweets on a silver platter, and each of the good figures, including many of the monkeys and bears, were fed. They looked properly serious now. Some of the rowdier elements of the crowd had already dispersed. But most of the audience remained, and accepted the leftover sweets as a sanctified offering. Even the demons got their share.

15.9

THE tazia procession from Baitar House to the city Imambara was a stately business. The Baitar House tazia was famous: it had been made many years before, and was a magnificent affair of silver and crystal. Each year on the ninth day of Moharram it was carried to the city Imambara, where it was displayed overnight and the next morning. Then, on the afternoon of the tenth day, together with all the other replicas of the tomb of the Imam Hussain, it was carried in a grand procession to the 'Karbala', the field outside Brahmpur specially designated for the burial of the tazias. But unlike those made of mere paper and glass, the silver Baitar House tazia (like a few others that were equally precious) was not smashed and buried in an open pit dug for the purpose. It was left on the field for an hour or so, its temporary ornaments of tinsel and kite-paper and mica were buried, and the tazia itself was taken back to the house by the servants.

The Baitar House procession this year consisted of Firoz (dressed in a white sherwani), a couple of drummers, six young men (three on each side) carrying the great tazia along on strong wooden poles, some of the house servants who beat their chests rhythmically and cried out the names of the martyrs (but did not use whips or chains), and a couple of constables to represent the forces of law and order. Their route from Pasand Bagh was rather long, so they started out early.

By early evening they had got to the street outside the Imambara which was the meeting place for the various tazia processions of the different guilds and neighbour-hoods and great houses. Here stood a tall pole, at least sixty feet high, with a green and black flag fluttering above. Here also stood the statue of a horse, Hussain's brave steed, richly decorated during Moharram with flowers and precious cloth. And here also, just outside the Imambara, near the wayside shrine of a local saint, was a busy fair – where the mourning of the processionists inter-mingled with the festive excitement of people buying or selling knick-knacks and holy pictures, and children eating all sorts of delicious street food, including sweets, ice-cream and candy-floss – coloured not only pink but also green for Moharram.

Most tazia processions were much less decorous than the one that represented the Nawab Sahib's family: their grief was loud, their drumbeats deafening, their self-flagella-tions bloody. Nor did they prize decorum above sincerity. The fervour of their feelings was what carried them on-wards. Unshod, naked above the waist, their backs a mess of blood from the chains with which they lashed themselves, the men accompanying the tazias panted and moaned as they took the name of Imam Hussain and his brother Hassan repeatedly, rhythmically, in plaintive or agonized lament. Some of the processions that were known to be the most fervent were accompanied by as many as a dozen policemen.

The routes of the tazia processions had been charted out with great care by the organizers and the police together. Hindu areas were to be avoided as far as possible, and in particular the area of the contested temple; low-lying branches of pipal trees were measured in advance against the heights of tazias, so that neither would be damaged; the processionists were enjoined from cursing the caliphs; and timings were matched so that by nightfall all the processions throughout the city would have arrived at the central destination.

Maan met Firoz, as agreed, a little before sunset near the statue of the horse by the Imambara.

'Ah, so you've come, you kafir.' Firoz was looking very handsome in his white sherwani.

'But only to do what all kafirs do,' replied Maan.

'And what is that?'

'Why don't you have your Nawabi walking-stick with you?' asked Maan, who had been looking Firoz up and down.

'It wouldn't have been appropriate for the procession,' replied Firoz. 'I'd have been expected to beat myself with it, no doubt. But you haven't answered my question.'

'Oh – what was that?'

'What is it that all kafirs do?'

'Is that a riddle?' asked Maan.

'It is not,' said Firoz. 'You just said that you'd come to do what all kafirs do. And I'm asking you what that is.'

'Oh, to prostrate myself before my idol. You said she'd be here.'

'Well, there she is,' said Firoz, jerking his head lightly in the direction of the nearby crossroads. 'I'm pretty sure.'

A woman dressed in a black burqa was standing at a booth, distributing sherbet to those who passed by in the tazia processions or who milled about the temporary market. They drank, they handed the glasses back, and these were dumped into a bucket of water by another woman in a brown burqa and given a cursory wash before being re-used. The stand was very popular, probably because it was known who the lady in black was.

'Quenching the thirst of Karbala,' added Firoz.

'Come,' said Maan.

'No, no, you go along. That other one's Bibbo, by the way, the one in a brown burqa. Not Tasneem.'

'Come with me, Firoz. Please. I really have no business to be here. I'll feel very awkward.'

'Nothing like as awkward as I felt when I went to her gathering last night. No, I'm going to see the tazias lined up. Most of them have arrived already, and each year there's something astonishing to see. Last year there was one in the shape of a double-storeyed peacock with a woman's head — and only half a dome to tell you it was meant to be a tomb. We're becoming Hinduized.'

'Well, if I come with you to see the tazias, will you accompany me to the sherbet-stand?'

'Oh — all right.'

Maan quickly got bored with the tazias, remarkable though they were.

Everyone around him appeared to be engaged in heated discussion about which one was the most elegant, the most elaborate, the most expensive. 'I recognize that one,' said Maan with a smile; he had seen it in the Imambara at Baitar House.

'Well, we'll probably use it for another fifty years,' said Firoz. 'I doubt we'll be able to afford to make anything like that again.'

'Come, now, keep your part of the bargain.'

'All right.'

Firoz and Maan walked over to the sherbet-stand.

'It's too unhygienic for words, Maan — you can't drink from those glasses.'

But Maan had gone forward, pushed his way through the crowd, and now held his hand out for a glass of sherbet. The woman in black handed it to him, but at the last moment, as her eyes suddenly registered who he was, she was so startled that she spilled the sherbet over his hands.

She took her breath in sharply and said, 'Excuse me, Sir,' in a low voice. 'Let me pour you another glass.'

There was no mistaking her voice. 'No, no, Madam,' protested Maan. 'Please do not trouble yourself. What is left in this glass will more than quench my thirst, however terrible.'

The woman in the brown burqa turned towards him upon hearing his voice. Then the two women turned towards each other. Maan sensed their tension, and he allowed himself a smile.

Bibbo may not have been surprised to see Maan, but Saeeda Bai was both surprised and displeased. As Maan had expected, she thought he had no business to be there; certainly he could not pretend to any lavish fondness for the Shia martyrs. But his smile only succeeded in making her angrier. She contrasted the flippancy of Maan's remark with the terrible thirst of the heroes of Karbala – their tents burning behind them, the river cut off in front of them – and, making no attempt this time to disguise her voice or her indignation, she said to Maan: 'I am running short of supplies. There is a booth half a mile further on where I would advise you to go when you have finished this glass. It is run by a lady of great piety; the sherbet is sweeter, and you will find the crowd less oppressive.'

And before Maan could respond with an appropriate conciliatory couplet, she had turned to the other thirsty men.

'Well?' said Firoz.

Maan scratched his head. 'No, she wasn't pleased.'

'Well, don't fret; it doesn't suit you. Let's see what the market has to offer.'

Maan looked at his watch. 'No, I can't. I have to go to watch the Bharat Milaap, or I'll lose my standing in the eyes of my nephew. Why don't you come along as well? It's very affecting. Everyone lines the lanes, cheering and weeping and showering flowers on the procession. Rama and company from the left, Bharat and company from the right. And the two brothers embrace in the middle – just outside the city of Ayodhya.'

'Well, I suppose there are enough people to manage without me here,' said Firoz. 'How far is it?'

'Misri Mandi – that's where Ayodhya's located this year. Only a ten minute walk from here – very close to Veena's house. She'll be pleasantly surprised to see you.'

Firoz laughed. 'That's what you thought Saeeda Bai would be,' he said, as they wandered hand in hand through the bazaar in the direction of Misri Mandi.

15.10

THE Bharat Milaap processions began on time. Since Bharat had merely to go to the outskirts of his city to meet his brother, he bided his time until the pandit gave him the signal; but Rama had a long journey to make to the holy capital of Ayodhya – to which he was returning in triumph after many years of exile – and just as it became dark he set out on this journey from a temple situated a good half-mile away from the stage where the brothers were at last to be united.

This stage had been festooned with strings of flowers suspended from the bamboo poles that rose from its four corners; it had been put together by almost the whole neighbourhood with much advice and many marigolds; and several cows that had attempted to eat the marigolds had been shooed off by the monkey army. The cows were normally welcome enough in the neighbourhood – their movements at least were unobstructed – and the poor trusting things must have wondered what had created such a sudden change in their popularity.

Today was a day of pure joy and celebration; for not only were Rama and Lakshman to be reunited with their brothers Bharat and Shatrughan, but it was the day when the people would see their Lord return to them, to rule over them and establish perfect righteousness not only in Ayodhya but in the entire world.

The procession began to wind its way through the narrow lanes of Misri Mandi to the sound of drums and shehnais and a raucous popular band. First came the lights, courtesy of Jawaharlal Light House, the same company that had provided the demons' red eyes the previous evening. The brilliant lights they held above them emitted an intense white glow from what looked like bulbs covered with gauze cloth.

Mahesh Kapoor held his hand against his eyes. He was here partly because his wife wanted him to be, partly because he was more and more coming around to the idea of rejoining the Congress Party and felt he should re-establish his links with his old constituency just in case.

'This light is too bright – I'm going blind –' he said. 'Kedarnath, do something about it. You're one of the organizers, aren't you?'

'Baoji, let's just let them pass. It'll be better later on,' said his son-in-law, who knew that once the procession had begun, there was almost nothing he could do about it. Mrs Mahesh Kapoor had cupped her hands over her ears, but was smiling to herself.

The brass band was deafening. After blaring out a few film songs, they switched to religious melodies. They made a striking sight in their cheap red trousers with white piping and their blue tunics with gold-coloured cotton braid. Every one of their trumpets, trombones and horns was out of tune.

Then came the principal noisemongers, the flat drummers, who had been roasting their instruments carefully over three small fires near the temple to heighten their pitch and crispness. They played as if they had gone mad – in unbelievably swift salvos of unbearable noise. They forced themselves aggressively upon anyone whom they recognized from the Ramlila Committee in a mixture of display and blackmail, compelling them to hand over coins and notes. They thrust their pelvises forward and moved their drums back and forth at a slant from their waists. These were good days for the drummers: they were in demand both by those who celebrated Dussehra and by those who observed Moharram.

'Where are they from?' asked Mahesh Kapoor.

'What?' asked Kedarnath.

'I said, where are they from?'

'I can't hear you because of these wretched drummers.'

Mahesh Kapoor cupped his hands and shouted into his son-in-law's ears: 'I said, where are they from? Are they Muslim?'

'They're from the market –' shouted Kedarnath, which was a way of admitting that they were.

Even before the swaroops – Rama, Lakshman, and Sita – could appear in their beauty and glory, the master of fireworks – who carried a massive sack on his shoulder – brought out a huge packet, tore off the coloured paper from it, ripped open the cardboard box inside, and rolled out another great red carpet of five thousand firecrackers. As they exploded in series, people drew back from the light and noise, their faces flushed with excitement, their hands clapped over their ears or their fingers inserted into them. The noise was so overwhelming that Mahesh Kapoor decided that even his obligation to be seen in his old constituency was not worth the loss of his hearing and sanity.

'Come,' he shouted to his wife, 'we're going home.'

Mrs Mahesh Kapoor could not hear a word of what he was saying, and kept smiling.

The monkey army, Bhaskar included, was next in the procession, and a great quiver of excitement went through the spectators; the swaroops were to follow shortly. The children started clapping; the old people were the most expectant of all, remembering perhaps the scores of Ramlilas they must have seen enacted in the course of their lives. Some children sat on a low wall along the route, others skilfully scrambled up to the ledges of houses, getting a foothold here or the help of an adult shoulder there. One father, kissing his two-year-old daughter's bare foot, pushed her up onto the flat top of a decorative pillar and held her there to help her get a better view.

And then at last Lord Rama appeared; and Sita, in a yellow sari; and Lakshman, smiling, his quiver glistening with arrows.

The eyes of the spectators filled with tears of joy, and they began showering flowers on the swaroops. The children clambered down from their perches and followed the procession, chanting 'Jai Siyaram' and 'Ramchandra ji ki jai!' and sprinkling rose-petals and water from the Ganga on them. And the drummers beat their drums with renewed frenzy.

Mahesh Kapoor, his face flushed with annoyance, seized his wife's hand and pulled her to one side.

'We are leaving,' he shouted directly into her ear. 'Can't you hear me? I have had enough.... Veena, your mother and I are leaving.'

Mrs Mahesh Kapoor looked at her husband, astonished, almost disbelieving. Tears filled her eyes when she understood what he had said, what she was to be deprived of. Once she had seen the Bharat Milaap at Nati Imli in Banaras, and she had never forgotten it. The tenderness of the occasion – with the two brothers who had remained in Ayodhya throwing themselves at the feet of their two long-exiled brothers – the throng of spectators, at least a lakh of people – the devotion in everyone's eyes as the small figures came onto the stage – everything came back to her. Whenever she saw the Bharat Milaap here in Brahmpur she thought of that occasion in all its charm and wonder and grace. How simple it was and how wonderful. And it was not merely the tender meeting of long-separated brothers but the first act of Ram Rajya, the rule of Rama when, unlike in these factious, violent, petty times, the four pillars of religion – truth, purity, mercy, and charity – would hold up the edifice of the world.

The words of Tulsidas, long known by heart, came back to her:

Devoted to duty, the people walked in the path of the

Vedas, each according to his own caste and stage of life, and enjoyed perfect happiness, unvexed by fear, or sorrow, or disease.

'Let us at least wait till the procession has reached Ayodhya,' Mrs Mahesh Kapoor pleaded with her husband.

'Stay if you want. I'm going,' snapped Mahesh Kapoor; and, forlornly, she followed. But she decided that tomorrow she would not persuade him to come for Rama's coronation. She would come alone and, not subject to his whims and commands, she would see it from beginning to end. She would not be prised away yet again from a scene that her soul thirsted for.

Meanwhile the procession wound its way through the labyrinthine alleys of Misri Mandi and the contiguous neighbourhoods. Lakshman stepped on one of the burnt-out bulbs from the Jawaharlal Light House, and yelped in pain. Since there was no water to be had immediately, Rama picked up some rose-petals that had been strewn in his path and crushed them against the burn. The people sighed at this sign of brotherly solicitude, and the procession moved on. The chief of fireworks now set off a few green-flared rockets that soared into the sky before exploding in a chrysanthemum of sparks. At this, Hanuman rushed forward, waving his tail, as if reminded of his own incendiary activities in Lanka. He was followed by the monkey throng, chattering and shouting with joy; they reached the marigold stage a couple of hundred yards before the three main swaroops. Hanuman, who today was even redder, plumper and jollier than he had been yesterday, leaped onto the stage, hopped, skipped, and danced for a few seconds, then jumped off. Now Bharat understood that Rama and Lakshman were approaching the river Saryu and the city of Ayodhya, and he too began to move towards the stage along the lane from the other side.

AND then suddenly Rama's procession stopped, and the sound of other drums was heard together with cries of terrible grief and lamentation. A group of about twenty men accompanied by drummers was trying to cut across the procession in order to get to the Imambara with their tazia. Some were beating their breasts in sorrow for Imam Hussain; in the hands of others were chains and whips tipped with small knives and razor-blades with which they lashed themselves mercilessly in jerky, compulsive motions. They were an hour-and-a-half behind time – their drummers had turned up late, they had got into a scuffle with another tazia procession – and now they were trying to push forward as fast as they could, desperate to get to their destination. It was the ninth night of Moharram. In the distance they could just make out the spire of the Imambara lit up with a string of lights. They moved forwards, tears coursing down their cheeks –

'Ya Hassan! Ya Hussain!' 'Ya Hassan! Ya Hussain!' 'Hassan! Hussain!' 'Hassan! Hussain!'

'Bhaskar,' said Veena to her son, who had grabbed her hand – 'Go home at once. At once. Where's Daadi ?–'

'But I want to watch –'

She slapped him once, hard, across his monkey-face. He looked at her unbelievingly, then, crying, backed out of the lane.

Kedarnath had moved forward to talk to the two policemen accompanying the tazia procession. Not caring what her neighbours might think, she went up to him, caught his hands in her own, and said:

'Let's go home.'

'But there's trouble here – I'd better –'

'Bhaskar's ill.'

Kedarnath, torn between two anxieties, nodded.

The two policemen accompanying the tazia-bearers tried to clear a path for them, but this was too much for the people of Misri Mandi, the citizens of the holy city of

Ayodhya who had waited so long and devotedly for a sight of Lord Rama.

The policemen realized that what would have been a safe path an hour previously was no longer safe. They ordered, then pleaded with the tazia procession to change its route, to halt, to go back, but to no avail. The desperate mourners thrust forward through the joyous celebrators.

This atrocious and violent interruption – this lunatic mourning that made a mockery of the enactment of Shri Ramachandra ji returning to his home, his brothers, his people, to establish his perfect reign – was not to be borne. The monkeys, who had just been leaping about in uncontrollable joy, angrily threw flowers onto the tazia, shouted and growled aggressively, and then stood threateningly around the intruders who were attempting to force themselves across the path of Rama, Sita and Lakshman.

The actor playing Rama himself moved forward in a motion that was half aggressive, half propitiatory.

A chain lashed out, and he staggered back, to lie gasping in pain against the ledge of a shop. Upon his dark blue skin a red stain formed and spread.

The crowd went berserk. What all the forces of Ravana had not succeeded in doing these bloodthirsty Muslims had managed to do. It was not a young actor, but God himself who lay wounded there.

Crazed by the sight of the wounded Rama, the man with the fireworks seized a lathi from one of the organizers and led the crowd in a charge against the tazia procession. Within seconds, the tazia, many weeks' work of delicate glass and mica and paper tracery, lay smashed on the ground. Fireworks were thrown onto it and it was set alight. The maddened crowd stamped on it and beat it with lathis until it was charred and splintered. Its horrified defenders slashed out with their knives and chains at these kafirs, leaping about like apes on the very eve of the great martyrdom, who had dared to desecrate the holy image of the tomb.

The sight of the crushed and blackened tazia made them mad.

Both sides now were filled with the lust to kill – what did it matter if they too suffered martyrdom?– to attack pure evil, to defend what was dear to them – what did it matter if they died?–whether to recreate the passion of Karbala or to re-establish Ram Rajya and rid the world of the murderous, cow-slaughtering, God-defiling devils.

'Kill the bastards – finish them off – the spawn of Pakistan –'

'Ya Hussain! Ya Hussain!' It was now a battlecry.

Soon even the crazed cries of the time of Partition – 'Allah-u-Akbar' and 'Har har Mahadeva' – were heard above the screams of pain and terror. Knives and spears and axes and lathis had appeared from the neighbouring houses, and Hindus and Muslims hacked at each other's limbs, eyes, faces, guts, throats. Of the two policemen, one was wounded in the back, the other managed to escape. But it was a Hindu neighbourhood and, after a few terrifying minutes of mutual butchery, the Muslims fled down side-lanes, most of them small and unfamiliar. Some were hunted down and killed, some escaped and rushed back in the direction from which they had come, some ran forward towards the Imambara by circuitous routes – guided from far off by its illuminated spire and festoons of light. They fled towards the Imambara as one would flee towards a sanctuary – where they would receive protection among those of their own religion and would find hearts that could understand their own fear and hatred and bitterness and grief – for they had seen their friends and relatives killed and wounded – and be inflamed by them in turn.

Soon Muslim mobs would be roaming around other parts of Brahmpur setting fire to Hindu shops and murdering any Hindu they could find. Meanwhile in Misri Mandi, three of the Muslim drummers who had been hired for the Bharat Milaap, who were not even Shias, and who did not care much more for the tazias than they did for the divinity of Rama, lay murdered by the wall of the temple, their drums smashed in, their heads half hacked off, their bodies doused in kerosene and set alight – all, doubtless, to the greater glory of God.

MAAN and Firoz were sauntering along through the dark lane of Katra Mast towards Misri Mandi when Maan stopped suddenly. The sounds he heard approaching them were not those he had expected. They were the sounds neither of a tazia procession – and surely it was too late for a tazia procession – nor the joyful sounds of Bharat Milaap. The sound of drums had stopped on either side – and neither 'Hassan! Hussain!' nor 'Jai Siyaram!' could be heard. Instead he made out the ominous, inchoate sounds of a mob, broken by screams of pain or passion – or shouts of 'Har har Mahadeva'. This aggressive invocation of Shiva would not have sounded out of place yesterday – but today it chilled his blood.

He let go of Firoz's hand and turned him around by the shoulders. 'Run!' he said, his mouth dry with fear. 'Run.' His heart was pounding. Firoz stared at him but did not move.

The crowd was rushing down the lane now. The sounds grew closer. Maan looked around him in desperation. The shops were all closed, their shutters down. There were no side-lanes within immediate reach.

'Get back, Firoz –' said Maan, trembling. 'Get back – run! There's nowhere to hide here –'

'What's the matter – isn't it the procession?' Firoz's mouth opened as he registered the terror in Maan's eyes.

'Just listen to me,' Maan gasped – 'Do as I say. Run back! Run back towards the Imambara. I'll delay them for a minute or two. That'll be enough. They'll stop me first.'

'I'm not leaving you,' said Firoz.

'Firoz, you fool, this is a Hindu mob. I'm not in danger. But I won't be all right if I come with you. God knows what will be happening there by now. If there's rioting going on, they'll be killing Hindus there.'

'No –'

'Oh God –'

By now the crowd had almost reached them, and it was too late to flee. Ahead of the pack was a young man, who looked as if he was drunk. His kurta was torn and he was bleeding from a cut along his ribs. He had a blood-stained lathi in his hand, and he made for Maan and Firoz. Behind him – though it was dark and difficult to see – must have been some twenty or thirty men, armed with spears and knives or flaming torches doused in kerosene.

'Mussalmans – kill them also –'

'We're not Mussalmans,' said Maan immediately, not looking at Firoz. He tried to control his voice, but it was high-pitched with terror.

'We can find that out quickly enough,' said the young man nastily. Maan looked at him – he had a lean, clean-shaven face – a handsome face, but one that was full of madness and rage and hatred. Who was he? Who were these people? Maan recognized none of them in the dark-ness. What had happened? How had the peacefulness of the Bharat Milaap suddenly turned into a riot? And what, he thought, his brain seizing up with fear, what was going to happen?

Suddenly, as if by a miracle, the fog of fear dispersed from his mind.

'No need to find out who we are,' he said in a deeper voice. 'We were frightened because we thought at first you might be Muslims. We couldn't hear what you were shouting.'

'Recite the Gayatri Mantra,' sneered the young man.

Maan promptly recited the few sacred syllables. 'Now go –' he said. 'Don't threaten innocent people. Be on your way. Jai Siyaram! Har har Mahadeva!' He could not keep the rising mockery out of his voice.

The young man hesitated.

Someone in the crowd cried: 'The other's a Muslim. Why would he be dressed like that?'

'Yes, that's certain.'

'Take off his fancy dress.'

Firoz had started trembling again. This encouraged them.

'See if he's circumcized.'

'Kill the cruel, cow-murdering haramzada – cut the sister-fucker's throat.'

'What are you?' said the young man, prodding Firoz in the stomach with his bloodstained lathi. 'Quick – speak – speak, before I use this on your head –'

Firoz flinched and trembled. The blood on the lathi had stained his white sherwani. He did not lack courage normally, but now – in the face of such wild, unreasoning danger – he found he had lost his voice. How could he argue with a mob? He swallowed and said: 'I am what I am. What's that to you?'

Maan was looking desperately around him. He knew there was no time to talk. Suddenly in the erratic, terrifying light of the blazing torches his eyes fell on someone he thought he recognized.

'Nand Kishor!' he shouted. 'What are you doing here in this gang? Aren't you ashamed of yourself? You're supposed to be a teacher.' Nand Kishor, a middle-aged, bespectacled man, looked sullen.

'Shut up –' said the young man to Maan viciously. 'Just because you like circumcized cocks do you think we'll let the Mussalman go?' Again he prodded Firoz and drew another smear of blood down his sherwani.

Maan ignored him and continued to address Nand Kishor. He knew that the time for dialogue was short. It was miraculous that they had been able to speak at all – that they were still alive.

'You teach my nephew Bhaskar. He's part of Hanuman's army. Do you teach him to attack innocent people? Is this the kind of Ram Rajya you want to bring about? We're doing no one any harm. Let us go on our way. Come!' he said to Firoz, grabbing him by the shoulder. 'Come.' He tried to shoulder his way past the mob.

'Not so fast. You can go, you sister-fucking traitor – but you can't,' said the young man.

Maan turned on him and, ignoring his lathi, caught him by the throat in sudden fury.

'You mother-fucker!' he said to him in a low growl that nevertheless carried to every man in the mob. 'Do you know what day this is? This man is my brother, more than my brother, and today in our neighbourhood we were celebrating Bharat Milaap. If you harm one hair of my brother's head – if even one hair of his head is harmed – Lord Rama will seize your filthy soul and send it flaming into hell – and you'll be born in your next life as the filthy krait you are. Go home and lick up your own blood, you sisterfucker, before I break your neck.' He wrenched the young man's lathi from his grasp and pushed him into the crowd.

His face flaming with anger, Maan now walked with Firoz unharmed through the mob, which seemed a little cowed by his words, a little uncertain of its purpose. Before it could think its way out again, Maan, pushing Firoz in front of him, had walked fifty yards and turned a corner.

'Now run!' he said.

He and Firoz ran for their lives. The mob was still dangerous. It was in effect leaderless for a few minutes and uncertain what to do, but it soon regrouped and, feeling cheated of its prey, moved along the alleys to hunt for more.

Maan knew that at all costs they had to avoid the route of the Bharat Milaap procession and still somehow get to his sister's house. Who knew what danger they might have to face on the way, what other mobs or lunatics they might encounter.

'I'll try to get back to the Imambara,' said Firoz.

'It's too late now,' said Maan. 'You're cut off, and you don't know this area. Stay with me now. We're going to my sister's. Her husband's on the Ramlila Committee, no one will attack their house.'

'But I can't. How can I –'

'Shut up!' said Maan, his voice trembling again. 'You've put us through enough danger already. Don't have any more stupid scruples. There's no purdah in our family, thank God. Go through that gate there and don't make a sound.' Then he put his arm around Firoz's shoulder.

He led Firoz through a small washermen's colony, and

they emerged in the tiny alley where Kedarnath lived. It was a mere fifty yards from where the stage had been set up for the Bharat Milaap. They could hear the sound of shouting and screaming from close by. Veena's house was in an almost entirely Hindu neighbourhood; no Muslim mobs could range here.

They stared at Firoz as he stumbled into the room in his bloodstained white sherwani – and at Maan, clutching the bloodstained lathi in his hand. Kedarnath stepped forward, the other three shrank back. Old Mrs Tandon clapped her hands to her mouth. 'Hai Ram! Hai Ram!' she gasped in horror.

'Firoz is staying here until we can get him out safely,' said Maan, looking at each of them in turn. 'There's a mob roaming around – and there'll be others. But everyone here is safe. No one will think of attacking this house.'

'But the blood – are you wounded?' asked Veena, turning to Firoz, her eyes distracted with concern.

Maan looked at Firoz's sherwani and his own lathi, and suddenly burst out laughing. 'Yes, this lathi did it, but I didn't – and it's not his blood.'

Firoz greeted his hosts as courteously as his own shock and theirs would allow.

Bhaskar, still tear-faced, seeing the effect of all this on his parents, looked strangely at Maan, who placed the long bamboo staff against the wall, and kissed his nephew on the forehead.

'This is the Nawab Sahib of Baitar's younger son,' said Maan to old Mrs Tandon. She nodded silently. Her mind had turned to the days of Partition in Lahore and her memories and thoughts were those of absolute terror.

15.13

FIROZ changed hurriedly out of his long coat into one of Kedarnath's kurta-pyjamas. Veena made them a quick cup of tea with plenty of sugar. After a while, Maan and Firoz climbed up to the roof, to the pots and plants of the small garden. Maan crushed a small tulsi leaf and put it in his mouth.

As they looked around them they saw that fires had already broken out here and there in the city. They could make out several of the main buildings of Brahmpur: the spire of the Imambara still ablaze with light – the lights of the Barsaat Mahal, the dome of the Legislative Assembly, the railway station, and – far beyond the Subzipore Club, the fainter glow of the university. But here and there in the old city it was not lights but fire that lit the sky. The muted din of drums came to them from the direction of the Imambara. And distant shouts, more distinct at times as the breeze changed, reached their ears, together with other sounds that could have been firecrackers, but were more likely the sounds of police firing.

'You saved my life,' said Firoz.

Maan embraced him. He smelt of sweat and fear.

'You should have had a wash before you changed,' he said. 'All that running in your sherwani – thank God you're safe.'

'Maan, I must get back. They'll be worried crazy about me at the house. They'll risk their own lives to look for me....'

Suddenly the lights went out at the Imambara.

Firoz said in quiet dread: 'What could have happened there?'

Maan said: 'Nothing.' He was wondering how Saeeda Bai would have got back to Pasand Bagh. Surely she must have remained in the safe area near the Imambara.

The night was warm, but there was a slight breeze. Neither of them said anything for a while.

A large glow now lit the sky about half a mile to the west. This was the lumberyard of a well-known Hindu trader who lived in a predominantly Muslim neighbourhood. Other fires sprang up around it. The drums were silent now, and the sounds of intermittent firing were very clear. Maan was too exhausted to feel any fear. A numbness and a terrible feeling of isolation and helplessness came over him.

Firoz closed his eyes, as if to shut out the terrible vision of the city in flames. But other fires beset his mind – the fire-acrobats of the Moharram fair; the embers of the trench dug outside the Imambara at Baitar House burning with logs and brushwood for ten days, the candelabra of the Imambara at the Fort blazing and guttering as Ustad Majeed Khan sang Raag Darbari while his father nodded with pleasure.

He suddenly got up, agitated.

Someone shouted from a neighbouring rooftop that curfew had been declared.

'How could it be declared?' asked Maan. 'People couldn't have got home by now.' He added softly, 'Firoz, sit down.'

'I don't know,' shouted the man. 'But it has just been announced on the radio that curfew has been declared and that in an hour police will have orders to shoot on sight. Before then, only if they see actual violence.'

'Yes, that makes sense,' Maan shouted back, wondering what if anything made sense any more.

'Who are you? Who's that with you? Kedarnath? Is everyone safe in your family?'

'It's not Kedarnath – it's a friend who came to see the Bharat Milaap. I'm Veena's brother.'

'Well, you'd better not move tonight, if you don't want to get your throat slit by the Muslims – or get shot by the police. What a night. Tonight of all nights.'

'Maan,' said Firoz quietly and urgently, 'can I use your sister's phone?'

'She doesn't have one,' said Maan.

Firoz looked at him with dismay.

'A neighbour's then. I have to get word back to Baitar House. If the news of the curfew is on the radio, my father will hear of it at the Fort in Baitar, and he will be terrified about what's happened here. Imtiaz might try to come back and get a curfew pass. For all I know Murtaza Ali might already be sending out search parties for me, and at a time like this that's crazy. Do you think you might phone from the house of one of Veena's friends?'

'We don't want anyone to know you're here,' said Maan. 'But don't worry, I'll find a way,' he said when he saw the look of sickening anxiety on his friend's face. 'I'll talk to Veena.'

Veena too had memories of Lahore; but her most recent memories were those of losing Bhaskar at the Pul Mela, and she could conceive the Nawab Sahib's agony of mind when he heard that Firoz had not returned home.

'How about trying Priya Agarwal?' said Maan. 'I could go over to her place.'

'Maan, you're not going anywhere,' said his sister. 'Are you mad? It's a five minute walk through the alleys – this isn't why I tied the rakhi around your wrist.' After a minute's thought she said: 'I'll go to the neighbour whose phone I use in an emergency. It's only two rooftops away. You met her that day – she's a good woman, the only trouble is that she is rabidly antiMuslim. Let me think. What's the number of Baitar House?'

Maan told her.

Veena came up to the roof with him, crossed over the connected rooftops, and descended the stairs to her neighbour's house.

Veena's large and voluble neighbour, out of her usual friendliness and curiosity, hung around while Veena made the call. The phone, after all, was in her room. Veena told her she was trying to get in touch with her father.

'But I just saw him at the Bharat Milaap, near the temple –'

'He had to go home. The noise was too much for him. And the smoke was not good for my mother either. Or for Pran's lungs – he didn't come. But Maan is here – he's had a lucky escape from a Muslim mob.'

'It must be providence,' said the woman. 'If they had got hold of him –'

The telephone was not a dialling machine; and Veena had to give the Baitar House number to the operator.

'Oh, you're not calling Prem Nivas?' said the woman, who knew that number from Veena's previous calls.

'No. Baoji had to visit friends later this evening.'

When a voice came on the line Veena said: 'I would like to speak to the Sahib.'

An aged voice at the other end said, 'Which Sahib? The Nawab Sahib or the Burré Sahib or the Chhoté Sahib?'

'Anyone,' said Veena.

'But the Nawab Sahib is in Baitar with the Burré Sahib, and Chhoté Sahib has not yet come home from the Imambara.'

The aged voice – it was Ghulam Rusool – was halting and agitated. 'They say there has been trouble in town, that you can see fires even from the roof of this house. I must g o now. There are arrangements –'

'Please be patient –' said Veena quickly. 'I will speak to anyone – put Sahib's secretary on the line – or anyone responsible. Call someone – anyone – to the line, please. This is Mahesh Kapoor's daughter Veena speaking, and I need to pass on an urgent message.'

There was silence for a few seconds, then the young voice of Murtaza Ali came on the line. He sounded both embarrassed and extremely anxious. He had sensed that perhaps there might be some news of Firoz.

Veena said, choosing her words with extreme care: 'I am Mahesh Kapoor's daughter. This is about Sahib's younger son.'

'The Nawab Sahib's younger son? The Chhoté Sahib?'

'Exactly. There is nothing to worry about. He is un-harmed, and quite safe, and staying in Misri Mandi to-night. Please inform Sahib of that in case he should inquire.'

'God is merciful!' came the quiet response.

'He will go home tomorrow when curfew is relaxed. Meanwhile, no search parties should be sent out for him. No one should go to the police station to get a curfew pass – or come here – or talk to anyone about his being here. Just say he is staying with me – with his sister.'

'Thank you, Madam, thank you for calling us – we were just about to set out in an armed party – it would have been terrible – we imagined the worst –'

'I must go now,' said Veena, knowing that the longer

she talked the more difficult it would be to maintain a protective ambiguity.

'Yes, yes,' said Murtaza Ali. 'Khuda haafiz.'

'Khuda haafiz,' replied Veena without thinking, and put down the phone.

Her neighbour looked at her strangely.

Unwilling to make further conversation with the curious woman, Veena explained that she had to go back home immediately because Bhaskar had sprained his ankle running about; and Maan and her husband needed to be fed; and old Mrs Tandon, with her memories of Pakistan, was in a panic and would need to be soothed.

15.14

BUT when she got back to the house, she found her mother-in-law, who was downstairs, almost incoherent with shock. Kedarnath had just gone out into the night, planning, no doubt, to calm down any people he found: to prevent them from harming others and, in case they had not heard about the curfew, themselves.

Veena almost fainted. She leaned against the wall and stared ahead of her. Finally her mother-in-law stopped sobbing and her words began to make more sense.

'He said that in this area there would be no risk from Muslims,' she whispered. 'He wouldn't listen to me. He said that it wasn't Lahore – that he would be back very shortly,' she continued, looking at Veena's face for comfort. '"Very shortly," he said. He said he would be back very shortly.' She broke down once again at the words.

Veena's mouth began to tremble. It was the phrase Kedarnath was fond of using when he went away on his interminable sales trips.

There was no comfort for the old lady to be found in Veena's face. 'Why didn't you stop him? Why didn't Maan stop him?' she cried. She was furious at her husband for this selfish and irresponsible heroism. Did she and Bhaskar and his mother not exist for him?

'Maan was on the roof,' said the old lady.

Now Bhaskar came down the stairs. Something had obviously been troubling him for a while.

'Why did Firoz Maama have so much blood all over him?' he demanded. 'Did Maan Maama beat him up? He said he didn't. But he was holding the lathi.'

'Be quiet, Bhaskar,' said Veena in a desperate voice. 'Go upstairs at once. Go upstairs and back to bed. Everything's all right. I'm here if you need me.' She gave him a hug.

Bhaskar wanted to know exactly what the matter was. 'Nothing,' said Veena. 'I have to prepare some food – don't get in my way.' She knew that if Maan got to know about what had happened he would immediately go out to look for his brother-in-law and would put himself at very grievous risk. Kedarnath at least did know exactly where the Hindu areas ended. But she was tormented with anxiety for him. Before Bhaskar had come down she had been on the verge of going out herself. Now she just waited – the most difficult thing of all.

She quickly heated some food for Maan and Firoz, and took it up, pausing on the stairs in order to appear calm.

Maan smiled when he saw her.

'It's quite warm,' said Maan. 'We'll sleep together on the roof. Just give us a mattress and a light quilt, and we'll be fine. Firoz will need a wash, and I could do with one too. Is something wrong?'

Veena shook her head. 'He almost gets killed, then asks me if something is wrong.'

She took a light quilt out of a trunk, and shook out from its folds the dried neem leaves that she used to preserve winter clothing from pests.

'Sometimes the night flowers on the roof attract insects,' she warned them.

'We'll be fine,' said Firoz. 'I am so grateful to you.'

Veena shook her head. 'Sleep well,' she said.

Kedarnath returned home five minutes before curfew. Veena wept, and refused to speak to him. She buried her face in his scarred hands.

For an hour or so Maan and Firoz remained awake. It

felt as if the world was trembling beneath them. The distant sound of gunfire had died down, probably as a result of the imposition of curfew, but the glow from the fires, especially to the west, continued through the night.

15.15

ON Sharad Purnima, the brightest night of the year, Pran and Savita hired a boat and went up the Ganga to look at the Barsaat Mahal. Curfew had been lifted that morning. Mrs Rupa Mehra had advised them not to go, but Savita said that no one could set fire to the river.

'And it isn't good for Pran's asthma either,' added Mrs Rupa Mehra, who believed that he should be confined to his bed and his rocking-chair, and not over-exert himself.

Pran had in fact slowly recovered from the worst of his illness. He was still not able to play cricket, but had built up his strength by walking, at first only around the garden, then a few hundred yards, and finally around campus or along the Ganga. He had avoided the incendiary festivities of Dussehra, and would have to avoid the firecrackers of Divali. But his trouble had not recurred in its acute form, and he had for the most part not allowed it to interfere with his academic work. Some days, when he was feeling weaker, he sat and lectured. His students were protective of him, and even his overworked colleagues on the disciplinary committee tried to relieve him of whatever duties they could.

Tonight, in particular, he felt much better. He reflected on Maan and Firoz's providential escape – and indeed Kedarnath's as well – and was inclined to minimize his own problems.

'Don't worry, Ma,' he reassured his mother-in-law. 'If anything, the river air will do me good. It's still quite warm.'

'Well, it won't be warm on the river. You should take a shawl each. Or a blanket,' grumbled Mrs Rupa Mehra.

After a pause, she said to Lata: 'Why are you looking like that? Do you have a headache?'

'No, Ma, I don't, please let me read.'

She had been thinking: thank God Maan is safe.

'What are you reading?' persisted her mother.

'Ma!'

'Bye, Lata, bye, Ma,' said Pran. 'Keep your knitting needles out of Uma's clutches.'

Mrs Rupa Mehra made a sound that was almost a grunt. She believed that one shouldn't mention such unspeakable dangers. She was knitting booties for the baby in the expectation of colder weather.

Pran and Savita walked down to the river, Pran leading the way with a torch, and helping Savita with a hand where the path was steep. He warned her to watch out for the roots of the banyan tree.

The boatman they hired from near the dhobi-ghat happened to be the same one who had taken Lata and Kabir to see the Barsaat Mahal some months previously at dawn. As usual he demanded an outrageous price. Pran brought it down slightly, but was in no mood for further haggling. He was glad Uma was too small to come with them; he was happy to be alone with Savita if only for an hour or two.

The river was still high, and a pleasant breeze was blowing.

'Ma was right – it is cold – you'd better hold onto me for warmth,' Pran said.

'Aren't you going to recite a ghazal by Mast for me?' asked Savita as she looked out, past the ghats and the Fort towards the vague silhouette of the Barsaat Mahal.

'Sorry, you've married the wrong brother,' said Pran.

'No, I don't think so,' said Savita. She leaned her head against his shoulder. 'What is that thing there with the walls and chimney – beyond the Barsaat Mahal?'

'Hmm – I don't know – perhaps the tannery or the shoe factory,' said Pran. 'But everything looks different from this side, especially at night.'

They were silent for a while.

'What's the latest on that front?' said Pran.

'You mean Haresh?'

'Yes.'

'I don't know. Lata's being secretive. But he does write and she does reply. You're the one who's met him. You said you liked him.'

'Well, it's impossible to judge someone on the basis of a single meeting,' said Pran.

'Oh, so you think so!' said Savita archly, and they both laughed.

A thought struck Pran.

'I suppose I too am going to be judged soon enough on the basis of a single meeting,' he said.

'Soon enough!' said Savita.

'Well, things really are going ahead at last –'

'Or so Professor Mishra assures you.'

'No, no – in a month or two at the latest they're going to have their interviews – someone who works in the Registrar's Office mentioned it to one of my father's ex-PAs. So let's see, it's the middle of October now –' Pran looked across towards the burning ghat. He lost the thread of his thoughts.

'How quiet the city looks,' he said. 'And when you think that Maan and Firoz could have been murdered –'

'Don't.'

'Sorry, darling. Anyway, what were you saying?'

'I've forgotten.'

'Oh, well.'

'I think,' said Savita, 'that you're in danger of becoming complacent.'

'Who – me?' said Pran, surprised rather than affronted. 'Why should I be complacent? A humble university lecturer with a weak heart, who will have to puff his way up the cliff at the end of this boat-ride.'

'Well, perhaps not,' said Savita. 'Anyway, what does it feel like to have a wife and child?'

'What does it feel like? It feels wonderful.'

Savita smiled into the darkness. She had fished for a compliment, and landed one.

'This is where you'll get the best view,' said the boatman, driving his long pole deep into the bed of the river. 'I can't go further back into the current. The river's too high.'

'And I suppose it must be quite pleasant to have a husband and child,' added Pran.

'Yes,' said Savita thoughtfully. 'It is.' After a while she said: 'Sad about Meenakshi.'

'Yes. But you've never been very fond of her, have you?'

Savita did not reply.

'Has her miscarriage made you like her more?' said Pran.

'What a question! It has, in a way. Well, let me think about that. I'll know immediately when I see her again.'

'You know,' said Pran, 'I don't look forward to staying with your brother and sister-in-law over the New Year.' He closed his eyes; there was a mild and pleasant breeze on the river.

'I'm not sure there'll even be room for all of us at Sunny Park,' said Savita. 'Ma and Lata can stay with them as usual. And you and I can camp in the garden. Rock-a-bye Baby can hang from the tree-top.'

Pran laughed. 'Well, at least the baby doesn't take after your brother, as I feared she might.'

'Which one?'

'Either. But I meant Arun. Well, they'll have to put us up somewhere – I suppose at the Chatterjis'. I liked that boy, what's his name –'

'Amit?'

'No, the other one – the holy man who was fond of Scotch.'

'Dipankar.'

'Yes, that's it. . . . At any rate, you'll meet him when we go to Calcutta in December,' said Pran.

'But I've already met him,' Savita pointed out. 'At the Pul Mela, most recently.'

'I meant Haresh. You can appraise him at your leisure.'

'But you were just talking about Dipankar.'

'Was I, dear?'

'Really, Pran, I wish you would keep track of your conversation. It's very confusing. I'm sure this isn't how you lecture.'

'I lecture rather well,' said Pran, 'even if I say so myself. But don't take my word for it. Ask Malati.'

'I have no intention of asking Malati how you lecture. The last time she listened to you, you were so overcome you fainted away.'

The boatman was getting tired of holding his boat steady against the current. 'Do you want to talk or to watch the Barsaat Mahal?' he asked. 'You're paying me good money to come here.'

'Yes, yes, of course,' said Pran vaguely.

'You should have come here three nights ago,' said the boatman – 'there were fires burning all along there. Beautiful it looked, and you couldn't smell it here on the Ganga. And the next day lots of corpses at the ghat there. Too many for one ghat to handle. The municipality has been planning another burning ghat for years now but they'll never get down to deciding where.'

'Why?' Pran couldn't resist asking.

'If it's on the Brahmpur side it'll face north like this one. Of course, by rights it should face south, in the direction of Yama. But that would put it on the other shore, and they'd have to ferry the bodies – and the passengers – across.'

'They. You mean you.'

'I suppose so. I wouldn't complain.'

For a while Pran and Savita looked at the Barsaat Mahal, lit in the full light of the full moon. Beautiful by itself, its reflection at night made it look lovelier than ever. The moon shivered gently in the water. The boatman said nothing further.

Another boat passed them. For some reason Pran shuddered.

'What's the matter, darling?'

'Nothing.'

Savita took a small coin out of her purse and put it in Pran's hand.

'Well, what I was thinking was how peaceful it all looks.'

Savita nodded to herself in the darkness. Pran suddenly realized she was crying.

'What's the matter, darling? What have I said?'

'Nothing. I'm so happy. I'm just happy.'

'How strange you are,' said Pran, stroking her hair.

The boatman released his pole and, guided only casually by him, the boat began to move downstream again. Quietly they moved down the calm and sacred river that had come down to earth so that its waters might flow over the ashes of those long dead, and that would continue to flow long after the human race had, through hatred and knowledge, burned itself out.

15.16

FOR the last few weeks Mahesh Kapoor had been in two minds – two uncertain and troubled minds – about whether to go back to the Congress Party. He, who was so full of definite, often dismissive, opinion, had found himself lost in a dust-storm of indecision.

Too many factors were whirling around in his head and each time they came to rest they formed a new configuration.

What the Chief Minister had said to him in his garden; what the Nawab Sahib had said to him at the Fort; the visit to Prem Nivas of the seceder from U.P. who had rejoined the Congress; Baba's advice in Debaria; Nehru's coup; Rafi Sahib's circuitous return to the fold; his own beloved legislation which he wanted to make sure did not merely moulder on the statute-books; irritatingly enough, even his wife's unspoken but palpable view of the whole matter: all these told him to go back to the party that, until his slow but thorough disillusionment, had unquestionably been his home.

Things had doubtless changed greatly since that disillusionment. And yet, when he thought about it deeply, how much had really changed? Could he belong in a party that contained – could he bear to belong to a government that might possibly be run by – the likes of the present Home Minister? The list of Congress candidates that was being drawn up in the state did nothing to dispel his disillusionment. Nor, after his talk with his old Parliamentary Secretary, could he honestly claim to himself that he sensed in Nehru any new surge of decisiveness. Nehru could not even ensure the passage of his favourite bill through Parliament. Compromise and muddle had reigned, and compromise and muddle would reign.

And having once made his break, thought Mahesh Kapoor, would he not be displaying the very indecisiveness he usually condemned by returning? After decades of loyalty to one party, he who believed in principle and firmness would have turned his coat twice in the course of a few months. Kidwai may have returned, but Kripalani had not. Whose had been the more honourable course?

Angry at himself for his own uncharacteristic dithering, Mahesh Kapoor told himself that he had had enough time and enough advice to determine twenty such matters. Whatever he decided, there would be aspects of his decision he would find difficult to live with. He should stop fretting, examine the nub of the matter, and once and for all say Yes or No.

Yet what, if anything, was the nub?

Was it the zamindari legislation? Was it his dread of communal hatred and violence? Was it the real and delicious possibility that he, not Agarwal, might become Chief Minister? Was it the fear that if he remained outside the Congress, he would lose his seat – that he could maintain his purity only in the wilderness? Surely all these things pointed in the same direction. What was really holding him back but uncertainty and pride?

He stared unseeingly out from his small office towards the garden of Prem Nivas.

His wife had his tea sent to him; it went cold.

She came to ask him if he was all right and brought

another cup for him herself. She said: 'So you have decided to return to the Congress? That's good.'

He responded with exasperation: 'I have decided nothing. What makes you think I have?'

'After Maan and Firoz nearly –'

'Maan and Firoz have nothing to do with it. I have been thinking this matter over for weeks without coming to any conclusion.' He looked at her in amazement.

She stirred his tea once more and placed it on the table, which was easier to do these days, since it was not covered with files.

Mahesh Kapoor sipped it and said nothing.

After a while he said, 'Leave me alone. I am not going to discuss this matter with you. Your presence is distracting me. I don't know where your farfetched intuitions come from. But they are more inaccurate and suspect than astrology.'

15.17

LESS than a week after the riots in Brahmpur, the Prime Minister of Pakistan, Liaquat Ali Khan, was shot at a public meeting that he was addressing at Rawalpindi. The murderer was done to death on the spot by the crowd.

At the news of his death, all government flags were lowered to half-mast in Brahmpur. The university court convened a meeting to express its condolences. In a city where the memory of rioting was only a week old, this had something of a sobering effect.

The Nawab Sahib was back in Brahmpur when he heard the news. He had known Liaquat Ali well, since both Baitar House and Baitar Fort had been meeting places for Muslim League leaders in his father's time. He looked at some of the old photographs of those conferences and read through some of the old correspondence between his father and Liaquat Ali. He realized – though he did not see what he could do about the fact – that he had begun to live increasingly in the past.

For the Nawab Sahib Partition had been a multiple tragedy: many of those he knew, both Muslim and Hindu, had been killed or injured or scarred by the terror of those days; he had lost two parts of his country; his family had been broken up by migration; Baitar House had come under attack through manipulations of the evacuee property laws; most of the great estate surrounding Baitar Fort was soon to be wrested from him under zamindari laws that would have been almost impossible to pass in a united India; the language of his ancestors and favourite poets was under siege; and he was conscious that even his patriotism was no longer readily accepted by many of his acquaintances. He thanked God that he still had friends like Mahesh Kapoor who understood him; and he thanked God that his son had friends like Mahesh Kapoor's son. But he felt beleaguered and beset by what was happening around him; and he reflected that if this was what he felt, it must be infinitely worse for those of his religion less insulated from the hardships of the world than himself.

I suppose I am getting old, he said to himself, and querulousness is a standard symptom of senility. He could not help grieving, though, for the cultivated, level-headed Liaquat Ali, whom he had personally liked. Nor, though he had hated the thought of Pakistan once, could he turn away from it with unconcern now that it actually existed. When the Nawab Sahib thought about Pakistan, it was about West Pakistan. Many of his old friends were there, many of his relatives, many of the places of which he had warm recollections. That Jinnah should have died in the first year of Pakistan's life, and Liaquat Ali early in its fifth was no happy augury for a country that needed, more than anything else, experience in its leadership and moderation in its polity, and appeared now to be bereft of both.

The Nawab Sahib, saddened by things and feeling a stranger in the world, phoned Mahesh Kapoor to invite him over for lunch the next day.

'Please persuade Mrs Mahesh Kapoor to come as well. I will get her food from outside, of course.'

'I can't. The mad woman will be fasting for my health

tomorrow. It's Karva Chauth, and she can't eat from sunrise till moonrise. Or drink a drop of water. If she does I'll die.'

'That would be unfortunate, Kapoor Sahib. There has been too much killing and dying of late,' said the Nawab Sahib. 'How is Maan, by the way?' he inquired fondly.

'Much the same. But recently I've stopped telling him three times a day to return to Banaras. There's something to be said for the boy.'

'There's a great deal to be said for the boy,' said the Nawab Sahib.

'Oh, it would have been the same the other way around,' said Mahesh Kapoor. 'Anyway, I've been thinking about my son's advice regarding constituencies. And your advice, of course, as well.'

'And about parties too, I hope.'

There was a long silence on the line.

'Yes, well, I've decided to rejoin the Congress. You're the first to know,' said Mahesh Kapoor.

The Nawab Sahib sounded pleased.

'Fight from Baitar, Kapoor Sahib,' he said. 'Fight from Baitar. You'll win, Inshallah – and with the help of your friends.'

'Let's see, let's see.'

'So you'll come for lunch tomorrow?'

'Yes, yes. What's the occasion?'

'No occasion. Just do me the favour of sitting silently through the meal and hearing me complain about how much better things were in the old days.'

'All right.'

'Give my greetings to Maan's mother,' said the Nawab Sahib. He paused. It would have been more proper to say 'Pran's mother' or even 'Veena's mother'. He stroked his beard, then continued: 'But, Kapoor Sahib, is it a sensible idea for her to fast in her present state of health?'

'Sensible!' was Mahesh Kapoor's response. 'Sensible! My dear Nawab Sahib, you are talking a language that is foreign to her.'

THIS language was also presumably foreign to Mrs Rupa Mehra, who stopped knitting the baby's booties on the day of Karva Chauth. Indeed, she locked up her knitting needles together with any sewing and darning needles that were lying about the house. Her reason was simple. Savita was fasting until moonrise for her husband's health and longevity, and touching a needle, even inadvertently, on that day would be disastrous.

One year an unfortunate young woman, famished during her fast, was persuaded by her anxious brothers that the moon had risen when all they had done was to light a fire behind a tree to simulate the moonglow. She had eaten a little before she had realized the trick, and soon enough the news was brought to her of her husband's sudden death. He had been pierced through and through by thousands of needles. By performing many austerities and making many offerings to the goddesses, the young widow had finally extracted their promise that if she kept the fast properly the next year her husband would return to life. Each day for the whole year she removed the needles one by one from her husband's lifeless body. The very last one, however, was removed on the day of Karva Chauth itself by a maidservant just as her master came back to life. Since she was the first woman he saw after opening his eyes, he believed that it was through her pains that he had revived. He had no choice but to discard his wife and marry her. Needles on Karva Chauth were therefore fearfully inauspicious: touch a needle and lose a husband.

What Savita, fortified in logic by law-books and grounded in reality by her baby, thought of all this, was not obvious. But she observed Karva Chauth to the letter, even going to the extent of first viewing the rising moon through a sieve.

The Sahib and Memsahib of Calcutta, on the other hand, considered Karva Chauth a signal idiocy, and were unmoved by Mrs Rupa Mehra's frantic implorations that Meenakshi – even if Brahmo by family – should observe it.

'Really, Arun,' said Meenakshi. 'Your mother does go on about things.'

One by one the Hindu festivals fell, some observed fervently, some lukewarmly, some merely noted, some entirely ignored. On five consecutive days around the end of October came Dhanteras, Hanuman Jayanti, Divali, Annakutam, and Bhai Duj. The day immediately following was observed most religiously by Pran, who kept his ear to the radio for hours: it was the first day of the first Test Match of the cricket season, played in Delhi against a visiting English side.

A week later the gods at last awoke from their four months' slumber, having wisely slept through a very boring and slow-scoring draw.

15.19

BUT though India vs England was humdrum in the extreme, the same could not be said for the University vs Old Brahmpurians match held that Sunday at the university cricket ground.

The university team was not quite as good as it might have been, owing to a couple of injuries. Nor were the Old Brahmpurians a push-over, for their side contained not merely the usual players rustled up from here and there, but also two men who had captained the university in the last ten years or so.

Among the rustled, however, was Maan. Among the uninjured was Kabir. And Pran was one of the umpires.

It was a brilliant, clear, crisp, early November day, and the grass was still fresh and green. The mood was festive, and – with exams and other woes a million miles away – the students were out in force. They cheered and booed and stood around the field talking to the outfielders and generally creating as much excitement off the field as on. A few teachers could be seen among them.

One of these was Dr Durrani; he found cricket curiously fertile. At the moment, unmoved by the fact that his son had just bowled Maan out with a leg-break, he was thinking about the hexadic, octal, decimal and duodecimal systems and attempting to work out their various advantages.

He turned to a colleague:

'Interesting, er, wouldn't you say, Patwardhan, that the number six, which, though "perfect", has a, well, an almost fugitive existence in mathematics – except, er, in geometry, of course, should um, be the – the presiding, one might say, the presiding, um, deity of cricket, wouldn't you say?'

Sunil Patwardhan nodded but would not say. His eyes were glued to the pitch. The next player was no sooner in than out; he had been dispatched on Kabir's next ball: a googly this time. A huge roar of delight rose from the crowd.

'Six balls to an, um, over, don't you see, Patwardhan, six runs to a boundary, a, a lofted boundary, of course, and, um, six stumps on the, er, field!'

The incoming player had hardly had time to pad up. The previous batsman was already back in the pavilion by the time he walked out onto the field, flexing his bat impatiently and aggressively. He was one of the two former captains, and he was damned if he was going to provide Kabir with a hat-trick. In he went and fiercely he glared, in a sweep that encompassed not only the tense but appraising bowler, but also his own batting partner, the opposite stumps, the umpire, and a few innocuous mynas.

Like Arjun aiming his arrow at the eye of the invisible bird, Kabir stared down single-mindedly at the invisible middle stump of his adversary. Straight down the pitch came the ball, but deceptively slowly this time. The batsman tried to play it. He missed; and the dull thump of the ball as it hit his pad was like the sound of muffled doom.

Eleven voices appealed in triumphant delight, and Pran, smiling, raised his finger in the air.

He nodded at Kabir, who was grinning broadly and accepting the congratulations of his team-mates.

The cheering of the crowd took more than a minute to

die down, and continued sporadically for the rest of Kabir's over. Sunil executed a few swift steps of joy — a sort of kathak jig. He looked at Dr Durrani to see what effect his son's triumph had had on him.

Dr Durrani was frowning in concentration, his eyebrows working up and down.

'Curious, though, isn't it, um, Patwardhan, that the number, er, six should be, um, embodied in one of the most, er, er, beautiful, er, shapes in all nature: I refer, um, needless to say, to the er, benzene ring with its single and, er, double carbon bonds. But is it, er, truly symmetrical, Patwardhan, or, um, asymmetrical? Or asymmetrically symmetrical, perhaps, like those, er, sub-super-operations of the, er, Pergolesi Lemma ... not really like the, er, rather unsatisfactory petals of an, um, iris. Curious, wouldn't you say ...?'

'Most curious,' agreed Sunil.

*

Savita was talking to Firoz:

'Of course, it's different for you, Firoz, I don't mean because you're a man as such, but because, well, you don't have a baby to distract you from your clients. Or perhaps that comes to the same thing.... I was talking to Jaya Sood the other day, and she tells me that there are bats — and I don't mean cricket bats! — in the High Court bathroom. When I told her I couldn't bear the thought, she said, "Well, if you're frightened of bats, why are you doing law in the first place?" But, do you know, though I never imagined I would, I actually find law interesting now, really interesting. Not like this awful sleepy game. They haven't made a run for the last ten minutes.... Oh no, I've just dropped a stitch, I always feel drowsy in the sun.... I simply can't see what Pran sees in it, or why he insists on ignoring all of us for five days with his ear glued to the radio, or being a referee and standing in the sun the whole day, but do you think my protests have any effect? "Standing in the sun is good for me," he insists.... Or Maan, for that matter. Before lunch he runs from one wicket to the

174

other seven times, and now after lunch he runs along the edge of the field for a few minutes at the most, and that's that: the whole Sunday's gone! You're very sensible to stick to polo, Firoz – at least that's over in an hour – and you do get some exercise.'

Firoz was thinking about Maan:
My dearest, dearest Maan, you've saved my life all right and I love you dearly, but if you keep nattering to Lata, your captain will forfeit your own.

Maan was talking to Lata:
'No, no, it's all right to talk, no ball ever comes my way. They know what a fantastic player I am, so they've put me here on the boundary where I can't drop any catches or overthrow the ball or anything. And if I go off to sleep, it doesn't matter. Do you know, I think you're looking very beautiful today, no, don't make a face. I've always thought so – green suits you, you know. You just merge with the grass like a ... a nymph! a peri in paradise.... No, no, not at all, I think we're doing tremendously well. All out for 219 isn't bad, after such a poor beginning, and now we've got them at 157 for 7. They've got hopeless people at the bottom of their batting order. I don't think they have a chance.... The Old Brahmpurians haven't won in a decade, so it'll be a great victory! The only danger is this wretched Durrani fellow, who's still batting on at ... what does the scoreboard say? 68.... Once we've forked him off the pitch we'll be home and dry....'

Lata was thinking about Kabir:

> O spirit of love! how quick and fresh art thou,
> That notwithstanding thy capacity
> Receiveth as the sea, nought enters there,
> Of what validity and pitch soe'er
> But falls into abatement and low price....

A few mynas were sitting on the field, their faces turned

towards the batsmen, and the mild, warm sun shone down on her as the sound of bat on ball continued drowsily – interspersed occasionally by a cheer – through the late afternoon. She broke off a blade of grass, and moved it gently up and down her arm.

Kabir was talking to Pran:
'Thanks; no, the light's fine, Dr Kapoor ... oh, thank you – well, it was just a fluke this morning....'

Pran was thinking about Savita:
I know our whole Sunday's gone, darling, but next Sunday I'll do whatever you want. I promise. If you wish, I'll hold a huge ball of wool instead, while you knit twenty booties for the baby.

*

Kabir had gone in fourth, higher up than usual in the batting order, but had more than justified himself there. He had noticed Lata in the crowd, but this had the effect, oddly enough, of steadying his nerves – or increasing his determination. His score mounted, mainly through boundaries, not a few of which got past Maan, and it now stood in the nineties.

One by one his partners had dropped away, however, and the fall of wickets told its own story: 140 for 4, 143 for 5, 154 for 6, 154 for 7, 183 for 8, and now 190 for 9. There were 29 runs to score for a tie, 30 for a win, and his new partner was the exceedingly nervous wicket-keeper! Too bad, thought Kabir. He's lived so long behind the stumps that he doesn't know what to do with himself when he's in front of them. Luckily it's the beginning of the over. Still, he'll be out the first ball he faces, poor chap. The whole thing's impossible, but I wonder if I'll at least manage to get my century.

The wicket-keeper, however, played an admirable second fiddle, and Kabir got the strategic singles that enabled him to keep the bowling. When the University stood at 199, with his own score at 98, on the last ball of the last-but-one over – with three minutes to go before end of play – he tried to make his usual single. As he and his partner passed each other, he said: 'We'll draw it yet!'

A cheer had gone up for the anticipated 200 while they were still running. The fielder hurled the ball at Kabir's wicket. It missed by a hair, but hurtled onwards with such force that poor Maan, who had begun, gallantly, to clap, realized too late what was happening. Too late did he run towards it, too late did he try to hurl himself at it as it sped past his extended length to the boundary.

A great cheer rose from the university ranks – but whether for Kabir's fortuitous five off a single ball, or for his century, or for the university's double-century, or for the fact that with sixteen, rather than twenty, runs to win in the last over, they suddenly felt they still had a chance, no one could say.

The captain of the Old Brahmpurians, a major from the cantonment, glared at Maan.

But now, to a background of cheers and jeers and shouts, Kabir faced the final over. He hit a grand cover drive for four, lofted the next ball just over long on for another, and faced the third ball to a complete and petrified silence from spectators of both sides alike.

It was a good-length ball. He hit it towards mid-wicket, but the moment he realized it was only worth a single, he waved his partner urgently back.

They ran two on the next ball.

It was now the last ball but one, with five runs to tie and six to win. No one dared to breathe. No one had the least idea of what Kabir was aiming to do – or the bowler for that matter. Kabir passed his gloved hand through his wavy hair. Pran thought he looked unnaturally calm at the crease.

Perhaps the bowler had succumbed to his tension and frustration, for amazingly enough his next ball was a full-toss. Kabir, with a smile on his face and happiness in his heart, hit it high in the air with all the force he could muster, and watched it as it sailed in a serene parabola towards victory.

High, high, high it rose in the air, carrying with it all the joy and hopes and blessings of the university. A murmur, not yet a cheer, arose all around, and then swelled into a shout of triumph.

But, as Kabir watched, a dreadful thing happened. For Maan, who too had been watching the red grenade ascend and then descend, and whose mouth was open in an expression of trance-like dismay, suddenly found himself at the very edge of the boundary, almost leaning backwards. And, to his considerable amazement, the ball lay in his hands.

The cheer became a sudden silence, then a great collective groan, to be replaced by an amazed shout of victory by the Old Brahmpurians. A finger moved skywards. The bails were taken off. The players stood dazed in the field, shaking hands and shaking heads. And Maan somersaulted five times for sheer joy in the direction of the spectators.

*

What a goof! thought Lata, watching Maan. Perhaps I should elope with him next April 1st.

'How's that? How's that? How's that?' Maan asked Firoz, hugging him, then rushed back to his team to be applauded as the hero of the day.

Firoz noticed Savita raise her eyebrows. He raised his eyebrows back at her; he wondered what she had made of the soporific climax.

'Still awake – just about,' Savita said, smiling at Pran as he came off the field a few minutes later.

A nice fellow – plucky under pressure, thought Pran, watching Kabir detach himself from his friends and walk towards them, his bat under his arm. A pity. . . .

'Fluke of a catch,' murmured Kabir disgustedly, almost under his breath, as he passed Lata on his way back to the pavilion.

15.20

THE Hindu festive season was almost over. But for Brahmpur one festival, observed much more devotedly here than almost anywhere in India, that of Kartik Purnima, remained. The full moon of Kartik brings to an end one of the three especially sacred months for bathing; and since Brahmpur lies on the holiest river of all, many pious people observe their daily dip throughout the month, eat their single meal, worship the tulsi plant, and hang lamps suspended from the end of bamboo poles in small baskets to guide departed souls across the sky. As the Puranas say: 'What fruit was obtained in the Perfect Age by doing austerities for one hundred years, all that is obtained by a bath in the Five Rivers during the month of Kartik.'

It is of course also possible that the city of Brahmpur could be said to have a special claim on this festival because of the god whose name the city bears. A seventeenth century commentator on the Mahabharata wrote: 'Brahma's festival is celebrated by all, and is held in autumn when the corn has begun to grow.' Certainly in Pushkar, the greatest living shrine to Brahma in all India (indeed, the only one of any great significance other than Gaya and – possibly – Brahmpur), it is Kartik Purnima that is the time of the great camel fair and the visit of tens of thousands of pilgrims. The image of Brahma in the great temple there is daubed with orange paint and decorated with tinsel by his devotees in the manner of other gods. Perhaps the strong observance of the festival in Brahmpur is a residue of the time when Brahma was worshipped here too, in his own city, as a bhakti god, a god of personal devotion, before he was displaced in this role by Shiva – or by Vishnu in one or other of his incarnations.

A residue is all it is, however, because for most of the year one would not suspect Brahma to be a presence in Brahmpur at all. It is his rivals – or colleagues – of the trinity who hold the limelight. The Pul Mela or the Chandrachur Temple speak of the power of Shiva, whether as the source of the Ganga or as the great sensual ascetic symbolized by the linga. As for Vishnu: the notable presence of numerous Krishna devotees (such as Sanaki Baba) and the fervent celebration (by those like Mrs Mahesh

Kapoor) of Janamashtami bear witness to his presence as Krishna; and his presence as Rama is unmistakable not only during Ramnavami early in the year but during the nine nights culminating in Dussehra, when Brahmpur is part of an island of Rama worship in a sea of goddess worship that extends from Bengal to Gujarat.

Why Brahma, the Self-Created or Egg-born, the overseer of sacrifice, the Supreme Creator, the old four-faced god who set in motion the triple world, should have suffered eclipse over the centuries is unclear. At one time even Shiva is shown cringing in the Mahabharata before him; and it is from a common root with Brahma himself that the words not only for 'brahmin' but also for 'brahman', the world-soul, derive. But by the time of the late Puranas, not to mention modern times, his influence had waned to a shadow.

Perhaps it was because – unlike Shiva or Rama or Krishna or Durga or Kali – he was never associated with youth or beauty or terror, those well-springs of personal devotion. Perhaps it was because he was too far above suffering and yearning to satisfy the longing of the heart for an identifiably human ideal or intercessor – one perhaps who had come down to earth to suffer with the rest of mankind in order that righteousness might be established. Perhaps it was because certain myths surrounding him – for instance his creation of mankind by intercourse with his own daughter – were too difficult to accept by a constant following over long ages and changing mores.

Or perhaps it was that, refusing to be turned on and off like a tap by requests for intercession, Brahma at last refused to deliver what was asked of him by millions of upraised hands, and therefore fell out of favour. It is rare for religious feeling to be entirely transcendent, and Hindus as much as anyone else, perhaps more so, are eager for terrestrial, not merely post-terrestrial, blessings. We want specific results, whether to cure a child of disease or to guarantee his IAS results, whether to ensure the birth of a son or to find a suitable match for a daughter. We go to a temple to be blessed by our chosen deity before a journey, and have our account books sanctified by Kali or Saraswati. At Divali, the words 'shubh laabh' – auspicious profit – are seen on the walls of every newly whitewashed shop; while Lakshmi, the presiding goddess, smiles from a poster as she sits on her lotus, serene and beautiful, dispensing gold coins from one of her four arms.

It must be admitted that there are those, mainly Shaivites and Vaishnavites, who claim that Brahmpur has nothing to do with the god Brahma at all – that the name is a corruption of Bahrampur or Brahminpur or Berhampur or some other such name, whether Islamic or Hindu. But for one reason or another these theories may be discarded. The evidence of coins, of inscriptions, of historical records and travellers' accounts from Hsuen Tsang to Al-Biruni, from Babur to Tavernier, not to mention those of British travellers, provide ample evidence of the ancient name of the city.

It should be mentioned in passing that the spelling Brumpore, which the British insisted on imposing on the city, was converted back to its more phonetic transcription when the name of the state itself was changed to Purva Pradesh under the Protected Provinces (Alteration of Name) Order, 1949, which came into operation a few months before the commencement of the Constitution. The spelling Brumpore was the source, however, of not a few errors by amateur etymologists during the two centuries of its prevalence.

There are even a few misguided souls who assert that the name Brahmpur is a variant of Bhrampur – the city of illusion or error. But the proper response to this hypothesis is that there are always people willing to believe anything, however implausible, merely in order to be contrary.

15.21

'PRAN darling, please turn off that light.'

The switch was near the door.

Pran yawned. 'Oh, I'm too sleepy,' was his response.

'But I can't sleep with it on,' said Savita.

'What if I had been sitting in the other room, working late? Wouldn't you have been able to do it yourself?'

'Yes, of course, darling,' yawned Savita, 'but you're closer to the door.'

Pran got out of bed, switched off the light, and staggered back.

'The moment Pran darling appears,' he said, 'a use is found for him.'

'Pran, you're so lovable,' said Savita.

'Of course! Anyone would be who dances attendance. But when Malati Trivedi finds me lovable....'

'As long as you don't find her lovable....'

And they drifted off to sleep.

At two in the morning the phone rang.

The insistent double ring pierced their dreams. Pran woke up with a shock. The baby woke up and started crying. Savita hushed her.

'Good heavens! Who could that be?' cried Savita, startled. 'It'll wake up the whole house – at – what's the time? – I hope it's nothing serious –'

Pran had stumbled out of the room.

'Hello?' he said, picking up the receiver. 'Hello, Pran Kapoor here.'

There was the sound of thick breathing at the other end. Then a voice rasped out:

'Good! This is Marh.'

'Yes?' said Pran, trying to keep his voice low. Savita had got out of bed. He shook his head to reassure her that it was nothing serious and when she left he closed the dining room door.

'This is Marh! The Raja of Marh.'

'Yes, yes, I understand. Yes, Your Highness, what can I do for you?'

'You know exactly what you can do for me.'

'I am sorry, Your Highness, but if this is about your son's expulsion, there's nothing I can tell you. You've received a letter from the university –'

'You – you – do you know who I am?'

'Perfectly, Your Highness. Now it is somewhat late –'

'You listen to me, if you don't want something to happen to you – or to someone who matters to you. You rescind that order.'

'Your Highness, I –'

'Just because of some prank – and I know that your brother is just as – my son tells me he turned him upside down and shook the money out of his pockets when he was gambling – you tell your brother – and your land-robbing father –'

'My father?'

'Your whole family needs to be taught a lesson –'

The baby started to cry again. A note of fury appeared in the voice of the Raja of Marh.

'Is that your baby?'

Pran was silent.

'Did you hear me?'

'Your Highness, I would like to forget this conversation. But if you phone me up again at this hour without cause, or if I receive any further threats from you, I will have to report the matter to the police.'

'Without cause? – you expel my son for a prank –'

'Your Highness, this was not some prank. The university authorities made the facts quite clear in their letter to you. Taking part in a communal riot is not a prank. Your son is lucky that he is still alive and out of jail.'

'He must graduate. He must. He has bathed in the Ganga – he is now a snaatak.'

'That was somewhat premature,' Pran said, trying to keep the scorn out of his voice. 'And your distress on that count cannot be expected to outweigh the decision of the committee. Goodnight, Your Highness.'

'Not so quick! You listen to me now – I know you voted to expel him.'

'That is neither here nor there, Your Highness – I saved him from trouble once before, but –'

'It is very much here and there. When my temple is completed – do you know that it will be my son, my son whom you are trying to martyr, who will lead the ceremonies – and that the wrath of Shiva –'

Pran put down the phone. He sat down at the dining table for a minute or two, staring at it and shaking his head.

'Who was that?' asked Savita when he returned to bed.

'Oh, no one, some lunatic who wanted to get his son admitted to the university,' said Pran.

15.22

THE CONGRESS PARTY was hard at work selecting its candidates. Throughout October and November the State Election Committees worked on, while festivals came and went, and disturbances erupted and subsided, and white-and-orange blossoms floated down from their twigs at dawn.

District by district they selected those they believed should be given Congress tickets for the Legislative Assemblies and for Parliament. In Purva Pradesh the well-packed committee guided by L.N. Agarwal did its best to keep the so-called seceders out of the running. They used every ploy imaginable – procedural, technical, and personal – in order to do so. With an average of six applicants for every ticket, there were grounds enough to tilt a decision towards candidates of one's own political persuasion without creating obvious evidence of bias. The board worked hard, and to good effect. It sat for ten hours a day for weeks on end. It balanced caste and local standing, money power and years spent in British jails. Most of all it considered whose faction a particular applicant belonged to and the chances of his (or, rarely, her) electoral success. L.N. Agarwal was well satisfied with the list. So was S.S. Sharma, who was happy to see the popular Mahesh Kapoor back but keen that he should not rejoin with too long a tail of followers.

Finally, with an eye towards the approval of the Prime Minister and the committees in Delhi which would screen their list, the P.P. Election Committee made a token gesture towards the seceders by inviting three of their representatives (among them Mahesh Kapoor) to the last two days of their meetings. When the seceders saw the list prepared by the committee, they were appalled. It contained almost no one from their group. Even sitting MLAs had been dropped as candidates if they belonged to the minority faction. Mahesh Kapoor himself had been deprived of his urban constituency and told that he could not have Rudhia either – it had been promised to a Member of Parliament who was returning to the state to rejoin the Legislative Assembly. If Mahesh Kapoor had not left the Congress (so the committee said) they would not have given his seat away; but by the time he rejoined the party it was too late, and they could do nothing. But instead of forcing him to accept a seat of their choosing, they would be accommodating and allow him a choice of the few seats still unsettled.

The three representatives of the seceders walked out of the meeting in disgust on the morning of the second day. They said that these meetings at the tail-end of the selection process, held in a hostile and partisan spirit when the list was almost complete, had been a waste of time – a farce aimed at duping Delhi into believing that they had been consulted. The election board for its part issued its own statement to the press, stating that it had sought the seceders' opinions earnestly and in a spirit of reconciliation. The board had 'given them every opportunity for co-operation and advice'.

It was not merely the seceders who were disgruntled. For every man or woman selected, there were five others who had had to be rejected, and many of them made haste to smear the names of their rivals before the scrutiny committees that met in Delhi to examine the lists.

The seceders too took their case to Delhi; there the bitterness continued. Nehru, among others, was almost sickened by the naked desire for power, the willingness to injure, and the unconcern for the effect on the party itself, that characterized the process of scrutiny and appeal. The Congress offices in Delhi were besieged by all manner of applicants and supporters who thrust petitions into influential hands and flung mud promiscuously about them. Even old and trusted Congress workers, who had spent years in jail, and had sacrificed everything for their country, now grovelled before junior clerks in the election office in an attempt to get a seat.

Nehru was on the side of the seceders, but the entire business had grown to be so filthy with ego, greed and ambition that his fastidiousness prevented him from championing them properly, from entering the gutter to wrestle with the entrenched powers in the state machines. The seceders grew alarmed and optimistic by turns. Sometimes it appeared to them that Nehru, exhausted by his earlier battle, would be happy to leave politics altogether and retire into his roses and reading. At other times Nehru tilted furiously at the state lists. At one point it appeared that an alternative list presented by the seceders from Purva Pradesh would actually displace the official list submitted by the State Election Committee. But after a talk with S.S. Sharma, Nehru changed his mind once again. Sharma, that wise psychologist, had offered to accept the unwelcome list and even to campaign for it if that was what Nehru wanted, but he begged in that case to be relieved of the office of Chief Minister or any other office in Government. This, as Nehru realized, would never do. Without S.S. Sharma's personal following and his adroitness at coalition-building and campaigning, the Congress Party in Purva Pradesh would be in deep trouble.

So factious and prolonged had been the selection of candidates at every stage that the Congress Party lists were finalized in Delhi just two days before the deadline for the filing of nominations in Purva Pradesh. Jeeps rushed around the countryside, telegraph wires hummed frantically, candidates rushed about in a panic from Delhi to Brahmpur or from Brahmpur to their allotted constituencies. Two of them even missed the deadline, one because his supporters were so keen to smother him with marigold garlands along his route to the station that he missed his train. The other entered the wrong government offices twice before he finally found the correct one and rushed inside, waving his nomination papers. It was two minutes past the deadline of three o'clock. He burst into tears.

But these were merely two constituencies. There were nearly four thousand in the country as a whole. The candidates for these had now been selected, the nominations had been filed, the party symbols chosen, the teeth bared. Already the Prime Minister had paid a few flying visits here and there to speak on behalf of the Congress Party; and soon electioneering in Purva Pradesh too would begin in earnest.

And then finally it would be the voters who mattered, the great washed and unwashed public, sceptical and gullible, endowed with universal adult suffrage, six times as numerous as those permitted to vote in 1946. It was in fact to be the largest election ever held anywhere on earth. It would involve a sixth of its people.

Mahesh Kapoor, having been denied Misri Mandi and Rudhia (West), had managed at least to be selected as the Congress candidate from Salimpur-cum-Baitar. He would never have imagined such an outcome a few months earlier. Now, because of Maan and L.N. Agarwal and the Nawab Sahib and Nehru and Bhaskar and S.S. Sharma and Jha and probably a hundred other known and unknown agents, he was about to fight for his political life and ideals from a constituency where he was a virtual stranger. To say that he was anxious was to put it mildly.

Part Sixteen

16.1

KABIR'S face lit up when he saw Malati enter the Blue Danube. He had drunk two cups of coffee already and had ordered a third. Outside the frosted glass the streetlights of Nabiganj glowed brightly but indistinctly, and the shadowy forms of pedestrians wandered past.

'Ah, so you've come.'

'Yes. Of course. I got your note this morning.'

'I haven't chosen a bad time for you?'

'No worse than any other,' said Malati. 'Oh, that sounds bad. What I meant was that life is so hectic I don't know why I don't simply collapse. When I was in Nainital and far away from anyone whom I knew I was quite at peace.'

'I hope you don't mind sitting in a corner? We could change.'

'No, I prefer it.'

'Well, what'll you have?' asked Kabir.

'Oh, just a cup of coffee, nothing more. I have to go to a wedding. That's why I'm so overdressed.'

Malati was wearing a green silk sari with a broad border in a darker green and gold. She was looking ravishing. Her eyes were a deeper green than usual.

'I like what you're wearing,' said Kabir, impressed. 'Green and gold – quite dazzling. And that necklace with those little green things and that paisley pattern.'

'Those little green things are emeralds,' said Malati, laughing a little, indignantly but delightfully.

'Oh, well, you see, I'm not used to this stuff. It looks lovely, though.'

The coffee came. They sipped it and talked to each other about the photographs of the play, which had come out well, about the hill stations they had both been to, about skating and riding, about recent politics and other events, including the religious riots. Malati was surprised how easy Kabir was to talk to, how likable he was, how very handsome. Now that he was no longer Malvolio, it was easier to take him seriously. On the other hand, since he had once been Malvolio, she felt something of a sense of guild solidarity with him.

'Did you know that there's more snow and ice in India than anywhere else in the world other than the poles?'

'Really?' said Malati. 'No I didn't.' She stirred her coffee. 'But I don't know lots of things. Such as, for instance, what this meeting's about.'

Kabir was forced to come to the point.

'It's about Lata.'

'I thought as much.'

'She won't see me, she won't answer my notes. It's as if she hates me.'

'Of course she doesn't, don't be melodramatic,' laughed Malati. 'She likes you, I think,' she said more seriously. 'But you know what the problem is.'

'Well, I can't stop thinking about her,' said Kabir, his spoon going round and round his cup. 'I'm always wondering when she'll meet someone else, just like she met me – whom she'll get to like more than me. Then I won't have any chance at all. I just can't stop thinking of her. And I feel so strangely low, it's no joke. I must have walked around the college grounds five times yesterday, thinking she was here – or she wasn't here – the bench, the slope down to the river, the steps of the exam hall, the cricket field, the auditorium – she's really getting me annoyed. That's why I want you to help me.'

'Me?'

'Yes. I must be crazy to love anyone so much. Not crazy, well. . . .' Kabir looked down, then continued quietly. 'It's difficult to explain, you know, Malati. With her I had a sense of joy – of happiness, which, really, I hadn't had for at least a year. But it lasted for no time at all. She's so cool towards me now. Tell her I'll run away with her if she wants – no, that's ridiculous, tell her – how can she – she's not even religious.' He paused. 'I'll never be able to forget the look on her face when she realized I was Malvolio! She was furious!' He started laughing, then sobered up again. 'So it's all up to you.'

'What can I do?' asked Malati, wanting to pat his head.

He seemed in his confusion to believe that she had endless power over Lata, which was quite flattering.

'You can intercede with her on my behalf.'

'But she's just gone to Calcutta with her family.'

'Oh.' Kabir looked thoughtful. 'Calcutta again? Well, write to her then.'

'Why do you love her?' asked Malati, looking at him strangely. In the course of a year, the number of Lata-lovers had shot up from zero to at least three. At this rate it would hit the double digits by next year.

'Why?' Kabir looked at Malati in amazement. 'Why? Because she has six toes. I have no idea why I love her, Malati – anyway, that's irrelevant. Will you help me?'

'All right.'

'All this is having the strangest effect on my batting,' continued Kabir, not even pausing to thank her. 'I'm hitting more sixes, but getting out sooner. But I performed well against the Old Brahmpurians when I knew she was watching. Odd, isn't it?'

'Very odd,' said Malati, trying to restrict her smile to her eyes.

'I'm not exactly an innocent, you know,' said Kabir, a bit piqued at her amusement.

'I should hope not!' said Malati, laughing. 'Good, I'll write to Calcutta. Just remain at the crease.'

16.2

ARUN managed to keep his mother's birthday party a secret from her. He had invited a few older ladies for tea – her Calcutta friends with whom she occasionally played rummy – and he had generously forborne from inviting the Chatterjis.

The tip of the tail of the cat was let out of the bag by Varun, however, who, ever since sitting for his IAS exams, had been feeling that he had fulfilled enough of his duty to last a decade. The Winter Season was on, and the beat of galloping hooves was pounding in his ears.

One day he looked up from the racing form and said: 'But I won't be able to go on that day, because that's when your party – oh!'

Mrs Rupa Mehra, who was saying, '3, 6, 10, 3, 6, 20,' looked up from her knitting and said, 'What is that, Varun? . . . You've disturbed my counting. What party?'

'Oh,' said Varun, 'I was talking to myself, Ma. My friends are, you know, well, throwing a party and it will interfere with a race-meeting.' He looked relieved that he had covered up so well.

Mrs Rupa Mehra decided that she wanted to be surprised after all, so she did not follow up the matter. But she was in a state of suppressed excitement for the next few days.

On the morning of her birthday she opened all her cards (a good two-thirds of which were illustrated with roses) and read each one out to Lata and Savita and Pran and Aparna and the baby. (Meenakshi had made good her escape.) Then she complained of eye-strain, and asked Lata to re-read them back to her. The one from Parvati read as follows:

Dearest Rupa,
   Your father and I wish you millions of happinesses on the occasion of your birthday, and hope that you are recovering well in Calcutta. Kishy joins me in saying Happy New Year in advance as well.
                                        With fondest affection,
                                        Parvati Seth

'And what am I supposed to be recovering from?' demanded Mrs Rupa Mehra. 'No, I don't want that one read again.'

In the evening, Arun left work early. He collected the cake that he had ordered from Flury's and a large number of pastries and patties. While waiting at an intersection, he noticed a man selling roses by the dozen. Arun rolled down his window and asked him the price. But the first price the man mentioned was so shocking that Arun yelled at him and began to roll up his window. He continued to glower even though the man was now shaking his head apologetically and pushing the flowers up against the pane.

But now that the car was moving, Arun thought of his mother again, and was almost tempted to tell the driver to halt. But no! it would have been intolerable to go back to the flower-seller and haggle with him. He had been absolutely mad angry, and he was still furious.

He thought of a colleague of his father's, about ten years his father's senior, who had recently shot himself out of rage just after his retirement. One evening his drink had been brought upstairs by his old servant, and he had flown into a fury because it had been brought without a tray. He had shouted at the servant, called his wife up, and told her to fire him immediately. This sort of thing had happened often enough in the past, and his wife told the servant to go down. Then she told her husband that she would speak to the servant in the morning, and that he should drink his whisky in the meantime. 'You only care for your servants,' he told her. She went down and, as was her habit, turned on the radio.

A few minutes later, she was startled by the sound of a shot. As she went upstairs, she heard another shot. She found her husband lying in a pool of blood. The first shot, applied immediately to his head, had glanced off and grazed his ear. The second had gone through his throat.

No one else in the Mehra family, when they heard the shocking news, had been able to understand the logic of it, least of all the appalled Mrs Rupa Mehra, who had known the man; but Arun felt that he understood it all too well. Rage did act like this. Sometimes he felt so angry that he wanted to kill himself or someone else, and he cared neither what he said nor what he did.

Once again Arun thought of what his life would have been like had his father been alive. A great deal more carefree than it was today, he thought – with everyone to support financially as he now had to; with Varun to place in a job somehow, since he was bound not to get through the IAS exam; with Lata to get married off to someone suitable before Ma got her married off to this Haresh fellow.

By now he had arrived home. He had the confectionery taken to the kitchen through the back. Then, humming to himself, he greeted his mother once again. Her eyes filled with tears and she hugged him. 'You came back early just for me,' she exclaimed. He noticed that she was wearing her rather nice fawn silk sari, and this puzzled him. But when the guests arrived, she displayed a very satisfying astonishment and delight.

'And I'm not even properly dressed – my sari's all crushed! Oh, Asha Di, how sweet of you to come – how sweet of Arun to have invited you – and I had no idea, none!' she exclaimed.

Asha Di was the mother, as it happened, of one of Arun's old flames, and Meenakshi insisted on telling her how domesticated Arun had become. 'Why, he spends half his evenings on the floor, doing jigsaw puzzles with Aparna.'

A wonderful time was had by all. Mrs Rupa Mehra ate more chocolate cake than her doctor would have advised. Arun told her that he had tried to get her some roses on the way home but had not succeeded.

When the guests had left, Mrs Rupa Mehra began opening her gifts. Arun, meanwhile, with only a word to Meenakshi, drove off in the Austin to try to locate the flower-seller again.

But when she opened the gift from Arun and Meenakshi she burst into injured tears. It was a very expensive Japanese lacquer box, which someone had given Meenakshi, and which Meenakshi had once, within earshot of her mother-in-law, described as being 'utterly ugly, but I suppose I can always give it away'.

Mrs Rupa Mehra had retreated from the drawing room and was sitting on her bed in the small bedroom with a hunted expression on her face.

'What's the matter, Ma?' said Varun.

'But the box is beautiful, Ma,' said Savita.

'You can keep the lacquer box, I don't care,' sobbed

Mrs Rupa Mehra. 'I don't care whether I have the flowers or not, I know what he was feeling, what love he has for me, you can say anything you like, but I know. You can say anything you like, now you all go away, I want to be by myself.'

They looked at her with incredulity – it was as if Garbo had decided to join the Pul Mela.

'Oh, Ma's just being difficult. Arun treats her much better than he treats me,' said Meenakshi.

'But, Ma –' said Lata.

'You also, go now. I know him, he is like his father. For all his tempers, his tantrums, his blow-ups, his fussiness, he has a big heart. But Meenakshi, for all her style, her thankyous, her goodbyes, her elegant laughter, her lacquer boxes, her Ballygunge Chatterjis, doesn't care for anyone. And least of all for me.'

'That's right, Ma –' said Meenakshi. 'If at first you don't succeed, cry, cry again.'

Impossible! she thought to herself, and walked out of the bedroom.

'But, Ma –' said Savita, turning the box around in her hands.

Mrs Rupa Mehra shook her head.

Slowly, with puzzled looks, her children filed out.

Mrs Rupa Mehra started weeping again and hardly noticed or cared. No one understood her, none of her children, no one, not even Lata. She wanted never to see another birthday. Why had her husband gone and died when she had loved him so much? No one would ever hold her again as a man holds a woman, no one would cheer her up as one cheers up a child, her husband was eight years dead, and soon he would be eighteen years dead, and soon twenty-eight.

She had wanted to have some fun in life when she was young. But her mother had died and she had had to take care of the younger children. Her father had always been impossible. She had had a few happy years of married life, and then Raghubir had died. Life had pressed in on her, a widow with too many encumbrances.

She was seized with anger against her late husband, who used to bring her an armful of red roses every birthday, and against fate, and against God. Where is there justice in this world, she said, when I have to observe our birthdays and our anniversary each year in loneliness that even my children can't understand? Take me soon from this horrible world, she prayed. Just let me see this stupid Lata married and Varun settled in a job, and my first grandson, and then I can die happily.

16.3

DIPANKAR stepped out of his hut in the garden after having meditated for an hour or so. He had come to a decision about the next step in his life. This decision was irrevocable unless he changed his mind.

The old gardener and the short, dark, cheerful young fellow who assisted him were at work among the roses. Dipankar stopped to talk to them, and heard disturbing complaints. The driver's ten-year-old son had been at his destruction again; he had lopped the heads off a few of the chrysanthemums that were still blooming against the creeper-covered fence which hid the servants' quarters. Dipankar, for all his non-violence and meditation, felt like cuffing the boy. It was so pointless and idiotic. Speaking to the boy's father had done no good. The driver had merely looked resentful. The fact was that the mother ruled the roost, and let the boy do what he wanted.

Cuddles bounded towards Dipankar, barking hoarsely. Dipankar, though his mind was on other matters, threw him a stick. Back bounded Cuddles, demanding affection: he was a strange dog, murderous and loving by turns. A bedraggled myna tried to dive-bomb Cuddles; Cuddles appeared to take this in his stride.

'Can I take him for a walk, Dada?' said Tapan, who had just come down the steps from the verandah. Tapan was looking, as he had been ever since he had returned for the winter holidays, even more disoriented than he usually did after the long train journey.

'Yes, of course. Keep him out of Pillow's way.... What's the matter with you, Tapan? It's been a fortnight since you returned, and you're still looking miserable. I know you haven't been calling Ma and Baba "Ma'am" and "Sir" for the past week –'

Tapan smiled.

'– but you're still keeping out of everyone's way. Come and help me in the garden if you don't know what to do with yourself, but don't just sit in your room reading comics. Ma says she's tried to talk to you but you say that nothing's the matter, that you just want to leave school and never go back again. Well, why? What's wrong with Jheel? I know you've had a few migraines these last few months, and they're very painful, but that could happen anywhere –'

'Nothing,' said Tapan, rubbing his fist on Cuddles' furry white head. 'Bye, Dada. See you at lunch.'

Dipankar yawned. Meditation often had this effect on him. 'So what if you've just got a bad report? Your last term's report wasn't much good either, and you weren't behaving like this. You haven't even spent a day with your Calcutta friends.'

'Baba was very stern when he saw my report.'

Mr Justice Chatterji's gentle reproof carried a great deal of weight with the boys in the family. With Meenakshi and Kuku, it was duck's water.

Dipankar frowned. 'Perhaps you should meditate a bit.'

A look of distaste spread across Tapan's face. 'I'm taking Cuddles for a walk,' he said. 'He looks restless.'

'You're talking to me,' said Dipankar. 'I'm not your Amit Da; you can't fob me off with excuses.'

'Sorry, Dada. Yes.' Tapan tensed.

'Come up to my room.' Dipankar had once been a prefect at Jheel School, and at one level knew how to exercise authority – though now he did it in a sort of dreamy way.

'All right.'

As they walked upstairs Dipankar said:

'And even Bahadur's favourite dishes don't seem to please you. He was saying yesterday that you snapped at him. He's an old servant.'

'I'm sorry.' Tapan really did look unhappy, and now that he was in Dipankar's room, almost trapped.

The room itself contained no chairs, just a bed, a variety of mats (including Buddhist prayer-mats), and a large painting that Kuku had made of the swamps of the Sundarbans. The single bookshelf contained religious books, a few economics textbooks, and a red bamboo flute – which Dipankar, when the mood took him, played very untunefully and fervently.

'Sit down on that mat,' said Dipankar, indicating a square blue cloth mat with a purple and yellow circular design in the middle. 'Now what is it? It's something to do with school, I know, and it isn't the report.'

'It's nothing,' said Tapan, desperately. 'Dada, why can't I leave? I just don't like it there. Why can't I join St Xavier's here in Calcutta, like Amit Da? He didn't have to go to Jheel.'

'Well, if you want –' shrugged Dipankar.

He reflected that it was only after Amit was well-ensconced at St Xavier's that some of Mr Justice Chatterji's colleagues had recommended Jheel School to him – so strongly, in fact, that he had decided to send his second son there. Dipankar had enjoyed it, and had done better than his parents had expected; and Tapan had therefore followed.

'When I told Ma I wanted to leave, she got annoyed and said that I should speak to Baba – and I just can't speak to Baba. He'll ask me for reasons. And there are no reasons. I just hate it, that's all. That's why I get those headaches. Apart from that, I'm not unfit, or anything.'

'Is it that you miss home?' asked Dipankar.

'No – I mean, I don't really –' Tapan shook his head.

'Has someone been trying to bully you?'

'Please let me go, now, Dada. I don't want to talk about it.'

'Well, if I let you go now you'll never tell me. So what is it? Tapan, I want to help you, but you've got to tell me what happened. I promise I won't tell anyone.'

He was distressed to notice that Tapan had started crying; and that now, enraged with himself, he was wiping away his tears and looking resentfully at his elder brother. To cry at thirteen was, he knew, a disgrace. Dipankar put his arm around his shoulder; it was angrily shrugged off. But slowly the story emerged, amid explosive outbursts, long silences, and furious sobs, and it was not a pleasant one, even to Dipankar, who had been to Jheel School years before, and was prepared for quite a lot.

A gang of three senior boys had been bullying Tapan. Their leader was the hockey captain, the seniormost prefect in the house other than the house captain. He was sexually obsessed with Tapan, and made him spend hours every night somersaulting up and down the long verandah as an alternative, he said, to somersaulting naked in his study four times. Tapan knew what he was after and had refused. Sometimes he was made to somersault in assembly because there was an imaginary spot of dust on his shoes, sometimes he had to run around the lake (after which the school was named) for an hour or more till he was near collapse — for no reason other than the prefect's whim. Protest was useless, since insubordination would carry its own penalties. To speak to the house captain was pointless; the solidarity of the barons would have ensured his further torture. To speak to the housemaster, a genial and ineffectual fool with his dogs and his beautiful wife and his pleasant don't-disturb-me life would have branded Tapan as a sneak — to be shunned and hounded even by those who now sympathized with him. And often enough his peers too could not resist teasing him about his powerful admirer's obsession, and implying that Tapan secretly enjoyed it.

Tapan was physically tough, and was always ready to use his fists or his sharp Chatterji tongue in his own defence; but the combination of major and minor cruelties had worn him down. He felt crushed by their cumulative weight and his own isolation. He had nothing and no one to tell him that he was right except a single Tagore song at Assembly, and this made his loneliness even deeper.

Dipankar looked grim as he listened; he knew the system from experience, and realized what pitiful resources a boy of thirteen could summon up against three seventeen-year-olds, invested with the absolute power of a brutal state. But he had no idea of what was to come; and Tapan became almost incoherent as he recounted the worst of it.

One of the nocturnal sports of the prefect's gang was to hunt the civet cats that roamed around under the roof of their house. They would smash their heads in and skin them, then break bounds with the connivance of the night-watchman and sell them for their skin and scent-glands. Because they discovered that Tapan was terrified of the things, they got a particular kick out of forcing him to open trunks in which they were lying dead. He would go berserk, run screaming at the senior boys and hit them with his fists. This they thought was hilarious, especially since they were also able to feel him up at the same time.

In one case they garotted a live civet cat, forced Tapan to watch, heated up an iron bar, and cut its throat from side to side with it. Then they played with its voice-box.

Dipankar stared at his brother, almost paralysed. Tapan was shuddering and gagging in dry heaves.

'Just get me out of there, Dada – I can't spend another term there – I'll jump off the train, I'm telling you – every time the morning bell rings I wish I was dead.'

Dipankar nodded and put his arm around his shoulder. This time it was not shrugged off.

'One day I'll kill him,' said Tapan with such hatred that Dipankar was chilled. 'I'll never forget his name, I'll never forget his face. I'll never forget what he did. Never.'

Dipankar's mind turned back to his own schooldays. There had been plenty of unpleasant incidents, but this psychopathic and persistent sadism left him speechless.

'Why didn't you tell me – why? – that school was like this?' said Tapan, still gasping. His eyes were full of misery and accusation.

Dipankar said: 'But – but school wasn't like that for me – my schooldays weren't unhappy for me on the whole. The food was bad, the omelettes were like lizards' corpses, but –' He stopped, then continued, 'I'm sorry, Tapan. . . . I was in a different house, and, well, times do change. . . . But that housemaster of yours should be sacked immediately. And as for those boys – they should be –'

He controlled himself with an effort, then went on:

'Gangs did terrorize the juniors, even in my time, but this –' He shook his head. 'Do other boys have it just as bad?'

'No –' said Tapan, then corrected himself. 'He picked on another boy earlier, but the boy gave in after a week's treatment, and went to his study.'

Dipankar nodded.

'How long has this been going on?'

'More than a year, but it's been worse since he was made a prefect. These last two terms –'

'Why didn't you tell me before?'

Tapan was silent. Then he burst out passionately:

'Dada, promise me, please promise me you won't tell anyone else.'

'I promise,' said Dipankar. His fists were clenched. 'No, wait; I'll have to tell Amit Da.'

'No!'

Tapan revered Amit, and could not bear that he should hear about his indignities and horrors.

'You've got to leave it to me, Tapan,' said Dipankar. 'We have to be able to convince Ma and Baba to take you out of school without letting them know the details. I can't do that by myself. Amit and I together may be able to. I'll tell Amit, but no one else.' He looked at Tapan with pity, affection, and dismay. 'Is that OK? Just Amit? No one else. I promise.'

Tapan nodded and got up, then started crying, and sat down again.

'Do you want to wash your face?'

Tapan nodded, and went off to use the bathroom.

'I'M writing,' said Amit crossly. 'Go away.' He looked up from his roll-top desk at Dipankar, and looked down again.

'Tell your Muse to go away instead, Dada, and to come back after we've finished.'

Amit frowned. Dipankar was rarely so abrupt. Something must be the matter. But he could feel his inspiration slipping away, and he wasn't pleased.

'Oh, what is it, Dipankar? As if Kuku isn't interruption enough. She came in to tell me something Hans had done that was singularly sweet. I can't even remember what it was now. But she had to tell someone, and you were in your hut. Well, what is it?'

'First, the good news,' said Dipankar tactically. 'I've decided to join a bank. So your Muse can keep visiting you.'

Amit jumped up from his desk and grabbed hold of his hands.

'You're not serious!'

'Yes. When I meditated today it all became clear to me. Crystal clear. It's irrevocable.'

Amit was so relieved that he didn't even ask Dipankar his reasons. In any case, he was sure they would be couched in the form of incomprehensible and capitalized abstractions.

'And how long will it remain irrevocable?'

Dipankar looked hurt.

'Well,' said Amit. 'I'm sorry. And it is very good of you to tell me.' He frowned and capped his pen. 'You're not doing this for me, are you? A sacrifice on the altar of literature?' Amit looked rather sheepishly grateful.

'No,' said Dipankar. 'Not at all.' But this was not entirely true; the effect of his decision on Amit's life had very much entered his thinking. 'But what I want to talk to you about is Tapan. Do you mind?'

'No, now that you've porlocked me already. He doesn't look very happy these days.'

'Oh, so you've noticed?'

Amit, in the throes of his novel, was insensitive to the feelings of his family in proportion to his sensitivity to the feelings of his characters.

'Yes, I have noticed. And Ma says he wants to leave school.'

'Do you know why?'

'No.'

'Well, that's what I want to discuss with you. Do you mind if I shut the door? Kuku –'

'Kuku can gurgle herself through any door; they're no obstacle to Kuku. But do, if you wish.'

Dipankar closed the door and sat down on a chair near the window.

He told Amit what Tapan had told him. Amit listened, nodding his head from time to time, and was sickened. At first he too could hardly speak.

'How long has Tapan had to go through all this?' he asked eventually.

'At least a year.'

'It makes my stomach turn – are you sure he's not – you know – imagining it – some of it? It seems so –'

'He's not imagining anything, Dada.'

'Why didn't he go to the school authorities?'

'It's not a day school, Dada, the boys would have made life worse hell for him – if you can imagine that.'

'This is terrible. This is really terrible. Where is he now? Is he all right?'

'In my room. Or he may have gone for a walk with Cuddles.'

'Is he all right?' repeated Amit.

'Yes,' said Dipankar. 'But he won't be if he has to go back to Jheel in a month.'

'Strange,' said Amit. 'I had no inkling of all this. None at all. Poor Tapan. He's never mentioned anything.'

'Well, Amit Da –' said Dipankar. 'Is that really his fault? He'd probably think we'd make a couplet out of it. No one ever talks to anyone in our family, we just exchange brilliances.'

Amit nodded.

'Does he want to go to another boarding-school?'

'I don't think so. Jheel is as good or as bad as any of them; they all breed conformists or bullies.'

'Well,' said Amit, 'Jheel bred you.'

'I'm talking about a general tendency, Amit Da, not about invariable effects. But it's up to us to do something. I mean the two of us. Ma will have hysterics if she hears about all this. And Tapan won't be able to face Baba if he thinks he's heard. As for Kuku, she sometimes has good ideas, but it would be idiocy to trust her to be discreet. And Meenakshi's out, obviously: the Mehras would know in a minute, and what Arun's mother knows today the world knows tomorrow. It was difficult enough to get Tapan to speak to me. And I promised him I'd tell only you.'

'And he didn't mind?'

Dipankar hesitated for a fraction of a second. 'No,' he said.

Amit uncapped his pen again, and drew a small circle on the poem he had been writing. 'Won't it be difficult for him to get admission somewhere else at this stage?' he asked, investing the circle with eyes and two large ears.

'Not if you talk to someone at St Xavier's,' replied Dipankar. 'It's your old school, and they're always telling you how proud they are of you.'

'True,' said Amit thoughtfully. 'And I did give a talk and a reading there earlier this year, which I very rarely do. So I suppose I could – but what reason could I give? Not his general health; you said he could swim across that lake and back. His headaches? Well, if they're brought on by travel, perhaps. Anyway, whatever I think of, getting him provisionally into another school would certainly counter one possible objection by Ma. A sort of fait accompli.'

'Well,' said Dipankar quietly, 'as Baba says, no fait is ever accompli until it's accompli.'

Amit thought of Tapan's misery and his own poem went out of his mind.

'I'll go over after lunch,' he said. 'Has the car been kuku'd?'

'I don't know.'

'And how will we convince Ma?' continued Amit, looking worried, almost grim.

'That's the problem,' said Dipankar. His decision to join a bank had made him quite decisive all around for an hour or so, but the effect was wearing off. 'What can he do here in Calcutta that he can't do at a boarding-school like Jheel? I suppose he couldn't develop a sudden interest in astronomy, could he, and be unable to live without a roof telescope. The thirst for knowledge, and so on. Then he'd have to live at home and attend a day school.'

Amit smiled. 'I can't see it going down too well with Ma: one poet, one seer, and one astronomer. Sorry, banker-cum-seer.'

'Headaches?'

'Headaches?' asked Amit. 'Oh, I see, his migraines. Yes, well, that'll help, but – let's try thinking not of Tapan, but of Ma. . . .'

After a few minutes, Dipankar suggested: 'How about Bengali culture?'

'Bengali culture?'

'Yes, you know, the Jheel School song book has one paltry song by Tagore, and no provision for teaching Bengali, and –'

'Dipankar, you're a genius.'

'Yes,' Dipankar agreed.

'That's just right. "Tapan is losing his Bengali soul in the swamp of the Great Indian Sensibility." She was complaining about his Bengali just the other day. Certainly it's worth a try. But you know, I'm not sure about letting matters rest here. If this is the state of affairs at Jheel, we ought to complain to the headmaster, and if necessary kick up a wider fuss.'

Dipankar shook his head. 'I'm afraid that if Baba gets involved, that is exactly what is going to happen. And I'm more concerned with Tapan at the moment than with undoing the general brutalities of Jheel. But Amit Da, do talk to Tapan. And spend a bit of time with him. He admires you.'

Amit accepted the implicit rebuke from his younger brother. 'Well, I'm impressed with us,' he said after a few moments of silence. 'We'd make a very practical team. Movers and Fixers. Wide experience of Law and Economics. Solutions while you wait: Intrepid, Immediate and Irrevocable –'

Dipankar cut him off. 'I'll talk to Ma at tea-time, then, Dada. Tapan has had to put up with this for months, he shouldn't have to put up with it for another day. If you and I – and, I hope, Ma – present a united front, and Tapan is so obviously unhappy at Jheel, Baba will give in. Besides, he won't mind having Tapan in Calcutta; he misses him when he's away. He's the only one of his children who isn't a Problem – except for his report card.'

Amit nodded. 'Well, wait for him to reach the age of responsibility before he displays his own variant of irresponsibility. If he's a Chatterji, he will.'

16.5

'BUT I thought you used to call him Shambhu,' said Mrs Chatterji to her gardener. She was referring to his young helper who had just gone off work at a little after five o'clock.

'Yes,' replied the old man, nodding his head vigorously. 'Memsahib, about the chrysanthemums –'

'But I just heard you call him Tirru when he left,' persisted Mrs Chatterji. 'Is he Shambhu or Tirru? I thought his name was Shambhu.'

'Yes, Memsahib, it is.'

'Well, what is Tirru then?'

'He doesn't use that name now, Memsahib,' continued the gardener candidly. 'He's on the run from the police.'

Mrs Chatterji was astonished.

'The police?'

'Yes, Memsahib. He hasn't done anything. The police

just decided to harass him. I think it's to do with his ration card. He may have had to do something illegal to get one, because he's from outside.'

'Isn't he from Bihar or somewhere?' asked Mrs Chatterji.

'Yes, Memsahib. Or Purva Pradesh. Or maybe even Eastern U.P. He seems reluctant to talk about it. But he's a good boy, you can see there's no harm in him.' He pointed with his hoe in the direction of the bed that Tirru had been weeding.

'But why here?'

'He thought a judge's house would be safest, Memsahib.'

Mrs Chatterji was nonplussed by the logic of this. 'But – ' she began, then thought better of it. 'What were you saying about the chrysanthemums?'

While the gardener explained the maraudings of the driver's son, Mrs Chatterji continued to nod without listening. How perplexing, she said to herself. I wonder if I should tell my husband. Oh, there's Dipankar. I'll ask him. She waved to him.

Dipankar came over. He was dressed in kurta-pyjamas, and was looking rather serious.

'Something extraordinary has happened, Dipankar,' said his mother. 'I want your advice.'

'And he does it to trees as well, Memsahib,' continued the gardener, seeing his ally approach. 'He broke all the lichis, then he broke the guavas, then he broke all the little jackfruit from the tree at the back. I got really annoyed. Only a gardener can understand the pain of a tree. We sweat for it and see it bear, and then this monster breaks them off with sticks and stones. I showed them to the driver and what did he say? No anger, not even a slap, just "Son, one doesn't do this sort of thing." If my child damaged his big white car,' continued the gardener, nodding forcefully, 'then he'd feel something.'

'Yes, yes, very sad,' said Mrs Chatterji vaguely. 'Dipankar, dear, do you know that that dark young man who helps around the garden is on the run from the police?'

'Oh?' said Dipankar philosophically.

'But aren't you upset?'

'Not yet. Why?'

'Well, we might all be murdered in our – well, in our beds.'

'What's he done?'

'It could be anything. The mali says it's to do with a ration card. But he's not sure. What should I do? Your father will be very upset if he hears that we've been harbouring a fugitive. And, as you know, he's not even from Bengal.'

'Well, he's a good fellow, this Shambhu –'

'Not Shambhu, Tirru. That's what he's called, apparently.'

'Well, we needn't upset Baba –'

'But a High Court Judge – with a wanted criminal working on his chrysanthemums –'

Dipankar looked beyond his hut to the large white chrysanthemums in the far bed – those few that the season and the driver's son had spared. 'I'd advise inaction,' he said. 'Baba will have enough on his plate now that Tapan is leaving Jheel.'

Mrs Chatterji continued: 'Of course, it isn't as if the police are always – what? What did you say?'

'And joining St Xavier's. It's a wise choice. And maybe, then, Ma, he can go on to Shantiniketan.'

'Shantiniketan?' Mrs Chatterji couldn't make out what that holy word had to do with the matter on hand. An image of trees came to her mind – great trees under which she had sat and partaken of the lessons of Gurudeb, her master, the waterer of the garden of the culture of Bengal.

'It's being parted from the soil of Bengal that's been making him so unhappy. He's a divided soul, can't you see, Ma?'

'Well, he certainly has two names,' said Mrs Chatterji, slipping down the wrong fork of the conversation. 'But what's this about Tapan and St Xavier's?'

Dipankar became soulful. His voice filled with a calm sadness, he said:

'It's Tapan I've been talking about, Mago. It's not the lake of Jheel that he needs, it's "your deep ponds, loving and cool as the midnight sky" that he misses. That's why he's been so low. That's why his reports have been so poor. That – and his longing for the songs of Tagore – Kuku and you singing Rabindrasangeet as the evening falls, at the cow-dust hour. . . .' Dipankar spoke with conviction, for he had convinced himself. Now he recited the magic words:

'Finally my homesickness grew too great to resist. . . .

I bow, I bow to my beautiful motherland Bengal!
To your river-banks, to your winds that cool and console;
Your plains, whose dust the sky bends down to kiss;
Your shrouded villages, that are nests of shade and peace;
Your leafy mango-woods, where the herd-boys play;
Your deep ponds, loving and cool as the midnight sky;
Your sweet-hearted women returning home with water;
I tremble in my soul and weep when I call you Mother.'

Mrs Chatterji was repeating the words together with her son. She was deeply moved. Dipankar was deeply moved.

(Not that Calcutta contained any of the above-mentioned features.)

'That is why he weeps,' he concluded simply.

'But he hasn't been weeping,' said Mrs Chatterji. 'Just scowling.'

'It has been to save you and Baba pain that he does not weep in front of you. But, Ma, I swear on my life and soul that he was weeping today.'

'Really, Dipankar,' said Mrs Chatterji, amazed and not entirely pleased at his fervour. Then she thought of Tapan, whose Bengali really had deteriorated since he had been to Jheel; and the thought of his unhappiness overwhelmed her.

'But which school will accept him at this stage?' she asked.

'Oh, that?' said Dipankar, brushing away the insignificant objection. 'I forgot to mention that Amit has already got St Xavier's to agree to take him in. All that is needed is his mother's consent.... "I tremble in my soul and weep when I call you Mother,"' he murmured to himself again.

At the word 'Mother', Mrs Chatterji, good Brahmo though she was, wiped away a tear.

A thought struck her. 'But Baba? –' she said. She was still overcome by events – in fact she wasn't certain she had comprehended them all. 'This is all so sudden – and the school fees – he really was crying? And it won't disturb his studies?'

'Amit has agreed to coach Tapan himself if necessary,' said Dipankar unilaterally. 'And Kuku will teach him one Tagore song a week,' he added. 'And you can improve his Bengali handwriting.'

'And you?' asked his mother.

'I?' said Dipankar. 'I? I will have no time to teach him anything, because I will be working at Grindlays from next month.'

His mother looked at him in amazement, hardly daring to believe what she had heard.

16.6

SEVEN Chatterjis and seven non-Chatterjis were seated for dinner at the long oval table in the Ballygunge house.

Luckily, Amit and Arun were not too close to each other. Both held strong opinions, Amit on some subjects, Arun on all; and Amit, being at home, would not be as reserved as he might otherwise be. The company, too, was the kind he felt comfortable in: the seven non-Chatterjis were all part of the clan by extension – or about to become so. They were Mrs Rupa Mehra and her four children, together with Pran (who was looking well) and the young German diplomat who was Kakoli's successful suitor. Meenakshi Mehra, when in Ballygunge, was included among the Chatterji count. Old Mr Chatterji had sent a message to say he would not be able to join them.

'It's nothing,' said Tapan, who had just returned from the garden. 'Perhaps he's tired of being tied up. Why don't I set him free? There aren't any other mushrooms around.'

'What? And have him bite Hans again?' said Mrs Chatterji. 'No, Tapan.'

Hans was looking grave and a little bewildered.

'Mushroom?' asked Hans. 'Please, what is a mushroom in this context?'

'You may as well know,' said Amit. 'Since you've been bitten by Cuddles, you are already virtually a blood-brother to us. Or a saliva-brother. A mushroom is a young man who is sweet on Kuku. They spring up everywhere. Some carry flowers, some just moon and mope. You had better be careful when you get married to her. I wouldn't trust any mushrooms, edible or otherwise.'

'No, indeed,' said Hans.

'How is Krishnan, Kuku?' asked Meenakshi, who had been following the conversation only partly.

'He is taking everything very well,' said Kuku. 'He will always have a special place in my heart,' she added defiantly.

Hans was looking even more grave.

'Oh, you needn't worry about that, Hans,' Amit said. 'That doesn't mean much. Kuku's heart is full of specially reserved places.'

'It is not,' said Kuku. 'And you have no right to talk.'

'Me?' said Amit.

'Yes, you. You are completely heartless; Hans takes all this flippant talk about affection very badly. He has a very pure soul.'

Meenakshi, who had had a bit too much to drink, murmured:

'Gentlemen that I allure,
They are always thinking pure.'

Hans blushed.

'Nonsense, Kuku,' said Amit. 'Hans is a strong man and can take anything. You can tell from his handshake.'

Hans flinched.

Mrs Chatterji found it necessary to intervene. 'Hans, you mustn't take what Amit says seriously.'

'Yes,' agreed Amit. 'Only what I write.'

'He gets into these moods when his writing is going badly. Have you had any news from your sister?'

'No, but I am expecting to hear from her any day,' said Hans.

'Do you think we are a typical family, Hans?' said Meenakshi.

Hans considered, then answered diplomatically: 'I would say you are an atypically typical family.'

'Not typically atypical?' suggested Amit.

'He's not always like this,' said Kuku to Lata.

'Isn't he?' asked Lata.

'Oh no – he's much less –'

'Less what?' demanded Amit.

'Less selfish!' said Kuku, annoyed. She had been trying to defend him before Lata. But Amit seemed to be in one of those moods where he cared about no one's feelings.

'If I tried to be more unselfish,' said Amit, 'I would lose all those qualities that make me a net joy-giver.'

Mrs Rupa Mehra looked at Amit, rather astounded.

Amit explained: 'I meant, Ma, that I would become completely sisterpecked and docile, and then my writing would suffer, and since my writing gives pleasure to many more people than I actually meet, there would be a net loss to the universe.'

This struck Mrs Rupa Mehra as astonishingly arrogant. 'Can you use that as a reason to behave badly to those around you?' she asked.

'Oh, yes, I think so,' said Amit, carried away by the force of his argument. 'Certainly, I demand meals at odd hours, and I never answer letters in time. Sometimes, when I'm in the middle of a patch of inspiration, I don't answer them for months.'

To Mrs Rupa Mehra this was sheer villainy. Not to answer letters was unforgivable. If this attitude spread, it would be the end of civilized life as she knew it. She glanced at Lata, who appeared to be enjoying the conversation, though not contributing to it at all.

'I'm sure none of my children would ever do that,' said Mrs Rupa Mehra. 'Even when I am away, my Varun writes to me every week.' She looked pensive.

'I'm sure they wouldn't, Ma,' said Kuku. 'It's just that we've pampered Amit so much that he thinks he can do anything and get away with it.'

'Quite right,' said Amit's father from the other end of the table. 'Savita's just been telling me how fascinating she finds the law and how much she looks forward to practising it. Why have a qualification if you make no use of it?'

Amit fell silent.

'Now Dipankar has settled down at last,' Mr Justice Chatterji added with approval. 'A bank is just the place for him.'

'A river-bank,' Kuku could not refrain from saying. 'With an Ideal to ply him with Scotch and type his ruminations for him.'

'Very amusing,' said Mr Justice Chatterji. He was pleased with Dipankar these days.

'And you, Tapan, you're going to become a doctor, are you?' said Amit with cynical affection.

'I don't think so, Dada,' said Tapan, who looked quite happy.

'Do you think I've made the right decision, Dada?' asked Dipankar uncertainly. He had made up his mind suddenly, having been struck by the insight that one had to be *of* the world before one could get away from it; but he was beginning to have second thoughts.

'Well –' said Amit, thinking of the fate of his novel.

'Well? Do you approve?' said Dipankar, looking with great concentration at the beautiful shell-shaped dish that had contained his baked vegetables.

'Oh, yes,' said Amit. 'But I'm not going to tell you I do.'

'Oh.'

'Because,' continued Amit, 'that would be the surest way of making you feel imposed upon – and then you'll change your mind. But – if this helps – you are certainly blinking less these days.'

'That's true,' said Mr Justice Chatterji with a smile. 'I'm afraid, Hans, you must think we're a very peculiar family.'

'Not so,' said Hans gallantly. 'Not very peculiar.' He and Kakoli exchanged affectionate glances.

'We hope to hear you sing after dinner,' continued Mr Justice Chatterji.

'Ah. Yes. Something from Schubert?'

'Who else is there?' said Kakoli.

'Well –' began Hans.

'For me there can only be Schubert,' said Kakoli giddily. 'Schubert is the only man in my life.'

At the far end of the table, Savita was talking to Varun, who had been looking downcast. As they talked, he cheered up perceptibly.

Meanwhile, Pran and Arun were engaged in a discussion of politics. Arun was lecturing Pran about the future of the country and how India needed a dictatorship. 'None of these stupid politicians,' he continued, unmindful of Pran's feelings. 'We really don't deserve the Westminster model of government. Nor do the British for that matter. We're still an advancing society – as our dhoti-wallahs are fond of telling us.'

'Yes, people are always making advances in our society,' said Meenakshi, rolling her eyes upwards.

Kuku giggled.

Arun glared and said in a low voice: 'Meenakshi, it's impossible to hold a sensible discussion when you're tight.'

Meenakshi was so unused to being ticked off by an Outsider in her parents' home that she did shut up.

After dinner, when everyone had adjourned to the drawing room for coffee, Mrs Chatterji took Amit to one side and said to him: 'Meenakshi and Kuku are right. She's a nice girl, though she doesn't say very much. She could grow on you, I suppose.'

'Mago, you make her sound like a fungus,' said Amit. 'I can see that Kuku and Meenakshi have won you over to their way of thinking. Anyway, I refuse not to talk to her just because you want me to. I'm not Dipankar.'

'Whoever said you were, darling?' said Mrs Chatterji. 'I do wish you had been nicer at dinner, though.'

'Well, anyone I like should be given the chance to see me at my best,' said Amit unrepentantly.

'I don't think that's a very useful way of looking at things, dear.'

'True,' admitted Amit. 'But looking at things in terms of a useful way of looking at things may not be a useful thing either. Why don't you talk to Mrs Mehra for a while? She was rather subdued at dinner. She didn't mention her diabetes once. And I'll talk to her daughter and apologize for my boorishness.'

'Like a good boy.'

'Like a good boy.'

16.7

AMIT walked over to Lata, who was chatting to Meenakshi.

'Sometimes he's terribly rude – and for no reason at all,' Meenakshi was saying.

'Talking about me?' said Amit.

'No,' said Lata, 'about my brother, not hers.'

'Ah,' said Amit.

'But the same certainly holds for you,' added Meenakshi. 'You've either been writing something strange or reading something strange. I can tell.'

'Well, you're right, I have. I was going to invite Lata to have a look at some books I promised to lend her but didn't post. Is this a good time, Lata? Or should we look at them some other time?'

'Oh, no, this is a good time,' said Lata. 'But when will they begin singing?'

'I shouldn't think for another fifteen minutes.... I'm sorry I was so rude at dinner.'

'Were you?'

'Wasn't I? Didn't you think so? Perhaps I wasn't. I'm not sure now.'

They were walking past the room where Cuddles had been confined, and he let out a growl.

'That dog should have his hypotenuse squared,' said Amit.

'Did he really bite Hans?'

'Oh, yes, quite hard. Harder than he bit Arun. Anyway, everything looks more livid on pale skin. But Hans took it like a man. It's a sort of rite of passage for our in-laws.'

'Oh. Am I within the bitable degrees?'

'I'm not sure. Do you want Cuddles to bite you?'

Upstairs, Lata looked at Amit's room in a new light. This was the room where 'The Fever Bird' had been written, she thought; and where he must have worked out his dedication to her. Papers lay scattered around in far worse disorder than the last time she had visited it. And piles of clothes and books lay on his bed.

'I shivered in the midnight heat,' thought Lata. Aloud she said: 'What sort of view do you get of that amaltas from here?'

Amit opened the window. 'Not a very good view. Dipankar's room is the best for that; it's just above his hut. But enough to see its shadow –'

'– Shake slightly on the moonlit grass.'

'Yes.' Amit didn't normally like his poetry quoted back at him, but with Lata he didn't mind. 'Well, come to the window, sweet is the night-air.'

They stood there together for a while. It was very still, and the shadow of the amaltas did not shake at all. Dark leaves and long dark podded beans hung from its branches, but no yellow clusters of flowers.

'Did it take you long to write that poem?'

'No. I wrote it out in a single draft when that damn bird kept me awake. Once I counted sixteen desperate triplets building upwards to fever pitch. Can you imagine: sixteen. It drove me crazy. And then I polished it over the next few days. I didn't really want to look at it, and kept making excuses. I always do. I hate writing, you know.'

'You – what –?' Lata turned towards him. Amit really puzzled her at times. 'Well, then, why do you write?' she asked.

Amit's face grew troubled. 'It's better than spending my life doing the law like my father and grandfather before me. And the main reason is that I often like my work when it's done – it's just the doing that is so tedious. With a short poem there's the inspiration of course. But with this novel I have to whip myself to my desk – To work, to work, Macbeth doth shirk.'

Lata remembered that Amit had compared the novel to a banyan tree. Now the image seemed somewhat sinister. 'Perhaps you've chosen too dark a topic,' she said.

'Yes. And perhaps too recent.' The Bengal Famine had taken place less than a decade ago, and was a very present memory to anyone who had lived through those times. 'But anyway, I can't go back now,' continued Amit. 'Returning is as tedious as go o'er – I'm two-thirds of the way through. Two-thirds, two-thirds; the fever-birds. Now, those books I promised to show you –' Amit stopped short suddenly. 'You have a nice smile.'

Lata laughed. 'It's a pity I can't see it.'

'Oh no,' said Amit. 'It would be wasted on you. You wouldn't know how to appreciate it – certainly not as much as me.'

'So you're a connoisseur of smiles,' said Lata.

'Far from it,' said Amit, suddenly plunged into a darker mood. 'You know, Kuku's right; I'm too selfish. I haven't asked you a single question about yourself, though I do want to know what's happened since you wrote to thank me for the book. How was your play? And your studies? And singing? And you said you had written a poem "under my influence". Well, where is it?'

'I've brought it along,' said Lata, opening her purse. 'But please don't read it now. It is very despairing, and would only embarrass me. It's only because you're a professional –'

'All right,' nodded Amit. He was completely tongue-tied all of a sudden. He had hoped to make some sort of declaration or indication of his affection to Lata, and he found that he did not know what to say.

'Have you written any poems recently?' asked Lata after a few seconds. They had moved away from the window.

'Here's one,' said Amit, looking through a pile of papers. 'One that does not bare my soul. It's about a family friend – you might even have met him at that party the last time you were in Calcutta. Kuku asked him upstairs to see her painting, and the first two lines suddenly occurred to her. He's rather fat. So she commissioned a poem from the resident poet.'

Lata looked at the poem, which was titled 'Roly Poly':

> Roly Poly Mr Kohli
> Toiling slowly up the stairs.
> Holy souly Mrs Kohli
> Tries to catch him unawares.
>
> Finger-wagging, fuming, frowning:
> 'Why you have not said your prayers?
> What means all this upping, downing?
> What is magic in the stairs?'
>
> Mr Kohli is Professor,
> Always doing complex sums.
> Answers mildly to aggressor,
> 'On the stairs the theory comes.'
>
> 'What a nonsense. Stop this summing.
> Come and eat. Your food is cold.'
> 'Just now only I am coming,'
> Says her husband, meek as gold.

Lata could not help smiling, though she thought it very silly. 'Is his wife all that fierce?' she asked.

'Oh, no,' said Amit, 'that's just poetic licence. Poets can create wives to suit their convenience. Kuku thinks that only the first stanza has any real force, and she's made up a second stanza of her own, which is much better than mine.'

'Do you remember it?' asked Lata.

'Well – you should ask Kuku to recite it.'

'It seems I won't be able to for a while,' said Lata. 'She's begun playing.'

From below the sound of the piano floated upwards, and Hans's baritone followed.

'We'd better go and join them,' said Amit. 'Toiling slowly down the stairs.'

'All right.'

There was no sound from Cuddles. Music or sleep had soothed him. They entered the drawing room. Mrs Rupa Mehra noted their entrance with a frown.

After a couple of songs, Hans and Kuku bowed, and the audience clapped.

'I forgot to show you the books,' said Amit.

'I forgot about them too,' said Lata.

'Anyway, you're here for a while. I wish you'd arrived on the 24th, as you had planned. I could have taken you to midnight mass at St Paul's Cathedral. It's almost like being back in England – unsettling.'

'My grandfather wasn't too well, so we postponed coming.'

'Well, Lata, are you doing anything tomorrow? I promised to show you the Botanical Gardens. Come see with me – the banyan tree – if you are free –'

'I don't think I'm doing anything –' began Lata.

'Prahapore.' It was Mrs Rupa Mehra's voice, from behind them.

'Ma?' said Lata.

'Prahapore. She is going to Prahapore tomorrow with the whole family,' said Mrs Rupa Mehra, addressing Amit. Then, turning to Lata she said: 'How can you be so thoughtless? Haresh has organized lunch for us at Prahapore, and you are thinking of gallivanting along to the Botanical Gardens.'

'I forgot, Ma – the date just slipped my mind for a moment. I was thinking of something else.'

'Forgot!' said Mrs Rupa Mehra. 'Forgot. You will forget your own name next.'

16.8

MUCH had happened in Prahapore since Haresh had got his job, indeed since his meeting with Arun and Meenakshi at the Chairman's mansion. He had plunged himself into his work, and become as much a Prahaman in spirit as the Czechs – though there was still not much love lost between them.

He did not mourn for his lost managerial status because he was the kind of man who preferred not to look back, and because in any case there was plenty of work to be done – and, what he liked most of all, battles to be fought, challenges to be overcome. As a foreman he had been put in charge of the Goodyear Welted line, which was the most prestigious line in the factory; Havel and Kurilla and the others knew that he could make this shoe-of-a-hundred-operations from scratch with his own rigid-thumbed hands, and would therefore be able to diagnose most problems in production and quality control.

But Haresh ran into problems almost immediately. He was not disposed to be friendly to Bengalis in general after his experience at CLFC, and now he decided fairly quickly that Bengali workmen were worse than Bengali bosses. Their slogan, which they made no secret of, was, 'Chakri chai, kaaj chai na': We want employment, not work. Their daily production was abysmal compared to what should have been possible, and there was a logic to this. They were attempting to establish a low working norm of about 200 pairs a day so that they could get incentive payments beyond that – or, if nothing else, the leisure to enjoy tea and gossip and samosas and paan and snuff.

They were also afraid, reasonably enough, of over-working themselves out of a job.

Haresh sat at his table near the production line, and bided his time for a few weeks. He noticed that the workmen on the entire line were often standing around idle because some machine or other was not working properly – or so they claimed. As a foreman he had the right to get them to clean the conveyor belt and the machines while they were doing nothing. But after the machines were gleaming, the workmen would saunter past him insolently and stand about in groups, chatting – while Praha and production suffered. It drove Haresh crazy.

Besides, almost all the workmen were Bengali and spoke Bengali, and he didn't understand much of it. He certainly understood when he was being insulted, however, because swear words like 'sala' are common to Hindi and Bengali. Despite his quick temper, he chose not to make an issue of it.

One day he decided that instead of grinding his teeth with frustration and sending for someone from the machinery department to repair a malfunctioning machine on site or to forklift it out, he would visit the machinery department himself. This was the beginning of what could be called the Battle of the Goodyear Welted Line, and it was fought on many fronts, against several levels of opposition, including that of the Czechs.

The mechanics were pleased to see Haresh. Normally foremen sent them slips asking them to repair their machines. Now a foreman, and that too the famous foreman who had got to live inside the white gates of the Czech compound, was visiting them and chatting to them on terms of equality, and even taking snuff with them. He was prepared to sit on a stool with them and talk and joke and share experiences, and look inside machines without caring if his hands got soiled with grease. And he called them 'Dada' out of respect for their age and abilities.

For once, they got the sense that they were part of the mainstream of production, not a mere auxiliary outfit in a forgotten corner of Praha. Most of the best mechanics were Muslims and spoke Urdu, so Haresh had no language problem. He was well-dressed, with a set of working overalls that he had adapted – sleeveless, collarless, extending no lower than the knee – to counter the heat and yet protect the front (if nothing else) of his cream silk shirt – perhaps a foppish appurtenance on the factory floor. But he had no airs of superiority when he talked to them, and this pleased them. Through their pleasure in exchanging the expertise of their trade, Haresh himself got interested in the mechanics of machines: how they worked, how they could be kept in good condition, how he might be able to make small innovations to improve their performance.

The mechanics told him, laughing, that the workmen on his conveyor belt were leading him a dance. Nine times out of ten, there wasn't even anything wrong with the machines.

This did not altogether surprise Haresh. But what could he do about it, he asked them? Because by this time they were friends, they said that they would tell him when something was really wrong – and they would repair his machines first when this was the case.

Now that the machines were out of action for shorter periods, production increased from 180 pairs a day to about 250, but this was still far below the 600 that was possible – or the 400 that Haresh was aiming for – as a realistic norm. Even 400 would have drawn cries of astonishment from his bosses; Haresh was convinced that it was doable, and that he was the man to do it.

The workmen, however, were not at all happy with 250 pairs, and found a new method to stop the conveyor belt. Men were allowed off the belt for five minutes at a time to answer a 'call of nature'. Now they staggered their calls of nature, and went off calmly to the bathroom by organized rotation – so that the conveyor belt was sometimes immobilized for half an hour at a time. By this time, Haresh had worked out who the gang-leaders were – they were usually the men doing the most cushy jobs. Despite his short temper, he did not behave in an unfriendly manner towards them, but a line had been clearly drawn, and each side was sizing up the other's strengths. A couple of months after he began his job, when production had plummeted to 160, Haresh decided that the time had come to play his hand.

He called the workmen into conference one morning,

and explained to them in a mixture of Hindi and rudimentary Bengali what had been simmering within him for a couple of months.

'I can tell you both from theory and from working with these machines that production should not be less than 400 pairs a day. That is what I would like to see from this line.'

'Oh?' said the man who pasted soles onto shoes – the easiest job on the line – 'Do show us, Sir.' And he nudged the operator to his left – a strapping fellow from Bihar who worked on the toughest job, the stitching of the welt to the lasted shoe.

'Yes, do show us, Sir,' said several other workmen, taking their cue from the sole-paster. 'Show us that it can be done.'

'Myself?'

'How else, Sir?'

Haresh fumed for a while, then thought that before any such demonstration, he needed to be certain that the workmen would not try to wriggle out of increasing production. He called together a few of the gang-leaders and said:

'What is it that you have against productivity? Are you really afraid that you will be thrown out if you increase production?'

One of them smiled and said: '"Productivity" is a word that management is very fond of. We are not so fond of it. Do you know that before the labour laws came into force last year, Novak would sometimes call people into his office, tell them they were fired and simply tear up their punch-in cards? That was that. And his reason used to be very simple: "We can do the same work with fewer people. We don't need you any more."'

'Don't talk about things that happened long before my time,' said Haresh impatiently. 'Now you have the new labour laws, and you're still deliberately keeping production down.'

'It will take time to build trust,' said the sole-paster philosophically and maddeningly.

'Well, what would induce you to produce more?' asked Haresh.

'Ah.' The man looked at his fellow-operators.

After a great deal of indirect discussion, Haresh came out of the meeting with the sense that if the workmen could get two assurances – that no one would be thrown out and that they would earn considerably more money than they were earning – they would not be averse to increasing production.

He next visited Novak, his old adversary, the fox-like head of Personnel. Would it be possible, he asked, for the workmen on his line to be rewarded with a higher grade – and thus a higher income – if they increased production to 400? Novak looked at him coldly and said, 'Praha cannot up grades for a particular line.'

'Why not?' asked Haresh.

'It would cause resentment among the other ten thousand workers. It cannot be done.'

Haresh had learned about the elaborate, sanctified hierarchy of Praha – it was worse than the Civil Service: there were eighteen different grades for workmen. But he felt that it could, without unhinging the universe, be given a tiny nudge here and there.

He decided to write a note to Khandelwal explaining his plan and asking for his approval. The plan had four elements. The workers would increase production to at least 400 pairs a day on the Goodyear Welted line. The management would raise the grades of these particular workmen by one level and thereby increase their weekly pay-packet. Beyond the figure of 400 pairs, incentives would be paid in proportion to any extra production. And instead of sacking anyone, a couple of new workmen would be hired at points where it was genuinely difficult to operate at the 400 pair level.

As it happened, about a month earlier, Khandelwal had sent Haresh on a two-day visit to Kanpur to help solve a labour reconciliation matter. An uneconomical depot was to be reduced in size and some workers laid off, and though Praha was acting strictly according to the new

Labour Manual, they had run into trouble; all the work-men had gone on strike. Khandelwal knew that Khanna had been at CLFC and was acquainted with affairs in Kanpur. He therefore sent him to help sort things out; and he had been pleased with the final result. Haresh had told the workmen who were to be laid off that they should accept Praha's offer. He had said, in effect: 'You idiots, you're getting good money by way of a settlement; take it and start your lives over again. No one is trying to con you.' The CLFC workers, who trusted Haresh and had been sorry to see him go, talked to the workers at the Praha depot; and matters had been settled amicably.

Haresh knew that he had won access to the Chairman's ear, and he decided to use his access immediately. He went to Calcutta one morning (before Khandelwal had had time to get to his whisky at the club) and placed a single sheet of paper in front of him. Khandelwal looked it over, followed the pricings, the costings, the benefits of the scheme, the loss of customers if production did not in-crease, the necessity of giving the workmen a higher grade. At the end of two minutes he said to Haresh:

'You mean to say you can actually double production?'

Haresh nodded. 'I believe so. Anyway, with your permis-sion, I can try.'

Khandelwal wrote two words across the top of the paper: 'Yes. Try,' and handed it back to Haresh.

16.9

HE said nothing to anyone; in particular he avoided the Czechs – especially Novak. Bypassing him – a step for which he was later to pay – he made a surprise move: he went to the union office and met the top union leaders of Prahapore. 'There is a problem in my department,' he said to them, 'and I want your help in solving it.' The Secretary-General of the union, Milon Basu, a man who was corrupt but very intelligent, looked at Haresh suspiciously.

'What do you propose?' he said.

Haresh told him only that he proposed a meeting the next day with his own workmen in the union offices. But it was not necessary to mention the matter to Novak until something had been worked out.

The next day was Saturday, a holiday. The workmen assembled in the union office.

'Gentlemen,' said Haresh, 'I am convinced that you can make 600 pairs a day. It is certainly within the capacity of your machines. I concede that you might need a couple of extra men at crucial points. Now tell me – which man here says that he cannot make 600 pairs?'

The sole-paster, who was the professional speaker, said belligerently: 'Oh, Ram Lakhan cannot do it.' He pointed to the strapping, mustachioed, good-natured Bihari who did the welt-stitching. All the toughest jobs on the conveyor, as well as elsewhere, were performed by Biharis. They stoked the furnaces; they were the policemen on night duty.

Haresh turned to Milon Basu and said: 'I am not asking for the opinion of a professional speaker. The man who has just spoken pastes the sock to the sole – in every other department his norm is 900 pairs a day. All he has to do is cement them and put them in. Let the man who is affected speak. If Ram Lakhan can't make 600 pairs a day, it's for him to speak out now.'

Ram Lakhan laughed and said: 'Sahib, you're talking about 600 pairs. I say that even 400 is impossible.'

Haresh said: 'Anyone else?'

Someone said: 'The capacity of the outsole stitcher isn't high enough.'

Haresh said, 'I have already conceded that. We'll put an extra man there. Anyone else?'

After a few seconds' silence, Haresh said to Ram Lakhan, who towered about a foot above him: 'Well, Ram Lakhan – if I make 400 pairs myself, how many will you make?'

Ram Lakhan shook his head. 'You will never be able to make 400 pairs, Sahib.'

'But if I do?'

'If you do – I'll make 450.'

'And if I make 500?'

'I'll make 550.' There was a recklessness in his answer and, indeed, a kind of intoxication to the challenge. Everyone was quiet.

'And if I make 600?'

'650.'

Haresh put up his hand and said – 'All right! It's done! Let's go into the battlefield!' There was no rationality to this exchange, merely a sense of drama, but it had been very impressive, and the issue had in effect been clinched.

'The matter has been decided,' said Haresh. 'On Monday morning I will don my overalls and show you what can be done. But let us talk for the moment of a mere 400. I am prepared to stand and tell you here and now that if our production rises to that level, not a single man will be fired. And the week that you regularly make 400 pairs a day I will fight for all of you to be promoted by one grade. And if this does not happen I am prepared to resign.'

There was a buzz of disbelief. Even Milon Basu thought that Haresh was a real fool. But he did not know of the two reassuring words: 'Yes. Try,' scrawled in the Chairman's hand on the sheet of paper in Haresh's pocket.

16.10

THE next Monday, Haresh donned his full overalls, not the natty, abridged ones he usually wore with his cream silk shirt, and told the workmen on his line to pile up the lasted shoes for welt-stitching. 600 shoes for an eight-hour day came to about ninety shoes an hour and still left an hour to spare. Each conveyor-rack contained five pairs of shoes. That meant eighteen racks an hour. The workmen gathered around, and those from other lines too could not resist betting on the odds of his succeeding.

Ninety pairs came and went before the hour struck. When it was over, Haresh wiped the sweat from his forehead and said to Ram Lakhan: 'Now I've done it – will you keep your side of the bargain?'

Ram Lakhan looked at the pile of welted shoes and said: 'Sahib, you've done it for an hour. But I have to do it every hour, every day, every week, every year. I will be finished, worn out, if I work at that rate.'

'Well, what do you want me to do to prove you won't?' said Haresh.

'Show me that you can do it for a whole day.'

'All right. But I'm not going to close the production line for a day. We won't stop the conveyor. Everyone will work at the same pace. Is that agreed?'

The conveyor was started up, and the work continued. The operators shook their heads at the unconventionality of it all, but they were amused and worked as hard as they could. Just over 450 pairs were made that day. Haresh was completely exhausted. His hands were trembling from having had to hold each lasted shoe against a needle going in and out of it at high speed. But he had seen people in a factory in England doing this with a single hand, turning the shoe casually around on the machine, and he had known it could be done.

'Well, Ram Lakhan? We have done 450. Now of course you'll make 500?'

'I said so,' said Ram Lakhan, stroking his moustache thoughtfully. 'I won't shift from that stand.'

After a couple of weeks Haresh got an extra man to assist Ram Lakhan with his crucial operation – mainly by handing him the shoes so that he wouldn't have to reach out for them – and the production level reached the final figure of 600.

What in Haresh's mind was the Battle of Goodyear Welted had been won. The Praha standard of production and profit was floating higher – and Haresh's own pennant too had ascended a notch. He was very happy with himself.

BUT not everyone was. One consequence of this whole business – and in particular the fact that Haresh had circumvented Novak – was that the Czechs, almost to a man, began to view him with intense suspicion. All kinds of rumours about him began to float around the colony. He had been seen allowing a driver to sit down in his house – to sit down on a chair as an equal. He was a communist at heart. He was a union spy, in fact the secret editor of the union paper *Aamaar Biplob*. Haresh could sense them cold-shouldering him, but he could do nothing about it. He continued to produce 3,000 pairs a week instead of the earlier 900 – and to pour his energy into every task within his direct control, down to the cleaning of his machines. And since he had given his own soul to the organization, he believed that Praha too – maybe in the distant form of Jan Tomin himself – would sooner or later do him justice.

He was in for a rude shock.

One day he went to the Design Centre in order to make a few suggestions that would help streamline the design and production of the shoes under his supervision. He discussed his ideas with the Indian who was the number two in the department. Just then Mr Bratinka, who ran the Design Centre, came in and stared at him.

'What are you doing here?' he said without even an attempt at civility and as if Haresh was trying to pollute his flock with the virus of rebellion.

'What do you mean, Mr Bratinka?' asked Haresh.

'Why are you here without permission?'

'I don't need permission to improve productivity.'

'Get out.'

'Mr Bratinka?'

'GET OUT!'

Mr Bratinka's assistant ventured to suggest that there was some merit in Mr Khanna's suggestions.

'Shut up,' said Mr Bratinka.

Both Bratinka and Haresh were furious. Haresh filed a

complaint in the open grievance book that Khandelwal had established for the redress of injuries. And Bratinka reported Haresh to his superiors.

The result was that Haresh was hauled up before the General Manager and a committee of four others: a regular Czech inquisition with all manner of odd allegations other than that he was in the Design Centre without permission.

'Khanna,' said Pavel Havel. 'You have been talking to my driver.'

'Yes, Sir, I have. He came to see me about a matter concerning his son's education.' Pavel Havel's driver was a quiet-spoken, extremely polite man, always spotlessly dressed: Haresh would have said that he was, in every sense that mattered, a gentleman.

'Why did he come to you?'

'I don't know. Perhaps because he thought that as an Indian I might be sympathetic – or would at least understand the difficulties of a young man's career.'

'What is that supposed to mean?' said Kurilla, whose Middlehampton comradeship with Haresh had helped him get his job in the first instance.

'Just what I said. Perhaps he thought I could help him.'

'And it was seen through your windows that he was sitting down.'

'He was,' said Haresh, annoyed. 'He is a decent man, and a much older man than me. As he was standing, I asked him to sit down. He was uncomfortable, but I insisted that he should take a seat. And we discussed the matter. His son has temporary work in the factory on daily wages, and I suggested that in order to improve his prospects he should attend night classes. I lent him a few books. That is all there is to the incident.'

Novak said: 'You think that India is Europe, Mr Khanna? That there is equality between managers and staff? That everyone is at the same level?'

'Mr Novak, I should remind you that I am not a manager. Nor am I a communist, if that is what you are implying. Mr Havel, you know your driver. I am sure you think he is a trustworthy man. Ask him what happened.'

Pavel Havel was looking a little shamefaced, as if he had implied that Haresh was not trustworthy. And what he next said rather proved it.

'Well, there have been rumours of your being the editor of the union newspaper.'

Haresh shook his head in amazement.

'You say you are not?' This was Novak.

'I am not. I don't even think I'm a union member – unless I have become one automatically.'

'You have been inciting the union people to work behind our back.'

'I have not. What do you mean?'

'You visited their offices and held a meeting with them secretly. I did not know of it.'

'It was an open meeting. There was nothing that was done secretly. I am an honest man, Mr Novak, and I do not like these aspersions.'

'How dare you speak like this?' exploded Kurilla. 'How dare you do these things? We are the providers of employment to Indians, and if you do not like this job and the way we run things, you can leave the factory.'

At this, Haresh saw red and said in a trembling voice:

'Mr Kurilla, you provide employment not only to Indians but also to yourselves. As for your second point, I may leave the factory, but I assure you that you will leave India before I do.'

Kurilla almost burst. That a chit of a junior should stand up to the mighty Czech Prahamen was something both incomprehensible and unprecedented. Pavel Havel calmed him down and said to Haresh: 'I think this inquiry is over. We have covered all the points. I will talk to you later.'

A day later he called Haresh to his office and told him to continue as before. He added that he was pleased with his job, especially with respect to production. Perhaps, thought Haresh, he's had a talk with his driver.

Amazingly enough, the Czechs, especially Kurilla, became fairly friendly towards Haresh after this incident. It had, in a way, cleared the air. Now that they believed he was not a communist or an agitator, they were neither panicky nor resentful. They were basically fair-minded men who believed in results, and his tripling of production, once it appeared in the official monthly figures, had the same sort of effect on them as the pair of Goodyear Welted shoes that Haresh had made – and which, as it happened, he had been facing throughout his inquisition in the General Manager's office.

16.12

AS Malati was walking out of the university library, en route to a meeting of the Socialist Party, one of her friends – a girl who studied singing at the Haridas College – got talking with her.

In the course of exchanging gossip, the friend mentioned that Kabir had been seen just a few days earlier at the Red Fox restaurant, in animated and intimate conversation with a girl. The girl who had seen them was entirely reliable, and had said –

But Malati cut her off. 'I'm not interested!' she exclaimed with surprising vehemence. 'I don't have the time to listen. I have to rush to a meeting.' And she turned away, her eyes flashing.

She felt as if she had been personally insulted. Her friend's information was always correct, so there was no point in doubting it. What infuriated Malati most of all was that Kabir must have met this girl at the Red Fox around the time that he was making his protestations of undying love in the Blue Danube. It was enough to put her into a Black Fury.

It confirmed everything she had ever thought about men.

O perfidy.

16.13

ON the evening before their meeting, while Lata had been at Ballygunge, Haresh was making last minute preparations at the Prahapore Officers' Club to entertain his guests the next day. The whole place was festooned with coloured crêpe for the Christmas season.

'So, Khushwant,' said Haresh in Hindi, 'there will be no problem if we are as much as half an hour late? They are coming from Calcutta and something might delay them.'

'No problem at all, Mr Khanna. I have been running the club for five years, and have grown used to adjusting to other people's schedules.' Khushwant had risen from being a bearer to becoming a cook-cum-bearer to becoming the virtual manager of the club.

'The vegetarian dishes will present no difficulty? I know that that is not usual at the club.'

'Please rest assured.'

'And the Christmas pudding with brandy sauce.'

'Yes, yes.'

'Or do you think it should be apple strudel?'

'No, the Christmas pudding is more special.' Khushwant knew how to prepare a variety of Czech desserts as well as dishes.

'No expense is to be spared.'

'Mr Khanna, at eighteen rupees a head instead of seven, there is no need to mention such matters.'

'It's a pity the swimming pool has no water at this time of year.'

Khushwant did not smile, but he thought that it was unlike Mr Khanna to be so concerned about things of this kind. He wondered what this special party was that he was being asked to cater for – at a lunch that would consume two weeks' worth of Mr Khanna's salary in two hours.

Haresh walked home thinking about his next morning's meeting rather than the Goodyear Welted line. It was a two minute walk to the small flat that he had been provided in the colony. When he got to his room, he sat at his desk for a while. He faced a small, framed photograph; it was the well-travelled picture of Lata that Mrs Rupa Mehra had given him in Kanpur.

He looked at it and smiled, then thought of the other photograph which used to travel with him. It had been left in its silver frame, but put away, lovingly and regretfully, in a drawer. And Haresh, after copying out in his small, slanting hand a few paragraphs and phrases from Simran's letters to him, had sent all her letters back to her. It would not be fair, he felt, to keep them.

The next day just at noon, two cars (the Chatterjis' white Humber which had been kuku'd by Meenakshi for the day, and Arun's little blue Austin) entered the white gates of the Prahapore Officers' Colony and stopped at House 6, Row 3. From the two cars emerged Mrs Rupa Mehra, together with two sons and a son-in-law, and two daughters and a daughter-in-law. The entire Mehra mafia was met and welcomed by Haresh, who took them upstairs to his little three-room flat.

Haresh had made sure that there would be enough beer, Scotch (White Horse, not Black Dog), and gin to keep everyone happy, as well as lots of nimbu pani and other soft drinks. His servant was a boy of about seventeen, who had been briefed that this was a very important occasion; he could not help grinning at the guests as he served them their drinks.

Pran and Varun had a beer, Arun a Scotch, and Meenakshi a Tom Collins. Mrs Rupa Mehra and her two daughters asked for nimbu pani. Haresh spent a lot of time fussing about Mrs Rupa Mehra. He was, most atypically and unlike his first meeting with Lata, quite nervous. Perhaps his meeting with Arun and Meenakshi at the Khandelwals' had given him the sense that they were critical of him. By now he and Lata had exchanged enough letters to make him feel that she was the woman for him. Her most affectionate letter had followed his announcement that he had lost his job; and he had been very moved by this.

Haresh made a few inquiries about Brahmpur and Bhaskar, and told Pran that he was looking very well. How were Veena and Kedarnath and Bhaskar? How was Sunil Patwardhan? He made a little polite conversation with Savita and Varun, whom he had never met before, and tried not to talk to Lata, who he sensed was equally nervous, perhaps even a little withdrawn.

Haresh was very conscious that he was under close family scrutiny, but he was not sure how to handle it. This was no Czech interview where he could talk about brass tacks and production. Some subtlety was required, and Haresh was not given to subtlety.

He talked a little about 'Cawnpore', until Arun said something denigratory about provincial industrial towns. Middlehampton too met with a similar response. Arun's amour propre and his habit of laying down his opinions as statute had clearly recovered from his setback at the Khandelwals'.

Haresh noticed that Lata was looking at his co-respondent shoes with what appeared almost to be distaste. But the moment he looked at her, she turned away a bit guiltily towards his small bookshelf with its maroon-bound set of Hardy novels. Haresh felt a little downcast; he had thought a great deal about what to wear.

But the grand luncheon was still to come, and he was sure that the Mehras would be more than impressed by the spread that Khushwant would lay on, as well as by the great wood-floored hall that constituted almost the entire premises of the Prahapore Officers' Club. Thank God he was not living outside the gates where the other foremen lived. The juxtaposition of those humble quarters with the pink silk handkerchief tucked into Arun's grey suit pocket, with Meenakshi's silvery laugh, with the white Humber parked outside, would have been disastrous.

By the time the party of eight was walking towards the club in the warm winter sunshine, Haresh's general optimism had reasserted itself. He pointed out that beyond the compound walls lay the river Hooghly and that the tall hedge that they were passing bounded the General Manager Havel's house. They walked past a small playground for children and a chapel. The chapel too was festooned for Christmas.

'The Czechs are good chaps at heart,' said Haresh expansively to Arun. 'They believe in results, in being shown rather than told something. I believe they'll even agree to my plan for brogues to be made in Brahmpur –

and not by the Praha factory there but by small-scale manufacturers. They're not like the Bengalis, who want to talk everything over the table and do as little work as possible. It is amazing what the Czechs have managed to create – and that too in Bengal.'

Lata listened to Haresh, quite astonished by his bluntness. She had had something of the same opinion about Bengalis, but once their family had become allied to the Chatterjis, she did not make or take such generalizations easily. And didn't Haresh realize that Meenakshi was Bengali? Apparently not, because he was continuing regardless:

'It's hard for them, it must be, to be so far away from home and not be able to go back. They don't even have passports. Just what they call white papers, which makes it difficult for them to travel. They're mostly self-taught, though Kurilla has been to university – and a few days ago even Novak was playing the piano at the club.'

But Haresh didn't explain who either of these two gentlemen were; he assumed that everyone else knew them. Lata was reminded of his explanations at the tannery.

By now they had got to the club, and Haresh, proud Prahaman that he had become, was showing them around with a proprietorial air.

He pointed out the pool – which had been drained and repainted a pleasant light blue, and a children's paddling pool nearby, the offices, the palm trees in pots, and the tables where a few Czechs were sitting outside under umbrellas, eating. There was nothing else to point out except the huge hall of the club. Arun, who was used to the subdued elegance of the Calcutta Club, was amazed by Haresh's bumptious self-assurance.

They entered the festooned hall; after the brightness outside, it was rather dark; there were a few groups here and there sitting down to lunch. Along the far wall was their own table for eight, created by joining three small square tables together.

'The hall is used for everything,' said Haresh. 'For dining, for dancing, as a cinema-hall, and even for important meetings. When Mr Tomin' – and here Haresh's voice took on a somewhat reverential note – 'when Mr Tomin came here last year, he gave a speech from the podium there. But these days it is used for the dance band.'

'Fascinating,' said Arun.

'How wonderful,' breathed Mrs Rupa Mehra.

16.14

MRS RUPA MEHRA was very impressed by all the arrangements. A thick white tablecloth and napkins, several sets of knives and forks, good glasses and crockery, and three flower arrangements consisting of an assortment of sweetpeas.

As soon as Haresh and his party entered, two waiters approached the table, and placed some bread on it, together with three dishes containing curlicues of Anchor butter. The bread had been baked under Khushwant's supervision; he had learned the technique from the Czechs. Varun, who had been walking a little unsteadily, was feeling quite peckish. After a few minutes, when the soup had not yet arrived, he took a slice. It was delicious. He took another.

'Varun, don't eat so much bread,' chided his mother. 'Can't you see how many courses there are?'

'Mm, Ma,' said Varun, his mouth full, and his mind on other things. When more beer was offered to him, he accepted with alacrity.

'How lovely the flower arrangements are,' said Mrs Rupa Mehra. Sweetpeas could never take the place of roses in her heart, but they were a lovely flower. She sniffed the air and took in the delicate colours: pale pink, white, mauve, violet, crimson, maroon, dark pink.

Lata was thinking that the sweetpeas made rather an odd arrangement.

Arun displayed his expertise on the subject of bread. He talked about caraway bread and rye bread and pumpernickel. 'But if you ask me,' he said (though no one had), 'there's nothing like the Indian naan for sheer delicacy.'

Haresh wondered what other kind of naan there was.

After the soup (cream of asparagus) came the first course, which was fried fish. Khushwant made quite a few Czech specialities, but only the simplest and most staple of English dishes. Mrs Rupa Mehra found that she was facing a cheese-covered vegetable bake for the second time in two days.

'Delicious,' she said, smiling at Haresh.

'I didn't know what to ask Khushwant to make for you, Ma; but he thought that this would be a good idea. And he has a treat for the second course, so he says.'

Tears threatened to come to Mrs Rupa Mehra's eyes at the thought of Haresh's kindness and consideration. Over the last few days she felt she had been starved of it. Sunny Park was like a zoo and Arun's explosions had been more frequent as a result. They were all staying together in the same small house, some of them sleeping on mattresses laid out at night in the drawing room. Though the Chatterjis had offered to put the Kapoors up in Ballygunge, Savita had felt that Uma and Aparna should be given the chance to get acquainted with each other. Also, she had quite unwisely wished to recreate the atmosphere of the old days in Darjeeling – or the railway saloons – when the four brothers and sisters had shared the same roof and pleasantly cramped quarters with their father and mother.

Politics was discussed. Results had started coming in from those states that had had early elections. According to Pran, the Congress would make a clean sweep of the elections. Arun did not contest the issue as he had the previous evening. By the end of the fish course politics was exhausted.

The second course was occupied mainly by Haresh impressing the assembled company with various facts of Praha history and production. He mentioned that Pavel Havel had praised him for 'working very hardly'. Although no communist, there was something in Haresh that resembled a cheerfully Stakhanovite Hero of Labour. He told them with pride that he was only the second Indian in the colony, and mentioned the weekly figure of 3,000 pairs to which he had increased production. 'I tripled it,' he added, very happy to share his sense of his own achievement. 'The welt-stitching operation was the real bottle-neck.'

A line from Haresh's tour of the tannery had stuck in Lata's mind. 'All the other processes – glazing, boarding, ironing and so on – are optional, of course.' She remembered it again now, and saw in front of her the soaking pits, where thin men with orange rubber gloves were pulling swollen hides out of a dark liquid with grappling hooks. She looked down at the delicious skin of her roast chicken. I can't possibly marry him, she thought.

Mrs Rupa Mehra, on the other hand, had moved several miles forward in the opposite direction, aided by a delicious mushroom vol-au-vent. She had decided not only that Haresh would make an ideal husband for Lata but that Prahapore, with its playground and sweetpeas and protective walls was the ideal place to bring up her grandsons.

'Lata has been saying how much she has been looking forward to seeing you in your smart new place,' Mrs Rupa Mehra fibbed. 'And now that we have seen it you must come for dinner on New Year's Day to our place in Sunny Park,' she added spontaneously. Arun's eyes opened wide, but he said nothing. 'And you must tell me if there is anything you particularly like to eat. I am so glad it is not Ekadashi today, otherwise I would not be allowed to have the pastry. You must come in the afternoon, that will give you a chance to speak to Lata. Do you like cricket?'

'Yes,' said Haresh, attempting to follow the ball of the conversation. 'But I'm not a good player.' He passed a puzzled hand across his forehead.

'Oh, I'm not talking about playing,' said Mrs Rupa Mehra. 'Arun will take you in the morning to see the Test Match. He has got several tickets. Pran also is so fond of cricket,' she continued. 'And then you can come over to the house in the afternoon.' She glanced at Lata, who, for some unknown reason, was looking quite upset.

What can be the matter with the girl? thought Mrs Rupa Mehra, irritated. Moody, that's what she is. She doesn't deserve her good fortune.

Perhaps she did not. At the moment her fortune, Lata couldn't help musing, was somewhat mixed. In immediate terms it consisted of meat curry and rice; Czech sentences floating across from another table followed by a heavy laugh; a Christmas pudding with brandy sauce that Arun took two helpings of and that Mrs Rupa Mehra took three helpings of, her diabetes notwithstanding ('But it's a special day'); coffee; Varun silent and swaying; Meenakshi flirting with Arun and bewildering Haresh with a discussion of the pedigree of Mrs Khandelwal's dogs; suddenly mentioning that her maiden name was Chatterji, to Haresh's consternation – from which he recovered by plunging into talk of Praha; too much, far too much talk of Praha and Messrs Havel, Bratinka, Kurilla, Novak; the sense of a pair of co-respondent shoes lurking invisibly under a thick white tablecloth; the sudden view of a pleasant smile – Haresh's eyes disappearing almost entirely. Amit had said something about a smile – her smile – just the other day – yesterday, was it? Lata's mind wandered off to the Hooghly beyond the wall, the Botanical Gardens on its banks – a banyan tree – boats on the Ganga – another wall near another Praha factory – a field fringed with bamboos and the quiet sound of bat against ball.... She suddenly found herself feeling very sleepy.

'Are you all right?' It was Haresh, smiling affectionately.

'Yes, thanks, Haresh,' said Lata unhappily.

'We haven't had the chance to talk.'

'It doesn't matter. We're meeting on New Year's Day.' Lata made an attempt at a smile. She was glad that her latest letters to Haresh had been quite non-committal. She was grateful, in fact, that he had hardly spoken to her at all. What could they talk about? Poetry? Music? Plays? Common friends or acquaintances or members of the family? She was relieved that Prahapore was fifteen miles away from Calcutta.

'That's a lovely salmon-pink sari you're wearing,' Haresh ventured.

Lata began to laugh. Her sari was a pale green. She laughed with pleasure and for the sheer relief of it.

Everyone else was amazed. What on earth had got into Haresh – and what on earth had got into Lata?

'Salmon-pink!' said Lata, happily. 'I suppose just "pink" isn't specific enough.'

'Oh,' said Haresh, suddenly looking uncomfortable. 'It isn't green, is it?' Varun gave a scornful snort, and Lata kicked him under the table.

'Are you colour-blind?' she asked Haresh with a smile.

'I'm afraid so,' said Haresh. 'But I can see nine out of ten colours accurately.'

'I'll wear pink the next time we meet,' said Lata. 'Then you can praise it without any uncertainty at all.'

Haresh saw the two cars off after lunch. He knew that he would be the topic of conversation for the next fifteen miles. He hoped that each car contained at least one of his supporters. He sensed once again that neither Arun nor Meenakshi wanted to have anything to do with him, but could not see what more he could have done to try to reconcile them to him.

About Lata he felt completely optimistic. He did not know of any rivals. Perhaps the lunch had been too filling, he thought; she had looked a bit sleepy. But it had gone off as well as expected. As for his colour-blindness, she would have had to find out about it sooner or later. He was glad that he had not asked them to come back to his flat for paan – Kalpana Gaur had warned him in a letter that the Mehras did not approve of paan. He had grown to like Lata so much that he wished he had had more time to speak with her. But he knew that it was not she but her family – and especially Ma – who was the target of today's exercise. 'Make 1951 the deciding year of your life,' he had written earlier in the year in one of his Action Points to himself. There were only three days to the new year. He decided to extend his deadline by a week or two, to the time when Lata would return to her studies in Brahmpur.

SAVITA had got into the front seat of the Austin; Arun was driving, and she wanted a word with him. Meenakshi sat at the back. The others went back to Calcutta in the Humber.

'Arun Bhai,' said the gentle Savita, 'what did you mean by behaving like that?'

'I don't see what you mean. Don't be a damned fool.'

Savita was the one person in the family who was not daunted by Arun's bullying tactics. There was to be no summary closure of debate.

'Why did you go out of your way to be unpleasant to Haresh?'

'Perhaps you should ask him that question.'

'I don't think he was particularly nasty to you.'

'Well, he certainly said that Praha was a household word in India and that the same couldn't be said for Bentsen Pryce.'

'It's a fact.'

'He had no call to say it even if it is.'

Savita laughed. 'He only said it, Arun Bhai, because you had gone on and on about the Czechs and their crude ways. It was self-defence.'

'I see you are determined to take his side.'

'That's not how I see it. Why couldn't you at least be civil? Don't you have any regard for Ma's feelings – or Lata's?'

'I most certainly do,' said Arun pompously. 'That is precisely why I think this thing should be nipped in the bud. He is simply the wrong sort of man. A shoemaker in the family!'

Arun smiled. When, on the recommendation of a former colleague of his father's, he had been asked to appear for an interview at Bentsen Pryce, they had had the wisdom instantly to perceive that he was the right sort of man. You either were or you weren't, reflected Arun.

'I don't see what's wrong with making shoes,' said Savita mildly. 'We're certainly happy to use them.'

Arun grunted.

'I think I have a bit of a headache,' said Meenakshi.

'Yes, yes,' continued Arun. 'I'm driving as fast as I can, considering I'm being distracted by my passenger. We'll be home soon.'

Savita was quiet for a couple of miles.

'Well, Arun Bhai, what do you have against him that you didn't have against Pran? You didn't have much to say about Pran's accent either when you first met him.'

Arun knew that he was treading on dangerous ground here, and that Savita would take no nonsense about her husband.

'Pran's all right,' conceded Arun. 'He's getting to know the ways of the family.'

'He has always been all right,' said Savita. 'It's just that the family has adjusted itself to him.'

'Have it your way,' said Arun. 'Just let me drive in peace. Or would you like me to pull over and continue this argument. Meenakshi has a headache.'

'Arun Bhai, this is not an argument. I'm sorry, Meenakshi, I have to have things out with him before he starts working on Ma,' said Savita. 'What is it you have against Haresh? That he isn't "one of us"?'

'Well, he certainly isn't,' said Arun. 'He's a dapper little man with co-respondent shoes, a grinning servant and a big head. I have rarely met anyone so arrogant, opinionated or self-satisfied – and with less cause to be.'

Savita merely smiled in reply. This irritated Arun even more than an answer.

'I don't know what you hope to achieve by this discussion,' he said after a few moments of silence.

'I just don't want you to ruin Lata's chances,' said Savita seriously. 'She isn't too certain about things herself, you know, and I want her to make up her own mind, not to have Big Brother deciding everything for her and laying down the law as usual.'

Meenakshi laughed from the back: a silvery, slightly steely laugh.

A huge lorry came towards them from the other side,

almost forcing them off the narrow road. Arun swerved and swore.

'Do you mind if we continue this conference at home?' he asked.

'There are hundreds of people at home,' said Savita. 'It will be impossible to make you see sense with all the interruptions. Don't you realize, Arun Bhai, that offers of marriage do not come raining down from the sky every day? Why are you determined to thwart this one?'

'There are certainly others who are interested in Lata – Meenakshi's brother for one.'

'Amit? Do you really mean Amit?'

'Yes, Amit. I do really mean Amit.'

Savita immediately thought that Amit would be most unsuitable, but did not say so. 'Well, let Lata decide for herself,' she said. 'Leave it to her.'

'With Ma fussing around her, she won't be capable of making up her own mind anyway,' said Arun. 'And Ma, as anyone can see, has been well wooed by the foreman. He hardly had a minute for anyone else the whole afternoon. I noticed that he didn't speak much to you, for example.'

'I didn't mind,' said Savita. 'I liked him. And I want you to behave decently on New Year's Day.'

Arun shook his head at the thought of Ma's sudden, unconsulted invitation to Haresh.

'Please let me out at New Market,' said Meenakshi suddenly. 'I'll join you later.'

'But your headache, darling?'

'It's all right. I have to buy a few things. I'll come home in a taxi.'

'Are you sure?'

'Yes.'

'We haven't upset you?'

'No.'

When Meenakshi had got down, Arun turned to Savita:

'You have quite needlessly upset my wife.'

'Oh don't be silly, Arun Bhai – and don't refer to Meenakshi as "my wife". I think she just can't face going home to a dozen people. And I don't blame her. There are too many of us in Sunny Park. Do you think Pran and Uma and I should take up the Chatterjis' invitation?'

'That's another thing. What did he mean by talking about Bengalis in that manner?'

'I don't know,' said Savita. 'But you do it all the time.'

Arun was quiet. Something was troubling him.

'Do you think she got down because she thought we were going to discuss Amit?'

Savita smiled at the thought of such unlikely delicacy on Meenakshi's part but simply said, 'No.'

'Well,' said Arun, still stung by the fact that Savita of all people was being so uncompromising in this matter of Haresh, and feeling a little uncertain as a result, 'you're getting quite a lot of courtroom practice out of me.'

'Yes,' said Savita, refusing to be jollied along. 'Now promise me you're not going to interfere.'

Arun laughed in an indulgent, elder-brotherly manner. 'Well, we all have our opinions – you have yours, and I have mine. And Ma can take whichever she likes. And Lata too, of course. Let's leave it at that, shall we?'

Savita shook her head, but said nothing.

Arun was trying to be winning, but she was not won.

16.16

MEENAKSHI made straight for the Fairlawn Hotel, where Billy was waiting for her in his room with a mixture of impatience and uncertainty.

'You know, Meenakshi, this thing makes me very anxious,' said Billy. 'I don't like it a bit.'

'I don't believe it makes you anxious,' said Meenakshi. 'Certainly not so anxious that it detracts from your wonderful –'

'– performance?' finished Billy.

'Performance. Just the word. Let's perform. But be nice to me, Billy. I'm sorry I'm late. I've had the most awful time and I have a headache as huge as *Buddenbrooks*.'

'A headache?' Billy was concerned. 'Shall I ask them to get you a couple of aspirin?'

'No, Billy,' said Meenakshi, sitting next to him. 'I think I have a better cure.'

'I thought women were supposed to say, "Not tonight, dear, I have a headache,"' said Billy, helping her with her sari.

'Some women, perhaps,' said Meenakshi. 'Does Shireen say that?'

'I'd rather not discuss Shireen,' said Billy stiffly.

By now Billy was as eager to cure Meenakshi as she was to be cured. About fifteen minutes later, he was lying, panting and pleasantly exhausted, upon her, his head nuzzling her neck. Meenakshi was much sweeter when she was making love than at any other time. She was almost affectionate! He began to withdraw.

'No, Billy, just stay where you are,' said Meenakshi in a sighing voice. 'You feel so nice.' Billy had been at his tenderly athletic best.

'All right,' Billy consented.

After a few minutes though, as he softened, he had to pull out.

'Whoops!' said Billy.

'That was lovely,' said Meenakshi. 'What was the "whoops" for?'

'I'm sorry, Meenakshi – but the thing's slipped off. It's still inside you.'

'But it can't be! I can't feel it.'

'Well, it's not on me, and I could feel it slip off.'

'Don't be ridiculous, Billy,' said Meenakshi sharply. 'It's never happened before – and do you think I wouldn't feel it if it was still there?'

'I don't know about that,' said Billy. 'I think you'd better go and check.'

Meenakshi went for a shower, and came out furious.

'How dare you?' she said

'How dare I what?' responded Billy, looking troubled.

'How dare you let it slip off! I'm not going through all that again,' said Meenakshi, and burst into tears. How horribly, horribly tawdry, she thought.

Poor Billy was very worried by now. He tried to console her by putting his arms around her wet shoulders, but she shook him off angrily. She was trying to work out if today fell within her most vulnerable week. Billy was a real fool.

'Meenakshi, I just can't go on with this sort of thing,' he was saying.

'Oh, do be quiet, and let me think. My headache's come back,' said Meenakshi.

Billy nodded contritely. Meenakshi was putting on her sari again – rather violently.

By the time she had worked out that she was probably safe anyway, she was in no mood to relinquish Billy. She told him so.

'But after Shireen and I are married –' began Billy.

'What does marriage have to do with it?' asked Meenakshi. 'I'm married, aren't I? You enjoy it, I enjoy it; that's all there is to it. Next Thursday, then.'

'But Meenakshi –'

'Don't gape, Billy. It makes you look like a fish. I'm trying to be reasonable.'

'But Meenakshi –'

'I can't stay to discuss all this,' said Meenakshi, putting the finishing touches to her face. 'I'd better be getting home. Poor Arun will be wondering what on earth's happened to me.'

16.17

'PUT off the light,' said Mrs Rupa Mehra to Lata as she came out of the bathroom. 'Electricity does not grow on trees.'

Mrs Rupa Mehra was seriously annoyed. It was New Year's Eve and, instead of spending it with her mother as she ought to, Lata was behaving like a Young Person and going out with Arun and Meenakshi for a round of parties. Mischief was afoot, and Mrs Rupa Mehra could sense it.

'Will Amit be going with you?' she demanded of Meenakshi.

'Well, Ma, I hope so – and Kuku and Hans too if we can persuade them,' Meenakshi added as camouflage.

Mrs Rupa Mehra was not deceived. 'Well, then, you will have no objection to Varun going as well,' she asserted. She promptly instructed her younger son to go along with them. 'And do not leave the party for a moment,' she warned him sternly.

Varun was not happy at all with this state of affairs. He had hoped to spend his New Year with Sajid, Jason, Hotends and his other Shamshuing and gambling acquaintances. But there was that in Mrs Rupa Mehra's eye which brooked no counter-squeak. 'And I do not want Lata to go off by herself,' said Mrs Rupa Mehra when she got Varun by himself for a moment. 'I do not trust your brother and Meenakshi.'

'Oh, why not?' asked Varun.

'They will be having much too good a time to keep an eye on Lata,' said Mrs Rupa Mehra evasively.

'I suppose I shouldn't have a good time myself,' said Varun with gloomy annoyance.

'No. Not if your sister's future is at stake. What would your father say?'

At the memory of his father Varun felt a sudden sense of resentment of the kind he often had towards Arun. Then, almost immediately, he felt bad about it, and was overcome by a sense of guilt. What kind of son am I? he thought.

Mrs Rupa Mehra and the rump of the family – Pran, Savita, Aparna and Uma – were to go over to Ballygunge that evening to spend New Year's Eve with the senior Chatterjis, including old Mr Chatterji. Dipankar and Tapan would be at home too. It would be a quiet family evening, thought Mrs Rupa Mehra, not like this endless gallivanting that seemed to be the craze these days. Frivolous, that was the word for Meenakshi and Kakoli; and their frivolity was a disgrace in a city as poor as Calcutta – a city moreover where Pandit Nehru had just arrived to talk about the Congress and the freedom struggle and socialism. Mrs Rupa Mehra told Meenakshi exactly what she thought.

Meenakshi's response was a couplet disguised as 'Deck the hall with boughs of holly', of which there had been a good deal too much on the radio recently:

> 'End the year with fun and frivol
> Fa-la-la-la-la, la-la-la-la!
> All the rest is drab and drivel.
> Fa-la-la-la-la, la-la-la-la!'

'You are a very irresponsible girl, Meenakshi, I can tell you that,' said Mrs Rupa Mehra. 'How dare you sing to me like that?'

But Mrs Arun Mehra was in too good a mood to be put off by her mother-in-law's ill-temper and, surprisingly and suddenly, gave her a kiss for New Year. Such a sign of affection was rare in Meenakshi, and Mrs Rupa Mehra accepted it with glum grace.

Then Arun, Meenakshi, Varun and Lata whizzed off to enjoy themselves.

They went to several parties, and landed up after eleven o'clock at Bishwanath Bhaduri's, where Meenakshi saw the back of Billy's head.

'Billy!' Meenakshi cooed in a carrying vibrato from halfway across the room.

Billy looked around and his face fell. But Meenakshi traversed the room and managed to detach him as blatantly and flirtatiously as possible from Shireen. When she had got him alone in a corner, she said:

'Billy, I can't make it on Thursday. The Shady Ladies just phoned to say they're having a special meeting.'

Billy's face expressed relief. 'Oh, I'm so sorry,' he said.

'So it will have to be Wednesday.'

'I can't!' pleaded Billy. Then he became annoyed. 'Why did you get me away from my friends?' he said. 'Shireen will begin to suspect me.'

'She will not,' said Meenakshi gaily. 'But it's good your back's turned to her at the moment. If she saw you looking so angry, she certainly would. And indignation doesn't suit you. In fact nothing suits you. Only your birthday suit.

Don't blush, Billy, or I shall be forced to kiss you passionately an hour before your New Year kiss is due. Wednesday
then. Don't evade your irresponsibilities.'

Billy was horribly unhappy, but he didn't know what to
do.

'Did you watch the Test Match today?' asked Meenakshi, changing the subject. Poor Billy, he looked so dejected.

'What do you think?' said Billy, cheering up at the
memory. India had not done too badly, having managed to
get England out for 342 in the first innings.

'So you'll be there tomorrow?' Meenakshi said.

'Oh, yes. I'm looking forward to seeing what Hazare
will do with their bowling. The MCC have sent a second-
rate team out to India, and I'll be happy to see them taught
a lesson. Well, it'll be a pleasant way to spend New Year's
Day.'

'Arun has a few tickets,' said Meenakshi. 'I think I'll go
and watch the match tomorrow.'

'But you aren't interested in cricket –' protested Billy.

'Ah – there's another woman waving at you,' said Meenakshi. 'You haven't been seeing other women, have you?'

'Meenakshi!' said Billy, so deeply shocked that Meenakshi was forced to believe him.

'Well, I'm glad you're still faithful. Faithfully unfaith-
ful,' said Meenakshi. 'Or unfaithfully faithful. No, it's
me she's waving at. Should I deliver you back to
Shireen?'

'Yes, please,' said Billy mutedly.

16.18

VARUN and Lata were talking to Dr Ila Chattopadhyay in
another part of the room. Dr Ila Chattopadhyay enjoyed
the company of all sorts of people – and the fact that they
were young did not count against them in her view. In fact
this was one of her strengths as a teacher of English.
Another was her devastating braininess. Dr Ila Chattopadhyay was as crazy and opinionated with her students as

with her colleagues. Indeed, she respected her students more than her colleagues. They were, she thought, much more intellectually innocent, and much more intellectually honest.

Lata wondered what she was doing at this party: was she also chaperoning someone? If so, she was performing her duties laxly. At the moment she was entirely absorbed in conversation with Varun.

'No, no,' she was saying, 'don't join the IAS – it's just another one of those Brown Sahib professions, and you'll turn into a variant of your odious brother.'

'But what should I do?' Varun was saying. 'I'm not good for anything.'

'Write a book! Pull a rickshaw! Live! Don't make excuses,' said Dr Ila Chattopadhyay with hectic enthusiasm, shaking her grey hair vigorously. 'Renounce the world like Dipankar. No, he's joined a bank, hasn't he? How did you do in your exams anyway?' she added.

'Terribly!' said Varun.

'I don't think you've done so badly,' said Lata. 'I always think I've done worse than I actually have. It's a Mehra trait.'

'No, I really have done terribly,' said Varun, pulling a morose face and gulping down his whisky. 'I'm sure I've failed. I shall certainly not be called for the interview.'

Dr Ila Chattopadhyay said: 'Don't worry. It could be far worse. A good friend of mine has just had her daughter die of TB.'

Lata looked at Ila Chattopadhyay in amazement. Next she'll say: 'Now don't worry. Just think – it could be far worse. A sister of mine has just had her two-year-old triplets decapitated by her alcoholic husband.'

'You have the most extraordinary expression on your face,' said Amit, who had joined them.

'Oh, Amit! Hello,' said Lata. It was good to see him.

'What were you thinking of?'

'Nothing – nothing at all.'

Dr Ila Chattopadhyay was telling Varun about the idiocy of Calcutta University in making Hindi a compulsory subject at the B.A. level. Amit joined the discussion for a bit. He sensed that Lata's thoughts were still quite far away. He wanted to talk to her a little about her poem. But he was accosted by a woman who said: 'I want to talk to you.'

'Well, here I am,' said Amit.

'My name is Baby,' said the woman, who looked about forty.

'Well, mine is Amit.'

'I know that, I know that, everyone knows that,' said the woman. 'Are you trying to impress me with your modesty?' She was in a quarrelsome mood.

'No,' said Amit.

'I love your books, especially *The Fever Tree*. I think of it all night. I mean *The Fever Bird*. You look smaller than your photographs. You must be very leggy.'

'What do you do?' asked Amit, not knowing what to make of her last few words.

'I like you,' said the lady decisively. 'I know whom I like. Visit me in Bombay. Everyone knows me. Just ask for Baby.'

'All right,' said Amit. He had no plans to go to Bombay.

Bishwanath Bhaduri came over to say hello to Amit. He ignored Lata almost completely. He even ignored the predatory Baby. He was in raptures about some new woman, whom he pointed out: someone who was dressed in black and silver.

'One feels she has such a beautiful soul,' said Bish.

'Repeat that,' said Amit.

Bishwanath Bhaduri drew back. 'One doesn't say such things in order to repeat them,' he said.

'Ah, but one doesn't get to hear such things very often.'

'You'll use it for your novel. One shouldn't, you know.'

'Why shouldn't one?'

'It's just Calcutta chitchat.'

'It's not chitchat – it's poetic; very poetic; suspiciously so.'

'You're making fun of me,' said Bishwanath Bhaduri. He looked around. 'One needs a drink,' he murmured.

'One needs to escape,' said Amit quietly to Lata. 'Two need to.'

'I can't. I have a chaperone.'

'Who?'

Lata's eyes indicated Varun. He was talking to a couple of young men, who were clinging to his words.

'I think we can give him the slip,' said Amit. 'I'll show you the lights on Park Street.'

As they walked behind Varun they heard him say: 'Marywallace, of course, for the Gatwick; and Simile for the Hopeful. I have no idea about the Hazra. And for the Beresford Cup it's best to go for My Lady Jean....'

They eluded him with ease and walked down the stairs, laughing.

16.19

AMIT hailed a taxi.

'Park Street,' said Amit.

'Why not Bombay?' asked Lata, laughing. 'To meet Baby.'

'She is a thorn in my neck,' said Amit, shaking his knees together rapidly.

'In your neck?'

'As Biswas Babu would say.'

Lata laughed. 'How is he?' she asked. 'Everyone talks about him, but I've never met him.'

'He's been telling me to get married – to produce, he hopes, a fourth generation of Chatterji judge. I suggested that Aparna was half a Chatterji and might easily rise to the bench, given her precocity. He said that that was a different kettle of tea.'

'But his advice ran off your back like duck's water.'

'Exactly so.'

They had been driving along Chowringhee, parts of which were lit up – especially the larger stores, the Grand Hotel, and Firpos. Now they were at the crossing of Park Street. Here a large reindeer complete with Santa and sled was illuminated by large coloured bulbs. Several people were strolling along the side of Chowringhee adjacent to the Maidan, enjoying the festive atmosphere. As the taxi turned into Park Street, Lata was taken aback by its unaccustomed brilliance. On both sides, multicoloured strings of lights and brightly coloured festoons of crêpe hung from the fronts of shops and restaurants: Flury's, Kwality's, Peiping, Magnolia's. It was lovely, and Lata turned to Amit with delight and gratitude. When they got to the tall Christmas tree by the petrol pump she said:

'Electricity growing on trees.'

'What was that?' said Amit.

'Oh, that's Ma. "Turn off the lights. Electricity doesn't grow on trees."'

Amit laughed. 'It's very nice to see you again,' he said.

'I feel the same way,' said Lata. 'Mutatis mutandis.'

Amit looked at her in surprise. 'The last time I heard that was at the Inns of Court.'

'Oh,' said Lata, smiling. 'I must have picked it up from Savita. She's always cooing such phrases to the baby.'

'By the way, what were you thinking of when I inter-rupted you and Varun?' asked Amit.

Lata told him about Dr Ila Chattopadhyay's remark.

Amit nodded, then said: 'About your poem.'

'Yes?' Lata grew tense. What was he going to say about it?

'I sometimes feel that it's a consolation in times of deep grief to know that the world, by and large, does not care.'

Lata was quiet. It was an odd sentiment, though a relevant one.

After a while she said: 'Did you like it?'

'Yes,' said Amit. 'As a poem.' He recited a couple of lines.

'The cemetery's on this street, isn't it?' said Lata.

'Yes.'

'Very different from the other end.'

'Very.'

'That was a curious sort of spiral pillar on Rose Aylmer's tomb.'

'Do you want to see it by night?'

'No! It would be strange, seeing all those stars. A night of memories and of sighs.'

'I should have pointed them out to you by day,' said Amit.

'Pointed what out?'

'The stars.'

'By day?'

'Well, yes. I can tell you roughly where the various stars are by day. Why not? They're still in the sky. The sun only blinds us to them. It's midnight. May I?'

And before she could protest, Amit had kissed her.

She was so surprised she didn't know what to say. She was also a bit annoyed.

'Happy New Year,' said Amit.

'Happy New Year,' she answered, hiding her annoyance. She had, after all, conspired to evade her chaperone. 'You didn't plan this, did you?'

'Of course not. Do you want me to deliver you back to Varun? Or should we take a walk by the Victoria Memorial?'

'Neither. I'm feeling tired. I'd like to go to sleep.' After a pause she said: '1952: how new it seems. As if each digit were polished.'

'A leap year.'

'I'd better go back to the party. Varun really will panic if he finds me gone.'

'I'll drop you back home, then go back to the party myself to tell Varun. How's that?'

Lata smiled to think of Varun's expression when he realized his charge had flown.

'All right. Thank you, Amit.'

'You aren't annoyed with me? New Year's licence. I couldn't help it.'

'So long as you don't claim poetic licence the next time.'

Amit laughed, and good relations were restored.

'But why don't I feel anything?' she asked herself. She did know that Amit was fond of her, but her chief emotion at the kiss was still astonishment.

She was home in a few minutes. Mrs Rupa Mehra had not yet returned. When she did come back half an hour later she found Lata asleep. Lata appeared restless – her head was turning from side to side on her pillow.

She was dreaming – of a kiss – but it was of Kabir that she was dreaming, the one who was absent, the one who above all others she should not meet, the most unsuitable boy of them all.

16.20

1952: the fresh and brilliant digits impressed themselves upon Pran's eye as he opened the morning newspaper. All the past grew veiled by the first of January, and all the future glistened ahead of him, emerging mysteriously from its grubby chrysalis. He thought about his heart and his child and Bhaskar's close brush with death, the mixed gifts of the previous year. And he wondered whether the coming year would bring him his readership – and a new brother-in-law – and possibly even see his father sworn in as the Chief Minister of Purva Pradesh. The last was by no means impossible. As for Maan, surely he would have to settle down sooner or later.

Although no one other than himself and Mrs Rupa Mehra was awake at six o'clock, there was a sudden storm of activity at seven. The time allowed in the two bathrooms was strictly rationed, and everyone was completely ready – and even breakfasted – by eight-thirty. The women had decided to spend the day at the Chatterjis' – perhaps they would go on to do a bit of shopping as well. Even Meenakshi, who at first appeared eager to come to the cricket match, decided against it at the last moment.

Amit and Dipankar arrived in the Humber at nine, and Arun, Varun and Pran went off with them to Eden Gardens to watch the third day of the Third Test. Just outside the stadium they met Haresh, as previously arranged, and the six of them made their way to the tier where their seats were located.

It was a wonderful morning. There was a clear blue sky, and dew still glistened on the outfield. Eden Gardens, with its emerald grass and surrounding trees, its huge scoreboard and new Ranji Stadium block, was a magnificent sight. It was packed solid, but luckily one of Arun's English colleagues at Bentsen Pryce, who had bought a bunch of season tickets for his family, was out sightseeing, and had offered his seats to Arun for the day. They were placed just next to the pavilion section, where VIPs and members of the Cricket Association of Bengal sat, and they had a fine view of the field.

India's opening batsmen were still at the crease. Since India had scored 418 and 485 in two previous innings in the series, and since England were all out for 342 in their first innings, there was a good chance that the hosts would be able to make something of the match. The Calcutta crowd – more knowledgeable and appreciative than any other in India – was looking forward to it with eager anticipation.

The chatter, which increased between overs, was reduced, but not quite to silence, every time the bowler came in to bowl. Leadbeater opened the bowling to Roy with a maiden, and Ridgway supported the attack from the other end, bowling to Mankad. Then, for the next over, instead of continuing with Leadbeater, the English skipper Howard brought Statham on.

This provoked a good deal of discussion among the group of six. Everyone started speculating as to why Leadbeater had been brought on for a single over. Amit alone said that it meant nothing at all. Perhaps, because Indian time was several hours ahead of England, Leadbeater had wanted to bowl the first English ball of 1952 and Howard had let him.

'Really, Amit,' said Pran with a laugh. 'Cricket isn't governed by poetical whims of that kind.'

'A pity,' said Amit. 'Reading old reports by Cardus always makes me think that it's just a variant of poetry – in six line stanzas.'

'I wonder where Billy is,' said Arun in rather a hangover-ish voice. 'Can't see him anywhere.'

'Oh, he's bound to be here,' said Amit. 'I can't imagine him missing a day of a Test.'

'We're off to a rather slow start,' said Dipankar. 'I hope this isn't going to be another awful draw like the last two Tests.'

'I think we're going to teach them a lesson.' This was Haresh's optimistic assessment.

'We might,' said Pran. 'But we should be careful on this wicket. It's a bowler's delight.'

And so it proved to be.

The quick loss of three of the best Indian wickets – including that of the captain – cast a chill on the stadium. When Amarnath – who had hardly had time to pad up – came onto the field to face Tattersall, there was complete silence. Even the women spectators stopped their winter knitting for a second.

He was bowled for a duck in that same fatal over.

The Indian side was collapsing like skittles. If the mayhem continued, India might be all out before lunch. High visions of a victory turned to the dread of an ignominious follow-on.

'Just like us,' said Varun morosely. 'We are a failure as a country. We can always snatch defeat out of the jaws of victory. I'm going to watch the racing in the afternoon,' he added disgustedly. He would have to watch his horses through the palings around the course rather than sit in these forty-rupee season-ticket seats, but at least there was a chance that his horse might win.

'I'm getting up to stretch my legs,' said Amit.

'I'll come with you,' said Haresh, who was annoyed by the poor show that India was putting on. 'Oh – who's that man there – the one in the navy-blue blazer with the maroon scarf – do any of you know? I seem to recognize him from somewhere.'

Pran looked across at the pavilion section and was completely taken aback.

'Oh, Malvolio!' he said, as if he had seen Banquo instead.

'What was that?' said Haresh.

'Nothing. I suddenly remembered something I had to teach next term. Cricket balls, my liege. Something just struck me. No, I – I can't say for sure that I recognize him – I think you'd better ask the Calcutta people.' Pran was not good at deception, but the last thing he wanted to encourage was a meeting between Haresh and Kabir. Any number of complications might ensue, including a visit by Kabir to Sunny Park.

Luckily, no one else recognized him.

'I'm sure I've seen him somewhere,' Haresh persisted. 'I'm bound to remember some time. Good-looking fellow. You know, the same thing happened to me with Lata. I felt I'd seen her before – and – I'm sure I'm not mistaken. I'll go and say hello.'

Pran could do nothing further. Amit and Haresh wandered over between overs, and Haresh said to Kabir: 'Good morning. Haven't we met somewhere before?'

Kabir looked at them and smiled. He stood up. 'I don't think we have,' he said.

'Perhaps at work – or in Cawnpore?' said Haresh. 'I have the feeling – well, anyway, I'm Haresh Khanna, from Praha.'

'Glad to meet you, Sir.' Kabir shook his hand and smiled. 'Perhaps we've met in Brahmpur, that is if you come to Brahmpur on work.'

Haresh shook his head. 'I don't think so,' he said. 'Are you from Brahmpur?'

'Yes,' said Kabir. 'I'm a student at Brahmpur University. I'm keen on cricket, so I've come down for a while to watch what I can of the Test. A pretty miserable show.'

'Well, it's a dewy wicket,' said Amit in mitigation.

'Dewy wicket my foot,' said Kabir with good-natured combativeness. 'We are always making excuses for ourselves. Roy had no business to cut that ball. And Umrigar did the same. And for Hazare and Amarnath to be bowled neck and crop in the same over: it's really too bad. They send over a team that doesn't include Hutton or Bedser or Compton or Laker or May – and we manage to disgrace ourselves anyway. We've never had a Test victory against the MCC, and if we lose this one, we don't ever deserve to win. I'm beginning to think it's a good thing I'm leaving Calcutta tomorrow morning. Anyway, tomorrow's a rest day.'

'Why, where are you going?' laughed Haresh, who liked the young man's spirit. 'Back to Brahmpur?'

'No – I've got to go to Allahabad for the Inter-'Varsity.'

'Are you on the university team?'

'Yes.' Kabir frowned. 'But I'm sorry, I haven't introduced myself. My name's Kabir. Kabir Durrani.'

'Ah,' said Haresh, his eyes disappearing. 'You're the son of Professor Durrani.'

Kabir looked at Haresh in amazement.

'We met for just a minute,' said Haresh. 'I brought young Bhaskar Tandon over to your house one day to meet your father. In fact, now I come to think of it, you were wearing cricket clothes.'

Kabir said: 'Good heavens. I think I do remember now. I'm terribly sorry. But won't you sit down? These two chairs are free – my friends have gone off to get some coffee.'

Haresh introduced Amit, and they all sat down.

After the next over Kabir turned to Haresh and said: 'I suppose you know what happened to Bhaskar at the Pul Mela?'

'Yes, indeed. I'm glad to hear he's all right now.'

'If he had been here, we wouldn't have needed that fancy Australian-style scoreboard.'

'No,' said Haresh with a smile. 'Pran's nephew,' he said to Amit by way of incomplete explanation.

'I do wish women wouldn't bring their knitting to the match,' said Kabir intolerantly. 'Hazare out. Plain. Umrigar out. Purl. It's like *A Tale of Two Cities*.'

Amit laughed at this pleasant young fellow's analogy, but was forced to come to the defence of his own city. 'Well, apart from our sections of the stadium, where people come to be seen as much as to see, Calcutta's a good place for cricket,' he said. 'In the four-rupee seats the crowd knows its stuff all right. And they start queueing up for day tickets from nine o'clock the previous night.'

Kabir nodded. 'Well, you're right. And it's a lovely stadium. The greenness of the field almost hurts the eyes.'

Haresh thought back for a moment to his mistake about colours, and wondered whether it had done him any harm.

The bowling changed over once again from the Maidan end to the High Court end.

'Whenever I think of the High Court end I feel guilty,' said Amit to Haresh. Making conversation with his rival was one way of sizing him up.

Haresh, who had no sense at all that he had any rival anywhere, answered innocently: 'Why? Have you done anything against the law? Oh, I'm forgetting, your father's a judge.'

'And I'm a lawyer, that's my problem. I should be working, according to him – writing opinions, not poems.'

Kabir half turned towards Amit in astonishment.

'You're not the Amit Chatterji?'

Amit had discovered that coyness made things worse once he was recognized. 'Yes, indeed,' he said. 'The.'

'Why – I'm – how amazing – I like your stuff – a lot of it – I can't say I understand it all.'

'No, nor do I.'

A sudden thought struck Kabir. 'Why don't you come to Brahmpur to read? You have a lot of fans there in the Brahmpur Literary Society. But I hear you never give readings.'

'Well, not never,' said Amit thoughtfully. 'I don't normally – but if I'm asked to come to Brahmpur, and can get leave of absence from my Muse, I might well come. I've often wondered what the town was like: the Barsaat Mahal, you know, and, of course, the Fort – and, well, other objects of beauty and interest. I've never been there before.' He paused. 'Well, would you care to join us there among the season-ticket holders? But I suppose these are better seats.'

'It's not that,' said Kabir. 'It's just that I'm with friends – they've invited me – and it's my last day in town. I'd better not. But I'm very honoured to meet you. And – well – you're sure you wouldn't take it amiss if you were invited to Brahmpur? It wouldn't interfere too much with your writing?'

'No,' said Amit mildly. 'Not Brahmpur. Just write to my publishers. It'll be forwarded to me.'

The game was continuing, a little more steadily than before. It would soon be lunchtime. No more wickets had fallen, which was a blessing, but India was still in perilous straits.

'It's a real pity about Hazare. His form seems to have deserted him after that knock on the head in Bombay,' said Amit.

'Well,' said Kabir, 'you can't blame him entirely. Ridgway's bouncers can be vicious – and he'd scored a century, after all. He was pretty badly stunned. I don't think he should have been forced back out from the pavilion by the Chairman of Selectors. It's demeaning for a skipper to be ordered back – and bad for morale all around.' He went on, almost in a dream: 'I suppose Hazare is indecisive – it took him fifteen minutes to decide whether to bat or to field in the last Test. But, well, I'm discovering that I'm quite indecisive myself, so I sympathize. I've been thinking of visiting someone ever since I arrived in Calcutta, but I can't. I find I just can't. I don't know what kind of bowling I'd have to face,' he added with a rather bitter laugh. 'They say he's lost his nerve, and I think I've lost mine!' Kabir's remarks were not addressed to anyone in particular, but Amit felt – for no very good reason – a strong sense of sympathy for him.

Had Amit identified him as the 'Akbar from *As You Like It*' of Meenakshi's imaginative description, he may not have felt quite so sympathetic.

16.21

PRAN did not question either Amit or Haresh about their meeting with Kabir. He waited for one or the other of them to mention that Kabir knew or had heard of either him or Arun; but since neither name had come up in their conversation, there was nothing as such to tell. He breathed a sigh of relief. Clearly Kabir would not be visiting Sunny Park and upsetting well-laid plans.

After a quick lunch of sandwiches and coffee the group of six – still dazed by India's sudden collapse and not optimistic about the afternoon's play – dispersed in cars and taxis. They had to thread their way through huge crowds that had begun to gather on the Maidan to hear Pandit Nehru speak. The Prime Minister – or, in this role, the President of Congress – was on one of his lightning election tours. Just the previous day he had spoken at Kharagpur, Asansol, Burdwan, Chinsurah and Serampore; and just before that he had been canvassing in Assam.

Varun asked to be put down near the smaller – but equally eager – crowds surrounding the race-track, and started to look around for his friends. After a while he began to wonder whether he shouldn't listen to Nehru's speech instead. But after a brief struggle, My Lady Jean and Windy Wold defeated Freedom Fighter by several lengths. I can always read about it in the newspapers, he told himself.

Haresh had meanwhile gone to visit distant relatives whom his foster-father had told him to look up in Calcutta. So involved had he been with production in Prahapore that he hadn't found the time to do so; but now he had a couple of hours to spare. When he got to his relatives' place he found them all glued to the radio listening to the cricket commentary. They tried to be hospitable, but their minds were clearly elsewhere. Haresh too joined them by the radio.

India was 257 for 6 at close of play. Disgrace at least had been miraculously averted.

Haresh was therefore in a good mood when he arrived at Sunny Park in time for tea. He was introduced to Aparna, whom he tried to humour and who treated him distantly as a result, and to Uma, who gave him an undiscriminating smile which delighted him.

'Are you being polite, Haresh?' asked Savita warmly. 'You're not eating anything at all. Politeness doesn't pay in this family. Pass the pastries, Arun.'

'I must apologize,' said Arun to Haresh. 'I should have mentioned it this morning but it slipped my mind entirely. Meenakshi and I will be out for dinner tonight.'

'Oh,' said Haresh, puzzled. He glanced at Mrs Rupa Mehra. She was looking flushed and upset.

'Yes. Well, we were invited three weeks ago, and couldn't cancel it at the last moment. But Ma and the rest will be here, of course. And Varun will do the honours. Both Meenakshi and I were looking forward to it, needless to say, but when we got home from Prahapore that day, we looked at our diary and – well, there it is.'

'We feel awful,' said Meenakshi gaily. 'Do have a cheese straw.'

'Thank you,' said Haresh, a little dampened. But after a few minutes he bounced back. Lata at least looked pleased to see him. She was indeed wearing a pink sari. Either that or she was very cruel! Today he'd certainly get a chance to talk to her. And Savita, he felt, was kind and warm and encouraging. Perhaps it was no bad thing that Arun wouldn't be there for dinner, though it would be odd to sit down at his table – and that too for the first time – in his host's absence. Haresh could feel muted pulses of antagonism emanating from his direction, and to some extent from the darkly radiant Meenakshi too, and he would not have felt entirely relaxed in their company. But it was certainly an odd response to the hospitality he had offered them.

Varun was looking unusually cheerful. He had won eight rupees at the races.

'Well, we didn't do so badly after all,' said Haresh to him.

'I'm sorry?'

'After this morning, I mean.'

'Oh, yes, cricket. What was the closing score?' asked Varun, who had got up.

'257 for 6,' said Pran, astonished that Varun hadn't been following it.

'Hmm,' said Varun, and went over to the gramophone.

'Don't!' thundered Arun.

'Don't what, Arun Bhai?'

'Don't put on that damn machine. Unless you want me to box your two intoxicated ears.'

Varun recoiled with murderous timidity. Haresh looked startled at the exchange between the brothers. Varun had hardly said a thing that day in Prahapore.

'Aparna likes it,' he said in a resentful tone, not daring to look at Arun. 'And so does Uma.' Unlikely though this was, it was true. Savita, whenever she found that legal Latin did not put Uma to sleep, would sing this song to her while rocking her to and fro.

'I do not care who likes what,' said Arun, his face reddening. 'You will turn it off. And at once.'

'I haven't turned it on in the first place,' said Varun in creeping triumph.

Lata hurriedly asked Haresh the first question that came into her head: 'Have you seen *Deedar*?'

'Oh, yes,' said Haresh. 'Thrice. Once by myself, once with friends in Delhi, and once with Simran's sister in Lucknow.'

There was silence for a few seconds.

'You must have enjoyed the film,' said Lata.

'Yes,' said Haresh. 'I like films. When I was in Middlehampton I sometimes saw two films a day. I didn't see any plays though,' he added rather gratuitously.

'No – I wouldn't have thought so,' said Arun. 'I mean – there's so little opportunity, as you once said. Well, if you'll excuse us, we'll get ready.'

'Yes, yes,' said Mrs Rupa Mehra. 'You get ready. And we have a few things to do. Savita has to put the baby to bed and I have a few New Year's letters to write, and Pran – Pran –'

'– has a book to read?' suggested Pran.

'Yes,' agreed Mrs Rupa Mehra. 'And Haresh and Lata can go into the garden.' She told Hanif to put on the garden light.

IT was not yet quite dark. The two walked around the small garden a couple of times, not knowing quite what to say. Most of the flowers had closed, but white stocks still perfumed one corner near the bench.

'Shall we sit down?' asked Haresh.

'Yes. Why not?'

'Well, it's been such a long time since we met,' said Haresh.

'Don't you count the Prahapore Club?' said Lata.

'Oh, that was for your family. You and I were hardly present.'

'We were all very impressed,' said Lata with a smile. Certainly, Haresh had been very much present, even if she hadn't.

'I hoped you would be,' said Haresh. 'But I'm not sure what your elder brother thinks of all this. Is he avoiding me? This morning he spent half the time looking around for a friend of his, and now he's going out.'

'Oh, he's just being Arun. I'm sorry about the scene just now; that too is typical of him. But he's quite affectionate sometimes. It's just that one never knows when. You'll get used to it.'

The last sentence had slipped out of its own accord. Lata was both puzzled at and displeased with herself. She did like Haresh, but she didn't want to give him any false hopes. Quickly she added: 'Like all his – his colleagues.' But this made things worse; it sounded cruelly distancing and a bit illogical.

'I hope I'm not going to become his colleague!' said Haresh, smiling. He wanted to hold Lata's hand, but sensed that – despite the scent of stocks and Mrs Rupa Mehra's tacit approval of their tête-à-tête – this was not the moment. Haresh was a little bewildered. Had he been with Simran, he would have known what to talk about; in any case they would have been talking in a mixture of Hindi, Punjabi and English. But talking to Lata was different. He did not know what to say. It was much easier to write letters. After a while he said:

'I've been reading one or two Hardys again.' It was better than talking about his Goodyear Welted line or how much the Czechs drank on New Year's Eve.

Lata said: 'Don't you find him a bit pessimistic?' She too was attempting to make conversation. Perhaps they should have kept on writing to each other.

'Well, I am an optimistic person – some people say too optimistic – so it's a good thing for me to read something that is not so optimistic.'

'That's an interesting thought,' said Lata.

Haresh was puzzled. Here they were, sitting on a garden bench in the cool of the evening with the blessing of her mother and his foster-father, and they could hardly piece together a conversation. The Mehras were a complicated family and nothing was what it seemed.

'Well, do I have grounds to be optimistic?' he asked with a smile. He had promised himself to get a clear answer quickly. Lata had said that writing was a good way to get to know each other, and he felt that their correspondence had revealed a great deal. He had perhaps detected a slight cooling off in her last two letters from Brahmpur, but she had promised to spend as much time as she could with him over the vacation. He could understand, however, that she might be nervous about an actual meeting, especially under the critical eye of her elder brother.

Lata said nothing for a while. Then, thinking in a flash over all the time she had spent with Haresh – which seemed to be no more than a succession of meals and trains and factories – she said: 'Haresh, I think we should meet and talk a little more before I make up my mind finally. It's the most important decision of my life. I need to be completely sure.'

'Well, I'm sure,' said Haresh in a firm voice. 'I've now seen you in five different places, and my feelings for you have grown with time. I am not very eloquent –'

'It's not that,' said Lata, though she knew that it was at least partly that. What, after all would they talk about for the rest of their lives?

'Anyway, I'm sure I will improve with your instruction,' said Haresh cheerfully.

'What's the fifth place?' said Lata.

'What fifth place?'

'You said we'd met in five places. Prahapore, Calcutta now, Kanpur, very briefly in Lucknow when you helped us at the station.... What's the fifth? It was only my mother you met in Delhi.'

'Brahmpur.'

'But –'

'We didn't meet exactly, but I was at the platform when you were getting onto the Calcutta train. Not this time – a few months ago. You were wearing a blue sari, and you had a very intense and serious expression on your face as if something had – well, a very intense and serious expression.'

'Are you sure it was a blue sari?' said Lata with a smile.

'Yes,' said Haresh, smiling back.

'What were you doing there?' asked Lata wonderingly; her mind was now already back on that platform and what she had been feeling.

'Nothing. Just leaving for Cawnpore. And then, for a few days after we met properly, I kept thinking, "Where have I seen her before?" Like today at the Test Match with that young fellow Durrani.'

Lata came out of her dream. 'Durrani?' she said.

'Yes, but I didn't have to wonder long. I discovered where I'd seen him within a few minutes of talking to him. That was in Brahmpur too. I'd taken Bhaskar to meet his father. Everything happens in Brahmpur!'

Lata was silent but looking at him with, he felt, great interest at last.

'Good-looking fellow,' continued Haresh, encouraged. 'Very well-informed about cricket. And on the university team. He's leaving tomorrow for the Inter-'Varsity somewhere.'

'At the cricket match?' said Lata. 'You met Kabir?'

'Do you know him?' asked Haresh, frowning a little.

'Yes,' said Lata, controlling her voice. 'We acted in

Twelfth Night together. How strange. What was he doing in Calcutta? How long has he been here?'

'I don't know,' replied Haresh. 'For the cricket mainly, I suppose. But it seems a pity to have to leave after three days of a Test. Not that this one is likely to end in a win for either side. And he might have come on business too. He did say something about wanting to meet someone but being uncertain about his reception when he met him.'

'Oh,' said Lata. 'Did he meet him eventually?'

'No, I don't think so. Anyway, what were we talking about? Yes, five towns. Brahmpur, Prahapore, Calcutta, Lucknow, Cawnpore.'

'I wish you wouldn't call it Cawnpore,' said Lata with a touch of irritation.

'What should I call it?'

'Kanpur.'

'All right. And if you wish I'll call Calcutta Kolkata.'

Lata didn't answer. The thought that Kabir was still in town, in Calcutta somewhere, but unreachable, and that he would be leaving the next day, made her eyes smart. Here she was, sitting on the same bench where she had read his letter – and with Haresh of all people. Certainly, if her meetings with Haresh were marked by meals, her meetings with Kabir were marked by benches. She felt like both laughing and crying.

'Is something the matter?' said Haresh, a little troubled.

'No, let's go in. It's getting a little chilly. If Arun Bhai has left by now it shouldn't be too difficult to get Varun to put on a few film songs. I feel in the mood for them.'

'I thought you were more fond of classical music.'

'I like everything,' said Lata brightly, 'but at different times. And Varun will offer you a drink.'

Haresh asked for a beer. Varun put on a song from *Deedar*, then left the drawing room; he had instructions from his mother to keep out of the way. Lata's eye fell on the book of Egyptian mythology.

Haresh was more than a little bewildered by her change of mood. It made him feel uneasy. He was being truthful when he wrote in his letters that he had grown to be in love with her. He was sure she too was fond of him. Now she was treating him in a baffling manner.

The record had run its three-minute course. Lata did not get up to change it. The room was quiet. 'I'm tired of Calcutta,' she said light-heartedly. 'It's a good thing I'm going to the Botanical Gardens tomorrow.'

'But I'd set tomorrow aside for you. I planned to spend it with you,' said Haresh.

'You never told me, Haresh.'

'You said – you wrote – that you wanted to spend as much time as possible with me.' Something had changed in their conversation at a certain point. He passed his hand across his forehead and frowned.

'Well, we still have five days before I leave for Brahmpur,' said Lata.

'My leave will be over tomorrow. Cancel your Botanical trip. I insist!' He smiled, and caught her hand.

'Oh, don't be mean –' said Lata.

He released her hand at once. 'I am not mean,' he said.

Lata looked at him. The colour had left his face, and the laugh too had been wiped away. He was suddenly very angry. 'I am not mean,' he repeated. 'No one has ever said that to me before. Don't ever use that word for me again. I – I am going now.' He got up. 'I'll find my way to the station. Please thank your family for me. I can't stay for dinner.'

Lata looked completely stunned, but did not try to stop him. 'Oh, don't be mean,' was an expression that the girls at Sophia Convent must have used twenty times a day to each other. Some of it had survived – especially in certain moods – in her present-day speech. It meant nothing particularly wounding, and she could not imagine for the moment why he was so wounded.

But Haresh, already troubled by something he could not lay his finger on, was stung to the depths of his being. To be called 'mean' – ungenerous, lowly, base – and that too by the woman he loved and for whom he was prepared to do so much – he could tolerate some things, but he would not tolerate that. He was not ungenerous – far less so than her cavalier brother who had had hardly a word of appreciation for his efforts a few days earlier and who did not have the decency to spend an evening with him in order to reciprocate his hospitality. As for being base, his accent might not have their polish nor his diction their elegance, but he came from stock as good as theirs. They could keep their Anglicized veneer. To be labelled 'mean' was something not to be borne. He would have nothing to do with people who held this opinion of him.

16.23

MRS RUPA MEHRA almost had hysterics when she heard that Haresh had gone. 'That was very, very rude of him,' she said, and burst into tears. Then she turned upon her daughter. 'You must have done something to displease him. Otherwise he would never have gone. He would never have gone without saying goodbye.'

It took Savita to calm her down. Then, realizing that Lata looked completely shell-shocked, she sat beside her and held her hand. She was glad that Arun had not been there to fling sawdust into the fire. Slowly she worked out what had happened, and what Haresh might have misconstrued Lata to have meant.

'But if we don't even understand each other when we speak,' said Lata, 'what possible future can we have together?'

'Don't worry about that for the moment,' said Savita. 'Have some soup.'

When all else fails, thought Lata, there is always soup.

'And read something soothing,' added Savita.

'Like a law-book?' There were still tears in her eyes, but she was trying to smile.

'Yes,' said Savita. 'Or – since Sophia Convent is what started this confusion in the first place – why not read your autograph book from school? It's full of old friends and eternal thoughts. I often look through mine when I'm feeling bad. I am quite serious. I'm not merely echoing Ma.'

It was good advice. A hot cup of vegetable soup appeared, and Lata, amused a bit by the idiocy of the suggested remedy, looked through her book. On the small pages of pink and cream and pale blue, in English and (from her aunts, and once from Varun in nationalistic mood) in Hindi, and even in Chinese (an unreadable but beautiful inscription from her classmate Eulalia Wong), the edifying or moving or amusing or facetious lines in their different inks and different hands stirred her memories and diminished her confusion. She had even pasted in a small fragment of a letter from her father, which ended with a rough pencil sketch of four little monkeys, his own 'bandar-log', as he used to call them. More than ever now she missed him. She read her mother's inscription, the first in the book:

When the world has been unkind, when life's troubles
                                              cloud your mind,
Don't sit down and frown and sigh and moon and mope.
Take a walk along the square, fill your lungs with
                                              God's fresh air,
Then go whistling back to work and smile and hope.

Remember, Lata darling, that the fate of each man (and woman) rests with himself.

Yours everloving,
Ma

On the next page a friend had written:

Lata —
Love is the star men look up to as they walk along, and marriage is the coal-hole they fall into.

Love and all good wishes,
Anuradha

Someone else had suggested:

It is not the Perfect but the Imperfect who have need of
Love.

Yet another had written on a page of blue in a hand that
sloped slightly backwards:

Cold words will break a fine heart as winter's first frost
does a crystal vase. A false friend is like the shadow on a
sun-dial which appears in very fine weather but vanishes
at the approach of a cloud.

Fifteen-year-old girls, thought Lata, took a serious view of
life.

Savita's own sisterly contribution was:

Life is merely froth and bubble.
Two things stand like stone:
Kindness in another's trouble,
Courage in our own.

To her own surprise, her eyes became moist again.

I am going to turn into Ma before I'm twenty-five,
thought Lata to herself. This quickly stemmed the last of
her tears.

The phone rang. It was Amit for Lata.

'So everything's ready for tomorrow,' he said. 'Tapan's
coming along with us. He likes the banyan tree. You can
tell Ma that I'll take good care of you.'

'Amit, I'm in a terrible mood. I'll be terrible company.
Let's go some other time.' Her voice, not yet quite clear,
sounded strange even to herself, but Amit did not comment
on it.

'That will be for me to decide,' he said. 'Or rather, for
both of us. If, when I come to pick you up tomorrow, you
decide not to go, I won't force the issue. How's that?
Tapan and I will go by ourselves. I've promised him now –
and I don't want to disappoint him.'

Lata was wondering what to say when Amit added: 'Oh, I myself have them often enough: breakfast blues, lunchtime lows, dinner doldrums. But if you're a poet, that's your raw material. I suppose that the poem you gave me must have had some such origin.'

'It did not!' said Lata, with some indignation.

'Good, good, you're on your way to recovery,' laughed Amit. 'I can tell.' He rang off.

Lata, still holding the receiver, was left with the thought that some people appeared to understand her far too little and others far too much.

16.24

DEAREST Lata,

I have been thinking of you often since you've been away, but you know how busy I always succeed in making myself, even in the holidays. Something, however, has happened which I feel I should write to you about. I have been torturing myself about whether to tell you, but I think the thing to do is simply to go ahead. I was so happy to get your letter and I dread the thought of making you unhappy. Maybe what with the election mail and the Christmas rush this letter will be delayed or will disappear entirely. I don't suppose I'll be sorry.

I'm sorry my thoughts are so scattered. I'm just writing on impulse. I was looking through my papers yesterday and came across the note you wrote to me when I was in Nainital, saying you had found the pressed flower again. I read it twice and suddenly thought of that day in the zoo, and tried to remember why I gave you that flower! I think it unconsciously was a seal to our friendship. It expressed my feelings for you, and I'm glad I can share my joys and sorrows with this wonderful, affectionate person who is so far away from me and yet so close.

Well, Calcutta isn't so far away really, but friends matter all the time, and it's good to know you haven't forgotten me. I was looking at the photographs of the play again while I was sorting things out in my mind, and was thinking how wonderfully you acted. It amazed me at the time and still amazes me – especially from someone who is sometimes so reserved, who doesn't often talk about her fears, fantasies, dreams, anxieties, loves and hates – and whom I would probably never have got to know if it hadn't been for the good luck of sharing the same hospital room – sorry! hostel room.

Well, I've avoided the subject long enough, and I can see your anxious face. The news I have to give you is about K, which – well, I should just give it and be done with it and I hope you'll find it in your heart to forgive me. I'm just doing the unpleasant duty of a friend.

After you left for Cal, K sent me a note and we met at the Blue Danube. He wanted me to get you to talk to him or write to him. He said all sorts of things about how much he cared for you, sleepless nights, restless wanderings, lovelorn longings, the lot. He spoke very convincingly, and I felt quite sorry for him. But he must be rather practised at that sort of thing, because he was seeing another girl – at the Red Fox – on about the same day. You told me he doesn't have a sister, and anyway, it's clear from my informant, who is completely reliable, that he wasn't behaving in a particularly brotherly way. I was surprised how furious I was to hear of this, but in a way I was glad that this made things quite clear. I made up my mind to fire him up face to face, but found he'd disappeared from town on some university cricket tour, and anyway now I don't think it's worth the stress and bother.

Now, please, Lata, don't let this open up all the old wounds. Just treat it as confirmation of the course of action you've chosen. I'm sure we women make things far worse for ourselves by dwelling endlessly on matters that are best pushed aside. This is my professional opinion too. Some moderate mooning is OK, but please, no perennial pining! He isn't worth it, Lata, and this proves it. If I were you, I would just crush him with the flat of my spoon into mashed potatoes and forget him entirely.

Now for other news.

What with elections coming up, everything is bubbling and swirling around here, and the Socialist Party is mapping out policies and strategies and quackeries and sorceries with the best of them. I attend all the meetings, and canvass and campaign, but I am rather disillusioned. Everyone is involved in pushing himself forward, spouting slogans, making promises, and not bothering about how these promises are to be paid for, let alone implemented. Even sensible people seem to have gone off their heads. One fellow here used to talk a good deal of sense before, but he froths so much and makes such 'big-big eyes' that I'm sure he is quite certifiable now.

And yes, women have been rediscovered: one pleasant side-effect of election fever. 'The time has come when Woman must be restored to the status she occupied in ancient India: we must combine the best of the past and the present, of the West and the East. . . .' Here, however, is our ancient lawbook, the Manusmriti. Take a deep breath:

'Day and night, women must be kept in dependence by the males of their families. In childhood, a woman must be subject to her father, in youth to her husband and in old age to her son; a woman must never be independent because she is innately as impure as falsehood. . . . The Lord created woman as one who is full of sensuality, wrath, dishonesty, malice and bad conduct.' (And, sadly, now, the vote.)

I don't suppose anything is going to bring you back here before the term begins, but I miss you a lot even though, as I said, things are so busy that I find it hard to think even half a thought through.

Love to you, and also to Ma, Pran, Savita and the baby – but you don't have to give them my love if you're afraid they'll start asking you all about my letter. Well, you can give Uma my love anyway.

Malati

P.S. Amongst the inmates of Paradise women will form the minority, and amongst the inmates of Hell a majority. I thought I'd be even-handed, and give you a quotation from the Hadith as well. 'Hit or myth': that, in a nutshell, is the attitude to women in every religion.

P.P.S. Since I'm in the mood for quotations, here is something from a short story in a women's magazine, which describes the symptoms I want you to avoid: 'She became an invalid, a moth-eaten flower.... A cloud of despair was roosting on her pale moon of a face.... A red and violent anger bubbled out of her. It emanated from the headache hatching in her heart.... Like a humbled monarch, bowing its head, the car cringed away, the swirling dust in its wake portraying her emotions.'

P.P.P.S. If you decide to sing him out of your system, I would recommend that you avoid your favourite 'serious' raags like Shri, Lalit, Todi, Marwa, etc, and sing something more melodious like Behag or Kamod or Kedar.

P.P.P.P.S. That's all, dearest Lata. Sleep well.

16.25

LATA did not sleep well. She lay awake for hours, racked with jealousy so intense it almost forced the breath out of her and misery so complete she could not believe it was she who was feeling it. There was no privacy in the house – there was no privacy anywhere – where she could go and be by herself for a week and wash away the image of Kabir that she had, despite herself, stored away with the most treasured of her memories. Malati had said nothing about who this woman was, what she looked like, what they had said, who had seen them. Had they met by chance just as she herself had met him? Was he taking her for dawn jaunts to the Barsaat Mahal? Had he kissed her? No, he couldn't have, he couldn't have kissed her, the thought was unbearable.

Thoughts of what Malati had told her in their discussions about sex came back to torment her.

It was past midnight, but it was impossible to sleep. Quietly, so as not to disturb her mother or the rest of the household, she entered the small garden. There she sat on the bench where in the summer she had sat among the spider-lilies and had read his letter. After an hour she found herself shivering from the cold, but she hardly cared.

How could he? – she thought, though she was forced to admit to herself that she had given him precious little encouragement or comfort. And now it was too late. She felt weak and exhausted, and finally went back and lay down on her bed. She slept, but her dreams were not calm. She imagined Kabir was holding her in his arms, was kissing her passionately, was making love to her, and that she was in ecstasy. But suddenly this disturbing ecstasy gave way to terror. For his face was now the deranged face of Mr Sahgal, and he was whispering, almost to himself, as he panted above her: 'You are a good girl, a very good girl. I am so proud of you.'

Part Seventeen

17.1

THAT Savita had been in Calcutta at all to advise Lata and counter Arun on the question of marriage was something that had not come about automatically. It had been the subject of a family dispute.

In the middle of December Pran had told Savita one morning in bed: 'I think, darling, that we should stay in Brahmpur. Baoji is far too busy with electioneering these days, and he needs all the help he can get.'

Uma was sleeping in her cot. This gave Pran another idea.

'Besides,' he continued, 'is it wise for the baby to go travelling just yet?'

Savita was still sleepy. She just about made sense of what Pran was saying. She thought a little about the repercussions of his suggestion, and said: 'Let's talk about this later.'

Pran, by now quite used to the way she phrased her disagreements, was quiet. After a while Mateen brought in the tea. Savita said: 'And perhaps you think you shouldn't be travelling at this time either?'

'No, perhaps not,' said Pran, pleased that things were going his way. 'And besides, Ammaji is not too well. I'm worried about her. I know you are too, darling.'

Savita nodded. But she felt that Pran had recovered quite rapidly, and was now well enough to travel. Moreover, he needed the holiday and change of scene badly. He should not, she felt, be imposed upon by his demanding father. The baby would be well taken care of in Calcutta. As for Savita's mother-in-law, she was, it was true, not very well, but was nevertheless taking part in election work among the women with the same robustness that had marked her relief work some years previously with the refugees from Punjab.

'So what do you say?' said Pran. 'It's only once in five years, these elections, and I know that Baoji wants me to help him.'

'How about Maan?'

'Well, of course, he'll help.'

'And Veena?'

'You know what her mother-in-law would say.'

They both sipped their tea. The *Brahmpur Chronicle* lay unopened on the bed.

'But how can you help?' asked Savita. 'I'm not going to have you travelling in jeeps and trains to Baitar and Salimpur and other barbaric places, getting all that dust and smoke into your lungs. You'd be asking for a relapse.'

Pran reflected that he probably couldn't visit his father's constituency, but that he could still be of some use to him. He said to Savita: 'I can stay in Brahmpur, darling, and handle things at this end. Besides, I'm a little worried about what Mishra will be doing to spoil my chances here. The selection committee is meeting in a month.'

It was evident that Pran was not keen to go to Calcutta. But he had put forward so many reasons that Savita could not tell whether it was his father or his mother or his baby or himself that he was most concerned about.

'How about me?' said Savita.

'You, darling?' Pran sounded surprised.

'Well, how do you think I will feel if Lata gets engaged to a man whom I haven't even seen?'

Pran paused before replying: 'Well, you got engaged to a man whom Lata hadn't seen.'

'That was quite different,' said Savita, neatly distinguishing the cases. 'Lata isn't my elder sister. I have a responsibility towards her. Arun and Varun aren't the best of advisers.'

Pran thought for a while, then said: 'Well, darling, why don't you go? I'll miss you, of course, but it will only be for a fortnight or so.'

Savita looked at Pran. He did not seem very perturbed at the thought of their separation. She got a little annoyed. 'If I go, the baby goes,' she said. 'And if the baby and I go, you go. And have you forgotten about the Test Match?'

So the three of them went to Calcutta with Lata and Mrs Rupa Mehra.

Their departure from Brahmpur was delayed for a couple of days by Dr Kishen Chand Seth falling ill. And their return to Brahmpur was brought forward by a couple of days because of sudden and devastating events. But these events were entirely unforeseeable, and arose neither out of electioneering nor out of anyone's illness nor out of Professor Mishra's manipulations. The events involved Maan; and as a result of them the family was never the same again.

17.2

IN the first week of December, Maan was still in Brahmpur. He had no plans whatsoever to go back to Banaras. As far as he was concerned, the entire city – ghats, temples, shop, fiancée, debtors, creditors and all – could have sunk into the Ganga and not a ripple would have been felt downstream. He wandered about Brahmpur quite happily, taking the occasional stroll through the old town to the Barsaat Mahal, passing through Tarbuz ka Bazaar on the way. He met the Rajkumar's university friends for an evening or two of poker. The Rajkumar himself, after his expulsion, had disappeared from Brahmpur for a while and returned to Marh.

Maan appeared erratically at meals at Prem Nivas and Baitar House, and his cheerful presence acted as a tonic on his mother. He visited Veena, Kedarnath and Bhaskar. He spent a little time with Firoz, though not as much as he would have liked: Firoz, after his work in the zamindari case had had a fair amount of success obtaining briefs. Maan also discussed campaign strategy with his father and with the Nawab Sahib, who had pledged Mahesh Kapoor his support in his candidacy. And he visited Saeeda Bai whenever he could.

In between ghazals one evening Maan said to her:

'I must meet Abdur Rasheed one of these days, Saeeda. But I understand he doesn't come here any more.'

Saeeda Bai looked at Maan thoughtfully, her head

slightly to one side, 'He has gone mad,' she stated simply. 'I can't have him here.'

Maan laughed and waited for her to elaborate. She did not.

'What do you mean, mad?' he said at last. 'You told me before that you thought he had an interest in Tasneem, but – surely –'

Saeeda Bai rather dreamily played an ornament on the harmonium, then said:

'He has been sending strange letters to Tasneem, Dagh Sahib, which naturally I don't allow the girl to read. They are offensive.'

Maan could not believe that Rasheed, whom he knew to be an upright man, particularly where it came to women or his sense of duty, could possibly have written letters of an offensive nature to Tasneem. Saeeda Bai, one of whose traits was the habitual exaggeration of nuance, was, to his mind, being over-protective of her sister. He did not say so, however.

'Why do you want to see him anyway?' asked Saeeda Bai.

'I promised his family I would,' said Maan. 'And I also want to talk to him about the elections. My father will be fighting from the constituency that includes his village.'

Now Saeeda Bai became cross. 'Has this entire city lost its senses?' she exclaimed. 'Elections! Elections! Is there nothing else in the world other than paper and boxes?'

Indeed, Brahmpur was talking of very little else. Campaigning had begun; most candidates, after filing their nomination papers, had remained in their constituencies and begun canvassing immediately. Mahesh Kapoor had decided to wait a few weeks in Brahmpur. Since he was Revenue Minister again, he had a great deal of work to do.

Maan, by way of apology, said: 'Saeeda, you know I have to help my father with these elections. My elder brother is not well and, besides, he has his teaching. And I know the constituency. But my exile will be short this time.'

Saeeda Bai clapped her hands and called for Bibbo.

Bibbo came running.

'Bibbo, are we on the voting list for Pasand Bagh?' she demanded.

Bibbo did not know, but she thought they were not. 'Should I try to find out?' she asked.

'No. It is not necessary.'

'Whatever you say, Begum Sahiba.'

'Where were you this afternoon? I was looking for you everywhere.'

'I had gone out, Begum Sahiba, to buy some matches.'

'Does it take an hour to buy matches?'

Saeeda Bai was becoming determinedly annoyed.

Bibbo was silent. She could not very well tell Saeeda Bai, who had been in such a flap about Rasheed, that she had surreptitiously been carrying letters to and fro between Firoz and Tasneem.

Saeeda Bai now turned briskly to Maan: 'Why are you lingering here?' she asked him. 'There are no votes to be had in this house.'

'Saeeda Begum –' protested Maan.

Saeeda Bai said sharply to Bibbo: 'What are you gawking at? Didn't you hear me tell you to go?'

Bibbo grinned and left. Suddenly Saeeda Bai got up and went into her room. She returned with three of the letters Rasheed had mailed Tasneem.

'His address is on these,' she said to Maan as she threw them onto the low table. Maan noted the address down in his unformed Urdu script, noticing, however, that Rasheed's writing was very much worse than he remembered it.

'There is something wrong with his head. You will find him a liability in your electoral endeavours,' said Saeeda Bai.

The rest of the evening was not a success. Public life had entered the boudoir, and together with it all Saeeda Bai's fears for Tasneem.

After a while she reverted to a kind of dreaminess again.

'When do you leave?' she asked Maan indifferently.

'In three days, Inshallah,' replied Maan as cheerfully as he could.

'Inshallah,' repeated the parakeet, responding to a phrase he recognized. Maan turned towards it and frowned. He was in no mood for the halfwitted bird. A weight had descended on him; Saeeda Bai, it appeared, did not care whether he stayed or left.

'I am tired,' said Saeeda Bai.

'May I visit you on the eve of my departure?'

'No longer did I desire to wander in the garden,' murmured Saeeda Bai to herself, quoting Ghalib.

She was referring to Maan and to the fickleness of men in general, but Maan thought she was referring to herself.

17.3

MAAN visited Rasheed's room the next day. It was located in a seedy and crowded part of the old city with narrow, unrepaired lanes and the stench of poor drainage. Rasheed was living alone. He could not afford to keep his family with him in Brahmpur. He cooked for himself whenever he could, he gave his tuitions, he studied, he was involved in some work for the Socialist Party, and he was trying to write a pamphlet – half popular, half scholarly – on the sanction for and meaning of secularism in Islam. He had run his life for months on will-power rather than on a combination of food and affection. When he saw Maan at his door Rasheed looked astonished and worried. Maan noticed with a shock that even more of his hair had gone white. His face was gaunt, but his eyes still held a sort of fire.

'Let us go for a walk,' Rasheed suggested. 'I have a tuition in an hour. There are too many flies here. Curzon Park is on the way. We can sit there and talk.'

In the mild December sunshine they sat in the park under a large, small-leafed ficus. Every time someone passed them, Rasheed would lower his voice. He looked extremely tired, but talked almost without stopping. Early on in the conversation it became apparent to Maan that Rasheed was not going to help his father in any sense. He was going to support the Socialist Party in the Salimpur-cum-Baitar constituency and he was, he said, going to campaign tirelessly for them and against the Congress throughout the university vacation. He talked endlessly about feudalism and superstition and the oppressive structure of society and especially the Nawab Sahib of Baitar's role in the system. He said that the leaders of the Congress Party – and presumably Mahesh Kapoor – were hand in glove with the large landlords, which was why landlords would be compensated for the lands that were to be taken over by the state. 'But the people will not be duped,' he said. 'They understand things only too well.'

So far Rasheed had spoken with great, perhaps slightly exaggerated, conviction, maybe even with excessive animus against the great landowner of the district, who he knew was Maan's friend; but there was nothing particularly odd about his manner of speaking or the logic of it. The word 'duped', however, acted as a kind of fault or fracture in his speech. He suddenly turned to Maan and said pointedly:

'Of course, people who are duped are wiser than you think.'

'Of course,' Maan agreed amiably, though he was rather disappointed. Rasheed, he thought, would have been very helpful to his father in the area around Debaria, and probably even in Salimpur town. If it had not been for Rasheed, he himself would not have known anything about the place.

'To be honest,' said Rasheed, 'I won't deny that I hated you as well as the others when I realized what you were trying to do.'

'Me?' said Maan. He could not see where he came into it, except that he was his father's son. And, anyway, why hatred?

'But I have put all that behind me,' continued Rasheed. 'Nothing is to be gained by hatred. But I must now ask for your help. Since you are partly responsible, you cannot deny me this.'

'What are you talking about?' asked Maan, bewildered. He had sensed, when he visited the village at Bakr-Id, that there was some tension involving Rasheed, but what had he to do with it?

'Please do not pretend ignorance,' said Rasheed. 'You know my family; you have even met Meher's mother – and yet you insisted on these events and these plans. You yourself are associated with the elder sister.'

What Saeeda Bai had said to Maan now clicked in his mind.

'Tasneem?' he asked. 'Are you talking about Saeeda Bai and Tasneem?'

A hard look passed over Rasheed's face – as if Maan had confirmed his own guilt. 'If you know it, what is the need to take her name?' he asked.

'But I don't know it – whatever it is,' protested Maan, amazed by the turn in the conversation.

Rasheed, attempting to be reasonable, said: 'I know that you and Saeeda Bai and others, including important people in the government, are trying to get me married to her. And she has decided on me. The letter she wrote – the looks she has given me – Suddenly one day in the middle of her lesson she made a remark which could only mean one thing. I cannot sleep for worry, for three weeks I have hardly slept a wink. I do not want to do this, but I am afraid for her sanity. She will go insane unless I return her love. But even if I undertake this – which I must do on the basis of humanity – even if I undertake this, I must have protection for my own wife and children. You will have to get complete confirmation from Saeeda Begum about this. I will only agree on certain clear conditions.'

'What on earth are you talking about?' said Maan a little sharply. 'I am part of no plot –'

Rasheed cut him off. He was so annoyed that he was trembling. But he tried to get a hold on himself. 'Please do not say that,' he said. 'I cannot accept it when you say this sort of thing to my very face. I know what is what. I have already said I bear no hatred towards you any longer. I have told myself that however mistaken your intentions, you were doing it for my good. But did you never give any thought to my wife and children?'

'I don't know about Saeeda Begum,' said Maan, 'but I doubt she wants Tasneem to marry you. As for myself, this is the first I'm hearing of it.'

A cunning look passed over Rasheed's face. 'Then why did you mention her name a minute ago?'

Maan frowned, trying to think back. 'Saeeda Begum said something about some letters you sent her sister,' he said. 'I wouldn't advise you to write any more. They will only annoy her. And,' he added, getting annoyed himself, but trying to contol his temper – for he was, after all, talking to his teacher, young though he was, and one who had, moreover, been his host in the village – 'I wish you would not imagine that I am part of some plot.'

'All right,' said Rasheed firmly. 'All right. I won't mention it. When you visited the patwari with my family did I ever criticize you? Let us close the chapter. I won't accuse you, and you will kindly not make these protests, these denials. All right?'

'But of course I will deny it –' said Maan, hardly even wondering where a patwari had entered all this. 'Let me tell you, Rasheed, that you are completely mistaken. I have always had the greatest respect for you, but I can't see where you have got these ideas from. What makes you think that Tasneem is in the least interested in you?'

'I don't know,' said Rasheed speculatively. 'Perhaps it is my looks, or my uprightness, or the fact that I have done so much in life already and will be famous some day. She knows I have helped so many people.' He lowered his voice. 'I did not invite any attentions. I have a religious attitude to life.' He sighed. 'But I know the meaning of duty. I must do what is necessary for her sanity.' He bowed his head in sudden exhaustion and leaned forward.

'I think,' said Maan after a while, patting him on the back in a puzzled manner, 'that you should take better care of yourself – or let your family do so. You should go back to the village as soon as the vacations begin, or even before – and let Meher's mother take care of you. Rest. Sleep. Eat properly. Do not study. And do not exhaust yourself by campaigning for any party.'

Rasheed lifted his head and looked at Maan mockingly. 'So that is what you would like?' he said. 'Then the path will be clear. Then you can farm my field again. Then you can send the police to break my head with a lathi. I may suffer some setbacks, but whatever I put my mind to doing, I do. I understand when things are connected with each other. It is not easy to dupe me, especially if your conscience is uneasy.'

'You are speaking in riddles,' said Maan. 'And I think it is getting late for your tuition. In any case, I don't want to hear anything more on this subject.'

'You must confirm or deny it.'

'What, for God's sake?' cried Maan in exasperation.

'When you visit Saeeda Begum next, tell her that I am willing to spread happiness in her home if she insists on my going ahead with all this, that I will undergo a simple ceremony, but that any children I have in my second marriage cannot usurp the rights of the children I already have. And the marriage with Tasneem must be kept secret, even from the rest of my family. There must be no rumour – she is, after all, the sister of, well – I have my reputation and that of my family. Only those who already know. . . .'

He drifted off.

Maan got up, looking at Rasheed in amazement and shaking his head. He sighed, then leaned against the trunk of the tree, continuing to stare at his former teacher and friend. Then he looked down at the ground and said:

'I am not going back to Saeeda Begum's, nor am I plotting against you. I am not interested in breaking anyone's head. I am leaving for Salimpur tomorrow with my father. You can send your own messages to – to Saeeda Begum, but I beg you not to. I cannot understand a quarter of what you have been saying. But if you wish, Rasheed, I will accompany you to your village – or to your wife's village – and make sure that you get there safely.'

Rasheed did not move. He pressed his right hand to his forehead.

'Well, what do you say?' asked Maan, concerned and angry. He had planned to go to Saeeda Bai's before leaving.

Now he felt obliged to mention to her his meeting with Rasheed and the disturbing turn it had taken. He fervently hoped that nothing harmful would come out of it, and he also hoped that it would not sour the evening of his departure.

'I will sit here,' said Rasheed after a while, 'and think.'

He made the word sound actively ominous.

17.4

MAAN had not been following Rasheed's activities. He was troubled by his talk of the patwari, though now he did recall faintly that someone – Rasheed's father or grand-father – had once mentioned something about a patwari to him. He knew that Rasheed had been moved to pity and indignation on behalf of the poorer people in the village: Maan's mind went back to the old man, destitute and dying, whom Rasheed had gone to visit, and because of whom he had taken up cudgels against the elders outside the mosque. But Rasheed was so rigid, expected so much of others and of himself, reacted so much in anger and pride, hammered away so powerfully in every direction he turned to, that – apart from putting other people's backs up – he must have worn himself out completely. Had he suffered from any specific shock that had caused him to crack in this way – to behave so sanely – at least at the beginning – and yet so deludedly? He still gave tuitions; did he still make ends meet? He was looking so poorly. And was he still the exacting, careful teacher, with his insistence on perfect, unbending alifs? What did his students and their families think of him?

And what did Rasheed's own family think? Did they know what had happened to him? If they knew, how could they be indifferent to his pitiable state? When he went to Debaria, Maan decided, he would ask them directly what they knew and tell them what they didn't. And where were Rasheed's wife and children?

Deeply disturbed, he mentioned to Saeeda Bai some of

the things that were on his mind. He could not understand how he had obtained either Rasheed's hatred or his conditional forgiveness. The image of Rasheed and his wild imaginings would haunt Maan for weeks.

Saeeda Bai, for her part, became so concerned about Tasneem's safety that she summoned the watchman and told him that under no circumstances was Tasneem's old Arabic teacher to be admitted to the house. When Maan mentioned Rasheed's belief that there was a plot to marry him against his will to the infatuated Tasneem, Saeeda Bai indignantly and with disgust in her voice read out a part of one of Rasheed's letters, which certainly gave Maan the impression that the overwhelming weight of passion was on Rasheed's side. He had written to Tasneem that he wanted to bury his face in the clouds of her hair and so on and so forth. Even his handwriting, about which he used to be so particular, had regressed to a scrawl under the force of his feelings. The letter, to judge from the excerpt that Saeeda Bai read, was alarming. When he added to this the whole bizarre conception of a plot with all its conditions and ramifications, about which Saeeda Bai had until then been ignorant, Maan could not help sympathizing with her agitation, her inability to concentrate on anything else – on music, on him, on herself. He tried in vain to distract her. So vulnerable did she seem to him that he longed to take her in his arms – but he sensed that hers was a volatile and explosive vulnerability and that he would be hurtfully rebuffed.

'If there is anything I can do at any time,' he told her, 'you have only to send for me. I don't know what to do or what to advise. I will be in Rudhia District, but they will keep track of me at the Nawab Sahib's house.' Maan did not mention Prem Nivas because Saeeda Bai was no longer persona grata there.

Saeeda Bai's face became pale.

'The Nawab Sahib has promised to assist my father's campaign,' Maan explained.

'Poor girl, poor girl,' said Saeeda Bai softly. 'O God,

what a world this is. Go now, Dagh Sahib, and may God keep you.'

'Are you sure –'

'Yes.'

'I will not be able to think of anything but you, Saeeda,' said Maan. 'At least give me a smile before I leave.'

Saeeda Bai gave him a smile, but her eyes were still sad. 'Listen, Maan,' she said, addressing him by his name, 'think of many things. Never place your happiness in one person's power. Be just to yourself. And even if I am not invited to sing at Holi in Prem Nivas, come here and I will sing for you.'

'But Holi is more than three months away,' said Maan. 'Why, I will see you in less than three weeks.'

Saeeda Bai nodded. 'Yes, yes,' she said absently. 'That's right, that's quite right.' She shook her head slowly a couple of times and closed her eyes. 'I don't know why I am so tired, Dagh Sahib. I don't even feel like feeding Miya Mitthu. God keep you in safety.'

17.5

THE electorate of Salimpur-cum-Baitar consisted of 70,000 people, about half Hindu and half Muslim.

Apart from the two smallish towns included in its name, the constituency encompassed over a hundred villages, including the twin villages of Sagal and Debaria where Rasheed's family lived. It was a single member constituency: only one candidate would be elected to the Legislative Assembly by the voters. Ten candidates in all were standing: six represented parties, and four were Independents. Of the former, one was Mahesh Kapoor, the Minister of Revenue, who was the candidate for the Indian National Congress. Of the latter, one was Waris Mohammad Khan, the candidate who had been put up as a dummy by the Nawab Sahib of Baitar in case his friend did not get the Congress ticket or chose not to stand or bowed out of the race for some reason or other.

Waris was delighted to be a candidate, even though he knew that he would be expected to throw his weight as actively as possible behind Mahesh Kapoor. Just the look of his name on the list of validly nominated candidates outside the office of the Returning Officer made him smile with pride. Khan came just below Kapoor in the list, which was arranged in the order of the English alphabet. Waris thought this significant: the two allies could almost be paired together by a bracket. Though everyone knew what his function in the election was, the fact that he was present on the same list as some of the better-known citizenry of the district – indeed, of the state – gave Waris a certain standing at the Fort. The munshi continued to order him about, but more cagily than before. And when Waris chose not to obey, he had the ready excuse that he was busy with election work.

When Maan and his father arrived at Baitar Fort, Waris reassured them:

'Now, Minister Sahib, Maan Sahib, leave everything in the Baitar area to me. I'll arrange everything – transport, meetings, drums, singers, everything. Just tell the Congress people to send us lots of those Nehru posters, and also a lot of Congress flags. We'll see that they are put up everywhere. And we won't let anyone go to sleep for a month,' he continued happily. 'They won't even be able to hear the azaan for the slogans. Yes. And I've made sure that the water for your bath is hot. Tomorrow morning I've arranged for a tour of some of the villages, and in the evening we return to the town for a meeting. And if Maan Sahib wants to hunt – but I fear there will be no time for that. Votes before nilgai. But first I have to make sure that a good many of our supporters attend the Socialist Party meeting this evening to heckle them properly. Those haram-zadas don't even think our Nawab Sahib should get compensation for the land that is going to be snatched from him – just imagine! What an injustice it is already. And now they want to add insult to injury – ' Waris suddenly stopped, the realization striking him that he was addressing the very author of the black act. 'What I mean is –' He finished with a grin, and shook his head vigorously, as if shaking the very thought out of his brain. They were, of course, allies now.

'Now I must see to things,' he said, and disappeared for a while.

Maan had a slow and relaxed bath, and came down to find his father waiting for him impatiently. They began to discuss the candidates, the support they could expect from people of different areas or religions or castes, their strategy with regard to women and other particular groups, election expenses and how to cover them, and the faint possibility that Nehru might be induced to give a speech in the constituency during his brief tour of Purva Pradesh in mid-January. What gave Maan a real sense of warmth was the fact that his father was far less dismissive of him than usual. Unlike Maan, he had not lived in this constituency, but Maan had expected that he might simply extrapolate his experiences of the Rudhia farm to this northern subdivision. But Mahesh Kapoor, though he did not believe in caste, and thought little of religion, was more than alive to their electoral implications, and listened with care to Maan's description of the demographic contours of this tricky terrain.

Among the Independent candidates – quite apart from Waris, who was a supporter – there was no one who presented much of a challenge to Mahesh Kapoor. And among the party candidates, because he happened to be the candidate of the Congress Party – anxious though he was about fighting from an unfamiliar constituency – he started out with an immense advantage. The Congress was the party of Independence and the party of Nehru, and it was far better funded, far more widely organized, and far more quickly recognized than the others. Its very flag – saffron, white and green, with a spinning wheel in the middle – resembled the national flag. The Congress Party had a worker or two in almost every village – workers who had been somewhat active in social service during the last few years, and would be very active indeed in election-eering in the coming couple of months.

The other five parties presented a mixed bag.

The Jan Sangh promised to 'advocate the spread and extension of the highest traditions of Bharatiya Sanskriti': a thinly veiled term for Hindu, rather than Indian, culture. It was more than willing to go to war with Pakistan over the issue of Kashmir. It demanded compensation from Pakistan for the property of Hindus who had been forced to migrate to India. And it stood for a United India which included the territory of Pakistan; presumably, it meant a forcibly re-united one.

The Ram Rajya Parishad appeared more peaceable if further removed from reality. It declared that its object was to bring about a state of affairs in the country similar to that of the idyllic age of Rama. Every citizen would be expected to be 'righteous and religious-minded'; artificial foodstuffs such as vanaspati ghee – a kind of hydrogenated vegetable oil – would be banned, as would obscene and vulgar films and the slaughter of cows. The ancient Hindu system of medicine would be 'recognized officially as the national system'. And the Hindu Code Bill would never be passed.

The three parties to the left of the Congress who were fighting from this constituency were the KMPP, the party that Mahesh Kapoor had joined and then left (and whose symbol was a hut); the Socialist Party (whose symbol was a banyan tree); and the Communist Party (whose symbol was a sickle and a few ears of corn). The Scheduled Castes Federation, the party of Dr Ambedkar (who had recently resigned from Nehru's Cabinet on the grounds of irreconcilable differences and the collapse of the Hindu Code Bill), had forged an electoral alliance with the socialists; they had no candidate of their own for this seat. They concentrated mainly on double-member constituencies where at least one member from the scheduled castes was bound by law to be elected to the legislature.

'It would have been good if your mother had been here,' said Mahesh Kapoor. 'It's even more important in this place than in my old constituency – even more of the women here are in purdah.'

'How about the Congress women's groups?' asked Maan.

Mahesh Kapoor clicked his tongue impatiently. 'It's not enough to have Congress women volunteers,' he said. 'What we need is a powerful woman speaker.'

'Ammaji isn't a powerful speaker,' Maan pointed out with a smile. He tried to imagine his mother on a podium and failed. Her speciality was quiet work behind the scenes, mainly in helping people, but sometimes – as in elections – in persuasion.

'No, but she's from the family, and that makes all the difference.'

Maan nodded. 'I think we should try to get Veena out to help,' he said. 'You'll have to talk to old Mrs Tandon, though.'

'The old lady doesn't like my godless ways,' said Mahesh Kapoor to his son. 'We'll have to get your mother to speak to her. You go back next week and tell her. And while you're at it, tell Kedarnath to speak to the jatavs he knows in Ravidaspur to contact the scheduled castes in this area. Caste, caste.' He shook his head. 'Oh yes, and one more thing. For the first few days we should travel around together. Then we can split forces to get more coverage. The Fort has two jeeps. You can go around with Waris and I'll go around with the munshi.'

'When Firoz comes, you should go around with him,' said Maan, who did not care much for the munshi and thought he might well lose his father votes. 'That will make a Hindu-Muslim pair in each jeep.'

'Well, what is keeping him away?' asked Mahesh Kapoor impatiently. 'It would have been much better if he had showed us around Baitar. I can understand why Imtiaz can't leave Brahmpur.'

'He's had a lot of work recently,' said Maan, thinking for a moment of his friend. He had been allotted Firoz's room as usual, high up in the Fort. 'And the Nawab Sahib?' he countered. 'What is his reason for deserting us?'

'He doesn't like elections,' said Mahesh Kapoor shortly. 'In fact, he doesn't like politics at all. And after his father's role in splitting up the country, I don't blame him. Well, he's put everything at our disposal. At least we are mobile. Can you imagine driving my car along these roads? Or going around on bullock-carts?'

'We're perfectly mobile,' said Maan. 'Two jeeps, a pair of bullocks, and a bicycle.' They both laughed. A pair of bullocks was the Congress symbol, and Waris's was a bicycle.

'A pity about your mother,' repeated Mahesh Kapoor.

'There's still a long way to go before the polls,' said Maan optimistically, 'and I'm sure she'll be well enough to give us a hand in a week or two.' He looked forward to the return to Brahmpur that his father had just suggested. It seemed to him that for almost the first time in his life his father trusted him; indeed, in some ways, depended on him.

Waris entered to announce that they were just on their way to the Socialist Party meeting in town. Did the Minister Sahib or Maan Sahib wish to come along?

Mahesh Kapoor thought that if Waris had organized some heckling it would be inappropriate for him to go. Maan was bound by no such scruples. He wanted to see everything there was to be seen.

17.6

THE meeting of the Socialist Party began forty-five minutes late under a huge red and green canopy on the playing fields of the government school in Baitar, where most important large meetings in town were held. A few men on the podium were trying to keep the crowd entertained and patient. Several people greeted Waris, and he was delighted to be the centre of a little knot of attention. He went around introducing Maan and greeting people with an adaab or a namasté or a hearty slap on the back. 'This is the man who saved the Nawabzada's life,' he announced so flamboyantly that even the robust Maan was embarrassed.

The socialist procession through the city had got held up somewhere. But now the roll of drums got closer, and soon the candidate was ascending the stage with his entourage. He was a middle-aged teacher who had been a member of the District Board for years. Not only was he known to be a good speaker himself but someone had also spread the false rumour that the great socialist leader Jayaprakash Narayan might possibly be coming to speak in Baitar – so there was a large crowd on the football field. It was seven in the evening, and beginning to get chilly; the almost entirely male audience, townsfolk and villagers alike, had brought shawls and blankets to wrap themselves up in. Cotton durries had been laid out on the ground by the organizers as protection against dust and dew.

Several local luminaries sat on the podium, which was lit in addition by several bright white lights. Behind them on a cloth wall was the huge image of a banyan tree, the socialists' symbol. The speaker, used perhaps to controlling rowdiness in his classroom, had such a powerful voice that the microphone was almost superfluous. In any case it alternately acted up and broke down. From time to time, especially when the candidate got carried away, it set up a vibrating wail. Having been introduced and garlanded, he was soon in the full flow of pure Hindi oratory:

'... And that is not all. This Congress government will not spend our taxes on pipes to bring us clean water to drink, but they will spend any amount of money on useless baubles. All of you have walked past that ugly statue of Gandhiji in the town square. I am sorry to say that however much we respect, however much we revere the man whom the statue is supposed to resemble, it is a shameful expense of public money. This great soul is enshrined in our hearts; why do we need to have him direct the traffic in the marketplace? But how can one argue with the government of this state? They would not listen, they had to go ahead. So the government spent this money on a useless statue that is good only for pigeons to defecate upon. If we had spent it instead upon public toilets, our mothers and sisters would not have to defecate in the open. And all this needless expense makes this useless government print more useless money, which in turn increases the prices of all the goods, all the necessities, that we poor people have to buy.' His voice rose in anguish. 'How can we cope? Some of us, like teachers and clerks, have fixed salaries, some of us depend on the mercy of the skies. How can we put up with this backbreaking expense – this inflation that is the true gift of the Congress to the people of this country in the last four years. What will help us take our boat across the river of life in these desperate times of reduced rations, of dwindling supplies of cloth, of the locusts of despair, of corruption and of nepotism? Why, I look at my students and weep –'

'Show us how you weep now! One, two, three, testing!' shouted a voice from the back of the crowd.

'– I will beg my respected and supposedly witty brothers at the back not to interrupt. We know from where they come, from what high nest they swoop down to help in the oppression of the people of this district. . . . I look at my students and weep. And why? Yes, I will tell you, if I may be permitted to by the firecrackers at the back. Because these poor students cannot get work, no matter how good, how decent, how intelligent, how hardworking they are. This is what the Congress has done, this is what it has driven the economy to. Think, my friends, think. Who among us does not know a mother's love? And yet today, that mother who, with tears streaming down her face, looked at her family jewels, her wedding bangles, her very mangalsutra for the last time – those precious things that are dearer to her even than life – and who sold them to support the education of her son – and who saw her son through school, through college, with such high hopes that he would do something worthwhile in life – she now finds that he cannot even get a job as a government clerk without knowing someone or bribing someone. Is this what we threw the British out for? Is this what the people deserve? Such a government that cannot make sure its people are fed, that cannot make sure that its students have jobs, such a government should die of shame, such a government should drown in a handful of water.'

The speaker paused for breath, and the organizers set up a shout:

'The MLA from Baitar, how should he be?'

His supporters in the crowd shouted back in rhyme:

'Ramlal Sinha, one such as he!'

Ramlal Sinha held up his hands in a humble namasté. 'But, my friends, my brothers, my sisters, let me speak further, let me unburden my heart of all the bitterness it has had to swallow these last four years of Congress misrule – I am not a man who likes to use strong language, but I tell you that if we are to prevent a violent revolution in this country, we must throw out the Congress. We must uproot it. This tree whose roots have sunk so deep, which has sucked all the water out of this soil, this tree has become rotten and hollow – and it is our duty – the duty of every one of us, my friends, to uproot this rotten and hollow tree from the soil of Mother India, and to throw it aside – and with it the inauspicious and rapacious owls that have made their dirty nests in it!'

'Get rid of the tree! Don't vote for the tree!' shouted a voice from the back. Maan and Waris looked at each other and laughed, and there was much laughter from the audience too, including the supporters of the Socialist Party. Ramlal Sinha, realizing the blunder in his imagery, thumped the table and shouted: 'This heckling is typical of Congress rowdyism.'

Then, realizing that anger would be counter-productive, he went on in a calm voice: 'Typical, my friends, typical. We fight these elections under this sort of disadvantage and in this sort of shadow. The whole state machinery is in the hands of the Congress Party. The Prime Minister flies around in a plane at state expense. The DMs and SDOs jump to the Congress tune. They hire hecklers to disrupt our meetings. But we must rise above all this and teach them that they can shout themselves hoarse, and we will still not be cowed. This is not some two-anna party they are dealing with, this is the Socialist Party, the party of Jayaprakash Narayan, of Acharya Narendra Deva, of fearless patriots, not venal goons. We will put our ballot papers in the box marked with the symbol of the – of the banyan, the true representation of the Socialist Party. This is the strong tree, the spreading tree, the tree that is neither hollow nor rotten, the tree that is symbolic of the strength and generosity and beauty and glory of this country of ours – the land of Buddha and Gandhi, of Kabir and Nanak, of Akbar and Ashoka, the land of the Himalayas and the Ganga, the land that belongs equally to all of us, Hindus, Muslims, Sikhs, and Christians alike, about which it was truly said, in the undying words of Iqbal,

> Better than all the world is this our Hindustan.
> We are its nightingales, it is our rose-garden.'

Ramlal Sinha, overcome by his rhetoric, coughed twice, and drank half a glass of water.

'Does the nightingale have any policies of its own, or does it merely want to smear the Congress statue from on high?' shouted a voice.

Get out of my class! Ramlal Sinha felt like shouting. Instead, he kept calm and said:

'I am delighted that the brainless buffalo from the back has asked that question. It comes very fittingly from one whose symbol ought, more appropriately, to consist of two water-buffaloes rather than two bullocks yoked together. Everyone can see how the Minister of Revenue has yoked himself to the biggest landlord in the whole of this district. If there was ever need for proof of collusion between the Congress Party and the zamindars, here it is. See them working together like the two wheels of a bicycle! See the zamindars grow still richer and fatter on the compensation that the government dispenses to them. Why is the Nawab Sahib not here to face the people? Is he afraid of their indignation? Or is he too proud, like those of his class – or too ashamed of the money of the poor, the public largesse that will soon be clinging to his hands? You ask me what are our policies. Let me tell you if you will allow me to.

The Socialist Party has given the agrarian problem far more thought than any other party. We are not, like the KMPP, a mere discontented tail of the Congress Party. We are not a doctrinaire tool of foreigners, like the communists. No, good people, we have our own independent views, our own policies.'

As he ticked off his points on his fingers, he winched up his voice in tandem: 'No peasant family will be allowed to possess land more than three times the size of an economic holding. No one who does not personally participate in cultivation will be allowed to possess land. The land will belong to the tiller. No one – not a Nawab, not a Maharaja, not a waqf or a temple trust – will be compensated for more than a hundred acres of appropriated land. The Right to Property in the Constitution will have to go: it is a barrier to just distribution of wealth. To the workers we promise Social Security which will include protection against disability, sickness, unemployment, and old age. To women we guarantee equal pay for equal work, effective universal education, and a civil code that will grant them equal rights.'

'Do you want to take our women out of purdah?' demanded an indignant voice.

'Let me finish; don't shoot your cannon before it's loaded. Listen to what I have to say, then I will happily answer any and all of your questions. To the minorities, let me say: we guarantee full protection, I repeat, full protection for your language, your script and your culture. And we must break our last ties with the British. We cannot remain in the anglophile Nehru's beloved colonialist and imperialist Commonwealth, in the name of whose head, King George, he himself was so often arrested, and whose boots he now desires to lick. Let us finish off with the old ways once and for all. Let us burn to ash once and for all the party of greed and favouritism, the Congress, that has brought the country to the edge of disaster. Take your ghee and sandalwood, my friends, if you can still afford it, or just bring yourselves and your families, and come to the cremation ground on the 30th of January, the day of the poll in this constituency, and let the corpse of the demon party be cremated there once and for all. Jai Hind.'

'Jai Hind!' roared the crowd.

'Baitar ka MLA kaisa ho?' cried someone from the podium.

'Ramlal Sinha jaisa ho!' shouted the crowd.

This antiphonal chant went on for a couple of minutes while the candidate folded his hands respectfully and bowed to the audience.

Maan looked at Waris, but Waris was laughing, and did not appear in the least worried.

'The town is one thing,' said Waris. 'It's in the villages that we will knock them out. Tomorrow our work begins. I will make sure you get a good dinner.'

He slapped Maan on the back.

17.7

BEFORE going to bed, Maan looked at the picture that Firoz kept on his table: the picture of the Nawab Sahib, his wife, and their three children, with Firoz in particular looking very intently at the camera with his head tilted. The owl called out, reminding Maan of the speech he had just heard. He realized with a mild sense of shock that he had forgotten to bring any whisky with him. But nevertheless, in a few minutes, he was fast asleep.

The next day was long and dusty and exhausting. They travelled by jeep along pitted and petering tracks to an endless succession of villages, where Waris introduced them to an endless number of headmen, Congress Party village-level workers, heads of caste 'biradaris' or communities, imams, pandits, and local bigwigs. Mahesh Kapoor's style of speech, in contrast to the political oiliness he detested, was clipped, abrupt, even somewhat arrogant, but quite straightforward; it was not taken amiss by most of those who met him. He gave short talks on various issues, and answered the questions of the villagers who had gathered to hear him. He asked very simply for their vote. Maan, Waris, and he drank innumerable cups of tea and sherbet. Sometimes the women came out, sometimes they stayed in and peeped out from behind the door. But wherever they went, the party was a superb spectacle for the village children. They tailed them in every village, and were even given rides on the jeep to the outskirts of the village when it departed for the next one.

Men of the kurmi caste in particular were very worried about the fact that women would inherit property under Nehru's threatened Hindu Code Bill. These careful agriculturalists did not want their lands to be divided into smaller, entirely uneconomic, holdings. Mahesh Kapoor admitted that he was in favour of the bill, but explained, as well as he could, why he thought it necessary.

Many of the Muslims were worried about the status of their local schools, their language, their religious freedom; they asked about the recent troubles in Brahmpur and, further afield, in Ayodhya. Waris reassured them that in Mahesh Kapoor they had a friend who could both read and write Urdu, who was a personal friend of the Nawab Sahib, and whose son – and here he pointed to Maan with great affection and pride – had actually saved the life of the younger Nawabzada in a religious riot at Moharram.

Some tenant farmers asked about the abolition of zamindari, but very tentatively, since Waris, the Nawab Sahib's man, was present. This caused a great deal of awkwardness all around, but Mahesh Kapoor grasped the nettle and explained people's rights under the new act. 'But this should not be seen as an excuse not to pay rent now,' he said. 'Four separate cases – from Uttar Pradesh, Purva Pradesh, Madhya Pradesh and Bihar – are at present before the Supreme Court, and it will decide quite soon whether the new zamindari laws are valid and can be put into effect. Meanwhile, no one is to be evicted forcibly from his land. And there are strict penalties for tampering with land records in order to benefit anyone – landlord or tenant. The Congress government has plans to move the village patwaris around every three years, so that they cannot form deep and profitable roots in one place. Every patwari must know that he will be most severely punished if he allows himself to be bribed into wrongdoing.'

To the totally landless labourers, most of whom were so cowed that they hardly dared to be present, let alone speak, Mahesh Kapoor promised distribution of surplus unused land where it was possible. But to these most unfortunate people he knew that he could be of little direct assistance – for his Zamindari Abolition Act did not even touch them.

In some places the people were so poor and underfed and ill that they looked like savages in rags. Their huts were in disrepair, their livestock half-dead. In others they were better off and could even afford to hire a school-teacher and construct a room or two for a small private school.

In a couple of places Mahesh Kapoor was surprised to be asked if it was true that S.S. Sharma was going to be called to Delhi and that he himself was going to be elected the next Chief Minister of Purva Pradesh. He denied the first rumour, and said that even if it were true, the second would not necessarily follow. They could rest assured that he would almost certainly be a Minister, but he was not asking them to vote him in because of that. He wanted them to vote for him simply as their MLA. In this he was entirely sincere, and it went down very well.

By and large, even those villagers who stood to benefit from the abolition of landlordism maintained an attitude of respect for the Nawab Sahib and his wishes. 'Remember,' said Waris, wherever they went, 'the Nawab Sahib is asking for your vote not in my name but in the Minister Sahib's. So put your ballot-paper in the box marked with the two bullocks, not in the one marked with a bicycle. And remember to put it inside the box, through the hole in the top. Don't just put it on the top of the box, or the next person who enters the booth will be able to put your ballot-paper into any box he chooses. Understand?'

The Congress volunteers and village-level workers, who were very pleased and honoured to see Mahesh Kapoor,

and who garlanded him repeatedly, told him which villages
they were going to canvass support in and where and when
he should try to appear, either with or – and they implied
that this was preferable – without Waris. They, being
unfettered by a retainer of the Nawab Sahib, were able to
play the powerful anti-zamindari card in a much more
fiery manner than the author of the Zamindari Abolition
Act himself. They walked about in groups of four or five
from village to village, with nothing more than a stick, a
water-bottle, and a handful of dried cereal, gathering potential voters together, singing party, patriotic, or even devotional songs, and dinning into any ears that were willing to
listen the great achievements of the Congress Party since
its inception. They spent the night in the villages, so that
no money was spent out of Mahesh Kapoor's accountable
funds. The one thing that disappointed them was that his
jeep had not come laden with Congress posters and flags,
and they made Mahesh Kapoor promise to provide these
in large numbers. They also filled him in on events and
issues that were important to particular villages, specific
caste structures in various areas, and – as important as
anything else – local jokes and references that would go
down well.

From time to time Waris would shout out various names,
almost at random, in order to stir up the crowd:

'Nawab Sahib –'

'Zindabad!'

'Jawaharlal Nehru –'

'Zindabad!'

'Minister Mahesh Kapoor Sahib –'

'Zindabad!'

'Congress Party –'

'Zindabad!'

'Jai –'

'Hind!'

After a few days of such electioneering in the cold and
heat and dust, everyone's voice was painfully hoarse. Finally, after promising to return to the Baitar area in due
course, Mahesh Kapoor and his son said goodbye to Waris

and, taking a jeep from the Fort with them, made for the Salimpur area. Here their headquarters was the home of a local Congress Party official, and here again they did the rounds of the caste leaders of the small qasbah town: the Hindu and Muslim goldsmiths who were the heads of the jewellery bazaar, the khatri who ran the cloth market, the kurmi who was the spokesman of the vegetable sellers. Netaji, who had inveigled himself onto the local Congress Committee, drove up on his motorcycle, pasted over with Congress flags and symbols, to greet Maan and his father. He embraced Maan like an old friend. One of his first suggestions was that the leaders of the chamars be sent two large tins of locally brewed liquor to sweeten their taste for the Congress. Mahesh Kapoor refused to do any such thing. Netaji looked at Mahesh Kapoor in astonishment, wondering how he had managed to become such a big leader with so little common sense.

That night Mahesh Kapoor confided in his son:

'What country is this that I have had the misfortune to be born into? This election is worse than any previous one. Caste, caste, caste, caste. We should never have extended the franchise. It has made it a hundred times worse.'

Maan said, by way of consolation, that he thought that other things mattered as well, but he could see that his father was deeply disturbed, not by his own chances of winning, which were virtually unassailable, but by the state of the world. He had begun to respect his father more and more as the days passed. Mahesh Kapoor worked as hard and straightforwardly and tactlessly at his campaign as he had worked at the various clauses of the Zamindari Bill. He worked cannily, but with a sense of principle. And this work, besides being much more physically gruelling than the work in the Secretariat, began at dawn and often ended after midnight. Several times he mentioned that he wished that Maan's mother had been there to help him; once or twice he even wondered about her health. But he never complained that circumstances had forced him out of the security of his constituency in Old Brahmpur into a rural district he had hardly even visited, let alone cultivated, before.

17.8

IF Mahesh Kapoor had been surprised by Maan's popularity during his Bakr-Id visit, not only he but Maan himself was amazed to discover how popular he now was in the area around Salimpur. While no word had leaked out in Baitar about his attack on the munshi, Maan's stay in Debaria earlier in the year had passed from fact into rumour into a kind of myth, and many exploits of his visit were recounted to him which he found hard to recognize. While in Salimpur he had looked up the spindly and sarcastic schoolteacher Qamar, and had introduced him to his father. Qamar had told Mahesh Kapoor laconically that he could count on his vote. What struck Maan as somewhat odd about this conversation was that neither Mahesh Kapoor nor Maan had asked him for his vote yet. He did not know that Netaji had mentioned rather contemptuously to Qamar Mahesh Kapoor's attitude towards bribing the chamars with liquor, and that Qamar had said forthwith that Mahesh Kapoor, though a Hindu, was the man he would vote for.

Mahesh Kapoor's own very brief visit to Salimpur at Bakr-Id was not forgotten. Although he was an outsider, people felt that he was not merely interested in them for their votes, a fickle migratory bird visible only at election time.

Maan enjoyed meeting people and asking for their votes on his father's behalf. At times he felt quite protective of him. Even when Mahesh Kapoor got annoyed, as he sometimes still did when he was very tired, Maan took it in good part. Perhaps I will become a politician after all, he thought. Certainly, I enjoy it more than most other things I've done. But even if I do manage to become an MLA or MP, what will I do once I get there?

Whenever he felt restless, Maan would take over from

the driver and hurtle the colourfully decorated flag-decked jeep at breakneck speed down roads that were meant at best for bullock-carts. This gave him an exhilarating sense of freedom and everyone else a physical and psychological shock. The jeep, which was meant to accommodate two passengers in front and at most four in the back, was often crammed with ten or a dozen people, food, megaphones, posters, and all sorts of other paraphernalia besides. Its horn blew unceasingly and it trailed impressive clouds of dust and glory. Once, when its radiator began to leak, the driver scolded it and mixed some turmeric into the water. This sealed the leak miraculously.

One morning, they drove towards the twin villages of Debaria and Sagal, which were on the agenda for the day. As they approached the village Maan fell into a sudden depression. He had remembered Rasheed on and off during these last few days, and was glad they had been so busy that the memory had not preyed on him even more. But now he thought of what he was going to have to say to Rasheed's family. Perhaps they already knew about him. Certainly, neither Netaji nor Qamar had asked about him. But then, when they had met, there had been very little time to enquire.

Some other questions came to Maan's mind, and instead of humming a ghazal, as he sometimes did when driving, he fell silent. Was Rasheed serious when he had spoken of canvassing for the Socialist Party? What had brought his disturbing rift of delusion about Tasneem to the surface? Again he thought back to the day when they had visited the old and sick man at Sagal. He felt that Rasheed was at heart a good man, not the calculating ogre of Saeeda Bai's fancy.

It was almost the end of the year, and Maan had not seen Saeeda Bai now for two weeks. During the days he was so busy that she did not often enter his mind. But at night, even though he was exhausted, and just before sleep took over, his mind would turn to her. He would think not of her steely tantrums but of her gentleness and softness, of her unhappiness about Tasneem, of the scent of attar of roses, of the taste of Banarasi paan on her lips, of the intoxicating atmosphere of her two rooms. How strange, he thought, that he had never met her anywhere other than in those two rooms – except twice. It had been nine months since Holi evening in Prem Nivas, when he had first quoted Dagh to her in light-spirited public banter. And it seemed ages since he had tasted the sherbet from her hands. Even for one who continued to feel tenderly towards almost all the women he had had affairs with, it was a new experience for Maan to be obsessed by one woman – sexually and emotionally – for so long.

'For God's sake, Maan, drive straight. Do you want to have the election cancelled?' said his father. There was a rule to the effect that if a candidate died before the poll, it would be countermanded and a new election declared.

'Yes, Baoji,' said Maan. 'Sorry.'

In the event, Maan did not have to say much to anyone about Rasheed. Baba, who had met Mahesh Kapoor on the last visit, took over the reins as soon as they arrived in the village.

'So you've rejoined the Congress,' he said to the Minister.

'Yes, I have,' said Mahesh Kapoor. 'It was good advice you gave me.'

Baba was pleased that Mahesh Kapoor had remembered.

'Well,' said Baba, fixing his eyes on the younger man, 'you'll have no problem winning by a large margin in this constituency, even if Nehru doesn't.' He spat a blob of reddish spittle onto the ground.

'Don't you think there's any threat to me at all?' asked Mahesh Kapoor. 'It's true that the Congress is winning hands down in all the states that have had early polls.'

'No threat at all,' said Baba. 'None. The Muslims are behind you and behind the Congress, the scheduled castes are behind the Congress whether they're behind you or not, a few of the upper caste Hindus will go for the Jan Sangh and that other party whose name I forget, but they don't form much of the population. The left is divided into three. And none of the Independents count for much. Do you really want me to take you around these villages?'

'Yes, if you don't mind,' said Mahesh Kapoor. 'If I have it all sewn up anyway, let me at least visit my future flock and find out about their needs.'

'Very well, very well,' said Baba. 'So, Maan, what have you been up to since Bakr-Id?'

'Nothing,' said Maan, wondering where all that time had disappeared.

'You must do something,' said Baba, vaguely but forcefully. 'Something that makes a mark on the world – something that people hear about and talk about.'

'Yes, Baba,' assented Maan.

'I suppose you've met Netaji recently,' snorted the old man, stressing his younger son's title.

Maan nodded.

'In Salimpur. He offered to come with us everywhere and do everything for everyone.'

'But you're not travelling with him?' chuckled Baba.

'Well, no. I think he rubs Baoji up the wrong way.'

'Good, good. Too much dust behind his motorcycle and too much self behind his selflessness.'

Maan laughed.

'The Nawab Sahib's jeep now,' said Baba with approval. 'That's swifter – and sounder.' Baba was pleased at the implicit connection it presented. It would help to keep people in the village in awe of him, and to make it clear to them that the Minister was not above coming to an understanding with certain landlords.

Maan looked across at his father, who was now eating paan and talking to Rasheed's father; he wondered how he would have taken Baba's remark, had he understood its implications.

'Baba –' he said, suddenly. 'Do you know about Rasheed?'

'Yes, yes,' said the old man sternly. 'He's been thrown out. We've forbidden him entrance to the house.' Noticing Maan's appalled look he went on. 'But don't worry. He won't go hungry. His uncle sends him some money every month.'

Maan could say nothing for a while, then burst out: 'But, Baba – his wife? and his children?'

'Oh, they're here. He's lucky we're so fond of Meher – and Meher's mother. He didn't think of them when he disgraced himself. Nor does he think of them now: does he stop to think of the feelings of his wife? She has suffered enough in life already.'

Maan did not quite understand the last part of this remark, but Baba did not give him time to ask for an explanation. He went on: 'In our family we don't marry four women at a time, we do it one by one. One dies, we marry another: we have the decency to wait. But he is talking about another woman now, and he expects his wife to understand. He writes to her saying he wants to marry again, but he wants her agreement first. Obtuse! Marry her, I say, marry her for God's sake, but don't torment your wife by asking for permission. Who this woman is, he doesn't write. We don't even know what family she comes from. He has grown secretive in everything he does. He was never cunning when he was a boy.'

Maan did not try in the face of Baba's indignation to defend Rasheed, about whom he himself had such mixed feelings now; but nor did he mention the wild accusations of conspiracy Rasheed had made against him.

'Baba,' he said, 'if he has trouble of this kind, how could it help to close your doors against him?'

The old man paused, as if uncertain. 'That is not his only offence,' he said, searching Maan's face. 'He has become a complete communist.'

'Socialist.'

'Yes, yes,' said Baba, impatient with such quibbling. 'He wants to take my land away without compensation. What kind of grandson have I produced? The more he studies, the stupider he becomes. If he had stuck to the one Book, his mind would have been more healthy.'

'But, Baba, these are just his views.'

'Just his views? Do you not know how he tried to put them into action?'

Maan shook his head. Baba, seeing no guile in his face,

sighed again, more deeply this time, and muttered something under his breath. Looking across at his son, who was still talking to Mahesh Kapoor, he said to Maan:

'Rasheed's father says that you remind him of his elder son.' He mused for a few seconds, then went on: 'I can see you know nothing about this sorry business. I will explain it all later. But now I must take your father round the village. You come as well. We'll talk after dinner.'

'Baba, there may not be time later,' Maan said, knowing Mahesh Kapoor's impatience to cover as much ground as possible. 'Baoji will want to move on long before dinner.'

Baba ignored this. The tour of the village began. The path was cleared by Moazzam (who clouted anyone younger than himself who dared impede the progress), Mr Biscuit (yelling 'Jai Hind!') and a motley gang of running, shouting village children. 'Lion, lion!' they screamed in simulated terror. Baba and Mahesh Kapoor strode energetically in front, their sons straggled along in the rear. Rasheed's father was friendly enough to Maan, but used his paan as protection against prolonged conversation. Though everyone greeted Maan with affection and friendliness, his mind was on what Baba had said to him and on what he had to say.

'I will not allow you to return to Salimpur tonight,' Baba told Mahesh Kapoor flatly after they had completed the circuit. 'You will eat with us and sleep here. Your son spent a month here, you will have to spend a day.'

Mahesh Kapoor knew when he had met superior force, and consented with good grace.

17.9

AFTER dinner, Baba took Maan aside. There was no privacy in the village itself, especially when such a tremendous event as the visit of a Minister was taking place. Baba got a torch and told Maan to put on something warm. They walked towards the school, talking along the way. Baba told Maan in brief about the incident of the patwari, how the family had got together to warn Rasheed, how he had refused to listen, how he had encouraged some of the chamars and other tenants to take matters up with revenue authorities higher than the patwari, and how his plans had backfired. Anyone who had dared to stray from the path of obedience had been thrown off his land. Rasheed, Baba said, had made troublemakers of some of their most faithful chamars, and he had shown no qualms about instigating this betrayal. The family had had no choice but to cut him off.

'Even Kachheru – do you remember him?' said Baba. 'The man who pumped the water for your bath –'

Alas, Maan remembered all too well now what at Bakr-Id had eluded him, the identity of the man whom Baba had shoved aside on the way to the Idgah.

'It's not easy to find permanent people,' continued Baba sadly. 'The young people find ploughing difficult. Mud, effort, sun. But the older ones have done it since childhood.'

They had by now reached the great tank near the school. On the other side of the water was a small cemetery for the dead of the two villages. The whitewashed tombs stood out at night. Baba said nothing more for a while, and nor did Maan.

Remembering what Rasheed had once said about how generation succeeds generation in working mischief, Maan now murmured to himself with a bitter smile: 'The rude forefathers of the hamlet sleep.'

Baba looked at him and frowned. 'I don't understand English,' he said quietly. 'We here are simple people. We do not have any great learning. But Rasheed treats us as if we are ignorant to the core. He writes us letters, threatening us and boasting of his own humanism. Everything has gone – logic, respect, decency; but his pride and his sense of self, lunatically, remain. When I read his letters I weep.' He looked towards the school. 'He had a classmate who became a dacoit. Even he treats his family with more respect.'

After a while he continued, looking past the school

towards Sagal. 'He says that we are deluded, that our god is money, that wealth and land is all we are interested in. That sick man whom he visited with you, Rasheed used to tell us we should help him, should support his legal rights, should make him start a court case against his brothers. Such madness, such unrealistic notions – to interfere in the family matters of others and bring about needless strife. Imagine what would have happened if we had taken his advice. The man is dead now but the feud between the villages would have gone on for ever.'

Maan said nothing; it was as if his mind was blocked. He hardly even registered the news of this death. His thoughts were still with that work-worn man who with such calm and cheerfulness used to pump water for his bath. Strange to think that even his paltry earnings had been undone by – by what? Perhaps by Maan's own father. The two knew nothing of each other as individuals, but Kachheru was the saddest case of the evil practised under the act, and Mahesh Kapoor was almost directly responsible for his utter devastation, his reduction to the forsaken status of a landless labourer. Linked though they were in this sense of the former's guilt and the latter's despair, if they were to pass each other in the street, thought Maan, neither would know the other.

No doubt the effect of the act would be substantially good, but that would be of no help to Kachheru. Nor, Maan realized, with a seriousness unusual in him, could he do anything about it. To intercede with Baba would be impossible, and to take it up with his father an unthinkable betrayal of trust. To have helped the old woman at the Fort – that was entirely another thing.

And Rasheed? Censorious, pitiable, worn out, torn between family shame and family pride, forced to choose between loyalty and justice, between trust and pity, what must he have been through? Was he too not a victim of the tragedy of the countryside, of the country itself? Maan tried to imagine the pressure and suffering he must have undergone.

But Baba was saying, as if he had read Maan's thoughts:

'You know, the boy is very disturbed. I don't like to think of it. He has almost no friends in the city as far as we can tell, no one to talk to except those communists. Why don't you talk to him and make him see sense? We don't know how it has happened that he has become so strange, so incoherent. Someone said that he got hit on the head during a demonstration. Then we found out that that was not so. But perhaps, as his uncle says, the immediate cause is not important. Sooner or later, what does not bend will snap.'

Maan nodded in the darkness. Whether or not the old man noticed, he continued: 'I am not against the boy. Even now if he mends his ways and repents we will take him back. God is not called the compassionate, the merciful, for nothing. He tells us to forgive those who turn away from evil. But Rasheed – you know – if he changes his mind, he will be as vehement facing south as he was facing north.' He smiled. 'He was my favourite. I had more energy then, when he was ten years old. I would take him to the roof of my pigeon-house, and he would point out all our lands, exactly which bits were ours, and when they came into the family. With pride. And yet this same boy....' The old man was silent. Then, in an almost anguished voice, he said: 'One never knows anyone in this world, one cannot read anyone's heart, one never knows whom to believe and whom to trust.'

A faint call was heard in the distance from Debaria, followed by a closer one from Sagal.

'That is the call to night prayer,' said Baba. 'Let's go back. I shouldn't miss it and I don't want to pray in this Sagal mosque. Come on, get up, get up.'

Maan remembered his first morning in Debaria when he had woken up to find Baba telling him to go to prayer. Then, his excuse had been his religion. Now he said, 'Baba, if it's all right, I'll just sit here for a while. I'll find my own way back.'

'You want to be alone?' asked Baba, his voice betraying his surprise at what was an unusual request, particularly from Maan. 'Here, take the torch. No, no, take it, take it. I only brought it along to guide you. I can cut across these fields blindfolded at midnight at the new moon of Id. Well, I will mention him again in my prayers. May it do him some good.'

Alone Maan sat and looked out over the expanse of water. Into its blackness fell the reflection of the stars. He thought of the Bear, and of how he had done something definite to help Rasheed, and he felt ashamed at his own inaction. Rasheed never rested from his endeavours, thought Maan, shaking his head, whereas he himself did nothing but; or at least would have liked to. He promised himself that when he returned to Brahmpur for a few days' break he would visit him, difficult though the encounter was bound to be. He had been deeply disturbed by his previous meeting, and he did not know if his perplexity had been enhanced or diminished by what Baba had told him.

So much lay beneath the placid surface of things, so much torment and danger. Rasheed was by no means his closest friend, but he had thought he knew him and understood him. Maan was given to trusting and being trusted, but, as Baba said, perhaps one could never read the human heart.

As for Rasheed, Maan felt that for his own sake he had to be made to see the world with all its evil in a more tolerant light. It was not true that one could change everything through effort and vehemence and will. The stars maintained their courses despite his madness, and the village world moved on as before, swerving only very slightly to avoid him.

17.10

TWO days later they drove back to Brahmpur for a brief rest. Mrs Mahesh Kapoor greeted them with unaccustomed tears in her eyes. She had helped a little in canvassing among women for local Congress candidates in Brahmpur. Mahesh Kapoor was annoyed when he heard that she had even canvassed in L.N. Agarwal's constituency. Now that Pran, Savita and Uma were in Calcutta, and Veena and Kedarnath were both busy and able only rarely to visit, she had been feeling quite lonely. Nor was she at all well. But she sensed immediately the new warmth of the relationship between her husband and her younger son, and this gave her great joy. She went into the kitchen in a little while to supervise Maan's favourite tahiri herself; and later, after a bath, to do puja and give thanks for their safe return.

Though Mrs Mahesh Kapoor did not have, or have cause to have, a particularly well-developed sense of humour, one object that she had recently added to her puja paraphernalia never failed to make her smile. It was a brass bowl filled with harsingar blossoms and a few harsingar leaves. The bowl rested on a Congress flag made of flimsy paper, and Mrs Mahesh Kapoor looked from one to another with pleasure, admiring the saffron, white and green first of this and then of that as she rang her small brass bell around them – and all the gods – in joint benediction.

The next morning Maan found his mother and sister shelling peas in the courtyard. He had demanded tahiri again, and they were obliging him. He pulled up a morha and joined them. He remembered how as a child he would often sit in the courtyard – on a small morha which was reserved for him – and watch his mother shelling peas while she told him some story or other about the gods and their doings. But now the talk was about more terrestrial matters.

'How is it going, Maan?'

Maan realized that this was probably the first proper news his mother would be getting about the new constituency. If she had asked his father, he would have dismissed her silliness and fobbed her off with a few generalities. Maan gave her as thorough a picture as he could.

At the end of it she said, with a sigh: 'I wish I could have helped.'

'You must take care of yourself, Ammaji,' said Maan, 'and not exert yourself too much. Veena should be the one to help with the women voters. The country air will do her good after the foetid alleys of the old city.'

'I like that!' said Veena. 'That's the last time you're invited to our house. Foetid alleys. And it sounds as if you have a sore throat from all that fresh country air. I know what canvassing among the women is like. Endless shy giggles, and how many children do I have, and why am I not in purdah? You should take Bhaskar along, not me. He's very enthusiastic to go and count all those heads. And he can help with the children's vote,' she added with a laugh.

Maan laughed too. 'All right, I'll take him along. But why can't you give us a hand as well? Does Kedarnath's mother really object so much?' He shelled a pea-pod, and thumbed the peas into his mouth. 'Delicious.'

'Maan,' said Veena reproachfully, with an imperceptible nod towards her mother, 'Pran and Savita are in Calcutta and will be there till the eighth of January. Who is left here in Brahmpur?'

Mrs Mahesh Kapoor said immediately: 'Don't use me as an excuse, Veena. I can take care of myself. You should help your father get out the vote.'

'Well, maybe in a week or two you can take care of yourself – and Pran will be back. But right now I'm not going. Even Savita's mother didn't leave for Calcutta when her father was unwell. Anyway, everything looks in very good shape in the constituency.'

'Yes, it does,' agreed Maan. 'But the real reason you're not going is that you're too lazy. That is what married life does to people.'

'Lazy!' said Veena, laughing. 'The pot calling the snow-flake black,' she added in English. 'And I notice you're eating more than you're shelling,' she continued in Hindi.

'So I am,' said Maan, surprised. 'But they're so fresh and sweet.'

'Have some more, son,' said Mrs Mahesh Kapoor. 'Don't listen to her.'

'Maan should learn to exercise some self-restraint,' said Veena.

'Should I?' asked Maan, popping a few more peas into his mouth. 'I can't resist delicious things.'

'Is that the disease or the diagnosis?' asked his sister.

'I am a changed man,' said Maan. 'Even Baoji's been paying me compliments.'

'I'll believe that when I hear one,' said Veena, popping a few more peas into her brother's mouth.

17.11

THAT evening Maan strolled along to Saeeda Bai's house. He had had a hair-cut and a bath. It was a cool evening, so he wore a bundi over his kurta; in a pocket of his bundi was a half-bottle of whisky; and on his head was a starched white cap worked in white.

It was good to be back. The mud roads of the country had their charms, no doubt, but he was a town man. He liked the city – at least this city. And he liked streets – at least this street, the street where Saeeda Bai's house stood – and of that house, he particularly liked Saeeda Bai's two rooms. And of those two rooms, he particularly liked the inner one.

A little after eight o'clock, he arrived at the gate, waved familiarly to the watchman, and was allowed in. Bibbo met him at the door, looked surprised to see him, and walked him up to Saeeda Bai's room. Maan's heart leapt up when he saw that Saeeda Bai was reading from the book that he had given her, the illustrated *Works of Ghalib*. She looked charming, her pale neck and shoulders leaning forward, the book in her hand, a bowl of fruit and a small bowl of water to her left, her harmonium to her right. The room was redolent with attar of roses. Beauty, fragrance, music, food, poetry, and a source of intoxication in his pocket: ah, Maan felt, as their eyes met, this is what happiness means.

She too looked surprised to see him, and Maan began to wonder if the watchman had admitted him by mistake. But she looked down quickly at the book, and idly turned a few pages.

'Come, Dagh Sahib, come, sit down, what time is it?'

'Just after eight, Saeeda Begum, but the year changed some days ago.'

'I was aware of it,' said Saeeda Bai, smiling. 'It will be an interesting year.'

'What makes you say that?' asked Maan. 'Last year was interesting enough for me.' He put out his hand and held hers. Then he kissed her shoulder. Saeeda Bai neither resisted nor responded.

Maan looked hurt. 'Is something the matter?' he said.

'Nothing, Dagh Sahib, that you can help me with. Do you remember what I said the last time we met?'

'I remember something of it,' said Maan – but all he could remember was the sense of the conversation, not the exact words: her fears for Tasneem, her look of vulnerability.

'Anyway,' said Saeeda Bai, changing the subject. 'I do not have much time with you this evening. I am expecting someone in a little while. God knows, I should have been reading the Quran, not Ghalib, but who knows what one will do from one moment to the next.'

'I met Rasheed's family,' said Maan, who was agitated at the thought that he would have no time with her this evening, and wanted to get his unpleasant duty of informing Saeeda Bai over and done with as soon as possible.

'Yes?' said Saeeda Bai almost indifferently.

'They don't know anything, it seems to me, about what is going on in his head,' said Maan. 'Nor do they care. All they are concerned about is that his politics shouldn't cause them any economic loss. That is all. His wife –'

Maan stopped. Saeeda Bai raised her head, and said: 'Yes, yes, I've known that he has one wife already. And you know I know. But I am not interested in all this. Forgive me, I must now ask you to go.'

'Saeeda – but tell me why –'

Saeeda Bai looked down at the book and started turning its pages in a distracted manner.

'A page is torn,' said Maan.

'Yes,' replied Saeeda Bai absently. 'I should have it mended better.'

'Let me do it for you,' said Maan. 'I can have it done. How did it get torn?'

'Dagh Sahib, do you not see what state I am in? I cannot answer questions. I was reading your book when you came in. Why do you not believe that I was thinking of you?'

'Saeeda,' said Maan helplessly. 'I can believe it. But what use is it to me that you should merely think of me when I am not here? I can see that you are distressed by something. But by what? Why don't you tell me? I don't understand it. I can't understand it – and I want to help you. Is there someone else you are seeing?' he said, suddenly sensing that her agitation could be caused by excitement as much as by distress. 'Is that it? Is that it?'

'Dagh Sahib,' said Saeeda Bai in a quiet, exhausted tone. 'This would not matter to you if you had more sakis than one. I told you that the last time.'

'I don't remember what you said the last time,' said Maan, feeling a rush of jealousy. 'Don't tell me how many sakis I should have. You mean everything to me. I don't care about what was said the last time. I want to know why I am being turned away by you this time with so little attempt at courtesy –' He paused, overcome, then looked at her, breathing hard. 'Why did you say this year would be so interesting for you? Why did you say that? What has happened since I've been away?'

Saeeda Bai leaned her head slightly at an angle. 'Oh, that?' she smiled, in a slightly mocking, even self-mocking, manner. 'Fifty-two is the number of a pack of cards. Things are complete. Fate is bound to have shuffled and dealt things in a comprehensive way this year. So far I have lifted the edge of only two cards that have fallen to me, a Queen and a Jack: a Begum and a Ghulam.'

'Of what suit?' asked Maan, shaking his head. Ghulam could mean either a young man or a slave. 'Are they of the same suit or are they antagonistic?'

'Paan, perhaps,' said Saeeda Bai, naming hearts. 'At any

rate I can see that they are both red. I can't see any more. But I do not care for this conversation.'

'Nor do I,' said Maan, angrily. 'At least there is no room this year for a joker in the pack.'

Suddenly Saeeda Bai started laughing in a desperate way. Then she covered her face with her hands. 'Now it is up to you to think what you like. Think that I too have gone mad. It is beyond me to say what is the matter.' Even before she uncovered her face Maan could tell that she was crying.

'Saeeda Begum – Saeeda – I am sorry –'

'Do not apologize. This is the easiest part of the night for me. I dread what is to come.'

'Is it the Raja of Marh?' said Maan.

'The Raja of Marh?' said Saeeda Bai softly, her eyes falling on the book. 'Yes, yes, perhaps. Please leave me.' The bowl of fruit was full of apples, pears, oranges, and even some unseasonal, wrinkled grapes. Impulsively she broke off a small bunch and gave them to Maan. 'This will nourish you better than what comes of it,' she said.

Maan put a grape in his mouth without thinking, then suddenly recalled eating peas that morning at Prem Nivas. For some reason, this made him furious. He crushed the rest of the grapes in his hand and dropped them into the bowl of water. His face red, he got up, stepped outside the threshold, put on his jutis, and walked downstairs. There he paused, and covered his face with his hands. Finally he went out and began walking homewards. But he had not gone a hundred yards when he stopped once more. He leaned against a huge tamarind tree and looked back towards Saeeda Bai's house.

17.12

HE took the bottle of whisky out of his pocket and began to drink. He felt as if his heart had been crushed. Every night for a fortnight he had thought of her. Every morning when he had woken up, whether at the Fort or in Salimpur,

326

he had lingered for a few minutes in bed, imagining that she was with him. No doubt his dreams too had been of her. And now, after these fifteen days away, she had granted him fifteen minutes of her time, and as good as given him to understand that someone else mattered far more to her than he ever could. But surely not the gross Raja of Marh.

Yet there was so much in her talk that he could not even remotely understand, even though Saeeda Bai at the best of times very rarely spoke except by indirection. If he himself was the slave or the young man whom she was referring to, what then? What did she mean by dread? Who would be coming to the house? Where did the Raja of Marh fit into all this? And what about Rasheed? By now Maan had drunk so much that he hardly cared what he did. He walked halfway back to her house and stood where he could not be observed by the watchman, but could see if anyone went in.

Though it was not late, the street was almost deserted; but then this was a quiet part of town. A car or two and a few bicycles and tongas passed along the road, and now and then a pedestrian walked by. An owl hooted calmly overhead. Maan stood there for half an hour. No car or tonga halted near her house. No one entered and no one left. Occasionally the watchman strolled up and down outside, or knocked the base of his spear hard against the pavement, or stamped his feet against the cold. A variable mist started to descend, obscuring his view from time to time. Maan began to feel that there was no one – no Bilgrami, no Raja, no Rasheed, no mysterious Other – whom Saeeda Bai was to meet. It was simply that she wanted to have nothing further to do with him. She had tired of him. He no longer meant anything to her.

Another pedestrian approached Saeeda Bai's house from the opposite direction, stopped by the gate, and was immediately admitted. Maan's blood ran cold with shock. At first he had been too far away to see him clearly. Then the mist had cleared slightly, and he thought that he recognized Firoz.

Maan stared. The door opened, and the man entered. Was it Firoz? It looked like him from this distance. His bearing was the same as that of his friend. He was carrying a walking-stick, but with a young man's air. His gait was that of Firoz. Gripped by disbelief and misery Maan started forward, then stopped. Surely, surely, it could not be Firoz.

And even if it were Firoz, could he not be visiting the younger sister whom he appeared to be so fascinated by? Surely someone else would be visiting Saeeda Bai in due course. But the minutes passed, and no one else stopped by the house. And Maan realized that whoever had entered would never have been admitted to meet Tasneem. It could only be Saeeda Bai whom he was going to see. Again Maan covered his face with his hands.

He had drunk more than half his bottle of whisky. He was unaware of the cold, unaware of what he was doing. He wanted to go to the door again, to enter and to find out who it was who had gone in and for what purpose. It cannot be Firoz, he thought to himself. And yet the man had looked so similar from this distance. The mist, the streetlights, the sudden illumination when the door opened: Maan tried to visualize once again what had happened just a few minutes before. But nothing became clearer.

No one else went in. Nor did anyone come out. After half an hour, Maan could bear it no longer. He walked across the street. When he got to the gate he blurted out to the watchman the first thing that came into his head: 'The Nawabzada asked me to bring his wallet in to him – and to take him a message.'

The watchman was startled, but, hearing Maan mention Firoz's title, he knocked at the door. Maan walked in without waiting for Bibbo to admit him. 'It's urgent,' he explained to the watchman. 'Has the Nawabzada arrived yet?'

'Yes, Kapoor Sahib, he went in some time ago. But can't I –?'

'No. I must deliver this personally,' said Maan.

He walked up the stairs, not glancing at the mirror. If he

had, he would have been shocked by the expression on his own face. Perhaps that glance in the mirror would have averted everything that was to happen.

There were no shoes outside the door. Saeeda Bai was alone in her room. She was praying.

'Get up,' said Maan.

She turned towards him and stood up, her face white. 'How dare you?' she began. 'Who let you in? Take your shoes off in my room.'

'Where is he?' said Maan in a low voice.

'Who –' said Saeeda Bai, her voice trembling with anger. 'The parakeet? His cage is covered up, as you can see.'

Maan looked quickly around the room. He noticed Firoz's stick in the corner and was seized by a fit of rage. Without bothering to reply, he opened the bedroom door. There was no one inside.

'Get out!' said Saeeda Bai. 'How dare you think – never come here again – get out, before I call Bibbo –'

'Where is Firoz?'

'He hasn't been here.'

Maan looked at the walking-stick. Saeeda Bai's eyes followed his.

'He's gone,' she whispered, agitated and suddenly fearful.

'Why did he come? To meet your sister? Is it your sister he is in love with?'

Suddenly, Saeeda Bai began to laugh as if what he had said was both bizarre and hilarious.

Maan could not stand it. He gripped her by the shoulders and began to shake her. She looked at him, terrified by the expression of fury in his eyes – but she could still not help her grotesque, mocking laughter.

'Why are you laughing? Stop it – stop it –' cried Maan. 'Tell me he came to see your sister –'

'No –' Saeeda Bai gasped out.

'He came to see you about your sister –'

'My sister! My sister!' Saeeda Bai laughed in Maan's face as if he had made some insane joke – 'it is not my *sister* he is in love with – it is not *my* sister he is in love with —' She tried to push Maan violently away. They fell onto the floor and Saeeda Bai screamed as Maan's hands went round her throat. The water in the bowl spilled over. The fruit bowl overturned. Maan noticed none of this. His mind was red with rage. The woman he loved had betrayed him with his friend, and now she was taking delight in mocking his love and his misery.

His hands tightened around her throat. 'I knew it,' he said. 'Tell me where he is. He's still here. Where is he hiding?'

'Dagh Sahib —' gasped Saeeda Bai.

'Where is he?'

'Help —'

'Where is he?'

Saeeda Bai reached with her right hand for the fruit knife, but Maan let go of her throat and wrenched it out of her hand.

They were still on the floor. He stared at the knife.

Saeeda Bai started shrieking for help. From below there was the sound of a door opening, frightened voices, people rushing upstairs. Maan got up. Firoz was the first to reach the door. Bibbo was behind him.

'Maan —' said Firoz, taking in the scene in an instant. Saeeda Bai was resting her head on a pillow and holding her throat with both her hands. She was gasping, and her chest was heaving. Horrible retching sounds were coming from her throat.

Maan looked at Firoz's guilty and agitated face and knew instantly that the worst was true. Again he was seized with blind rage.

'Look here, Maan,' said Firoz, moving gradually towards him. 'What is the matter? Let's talk this over — easy does it —'

Suddenly he lunged forward and tried to disarm Maan. But Maan was too quick for him. Firoz clutched at his stomach. Blood began to stain his waistcoat, and he stumbled onto the floor. He cried out in pain. Blood fell on the white sheet spread on the floor. Maan looked at it like a stupefied ox, then at the knife still in his hands.

For a minute no one said a word. There was no sound apart from Saeeda Bai's attempts to breathe, and Firoz's stifled cries of pain, and Maan's long and bitter sobs.

'Put it down on the table,' said Bibbo quietly.

Maan put the knife down, and knelt by Firoz.

'Leave at once,' said Bibbo.

'But a doctor –'

'Leave at once. We will manage everything. Leave Brahmpur. You have not been to this house this evening. Go.'

'Firoz –'

Firoz nodded.

'Why?' said Maan in a broken voice.

'Go – quick –' said Firoz.

'What have I done to you? What have I done?'

'Quick –'

Maan took one final look around the room and rushed downstairs and out. The watchman was pacing up and down outside the outer gate. He had heard nothing to agitate him. He saw Maan's face and said: 'What is the matter, Sahib?'

Maan did not reply.

'Is something the matter? I heard voices – do they want me?'

'What?' said Maan.

'Do they want me, Sahib? Inside, I mean.'

'Want? No, no – goodnight.'

'Goodnight, Sahib,' said the watchman. He stamped his feet a few times as Maan hurried away into the mist.

17.13

TASNEEM appeared at the door of Saeeda Bai's room.

'What is the matter, Apa? Oh my God –' she cried, her eyes taking in the horrible scene: blood, crushed fruit, spilled water, her sister leaning, gasping against the couch, Firoz lying wounded on the floor, the knife on the table.

Firoz saw her and felt that he was about to pass out.

Then the true horror of all that had happened that evening swam into his mind.

'I am going,' he said, to no one in particular.

Saeeda Bai was incapable of speaking. Bibbo said: 'The Nawabzada cannot leave like this. He is badly injured. He needs a doctor.'

Firoz got up with an effort. The pain made him gasp. He looked around the room and shuddered. He saw his walking-stick.

'Bibbo, give me the stick.'

'The Nawabzada must not —'

'The stick.'

She handed it to him.

'Take care of your mistress. Your mistresses,' he added bitterly.

'Let me help you down the stairs,' said Tasneem.

Firoz stared into her face with a glazed look. 'No,' he said gently.

'You need help,' she said, her lips trembling.

'No!' he cried with sudden vehemence.

Bibbo saw that Firoz was determined to have his way. 'Begum Sahiba — that shawl?' she asked. Saeeda Bai nodded, and Bibbo put a shawl around Firoz's shoulders. She walked downstairs with him to the door. It was still misty outside. Firoz leaned against his stick, hunched forward like an old man. He kept saying to himself: 'I cannot stay here. I cannot stay here.'

Bibbo said to the watchman: 'Go immediately to Dr Bilgrami's. Tell him that the Begum Sahiba and another person have been taken ill.' The watchman stared at Firoz.

'Go. Go quickly, you dolt —' said Bibbo with authority.

The watchman stomped off.

Firoz made to move towards the gate. The night was thick with mist.

'The Nawabzada is in no state to go — please, please wait here — look at the night and at yourself. I have called the doctor. He will be here any minute,' cried Bibbo, holding him back.

'You cannot go —' This time it was Tasneem, who had

run downstairs to prevent him from leaving. She was standing – for the first time in her life – at the open door, not daring, however, to go further. Had there been no fog she would have been visible from the road.

He was unable to control his tears of pain and shock as he walked along.

Why Maan had stabbed him – what had happened between Maan and Saeeda Bai – he could not even think. But nothing was worse than what had happened before. Saeeda Bai had intercepted one of his letters, and had summoned him. Curtly she had forbidden him to write to Tasneem, to have anything to do with her. When he had protested, she had told him the truth.

'Tasneem is not my sister,' she had said as factually as possible. 'She is yours.'

Firoz had stared at her in horror. 'Yes,' Saeeda Bai had continued. 'She is my daughter, God forgive me.'

Firoz had shaken his head.

'And God forgive your father,' she had continued. 'Now go in peace. I must say my prayers.'

Firoz, speechless with disgust and torn between belief and disbelief, had left her room. Downstairs he told Bibbo he had to see Tasneem.

'No –' said Bibbo. 'No – how can the Nawabzada presume –'

'You have known all along,' he said to her, clutching her arm.

'Known what?' protested Bibbo, shaking him off.

'If you haven't known it, it can't be true,' said Firoz. 'It is a cruel lie. It cannot be true.'

'True? True?' said Bibbo. 'The Nawabzada has taken leave of his senses.'

'I must see Tasneem. I must see her,' Firoz had cried in desperation.

Hearing her name, Tasneem had come out of her room and looked at him. He had gone up to her and stared at her face till tears of embarrassment and misery ran down her cheeks.

'What is the matter? Why is the Nawabzada looking at

me in this manner?' she asked Bibbo, turning her face away.

'Go back to your room or your sister will be furious with you,' said Bibbo. Tasneem had turned back.

'I must talk with you,' said Firoz, following Bibbo into another room.

'Then keep your voice low,' said Bibbo curtly. But his questions had been so wild and strange – and so full of guilt and shame – that she had looked at him in real perplexity. 'I can see no resemblance to anyone – to Zainab, to my father –' he had said. She had still been trying to make sense of his words when they had heard the sounds upstairs – of someone falling, and Saeeda Bai crying for help.

The night had become bitterly cold. Firoz stopped, and walked, and stopped again. The mist thinned out here and there, then wound itself around him. The shawl was soaked in blood. His thoughts, his pain, the mist all dispersed and concentrated about him as if at random. His hands were wet with blood where he had clutched his side. The walking-stick slipped in his hand. He did not know if he would be able to get home like this. And if he got home, he thought, how could he bear to look at his father's old and beloved face?

He had hardly walked a hundred yards when he felt that he would not be able to make it. The loss of blood, the physical pain, and the terrible thoughts that oppressed his mind had brought him almost to collapse. A tonga loomed up out of the mist. He raised his stick and tried to hail it, and collapsed onto the pavement.

17.14

IT was a quiet night at the Pasand Bagh Police Station, and the station house officer, who was a Sub-Inspector, was yawning, writing up reports, drinking tea, and cracking jokes with his subordinates.

'This is a very subtle one, Hemraj, so listen carefully,' he addressed a writer-constable who was making an entry in the daily diary. 'Two masters each said that their servant was stupider than the other's. So they had a bet. One summoned his servant and said: "Budhu Ram, there's a Buick for sale in a shop on Nabiganj. Here is ten rupees. Go and buy it for me." So Budhu Ram took the ten rupees and went out.'

A couple of the constables burst out laughing, and the Sub-Inspector shut them up. 'I have hardly begun telling you the joke and you idiots start braying. Shut up and listen.... So the other master said: "You may think that's stupid, but my servant, Ullu Chand, is even stupider. I'll prove it." He summoned Ullu Chand and said: "Now look here, Ullu Chand, I want you to go to the Subzipore Club and see if I'm there. It's urgent." Ullu Chand immediately went off to do as he was told.'

The constables started laughing uncontrollably. 'See if I'm there –' one said, rolling about. 'See if I'm there.'

'Shut up, shut up,' said the Sub-Inspector. 'I haven't finished.' The constables promptly shut up. The Sub-Inspector cleared his throat. 'On the way, one servant met the other and said –'

A bewildered tonga-wallah entered the room, and mumbled, in obvious distress: 'Daroga Sahib –'

'Oh, shut up, shut up,' said the Sub-Inspector genially. 'So one servant met the other and said: "I say, Ullu Chand, my master is a complete idiot. He gave me ten rupees and told me to buy a Buick. But doesn't he know that today is Sunday and the shops are closed?"'

At this point everyone burst out laughing, including the Sub-Inspector himself. But he hadn't finished yet, and, when the laughter had died down, he continued:

'And the other servant said: "Well, that may be stupid, Budhu Ram, but it's nothing compared to the idiocy of my master. He asked me to find out urgently if he was at the club. But if it was so urgent, why didn't he simply go to the other room and use the telephone?"'

At this the entire room resounded with hoots and shrieks of laughter, and the Sub-Inspector, very pleased, took a loud sip of tea, some of which wet his moustache. 'Yes, what do you want?' he said, noticing the tonga-wallah, who appeared to be trembling.

'Daroga Sahib, there's a body lying on the pavement on Cornwallis Road.'

'It's a bad night. Must be some poor fellow who's succumbed to the cold,' said the Inspector. 'But Cornwallis Road?'

'He's alive,' said the tonga-wallah. 'He tried to hail me, then collapsed. He's covered in blood. I think he's been stabbed. He looks as if he's from a good family. I didn't know whether to leave him or to bring him – to go to the hospital or the police. Please come quickly. Did I do the right thing?'

'You idiot!' cried the Sub-Inspector. 'You've been standing here all this while. Why didn't you speak earlier?' He addressed the others: 'Get some bandages. And you, Hemraj, phone the government doctor at the night clinic. Get the police kit together quickly, and bring a couple of extra torches. And you' – he addressed the tonga-wallah – 'come with us and show us where he's lying.'

'Did I do the right thing?' asked the tonga-wallah fearfully.

'Yes, yes, yes – you didn't disturb him, did you?'

'No, Daroga Sahib, I just turned him over to see – to see, well, if he was alive.'

'For God's sake, what is taking you so long?' said the Sub-Inspector impatiently to his subordinates. 'Come on. How far is it from here?'

'Just two minutes away.'

'Then we'll go in your tonga. Hemraj, use the police jeep to get the doctor. Don't fill in more than a line in the daily diary. I'll do the rest later. If he's still alive maybe I'll get an FIR from him rather than from the tonga-wallah. I'm taking Bihari with me. The other Assistant Sub-Inspector will handle the station while I'm gone.'

Within two minutes they had got to Firoz. He was semi-conscious and still bleeding. It was immediately clear to the Sub-Inspector that if his life was to be saved there was no question of first aid and bandages. Time was of the essence. He should be moved to the hospital forthwith.

'Bihari, when the doctor comes, tell him to hurry to the Civil Hospital. We're going there by tonga. Yes, give me the bandages – I'll see what I can do on the way to stop the blood. Oh, yes, follow the blood if you can: keep two torches, I'll take one. I'll take statements from the tonga-wallah and the injured man. Check the walking-stick for a hidden blade. See if the weapon's lying around, and so on. His wallet is on him – it doesn't seem as if he's been robbed. But maybe someone tried to rob him and he managed to get away. On Cornwallis Road!' The Sub-Inspector shook his head, licked the right side of his moustache, and wondered what Brahmpur was coming to.

They lifted Firoz into the tonga and got in themselves, and it clopped off into the mist. The Sub-Inspector shone his torch carefully at Firoz's face. Even with the wavering torchlight shining on his pale and distorted features, Firoz's face looked familiar. The Inspector noticed that he was wearing a woman's shawl and frowned. Then he opened his wallet, and saw the name and address on his driving licence; and his frown became one of real concern. He shook his head slowly. This case was going to mean trouble and would have to be handled carefully. As soon as they got to the hospital and put Firoz in the hands of the emergency ward staff, the Sub-Inspector telephoned the Superintendent of Police, who himself undertook to inform Baitar House.

17.15

THE emergency ward – which had recently been renamed the casualty department – represented a scene of organized chaos. A woman, clutching her stomach, was screaming in pain in a corner. Two men were brought in with head injuries from a lorry accident – they were still living, but there was no hope for them. A few people had minor cuts of one kind or another, bleeding to a greater or lesser degree.

Two young house surgeons examined Firoz. The Sub-Inspector filled them in on the background: where he had been found, and his name and address.

'This must be Dr Imtiaz Khan's brother,' said one of them. 'Has the police informed him? We would like to have him on hand, especially if permission is needed for an operation. He works at the Prince of Wales College Hospital.'

The Sub-Inspector told them that the SP was getting in touch with Baitar House. Meanwhile, could he speak to the patient? He needed to file a First Information Report.

'Not now, not now,' said the doctors. They checked Firoz's pulse, which was shallow and irregular, his blood pressure, which was low, his respiration, which was rather fast, and the responses of his pupils, which were normal. He was pale and his forehead was clammy. He had lost a lot of blood and appeared to be in shock. He was still speaking a few words, but they were incoherent. The Sub-Inspector, who was an intelligent man, tried to make what sense of them he could. In particular he noted Saeeda Bai's name, the words 'Prem Nivas', and several agitated mentions of a sister or sisters. These might help him to discover what had happened.

He turned to the doctors. 'You mentioned he had a brother. Does he also have a sister?'

'Not that I know,' said one doctor, shortly.

'I believe he does,' said the other. 'But she doesn't live in Brahmpur. He's lost too much blood. Sister, get a drip ready. Normal saline.'

They removed Firoz's shawl and cut away part of his kurta and vest. All his clothes were covered with blood.

The policeman murmured: 'I'll have to get you to write a medical report.'

'I can't find a vein in the arm,' said one of the doctors, ignoring what the Sub-Inspector was saying. 'We'll have to cut down.' They cut a vein in Firoz's ankle, drew out a little blood, and inserted a drip. 'Sister, please take this to the lab for tests, and for grouping and matching. Pretty shawl, that. Dyeing doesn't improve it.'

A few minutes passed. Blood was still seeping from Firoz's wound, and his moments of speech, incoherent as they were, were becoming rarer. He appeared to be sinking into deeper shock.

'There's a little dirt around the wound,' said one of the house surgeons. 'We'd better give him an anti-tetanus shot.' He turned to the policeman. 'Did you recover the weapon? How long was it? Was it rusty at all?'

'We haven't recovered the weapon.'

'Sister, some iodine and cetavlon – please swab the area around the wound.' He turned to his colleague. 'There's blood in the mouth. It's got to be internal injury: stomach possibly, or upper intestine. We can't handle this. Better call the registrar and alert the senior surgeon on duty. And, Sister, please get the lab to hurry up with that blood report, especially the haemoglobin count.'

The senior surgeon, when he came down, took one look at Firoz and at the lab report and said: 'We will have to do an exploratory laparotomy immediately.'

'I need to get an FIR –' said the Sub-Inspector aggressively, nudging his moustache with the back of his fist. The First Information Report was often the most important document in the case, and it was good to have a solid one, preferably from the victim's mouth.

The senior surgeon looked at him in cold incredulity. 'This man is not capable of speech now, nor will he be capable of speech for another twelve hours once he is under anaesthetic. And even after that – assuming he lives – you will not be allowed to examine him for at least twenty-four hours. Get your FIR from whoever found him. Or else wait. And, if you wish, hope.'

The Sub-Inspector was used to the rudeness of doctors, having come into contact – as had most policemen in Brahmpur at one time or other – with Dr Kishen Chand Seth. He took no offence. He knew that doctors and policemen viewed 'cases' in a different light. Besides, he was a realist. He had told the tonga-wallah to wait outside. Now that he knew that Firoz would not be able to speak further, he decided that he would get his First Information Report from the man who had in fact given him his first information.

'Well, thank you, Doctor Sahib, for the advice,' said the Sub-Inspector. 'If the police doctor comes, could he examine the patient for the medical report?'

'We'll do all that ourselves,' said the senior surgeon, unmollified. 'The patient has to be saved, not endlessly examined. Leave the forms here.' He said to the Sister: 'Who is the anaesthetist on duty? Dr Askari? The patient is in shock, so we'd better use atropine for pre-anaesthetic. We'll wheel him into the theatre now. Who did the cut down procedure?'

'I did, Sir,' said one of the house surgeons proudly.

'Untidy job,' said the senior surgeon bluntly. 'Has Dr Khan come yet? Or the Nawab Sahib? We need signatures on those permissions.'

Neither Firoz's brother nor father had yet arrived.

'Well, we can't wait,' said the senior surgeon. And Firoz was wheeled through the corridors of the Civil Hospital into the operating theatre.

The Nawab Sahib and Imtiaz arrived too late to see him being wheeled in. The Nawab Sahib was virtually in a state of shock himself.

'Let me see him,' he said to Imtiaz.

Imtiaz put his arm around his father's shoulder, and said: 'Abba-jaan, that's not possible. He'll be all right, I know. Bhatia is doing the operation. Askari is the anaesthetist. They're both very good.'

'Who would want to do this to Firoz?' said the old man.

Imtiaz shrugged. His face was grim. 'He didn't tell you where he was going this evening, did he?' he asked his father.

'No,' said the Nawab Sahib. After a pause he said, 'But Maan's in town. He might know.'

'All in good time, Abba-jaan. Don't agitate yourself.'

'On Cornwallis Road,' said the Nawab Sahib incredulously. Then he covered his face with his hands and started weeping softly. After a while he said: 'We should tell Zainab.'

'All in good time, Abba-jaan, all in good time. Let's wait till the operation is over and we know how things have gone.'

It was almost midnight. The two of them remained outside the operating theatre. The smell of the hospital began to panic the Nawab Sahib. Occasionally a colleague would walk past and greet Imtiaz or commiserate with him and his father. The news of the attack on Firoz must have got around, because a reporter from the *Brahmpur Chronicle* turned up at just after midnight. Imtiaz was tempted to tell him to buzz off, but decided to answer a few short questions instead. The more publicity Firoz got, he decided, the more likely it was that someone who may have noticed something would come forward with a clue.

At about one o'clock, the doctors emerged from the operating theatre. They looked tired. It was impossible to read Dr Bhatia's expression. But when he saw Imtiaz, he drew a deep breath and said:

'It's good to see you, Dr Khan. I hope it will be all right. He was in severe shock when we operated, but we couldn't wait. And it's a good thing we didn't. We did the usual laparotomy. There was severe laceration of the small intestine, and we had to perform several anastomoses, apart from cleaning out the abdominal cavity. That's why it took us so long.' He turned to the Nawab Sahib. 'Your handsome son is now the proud possessor of a handsome seven-inch scar. I hope he will be all right. I am sorry we couldn't wait for your permission to anaesthetize and operate.'

'May I —' began the Nawab Sahib.

'What about —' said Imtiaz simultaneously.

'What about what?' said Bhatia to Imtiaz.

'What about the danger of sepsis, of peritonitis?'

'Well, let us pray that that has been averted. There was quite a mess inside. But we will keep a close watch. We

341

have given him penicillin. I am sorry, Nawab Sahib, what were you about to say?'

'May I speak to him?' said the old man falteringly. 'I know he will want to speak to me.'

Dr Bhatia smiled. 'Well, he is still under chloroform. If he does say something, you may not be able to make much sense of it. But you might find it interesting. Indeed, people have no idea what interesting things they say under anaesthesia. Your son kept talking about his sister.'

'Imtiaz, you must call Zainab,' said the Nawab Sahib.

'I'll do that at once, Abba. Dr Bhatia, we cannot thank you enough.'

'Not at all, not at all. I only hope they get whoever did this. A single incision, the work of a second, and I don't mind telling you, Dr Khan, if they hadn't brought him to us directly, we would not have been able to save him. Indeed –' He stopped.

'Indeed, what?' said Imtiaz sharply.

'Indeed, it's odd that what one person does in a second can take seven of us – and all this – three hours to undo.'

'What did he say?' said the Nawab Sahib to Imtiaz when Dr Bhatia had taken his leave. 'What did they do to Firoz?'

'Nothing very exciting, Abba,' said Imtiaz, attempting reassurance. 'They cut out the injured parts of his intestinal loops, and joined the healthy parts together again. But we have yards and yards of the stuff, so Firoz won't miss what he's lost.'

In the event, his reply sounded flippant, and far from reassuring to his father.

'So he's all right?' said the Nawab Sahib, searching Imtiaz's face.

Imtiaz paused, then said: 'His chances are good, Abba. There were no complications. The only concern now is infection, and we can deal with that much better now than we could just a few years ago. Don't worry. I am sure he will be well. Inshallah.'

THE Sub-Inspector would have followed up the trail of Firoz's words the next morning if it had not been the case that a trail of his blood led to within a few yards of Saeeda Bai's gate. When informed of this, he decided to act at once. Together with Bihari and another constable, he arrived at Saeeda Bai's door. The watchman, who had been questioned in a threatening manner by the policemen earlier, and who had himself been perplexed and worried by the events of the night, admitted that he had seen both the Nawabzada and Kapoor Sahib from Prem Nivas earlier in the evening, as well as Dr Bilgrami.

'We will need to speak with Saeeda Bai,' said the Sub-Inspector.

'Daroga Sahib, why not wait till morning?' suggested the watchman.

'Did you not hear me?' said the Sub-Inspector, smoothing his moustache like a movie villain.

The watchman knocked and waited. There was no reply. He rapped at the door a few times with the blunt end of his spear. Bibbo emerged, saw the police, shut the door promptly and latched it.

'Let us in at once,' said the Sub-Inspector, 'or we will break down the door. We have questions to ask you about a murder.'

Bibbo opened the door again. Her face was white. 'A murder?' she said.

'Well, an attempt at it. You know what we are talking about. It's pointless to deny it. The Nawab's son might have been dead by now but for our prompt action. For all we know he might be dead anyway. We want to talk with you.'

'I know nothing –'

'He was here this evening, and so was Kapoor.'

'Oh – Dagh Sahib,' said Bibbo, looking daggers at the watchman, who shrugged his shoulders.

'Is Saeeda Bai awake?'

'Saeeda Begum is taking her rest, as any respectable citizen of Brahmpur would be doing at this time of night.'

The Sub-Inspector laughed. 'As any respectable citizen –' Again he laughed, and the constables joined in. 'Wake her up. We have to speak with her here. Unless she would like to come down to the police station.'

Bibbo made a quick decision. She closed the door once again, and disappeared. About five minutes later, during which time the Sub-Inspector asked the watchman a few questions, she came out again.

'Saeeda Begum will see you upstairs. But she has a bad throat, and cannot speak.' Saeeda Bai's room was, as always, in impeccable order, with a clean white sheet laid out on the floor. There was no bowl of fruit, no fruit knife. The three khaki uniforms contrasted absurdly with the scent of attar of roses.

Saeeda Bai had dressed hastily in a green sari. Her throat was wrapped around with a dupatta. Her voice was a croak, and she tried to avoid speaking. Her smile was as charming as ever.

At first she denied that there had been any quarrel. But when the Sub-Inspector said that Firoz had mentioned Prem Nivas, and that his presence at Saeeda Bai's had been corroborated not only by the watchman, who had described his crippled bearing when he had emerged from the house, but also by the physical evidence of an irregular trail of blood, she saw that denial was useless. She agreed that there had been a fight.

'Where did it take place?'

'In this room.'

'Why is there no blood here?'

Saeeda Bai did not answer.

'What was the weapon?'

Saeeda Bai remained silent.

'Answer these questions, please. Or else come down to the police station and make your statement there. In any case, we will ask you to confirm these statements in writing tomorrow.'

'It was a fruit knife.'

'Where is it?'

'He took it with him.'

'Who did? The attacker or the victim?'

'Dagh Sahib,' she managed to croak out. Her hands went to her throat and she looked pleadingly at the policeman.

'What is all this about Prem Nivas?'

Bibbo intervened: 'Please, Sub-Inspector Sahib, Saeeda Begum can hardly speak. She has been singing so much, and the weather has been so bad these last few days, what with the dust and the mist, that her throat is very sore.'

'What is all this about Prem Nivas?' insisted the Sub-Inspector.

Saeeda Bai shook her head.

'That is where Kapoor lives, is it not?'

Saeeda Bai nodded.

'It is the Minister Sahib's house,' added Bibbo.

'And what is all this about a sister?' asked the Sub-Inspector.

Saeeda Bai's body went rigid for a moment, and she began to tremble. Bibbo gave her a sharp and puzzled glance. Saeeda Bai had turned away. Her shoulders were shaking, and she was crying. But she did not say a word.

'What is all this about a sister?' repeated the policeman with a yawn.

Saeeda Bai shook her head.

'Haven't you had enough?' cried Bibbo. 'Haven't you had enough of torturing Saeeda Begum? Why can't this wait till morning? We will complain to the SP about this. Disturbing decent and respectable citizens —'

The Sub-Inspector did not mention that the SP had told him to treat this case like any other, but with greater urgency and dispatch. Nor did he make a sarcastic comment, though it did come to his mind, about decent and respectable citizens stabbing each other in their salons.

But perhaps this specific line of questioning could wait till morning, he thought. Even if matters were not entirely clear, it now was obvious enough to him that Maan Kapoor, the younger son of Mahesh Kapoor, had perpetrated the attack on the Nawabzada. But the Sub-Inspector was in two minds about whether to attempt to arrest him tonight. On the one hand, Prem Nivas, like Baitar House, was one of the great houses of Pasand Bagh, and Mahesh Kapoor one of the great names of the province. For a mere Sub-Inspector to think of rousing that august household in the early hours – and for such a purpose – could be interpreted as the greatest insolence and disrespect. But on the other hand the case was a most serious one. Even if the victim lived, the facts spoke of an attempt at culpable homicide, possibly attempted murder, and certainly grievous hurt.

He had already gone over several levels of authority to telephone the SP earlier in the night. He could not wake him up now to ask him for further instructions. An additional consideration occurred to the Sub-Inspector and determined his course of action. There was, in cases such as these, the danger of the criminal panicking and absconding. He decided to make the arrest at once.

17.17

'PANICKING and absconding' was in fact an accurate description of what Maan was doing. He was not at home. It was three o'clock in the morning when the household at Prem Nivas was woken up. Mahesh Kapoor had just come back to town, and was exhausted and irritable. At first he almost threw the police out of his house. But then his indignation turned to disbelief and finally to an appalled concern. He went to call Maan, but did not find him in his room. Mrs Mahesh Kapoor – equally horrified by what had happened to Firoz and fearful for her son – wandered through the house, not knowing what she would do if she found him. Her husband, however, was clear in his mind. He would cooperate with the police. He was surprised that a more senior officer had not come to his house to look for Maan, but the lateness of the hour and the suddenness of events must account for this.

He allowed the policeman to search Maan's room. The bed had not been slept in. There was no sign of anything remotely resembling a weapon.

'Have you found anything to interest you?' asked Mr Mahesh Kapoor. He kept thinking back to the searches and arrests that he and Prem Nivas had undergone in the time of the British.

The Sub-Inspector looked around as quickly as possible, apologized profusely, and left. 'If Mr Maan Kapoor does return, would Minister Sahib ask him to come to the Pasand Bagh Police Station? It would be better than the police coming here again,' he said. Mahesh Kapoor nodded. He was stunned, but did not appear to be anything but calm and sarcastic.

When they had left, he tried to console his wife with the thought that there had been some mistake. But Mrs Mahesh Kapoor was convinced that something disastrous had indeed happened – and that Maan, somehow, in his impetuousness, had caused it. She wanted to go at once to the Civil Hospital to see how Firoz was, but Mahesh Kapoor said that it would be best to wait till morning. Anyway, in her state of health, it was perhaps best if she did not see Firoz.

'If he comes home, we can't give him up,' she said.

'Don't be stupid,' said Mahesh Kapoor impatiently. Then he shook his head. 'You must go to bed now.'

'I won't be able to sleep.'

'Well, then, pray,' said Mahesh Kapoor impatiently. 'But keep yourself covered up. Your chest sounds bad. I will call a doctor in the morning.'

'Call a lawyer for him, not a doctor for me,' said Mrs Mahesh Kapoor, who was in tears. 'Can't we get him bail?'

'He hasn't been arrested yet,' said Mahesh Kapoor. Then a thought occurred to him. Though it was the middle of the night, he phoned up the middle Bespectacled Bannerji, and asked him about anticipatory bail. The lawyer was irked to be woken up at this amazing hour, but when he recognized Mahesh Kapoor's voice and heard an account of what the police said had happened, he did his best to explain matters.

'The problem, Kapoor Sahib, is that neither attempted murder nor grievous hurt with a dangerous weapon is a bailable offence. Is it, well, feasible, I mean, possible, that the charge might be considered to be ordinary grievous hurt? Or attempted culpable homicide? Those are bailable charges.'

'I see,' said Mahesh Kapoor.

'Or simple hurt?'

'No, I don't think that is possible.'

'You said a Sub-Inspector came to the house. Not even an Inspector. I am astonished.'

'Well, that's who it was.'

'Perhaps you should have a word with the Deputy Superintendent of Police or the SP – to clarify things.'

'Thank you for your explanations and, well, suggestion,' said Mahesh Kapoor disapprovingly. 'I am sorry to have woken you up at this hour.'

There was a pause at the other end. 'Not at all, not at all. Please feel free to call me up at any time.'

When he returned to his room Mahesh Kapoor found his wife praying, and he wished he could have prayed as well. He had always been very fond of his reckless son, but had only realized in these last few weeks how dearly he loved him.

Where are you? he thought, irritated and upset. Don't for God's sake do anything even more stupid than you've already done. At this thought his irritation disappeared, and was replaced with a profound anxiety both for his son and for the son of his friend.

17.18

MAAN had disappeared into the mist and reappeared at Brahmpur Railway Station. He knew he had to get out of Brahmpur. He was drunk, and he was not certain why he had to escape. But Firoz had told him to, and Bibbo had told him to. He pictured the scene in his mind. It was terrible. He could not believe what he had done. There had been a knife in his hand. And then his friend had been lying on the ground, wounded and bleeding. Wounded? But Firoz – Firoz – that he and Saeeda Bai – Maan relived the wretchedness of his feelings. What tormented him more than anything was the deception. 'It is not my sister he is in love with' – he thought of the near-hysterical words and realized how much Saeeda Bai must have been obsessed with Firoz. And again he chided himself for having been duped by his own love for her, and his love for his friend. Oh, what a fool I am, he thought. Oh, what a fool. He looked at his own clothes. There was no blood anywhere – not even on his bundi. He looked at his hands.

He bought a ticket to Banaras. He was almost weeping at the counter, and the clerk looked at him strangely.

On the train he offered the remnants of his bottle of whisky to a young man who happened to be awake in the compartment. The man shook his head. Maan looked at the sign near the alarm handle – *To Stop Train Pull Chain* – and began to tremble violently. By the time he got to Banaras, he had gone off to sleep. The young man woke him up and made sure he got off.

'I'll never forget your kindness – never –' said Maan, as the train steamed off.

Dawn was breaking. He walked along the ghats, singing a bhajan which his mother had taught him when he was ten years old. Then he went to the house where his fiancée lived, and started battering on the door. Those good people got alarmed. When they saw Maan there, they became very angry: they told him to go away and not to make an exhibition of himself. He next went to some people to whom he had lent money. They were not keen to see him at all. 'I've killed my friend,' Maan told them. 'Nonsense,' they replied.

'You'll see – it'll be in all the papers,' Maan said, distraught. 'Please hide me for a few days.'

They thought it a wonderful joke. 'What are you doing in Banaras?' they said. 'Are you here on business?'

'No,' said Maan.

Suddenly he could bear it no longer. He went to the local police station to give himself up.

'I was the man – I –' he said, hardly able to speak coherently.

The policemen humoured him for a while, then grew annoyed, and finally wondered whether there might not be some truth to what he was saying. They tried to telephone Brahmpur but could not get through. Then they sent an urgent telegram. 'Please wait,' they told Maan. 'We'll arrest you if we can.'

'Yes – yes –' said Maan. He was feeling very hungry. All he had had that day was a few cups of tea.

Finally the police got a message back that stated that the younger son of the Nawab Sahib of Baitar had been found seriously wounded on Cornwallis Road in Brahmpur, and that the principal suspect was Maan Kapoor. They looked at Maan as if he was mad, and arrested him. Then, in a few hours, they handcuffed him, and put him on the train back to Brahmpur under the escort of two constables.

'Why must you handcuff me? What have I done?' said Maan.

The station house officer was so tired of Maan, so annoyed with the needless work he had caused him, and so exasperated by his latest and most ludicrous protest that he wanted to beat him up. 'These are the regulations,' he said.

Maan got along better with the constables.

'I suppose you have to be very alert in case I escape,' he said. 'In case I break free and jump from the train.'

The constables laughed good-humouredly. 'You won't escape,' they said.

'How do you know?'

'Oh, you can't,' one of them said. 'We keep the key-holes on top, so that you can't open the handcuffs by striking them on – well, on those window-bars, for instance. But if you want to go to the bathroom, you should tell us.'

'We're very careful about our handcuffs,' said the other.

'Yes, we unlock them when they aren't in use. Otherwise the springs can get weak.'

'Can't have that,' said the other constable. 'Why did you give yourself up?' he asked curiously. 'Are you really the son of a Minister?'

Maan shook his head miserably. 'Yes, yes,' he said, and went off to sleep.

He dreamed of a vast and varicose Victoria, like the one in the portrait in the dining room of Baitar Fort. She was removing layer after layer of her regalia and calling to him enticingly. 'I have left something behind,' she was saying. 'I must go back.' The dream was unbearably disturbing. He woke up. Both the constables were asleep, although it was only early evening. When the train approached Brahmpur, they woke up by instinct, and delivered him into the hands of a party from the Pasand Bagh Police Station that was waiting at the platform.

'What will you do?' Maan asked his escorts.

'We'll take the next train back,' they replied.

'Look us up when you are next in Banaras,' one of them said.

Maan smiled at his new escorts, but they were much less inclined to humour him. The mustachioed Sub-Inspector, in particular, appeared very serious. When they got to the police station, he was given a thin grey blanket and put in the lock-up. It was a small, cold, filthy cell – a barred room with nothing but a few pieces of jute on the floor – no straw or mattress or pillow. It stank. In place of a toilet there was a large clay vessel in the corner. The other man in the cell looked tubercular and was drunk. His eyes were red. He stared in a hunted way at the police and, when the door clanged shut, at Maan.

The Sub-Inspector apologized to Maan curtly. 'You will have to stay here tonight,' he said. 'Tomorrow we will decide whether to remand you into judicial custody or not. If we get a proper statement from you we won't need to hold you here much longer.'

Maan sat down on the floor on a piece of jute matting and covered his head with his hands. For a second he imagined the scent of attar of roses, and he began to cry bitterly. More than anything he regretted that the last day had existed. If only he had remained ignorant, he thought. If only he had not known.

17.19

APART from Firoz, who was still not conscious, there were two people sitting in the room in the ward. One was an Assistant Sub-Inspector, who nodded off because there was nothing for him to take down; the police had insisted on, and the hospital had acquiesced in, his presence. The other was the Nawab Sahib. Imtiaz, because he was a doctor, was not prevented from coming in, and did so from time to time. But it was the Nawab Sahib who kept vigil by the bedside of his son. His servant, Ghulam Rasool, was given a pass so that he could bring the Nawab Sahib his food and a daily change of clothes. At night the Nawab Sahib slept on a couch in the same room; he insisted that it was not a problem for him. Even in winter he was used to sleeping with a single blanket. At the appointed hours, he spread a small rug on the floor and prayed.

On the first day Firoz was not allowed visitors even during visiting hours. Imtiaz did manage to get Zainab into the hospital; she was in purdah. When she saw Firoz – his face pale, his thick curly hair matted to his forehead, the tube of a saline drip stuck in the crook of his right arm (they had moved it from his ankle) – she was so upset that she decided that she would not bring her children to see him until he was better. Nor would it do them any good to see their grandfather so desperate and tearful. But agitated though she was, she was convinced that Firoz would get better. It was the usually optimistic Imtiaz who thought of all the possible complications and was worried.

Whoever came to relieve the policeman on duty usually brought some news for the Nawab Sahib from the police station. By now he knew that Firoz had not been stabbed by a stranger on the street, but that there had been a fight at Saeeda Bai's between Maan and Firoz, and that it was Maan who had nearly killed him. He had not believed this at first. But Maan had been arrested, and had confessed, and there was no question of not believing it now.

Sometimes he would get up and wipe Firoz's forehead with a towel. He would take his name, not so much to wake him as to reassure himself that the name still meant someone living. He remembered Firoz's childhood and thought of his wife, whose features were so like his. Even more than Zainab, Firoz was his link to her. Then he would begin to upbraid himself because he had not prevented Firoz from visiting Saeeda Bai's. He should have known from the experience of his own youth the attraction of places of that kind. But since his wife's death it had grown difficult to speak to his children; his library had more and more taken over his world. Only once had he ordered his secretary not to give Firoz an easy excuse to go to that place. If only, he thought, he had explicitly forbidden Firoz from going there. But what good would it have done? he reflected. In Maan's company he could well have gone regardless – that unthinking young man would have cared as little for the behests of his friend's father as for those of his own.

Now and then, listening to the doctors, and looking at Imtiaz's worried expression as he consulted with them, the Nawab Sahib felt that he was going to lose his son. Then he was overwhelmed with despair, and in bitterness of spirit wished every ill and pain on Maan – even on his family. He wished Maan to suffer as he had made his son suffer. He could not conceive what Firoz could possibly have done to have been stabbed with a knife by the friend who he thought had loved him.

When he prayed, he felt ashamed of these feelings, but he could not control them. That Maan had saved his son's life once seemed to be a fact so hazy, so distant from this present jeopardy, as to be almost irrelevant.

His own connection with Saeeda Bai too had sunk so far back in his consciousness that he did not think of her any more with reference to himself. He did not know where and how she fitted into these events. He felt only the dimmest anxiety in her regard, not the possibility of any revelation of the past. The present provision he made for her and for the daughter who she claimed was his own, this was a duty he accepted as a necessary act of decency, the partial expiation of an old and half-forgotten sin. And it was understood that for her part nothing would ever be said to anyone about what had happened two decades ago between a married man of almost forty and a girl of fifteen. The child who had later been born was never told that she was anything but Saeeda Bai's younger sister; or so the Nawab Sahib had been given to understand. Apart from Saeeda Bai herself, only her mother had truly known what had happened, and she was long since dead.

Firoz was now speaking a few words, and, incoherent as they were, for his father they were as miraculous as the words of someone who had returned from the dead. He pulled his chair closer to the bed and held Firoz's left hand. It was reassuringly warm. The policeman too became more alert. 'What is your son saying, Nawab Sahib?' he asked.

'I don't know,' said the Nawab Sahib, smiling. 'But it appears to me to be a good sign.'

'Something about his sister, I think,' said the policeman, his pencil poised over a new page.

'She was here before you took over,' said the Nawab Sahib. 'But, poor girl, she was distressed to see him in this state and did not stay long.'

'Tasneem –' It was Firoz's voice.

The Nawab Sahib heard and flinched. That was her name, the name of Saeeda Bai's daughter. He had spoken it with a terrifying tenderness.

The policeman continued to jot down whatever Firoz said.

The Nawab Sahib looked upwards in sudden fear. A lizard was climbing up the wall in an irregular wriggle, stopping and starting. He stared at it, transfixed.

'Tasneem –'

The Nawab Sahib sighed very slowly, as if the effort of

drawing and releasing breath had suddenly become painful. He released Firoz's hand, and unconsciously joined both his own together. Then he let them fall to his side.

He tried, in his fear, to piece the words together. His first feeling was that Firoz had somehow come to learn the truth, or some part of the truth. The thought caused him such pain that he had to lean back in his chair and close his eyes. He had longed for his son to open his eyes and to see him sitting by his side. But now the thought was terrifying. When his eyes open and he finds me sitting here, what will he say to me or I to him?

Then he thought of the policeman's dutiful note-taking. What would happen if ever anyone else pieced together the fragments of the truth? Or if they heard about the past from whoever had told Firoz about it? Things that had long been dead would rear themselves out of the grave; and matters so little known that they had almost lost their sense of existence would become the business of the world at large.

But perhaps no one had said anything at all. Perhaps Firoz did not know anything. The Nawab Sahib reflected that possibly in his own guilt he had merely conjoined a few innocent fragments into a frightening whole. Perhaps Firoz had merely met the girl at Saeeda Bai's.

'In the name of God, the Merciful, the Compassionate,' he began hurriedly.

'Praise belongs to God, the Lord of all Being,
  the All-Merciful, the All-Compassionate,
    the Master of the Day of Doom.

Thee only we serve; to Thee alone we pray for succour.
    Guide us in the straight path –'

The Nawab Sahib stopped. If it was in fact the case that Firoz did not know, that was no cause for relief at all. He would have to know. He would have to be told. The alternative was too terrible to imagine. And it was he who would have to tell him.

VARUN was reading the racing results in the *Statesman* with great interest. Uma, who was in Savita's arms, had grabbed a handful of his hair and was tugging at it, but this did not distract him. Her tongue was poking out between her lips.

'She will be a tell-tale when she grows up,' said Mrs Rupa Mehra. 'A little chugal-khor. Whom will we tell tales on? Whom will we tell tales on? Look at her little tongue.'

'Ow!' said Varun.

'Now, now, Uma,' said Savita in mild reproof. 'I find her very exhausting, Ma. She's so good-natured as a rule, but last night she kept on crying. Then this morning I discovered she was wet. How does one sort out the tantrums from the genuine tears?'

Mrs Rupa Mehra would hear nothing against Uma. 'There are some babies who cry several times in the night until they're two years old. Only their parents have a right to complain.'

Aparna said to her mother: 'I'm not a cry-baby, am I?'

'No, darling,' said Meenakshi, flipping through the *Illustrated London News*. 'Now play with the baby, why don't you?'

Meenakshi, whenever she gave the matter any thought, still could not quite figure out how Uma had succeeded in becoming so vigorous, born as she had been in a Brahmpur hospital that was, as Meenakshi saw it, simply seething with septicaemia.

Aparna turned her head down sideways, so that her two eyes were in a vertical line. This amused the baby, and she gave her quite a generous smile. Simultaneously she yanked Varun's hair once more.

'Cracknell's done it again,' murmured Varun to himself. 'Eastern Sea in the King George VI Cup. By just half a length.'

Uma grasped the paper and drew a handful of it towards herself. Varun tried to disengage her clasp. She latched onto one of his fingers.

'Did you bet on the winner?' asked Pran.

'No,' said Varun glumly. 'Need you ask? Everyone else has all the luck. My horse came in fourth, after Orcades and Fair Ray.'

'What peculiar names,' said Lata.

'Orcades is one of the Orient Line boats,' said Meenakshi lazily. 'I am so looking forward to going to England. I shall visit Amit's college at Oxford. And marry a duke.'

Aparna straightened her head. She wondered what a duke was.

Mrs Rupa Mehra did not care for Meenakshi's brand of idiocy. Her hardworking elder son was slaving himself to the bone to support the family, and in his absence his empty-headed wife was making jokes in poor taste. She was a bad influence on Lata.

'You're married already,' Mrs Rupa Mehra pointed out.

'Oh, yes, silly me,' said Meenakshi. She sighed. 'How I wish something exciting would happen. Nothing ever happens anywhere. And I was so looking forward to something happening in 1952.'

'Well, it's a leap year,' said Pran encouragingly.

Varun had reached the end of the racing results and turned to another inside page. Suddenly he exclaimed 'My God!' in such a shocked tone that everyone turned towards him.

'Pran, your brother's been arrested.'

Pran's first instinct was to consider this another joke in dubious taste, but there was something in Varun's voice that made him reach for the paper. Uma tried to grab it on the way, but Savita held her off. As Pran read the few lines dated 'Brahmpur. January 5' his face grew taut.

'What is it?' said Savita, Lata and Mrs Rupa Mehra almost simultaneously. Even Meenakshi raised a languid head in surprise.

Pran shook his head from side to side in agitation. He quickly and silently read about the attack on Firoz – and that he was still in critical condition. The news was worse than he could possibly have imagined. But no telephone call or telegram had come from Brahmpur to inform him or warn him or summon him. Perhaps his father was still campaigning in his constituency. No, thought Pran. He would have heard within hours and rushed back to Brahmpur. Or perhaps he had tried to get through by phone to Calcutta and failed.

'We will have to leave for Brahmpur immediately,' he said to Savita.

'But what on earth has happened, darling?' asked Savita, very alarmed. 'They haven't really arrested Maan? And what for? What does it say?'

Pran read the few lines out aloud, hit his forehead with the palm of his hand and said: 'The idiot – the poor, unthinking, crazy idiot! Poor Ammaji. Baoji has always said –' He stopped. 'Ma, Lata – you should both remain here –'

'Of course not, Pran,' said Lata, very concerned. 'We were due to return in a couple of days anyway. We'll all travel together. How terrible. Poor Maan – I'm sure there's an explanation – he couldn't have done it. There must be –'

Mrs Rupa Mehra, thinking first of Mrs Mahesh Kapoor and then of the Nawab Sahib, felt tears start to her eyes. But tears, she knew, were not helpful, and she controlled herself with an effort.

'We'll go directly to the station,' said Pran, 'and try to get a ticket on the Brahmpur Mail. We only have an hour-and-a-half to pack.'

Uma burst into a happy and meaningless chant. Meenakshi volunteered to hold her while they packed, and to call Arun at the office.

17.21

WHEN Firoz came round from the effect of the anaesthesia, his father was asleep. He was at first uncertain where he was – then he moved, and a stab of terrible pain pierced his side. He noticed the tube in his arm. He turned his head to the right. There was a khaki-clad policeman with a notebook beside him, asleep in a chair. The light of a dim lamp fell on his dreaming face.

Firoz bit his lip, and tried to understand this pain, this room, and why he was here. There had been a fight – Maan had had a knife – he had been stabbed. Tasneem came into it somewhere. Someone had covered him with a shawl. His walking-stick had been slippery with blood. Then a tonga had reared out of the mist. Everything else was dark.

But the sight of his father's face disturbed him greatly. He could not understand why. There had been something said by someone – what it was he could not for the moment remember – something about his father. His memory of what had happened was like the map of an unexplored continent – the edges were clearer than the core. Yet there was something at that core that he shrank away from even as he approached it. Thinking was an effort, and he kept lapsing into a quiet darkness and emerging once again into the present.

Lying flat on his back he noticed a lizard on the upper reaches of the wall in front of him – one of the permanent denizens of this ward. Firoz found himself wondering what it must be like to be a lizard – what strange surfaces it lived on, where it needed more effort to move in one direction than in another. He was still staring at the lizard, when he heard the policeman say, 'Ah, Sahib, you've woken up.'

'Yes,' Firoz heard himself say. 'I've woken up.'

'Do you feel well enough to make a statement?'

'Statement?' said Firoz.

'Yes,' said the policeman. 'Your assailant has been arrested.'

Firoz looked at the wall. 'I am tired,' he said. 'I think I'll sleep a little longer.'

The Nawab Sahib had woken at the sound of his son's voice. He looked silently at Firoz now, and Firoz at him. The father appeared to be pleading with the son, the son frowning in unhappy concentration. Then he closed his eyes for a while, leaving the Nawab Sahib baffled and disturbed.

'I think he will be able to speak clearly in an hour or so,' said the policeman. 'It is important to get a statement as soon as possible.'

'Please do not disturb him,' said the Nawab Sahib. 'He looks very tired and he needs to rest.'

The Nawab Sahib could not go back to sleep. He got up after a while and paced about the room. Firoz was sound asleep, and did not take anyone's name. After about an hour he woke up again.

'Abba –' he said.

'Yes, son.'

'Abba – there is something –'

His father was silent.

'What is all this?' Firoz said suddenly. 'Did Maan attack me?'

'So it seems. They found you on Cornwallis Road. Do you remember what happened?'

'I am trying to –'

The policeman interrupted: 'Do you remember what happened at Saeeda Bai's?'

Firoz saw his father start at the name, and suddenly he saw the blinding core of what he had been trying to touch, to approach, to remember. He turned towards his father and looked at him with an expression of pain and reproach that pierced him to the heart. The old man could not hold his gaze, and turned away.

17.22

SAEEDA BAI had not been idle in the face of calamity. Despite the terror and shock of Maan's attack on her and on Firoz, she – and Bibbo too – had managed, after the initial shock and reaction, to keep their heads. The house had to be protected, and Maan had to be saved from the effect of his own actions. The law might define things as it chose, but Saeeda Bai knew that Maan was not a criminal.

And she blamed herself and her own excitability too for his tragic outburst of violence.

For herself, once Dr Bilgrami had examined her, she almost forgot her concern. She knew she would live; what happened to her voice was in God's hands. For Tasneem, however, she felt the clutch of a cold fear. The child she had conceived in terror, had carried in shame, and had borne in pain had been given the name of that paradisal spring which could, if anything could, wash antecedence into nonexistence and torment into calm. Yet now again that antecedence and that torment were knocking at the door of the present. Saeeda Bai longed once more for her mother's advice and strong comfort. Mohsina Bai had been a harder, more independent woman than Saeeda; without her courage and persistence Saeeda Bai herself would by now be merely another ageing and impoverished whore from Tarbuz ka Bazaar — and Tasneem a younger version of the same.

That first night, half-expecting a visit from the police or a message from the Nawab Sahib, and sick with fear and pain, she had remained at home, making sure that everything in her room, along the bloodstained stairs, indeed everywhere in the house was as it should be. Sleep, she told herself; sleep; and if you can't sleep, lie in bed and pretend that this is just a night like any other. But she had been seized with restlessness. If it had been possible, she would have got down on her knees and scrubbed clean each drop of blood on the street that led to her door.

As for the man from whose side this blood had flowed, and whose face reminded her not of his mother, whom she had never seen, but most disturbingly of his father, Saeeda Bai felt nothing, a mere coldness, halfbrother to her daughter though he was. She hardly cared if he lived or died except in so far as it would affect Maan. And yet, when the police had come, she had been terrified into giving testimony that might — she saw it all too clearly now — that might lead her beloved Dagh Sahib to the scaffold.

For Maan, who had almost killed her, her anxiety, her terrified tenderness, knew no limits — but what could she do? And she began now to think as her mother would have thought. Whom did she know? And how well? And whom did they know? And how well? Soon Bilgrami Sahib became the emissary of elliptical communications from Saeeda Bai to a rising Minister of State, to a Joint Secretary in the Home Department, to the kotwal of Brahmpur. And Bilgrami Sahib himself used his own contacts judiciously and persistently in a generous attempt to save his rival – persistently, because he feared for Saeeda Bai's health and spirit if something terrible were to happen to Maan, and judiciously, because he feared that Saeeda Bai, in her attempt to spread the web of her influence too wide, might tempt some contrary spirit to rip it from end to end.

17.23

'PRIYA, promise me you'll talk to your father.'

This time it had been Veena who had suggested going up onto the roof. She could not bear the looks of satisfaction, distaste, and pity that she had had to face in the Goyal household below. It was a cold afternoon, and they were both wearing shawls. The sky was slate-coloured, except for an area across the Ganga where the sands had been whipped up by the wind into a dirty yellow-brown haze. Veena was crying blindly and pleading with Priya.

'But what good will it do?' said Priya, wiping the tears from her friend's face and her own.

'All the good in the world if it saves Maan.'

'What is your father doing?' asked Priya. 'Hasn't he spoken to anyone?'

'My father,' said Veena bitterly, 'cares more for his image as a man of principle than for his family. I spoke to him; do you think it had any effect? He told me that I should be thinking of my mother, not of Maan. Only now do I realize what a cold man he really is. Maan will be hanged at eight o'clock, and he'll be signing his files at nine. My mother is beside herself. Promise me you'll speak

to your father, Priya, promise me. You're his only child,
he'll do anything for you.'

'I'll speak to him,' said Priya. 'I promise.'

What Veena did not know – what Priya did not have the
heart to tell her – was that she had spoken to her father
already, and that the Home Minister had told her that
there was nothing he would do to interfere. This was, in
his words, an unimportant matter: one ruffian trying to
kill another in an infamous establishment. That their fa-
thers were who they were had nothing to do with the
business. It touched upon no affairs of state; it provided
no excuse for intervention; the local police and magistracy
could handle it adequately. He had even gently upbraided
his daughter for attempting to use his influence in this
manner, and Priya, who was not used to being upbraided
by her father, had felt both unhappy and ashamed.

17.24

MAHESH KAPOOR was unable to bring himself to do what
had been suggested to him over the phone: to try to bring
pressure to bear directly or from above on the investigating
officer, in this case the Sub-Inspector in charge of the
Pasand Bagh Police Station. It went against his grain to do
so. Indeed, the just implementation of his own Zamindari
Abolition and Land Reforms Act would depend on how
far he could prevent landlords from bringing their influence
to bear on village record-keepers and local officers. He did
not relish the way the politician Jha was undermining the
administration near Rudhia town, and he did not see
himself as ever being tempted to do the same. So when his
wife asked him whether he could not 'talk to someone,
even to Agarwal', Mahesh Kapoor told her abruptly to be
quiet.

For her the shock and grief of the last two days had
been almost unbearable. When she thought of Firoz lying
in hospital and Maan in the police lock-up, she could not
sleep. Once Firoz had become conscious he had been

allowed a very few visitors – including his aunt Abida and his sister Zainab. Mrs Mahesh Kapoor had begged her husband to speak to the Nawab Sahib – to express his grief and regret, and to ask if they could visit Firoz. This he had tried to do. But the Nawab Sahib, being in the hospital, was not available on the phone. And his apologetic, embarrassed, excessively polite secretary Murtaza Ali had made it clear that the Nawab Sahib had indicated from his remarks that a visit by Maan's family at this time would be unwelcome.

The rumour mills, meanwhile, were busy. What was a mere paragraph in the Calcutta papers was the staple of the Brahmpur press and Brahmpur conversation, and would continue to be so for days, despite the alternative attractions of elections and electioneering. The police were still unconscious of the connection between Saeeda Bai's establishment and the Nawab Sahib's. They had still not learned of the monthly stipend. But Bibbo had begun to put two and two together, and was unable to resist casting dark and proud hints about Tasneem's ancestry in the strictest (and thus leakiest) confidence to a couple of her closest friends. And a reporter from the Hindi press who was well known for muck-raking had interrogated an old and retired courtesan who had known Saeeda Bai's mother in the days when they had been part of a joint establishment in Tarbuz ka Bazaar. This old woman was induced by money and the promise of more money to describe all she knew about Saeeda Bai's early life. Some of her facts were true, some embroidered, some false, almost all interesting to the journalist. She stated calmly and authoritatively that Saeeda Bai had lost her virginity when she had been raped at the age of fourteen or fifteen by a prominent citizen who had been drunk; it was Saeeda Bai's mother who had told her so. What lent some likelihood to this particular assertion was that the old woman admitted that she did not know who this man was. She had her ideas, that was all.

For every fact or imagined fact that appeared in print, there were ten rumours that hovered about like wasps over a rotting mango. Neither family escaped the whispered voices, the pointed fingers that followed them wherever they went.

Veena, partly to be with her mother at this hard time, and partly to flee from her kindly but insatiable neighbours, moved into Prem Nivas for a few days. That same evening Pran and the Calcutta party returned to Brahmpur.

Within twenty-four hours of his arrest, Maan had been produced before a local magistrate. His father had hired a District Court lawyer to ask for bail or at least a transfer from the lock-up into a proper jail, but the charges that were being investigated did not admit of the former, and the police opposed the latter. The investigating officer, who had been frustrated by his inability to find a weapon and by Maan's lapses of memory about this and other details, had asked that Maan be kept in police custody for a few more days on the grounds that they needed to interrogate him further. The magistrate had allowed the police to keep him for two more days in the lock-up, after which he would be transferred to the comparative decency of the district jail.

Mahesh Kapoor had visited Maan in the police station twice. Maan complained about nothing in his cell – the filth, the discomfort, the cold. He appeared to be so shocked and so remorseful that his father could not find it in his heart to reproach him further for what he had done to himself and to Firoz and to the Nawab Sahib; and indeed to Mahesh Kapoor's own future.

Maan kept asking for information about Firoz – he was in terror that he might die. He asked his father if he had visited him in hospital, and Mahesh Kapoor was forced to admit that he had not been permitted to.

Mahesh Kapoor had told his wife not to visit Maan until he was in jail – the conditions in the police lock-up would, he thought, upset her too much. But finally Mrs Mahesh Kapoor could bear it no longer. She said that if necessary she would go alone. In exasperation her husband finally gave in and asked Pran to take her there.

She saw Maan and wept. Nothing in her life had approached in degradation her experience of these last few days. The police at the door of Prem Nivas, the searches for incriminating evidence, the arrest of someone she loved – these she had known from the time of the British. But she had not been ashamed of the man whom they had hauled off to jail as a political prisoner. Nor had he had to undergo such filth and squalor as this.

As painful as anything to her had been the fact that she had not been granted permission to visit Firoz and expiate with her affection some of the terrible guilt and sadness she felt towards him and his family.

Maan no longer looked like her handsome son but a dirty and unkempt man, one whose looks spoke of shame and desperation.

She hugged him and wept as if her heart would break. Maan wept too.

17.25

IN the midst of his regret and repentance, Maan still felt he had to see Saeeda Bai. He could not mention this to his father, and he did not know whom to ask to convey a message to her. Only Firoz, he thought, would have understood. When his mother returned to Prem Nivas by car, Pran remained for a few minutes. Maan asked him to get Saeeda Bai to see him somehow. Pran tried to explain that it was impossible: she would be a material witness in the case, and she would not be allowed to visit him.

Maan seemed hardly to understand his own jeopardy – or the fact that attempted murder or even grievous hurt with a dangerous weapon carried a maximum sentence of life imprisonment. He seemed to believe that it was inexplicably unjust to keep him away from Saeeda Bai. He asked Pran to convey to her his bitter regret and continuing love. He scrawled out a couple of lines in Urdu to that effect. Pran was very unhappy with his mission, but agreed to perform it, and gave the note to the watchman within the hour.

When he returned to Prem Nivas in the late afternoon, he saw his mother lying on a sofa on the verandah. She was facing the garden, which was full of early flowers: pansies, calendulas, gerberas, salvias, cosmos, phlox and a few California poppies. The beds, where they met the lawn, were fringed with sweet alyssum. Bees were buzzing around the first few lemon-scented blossoms on the pomelo tree, and a small, glossy, blue-black sunbird flitted in and out of its branches.

Pran paused for a minute near the pomelo tree and breathed in its scent. It reminded him of his childhood; and he thought sadly of the dramatic changes that had occurred to Veena and himself and Maan since those uncertain but comparatively carefree days. Veena's husband had since become an impoverished refugee from Pakistan, he himself was a cardiac patient, and Maan was lying in jail awaiting a charge-sheet. Then he thought of Bhaskar's miraculous escape and of Uma's birth, of his life with Savita, of his mother's sustaining goodness, of the continuing peace of this garden; and he was swayed a little towards accepting that some good of some kind had been gained or retained.

He walked slowly across the lawn to the verandah. His mother was still lying down on the sofa and looking out at the garden.

'Why are you lying down, Ammaji?' he asked. She would normally have sat up to talk to him. 'Are you feeling tired?'

She sat up immediately.

'Can I get you something?' he asked. He noticed she was trying to say something, but he could not make out what she was saying. Her mouth was open, and had drooped to one side. He understood with difficulty that she wanted tea.

Worried now, he called out for Veena. A servant said she had gone out somewhere with his father in the car. Pran ordered some tea. When it came he gave it to his mother to drink. She began to splutter as she drank it, and he realized that she had had a stroke of some kind.

His first thought was to contact Imtiaz at Baitar House. Then he decided to contact Savita's grandfather. Dr Kishen Chand Seth was not in either. Pran left a message for him saying that his mother was ill, and that Dr Seth should phone Prem Nivas immediately he returned. He tried a couple of other doctors, but could not get through to anyone. He was about to order a taxi to go to the hospital to find someone when Dr Seth called back. Pran explained what had happened.

'I'll come over,' said Dr Kishen Chand Seth. 'But get Dr Jain – he's the expert at this sort of thing. His telephone number is 873. Tell him I asked him to come immediately.'

When he arrived, Dr Seth said that he thought it was a case of facial paralysis, and made Mrs Mahesh Kapoor lie down flat. 'But this is very far from my speciality,' he added.

At about seven o'clock, Veena and her father returned. Mrs Mahesh Kapoor's voice was slurred but she was making an effort to communicate.

'Is it about Maan?' asked her husband.

She shook her head. In a little while they understood that what she wanted was her dinner.

She tried to drink her soup. Some went down, but she coughed some of it up. They tried to feed her some rice and daal. She took a little into her mouth, chewed it, and asked Veena to give her some more. But it soon became apparent that she was storing it in her mouth and not swallowing it. Very slowly, with sips of water, she was able to take it down.

Dr Jain arrived about half an hour later. He examined her thoroughly, and said: 'This is a serious condition, you see. I am worried that her seventh, tenth and twelfth nerves are affected.'

'Yes, yes –' said Mr Mahesh Kapoor, at the end of his tether. 'What does all this mean?'

'Well, you see,' said Dr Jain, 'these nerves are connected to the main area of the brain. I am worried that the patient's ability to swallow might fail. Or there could be a second stroke. That would be the end. I suggest that the patient should be removed to hospital immediately.'

Mrs Mahesh Kapoor reacted violently to the word 'hospital'. She refused to go. Her speech was slurred and her senses somewhat dulled, but there was no doubt about her will. She gave them to understand that if she was dying, she wanted to die at home. Veena made out the words 'Sundar Kanda'. She wanted her favourite part of the Ramayana to be read out to her.

'Dying!' said her husband, impatiently. 'There is no question of your dying.'

But Mrs Mahesh Kapoor for once defied her husband and did die that night.

17.26

VEENA was sleeping in her mother's room when she heard her mother suddenly cry out in pain. She turned on the light. Mrs Mahesh Kapoor's face was shockingly distorted, and her whole body appeared to be undergoing a violent spasm. Veena ran to fetch her father. He came. Soon the household was roused. Pran and the doctors were called, and Kedarnath's neighbours were asked to tell him to come over immediately. Pran had no doubt of the seriousness of the matter. He told Savita, Lata and Mrs Rupa Mehra that he thought his mother was dying. They came over. Savita brought the baby too, in case her grandmother wanted to see her.

Within half an hour everyone had gathered around. Bhaskar looked on uneasily. He asked his mother if Nani was indeed dying, and she replied tearfully that she thought so, though everything was in God's hands. The doctor said that there was nothing that could be done. Mrs Mahesh Kapoor too, having asked with incoherent sounds and gestures to have Bhaskar brought close to her, now indicated that she wished to be lowered from her bed onto the ground. At this, all the women began to weep. Mr Mahesh Kapoor, angry, disappointed, and upset, looked at his wife's face, which had grown calm, with irked affection – as if she had deliberately failed him. A small mud lamp was lit and placed in the palm of her hand. Old Mrs Tandon took the name of Rama, and Mrs Rupa Mehra recited from the Gita. A short while afterwards Mrs Mahesh Kapoor struggled to say a word which sounded like 'Maa –'. She could have meant either her mother, who was long dead, or her younger son, whom she could not see among those gathered around her. She closed her eyes. A few tears appeared at the corners of her eyelids, but again her face, so distorted earlier, became calm. A little later, almost at the time she usually woke up, she died.

In the morning a stream of visitors came through the house to pay their last respects. Among them were many of Mahesh Kapoor's colleagues, all of whom, no matter what they thought of him, had had nothing but affection for this decent, kind, and affectionate woman. They had known her as a quiet, bustling wife, untiring and warm in her hospitality, who had compensated with her gentleness for the worst of her husband's acerbity.

Now she lay on the ground on a sheet, her nostrils and mouth lightly plugged with cotton-wool, a bandage tying her head to her jaw. She was dressed in red, as she had been at her wedding many years ago, and there was sindoor in the parting of her hair. Incense was burning in a bowl at her feet. All the women, including Savita and Lata, were sitting beside her, and some were weeping, Mrs Rupa Mehra as much as anyone.

S.S. Sharma removed his shoes and entered. His head was trembling slightly. He folded his hands, said a few words of comfort, and went away. Priya comforted Veena. Her father, L.N. Agarwal, took Pran aside, and said:

'When is the cremation?'

'At eleven o'clock at the ghat.'

'What about your younger brother?'

Pran shook his head. His eyes filled with tears.

The Home Minister asked to use the phone, and called the Superintendent of Police. On hearing that Maan was due to be moved from police custody to judicial custody that afternoon, he said:

'Tell them to do it this morning instead, and to take him past the cremation ghat. His brother will go to the police station and join the escort party. There is no danger of the prisoner escaping, so handcuffs will not be necessary. Have the formalities completed by ten o'clock or so.'

The Superintendent said: 'It will be done, Minister Sahib.'

L.N. Agarwal was about to put down the phone, when he thought of something else. He said: 'Also, would you tell the station house officer to make a barber available in case it is necessary – but not to break any news to the young man himself. His brother will do that.'

In the event, when Pran went over to the lock-up to see Maan, he did not have to say a word. When Maan saw his brother's shaven head he knew by some instinct that it was his mother who had died. He burst into horrible, tearless weeping and began to hit his head against the bars of his cell.

The policeman with the keys was bewildered in the face of this display; the Sub-Inspector snatched the keys from him and let Maan out. He fell into Pran's embrace, and kept making these terrible, animal sounds of grief.

After a while, Pran calmed him down by talking continuously and gently to him. He turned to the police officer and said:

'I understand you have got a barber here to shave my brother's head. We should be leaving for the ghat soon.'

The Sub-Inspector was apologetic. A problem had arisen. One of the ticket clerks at the Brahmpur Railway Station was going to be asked to try to pick Maan out at an identification parade in the jail. Under these circumstances, he could not let Maan's head be shaved.

'This is ridiculous,' said Pran, looking at the policeman's moustache and thinking he had a great deal too much hair himself. 'I heard the Home Minister himself say that –'

'I spoke to the SP ten minutes ago,' said the Sub-Inspec-

tor. Clearly, for him, the SP was more important than
even the PM.

They got to the ghat by eleven. The policemen stood
some distance away. The sun was high, the day unseason-
ably warm. Only the men were there. The cotton-wool
was removed from the face, the yellow cloth and the
flowers were removed from the bier, the body was moved
onto two long logs and covered with others.

Her husband performed all the necessary rites under the
guidance of a pandit. What the rationalist in him thought
of all the ghee and sandalwood and swahas and the demands of the doms who worked at the pyre was not
betrayed by his face. The smoke of the pyre was oppressive,
but he did not appear to sense it. No breeze blew from the
Ganga to disperse it quickly.

Maan stood next to his brother, who almost had to
support him. He saw the flames rise and lap over his
mother's face – and the smoke cover his father's.

This is my doing, Ammaji, he thought, though no one
had said any such thing to him. It is what I did that has led
to this. What have I done to Veena and Pran and Baoji? I
will never forgive myself and no one in the family will ever
forgive me.

17.27

ASH and bones, that was all Mrs Mahesh Kapoor was
now, ash and bones, warm still, but soon to cool, and be
collected, and sunk in the Ganga at Brahmpur. Why not at
Hardwar, as she had wished? Because her husband was a
practical man. Because what are bones and ash, what even
are flesh and blood and tissue when life has gone? Because
it made no difference, the water of the Ganga is the same
at Gangotri, at Hardwar, at Prayag, at Banaras, at Brahmpur, even at Sagar to which it was bound from the moment
it dropped from the sky. Mrs Mahesh Kapoor was dead,
and felt nothing, this ash of hers and sandalwood and
common wood could be left to the doms at the cremation

ghat to sift for the few pieces of jewellery which had melted with her body and were theirs by right. Fat, ligament, muscle, blood, hair, affection, pity, despair, anxiety, illness: all were no more. She had dispersed. She was the garden at Prem Nivas (soon to be entered into the annual Flower Show), she was Veena's love of music, Pran's asthma, Maan's generosity, the survival of some refugees four years ago, the neem leaves that would preserve quilts stored in the great zinc trunks of Prem Nivas, the moulting feather of some pond-heron, a small unrung brass bell, the memory of decency in an indecent time, the temperament of Bhaskar's great-grandchildren. Indeed, for all the Minister of Revenue's impatience with her, she was his regret. And it was right that she should continue to be so, for he should have treated her better while she lived, the poor, ignorant, grieving fool.

17.28

THE chautha was held in the afternoon three days later under a small canopy on the lawn of Prem Nivas. The men sat on one side of the aisle, the women on another. The area under the canopy quickly filled up, and then the aisle itself, and finally people spilled out onto the lawn, some of them as far as the flowerbeds. Mahesh Kapoor, Pran and Kedarnath received them at the entrance to the garden. Mahesh Kapoor was amazed by how many people had come to attend the chautha of his wife, whom he had always thought of as being a silly, superstitious and limited woman. Refugees she had helped during the days of Partition in the relief camps, their families, all those to whom she had given kindness or shelter from day to day, not merely the Rudhia relatives but a large group of ordinary farmers from Rudhia, many politicians who might well have paid only perfunctory or hypocritical homage if he himself had passed away, and scores of people whom neither he nor Pran recognized, all felt that they had to attend this service in her memory. Many of them folded their hands in respect before the photograph of her that stood, garlanded with marigolds, on a table on the long white-sheeted platform at one end of the shamiana. Some of them tried to utter a few words of condolence before being overcome themselves. When Mahesh Kapoor himself sat down, his heart was even more disturbed than it had been these last four days.

No one from the Nawab Sahib's family came to the chautha. Firoz had taken a turn for the worse. He was suffering from a low infection, and he was being given stronger doses of penicillin to check and suppress it. Imtiaz – aware both of the possibilities and limitations of this comparatively recent form of treatment – was worried sick; and his father, seeing his son's illness as punishment for his own sins, pleaded with God more than five times a day to spare Firoz and take away his own life instead.

Perhaps, too, he could not face the rumours that followed him now wherever he went. Perhaps he could not face the family, friendship with whom had caused him such grief. At any rate, he did not come.

Nor could Maan be present.

The pandit was a large man with a full, oblong face, bushy eyebrows, and a strong voice. He began to recite a few shlokas in Sanskrit, especially from the Isha Upanishad and from the Yajurveda, and to interpret them as a guide to life and to righteous action. God was everywhere, he said, in each piece of the universe; there was no permanent dissolution; this should be accepted. He talked about the deceased and how good and godfearing she had been and how her spirit would remain not only in the memories of those who knew her, but in the very world that surrounded them – in this garden, for instance; in this house.

After a while the pandit told his young assistant to take over.

The assistant sang two devotional songs. For the first one the audience sat silent, but when he began to sing the slow and stately 'Twameva Mata cha Pita twameva' – 'You are both mother and father to us' – almost everyone joined in.

The pandit asked people to move forward in order to let people at the back squeeze in under the canopy. Then he asked whether the Sikh singers had arrived. Mrs Mahesh Kapoor had been very fond of their music, and Veena had convinced her father to ask them to sing at the chautha. When the pandit was told that they were on their way, he smoothed his kurta and began a story, which he had told many times before and which went as follows:

There was once a villager who was very poor, so poor that he did not have enough money to pay for his daughter's wedding and had nothing to borrow against. He was in despair. At last someone said: 'Two villages away there is a money-lender who believes in humanity. He will not need any security or property. Your word will be your bond. He lends to people according to their need, and he knows whom to trust.'

The man set out in hope, and reached the money-lender's village by noon. On the outskirts of the village he noticed an old man who was ploughing a field, and a woman, her face covered, who was bringing food out for him, her utensils balanced on her head. He could tell from her gait that she was a young woman and he overheard her say in a young woman's voice: 'Baba, here is some food for you. Eat it, and then please come home. Your son is no more.' The man looked up at the sky and said: 'As God wills.' He then sat down to eat the food.

The villager, puzzled and disturbed by this conversation, tried to make sense of it. He thought to himself: If she were the old man's daughter, why would she cover her face before him? She must be his daughter-in-law. But then he was worried by the identity of the dead man. Surely, if it had been one of her husband's brothers who had died, she would have referred to him as 'jethji' or 'devarji', rather than 'your son'. So it must have been her husband who had died. The calm manner in which both father and wife had accepted his death was unusual, not to say shocking.

At any rate, the villager, considering his own purposes and his own problems, went on to the money-lender's shop. The money-lender asked him what he wanted. The villager told him that he needed some money for his daughter's wedding and had nothing to pledge in exchange.

'That is all right,' said the money-lender, looking at his face. 'How much do you want?'

'A lot,' said the man. 'Two thousand rupees.'

'Fine,' said the money-lender, and asked his accountant to count it out immediately.

While the accountant was counting out the money, the poor villager felt obliged to make some conversation. 'You are a very good man,' he said gracefully, 'but the other people in your village seem peculiar to me.' And he re-counted what he had seen and heard.

'Well,' said the money-lender. 'How would the people in your village have reacted to such news?'

'Well, obviously,' said the poor man, 'the whole village would have gone to the family's house to mourn with them. There would have been no question of ploughing your fields, let alone eating anything till the body was disposed of. People would have been wailing and beating their breasts.'

The money-lender turned to the accountant and told him to stop counting out the money. 'It is not safe to lend anything to this man,' he said.

The man, appalled, turned to the money-lender. 'But what have I done?' he asked.

The money-lender replied: 'If you weep and wail so much about returning what has been given to you in trust by God, you will not be happy about returning what is given to you in trust by a mere man.'

While the pandit told this story there was silence. No one knew what to expect, and at the end of it they felt that they had been reproached for their grief. Pran found himself feeling upset rather than consoled: what the pandit had said was perhaps true, he thought, but he wished the Sikh ragis had come earlier.

Still, here they were now, all three of them, dark and full-bearded, their white turbans set off by a blue headband.

One of them played the tabla, the other two the harmonium, and all three closed their eyes while they sang songs from Nanak and Kabir.

Pran had heard them before; his mother asked the ragis about once a year to sing at Prem Nivas. But now he thought not of the beauty of their singing or of the words of the saints, but of the last time he had heard tabla and harmonium in Prem Nivas: when Saeeda Bai had sung on the evening of Holi last year. He glanced across to where the women were sitting. Savita and Lata were sitting together, as they had been that other evening as well. Savita's eyes were closed. Lata was looking at Mahesh Kapoor, who seemed once again to have distanced himself from what was going on. She had not seen Kabir, who was sitting far behind her, at the back of the covered area.

Her thoughts had wandered to the life of this woman, Pran's mother, whom she had greatly liked but not much known. Had hers been a full life? Could her marriage be said to have been happy or successful or fulfilled: and if so, what did those words mean? What was at the centre of her marriage: her husband, her children, or the small puja room where every morning she prayed, allowing routine and devotion to create a purpose and imply an order in her daily and annual round? Here sat so many people who were affected by her death, and there sat her husband, the Minister Sahib, transparently fretful about the long proceedings. He was trying to indicate to the pandit that he had had enough, but was unable to catch his eye.

The pandit said: 'I understand that the women would now like to sing some songs.' No one came forward. He was about to speak again, when old Mrs Tandon said: 'Veena, come forward, sit here.' The pandit asked her to sit on the platform where the ragis had been singing, but Veena said, 'No; down here.' She was very simply dressed, as was her friend Priya and another young woman. Veena had on a white cotton sari with a black border. A very thin gold chain, which she kept touching, hung around her neck. Her dark red tika was smudged. There appeared to be tears on her cheeks, and especially in the dark, puffy rings around her eyes. Her plump face looked sad and strangely placid. She took out a small book, and they began singing. She sang clearly, and from time to time moved her hand slightly in response to the words of the song. Her voice was natural and very affecting. After the first song was over she began, without even a pause, her mother's favourite hymn, 'Uth, jaag, musafir':

> 'Rise, traveller, the sky is light.
> Why do you sleep? It is not night.
> The sleeping lose, and sleep in vain.
> The waking rise, and rise to gain.
>
> Open your eyelids, you who nod.
> O heedless one, pay heed to God.
> Is this your way to show your love?
> You sleep below, he wakes above.
>
> What you have done, that you must bear.
> Where is the joy in sin then, where?
> When on your head your sins lie deep,
> Why do you clutch your head and weep?
>
> Tomorrow's task, enact today.
> Today's at once; do not delay.
> When birds have robbed the standing grain
> What use to wring your hands in vain?'

Somewhere in the middle of the second stanza she stopped singing – the others continued – and began crying quietly. She tried to stop but couldn't. She started to wipe her tears with the pallu of her sari and then simply wiped them away with her hands. Kedarnath, who was sitting in front, took out his handkerchief and threw it into her lap, but she didn't notice. She slowly looked up, her eyes a little above the crowd, and continued singing. Once or twice she coughed. By the time she was singing the first verse again, her voice was clear; but now it was her irritable father who was in tears.

The song, taken from the hymn-book of Mahatma Gandhi's ashram, brought home to him like nothing else had his unrealized loss. Gandhi was dead, and with him his ideals. That preacher of nonviolence whom he had followed and revered had died violently, and now Mahesh Kapoor's own son – more beloved for the danger he was in – was lying in prison for violence of his own. Firoz, whom he had known from childhood, might die. His friendship with the Nawab Sahib, that had stood so much and so long, had shattered under the sudden power of grief and rumour. The Nawab Sahib was not here today, and he had prevented the two of them from visiting Firoz. That visit would have meant much to the dead woman. The lack of it had enhanced her grief and – who knew the workings of sorrow on the brain? – may have hastened her death.

Too late, and perhaps because of the love that everyone else around him so clearly bore her, he began to realize fully what he had lost, indeed, whom he had lost – and how suddenly. There was so much to do, and no one to help him, to advise him quietly, to check his impatience. His son's life and his own future both seemed to him to be in hopeless straits. He wanted to give up and let the world take care of itself. But he could not let Maan go; and politics had been his life.

She would not be there, as she had always been, to help. The birds had robbed the standing grain, and here he was wringing his empty hands. What would she have said to him? Nothing direct, but possibly a few words of circuitous comfort, something that might, a few days or a few weeks later, have taken the edge off his despair. Would she have told him to withdraw from the election? What would she have asked him to do about his son? Which of his several duties – or conceptions of duty – would she have expected him to follow or have anticipated that he would follow, and which would she have wished him to? Even if in the weeks ahead it became clear to him, he did not have those weeks, but only days, and, indeed, very few of those.

WHEN Maan was admitted to jail after the cremation, he was required to wash himself and his clothing, and he was provided with a cup and a plate. He was examined by the medical officer and weighed. A note was made of the condition of his hair and beard. As an unconvicted prisoner with no previous convictions he was supposed to be kept separate from those undertrial prisoners who had previous convictions, but the district jail was crowded, and he was accommodated in a ward which contained a couple of undertrial prisoners who knew about jail life from experience and set out to educate the others about it. Maan they treated as a great curiosity. If he was really a Minister's son – and the one newspaper they were permitted confirmed that indeed he was – what was he doing there? Why had he not managed to get bail on one pretext or another? If the charge being investigated was nonbailable, why had the police not been told to lessen the charge?

If Maan had been in anything resembling his normal state of mind, he would have made friends with a few of his present colleagues. Now he hardly sensed their existence. He could think of no one except those whom he could not see: his mother, and Firoz, and Saeeda Bai. His life, though not easy, was luxury compared to what it had been in the lock-up. He was allowed to receive food and clothes from Prem Nivas; he was allowed to shave his face and to exercise. The jail was comparatively clean. Since he was a 'superior class' prisoner, his cell was equipped with a small table, a bed, and a lamp. They sent him oranges, which he ate in a daze. They sent a quilt of kingfisher blue from Prem Nivas to protect him against the cold. It protected him and it comforted him, while at the same time it reminded him of home – and all that he had destroyed or lost.

Again, as a superior class prisoner, he was shielded from the worst degradations of jail life – the crowded cells and barracks where assorted horrors were perpetrated by the prisoners on one another. The Superintendent of the jail was also aware of whose son he was, and kept an eye on him. He was liberal in permitting him visits.

Pran visited him, and Veena, and his father too before he returned, heartsick, to campaign in his constituency. No one knew what to talk about to Maan. When his father asked him what had happened, Maan started trembling and could say nothing. When Pran said, 'But why, Maan, why?' he stared at him in a hunted manner and turned away.

There were not many safe subjects. Sometimes they talked about cricket. England had just defeated India in the fourth Test Match of the series, the first match that had not ended in a draw. But though Pran could spin out cricket talk even in his sleep, Maan began to yawn after a few minutes.

Sometimes they talked about Bhaskar or Pran's baby, but even these conversations took painful turns.

Maan would talk most easily about jail routine. He said that he wanted to work a bit, though it was not compulsory: perhaps in the jail vegetable garden. He asked about the garden in Prem Nivas, but when Veena began to describe it he started weeping.

He yawned a great deal during conversations without knowing why, sometimes when he wasn't even tired.

The lawyer who was sent to visit him by his father often returned frustrated. Maan, when asked anything, said that he had talked about it all with the police and would not go over it again. But this was not true. When the Sub-Inspector and a few other policemen came to the jail to ask him questions, to get him to elaborate on his confession, he insisted that he had nothing more to say to them either. They asked him about the knife. He said he couldn't remember if he had left it at Saeeda Bai's or taken it along with him; he thought the latter. Meanwhile, the case against him grew through a combination of statements and circumstantial evidence.

No one who visited him mentioned Firoz's turn for the worse, but he learned about it from the ward newspaper, the local Hindi paper, *Adarsh*. He also learned, from gossip among the prisoners, about the rumours floating around the Nawab Sahib and Saeeda Bai. He had fits of almost suicidal misery, from the worst of which he was guarded by the ritual of jail life.

Routine took over his days. The *Jail Manual*, to which the Brahmpur District Jail approximately adhered, read as follows:

To perform morning ablutions, etc:	After unlocking up to 7 a.m.
To be on parade in the enclosure:	7 a.m. to 9 a.m.
To be locked up in cell or barracks:	9 a.m. to 10 a.m.
To bathe and take the midday meal:	10 a.m. to 11 a.m.
To be locked up in cell or barracks:	11 a.m. to 3 p.m.
To take exercise, have evening meal, and be searched and locked up:	3 p.m. to locking up.

He was a model prisoner, and never complained about anything. Sometimes he sat at the table in his cell and looked at a piece of paper on which he planned to write a letter to Firoz. But he could never begin it. He took to doodling instead. Having hardly slept in the lock-up, he slept for long hours in his jail cell.

Once he was lined up for an identification parade, but he was not told whether it was to be for himself or for some other prisoner. When he saw that his lawyer was present, he realized it was for himself. But he did not recognize the self-important looking clerk who walked down the line and paused a little longer when he came to him. And he did not care whether he had been identified or not.

'If he dies, you could well be hanged,' said one experienced prisoner with a sense of humour. 'If that happens we'll all be locked up for the morning, so I'm counting on you to spare us the inconvenience.'

Maan nodded.

Since he was not responding satisfactorily, the prisoner went on: 'After every execution do you know what they do with the ropes?'

Maan shook his head.

'They dress them with beeswax and ghee to keep them smooth.'

'In what proportions?' asked another prisoner.

'Oh, half and half,' said the knowledgeable one. 'And they add a bit of carbolic acid to the mixture to keep off the insects. It would be a pity if white ants or silverfish chewed them away. What do you think?' he asked Maan.

Every one turned to look at Maan.

Maan, however, had stopped listening. Neither had the man's sense of humour amused him nor had his cruelty upset him.

'And in order to preserve them from rats,' continued the expert, 'they put the five ropes – they have five ropes in this jail, don't ask me why – they put all five ropes in a clay pot, stop up the top, and suspend it from the roof of the store room. Think about that. Five manilla ropes, one inch in diameter, each fattened on a diet of ghee and blood slithering about like snakes in a pot, waiting for their next victim –'

He laughed delightedly and looked at Maan.

17.30

MAAN may have paid no attention to any distant hazard to his neck, but it was impossible for Saeeda Bai not to be conscious of what had happened to hers. For days afterwards she could hardly speak except in a croak. Her worlds had fallen apart around her: both her own world of nuance and attraction, and her daughter's world of innocence and protection.

For Tasneem was now branded by the rumours. She herself continued to be less than fully aware of them; this was not through lack of intelligence but rather because the outside world had once again been cut off from her. Even Bibbo, whose taste for both intrigue and gossip had caused enough damage already, pitied Tasneem, and did not say anything that could hurt her. But after what had happened in front of Tasneem's eyes to the Nawabzada, the only man whom she had ever felt any deep emotion for, she felt it was safest to withdraw into herself, into her novels and household work. He was in severe danger still; she could tell from the answers that Bibbo gave her that his life was in danger. She could do nothing for him; he was a distant and retreating star. She assumed he had been injured trying to disarm the drunken Maan, but she did not ask what had impelled Maan to become so drunken and murderous. Of the other men who had shown some interest in her, she heard nothing, nor did she wish to hear anything. Ishaq, increasingly influenced by Majeed Khan, retreated from the scandal and neither wrote nor visited. Rasheed wrote another crazy letter to her; but Saeeda Bai tore it up before it reached Tasneem.

More fiercely than ever before, Saeeda Bai tried to protect – and harry – Tasneem. Tender and furious by turns, she once again re-lived the long torment of having to be a sister to her daughter, of suffering her own strong-willed mother to determine both the course of her own life and the course of the life that Saeeda had been forced, in shame and agony, to relinquish to her.

Saeeda Bai could not now sing, and it seemed to her that she would never again be able to, even if her throat allowed it. The parakeet, however, unmindful of her trauma, burst into a blaze of speech. He took on a sort of grotesque croak in imitation of the mistress of the house. This was one of Saeeda Bai's consolations. The other was Bilgrami Sahib, who not only helped her medically but stood by her through this ordeal of press and police, of fear and distress and pain.

She realized now that she loved Maan.

When his two lines of misspelt Urdu came to her, she wept bitterly, oblivious to the feelings of Bilgrami Sahib, who was at her side. She imagined the guilt and trauma of his imprisonment, and was terrified to think of where it might end. When she heard of the death of his mother, she again wept. She was not the kind of woman who thrives on ill-treatment or values those who misprize her, and she could not understand why Maan's attack should have caused her to feel what she did. But perhaps it had merely forced her to realize what she had felt before, but had not known. His note to her said nothing except how sorry he was and how much he loved her still.

When the next instalment of the stipend came from Baitar House, Saeeda Bai, who needed the money, returned it unopened. Bilgrami Sahib, when she told him what she had done, said that he would not have advised it, but that it was well done. For anything she needed now, she should depend on him. She accepted his help. He once again asked her to be his wife and to give up her singing and her profession. Although she did not know if she would ever regain her voice, she refused him once again.

As Bilgrami Sahib had feared, their attempt to bring influence into play had attracted the attention of the Raja of Marh, who quite blatantly began to pay journalists to dig up what dirt they could about the scandal – and particularly to attempt to prevent any subversion of justice by Maan's friends and family. He had also attempted to fund a couple of the Independent candidates who were standing against Mahesh Kapoor in the elections, but this had proved to be a less fruitful investment.

One night the Raja of Marh came with a gang of three guards and virtually forced his way into Saeeda Bai's house. He was delighted by recent events. Mahesh Kapoor, the plunderer of his rightful lands and the derider of his great temple, had been humbled; Maan – whom he saw both as his competitor and as the brother of the man who had expelled his son – was locked safely away; the Nawab Sahib – whose religion and high cultural airs he equally loathed – was stricken with shame and with fear and grief for his son; and Saeeda Bai had been disgraced further before the world and would doubtless abase herself to his, the Raja of Marh's, commands.

'Sing!' he commanded her. 'Sing! I hear your voice has gained a richer tone since your neck was wrung.'

It was fortunate for both him and Saeeda Bai that the watchman had alerted the police. They came in, and he was forced to leave. He did not know, either then or afterwards, how close he had come to becoming that well-washed fruit knife's second victim.

17.31

FIROZ lay between life and death for several days. Eventually the Nawab Sahib grew so exhausted that he was ordered home by his elder son.

It was the fear of Firoz's death that finally forced Mahesh Kapoor, that upright and law-abiding man, to speak to the Superintendent of Police. He knew what he was doing: he did it with his eyes open, and he was ashamed, but he did it. He had lost his wife, he could not bear to lose his son. If Firoz died, and the investigating officer and committal magistrate saw fit, Maan might be tried under Section 302 of the Indian Penal Code – and this thought was so horrific – and to his mind, unjust – that he could not bear it. The SP for his part was a man who knew how many ways bread could be buttered. He said that it was a difficult problem now that matters had been aired so openly in the press, but that he would do what he could. He repeated several times that he had always had the greatest respect for Mahesh Kapoor. Mahesh Kapoor repeated, though the words tore at his sense of his own integrity, that his feelings towards the SP were very similar.

He visited Maan once more in jail. Once again, father and son did not have much to say to each other. He then left for Salimpur for a few days. He did not tell anyone what he had done, and he reproached himself both for having done it and for not having done it earlier.

Maan had begun working in the jail garden, and this did help him somewhat. Even now, he found the visits of his brother and sister painful. Once he asked Pran to send some money anonymously to Rasheed and gave him his address. Once he asked for a few harsingar flowers from the garden of Prem Nivas and Veena told him that the season was over. For the most part Maan did not know what to say to them. He continued to feel that the shock of his crime had killed their mother, and that they felt the same. But time passed, and exhaustion eased his mind.

Firoz too became better. The advances in medicine of the previous ten years had saved his life, but only just. Had antibiotics not been available in Brahmpur, or had doctors not been sufficiently skilled in their administration, he would surely not have gazed at that lizard again. But despite the wound and the infections, whether he wished to or not, he lived.

A change came over Maan too with the slow recovery of his friend. It was as if he had come out of the valley of the shadow of his own death. If his own danger had caused Saeeda Bai to realize how much she loved him, the danger Firoz had been in had given him a similar insight. He cheered up as soon as Pran told him that Firoz was finally and definitely on the mend. His appetite recovered. He asked for certain kinds of food to be brought from Prem Nivas. He joked about rum chocolates, which a friend had once brought from Calcutta, as a means of smuggling alcohol into jail. He asked for certain visitors: not his immediate family, but people who would bring him a sense of something different: Lata (if she wouldn't mind paying him a visit) and one of his old girlfriends, who was now married. Both came, on consecutive days: one with Pran (after she had overcome Mrs Rupa Mehra's objections), one with her husband (after she had overcome his).

Lata, despite the sad and, in some ways, sinister venue, was pleased to see Maan. It was true that their worlds hardly intersected. It had amazed her that Pran had been able, last April Fool's, to convince her mother of their elopement. But she remembered Maan as she always had – jovial and affectionate – and she was glad to think that he had remembered her. She was not determinedly cheerful, but she could see that talking with her was doing Maan good. They talked about Calcutta, particularly the Chatterjis, and – partly because she wanted to keep him interested – she talked a great deal more freely with him than she normally would have, or than she ordinarily did with Pran.

The jail officers sat out of clear hearing, but they looked at them curiously when they burst out laughing. They were not accustomed to that sound in the visiting room.

The next day they heard more of the same. Maan was visited by his old friend Sarla and her husband, who for some reason was called Pigeon by all his friends. Sarla, who had not seen Maan for months, regaled him with a description of a New Year's party that she and Pigeon had been to. It had been organized by Pigeon's friends.

'In order to add a little spice to the gathering,' said Sarla, 'they decided this year to be bold and hire a cabaret dancer – from a cheap hotel in Tarbuz ka Bazaar – one of those hotels that advertises stripteases with a new Salome every week and is constantly being raided by the police.'

'Lower your voice,' laughed Maan.

'Well,' said Sarla, 'she danced, and took off a few of her clothes, and danced some more – and all so suggestively and lasciviously that the women were appalled. The men – well, they had mixed emotions. Pigeon, for instance.'

'No – no,' said Pigeon.

'Pigeon, she sat on your lap, and you didn't stop her.'

'How could I?' said Pigeon.

'Yes, he's right – it isn't easy,' said Maan.

Sarla gave Maan a look, and continued: 'Well, anyway, she then set upon Mala and Gopu, and began to caress Gopu in all kinds of ways. He was quite tipsy, and didn't object. But you know how possessive Mala is of her husband. She pulled him away. But the other woman pulled him back. Quite shameless. Gopu got scolded badly the next day, and all the wives vowed: Never again.'

Maan burst out laughing, Sarla joined in, and even Pigeon smiled, a little guiltily.

'But you haven't heard the best part,' said Sarla. 'A week later the police raided that Tarbuz ka Bazaar hotel, and it was discovered that the cabaret dancer was a boy! Well, we teased those two unmercifully after that! I can still hardly believe it. He had us all fooled – the voice, the eyes, the gait, the feel of the whole situation – and all along it was a boy!'

'I suspected it all along,' said Pigeon.

'You didn't suspect anything,' said Sarla. 'If you did and still behaved the way you did I'd be even more worried.'

'Well, not all along,' said Pigeon.

'He must have enjoyed himself,' said Sarla. 'Fooling us like that. No wonder he could act so shamelessly. No girl would!'

'Oh no,' said Pigeon sarcastically. 'No girl would. Sarla thinks all women are paragons.'

'Well, compared to men we certainly are,' said Sarla. 'The trouble is, Pigeon, you don't appreciate us. Well, most of you don't. Maan's an exception; he always did. You'd better come out of jail fast and rescue me, Maan. What do you say, Pigeon?'

As their time was up, her husband was spared from having to think of an answer. But for half an hour after they left, Maan kept picturing the scene she had conjured up, and kept laughing to himself in his cell. His fellow prisoners could not think what had got into him.

17.32

TOWARDS the end of January Maan's case came up for committal proceedings before a magistrate. The question at issue was what charges were to be preferred against him, if any.

Clearly, there would have to be a charge-sheet; no policeman, however dedicated he might be to undo his duty or to misuse his discretion, could easily have spoiled such a case sufficiently to issue a 'final report', which would have stated that there was no case to answer. The Sub-Inspector could perhaps have tried to go around winning over witnesses in such an attempt, but as investigating officer he had done his job well; and he was unhappy enough as it was that his investigation was being interfered with by his superiors. He knew that the matter was still in the public eye, and he also knew who the scapegoat would be if there was any suggestion of interference with the course of justice.

Maan and his lawyer were both present at the committal proceedings.

The Sub-Inspector stood before the committal magistrate and described the events that had led to the investigation, provided a summary of the investigation itself, submitted the documents relevant to the case, stated that the victim was now definitely out of danger, and asserted in conclusion that Maan should be charged with voluntarily causing grievous hurt.

The magistrate was puzzled.

'What about attempted murder?' he said, looking the policeman in the eye, and avoiding Maan's.

'Attempted murder?' said the policeman unhappily, tugging a little at his moustache.

'Or at least attempted culpable homicide,' said the magistrate. 'But from these statements, I am not sure the former charge cannot be made out. Even if there had been grave and sudden provocation, it was not given by the victim. Nor does it appear prima facie that the wound was inflicted by mistake or accident.'

The policeman was silent, but nodded his head.

Maan's lawyer whispered to Maan that he thought they were in trouble.

'And why section 325 instead of section 326?' continued the magistrate.

The former section dealt with grievous hurt; when the case came up for trial, the maximum sentence that could be imposed would be seven years; but for the moment Maan could be let out on bail. The latter section also dealt with grievous hurt, but with a dangerous weapon. This was not bailable, and the maximum punishment was life imprisonment.

The Sub-Inspector mumbled something about the weapon not having been discovered.

The magistrate looked at him severely. 'Do you think these injuries' – he looked down at the medical certificate – 'these lacerations of the intestine and so on were caused by a stick?'

The Sub-Inspector said nothing.

'I think you should, well, investigate further,' said the magistrate. 'And re-examine your own evidence and the charges that suggest themselves.'

Maan's lawyer stood up to propose that such matters were within the discretion of the investigating officer.

'I am aware of that,' snapped the magistrate, who was disgusted with the proceedings. 'I am not telling him what charge to prefer.' He reflected that if it had not been for the medical certificate, the Sub-Inspector would probably have put forward a charge of simple hurt.

Glancing at Maan, the magistrate noticed that he looked unaffected enough by events. Presumably he was one of those criminals who learned nothing from their crimes.

Maan's lawyer asked that Maan be let out on bail, since the only present charge against him was bailable. The magistrate granted this, but it was clear that he was very annoyed. Part of his annoyance stemmed from the lawyer's reference to 'my client's grievous distress consequent on the demise of his mother'.

Maan's lawyer whispered: 'Thank God you won't be tried by him.'

Maan, who had begun to take an interest in his defence, said: 'Am I free?'

'Yes; for the moment.'

'What will I be charged with?'

'I'm afraid that isn't clear. This magistrate for some reason is after your blood, and is out to – well, to do you grievous hurt.'

The magistrate, however, was not interested in Maan's blood but merely in upholding the law. He would not be a party to the subversion of justice by influential people, and that is what he suspected this to be. He knew of courts where this might be possible, but his was not one of them.

'NO person shall vote at any election if he is confined in a prison, whether under a sentence of imprisonment or transportation or otherwise, or is in the lawful custody of the police.'

The Representation of the People Act, 1951, was quite unambiguous about this, and so it happened that Maan was not able to vote in the great General Election for which he had fought so hard. He was registered in Pasand Bagh, and elections for the Brahmpur (East) constituency for the Legislative Assembly were held on the 21st of January.

Curiously enough, had he been a resident of Salimpur-cum-Baitar, he would have succeeded in voting; for, owing to a shortage of trained personnel, voting in different constituencies was staggered, and the Legislative Assembly elections there were held on the 30th of January.

The fight now was an extremely harsh one. Waris was as bitter a rival to Mahesh Kapoor as he had been a doughty supporter. Everything had changed; and the Zamindari Act, rumours and scandals, pro- and anti-Congress feeling, religion, nothing was left unexploited in the mauling battle that led up to the polls.

The Nawab Sahib had not stated as such that Waris should fight against Mahesh Kapoor, but it was clear that he did not want him to support him. And Waris, who saw Maan no longer as the saviour but as the attempted murderer of the young Nawabzada, was passionate in his denunciation of him and his father, his clan, his religion, and his party. When the local Congress office belatedly sent a large number of posters and flags to Baitar Fort, he made a bonfire of them.

Waris spoke powerfully because he was so aroused. Already well-liked in the area, he now rose on a great wave of popularity. He was the Nawab Sahib's champion, and the champion of his injured son, who even now (so it was convenient to assert) lay at the point of death owing to the treachery of his seeming friend. The Nawab Sahib had to remain in Brahmpur, claimed Waris, but if he could have campaigned, he would have exhorted the people from every podium in the district to throw the betrayer of the salt of his hospitality, the vile Mahesh Kapoor and all he stood for out of the constituency into which he had so recently crawled.

And what did Mahesh Kapoor and the Congress stand for? continued Waris, who had begun to enjoy his role as a political and feudal leader. What had they given the people? The Nawab Sahib and his family had worked for the people for generations, had fought the British in the Mutiny – long before the Congress had even been conceived – had died heroically, had suffered with the people's sufferings, had taken pity on their poverty, had helped them in every way they could. Look at the power station, the hospital, the schools founded by the Nawab Sahib's father and grandfather, said Waris. Look at the religious trusts they had either established or contributed to. Think of the great processions at Moharram – the grand climax of the festivities of the Baitar year – which the Nawab Sahib paid for out of his own pocket as an act of public piety and private charity. And yet Nehru and his ilk were trying to destroy the man who was so well-beloved, and replace him with what? A voracious pack of petty government officials who would eat the very vitals of the people. To those who complained that the zamindars exploited the people he suggested that they compare the state of the peasants on the Baitar estate with those of a certain village just outside, where they were sunk in destitution which aroused not pity so much as horror. There the peasants – especially the landless chamars – were so poor that they sifted the bullocks' droppings on the threshing floor for residual grain – and washed it and dried it and ate it. And yet many chamars were going to vote blindly for the Congress, the party of the government that had oppressed them for so long. He begged his scheduled caste brothers to see the light and to vote for the bicycle they might aspire to and not for the pair of bullocks, which should only remind them of the degrading scenes they knew so well.

Mahesh Kapoor found himself entirely on the defensive. In any case, his heart lay in Brahmpur now: in a prison cell, in a hospital ward, in the room in Prem Nivas where his wife no longer slept. Increasingly, the fight, which had begun as an irregular ten-pointed star with one huge gleaming point, his own, had polarized into a struggle between two men: the man who tried to project himself as the Nawab Sahib's candidate and the man who realized that his only chance of victory lay in suppressing his individuality and projecting himself as the candidate of Jawaharlal Nehru.

He talked not about himself now but about the Congress Party. But he was heckled at every meeting and asked to explain the actions of his son. Was it true that he had used his influence to try to get him off? What if the young Nawabzada died? Was this a plot to wipe out the leaders of the Muslims one by one? For one who had spent his life fighting for communal amity, such accusations were hard to bear. If he had not been sick at heart, he would have responded as furiously as he usually did in the presence of aggressive stupidity, and this would have done him less good still.

Not once, either by studied implication or in a fit of anger, did he mention the rumours gathering around the Nawab Sahib. Yet now these rumours too began to float around Salimpur and Baitar and the hinterland of the two small towns. They were more damaging morally than those that touched Mahesh Kapoor, even though what they imputed was two decades old; and the Hindu communalist parties tried to use them as well as they could.

But many people, particularly around Baitar, refused to believe these rumours of illegitimacy and rape. And some, who believed them, held that the Nawab Sahib had been punished enough by God through his grief for his son; and that charity suggested that there was a statute of limitations on one's sins.

In practical terms too, Mahesh Kapoor was at his wit's end. He no longer had two jeeps but only one broken-down vehicle provided by the Congress office. His son was no longer with him to provide him with help and support and introductions. His wife, who could have helped him, who could have talked to the shy women of the constituency, was dead. He had hoped at one stage that Jawaharlal Nehru might make time on his whirlwind tour of Purva Pradesh to visit Salimpur, but so certain had his election appeared that he had not pressed his case. And now it seemed that only a visit from Nehru could save him. He telegrammed Delhi and Brahmpur and asked that Nehru's great progress be diverted his way for just a few hours; but he knew that half the Congress candidates in the province were making similar pleas, and that his chances of persuasion were utterly remote.

Veena and Kedarnath came out to help for a few days. Veena felt that her father needed her more than Maan, whom at best she could visit for a few minutes every other day. Her arrival had some effect in the towns, especially in Salimpur. Her homely but lively face, her warm-hearted manner, and the dignity of her sorrow – for her mother, for her brother, for her beleaguered father – affected the hearts of many women. When she spoke, they even attended public meetings. Because of the expansion of the franchise, they now formed half the electorate.

The Congress village-level workers campaigned as hard as they could, but many of them had begun to feel that the tide had turned irreversibly against them, and they were not able to disguise how disheartened they were. They could not even be certain of the scheduled caste vote because the socialists were trumpeting their electoral alliance with Dr Ambedkar's party.

Rasheed had returned to his village to campaign for the socialists. He was disturbed and excitable and he even looked unstable. Every second day he rushed off to Salimpur. But whether he was an asset or a liability to Ramlal Sinha's campaign was difficult to ascertain. He was Muslim, and religious, and that helped; but he had been disowned by almost everyone in his own village of Debaria – from Baba down to Netaji – and he had no particular standing anywhere. The elders of Sagal in particular mocked his pretensions. One joke that was doing the rounds was that 'Abd-ur-Rasheed' or 'The Slave of The Director' thought he had lost the head of his name when he had merely lost his own. Sagal had gone solidly into the Independent camp of Waris Khan.

In Debaria the picture was more complicated. This was partly because there were many more Hindus there: a small knot of brahmins and banias and a large group of jatavs and other scheduled castes. Every party – the Congress, the KMPP, the socialists, the communists, and the Hindu parties – could hope to garner votes here. Among the Muslims, matters were complicated by Netaji's sporadic presence. He exhorted people to vote for the Congress candidate for Parliament, leaving open the question of the race for the Legislative Assembly; but there was bound to be some spillover in the resulting vote. A villager who placed his parliamentary ballot-paper in a green box that carried the symbol of yoked oxen would be very likely to place his other ballot-paper in a brown box carrying the same symbol.

When Mahesh Kapoor, after long and dusty hours of campaigning, arrived in Debaria with Kedarnath one evening, Baba met him and greeted him hospitably, but told him plainly that the situation had greatly changed.

'And what about you?' asked Mahesh Kapoor. 'Have you changed? Do you believe that a father should be punished for an offence of his son's?'

Baba said: 'I have never believed that. But I do believe that a father is responsible for the manner in which his son behaves.'

Mahesh Kapoor forbore from remarking that Netaji had not proved a great credit to Baba. The point was irrelevant, and he had no energy to argue. It was perhaps at that moment that he felt most acutely that he had lost the fight.

When he got back to Salimpur late at night, he told his son-in-law that he wished to be alone. The electricity in the room was weak, the bulbs low and flickering. He ate by himself and thought about his life, attempting to dissociate his family life from his public life, and to concentrate on the latter. Now more than ever he felt that he should have dropped out of politics in 1947. The sense of determination he had had when fighting the British had dissipated in the uncertainties and feeblenesses of Independence.

After dinner he looked through his post. He picked up a large envelope containing details of local electoral rolls. Then he picked up another local letter, and was startled to see King George VI's face on the stamp.

For a minute he stared at it, completely disoriented, as if he had seen an omen. Very carefully he placed the envelope down upon the postcard below: a postcard displaying a portrait of Gandhi. He felt as if he had unconsciously trumped his own best card. He stared once again at the stamp.

There was a simple explanation, but it did not occur to him. The Posts and Telegraph Department, under pressure of the great demands of election mail, and concerned about possible shortages, had issued instructions that old stocks of the King George series be put on sale at post offices. That was all. King George VI, from his sick-bed in London, had not visited Mahesh Kapoor in the watches of the night to predict that he would see him again at Philippi.

17.34

THE next morning Mahesh Kapoor arose before dawn, and took a walk through the unwoken town. The sky was still starry. A couple of birds had just begun to sing. A few dogs barked. Over the faint voice of the muezzin's call to prayer, a cock crowed. Then again everything was silent except for the occasional birdsong.

> 'Rise, traveller, the sky is light.
> Why do you sleep? It is not night.'

He hummed the tune to himself, and felt a renewal, if not of hope, at least of determination.

He looked at the watch that Rafi Sahib had given him, thought of the date, and smiled.

Later that morning, he was about to set out on the election round, when the Sub-Divisional Officer of Salimpur came up to him in a great hurry.

'Sir, the Prime Minister will be coming here tomorrow afternoon. I was instructed by telephone to inform you. He will be speaking at Baitar and at Salimpur.'

'Are you sure?' said Mahesh Kapoor impatiently. 'Are you absolutely sure?' He looked amazed, as if his improvement of mood had of itself brought about an improvement of fortune.

'Yes, indeed, Sir. I am sure.' The SDO looked both excited and extremely anxious. 'I have made no arrangements at all. None at all.'

Within an hour the extraordinary news was all over town, and by midday had percolated into the villages.

Jawaharlal Nehru, amazingly young-looking for his sixty-two years, dressed in an achkan which was already taking on the colour of the dust of the constituency roads, met Mahesh Kapoor and the Congress parliamentary candidate in the Circuit House at Baitar. Mahesh Kapoor could still hardly believe it.

'Kapoor Sahib,' said Nehru, 'they told me I shouldn't come here because it was a lost battle. That made me even more determined to come. Take these things away,' he said irritably to a man standing near him, as he bent his neck and freed himself of seven marigold garlands. 'Then they told me some nonsense about some trouble your son had got himself into. I asked if it had anything to do with you – and it clearly hadn't. People put too much emphasis on the wrong things in this country.'

'I cannot thank you enough, Panditji,' said Mahesh Kapoor with grateful dignity; he was very moved.

'Thank? There is nothing to thank me for. By the way, I am very sorry about Mrs Kapoor. I remember meeting her in Allahabad – but that must have been – what? – five years ago.'

'Eleven.'

'Eleven! What is the matter? Why are they taking so much time to set things up? I'll be late in Salimpur. He popped a pastille into his mouth. 'Oh, I meant to tell you. I am asking Sharma to come and join my Cabinet. He can't keep refusing me. I know he likes being Chief Minister, but I need a strong team in Delhi too. That is why it is so important that you win here and help to handle things in Purva Pradesh.'

'Panditji,' said Mahesh Kapoor with surprise and pleasure, 'I will do my best.'

'And of course we cannot have reactionary forces winning sensitive seats,' said Nehru, pointing in the general direction of the Fort. 'Where is Bhushan – is that his name? Can't they organize anything?' he continued impatiently. He stepped onto the verandah and shouted for the man from the District Congress Committee who was in charge of logistics. 'How can we expect to run a country if we can't get together a microphone and a platform and a few policemen?' When he heard that the irksome and interminable security arrangements were finally secure, he ran down the steps of the Circuit House two at a time and jumped into the car.

The cavalcade was stopped every hundred yards or so by adoring crowds. When they reached the grounds where he was due to talk, he ran up the steps of the flower-strewn podium before doing namasté to the vast throng gathered below. The people – townsfolk and villagers alike – had been waiting for him with growing anticipation for more than two hours. When they sensed his arrival, even before they saw him, an electric shiver ran through the huge, excited audience, and they shouted:

'Jawaharlal Nehru Zindabad!'
'Jai Hind!'
'Congress Zindabad!'
'Maharaj Jawaharlal ki jai!'
This last was too much for Nehru.
'Sit down, sit down, don't shout!' he shouted.
The crowd laughed delightedly and kept cheering. Nehru

got annoyed, jumped down from the podium before anyone could stop him, and started physically pushing people down. 'Hurry up, sit down, we don't have all the time in the world.'

'He gave me a push – a hard push!' said one man proudly to his friends. He was to boast about it ever afterwards.

When he returned to the podium, a Congress bigwig started introducing and seconding someone else on the platform.

'Enough, enough, enough of all this, start the meeting,' said Nehru.

Then someone started talking about Jawaharlal Nehru himself, how flattered, honoured, privileged, blessed they were to have him with them, how he was the Soul of Congress, the Pride of India, the jawahar and lal of the people, their jewel and their darling.

All this got Nehru very angry indeed. 'Come on, don't you have anything better to do?' he said under his breath. He turned to Mahesh Kapoor. 'The more they talk about me, the less use I am to you – or to the Congress – or to the people. Tell them to be quiet.'

Mahesh Kapoor hushed up the speaker, who looked hurt; and Nehru immediately launched into a forty-five minute speech in Hindi.

He held the crowd spellbound. Whether they understood him or not was hard to say, because he rambled on in an impressionistic manner from idea to idea, and his Hindi was not much good, but they listened to him and stared at him with rapt attention and awe.

His speech went something like this:

'Mr Chairman, etc, – brothers and sisters – we are gathered here at a troubled time, but it is also a time of hope. We do not have Gandhiji with us, so it is even more important that you have confidence in the nation and in yourselves.

The world is also going through a hard time. We have the Korean crisis and the crisis in the Persian Gulf. You have probably heard about the attempt of the British to bully the Egyptians. This will lead to trouble sooner or later. This is bad, and we cannot have it. The world must learn to live in peace.

Here at home also, we must live in peace. As tolerant people we must be tolerant. We lost our freedom many years ago because we were disunited. We must not let it happen again. Disaster will strike the country if religious bigots and communalists of all descriptions get their way.

We must reform our way of thinking. That is the main thing. The Hindu Code Bill is an important measure which must be passed. The Zamindari Bills of the various states must be implemented. We must look at the world with new eyes.

India is an ancient land of great traditions, but the need of the hour is to wed these traditions to science. It is not enough to win elections, we must win the battle of production. We must have science and more science, production and more production. Every hand has to be on the plough and every shoulder to the wheel. We must harness the forces of our mighty rivers with the help of great dams. These monuments to science and modern thinking will give us water for irrigation and also for electricity. We must have drinking water in the villages and food and shelter and medicine and literacy all around. We must make progress or else we will be left behind. . . .'

Sometimes Nehru was in a reminiscent mood, sometimes he waxed poetic, sometimes he got carried away and scolded the crowd. He was, as they had sensed in their earlier slogans, rather an imperious democrat. But they applauded him, almost regardless of what he said. They cheered when he talked about the size of the Bhakra dam, they cheered when he said that the Americans must not oppress Korea — whatever Korea was. And they cheered most of all when he requested their support, which he did almost as an afterthought. In the eyes of his people, Nehru

– the prince and hero of Independence, the heir of Mahatma Gandhi – could do no wrong.

Only in the last ten minutes or so of any speech did he spend time asking for their votes – for the Congress, the party which had brought freedom to the country and which, for all its faults, was the only party that could keep India together; for the Congress parliamentary candidate 'who is a decent man' (Nehru had forgotten his name); and for his old comrade and companion Mahesh Kapoor, who had undertaken such a heavy task for the whole state by framing the crucial zamindari laws. He reminded the audience of certain anachronisms in an age of republicanism who were attempting to misuse feudal loyalties for their own personal ends. Some of them were even standing for election as Independents. One of them, who owned a huge estate, was even using the humble bicycle as his symbol. (This local reference went down well.) But there were many such, and the lesson was a general one. He asked the audience not to swallow the present professions of idealism and humility of such notables, but to contrast these with their ugly past record, a record of oppression of the people and of faithful service to their British overlords who had protected their domains, their rents and their misdeeds. The Congress would have no truck with such feudalists and reactionaries, and it needed the support of the masses to fight them.

When the crowd, carried away with enthusiasm, shouted 'Congress Zindabad!' or, worse still, 'Jawaharlal Nehru Zindabad!' Nehru ticked them off sharply and told them to shout 'Jai Hind!' instead.

And thus his meetings ended, and on he went to the next one, always late, always impatient, a man whose greatness of heart won the hearts of others, and whose meandering pleas for mutual tolerance kept a volatile country, not merely in those early and most dangerous years but throughout his own lifetime, safe at least from the systemic clutch of religious fanaticism.

THE few hours that Jawaharlal Nehru spent in the district had an enormous effect on all the electoral campaigns there, and on none more so than Mahesh Kapoor's. It gave him new hope and it gave the Congress workers new heart. The people too became perceptibly more friendly. If Nehru, who was indeed perceived by the ordinary people as the Soul of Congress and the Pride of India had put his stamp of approval on his 'old comrade and companion', who were they to doubt his credentials? Had the elections been held the next day instead of two weeks later, Mahesh Kapoor would probably have flown home with a large majority on the hem of Nehru's dusty achkan.

Nehru had also partially drawn the communal sting. For among Muslims throughout the country he was perceived as their true champion and protector. This was the man who at the time of Partition had jumped down from a police jeep in Delhi and rushed unarmed into the midst of fighting mobs in order to save lives, no matter whether the lives were Hindu or Muslim. This was the man whose very dress spoke of nawabi culture, however much he fulminated against Nawabs. Nehru had been to the shrine of the great sufi saint Moinuddin Chishti at Ajmer, and had been honoured with the gift of a gown; he had been to Amarnath, where the Hindu priests had honoured him with puja. The President of India, Rajendra Prasad, would have gone to the latter but not to the former. It gave the frightened minorities heart that the Prime Minister saw no essential difference between the two.

Even Maulana Azad, the most notable leader among the Muslims after Independence, was a moon compared to Nehru's sun; his brightness was largely that of reflection. For it was in Nehru – though he was not a man who was in love with it, and though he did not make the most effectual use of it – that popularity – and national power – was vested.

There were even some – both Hindus and Muslims – who said half-jokingly that he would have made a better leader of the Muslims than Jinnah. Jinnah had no sympathy for them – it was his will that had held them in his sway and led them towards Pakistan. But here was a man who was positively bubbling with sympathy, and who, unembittered by the partition of his country, continued, unlike others, to treat them – as he treated people of all religions or none – with affection and respect. They would have felt a great deal less secure and more fearful if someone else had been ruling in Delhi.

But, as the saying goes, Delhi is far away. And Brahmpur too for that matter – and even the district headquarters of Rudhia. As the days passed, once again local loyalties, local quarrels, local issues, and the local configurations of caste and religion began to reassert themselves. Gossip about Mahesh Kapoor's son and the Nawabzada, about Saeeda Bai and the Nawab Sahib, continued to be exchanged at the small barber's shop in Salimpur – more a pavement stall than a shop – in the vegetable market, over an evening hookah in a village courtyard, and wherever people met and talked.

Many upper-caste Hindus decided that Maan had lost his caste by associating with – and, worse still, falling in love with – that Muslim whore. And with Maan's loss of caste his father had lost his claim on their vote. On the other hand, with the passage of time, many of the poorer Muslims – and most of them were poor – rethought the question of where their interests lay. Though they had a traditional loyalty to the Nawab Sahib, they began to fear what would happen if they elected his man Waris to the Legislative Assembly. What if not only he but other feudal Independents were elected? What if the Congress did not get a clear majority? Would the Zamindari Act – or at least its implementation – not then be at hazard, even if it passed the barrier of the Supreme Court? The danger of permanent tenantry under the cruel control of the munshi and his enforcers held few attractions compared to the possibility of independent ownership, however encumbered, of their own land.

Meanwhile, Kedarnath had some success with the jatavs

of Salimpur and the villages around; unlike most upper-caste or even comparatively lower-caste Hindus, he did not refuse to eat with them, and they knew through their relatives or acquaintances in Brahmpur, such as Jagat Ram of Ravidaspur, that he was one of the few footwear traders in Misri Mandi who treated their caste-brethren tolerably well. Nor had Mahesh Kapoor, unlike L.N. Agarwal with his police charge, done anything to dilute their natural affinity for the Congress. Veena for her part continued to go from house to house and village to village with the Congress women's committees to canvass for her father. She was glad of the work, and she was glad that her father was once again immersed in his campaign. It took his mind off matters which would have been too painful to contemplate. Old Mrs Tandon was running Prem Nivas these days, and Bhaskar was staying there. Veena missed him, but there was nothing she could do about it.

The race was now almost a straight contest between Nehru's old comrade-in-arms and the lackey of the reactionary Nawab Sahib; or, equally plausibly, between the father of the villainous Maan and the stout and faithful Waris.

The walls of both Baitar and Salimpur were covered with handbills carrying Nehru's portrait, many defaced with a large green bicycle, whose two wheels covered his two eyes. Waris had been appalled by Nehru's remarks about his master, whom he revered, and he was determined to avenge both that verbal attack and Maan's physical attack on the gallant Firoz. He was not excessively nice about his methods. He would use legitimate means where he could, and anything else where he could not. He coaxed money out of the tight-fisted munshi, he threw feasts and distributed sweets and liquor, he coerced whoever he could and cajoled whoever he could, he promised whatever was necessary, he took the Nawab Sahib's name and God's, certain that he was speaking on their joint behalf and heedless of the possibility of their future disapproval. Maan, whom he had once instinctively liked and who had proved such a false and dangerous friend, was his arch-enemy. But now, after the disruptive magic of the Nehruvian wand, Waris could not be certain that he would defeat his father.

On the day before the election, when it would be too late for any effective refutation, appeared a small handbill in Urdu, printed in the thousands on flimsy pink paper. It carried a black border. It appeared to have no author. There was no printer's name at the bottom. It announced that Firoz had died the previous night, and called upon all faithful people, in his grieving father's name, to cast their vote in such a way as to express their indignation against the author of this great misfortune. The murderer even now walked the streets of Brahmpur, free on bail, free to strangle more helpless Muslim women and slaughter the flower of Muslim manhood. Where could such an abomination occur, such a prostitution of the ideals of justice, than under Congress Raj? It was being said that no matter who or what stood for election as a Congress candidate – even a lamp-post or a dog – they would be bound to win. But the people of this constituency should not vote for the shameless lamp-post or the foul dog. They should remember that if Mahesh Kapoor got into power, no one's life or honour would be safe.

The fatal flier – for such it was intended to be – appeared, as befitted its flimsiness – to travel on the wind; for by that evening, when all overt electioneering had ceased, it had found its way to almost every village in the constituency. The next day was the vote, and it was too late to suppress or counter the lie.

17.36

'WHOSE wife are you?' asked Sandeep Lahiri, who was Presiding Officer at one of the many polling stations in Salimpur.

'How can I take his name?' asked the burqa-clad woman in a shocked whisper. 'It is written on that slip of paper which I gave you before you left the room just now.'

Sandeep looked down at the slip of paper, then once

more at the voting list. 'Fakhruddin? You are Fakhruddin's wife? From the village Noorpur Khurd?'

'Yes, yes.'

'You have four children, don't you?'

'Yes, yes, yes.'

'Out!' said Sandeep sternly. He had already ascertained that the real woman in question had two children. Strictly speaking, he should have handed the woman over to the police, but he didn't feel her offence merited such stern action. Only once had he had recourse to the police in this election. That had been a few days earlier when a drunken man in Rudhia had threatened a member of his polling party and had tried to tear up a copy of the electoral rolls.

Sandeep enjoyed being away from Brahmpur. His work in the Department of Mines was dull and desk-bound compared to his earlier responsibilities out in the subdivision. This election work – though for the most part also performed at a desk – provided a refreshing respite, and he got to see once again the areas that, for all their backwardness, he had grown to feel such affection for. He looked around the room at a torn map of India and a chart of the Hindi alphabet. The polling station happened to be in a local school.

There were sounds of an argument from the adjoining classroom, where the men's booth was located. Sandeep got up to find out what the matter was and was faced with an unusual sight. A beggar who had no hands was intent on casting his vote, and on doing so unaided by anyone. He refused to be accompanied into the curtained area, insisting that the officer would reveal whom he had voted for. The polling officer was arguing with him, but to no avail, and the flow of voters had halted outside the classroom while voices rose hotly from within. The beggar said that the polling officer should fold his ballot-paper for him and put it between his teeth. Then he himself would go behind the curtain and insert it in the box of his choice.

'I can't do that,' said the officer.

'Why not?' insisted the beggar. 'Why should I let you

come in with me? How do I know you are not one of the Nawab Sahib's spies? Or the Minister's?' he added hastily.

Sandeep made a quiet gesture to the polling officer, indicating that he should allow the man's request. The beggar performed his electoral duty for both Parliament and the Legislative Assembly. When he emerged for the second time, he gave the officer a contemptuous snort. The officer was quite miffed.

'Wait a second,' said another officer. 'We forgot to mark you with the ink.'

'You'll recognize me if you see me again,' said the beggar.

'Yes, but you might try to vote somewhere else. It's a rule. Everyone has to have their left forefinger marked.'

The beggar snorted again. 'Find my left forefinger,' he said.

The entire polling party appeared to be held at bay by one man. 'I have the answer to that,' Sandeep told his officer with a smile, turned to a page of his instructions, and read out:

'Any reference in this rule or in rule 23 to the left fore-finger of an elector shall, in the case where the elector has his left fore-finger missing, be construed as a reference to any other finger of his left hand, and shall, in the case where all the fingers of his left hand are missing, be construed as a reference to the fore-finger or any other finger of his right hand, and shall, in the case where all his fingers of both the hands are missing, be construed as a reference to such extremity of his left or right arm as he possesses.'

He dipped the glass rod into the phial of ink, and smiled weakly at the beggar, who, defeated by the labyrinthine brains of the Raj-trained drafters of the Ministry of Law, held out his left stump with very bad grace.

Polling was fairly brisk. By noon, about three in every ten names on the voting list had been crossed off. After an hour's break for lunch came the second four-hour voting period. By the time the polls closed at five, fifty-five per cent or so of those eligible to vote at that polling station had cast their votes. This represented a very good turnout, Sandeep thought. He knew from his experience of the last few days that – contrary to what he had expected – the urban turnout in most areas was lower than the rural one.

At five o'clock, the school gates were closed, and signed paper slips were given to those already in the queue. When they too had cast their votes, the slits of the ballot-boxes were closed with a paper seal, and stamped with a red seal of lac. The polling agents of the various candidates added their own seals. Sandeep made arrangements for the ballot-boxes to be locked in the schoolroom overnight and posted a guard over them. The next day these boxes, along with others, were taken under the care of the SDO of Salimpur to the Collectorate at Rudhia, where they were locked up, together with ballot-boxes that had begun to arrive from all over the district, in the government treasury.

Because the voting itself had been staggered, the counting of votes too was staggered, with the constituencies that had gone to the polls first being counted first. Some of the polling parties now became counting parties. As a result of this schedule, seven to ten days generally elapsed between the poll and the count in a typical constituency in Purva Pradesh in the General Elections of 1952.

These were days of tormenting anxiety for any candidate who fancied that he or she might have a chance of winning. Certainly, it was so for Waris Khan, though no one would have thought it would be otherwise. But despite his many other anxieties, it was true for Mahesh Kapoor as well.

Part Eighteen

18.1

LATA was not an active participant in the dramatic events of January. She reflected, however, on Meenakshi's prediction, or at least expectation, of excitement in the New Year. Had Brahmpur been Calcutta and Savita's family hers, Meenakshi could not have been entirely disappointed by events: a stabbing, a scandal, a death, a vicious election – and all in a family that was for the most part used to nothing more exciting than strong words between a mother and a daughter – or stronger words between a father and a son.

This was the term that would culminate in her final exams. Each day Lata attended her lectures, her mind only half on what was being said about old novels and older plays. Most of her fellow students, including Malati, were concentrating on their studies; there were very few extra-curricular activities, certainly no plays or anything that required an investment of time. The weekly meetings of the Brahmpur Literary Society continued as before, but Lata had no heart to attend them. Maan had very recently been released from prison on bail, which was a relief, but it appeared that the final charge-sheet was going to be more serious than they had come to hope it might.

Lata enjoyed managing Uma, who was a very obliging baby, and whose smiles made her forget that there was a sorrowing or troubled world around her. The baby had inexhaustible energy, and a determined grip on life, her surroundings, and any hair within reach. She had taken to singing and to dictatorially thumping the edge of her wicker cot.

Uma, Lata noticed, had a pacifying effect on Savita and even on Pran. Her father, when he dandled her in his arms, was unconscious for a few moments of his own father – smarting between grief and anger; or his brother, caught equally in the toils of love and the law; or his wife; or his late mother; or his own health and work and ambitions. Pran had learned 'The Lady Baby' by heart, and would declaim it to Uma from time to time. Mrs Rupa Mehra, who had undertaken enormous quantities of winter knitting, would look up, half delighted and half suspicious, whenever Pran began one of his recitations.

Kabir had made no attempt to contact Lata in Calcutta. He did not meet her in Brahmpur either. He saw her at the chautha, and once from a distance on the college campus. She looked quietly unapproachable. With all the recent uproar in the press he could imagine that she, like Pran, would be unable to escape endless expressions of sympathy and curiosity from friends, acquaintances, and strangers.

He reflected unhappily that their meetings had always had a somewhat illogical, incomplete, and insubstantial feel about them. They always met for a very short time, were constantly aware of the risk of discovery, and so, even during the brief while that they were together, seemed extremely awkward with each other. Kabir was straightforward in his conversations with everyone except Lata, and he wondered if she too might not be at her most complex and difficult when she was with him.

He did not expect any longer that she would be thinking much about him. Even if she had not been at the unsettled periphery of so many distractions and distresses, he would not have expected it. He could not know she had heard that he had been in Calcutta. He had no idea of Malati's letter. He too was involved in his studies, and he too had his private sadnesses and consolations. His weekly visit to his mother was an unavoidable sadness – and he found his own solace in whatever interests he could: in playing cricket, for example, or in further news of the Test series with England, the last match of which was still to be played in Madras. Recently, with Mr Nowrojee's active enthusiasm, he had arranged for the poet Amit Chatterji to come to Brahmpur to read and discuss his work at a meeting of the Brahmpur Literary Society. This was due to take place in the first week of February. He hoped, but did not expect, that Lata would be there. He assumed she had heard of Chatterji's work.

At ten past five on the appointed day, there was an air of great excitement at 20 Hastings Road. The stuffed chairs with their flowery prints were all occupied. Glasses of water covered with lace doilies stood on the table from which Mr Nowrojee would introduce the speaker and Amit would recite his poetry. Mrs Nowrojee's rock-like delicacies lurked in a nearby room. The late light fell gently on the translucent skin of Mr Nowrojee, as he looked out with a melancholy tremor at his sundial and wondered why the poet Chatterji had not yet appeared. Kabir was sitting at the back of the room. He was dressed in whites, having just played a friendly match between the History Department and the Eastern India Railway Cricket Club. He had cycled over and was still sweating. The booming poetess, Mrs Supriya Joshi, sniffed the air daintily.

She turned to Mr Makhijani, the patriotic poet.

'I always feel, Mr Makhijani,' she murmured in her resonant voice, 'I always feel –'

'Yes, yes,' said Mr Makhijani fervently. 'That is the ticket. One must feel. Without feeling, wherefrom would the Muse strike?'

Mrs Supriya Joshi continued: 'I always feel that one should approach poetry in a spirit of purity. One must have a freshness of mind, a cleanliness of body. One must lave oneself in sparkling springs –'

'Lave – ah, yes, lave,' said Mr Makhijani.

'Genius may be ninety-nine per cent perspiration, but ninety-nine per cent perspiration is the prerogative of genius.' She looked pleased with her formulation.

Kabir turned to Mrs Supriya Joshi. 'I'm so sorry,' he said. 'I was just playing a match.'

'Oh,' said Mrs Supriya Joshi.

'May I say how very glad I was where I happened to be when you read your remarkable poetry a few months ago.' Kabir beamed at her; she looked smitten. It was not for nothing that he planned to join the diplomatic service. The smell of his sweat had suddenly become aphrodisiac. Indeed, thought Mrs Supriya Joshi, this young man is very good-looking and very courteous.

'Ah –' she whispered. 'Here comes the young master.'

Amit had just entered with Lata and Pran. Mr Nowrojee immediately began to talk to Amit earnestly and inaudibly.

Kabir noticed that Lata was looking around for a place to sit in the crowded room. In the gladness and surprise of seeing her, he did not even wonder why she had come in together with Amit.

He stood up. 'There's a place here,' he said.

Lata's mouth opened a little and she took in a quick breath. She glanced at Pran, but his back was turned. Without a word, she joined Kabir, squeezing in between him and Mrs Supriya Joshi, who did not look at all pleased. Far too courteous, she thought.

18.2

MR NOWROJEE, now smiling in wintry relief at the distinguished guest and the distinguished audience − which included the Proctor, Mr Sorabjee, as well as the eminent Professor Mishra − removed Amit's doily and his own, and took a sip of water before declaring the meeting open.

He introduced the speaker as 'not the least of those who have merged the vigour of the West with a sensibility distinctly Indian' and then proceeded to treat his audience to a disquisition on the word 'sensibility'. Having touched on several senses of the word 'sensible', he continued to other adjectives: sensitive, sensile, sensate, sensuous and sensual. Mrs Supriya Joshi grew restless. She said to Mr Makhijani:

'Such long long speeches he loves to give.'

Her voice carried, and Mr Nowrojee's cheek, already flushed as a result of his discussion of the last two adjectives, took on a darker tinge of embarrassment.

'But I do not mean to deprive you of the talents of Amit Chatterji with my own poor meanderings,' he stated in a stricken manner, sacrificing the brief history of Indian Poetry in English that he had planned to deliver (it was to have climaxed in a triolet to 'our supreme poetess Toru

Dutt'). Mr Nowrojee continued: 'Mr Chatterji will read a selection of his poems and then answer questions about his work.'

Amit began by saying how pleased he was to be in Brahmpur. The invitation had been extended at a cricket match; he noticed that Mr Durrani, who had invited him, was still dressed for cricket.

Lata looked astonished. Amit had told her when he arrived the previous day from Calcutta that he had been invited by the Literary Society, and Lata had simply assumed that it was Mr Nowrojee who had initiated the process. She turned to Kabir and he shrugged. There was a scent of sweat to him that reminded her of the day when she had watched him practising at the nets. He was behaving all too coolly. Was he like this with this other woman? Well, Lata told herself, two could be cool.

Amit for his part, noticing this unconscious and intimate look pass between them, realized that Lata must know Kabir quite well. He lost the thread of his thoughts for a moment, and improvised some guff about the resemblance between cricket and poetry. He then continued to say what he had meant to, which was that it was an honour to be reading in the city associated with the name of the Barsaat Mahal and the Urdu poet Mast. Perhaps it was not widely known that Mast, apart from being a famous writer of ghazals, was also a satirist. What exactly he would have made of the recent elections one could not tell, but he would certainly have made something of the unscrupulous energy with which they had been conducted, nowhere more so than in Purva Pradesh. Amit himself had been inspired to write a short poem after reading the morning's edition of the *Brahmpur Chronicle*. In lieu of Vande Mataram or any such patriotic opening hymn he would lay his poem before this audience as a Victory Hymn to their elected or soon-to-be-elected sovereigns.

He took a sheet of paper out of his pocket and began.

'God of pebbles, help us, now the poll is past,
Not to spurn the small bribes but to snatch the vast,

> To attack the right cause, to defend the wrong,
> To exploit the helpless and protect the strong.
> To our peculations and our victims add.
> Mighty Lord, we pray thee, make us very bad. . . .'

There were three more stanzas, referring among other things to a few local contests that Amit had read about in the newspaper – one of which made both Pran and Lata sit up: it referred in a flippant manner to a landowner and a land-snatcher who had first come together and then bounced apart like billiard balls in the cause of garnering the vote.

Most of the audience enjoyed the poem, especially the local references, and laughed. Mr Makhijani, however, was not amused.

'He is making mockery of our Constitution. He is making mockery,' said the patriotic bard.

Amit went on to read a dozen poems, including 'The Fever Bird', which had so haunted Lata when she first read it. Professor Mishra too thought it very good, listened intently, and nodded his head.

Several of the poems Amit read were not to be found in his books; for the most part they had been written more recently. One, however, about the death of an old aunt of his, which Lata found very moving, had been composed some time before. Amit had kept it aside and rarely read it. Lata noticed that Pran's head was bowed as he listened to this poem, and indeed the whole audience was quite still.

After the reading and applause was over, Amit said that he would be happy to answer any questions.

'Why is it that you do not write in Bengali, your mother tongue?' asked a challenging voice. The young man who spoke appeared to be quite angry.

Amit had been asked this question – and had asked himself this question – many times before. His answer was that his Bengali was not good enough for him to be able to express himself in the manner he could in English. It wasn't a question of choice. Someone who had been trained all his life to play the sitar could not become a sarangi player because his ideology or his conscience told him to. 'Besides,' Amit added, 'we are all accidents of history and must do what we are best at without fretting too much about it. Even Sanskrit came to India from outside.'

Mrs Supriya Joshi, the songbird of free verse, now stood up and said:

'Why do you use rhyming? Moon, June, Moon, June? A poet must be free – free as a bird – a fever bird.' Smiling, she sat down.

Amit said he rhymed because he liked to. He liked the sound, and it helped give pith and memorability to what might otherwise become diffuse. He no more felt chained by it than a musician felt chained by the rules of a raag.

Mrs Supriya Joshi, unconvinced, remarked to Mr Makhijani: 'All is rhyming, chiming, in his poems, like Nowrojee's triolets.'

Professor Mishra asked a question about Amit's influences: did he detect the shadow of Eliot in his writing? He referred to several lines in Amit's poetry, and compared them to lines of his own favourite modern poet.

Amit tried to answer the question as well as he could, but he thought that Eliot was not one of his major influences.

'Have you ever been in love with an English girl?'

Amit sat up sharply, then relaxed. It was a sweet, anxious old lady from the back of the room.

'Well, I – I don't feel I can answer that before an audience,' he said. 'When I asked for questions, I should have added that I would answer any questions so long as they were not too private – or, for that matter, too public. Government policy, for instance, would be out.'

An eager young student, blinking in adoration, and unable to restrain the nervousness in his voice, said: 'Of the 863 lines of poetry in your two published books, thirty-one refer to trees, twenty-two have the word "love" or "loving" in them, and eighteen consist of words of only one syllable. How significant is this?'

Lata noticed Kabir smile; she was smiling herself. Amit attempted to extricate an intelligent question out of what had just been said and talked a little about his themes. 'Does that answer the question?' he asked.

'Oh, yes,' nodded the young man happily.

'Do you believe in the virtue of compression?' asked a determined academic lady.

'Well, yes,' said Amit warily. The lady was rather fat.

'Why, then, is it rumoured that your forthcoming novel – to be set, I understand, in Bengal – is to be so long? More than a thousand pages!' she exclaimed reproachfully, as if he were personally responsible for the nervous exhaustion of some future dissertationist.

'Oh, I don't know how it grew to be so long,' said Amit. 'I'm very undisciplined. But I too hate long books: the better, the worse. If they're bad, they merely make me pant with the effort of holding them up for a few minutes. But if they're good, I turn into a social moron for days, refusing to go out of my room, scowling and growling at interruptions, ignoring weddings and funerals, and making enemies out of friends. I still bear the scars of *Middlemarch*.'

'How about Proust?' asked a distracted-looking lady, who had begun knitting the moment the poems stopped.

Amit was surprised that anyone read Proust in Brahmpur. He had begun to feel rather happy, as if he had breathed in too much oxygen.

'I'm sure I'd love Proust,' he replied, 'if my mind was more like the Sundarbans: meandering, all-absorptive, endlessly, er, sub-reticulated. But as it is, Proust makes me weep, weep, weep with boredom. Weep,' he added. He paused and sighed. 'Weep, weep, weep,' he continued emphatically. 'I weep when I read Proust, and I read very little of him.'

There was a shocked silence: why should anyone feel so strongly about anything? It was broken by Professor Mishra.

'Needless to say, many of the most lasting monuments of literature are rather, well, bulky.' He smiled at Amit. 'Shakespeare is not merely great but grand, as it were.'

'But only as it were,' said Amit. 'He only looks big in

bulk. And I have my own way of reducing that bulk,' he confided. 'You may have noticed that in a typical *Collected Shakespeare* all the plays start on the right-hand side. Sometimes, the editors bung a picture in on the left to force them to do so. Well, what I do is to take my pen-knife and slit the whole book up into forty or so fascicles. That way I can roll up *Hamlet* or *Timon* – and slip them into my pocket. And when I'm wandering around – in a cemetery, say – I can take them out and read them. It's easy on the mind and on the wrists. I recommend it to everyone. I read *Cymbeline* in just that way on the train here; and I never would have otherwise.'

Kabir smiled, Lata burst out laughing, Pran was appalled, Mr Makhijani gaped and Mr Nowrojee looked as if he were about to faint dead away.

Amit appeared pleased with the effect.

In the silence that followed, a middle-aged man in a black suit stood up. Mr Nowrojee began to tremble slightly. The man coughed a couple of times.

'I have formulated a conception as the result of your reading,' he announced to Amit. 'It has to do with the atomic age and the place of poetry, and the influence of Bengal. Many things have happened since the War, of course. I have been listening for an hour to the very scintillation of India, that is what I said to myself when I formulated my conception. . . .'

Immensely pleased with himself, he continued in this vein for the verbal equivalent of about six paragraphs, punctuated with 'You understand?' Amit nodded, less amiably each time. Some people got up, and Mr Nowrojee in his distress pounded an imaginary gavel on the table.

Finally the man said to Amit: 'Would you care to comment?'

'No thank you,' said Amit. 'But I appreciate your sharing your remarks with us. Any other questions?' he asked, emphasizing the last word.

But there were no more questions. It was time for Mrs Nowrojee's tea and her famous little cakes, the delight of dentists.

18.3

AMIT had hoped to talk to Lata a little, but he was mobbed. He had to sign books, he had to eat cake for fear of offending, and the sweet old lady, foiled once, insisted on asking him again whether he had been in love with an English girl. 'Now you can answer, there is no audience now,' she said. Several other people agreed with her. But Amit was spared: Mr Nowrojee, murmuring that his defence of rhyme had been so very heartening and that he himself was an unashamed devotee of rhyme, pressed into Amit's hand the suppressed triolet, and asked Amit to read it and tell him what he thought. 'Now, please be quite honest. Honesty such as yours is so refreshing, and only honesty will do,' said Mr Nowrojee. Amit looked down at the poem in Mr Nowrojee's thin, small, careful, upright handwriting:

A TRIOLET TO THE SONGSTER OF BENGAL

Fate snatched away sweet Toru Dutt
   At the soft age of twenty-two.
The casuarina tree was cut.
Fate snatched away sweet Toru Dutt.
No bulbuls haunt its branches but
   Her poems still haunt me and you.
Fate snatched away sweet Toru Dutt
   At the soft age of twenty-two.

Meanwhile, Professor Mishra was talking to Pran in another corner of the room. 'My dear boy,' he was saying. 'My commiserations go deeper than words. The sight of your hair, so short still, reminds me of that cruelly abridged life....'

Pran froze.

'You must take care of your health. You must not undertake new challenges at a time of bereavement – and, of course, family anxiety. Your poor brother, your poor brother,' said Professor Mishra. 'Have a cake.'

'Thank you, Professor,' said Pran.

'So you agree?' said Professor Mishra. 'The meeting is too soon, and to subject you to an interview –'

'Agree to what?' said Pran.

'To withdrawing your candidature, of course. Don't worry, dear boy, I will handle all the formalities. As you know, the selection committee is meeting on Thursday. It took so long to arrange a date,' he went on. 'But finally, in the middle of January, I succeeded in fixing one. And now, alas – but you are a young man, and will have many more opportunities for advancement, here in Brahmpur or elsewhere.'

'Thank you for your concern, Professor Mishra, but I believe I will feel well enough to attend,' said Pran. 'That was an interesting question you asked about Eliot,' he added.

Professor Mishra, his pallid face still frozen in disapproval at Pran's unfilial attitude and tempted almost to refer to funeral baked meats, was silent for a while. Then he pulled himself together and said: 'Yes, I gave a paper here a few months ago entitled "Eliot: Whither?" It is a pity you were unable to attend.'

'I didn't hear about it till later,' said Pran. 'I regretted it for weeks afterwards. Do have a cake, Professor Mishra. Your plate is empty now.'

Meanwhile Lata and Kabir were talking.

'So you invited him when you came to Calcutta?' said Lata. 'Did he come up to your expectations?'

'Yes,' said Kabir. 'I enjoy his poetry. But how did you know I went to Calcutta?'

'I have my sources,' said Lata. 'And how do you know Amit?'

'Amit, is it?'

'Mr Chatterji, if you like. How do you know him?'

'I don't – I mean, I didn't,' said Kabir, correcting himself. 'We were introduced by someone.'

'By Haresh Khanna?'

'You really do have your sources,' said Kabir, looking straight into Lata's eyes. 'Perhaps you would care to tell me what I was doing this afternoon.'

'That's easy,' said Lata. 'You were playing cricket.'

Kabir laughed. 'That was too easy,' he said. 'Yesterday afternoon?'

'I don't know,' said Lata. 'I really can't eat this cake,' she added.

'I've put up with some of this cake in the past in the hope of seeing you,' said Kabir. 'But you're worth any amount of chipped enamel.'

Very charming, thought Lata coldly, and did not respond. Kabir's compliment seemed rather too facile.

'So, how do you know Amit — I mean Mr Chatterji?' continued Kabir. His voice had an edge to it.

'What is this, Kabir, an interrogation?'

'No.'

'Well, what is it then?'

'A civil question, which might merit a similar answer,' said Kabir. 'I asked out of interest. Do you want me to withdraw it?'

Lata reflected that the tone of the question had not been civil. It had been jealous. Good!

'No. Let it stand,' she said. 'He's my brother-in-law. I mean,' — and here she flushed — 'he's not my own brother-in-law but my brother's.'

'And I imagine you've had plenty of opportunity of meeting him in Calcutta.'

The word Calcutta was like a goad.

'Just what are you trying to get at, Kabir?' said Lata angrily.

'Just that I've been watching him for the last few minutes and during the reading too, and everything he does seems to be aimed at you.'

'Nonsense.'

'Look at him now.'

Lata turned instinctively; and Amit, who had had half an eye on her while he was attempting not too dishonestly to comment on Nowrojee's triolet, gave her a smile. Lata smiled back weakly. Amit, however, was soon obscured by the bulk of Professor Mishra.

'And I suppose you take walks?'

'Sometimes –'

'Reading *Timon* to each other in cemeteries.'

'Not exactly.'

'And I suppose you go up and down the Hooghly on a boat at dawn.'

'Kabir – how dare you, you of all people –'

'And I suppose he writes you letters as well?' continued Kabir, who looked as if he wanted to shake her.

'What if he did?' said Lata. 'What if he does? But he doesn't. It's the other man you met, Haresh, who writes to me – and I write back.'

The colour drained from Kabir's face. He grabbed her right hand and held it tight.

'Let go,' whispered Lata. 'Let me go at once. Or I'll drop this plate.'

'Go ahead,' said Kabir. 'Drop it. It's probably a Nowrojee heirloom.'

'Please –' said Lata, tears starting to her eyes. He was actually hurting her physically, but she was very annoyed about her tears. 'Please don't, Kabir –'

He released her hand.

'Ah, Malvolio's revenge –' said Mr Barua, coming up to them. 'Why have you made Olivia cry?' he asked Kabir.

'I haven't made her cry,' said Kabir. 'No one has an obligation to cry. Any crying of hers is purely voluntary.'

And with that he left.

18.4

LATA, refusing to explain anything to Mr Barua, went to wash her face. She did not return to the room until she felt that it would not be obvious that she had been in tears. But the crowd had thinned, and Pran and Amit were ready to take their leave.

Amit was staying at the home of Mr Maitra, the retired Superintendent of Police; but he was having dinner with Pran, Savita, Mrs Rupa Mehra, Lata, Malati and Maan.

Though Maan, out on bail, was living once again at

Prem Nivas, he could not bear to take his meals there. The polls were over, and his father had returned to Brahmpur. He was an angry and grieving man – and wanted Maan with him all the time. He did not know what would happen to his son once a proper charge-sheet was delivered. Everything was collapsing about Mahesh Kapoor's ears. He hoped that he might at least retain his power in politics. But if he did not succeed even in winning his own seat, he knew how drastically this would weaken his following.

Not being a Minister, he had no immediate activity to lose himself in. Some days he received visitors, on other days, he sat and looked out at the garden, saying nothing. The servants knew that he did not wish to be disturbed. Veena would bring him tea. The counting of the vote for his constituency was due to take place a few days from now; he would go to Rudhia for the day. By the evening of the 6th of February he would know if he had won or lost.

Maan was riding in a tonga to Pran's house for dinner when he saw Malati Trivedi walking along. He greeted her. She said hello, then suddenly looked awkward.

'What's the matter?' said Maan. 'I haven't been convicted yet. And Pran says you're having dinner with us. Get in.'

Malati, feeling ashamed of her hesitancy, did get in, and they rode towards the university together, not saying much for two such outgoing people.

Maan had met three of the Chatterjis – Meenakshi, Kakoli and Dipankar – at various times. He remembered Meenakshi most of all: she had stood out at Pran's wedding – and had made even a hospital room appear a glamorous backdrop for her own dramatic presence. He now looked forward to meeting their brother, whom Lata had mentioned to him during her jail visit. Amit greeted him in a sympathetic and curious manner.

Maan looked worn and knew it. Sometimes he still couldn't believe where he had been; at other times he couldn't believe that he was, at least for a while, free again.

'We hardly meet these days,' said Lata, who had not been able to concentrate on conversation for the last hour.

Maan began to laugh. 'No, we hardly do,' he said.

Malati could see that something was the matter with Lata. She attributed it to the presence of the Poet. Malati had been keen to examine this contender for Lata's hand. She decided that Amit was not very impressive: he was bent on making small talk. The Cobbler, who (as Malati had been told) had got angry when called mean, had shown far more spirit – even if, she decided, of a rather zany kind.

Malati did not know that Amit, especially after reading his poems or writing a serious one, would often switch into an entirely different mood: cynical and sometimes trivializing. He had been leached of any pretence at profundity. Though no Kuku-couplets flapped away like freed pigeons from his mouth this evening, he began to talk in a light-hearted manner about elected politicians and the way they subverted the system by winning favours for themselves and their families. Mrs Rupa Mehra, who switched off whenever the talk turned to politics, had gone into the other room to put Uma to bed.

'Mr Maitra, with whom I'm staying, has been explaining to me his prescription for Utopia,' said Amit. 'The country should be run by only children – unmarried only children – whose parents are dead. At any rate, he says, all Ministers should be childless.'

Noticing that no one was taking up the subject, Amit continued: 'Otherwise, of course, they're bound to try to get their children out of whatever scrapes they've got themselves into.' He stopped, suddenly realizing what he was saying.

Since everyone was looking at him without speaking, he quickly added: 'Of course, Ila Kaki says it isn't just in politics that this sort of thing happens – academia is just as bad – full of – how does she put it? – "sordid nepotisms and antagonisms". It sounds just like the literary world.'

'Ila?' said Pran.

'Oh, Ila Chattopadhyay,' said Amit, relieved that the

points had been switched on the tracks. 'Dr Ila Chattopadhyay.'

'The one who writes about Donne?' asked Pran.

'Yes. Didn't you meet her when you were in Calcutta? Not even at our place? I suppose not. Anyway, she was telling me about a textbook scandal at some university where a professor got a book prescribed as a compulsory textbook when he himself had written it under a pseudonym. She got extremely excited about the whole business.'

'Doesn't she tend to?' asked Lata with a smile.

'Oh, yes,' said Amit, pleased that Lata was at last taking part in the conversation. 'Yes, she does. She's coming to Brahmpur in a few days, as it happens, so you'll have a chance to meet,' he added to Pran. 'I'll tell her to look you up. You'll find her very interesting.'

'The baby's sleeping,' said Mrs Rupa Mehra, returning to the room. 'Very soundly, very sweetly.'

'Well, I thought her book on Donne was very good,' said Pran. 'What's she coming here for?'

'She's sitting on some committee or other – I don't think she mentioned what,' said Amit. 'And I'm not sure, given her erratic ways, that she herself will remember.'

Mrs Rupa Mehra said: 'Yes, she is one of these very intelligent women. Very modern in her views. She was advising Lata against getting married.'

Pran hesitated before saying: 'Was it a selection committee by any chance?'

Amit tried to remember. 'I think so. I'm not sure, but I think that's what it was. Yes, she was talking about the poor calibre of most of the candidates, so it must have been.'

'I don't think I'd better meet her, in that case,' said Pran. 'She'll probably be deciding my fate. I think I'm one of those candidates she was referring to.'

In the straits in which the family now found itself, Pran's possible promotion had become still more important. Even his retention of this house, the conferral of which had been rather ad hoc, could well depend on it.

'Your fate! That sounds very dramatic,' said Amit. 'I

should think that with Professor Mishra firmly on your side, Fate would think twice about misbehaving with you.'

Savita leaned forward eagerly. 'What did you say? Professor Mishra?'

'Yes, indeed,' said Amit. 'He spoke most fulsomely about Pran when I told him I was having dinner here.'

'There, darling,' said Savita.

Pran said: 'If I had been born a cockroach, I wouldn't wonder: "What will the selection committee decide?" "What's happening to India?" "Is the cheque in the mail?" "Will I live to see my daughter grow up?" Why on earth am I so concerned about all these things?'

Everyone except Amit looked at Pran with varying degrees of surprise and concern.

'Don't you care what happens to me?' Maan asked suddenly.

'Yes, I do,' said Pran, taking his argument through its paces. 'But I doubt a cockroach would care about what happened to his brother. Or father for that matter.'

'Or mother,' added Maan, getting up immediately to go. He looked as if he could not bear any more such talk.

'Maan,' said Savita, 'don't take it like that. Pran too has been under a lot of strain. And he didn't mean any harm by that remark. Darling, please don't talk like that. It was quite a peculiar thing to say, and it's not like you at all; I'm not surprised Maan's upset.'

Pran, with a look of tired affection, yawned and said: 'I'll try to be careful about what I say. In my own house and with my own family.'

Seeing Savita's expression of hurt he wished he had left the second sentence unsaid. She, after all, succeeded in being careful without appearing constricted, without at all losing her sense of ease. She had never known him in perfect health. Even before the baby had been born, he could sense how much she loved him by the quiet of her footsteps in the room where he was sleeping – by the fact that she might begin to hum and suddenly become quiet. She would never have considered this to be a constraint. Sometimes he used to keep his eyes closed even though he was awake – just for the pleasure of feeling that someone cared for him so much. He supposed she was right: his remark had been a thoughtless one. Perhaps even childish.

Lata was looking at Savita and thinking: Savita was made to be married. She's happy to do all the things a house and a family require, all the small and serious things of life. She's only taken up law because it's been forced upon her by Pran's health. Then the thought struck her that Savita would have loved anyone whom she had married, anyone who was basically a good man, no matter how difficult he was, no matter how different he was from Pran.

18.5

'WHAT were you thinking?' Amit asked Lata after dinner, lingering over his coffee. The other guests were being seen to the door by Pran and Savita, and Mrs Rupa Mehra had gone into her room for a few minutes.

'That I really liked your reading,' said Lata. 'It was very affecting. And I enjoyed the question-and-answer session afterwards. Especially the statistical appendix – and the tearing of the tomes. You should advise Savita to deal as brutally with her law-books.'

'I didn't know you knew young Durrani,' said Amit.

'I didn't know he'd invited you.'

There was a few seconds' pause. Then Amit said: 'I meant, what were you thinking just now.'

'When?' said Lata.

'When you were looking at Pran and Savita. Over the pudding.'

'Oh.'

'Well, what?'

'I can't remember,' said Lata with a smile.

Amit laughed.

'Why are you laughing?' asked Lata.

'I like making you feel uncomfortable, I suppose.'

'Oh. Why?'

'– Or happy – or puzzled – just to see your change of mood. It's such fun. I pity you!'

'Why?' said Lata, startled.

'Because you'll never know what a pleasure it is to be in your company.'

'Do stop talking like that,' said Lata. 'Ma will come in any minute.'

'You're quite right. In that case: will you marry me?'

Lata dropped her cup. It fell on the floor and broke. She looked at the broken pieces – luckily, it had been empty – and then at Amit.

'Quick!' said Amit. 'Before they come running to see what's happened. Say yes.'

Lata had knelt down; she was gathering the bits of the cup together and placing them on the delicately patterned blue-and-gold saucer.

Amit joined her on the floor. Her face was only a few inches away from his, but her mind appeared to be somewhere else. He wanted to kiss her but he sensed that there was no question of it. One by one she picked up the shards of china.

'Was it a family heirloom?' asked Amit.

'What? I'm sorry –' said Lata, snapped out of her trance by the words.

'Well, I suppose I'll have to wait. I was hoping that by springing it on you like that I'd surprise you into agreeing.'

'I wish –' said Lata, putting the last piece of the shattered cup onto the saucer.

'What?' asked Amit.

'I wish I would wake up one day and find I'd been married to someone for six years. Or that I had a wild affair with someone and never got married at all. Like Malati.'

'Don't say that,' said Amit. 'Ma might come in at any moment. Anyway, I wouldn't advise an affair with Malati,' he added.

'Do stop being idiotic, Amit,' said Lata. 'You're so brilliant, do you have to be so stupid as well? I should only take you seriously in black and white.'

'And in sickness and health.'

Lata laughed: 'For better and for worse,' she added. 'Far worse, I suppose.'

Amit's eyes lit up. 'You mean yes?'

'No, I don't,' said Lata. 'I don't mean anything. And nor, I assume, do you. But why are we kneeling here facing each other like Japanese dolls? Get up, get up. Here comes Ma, just as you said.'

18.6

MRS RUPA MEHRA was less sharp with Amit, however, than he had expected, for she was having second thoughts about Haresh.

For fear of having her own judgment called into question, she did not speak her thoughts out aloud. But she was not skilled in dissimulation; and over the next few days, when Amit had left Brahmpur, it was her want of enthusiasm for, rather than her actual criticism of Haresh that indicated to Lata that all was not at ease in her mind with respect to her former favourite.

That he had been so upset by Lata calling him 'mean' bewildered Mrs Rupa Mehra. On the other hand, it must have been Lata's fault in some way, she decided. What she could not understand was that Haresh had not said good-bye to her, Mrs Rupa Mehra, his self-appointed mother-in-law-to-be. Several days had passed between the altercation and their hurried return to Brahmpur; yet during that time he had not visited or telephoned or written. It was not right; she was hurt; and she did not see why he should have continued to treat her so insensitively. If only he had called, she would have forgiven him immediately and tearfully. Now she was not in a forgiving mood at all.

It also struck her that some of her friends, when she had mentioned that Haresh was involved in the shoe trade, had made remarks such as, 'Well, of course, things have changed nowadays,' and 'Oh! Dear Rupa – but everything is for the best, and Praha is of course Praha.' In the first flush of vicarious romance, such veiled or consolatory comments had not struck home. But now the memory of them caused her to suffer a rush of embarrassment. Who could have predicted that the daughter of the potential Chairman of the Railway Board might be linked to the lowly lineage of leather?

'But such is Fate,' said Mrs Rupa Mehra to herself; and this led to a thought which an advertisement in the next morning's *Brahmpur Chronicle* translated into action. For there she noticed, under the heading 'Astrologer-Royal: Raj Jyotishi', the photograph of a plump and beaming middle-aged man, his hair cut short and parted in the middle. Underneath were the words:

The greatest Astrologer, Palmist and Tantrik. Pandit Kanti Prasad Chaturvedi, Jyotishtirtha, Tantrikacharya, Examiner, Government Board of Astrological Studies. Highly praised and honoured with unwanted testimonials. Very speedy results.

Very speedily – in fact the same afternoon – Mrs Rupa Mehra made her way to the Astrologer-Royal. He was unhappy that she knew only the place and date of Haresh's birth, not the exact time of day. But he promised to see what he could do. It would require certain extra assumptions, certain extra calculations, and even the use of the adjustment factor of Uranus, which was not standard in Indian astrology; and the use of Uranus was not costless. Mrs Rupa Mehra paid up and he told her to return two days later.

She felt quite guilty about these proceedings. After all, as she had complained to Lata when Mrs Mahesh Kapoor had asked for Savita's horoscope: 'I don't believe in all this matching. If it had been true, my husband and I....' But now she told herself that perhaps the fault lay in the lack of skill of particular astrologers, not in the science itself. And the Astrologer-Royal had been very persuasive. He had explained why her gold wedding ring would 'reinforce and concentrate the power of Jupiter'; he had advised her to wear a garnet because it would control the ecliptic node of Rahu and confer mental peace; he had praised her wisdom, which was patent to him from both her palm and her expression; and a large silver-framed photograph on his desk, facing clientwards, showed him shaking hands with the Governor himself.

When they next met, the Astrologer-Royal said: 'You see, in this man's seventh house, the Jupiter is aspected by Mars. The whole impression is yellow and red, which in combination you may consider to be orange or golden, therefore his wife will be very beautiful. Then you see, the moon is surrounded by lots of planets, that is also a sign of the same thing. But the seventh house has Aries in it, who is very stubborn, and Jupiter, who is strong, which will enhance the stubbornness. So therefore he will marry a beautiful but difficult woman. Is your daughter such a one?'

Mrs Rupa Mehra thought about the matter for a few seconds, then, hoping for better luck elsewhere, said: 'But what about all the other houses?'

'The seventh house is the House of the Wife.'

'But are there no problems at all? In the matching of the two horoscopes, I mean?' His eyes were very piercing, and she was forced to concentrate on the middle parting in his hair.

The Astrologer-Royal looked at her for a few seconds, smiling speculatively, then said: 'Yes, certain problems surely exist. I have examined the totality of the picture, taking into consideration the information of both your daughter and the Prospective. It is quite problematical, I would say. Kindly come and collect the problematical details this evening. I will write them down.'

'And Uranus?' asked Mrs Rupa Mehra. 'What does Uranus say?'

'The effect did not prove to be significant,' said the Astrologer-Royal. 'But of course the calculations had to be made anyway,' he added hastily.

18.7

AS they entered the Haridas College of Music together,
Malati's friend said: 'Well, there have been no more sight-
ings of the quarry. But if there are, I'll keep you informed.'

'What are you gabbling about?' asked Malati. 'I hope
we're not too late.' Ustad Majeed Khan was in an impatient
mood these days.

'Oh, you know, the woman he met at the Blue Danube.'

'Who met?'

'Kabir, of course.'

Malati stopped and turned towards her friend:

'But you said the Red Fox.'

Her friend shrugged. 'Did I? I might have. It's quite
confusing. But what difference does it make whether you
shoot someone in Chowk or in Misri Mandi?.... What's
the matter with you?'

For Malati had seized her friend's arm; her face had
gone white.

'What was this woman like? What was she wearing?'
she asked.

'Amazing! You didn't want to know anything then, but
now –'

'Tell me. Quickly.'

'Well, I wasn't there, but this girl Purnima – I don't
think you know her, she's from Patna and she's doing
history – it was she who noticed them. She was sitting a
few tables away, though, and you know what it's like with
these dimmed lights –'

'But what was she wearing? The woman, I mean, not
this wretched girl.'

'Malati, what's the matter with you? It's been weeks –'

'What was she wearing?' asked Malati desperately.

'A green sari. Wait, I'd better make sure I get my
colours right this time, or you'll kill me. Yes, Purnima
said she was wearing a green sari – and lots of flashy
emeralds. And she was tall and quite fair – that's about
all –'

'Oh, what have I done –' said Malati. 'Oh, poor fellow –

poor Kabir. What a terrible mistake. What have I done, what have I done?'

*

'Malati,' said Ustad Majeed Khan, 'carry the tanpura with respect, with both hands. It isn't the offspring of a cat. What is the matter with you?'

*

'What's the matter with you?' asked Lata, as Malati burst into her room.

'It was me he was with –' said Malati.

'Who?'

'Kabir – that day in the Red Fox, I mean the Blue Danube.'

A pang of literally green-eyed jealousy shot through Lata.

'No – I don't believe it. Not you!'

The cry was so vehement that Malati was taken aback. She almost feared Lata would attack her.

'I don't mean that – I don't mean that at all,' said Malati. 'I mean that he wasn't seeing some other girl. He hasn't been seeing anyone else. I was told the name of the wrong place. I should have waited to hear more. Lata, I blame myself. It's entirely my fault. I can imagine what you've gone through. But please, please don't take my mistake out on him – and on yourself.'

Lata was silent for a minute. Malati expected her to burst into tears of relief or frustration, but no tears came. Then she said: 'I won't. But Malu, don't blame yourself.'

'I do, I do. Poor fellow – he was entirely sincere all along.'

'Don't,' said Lata. 'Don't. Don't. I'm glad Kabir wasn't lying to you – I can't tell you how glad. But I've – well, I've learned something as a result of all this wretchedness – I have, Malu, I really have – about myself – and about, well, the strength of – really, the strangeness of my own feelings for him.'

Her voice seemed to come from a no-man's-land between hope and despair.

18.8

PROFESSOR MISHRA, frustrated that he had not got Pran to withdraw either his application for the readership or his harebrained schemes of syllabus reform, was grateful nevertheless that things were not going at all well for his father. Opinion in the press was strongly critical of the means deployed by his opponents, but on the question of whether he would win or lose the election, most people were agreed that he had almost certainly lost. Professor Mishra took a lively interest in politics, and almost all his informants told him that he should work on the assumption that Pran's father would not be in a position to wield much power to undo or avenge any injustice done to his son in the matter of the readership.

Professor Mishra was also pleased that he would know this fact for certain by the time the selection committee met. Counting in Mahesh Kapoor's constituency was due to he held on the 6th of February, and the selection committee was to meet on the 7th. He would thus be secure in the knowledge that he could safely stiletto the young lecturer who was proving to be such an obstacle in the smooth running of the department.

At the same time, since one of the prospective candidates, and by no means the worst one, was the nephew of the Chief Minister, Professor Mishra could ingratiate himself further in the eyes of S.S. Sharma by helping him out in this small particular. And Professor Mishra expected that when any committee assignments in the government, particularly — but not necessarily — in the field of education, opened up, the name of the by-then-retired Professor O.P. Mishra would be considered in a not unfavourable light by the reigning powers.

What if S.S. Sharma were called to Delhi, as it was rumoured that Nehru had not merely requested but virtually demanded of him? Professor Mishra reflected that it was not likely that even Nehru would succeed in dislodging so wily a politician as S.S. Sharma from his happy fief. And if he were to go and take charge of a ministry in Delhi, well, plums could fall from Delhi too, not merely from the Secretariat at Brahmpur.

What if S.S. Sharma went to Delhi and Mahesh Kapoor became Chief Minister in Brahmpur? This prospect was horrible, but it was utterly remote. Everything was against it: the scandal surrounding his son, his own recent widower-hood, the fact that his political credibility would be damaged as soon as it was known and published that he had lost his own seat. Nehru liked him, it was true; and was particularly impressed by his work on the Zamindari Act. But Nehru was not a dictator, and the Congress MLAs of Purva Pradesh would elect their own Chief Minister.

That it would be the great, baggy, faction-ridden Congress Party that would continue to run the country and the state was by now entirely clear. Congress, riding high on the popularity of Jawaharlal Nehru, was in the process of winning a landslide across the country. True, the party was garnering less than half the actual vote nationwide. But opposition to Congress was so fragmented and disorganized in most constituencies that it looked – from all the early returns – that Congress would be first-past-the-post in about three-quarters of the parliamentary seats, and in about two-thirds of the seats in the various state legislatures.

That Mahesh Kapoor's candidacy had collapsed for personal and special reasons relating to his constituency and his family, including the great popularity of the man whose agent he was seen to be opposing, would not help the ex-Minister of Revenue after the elections. If anything, he would be seen to be one of the exceptional electoral failures in a sea of successes. Sympathy for losers counts for little in politics. Mahesh Kapoor would, Professor Mishra devoutly hoped, be finished; and his upstart, Joyce-loving, professor-baiting son would come to realize in due course that he had no future prospects in this

438

department – any more than his younger brother had in civilized society.

And yet – and yet – could anything go wrong in Professor Mishra's plans? The five-person selection committee included himself (as Head of Department); the Vice-Chancellor of the university (who chaired the committee); the Chancellor's nominee (who happened that year to be a distinguished but rather feeble retired professor of history); and two outside experts from the panel of experts approved by the Academic Council. Professor Mishra had looked carefully through the panel and chosen two names, which the Vice-Chancellor had accepted without discussion or demur. 'You know what you are doing,' he had told Professor Mishra encouragingly. Their interests lay in the same direction.

The two experts, who at this moment were travelling from different directions to Brahmpur were Professor Jaikumar and Dr Ila Chattopadhyay. Professor Jaikumar was a mild-mannered man from Madras, whose specialism was Shelley, and who, unlike that volatile and fiery spirit, believed firmly in the stability of the cosmos and the absence of intra-departmental friction. Professor Mishra had taken him around the department on the day when Pran had had his fortuitous collapse.

Dr Ila Chattopadhyay would present no problem; she was beholden to Professor Mishra. He had sat on the committee that had made her a university reader some years ago, and he had immediately afterwards and on numerous subsequent occasions emphasized to her how instrumental he had been in the process. He had praised her work on Donne with great unctuousness and assiduity. He was certain that she would be compliant. When her train arrived at Brahmpur Station he was there to meet her and escort her to the Brahmpur University guest house.

On the way he tried to veer the conversation prematurely around to the next day's business. But Dr Ila Chattopadhyay did not appear to be at all keen to discuss the various candidates beforehand, which disappointed Professor

Mishra. 'Why don't we wait till the interviews?' she suggested.

'Quite so, quite so, dear lady, that is just what I would have suggested myself. But the background – I was sure you would appreciate being informed about – ah, here we are.'

'I am so exhausted,' said Dr Ila Chattopadhyay, looking around. 'What a horrible place.'

There should have been nothing exceptionally horrible about the room to one who had been to such places often before, but it was indeed fairly depressing, Professor Mishra had to agree. The university guest house was a dark series of rooms connected by a corridor. Instead of carpets there was coir matting, and the tables were too low to write at. A bed, two chairs, a few lights that did not work well, a tap that was over-generous with water even when turned off, and a flush that was miserly with it even when tugged violently: these were some of the appurtenances. As if to compensate for this, there was a great deal of dingy and unnecessary lace hanging everywhere: on the windows, on the lampshades, on the backs of the chairs.

'Mrs Mishra and I would be delighted if you would come for dinner to our place,' murmured Professor Mishra. 'The facilities for dining here are, well, adequate at best.'

'I've eaten,' said Dr Ila Chattopadhyay, shaking her head vigorously. 'And I'm really exhausted. I need to take an aspirin and go straight to bed. I'll be on that wretched committee tomorrow, don't worry.'

Professor Mishra went off, rather perturbed by Dr Ila Chattopadhyay's extraordinary attitude.

If it had not been open to misconstruction he would have invited her to stay at his house. When Professor Jaikumar arrived, he did precisely that.

'This is extremely – infinitely kind,' said Professor Jaikumar.

Professor Mishra winced, as he almost invariably did when talking to his colleague. Professor Jaikumar had prefixed a 'y' to both adverbs. The Mask of Yenarchy! thought Professor Mishra.

'Not at all, not at all,' he assured his guest blandly. 'You are the repository of the future stability of our department, and the least we can do is to make you welcome.'

'Yes, welcome, welcome,' said Mrs Mishra meekly and rapidly, doing namasté.

'I am sure you have looked through the candidates' applications and so on,' said Professor Mishra jovially.

Professor Jaikumar looked very slightly surprised. 'Yes, indeed,' he said.

'Well, if I may just indicate a couple of lines of thought that might smoothen the process tomorrow and make everyone's task easier –' began Professor Mishra. 'A sort of foretaste, as it were, of the proceedings. Merely to save time and bother. I know you have to catch the seven o'clock train tomorrow night.'

Professor Jaikumar said nothing. Courtesy and propriety struggled in his breast. Professor Mishra took his silence for acquiescence, and continued. Professor Jaikumar nodded from time to time but continued to say nothing.

'So –' said Professor Mishra finally.

'Thank you, thank you, most helpful,' said Professor Jaikumar. 'Now I am fore-warned and fore-armed for the interviews.' Professor Mishra flinched at the last word. 'Yes – most helpful,' continued Professor Jaikumar in a noncommital manner. 'Now I must do a little puja.'

'Of course, of course.' Professor Mishra was taken aback by this sudden piety. He hoped it was not a purificatory rite.

18.9

A little before eleven the next morning the committee gathered in the glum-panelled and well-appointed office of the Vice-Chancellor. The Registrar was present too, though not as a participant. A few of the candidates were already waiting in the ante-room outside. After some tea and biscuits and cashew nuts and a little casual social chitchat, the Vice-Chancellor looked at his watch and nodded at the Registrar. The first candidate was brought in.

Professor Mishra had not been feeling entirely happy about the way preliminary matters were going. Apart from Dr Ila Chattopadhyay, who had continued in her abrupt vein this morning, there was something else that was bothering him. He did not yet know for certain what had happened to Pran's father. He knew that for some reason the counting had not finished by the time of the local news bulletin on the radio the previous evening, for if it had, the name of the winning candidate would have been announced. But that was all he knew, and he had not been able to get in touch with his own informant. He had left instructions at home that he was to be called as soon as any news on the matter was received. Any excuse would do; and if necessary the information could be noted down, sealed in an envelope, and sent in to him. There would be nothing unusual in this. The Vice-Chancellor himself, who was – and took pride in being seen to be – a busy man, was forever interrupting committee meetings by taking telephone calls, and indeed sometimes signing letters that peons brought in.

The interviews went on. The clear February sunlight pouring through the window helped dissipate the grand but dampening atmosphere of the office. The interviewees – thirteen men and two women, all of them lecturers, were, for the most part, treated not as colleagues but as suppliants by the ViceChancellor; the nephew of the Chief Minister, on the other hand, was treated with excessive deference by both him and Professor Mishra. Every so often a telephone call would interrupt the proceedings. At one point Dr Ila Chattopadhyay found it necessary to say:

'Vice-Chancellor, can't you take your phone off the hook?'

The Vice-Chancellor looked absolutely amazed.

'My dear lady,' said Professor Mishra.

'We have travelled a very considerable distance to be here,' said Dr Ila Chattopadhyay. 'At least two of us have. These selection committees are a duty, not a pleasure. I haven't seen one decent candidate so far. We are due to go back tonight, but I'm not sure we will be able to at this rate. I do not see why our torment should be further prolonged by these endless interruptions.'

Her outburst had its effect. For the next hour, the Vice-Chancellor told whoever called that he was in the middle of an urgent meeting.

Lunch was served in a room adjoining the Vice-Chancellor's office, and a little academic gossip was exchanged. Professor Mishra begged leave to go home. One of his sons was not very well, he said. Professor Jaikumar looked a little surprised.

Once home, Professor Mishra phoned his informant.

'What is the matter, Badri Nath?' he said impatiently. 'Why have you not got in touch with me?'

'Because of George the Sixth, of course.'

'What are you talking about? George the Sixth is dead. Don't you listen to the news?'

'Well, there you are.' There was a cackle at the other end.

'I can't get any sense out of you, Badri Nath ji. Yes, I have heard you. George the Sixth is dead. I know that. I heard it on the news, and all the flags are at half-mast. But what does that have to do with me?'

'They've stopped the counting.'

'They can't do that!' exclaimed Professor Mishra. This was madness.

'Yes — they can. They began the counting late — I think the DM's jeep broke down — so they didn't finish it by midnight. And at midnight they suspended the counting. All over the country. As a mark of respect.' The thought struck Badri Nath as droll, and he cackled again.

It did not strike Professor Mishra as being in the least droll. The former King-Emperor of India had no business dying at a time like this.

'How far did they get in the counting?' he asked.

'That's what I'm trying to find out,' said Badri Nath.

'Well, find out, please. And tell me the trend.'

'What trend?'

'Can't you at least tell me who's ahead in the race?'

'There's no ahead or behind in this, Mishraji. They don't count the vote polling station by polling station. They count all the boxes of the first candidate first, and then go on down the line.'

'Oh.' Professor Mishra's head had begun to throb.

'Don't worry, though – he's lost. Take it from me. All my sources say so. I guarantee it,' said Badri Nath.

Professor Mishra wanted with all his heart to believe him. But some gnawing little doubt prompted him to say: 'Please call me at four o'clock at the Vice-Chancellor's office. His number is 623. I must know what is happening before we begin our discussion of the candidates.'

'Who would have thought it!' said Badri Nath, laughing. 'The English still run our lives.'

Professor Mishra put down the phone. 'Where is my lunch?' he said coldly to his wife.

'You said that you –' she began, then saw the look on his face. 'I'll just get something ready,' she said.

18.10

PRAN'S interview was scheduled for the early afternoon. The Vice-Chancellor asked him the usual questions about the relevance of teaching English in India. Professor Jaikumar asked him a careful question about *Scrutiny* and F.R. Leavis. Professor Mishra asked tenderly after his health and fussed about the onerous burdens of academia. The old history professor who was the Chancellor's nominee said nothing at all.

It was with Dr Ila Chattopadhyay that Pran got along really well. She drew him out on the subject of *The Winter's Tale*, one of Pran's favourite plays, and they both got carried away, talking freely of the implausibilities of the plot, the difficulties of imagining, let alone performing, some of the scenes, and the absurd and deeply moving climax. They both thought it should be on every syllabus. They agreed with each other violently and disagreed with each other pleasurably. At one point Dr Chattopadhyay told him outright that he was talking nonsense, and Professor Mishra's troubled face wreathed itself in a smile. But even if she thought that the point Pran had just made was nonsense, it was obviously very stimulating nonsense; her attention was entirely engaged in rebutting it.

Pran's interview – or, rather, his conversation with her – lasted twice as long as the time allotted to him. But, as Dr Chattopadhyay remarked, some of the other candidates had been disposed of in five minutes, and she looked forward to other candidates of Pran's calibre.

By four o'clock the interviews were over, and they broke off for a short tea-break. The peon who brought in the tea was not deferential to anyone except the Vice-Chancellor. This irked Professor Mishra, whose afternoon tea was usually sweetened by a little cringing.

'You are looking very pensive, Professor Mishra,' said Professor Jaikumar.

'Pensive?'

'Yes, indeed.'

'Well, I was wondering why it was that Indian academics publish so little. So few of our candidates have worthwhile publications to their name. Dr Chattopadhyay, of course, is a remarkable exception. Many moons ago, my dear lady,' – he turned towards her – 'I remember how impressed I was by reading your work on the Metaphysicals. That was long before I sat on the committee which –'

'Well, we're neither of us young now,' interrupted Dr Ila Chattopadhyay, 'and neither of us has published anything of worth in the last ten years. I wonder why that is.'

While Professor Mishra was still recovering from this remark, Professor Jaikumar put forth an explanation which caused him a different kind of pain. 'Our typical young university teacher,' he began, 'is overworked when he is junior – he has to teach yelementary prose and compulsory Yinglish. If he is yinnately conscientious, he has no time for yennything else. By then the fire is out –'

'If it was ever there,' added Dr Ila Chattopadhyay.

'– and the family is growing up, yemoluments are small,

and making yends meet is a problem. Luckily,' added Professor Jaikumar, 'my wife was yeconomical in her habits, and I got the opportunity to go to Yingland and that is how I managed to develop my yinterest in Shelley.'

Professor Mishra, his mind distracted by Professor Jaikumar's almost instinctive choice of words beginning with dangerous vowels, said: 'Yes, but I really fail to see why, once we have riper academic experience and more leisure —'

'But by then we have yimportant committees like this one to take up our time,' Professor Jaikumar pointed out. 'And also we may know too much by then and have no yexpress motivation for writing. Writing is yitself discovery. Yexplication is yexploration.' Professor Mishra shuddered inwardly while his colleague continued: 'Ripeness is not all. Perhaps, ripe in years, and thinking he academically now knows yevrything, our university teacher turns from knowledge to religion that goes beyond knowledge — from gyaan to bhakti. Rationality has a very tenuous hold on the Indian psyche.' (He rhymed it with bike.) 'Even the great Shankara, Adi-Shankara, who said in his advaita that the great yinfinite idea was that of Brahman — which needed to be brought down by uncomprehending Man to mere Ishvara, whom did he pray to? To Durga!' Professor Jaikumar nodded his head around the room and in particular to Dr Ila Chattopadhyay. 'To Durga!'

'Yes, yes,' said Dr Ila Chattopadhyay. 'But I have a train to catch.'

'Well,' said the Vice-Chancellor. 'Let us then make our decision.'

'That shouldn't take us long,' said Dr Ila Chattopadhyay. 'That thin, dark fellow, Prem Khanna, is head and shoulders above everyone else.'

'Pran Kapoor,' Professor Mishra corrected her, pronouncing the syllables with delicate distaste.

'Yes, Prem, Pran, Prem, Pran: I'm always getting things like this wrong. Really, I sometimes wonder what has happened to my brain. But you know whom I mean.'

'Indeed.' Professor Mishra pursed his lips. 'Well, there

might be certain difficulties there. Let us look at a few more possibilities – in justice to the other candidates.'

'What difficulties?' said Dr Ila Chattopadhyay bluntly, thinking of the prospect of another night amid lace and coir, and determined not to let this discussion go on at any great length.

'Well, he has had a bereavement recently. His poor mother. He will be in no condition to undertake –'

'Well, he certainly didn't let the thought of his dead mother get in the way of his duelling this afternoon.'

'Yes, when he said that Shakespeare was implausible,' said Professor Mishra, pursing his lips to indicate his sense of how unsound and even sacrilegious Pran's opinions were.

'Nonsense!' said Dr Ila Chattopadhyay, looking quite fierce. 'He said that the plotting of *The Winter's Tale* was implausible. And so it is. But seriously, this question of duty and bereavement is surely none of our concern.'

'Dear lady,' said Professor Mishra in exasperation, 'I am the one who has to run this department. I must see that everyone pulls his weight. Professor Jaikumar will, I am sure, agree that one must not rock the boat.'

'And I suppose that those whom the captain deems unfit for first-class accommodation must be kept firmly, by whatever means necessary, in the steerage,' said Dr Ila Chattopadhyay.

She had sensed that Professor Mishra did not like Pran. In the subsequent heated discussion she discovered that he and the Vice-Chancellor had a favourite candidate, one whom she had judged very ordinary, but to whom, she recalled, they had been excessively courteous during the interview.

Assisted by the Vice-Chancellor and with the extremely tacit acquiescence of the Chancellor's nominee, Professor Mishra built up a case for this candidate. Pran was tolerable as an academic, but not very cooperative in the running of the department. He needed to mature. Perhaps, in two years' time, they could consider him again. This other candidate was equally good and a greater asset.

Besides, Pran had the strangest views about the syllabus. He thought that Joyce — yes, Joyce — should be thrust down people's throats. His brother was a bad lot and would bring scandal to the name of the department; these might seem to outsiders to be extraneous matters, but one had to observe certain proprieties. And his health was poor; he came late for classes; why, Professor Jaikumar himself had once seen him collapse in mid-lecture. And there had been complaints that he was involved with a certain woman student. In the nature of things, it would be unreasonable to expect concrete evidence for these complaints, but they had to be considered.

'Yes, and I suppose he drinks as well?' said Dr Ila Chattopadhyay. 'I was wondering when the passes-classes-glasses argument was going to come up.'

'Really!' exclaimed the Vice-Chancellor. 'Do you need to cast aspersions on Professor Mishra's motives? You should accept with grace —'

'I will not accept with grace what is a disgrace,' said Dr Ila Chattopadhyay. 'I don't know what is going on but something certainly is, and I am not going to be a part of it.' She had as acute a nose for what she called 'intellectual squalor and academic sordor' as for faulty plumbing.

Professor Mishra was staring at her in outrage. Her treasonous ingratitude to him was beyond belief.

'I think you should discuss matters coolly,' he spluttered.

'Coolly?' cried Dr Ila Chattopadhyay. 'Coolly? If there is one thing I cannot stand, it is rudeness!' Seeing that Professor Mishra had been floored by this remark, she continued: 'And if there is one thing I refuse to deny, it is merit. That young man has merit. He knows his subject. I am sure he makes a very stimulating teacher. And from his folder and the number of committees he is sitting on and the extra-curricular activities he is involved in, it does not appear to me that he does not pull his weight in the department or the university. Rather the opposite. He should get the job. Outside panellists like Professor Jaikumar and myself are here as a check on academic —' she was about to say 'rascality' but changed it in mid-flight to 'irresponsibility', before continuing – 'I am sorry, I am a very stupid woman, but one thing I have learned is that when it is necessary to speak, one must. If we cannot come to a proper decision and you force your candidate through, I will insist that you put down in your report that the experts disagreed with you –'

Even Professor Jaikumar looked shocked. 'Self-control leads to heaven,' he murmured to himself in Tamil, 'but uncontrolled passion is the road to endless darkness.' No one ever voted on these matters. They were decided by consensus. Voting meant that the matter would have to be put up to the Executive Council of the university for a decision, and no one wanted that. This was rocking the boat with a vengeance. It would mean the end of all stability, all order. Professor Mishra looked at Dr Ila Chattopadhyay as if he would not mind jettisoning her forthwith – and hoped that the water was infested with jellyfish.

'Yif I may speak –' It was Professor Jaikumar, actually interrupting, which was something he almost never did. 'I do not feel a minority report by the outside yexperts is called for. But there should be a proper decision.' He paused. He was a genuinely learned man of deep and unflamboyant probity, and he had been greatly upset by his tête-à-tête with his host the previous evening. He had decided there and then that whoever he selected, it would not be the man who had been so irregularly recommended to him. 'Should we not think of a third candidate?'

'Of course not,' said Dr Ila Chattopadhyay, in whom the zest of battle now raged warmly: 'Why select someone third-rate as a compromise when we have a first-rate man at hand?'

'Certainly, yit is true,' said Professor Jaikumar, 'as it says in the Tirukukural' – and here he paused to translate – 'that after assessing that this man can do this task because of this competence he has, and this tool he can use, that task must be assigned to that man. But yit also says: "Yit

is a part of wisdom to conform to the ways of the world."
But in yet another place yit says –'

The telephone rang. Professor Mishra sprang up. The
Vice-Chancellor reached out for the phone. 'Vice-Chancel-
lor here. . . . I'm sorry, I'm in a meeting. . . . oh, it's for you,
Professor Mishra. Were you expecting a call?'

'Er, yes, I asked the doctor to call me – well, yes –
Mishra speaking.'

18.11

'YOU old jackal!' said Badri Nath on the phone. 'I heard
all that.'

'Er, yes, Doctor, well, what news?' said Professor Mishra
in Hindi.

'Bad.'

Professor Mishra's jaw dropped. Everyone looked at
him. The others in the room tried to talk, but it was
impossible for them not to listen to his side of the
conversation.

'I see. How bad?'

'The counting went alphabetically. It stopped after
Kapoor and just before Khan.'

'Then how do you know who –'

'Mahesh Kapoor got 15,575 votes. There aren't enough
votes left for Waris Khan to defeat him. Mahesh Kapoor is
bound to win.'

Professor Mishra's free hand went to his forehead. Beads
of sweat began to form on it.

'What do you mean? How do you know? Could you go
a little slowly for me? I'm not used to the terminology.'

'All right, Professor. You will need to ask the Vice-
Chancellor for a pen and some paper.' Badri Nath, though
obviously unhappy about the result of his inquiries, was
nevertheless extracting what little enjoyment he could out
of the situation.

'I have them here,' said Professor Mishra. He took a pen
and an envelope out of his pocket. 'Please go slowly.'

Badri Nath sighed. 'Why don't you simply accept what I'm saying?' he asked.

Professor Mishra wisely refrained from replying: 'Because you told me this very morning to accept that he'd lost, and now you're telling me to accept that he's won.' He said: 'I'd like to know how you came to this conclusion.'

Badri Nath relented. After another sigh, he said, very slowly and carefully: 'Please listen carefully, Professor. There are 66,918 voters. Given a very high turn-out for this part of the country, say, fifty-five per cent, that would mean a total of 37,000 votes cast in the election. Shall I go on? The first five candidates have been counted. Their total comes to 19,351. That leaves about 18,700 for the last five candidates. Apart from Waris, the other four are bound to get at least 5,000 votes: they include the socialist and the Jan Sangh candidate as well as a fairly popular and well-funded Independent. So what does that leave for Waris Khan, Professor Sahib? Less than 14,000. And Mahesh Kapoor has already got 15,575.' He paused, then continued: 'Too bad. Chacha Nehru's visit turned the tide. Do you want me to repeat the figures?'

'No, no, thank you. When does – when does it resume?'

'When does what resume? You mean the counting?'

'Yes. The treatment.'

'Tomorrow.'

'Thank you. May I call you later this evening?'

'Yes, of course. I'll be in the casualty department,' cackled Badri Nath, and put down the phone.

Professor Mishra sat down heavily in his chair.

'Not bad news, I hope,' said Professor Jaikumar. 'Both your sons looked so well yesterday.'

'No, no –' said Professor Mishra bravely, mopping his forehead. 'We all have our private crosses to bear. But we must press on with our duty. I am so sorry for keeping you all waiting.'

'Not at all,' said Dr Ila Chattopadhyay, thinking that she'd been a bit rough on the poor, pulpy fellow who had, after all, once encouraged her. Really, though, she thought to herself, he can't be allowed to get away with this.

But it now appeared that Professor Mishra was no longer vociferously opposed to Pran. He even found one or two good things to say about him. Dr Ila Chattopadhyay wondered if, in the face of possible minority dissension and scandal, he had merely succumbed to the inevitable – or if perhaps his son's ill health had brought him face to face with his own uncertain soul.

By the end of the meeting, Professor Mishra had regained some of his air of placidity; he was still staggered, however, by the turn of events.

'You have left your telephone numbers behind,' said Professor Jaikumar, handing him his envelope as he walked to the door.

'Oh, yes –' said Professor Mishra. 'Thank you.'

Later, when he was packing hurriedly for his train, Professor Jaikumar was startled to see both Professor Mishra's sons playing about outside, looking as robust as ever.

At the station Professor Jaikumar recalled, apropos of nothing, that telephone numbers in Brahmpur had three, not five, digits.

How peculiar, he said to himself. But he was never to solve either mystery.

Professor Mishra, pleading a previous appointment, had not gone with him to the railway station. Instead, after a few words in private with the Vice-Chancellor, he had walked over to Pran's house. He was resigned to congratulating him.

'My dear boy,' he said, taking both Pran's hands in his. 'It was a close thing, a very close thing. Some of the other candidates were truly excellent, but, well, I believe we have an understanding, you and I, an equation, as it were, and – well, I should not be telling you this until the seal of the envelope containing our decision is broken in the Academic Council – not that your own excellent, er, performance, did not contribute as much to our decision as my own humble words on your behalf –' Professor Mishra sighed before continuing: 'There was opposition. Some people said you were too young, too untried. "The atrocious crime of being a young man ..." etcetera. But quite apart from the question of merit, at such a sad time for your family one feels a sense of obligation, one feels one has to do one's bit. I am not one who talks of humanity in exaggerated terms, but, well – was it not the great Wordsworth who talked about those "little nameless unremembered acts of kindness and of love"?'

'I believe it was,' said Pran, slowly and wonderingly, as he shook Professor Mishra's pale and perspiring hands.

18.12

MAHESH KAPOOR was at the Collectorate at Rudhia when the count for the Salimpur-cum-Baitar election opened. He had got there late, but the District Magistrate had himself been unavoidably delayed; owing to a problem with the ignition his jeep had broken down. The counting officers, having grouped all the ballot-boxes of each candidate together, now began with the first candidate, who was an Independent named Iqbal Ahmad. They emptied one of his ballot-boxes onto each of several tables, and – watched carefully by the counting agents of all the candidates – began simultaneously to count his votes.

Secrecy was enjoined on everyone under the canopy, but of course nothing was secret, and news soon leaked out that Iqbal Ahmad was doing as badly as expected. Since the ballot-papers in the first General Election were not stamped by the voter but simply placed in a candidate's box, very few ballot-papers were rejected as spoiled. Counting continued briskly, and, had it begun on time, should have been over by midnight. But it was now eleven o'clock, everyone was exhausted, and the Congress candidate's ballot-boxes had not yet been completely counted. He was making an unexpectedly good showing: over 14,000 votes, and several more boxes to go.

In some of Mahesh Kapoor's boxes, astonishingly, there

was even, in addition to the ballot-papers, a little red powder and a few coins. Presumably, some pious peasants, seeing the holy cattle featured on his box, had placed small offerings inside the slot together with their vote.

While the count was continuing under the careful supervision of the District Magistrate and the Sub-Divisional Officer, Mahesh Kapoor walked over to Waris, who was looking very worried, and said: 'Adaab arz, Waris Sahib.'

'Adaab arz,' replied Waris pugnaciously. The 'Sahib' had surely been ironic.

'Is everything all right with Firoz?'

It was said without any rancour, but Waris felt a burning sense of shame; he thought immediately of the pink fliers.

'Why do you ask?' he demanded.

'I wanted to know,' said Mahesh Kapoor sorrowfully. 'I have very little news of him, and I thought you would. I do not see the Nawab Sahib anywhere. Does he plan to come?'

'He is not a candidate,' said Waris bluntly. 'Yes, Firoz is fine.' He turned his eyes downwards, unable to look Mahesh Kapoor in the face.

'I am glad,' said Mahesh Kapoor. He was about to send his good wishes, then thought better of it and turned away.

A little before midnight, the results stood as follows:

1. Iqbal Ahmad	Independent	608
2. Mir Shamsher Ali	Independent	481
3. Mohammed Hussain	KMPP	1,533
4. Shanti Prasad Jha	Ram Rajya Parishad	1,154
5. Mahesh Kapoor	Congress	15,575

At midnight, just after Mahesh Kapoor's boxes had all been counted, the District Magistrate, as Returning Officer, declared the poll temporarily suspended as part of a nationwide mark of respect for King George VI. He had told the candidates and their counting agents a couple of hours earlier that he had orders to this effect, and asked for their patience. The suspense was terrible, especially since Waris Khan came immediately after Mahesh Kapoor alphabetically; but, owing to the timely warning, there were no protests. He got the counted ballots and the uncounted ballot-boxes locked up separately under his own seal in the treasury, and announced that they would be unlocked and the count resumed on the 8th of February.

The results so far determined were bound to leak out, and in both Brahmpur and the constituency most people made the same sort of reckoning that Professor Mishra's informant had. Mahesh Kapoor too was optimistic. He stayed on his farm at Rudhia, talking to his farm manager as he walked around the wheat fields.

On the morning of the 8th, he woke up with a sense of freshness and thankfulness, a sense that at least one of his burdens had been lifted off his shoulders.

18.13

THE count proceeded once more, and by the time Waris's vote had reached 10,000, it began to appear that the contest would in fact be close. Apparently, in the areas immediately surrounding Baitar town, the voting rate had been far in excess of fifty-five per cent – a figure which, to go by other elections whose results had been announced earlier in the week, was itself very high.

By the time it had reached 14,000 and there were a number of ballot-boxes still to be counted, a great sense of unease overtook the Congress camp. The District Magistrate had to tell everyone to be quiet and to let his counting agents proceed; if not, he would have to suspend the count again.

This had some effect, but by the time the vote had reached 15,000 there was a tremendous hubbub. Some of the more feisty Congress workers had started challenging entire ballot-boxes. Mahesh Kapoor told them sharply to stop their antics. But his face betrayed his dismay, for by now he feared he would lose. The other side had begun cheering in anticipation of surpassing the magic number. They did not have long to wait.

There were still several of Waris's boxes left to count when the tally reached 15,576. Waris jumped onto a table and shouted for joy. He was raised high on the shoulders of his supporters, and outside the District Headquarters they began to shout to the well-known pattern:

'The MLA from Baitar, who should he be?'

'Waris Khan Sahib, one such as he!'

Waris, delighted to win, delighted to have 'Khan Sahib' appended to his name, and delighted to have avenged the young Nawabzada, was grinning away, having in the flush of victory forgotten his dirty trick with the posters.

He was soon brought literally down to earth by the District Magistrate, who threatened to throw him out of the Collectorate unless his supporters stopped the ruckus. Waris calmed his followers down, and told one or two of them: 'Let's see, let's see, now that I'm an MLA, who gets thrown out of the Collectorate first, him or me.'

Several Congressmen now urged Mahesh Kapoor, who so far had not lodged a complaint or an election petition, to do so immediately – to challenge the election result. It was clear that, even if nowhere else, in the hinterland of Baitar town the false and flimsy posters announcing Firoz's death had had a devastating effect in getting people out of their huts and houses to vote for Waris.

But Mahesh Kapoor, bitter and disillusioned, and not wishing to create further bitterness, refused to lodge an election petition. Waris had got 16,748 votes; the difference was too great to justify even requesting a re-count. After a while he went over to congratulate his rival; he looked shattered, the more so because of his premonition that morning. Waris accepted his congratulations graciously and calmly. Victory had wiped out his sense of shame.

Only after the counting of all the candidates' votes was complete did the District Magistrate officially declare Waris Khan the winner. The radio announced the news in the evening. The final result was as follows:

SALIMPUR-CUM-BAITAR (District Rudhia, Purva Pradesh)
LEGISLATIVE ASSEMBLY ELECTION

No. of seats: 1
No. of candidates: total: 10   contesting: 10
No. of electors: 66,918
Total no. of valid votes polled: 40,327
Voting rate: 60.26%

NAME (in English) alphabetical order)	PARTY/ INDEPENDENT	VOTES	% OF VOTES
1. Iqbal Ahmad	Independent	608	1.51
2. Mir Shamsher Ali	Independent	481	˜1.19
3. Mohammed Hussain	KMPP	1,533	3.80
4. Shanti Prasad Jha	Ram Rajya Parishad	1,154	2.86
5. Mahesh Kapoor	Congress	15,575	38.62
6. Waris Mohammad Khan	Independent	16,748	41.53
7. Mahmud Nasir	Communist	774	1.92
8. Madan Mohan Pandey	Independent	1,159	2.87
9. Ramlal Sinha	Socialist	696	1.73
10. Ramratan Srivastava	Jan Sangh	1,599	3.97

Name of successful candidate: Waris Mohammad Khan

18.14

AT Baitar Fort that night there was jubilation.

Waris had an immense bonfire built in the grounds, ordered a dozen sheep and a dozen goats to be slaughtered, invited everyone who had helped him or voted for him to come to the feast, and then added that even the bastards who had voted against him were welcome to join in. He was cautious enough not to serve alcohol, but he himself greeted his guests royally drunk, and made a speech – he was by now proficient at speechmaking – about the nobility of the house of Baitar, the excellence of the electorate, the glory of God and the wonder of Waris.

About what he planned to do in the State Assembly he was silent; but in his own mind he was certain that he would learn the legislative ropes as quickly as he had mastered the pulling of electoral strings.

The oily munshi sanctioned all the expenses he demanded, had the grand archway of the Fort festooned with flowers, and greeted Waris with folded hands and tears in his eyes. He had always loved Waris, he had always known of the hidden greatness in him, and now at last his prayers for him had been answered. He fell at his feet and begged Waris for his blessings, and Waris, slurred and benevolent, said:

'All right, you sister-fucker, I bless you. Now get up or I'll be sick all over you.'

18.15

MAHESH KAPOOR sat in his garden at Prem Nivas one afternoon a few days after the count. He was talking to Abdus Salaam, his former Parliamentary Secretary. He looked very weary. The many implications of his loss were coming home to him. He felt that his occupation was gone, the thing that gave his life vigour and direction and the capacity to do good. His wing of the state Congress Party would have to do without his guidance in the legislature. His loss of power affected not only his own pride but would affect his ability to help his son, soon to be charged with he knew not what. The loss of his friendship with the Nawab Sahib was another bitter blow; he felt sad and ashamed of what had happened to Firoz – and to the Nawab Sahib himself. And every moment he spent in Prem Nivas, especially in the garden, could not fail to remind him of the loss of his wife.

He looked at the sheet of paper in his hand; it contained the various figures describing the election he had fought. For a few minutes he succeeded in discussing them with Abdus Salaam with something of his old interest and objectivity. If the KMPP had dissolved itself and rejoined the Congress, as Mahesh Kapoor himself had, their combined votes would have defeated Waris. If his wife had been able to help him, she would have made the quiet difference she always did – a couple of thousand votes, if not more. If the poster about Firoz had not been published, or had been published when it was not too late to refute it with the facts, he would still have won. Whatever other rumours Mahesh Kapoor had come to believe about his friend, he refused to believe that the Nawab Sahib had sanctioned that poster. That was Waris and Waris alone; it had to be.

But every thread of his analysis, objective though he attempted to make it, led him back to his own unhappy situation. After a while he closed his eyes and said nothing.

'Waris is an interesting phenomenon,' said Abdus Salaam. '"I know what is moral and yet I do not have the inclination for it, and I know what is immoral and yet do not have an aversion from it" – as Duryodhana said to Krishna.'

A faint look of exasperation crossed Mahesh Kapoor's face. 'No,' he said, opening his eyes. 'Waris is a different kind of man. He has no sense of evil or immorality as such. I know him. I've been fighting with him and against him. He's the kind who would murder someone over a woman or land or water or a feud – and then give himself up, boasting, "I finished him off!" – and expect everyone to understand.'

'You will remain in politics,' predicted Abdus Salaam.

Mahesh Kapoor laughed shortly. 'Do you think so?' he said. 'I had thought, after my conversation with Jawaharlal, that I might even become Chief Minister. What ambitions! I am not even an MLA. Anyway, I hope you don't let them fob you off with any minor post; you might be a young man, but you've done excellent work and this is your second term. And they'll want two or three Muslims in the Cabinet, no matter whether it's Sharma or Agarwal who is CM.'

'Yes, I suppose that's so,' said Abdus Salaam. 'But I don't think that Agarwal would choose me even at the point of a bayonet.'

'So Sharma is going to Delhi after all?' Mahesh Kapoor noticed a few mynas walking about on the lawn.

'No one knows,' replied Abdus Salaam. 'I don't, anyway. For every rumour, there's an equal and opposite rumour.' He was glad that Mahesh Kapoor was showing at least sporadic interest in the political scene. 'Why don't you go to Delhi for a few days?' he suggested.

'I will stay here,' said Mahesh Kapoor quietly, looking around the garden. Abdus Salaam remembered Maan, and said nothing.

After a while he spoke. 'What happened to your other son and his promotion?' he said.

Mahesh Kapoor shrugged his shoulders. 'He was here this morning with my granddaughter. I asked him. He said he thought things had gone quite well at the interview, that was all.'

Pran, fearing that Professor Mishra might yet be up to something unfathomable, and not daring to believe his report, had decided not to tell anyone – not even Savita – of his supposed selection by the committee. He was afraid of the greater disappointment of his family if the good news turned out to be unfounded. He wished he could have told his father, though. In his black mood it might have done him a little good.

'Well,' said Abdus Salaam. 'You need something good to happen to you now. God brings relief to those who suffer.'

The Arabic word Abdus Salaam naturally used for God reminded Mahesh Kapoor of the use to which religion had been put in his own election battle. Again he closed his eyes and said nothing. He felt sick at heart.

Abdus Salaam uncannily sensed what he was thinking, or so his next remark appeared to indicate. 'Waris's election was determined by prejudice,' he stated. 'You would have felt ashamed to say one word to inflame anyone on the grounds of religion. Waris may at first merely have been a loyal man, but from his use of that poster I would have to say that he became a bad one.'

Mahesh Kapoor sighed again. 'That is a pointless speculation. Anyway, "bad" is too strong a word. He is fond of Firoz, that's all. He's served that family all his life.'

'He will become just as fond of his own position in time,' said Abdus Salaam. 'I will have to face him across the floor of the House soon enough. But what I am curious about is this: how soon will he assert his position against the Nawab Sahib?'

'Well,' said Mahesh Kapoor after a while. 'I don't think he will. But if he does, there's nothing to be done about it. If he's bad, as you say, he's bad.'

Abdus Salaam said: 'Anyway, it is not the prejudices of bad people that are the problem.'

'Ah, and what is the problem then?' said Mahesh Kapoor with a slight smile.

'If only bad people were prejudiced, that would not have such a strong effect. Most people would not wish to imitate them – and so, such prejudices would not have much effect – except in exceptional times. It is the prejudices of good people that are so dangerous.'

'That is too subtle,' said Mahesh Kapoor. 'You should give blame where blame is due. The inflammatory ones are the bad.'

'Ah, but many of the inflammable ones are the otherwise good.'

'I won't argue with you.'

'That is just what I want you to do.'

Mahesh Kapoor made an impatient sound but said nothing.

'The Congress will win seventy per cent of the assembly seats in P.P. You'll soon come back in a by-election,' said Abdus Salaam. 'I suppose people are surprised that you aren't submitting an election petition against the Salimpur result.'

'What people think –' began Mahesh Kapoor, then shook his head.

Abdus Salaam tried one final time to shake his mentor out of his listlessness. He began one of his ruminations, partly because he enjoyed them, mainly because he wanted to strike some spark from the Minister Sahib.

'It is interesting to see how, after just four years of Independence, the Congress has changed so much,' he began. 'Those people who broke their heads fighting for freedom are now breaking each other's. And we have new entrants to the business. If I were a criminal, for example, and I could get into politics profitably and without too much difficulty, I would not say: "I can deal in murder or drugs, but politics is sacred." It would be no more sacred to me than prostitution.'

He looked towards Mahesh Kapoor, who had closed his eyes again. Abdus Salaam went on: 'More and more money is required to fight elections, and politicians will be forced to demand more and more money from business-men. Then, being corrupt themselves, they won't be able to wipe out corruption in the civil service. They won't even want to. Sooner or later the appointments of judges, election commissioners, the top civil servants and police-men, will be decided by these same corrupt men, and all our institutions will give way. The only hope,' continued Abdus Salaam treasonously, 'is that the Congress will be wiped out two elections from now....'

As at a concert a single false note sung outside the strict scope of a raag can wake up a listener who is apparently asleep, so too Abdus Salaam's last assertion made Mahesh Kapoor open his eyes.

'Abdus Salaam, I am not in a mood to argue with you. Don't make idle statements.'

'Everything I have said is possible. I would say probable.'

'The Congress won't be wiped out.'

'Why not, Minister Sahib? We have got less than fifty per cent of the vote. Next time our opponents will under-stand electoral arithmetic better and will band together.

And Nehru, our vote-catcher, will be dead by then, or retired. He won't last five years more in this job. He will be burned out.'

'Nehru will outlive me, and probably you,' said Mahesh Kapoor.

'Should we take a bet on that?' said Abdus Salaam.

Mahesh Kapoor stirred restlessly. 'Are you trying to get me angry?' he said.

'Just a friendly bet.'

'Now please leave.'

'All right, Minister Sahib. I'll come by again tomorrow at the same time.' Mahesh Kapoor said nothing.

After a while he looked out at the garden. The kachnar tree was just coming into blossom: the buds looked like long green pods with a slight hint of deep mauve where the flowers would burst forth. Scores of small squirrels were either running around or on the tree, playing with each other. The sunbird, as usual, was flying in and out of the pomelo tree; and from somewhere a barbet was calling insistently. Mahesh Kapoor did not know either the Hindi or the English names of the birds and flowers that surrounded him, but perhaps in his present state of mind he enjoyed the garden more truly for that. It was his only refuge, and a nameless, wordless one, with bird-song its only sound – and it was dominated, when he closed his eyes, by the least intellectualizable sense – that of scent.

When his wife had been alive she had occasionally asked him for his opinion before laying out a new bed or planting a new tree. This had only served to annoy Mahesh Kapoor. 'Do whatever you want,' he had snapped. 'Do I ask you for your opinion on my files?' After a while she had ceased to ask for his advice.

But to Mrs Mahesh Kapoor's great if quiet delight and to the frustration of her various more imposing competitors, who could not understand what she had over them by way of resources or expertise or foreign seeds, the garden at Prem Nivas had won numerous prizes in the Flower Show year after year; and this year would win the First

Prize as well, for the first and, needless to say, the last time.

18.16

ON the front wall of Pran's house, the yellow jasmine had begun to bloom. Inside, Mrs Rupa Mehra muttered, 'Plain, purl, plain, purl. Where's Lata?'

'She's gone out to buy a book,' said Savita.

'Which book?'

'I don't think she knows yet. A novel, probably.'

'She shouldn't be reading novels but studying for her exams.'

This was, as it happened, what the bookseller was telling Lata at almost the same moment. Luckily for his business, students rarely took his advice.

He reached out for the book with one hand, and extracted wax from his ear with the other.

'I've studied enough, Balwantji,' said Lata. 'I'm tired of my studies. In fact, I'm tired of everything,' she ended dramatically.

'You look just like Nargis when you say that,' said Balwant.

'I am afraid I only have a five-rupee note.'

'Don't worry,' said Balwant. 'Where is your friend Malatiji?' he continued. 'I never see her these days.'

'That's because she's not wasting her time buying novels,' said Lata. 'She's studying hard. I hardly see her myself.'

Kabir entered the shop, looking quite cheerful. He noticed Lata and stopped.

The whole of their last meeting flashed before Lata's eyes – and, immediately afterwards, their first meeting in the bookstore. They looked at each other for a few seconds before Lata broke the silence with a hello.

'Hello,' replied Kabir. 'I see you're on your way out.' Here was another meeting brought about by coincidence, and to be governed, no doubt, by awkwardness.

'Yes,' said Lata. 'I came in to buy a Wodehouse, but I've bought myself a Jane Austen instead.'

'I'd like you to have a coffee with me at the Blue Danube.' It was a statement more than a request.

'I have to get back,' said Lata. 'I told Savita I'd be back in an hour.'

'Savita can wait. I was going to buy a book, but that too can wait.'

'Which book?' asked Lata.

'What does it matter? replied Kabir. 'I don't know. I was just going to browse. Not in Poetry or Mathematics, though,' he added.

'All right,' said Lata recklessly.

'Good. The cake will be better, at least. Of course, I don't know what excuse you'll make if someone you know walks in.'

'I don't care,' said Lata.

'Good.'

The Blue Danube was just a couple of hundred yards along Nabiganj. They sat down and placed their orders.

Neither spoke. Finally Lata said:

'Good news about the cricket.'

'Excellent.' India had just won the fifth Test Match against England in Madras by an innings and eight runs, and no one could quite believe it.

After a while the coffee came. Stirring it slowly, Kabir said: 'Were you serious?'

'About what?'

'You are writing to this man?'

'Yes.'

'How serious is it?'

'Ma wants me to marry him.'

Kabir said nothing, but looked down at his right hand as it kept stirring the coffee.

'Aren't you going to say something?' she asked him.

He shrugged.

'Do you hate me?' asked Lata. 'Don't you care whom I marry?'

'Don't be stupid.' Kabir sounded disgusted with her.

'And please stop those tears. They won't improve your coffee or my appetite.' For again, though she was half unconscious of them, tears had slowly filled Lata's eyes and were falling down her cheeks one by one. She did not try to wipe them away, nor did she take her eyes off Kabir's face. She did not care what the waiters or anyone else thought. Or even he, for that matter.

He continued to stir his coffee with a troubled look.

'I know of two mixed marriages –' he began.

'Ours wouldn't work. No one else will let it work. And now I can't even trust myself.'

'Then why are you sitting here with me?' he said.

'I don't know.'

'And why are you crying?'

Lata said nothing.

'My handkerchief is dirty,' said Kabir. 'If you haven't brought a handkerchief, use that napkin.'

Lata dabbed at her eyes.

'Come on, eat your cake, it'll do you good. I'm the one who's been rejected, and I'm not sobbing my poor little heart out.'

She shook her head. 'Now I must go,' she said. 'Thank you.'

Kabir did not try to dissuade her.

'Don't leave your book behind,' he said. '*Mansfield Park*? I haven't read that one. Tell me if it's any good.'

Neither of them turned around to look at the other as Lata walked towards the door.

18.17

SO unsettled was Lata by her meeting with Kabir – but when was she not unsettled by a meeting with him? she wondered – that she took a long walk near the banyan tree. She sat down on the great, twisted root, remembered their first kiss, read some poetry, fed the monkeys, and fell into a reverie.

Walks are my panacea, she thought, bitterly; and my substitute for any decisive action.

The next day, however, she took action of the most decisive kind.

Two letters arrived for Lata by the morning post. She sat on the verandah with its trellis of yellow jasmine and slit open both envelopes. Mrs Rupa Mehra was not at home when they arrived, or she would have recognized the handwriting on the envelopes and demanded to know what news they contained.

The contents of the first envelope consisted of eight lines and a heading, typewritten and unsigned:

A MODEST PROPOSAL

As you've asked for black and white,
May I send these lines to you
In the tacit hope you might
Take my type at least as true.

Let this distance disappear
And our hearts approach from far
Till we come to be as near
As acrostically we are.

Lata began to laugh. The poem was a little trite, but it was skilful and entirely personalized, and it pleased her. She tried to recall exactly what she had said; had she really asked for black and white or merely told Amit that that was all she would believe? And how serious was this 'modest' proposal? After thinking the matter over, she was inclined to believe it was serious; and, as a result, it pleased her somewhat less.

Would she have preferred it to be determinedly sombre and passionate – or not to have been written in the first place? Would a passionate proposal have been in Amit's style at all – or at least in his style with her? Many of his poems were far from light in either sense of the word, but it seemed almost as if he hid that side of himself from her for fear that looking into that dark, pessimistic cynicism might trouble her too greatly and make her shy away.

And yet, what was it he had said about her own poem, the despairing one that she had hesitantly shown him? That he had liked it – but only, he had implied, as a poem. If he disapproved of gloom, what was he doing as a poet? Would he not – at least for his own sake – have been far better off in the practical profession of law? But perhaps he did not disapprove of gloom as such in himself or others, only on the fruitless dwelling on it – which, she had to admit, that poem of hers had been guilty of. Clearly, the unhappiness or unease of Amit's own strongest poems was typical not of his daily behaviour but of certain moments of intensity. Still, Lata felt that high hills rarely rise direct and isolated from the plains, and that there had to be some deeper organic connection between the poet of 'The Fever Bird' and Amit Chatterji as she knew him than he himself encouraged herself or others to believe.

And what would it be like to be married to such a man? Lata got up and paced restlessly about the verandah. How could she consider him seriously – Meenakshi and Kuku's brother, her own friend and guide to Calcutta, the purveyor of pineapples, the castigator of Cuddles? He was just Amit – to convert him into a husband was absurd – the thought of it made Lata smile and shake her head. But again she sat down, and again she read the poem, and she looked out beyond the hedge to the campus, from where the sloped and slated roof of the examination hall was distantly visible. She realized that she had the poem by heart already – as she had his earlier acrostic, and 'The Fever Bird', and other poems besides. Without any attempt on her part to learn them, they had become a part of herself.

18.18

THE second letter was from Haresh.

My dearest Lata,
I hope everything is well with you and with the family. I have been so busy with work these last few

weeks that I have come home exhausted, and not been in that state of mind in which you deserve to hear from me. But the Goodyear Welted line is going from strength to strength, and I have even persuaded the management to take on a new scheme of mine, by which entire uppers can be made outside and assembled for final manufacture here at Praha. Of course, that would be in other lines, such as brogues. All in all, I think I have already shown them that it was not a mistake to take me on, and that I am not merely someone imposed on them by Mr Khandelwal.

I have some good news to convey. There is talk of promoting me to Group Foreman soon. If so, it will not come a moment too soon, as I find it difficult to keep down my expenses. I am a bit lavish by nature, and it will be good if someone helps me to curb it. If that is so, then it will certainly be true what they say, that two can live cheaper than one.

I have talked to Arun and Meenakshi a few times on the phone, although the line from Prahapore to Calcutta is not as clear as it could be. They have unfortunately been busy with various engagements, but they have promised to make time to come for dinner sometime in the near future.

My own family is well. My doubting Uncle Umesh has been impressed by my obtaining a job like this one so quickly. My foster-mother, who is really like a real mother to me, is also pleased. I remember when I went to England first, she said: 'Son, people go to England to become doctors, engineers, barristers. Why do you need to go all the way to become a cobbler?' I could not help smiling at the time, and even now I smile when I think of it. I am happy, however, that I am not a burden on them, that I am standing on my own two feet, and that my work is useful in its own circle.

You will be glad to know that I have given up eating paan. I was warned by Kalpana that your family does not think it attractive, and, whatever I think about it, I have decided to be accommodating in this respect. I hope you are impressed by all these efforts of mine to Mehra-ise myself.

There is something I have not touched upon in either of my last two letters, and it is good of you not to have mentioned its absence. As you know, I was very upset about a word you used, which I realize in retrospect you did not intend as I took it. I wrote to Kalpana about it that same evening, because I felt the need to unburden myself. For some reason I was also uneasy in general. She ticked me off for my 'thickskinned sensitivity' (she had a way with words even in college) and told me I should apologize at once and not be truculent. Well, I did not feel sorry, so I did not write it. But now with the passing of the weeks I realize that I was in the wrong.

I am a practical man and I am proud of it – but sometimes I come across situations that I do not know how to handle despite my wellformed opinions, and I find that after all perhaps there is less reason to be proud than I thought. So please accept my apologies, Lata, and forgive me for ending New Year's Day in such an unpleasing manner.

I hope that when we get married – I am hoping that it is *when*, and not *if* – you will tell me, with that lovely quiet smile of yours, whenever I take things amiss that are not badly intended.

Baoji has been asking me about my marriage plans, but on that score I have not been able to reassure him as yet. As soon as you are sure in your mind that I would make you the right husband, please do tell me. I give thanks every day that I should have met you and that you and I should have got to know each other through words and meetings. The feelings I have for you increase every day, and, unlike my shoes, do not take Saturday and Sunday off. Needless to say, I have your framed photograph on my desk before me, and it brings to me tender thoughts of the original.

Apart from what one sometimes reads in the Calcutta papers, I have had a little news of the Kapoor family in the course of some business dealings with Kedarnath, and my deep sympathy goes to all of them. It must be a terrible time for everyone. He says that Veena and Bhaskar are most agitated, but he makes light of his own anxieties. I can also imagine how hard it is for Pran, with his brother's difficulties and the death of his mother coming side by side. It is good that Savita has her baby and her law studies to provide other thoughts, but it could not be easy to concentrate, especially on some subject as hard as law. I do not know what I can do to help in any way, but if there is anything I can do, please tell me. Some things – the latest law-books and so on – are available in Calcutta more easily than in Brahmpur, I think.

I hope you are studying somehow through all this. I am keeping my fingers crossed for you and am very confident, my Lata, that you will come out in flying colours.

My love to Ma, whom I often thank in my mind for bringing you to Kanpur, and to Pran and Savita and the baby. Please tell Kedarnath if you happen to meet him that I will be writing to him very shortly, probably within the week, depending on certain consultations at this end.

With all my love,
Your own,
Haresh

18.19

AS Lata read, she smiled to herself from time to time. He had crossed out 'Cawnpore' to write 'Kanpur'. When she came to the end she read it through once more. She was glad to hear about Umesh Uncle and his resolved doubts. She could imagine Haresh's father demanding a similar resolution to his own.

Over the months her world had begun to be populated by the various people Haresh continually mentioned. She even missed Simran; Haresh had probably left her out of this letter for fear of treading on her sensitivities. But Lata realized with a start that, however much she liked Haresh, she was not jealous of Simran.

And who were these people in reality? She thought of Haresh: generous, robust, optimistic, impatient, responsible. There he stood in Prahapore, as solid as a pair of Goodyear Welted shoes, twinkling his eyes affectionately at her from the pages of his letter and telling her as well as he could that he was lonely without her.

But Haresh stood alone: Umesh Uncle, Simran, his foster-father, all these figures whom she felt she knew, could turn out to be entirely different from what she had imagined. And his family of conservative Old Delhi khatris: how could she possibly behave with them as she behaved with Kuku or Dipankar or Mr Justice Chatterji? What would she talk about to the Czechs? But there was something adventurous in losing herself entirely in a world that she did not know with a man whom she trusted and had begun to admire – and who cared for her so deeply and steadily. She thought of a paan-less Haresh, smiling his open smile; she sat him down at a table so that she could not see his co-respondent shoes; she ruffled his hair a bit, and – well, he was quite attractive! She liked him. Perhaps, given time and luck, she could even learn to love him.

18.20

A letter from Arun arrived in the afternoon post and helped clarify her thoughts:

My dear Lata,
    You will not mind if I take an elder brother's prerogative to write to you on a matter of great importance to your future and to the future of the family. We are, as such things go, an exceptionally close family, and perhaps as a result of Daddy's death we have been forced even closer together. I, for example, would not have taken on the responsibilities that I have, had Daddy

472

been alive. Varun would probably not have been staying with me, nor would I feel it incumbent on myself to advise him about finding a direction in life, something that left to himself he would, I am afraid, be disinclined to do. Nor would I have the sense that I am, in a manner of speaking, in loco parentis to you.

I imagine you have already guessed the matter I am referring to. Suffice it to say that I have thought about it from every possible angle, and I find myself in disagreement with Ma's judgment on the subject. Hence this letter. Ma has too great a tendency to be swayed by sentiment, and she appears to have taken an irrationally strong liking to Haresh – as well as a strong antipathy – irrational or otherwise – to other people. I experienced something similar in her attitude to my own marriage, which, contrary to her expectations, has turned out to be a happy one based on mutual affection and trust. I believe that as a result I have gained a more objective sense of the choices facing you.

Apart from your temporary infatuation with a certain person in Brahmpur, about which the less said the better, you do not have much experience of the tangled thickets of life, nor have you had the chance to develop criteria for judging the alternatives unguided. It is in this context that I am proffering my advice.

I believe that Haresh has some excellent qualities. He is hardworking, he is in some sense self-made, and he has been educated at – or has at least obtained a degree from – one of the better colleges in India. He is, from all accounts, competent at the trade he has chosen. He has confidence, and he is unafraid to speak his mind. One must give the man his due. That said, however, let me make it clear that I believe that he would not make a suitable addition to our family, and for the following reasons:

1. Despite his having studied English at St Stephen's and having lived in England for two years, his use of the English language leaves a great deal to be desired. This is no trivial point. Conversation between man and wife

is the staple of a marriage based on true understanding. They must be able to communicate, to be, as they say, on the same wave-length. Haresh is simply not on the same wave-length as you – or any of us for that matter. This is not merely a question of his accent, which immediately betrays the fact that English is very far from being his first language; it is a question of his idiom and diction, of his very sense, sometimes, of what is being said. I am glad I was not present at home when that ludicrous fracas about the word 'mean' took place but, as you know, Ma informed me (with many tears and in great detail) about what had occurred the moment Meenakshi and I returned home. If you take the view that Mother knows best, and become engaged to this man, you will continually face painful and absurd situations of this kind.

2. A second, not unrelated, point, is that Haresh does not, and can never aspire to, move in the same social circles as we do. A foreman is not a covenanted assistant, and Praha is simply not Bentsen Pryce. The smell of leather clings rather too closely to the name; the Czechs, who are his bosses, are technicians, sometimes barely literate in English, not graduates from the best universities in England. In a certain sense, by choosing a trade rather than a profession after his graduation from St Stephen's, Haresh has downgraded himself. I hope you do not mind my speaking frankly on a matter of such importance to your future happiness. Society matters, and society is exacting and cruel; you will find yourself excluded from certain circles simply by virtue of being Mrs Khanna.

Nor can Haresh's own background or demeanour counteract the Praha trademark. Unlike say, Meenakshi or Amit, whose father and grandfather have been High Court judges, his family are small people from Old Delhi, and are, to put it bluntly, entirely undistinguished. Certainly, it does him credit that he has brought himself to where he is; but, being a self-made man, he has a tendency to be rather pleased with himself – indeed, a little bumptious. I have noticed that this is often true of short people; he may well have an additional chip on his shoulder as a result of this. I know that Ma thinks of him as a rough diamond. All I can say is that the cut and polish of a stone matter. One does not wear a rough diamond – or one that is chipped – in a wedding ring.

Family, if I may put it plainly, will out. It shows in Haresh's manner of dress, in his liking for snuff and paan, in the fact that, despite his stint in England, he lacks the small social graces. I warned Ma about family background at the time of Savita's engagement to Pran, but she would not listen; and the result, socially speaking, has been the disgraceful connection, through us, of the family of a jailbird to the family of a judge. This is another reason why I feel it is my duty to speak to you before it is too late.

3. Your future family income will in all likelihood not permit you to send your children to the kind of school – for example, St George's or St Sophia's or Jheel or Mayo or Loreto or Doon – that our children – Meenakshi's and mine – will go to. Besides, even if you could afford it, Haresh may have very different views from you about the upbringing of his children or the proportion of the family budget to be devoted to education. With respect to Savita's husband, since he is an academic, I have no concerns on this particular count. But with Haresh I do, and I have to put them to you. I wish the family to remain close, indeed, I feel responsible for the maintenance of this closeness; and differences in the upbringing of our children are bound to draw us apart in time, and to cause you a great deal of heartache besides.

I must ask you to treat this letter as a personal one; to think deeply about it, as befits its contents, but not to show it around the family. Ma would no doubt take it amiss, and, I suppose, so would Savita. As for the subject of this letter, I will only add that he has been pestering us with offers of hospitality; we have been cool to him, and have so far avoided going to Prahapore for another gargantuan lunch. He should, we believe, not presume to be considered part of the family unless he in fact becomes part of it. Needless to say, the choice is yours, and we would welcome your husband, whoever he happened to be, in our private capacity. But it is no use meaning well if you cannot also speak freely, and that is what I have done in this letter.

Rather than add news and small talk, which can wait for another occasion, I will simply end with my love and fondest hopes for your future happiness. Meenakshi, who agrees with me on all points, does the same.

Yours,
Arun Bhai

Lata read the letter through several times, the first time – owing mainly to Arun's wildly erratic handwriting – very slowly; and, as instructed, she pondered its contents deeply. Her first instinct was to have a heart-to-heart talk with Savita, or Malati, or her mother – or with each of them. Then she decided that it would make no difference and would, if anything, only serve to confuse her. This decision was hers to make.

She wrote to Haresh the same evening, accepting with gratitude – and, indeed, warmth – his often repeated offer of marriage.

18.21

'NO!' cried Malati, staring at Lata. 'No! I refuse to believe it. Have you posted the letter yet?'

'Yes,' said Lata.

They were sitting in the shadow of the Fort on the Pul Mela sands, looking out over the warm, grey Ganga, which was glinting in the sunlight.

'You are mad – absolutely mad. How could you do it?'

'Don't be like my mother – "O my poor Lata, O my poor Lata!"'

'Was that her reaction? I thought she was keen on

Haresh,' said Malati. 'Trust you to do just what Mummy says. But I won't have it, Lata, you can't ruin your life like this.'

'I'm not ruining my life,' said Lata heatedly. 'And yes, that might well be her reaction. She's taken against Haresh for some reason. And Arun's been against him from the beginning. But no, Mummy didn't say. In fact, Mummy doesn't even know. You're the first person I'm telling, and you shouldn't be trying to make me feel miserable.'

'I should. I should. I hope you feel really miserable,' said Malati, her eyes flashing green fire. 'Then perhaps you'll see some sense and undo what you've done. You love Kabir, and you must marry him.'

'There's no must about it. Go and marry him yourself,' said Lata, her cheeks red. 'No – don't! Don't! I'll never forgive you. Please don't talk about Kabir, Malu, please.'

'You're going to regret it bitterly,' said Malati. 'I'm telling you that.'

'Well, that's my look-out,' said Lata, struggling to control herself.

'Why didn't you ask me before you decided?' demanded Malati. 'Whom did you consult? Or did you just make up your silly mind by yourself?'

'I consulted my monkeys,' said Lata calmly.

Malati had the strong urge to slap Lata for making stupid jokes at such a time.

'And a book of poetry,' added Lata.

'Poetry!' said Malati with contempt. 'Poetry has been your complete undoing. You have too good a brain to waste on English literature. No, perhaps you don't, after all.'

'You were the first person to tell me to give him up,' said Lata. 'You told me. Or have you forgotten all that?'

'I changed my mind,' said Malati. 'You know I did. I was wrong, terribly wrong. Look at the danger caused to the world by that sort of attitude –'

'Why do you think I'm giving him up?' asked Lata, turning towards her friend.

'Because he's Muslim.'

Lata didn't answer for a while. Then she said:

'It's not that. It's not just that. There isn't any single reason.'

Malati gave a disgusted snort at this pathetic prevarication.

Lata sighed. 'Malati, I can't describe it – my feelings with him are so confused. I'm not myself when I'm with him. I ask myself who is this – this jealous, obsessed woman who can't get a man out of her head – why should I make myself suffer like this? I know that it'll always be like this if I'm with him.'

'Oh, Lata – don't be blind –' exclaimed Malati. 'It shows how passionately you love him –'

'I don't want to,' cried Lata, 'I don't want to. If that's what passion means, I don't want it. Look at what passion has done to the family. Maan's broken, his mother's dead, his father's in despair. When I thought that Kabir was seeing someone else, what I remember feeling was enough to make me hate passion. Passionately and forever.'

'It's my fault,' said Malati bitterly, shaking her head from side to side. 'I wish to God I'd never written that letter to Calcutta. And you're going to wish the same.'

'It isn't, Malati. And I'm not. Thank God you did.'

Malati looked at Lata with sick unhappiness. 'You just don't realize what you're throwing away, Lata. You're choosing the wrong man. Stay unmarried for a while. Take your time to make up your mind again. Or simply remain unmarried – it's not so tragic.'

Lata was silent. On the side that Malati could not see, she let a handful of sand pass through her fingers.

'What about that other chap?' said Malati – 'that poet, Amit? How has he put himself out of the running?'

Lata smiled at the thought of Amit. 'Well, he wouldn't be my undoing, as you put it, but I don't see myself as his wife at all. We're too alike. His moods veer and oscillate as wildly as mine. Can you imagine the life of our poor children? And if his mind's on a book I don't know if he'll have any time for me. Sensitive people are usually very insensitive – I should know. As a matter of fact, he's just proposed to me.'

Malati looked shocked and angry.

'You never tell me anything!'

'Everything happened all of a sudden yesterday,' said Lata, fishing Amit's acrostic out of the pocket of her kameez. 'I brought this along, since you usually like to see the documents in the case.'

Malati read it in silence, then said: 'I'd marry anyone who wrote me this.'

'Well, he's still available,' laughed Lata. 'And I won't veto that marriage.' She put her arm around Malati's shoulder before continuing: 'For me, marrying Amit would be madness. Quite apart from everything else, I get more than enough of my brother Arun. To live five minutes away from him would be the ultimate lunacy!'

'You could live somewhere else.'

'Oh no –' said Lata, picturing Amit in his room overlooking the laburnum in bloom. 'He's a poet and a novelist. He wants things laid on for him. Meals, hot water, a running household, a dog, a lawn, a Muse. And why not? After all, he did write "The Fever Bird"! But he won't be able to write if he has to fend for himself away from his family. Anyway, you seem to be happy with anyone but Haresh. Why? Why are you so dead-set against him?'

'Because I see nothing, nothing, nothing at all in common between you two,' said Malati. 'And it's completely obvious you don't love him. Have you thought this thing through, Lata, or are you just making up your mind in a sort of trance? Like that nun business that Ma keeps talking about. Think. Do you like the idea of sharing your possessions with this man? Of making love with him? Does he attract you? Can you cope with the things that irritate you about him – Cawnpore and paan and all that? Please, please, Lata, don't be stupid. Use your brains. What about this Simran woman – doesn't that bother you? And what do you want to do with yourself after your marriage – or are you just content to be a housewife in a walled compound full of Czechs?'

'Do you think I haven't thought about any of this?' said

Lata, removing her arm, annoyed once more. 'Or that I haven't tried to visualize what life will be like with him? It'll be interesting, I think. Haresh is practical, he's forceful, he isn't cynical. He gets things done and he helps people without making a fuss about it. He's helped Kedarnath and Veena a great deal.'

'So what? . . . Will he let you teach?'

'Yes, he will.'

'Have you asked him?' pressed Malati.

'No. That's not the best idea,' said Lata. 'But I'm sure of it. I think I know him well enough by now. He hates to see anyone's talent wasted. He encourages them. And he's really concerned about people – about me, about Maan, about Savita and her studies, about Bhaskar –'

'– who, incidentally, is alive today only because of Kabir,' Malati could not resist interposing.

'I don't deny it.' Lata sighed deeply, and looked at the warm sands all around.

For a while neither said anything. Then Malati spoke.

'But what has he done, Lata?' she said quietly. 'What has he done that is wrong – that he should be treated like this? He loves you and he never deserved to be doubted. Is it fair? Just think, is it fair?'

'I don't know,' said Lata slowly, looking over towards the far shore. 'No, it isn't, I suppose. But life isn't always a question of justice, is it? What is that line? – "Use every man after his desert, and who should 'scape whipping?" But it's true the other way around as well. Use every man after his desert and you'll become a complete emotional bankrupt.'

'That's a really mean-spirited view of the world,' said Malati.

'Don't call me mean,' cried Lata passionately.

Malati looked at her in astonishment.

Lata shivered. 'All I meant was, Malati, that when I'm with Kabir, or even away from him but thinking about him, I become utterly useless for anything. I feel I'm out of control – like a boat heading for the rocks – and I don't want to become a wreck.'

'So you're going to instruct yourself not to think of him?'

'If I can,' said Lata, almost to herself.

'What did you say? Speak up,' demanded Malati, wanting to shake her into seeing sense.

'If I can,' said Lata.

'How can you deceive yourself like this?'

Lata was silent.

'Malu, I'm not going to quarrel with you,' she said after a while. 'I care for you as much as I care for any of these men, and I always will. But I'm not going to undo what I've done. I do love Haresh, and –'

'What?' cried Malati, looking at Lata as if she were an imbecile.

'I do.'

'You're full of surprises today,' said Malati, very angry now.

'And, well, you're full of incredulities. But I do. Or I think I do. Thank God it isn't what I feel for Kabir.'

'I don't believe you. You're just making that up.'

'You must. He's grown on me, he really has. I don't find him unattractive. And there's something else – I won't feel I'll be making a fool of myself with him – with regard to, well, with regard to sex.'

Malati stared at her. What a crazy thing to say.

'And with Kabir you will?'

'With Kabir – I just don't know –'

Malati said nothing. She shook her head slowly, not looking at Lata, half lost in her own thoughts.

Lata said: 'Do you know those lines of Clough that go: "There are two different kinds, I believe, of human attraction"?'

Again Malati said nothing but merely shook her head.

'Well, they go something like this:

There are two different kinds, I believe, of human attraction.
One that merely excites, unsettles, and makes you uneasy;
The other that –

Well, I can't remember exactly, but he talks about a calmer, less frantic love, which helps you to grow where you were already growing, "to live where as yet I had languished" – I just read it yesterday, it isn't in my head yet, but it said everything that I couldn't express on my own. Do you understand what I mean? . . . Malati?'

'All I understand,' said Malati, 'is that you can't live on other people's words. You're throwing away the golden casket and the silver one, and you seem to think that you'll be as lucky with the bronze casket as your English literature tells you you'll be. Well, I hope you will, I really hope you will. But you won't be. You won't.'

'You'll grow to like him too, Malu.'

Malati didn't answer.

'You haven't even met him,' continued Lata with a smile. 'And I remember at first you refused to like Pran.'

'I hope you're right.' Malati sounded weary. Her heart was sick for both Lata and Kabir.

'It's more like Nala and Damyanti than Portia and Bassanio,' said Lata, trying to cheer her up. 'Haresh's feet touch the ground, and he has dust and sweat and a shadow. The other two are a bit too God-like and ethereal to be any good for me.'

'So you're at ease,' said Malati, searching her friend's face. 'You're at ease with yourself. And you know exactly what you're going to do. Well, tell me, out of curiosity, before you write him off, are you at least going to drop a line to Kabir?'

Lata's lips began to tremble.

'I'm not at ease – I'm not –' she cried. 'It's not easy – Malu, how can you think it is? I hardly know who I am or what I'm doing – I can't study or even think these days – everything is pressing in on me. I can't bear it when I'm with him, and I can't bear not to see him. How do I know what I may or may not do? I only hope I have the courage to stick to my decision.'

18.22

MAAN sat at home or in the garden with his father or visited Pran or Veena. Other than that he did very little. He had been eager to visit Saeeda Bai when he was in jail, but now that he was out of jail, he found that he had inexplicably lost his eagerness to do so. She sent him a note, which he did not reply to. Then she sent him another, more urgent one, upbraiding him for his desertion of her, but to no effect.

Maan was not very fond of reading, but these days he spent whole mornings with the newspapers, reading everything from the international news to the advertisements. Now that Firoz was out of danger he had begun to worry about himself and what was going to happen to him once the charge-sheet was prepared.

Firoz had remained in hospital for about twenty days before the doctors consented to his being moved back to Baitar House. He was physically weak, but on the mend. Imtiaz took charge of him, Zainab stayed on in Brahmpur to nurse him, and the Nawab Sahib watched over him and prayed for his full recovery. For his mind was still clouded and agitated, and he would sometimes cry out in his sleep. These fragments of speech, which would have meant nothing to anyone earlier, could now be fitted into the frame of the rumours by anyone who sat by his bedside.

The Nawab Sahib had turned to religion almost two decades ago partly as the result of his appalled realization of what he had done when he emerged from the worst of his drunken binges, and partly because of the quiet influence of his wife. He had always had a taste for scholarly and analytical pursuits but, being a sensualist, had allowed these to be overlaid by his more urgent needs and pleasures. The change in his life had been sudden; and he had hoped to save his own children from the sins and the repentance that he himself had undergone. The boys knew he did not approve of their drinking, and they never did so in his presence. As for his grandchildren, they would never have been able to imagine him as a young – or even a middle-aged – man. They had known their Nana-jaan throughout their lives as a quiet, pious old man whom only they were permitted to disturb in his library – and who could easily be persuaded to grant them a respite from bedtime by the telling of a ghost story. The Nawab Sahib understood all too well the infidelities of their father and, while his heart went out to his daughter, he was reminded of the suffering he had in his own time inflicted on his own wife. Not that Zainab would have wanted him to speak to her husband. She had needed comfort, but had not expected relief.

The Nawab Sahib now suffered once again, but this time not only from the memory of the past but from the present opinion of the world, and – worst of all – from the sense of what his children must think of him. He did not know what interpretation to place upon the rejection of his continuing financial help to Saeeda Bai. He was more troubled by it than relieved. He did not really think of Tasneem as his daughter, or feel any affection for this unseen being, but he did not want her to suffer. Nor did he wish Saeeda Bai now to feel free to publish to the world whatever it suited her convenience to publish. He begged God to forgive him for the unworthiness of this concern, but he was unable to put it aside.

He had shrunk further into his library in the course of the last month, but every visit to Firoz's bedside and every appearance at meal-time was infinitely painful to him. His children, however, understood this, and continued to be outwardly as respectful towards him as before. Firoz's illness or the acts of the distant past were not to be allowed to split the shell of the family. The grace was said, the meat stew was passed, the kababs served, the permission to rise accepted with routine decorum. Nothing was said or shown to him that might add to his disequilibrium. He had still not heard about the fliers announcing that Firoz had died.

And if I had died, thought Firoz to himself, what would it have mattered to the universe? What have I ever done for anyone? I am a man without attributes, very handsome, very forgettable. Imtiaz is a man of substance, of some use to the world. All that would be left of me is a walking-stick, the grief of my family, and terrible danger for my friend.

He had asked to see Maan once or twice, but no one had passed the message on to Prem Nivas. Imtiaz could see no good coming of the meeting, either for his brother or for his father. He knew Maan well enough to realize that the attack had been a sudden one, unpremeditated, almost unintentional. But his father did not see it that way; and Imtiaz wanted to spare him any avoidable shock of emotion, any access of hatred or recrimination. Imtiaz believed that Mrs Mahesh Kapoor's death had indeed been hastened by the sudden and terrible events that had struck their two houses. He would insulate his father from anything similar, and his brother from any agitation about Maan or, through the revival of his memory of that night, about Tasneem.

Tasneem, though she was no doubt his half sister, meant nothing to Imtiaz at all. Zainab too, though she was curious, realized that wisdom lay in closing the door of interpretation.

Finally, Firoz wrote a note to Maan, which read simply: 'Dear Maan, Please visit me. I'm well enough to see you. Firoz.' He half-suspected his brother of mollycoddling him, and he had had enough of it. He gave the note to Ghulam Rusool, and told him that he was to see that it got to Prem Nivas.

Maan received the note in the late afternoon and did not hesitate. Without telling his father, who was sitting on a bench reading some legislative papers, he walked over to Baitar House. Perhaps this call, rather than a summons from the court of the committal magistrate, was what in his state of idle tension he had been waiting for all along. As he approached the grand main gates, he looked instinctively about him, thinking of the she-monkey who had attacked him here earlier. This time he carried no stick.

A servant asked him to enter. But the Nawab Sahib's secretary, Murtaza Ali, happened to be passing by, and asked him, with stern courtesy, what he imagined he was doing there. He had been given strict orders not to admit anyone from Mahesh Kapoor's family. Maan, whose instinct not very long ago would have been to tell him to go hang himself, had been shaken by his jail life into responding to the orders of his social inferiors. He showed him Firoz's note.

Murtaza Ali looked worried but thought quickly. Imtiaz was at the hospital, Zainab was in the zenana, and the Nawab Sahib was at his prayers. The note was unambiguous. He told Ghulam Rusool to take Maan up to see Firoz for a few minutes and asked Maan if he would like something to drink.

Maan would have liked a gallon of whisky to fortify himself. 'No, thank you,' he replied.

Firoz's face lit up when he saw his friend. 'So you've come!' he said. 'I feel I'm in jail here. I've been asking for you for a week, but the Superintendent won't let messages out. I hope you've brought me some whisky.'

Maan started weeping. Firoz looked so pale – really, as if he had just returned from death.

'Have a look at my scar,' Firoz said, trying to lighten the situation. He pushed the bedsheet down and pulled up his kurta.

'Impressive,' said Maan, still in tears. 'Centipede.'

He went to Firoz's bedside, and touched his friend's face.

They talked for a few minutes, each attempting to avoid what might cause the other pain except in such a way as would more probably defuse it.

'You're looking well,' said Maan.

'How poorly you lie,' said Firoz. 'I wouldn't take you on as a client.... These days I find I lack concentration. My mind wanders,' he added with a smile. 'It's quite interesting.'

They were silent for a minute. Maan put his forehead to Firoz's and sighed painfully. He did not say how sorry he was for all he had done.

He sat down near Firoz.

'Does it hurt?' he asked.

'Yes, at times.'

'Is everyone at home all right?'

'Yes,' said Firoz. 'How are – how is your father?'

'As well as can be expected,' said Maan.

Firoz did not say how sorry he was about Maan's mother, but shook his head in regret, and Maan understood.

After a while he got up.

'Come again,' said Firoz.

'When? Tomorrow?'

'No – in two or three days.'

'You'll have to send me another note,' said Maan. 'Or I'll be thrown out.'

'Here, give me the old note. I'll re-validate it,' said Firoz with a smile.

As Maan walked home, it struck him that they had avoided talking directly about Saeeda Bai or Tasneem or his experience of prison or the forthcoming case against him, and he was glad.

18.23

THAT evening, Dr Bilgrami came over to Prem Nivas to have a word with Maan. He told him that Saeeda Bai wished to see him. Dr Bilgrami looked exhausted, and Maan went along with him. The meeting was a painful one.

Saeeda Bai's voice was still not itself, though she had recovered her looks. She reproached Maan for not having visited her since his release from jail. Had he changed so much? she asked with a smile. Had she changed? Had he not received her notes? What had kept him away? She was ill, she was desperate to see him. Her voice broke. She was going mad without him. She impatiently waved Dr Bilgrami away, and turned to Maan with longing and pity. How was he? He looked so thin. What had they done to him?

'Dagh Sahib – what has happened to you? What will happen to you?'

'I don't know.'

He looked around the room. 'The blood?' he asked.

'What blood?' she asked. It had been a month ago.

The room smelt of attar of roses and of Saeeda Bai herself. Sadly and sensuously she leaned back on her cushions against the wall. But Maan thought he saw a scar on her face, and the face itself turned into a portrait of the varicose Victoria.

So shattering had been his mother's death, Firoz's danger, his own disgrace, and his terrible sense of guilt that he had begun to suffer a violent revulsion of feeling against himself and Saeeda Bai. Perhaps he saw her too as a victim. But his greater understanding of events gave him no greater control over his feelings. He had been too deeply scoured by what had occurred, and his present vision of her horrified him. He stared at her face.

I am becoming like Rasheed, he thought. I'm seeing things that don't exist. He stood up, his face pale. 'I am going,' he said.

'You aren't well,' she said.

'No – no, I'm not,' he said.

Hurt and frustrated by his behaviour, she had been about to rebuke him for his attitude towards her, for what he had done to her household, to her reputation, to Tasneem. But one look at his bewildered face told her it would be no use. He was in another world – beyond the reach of her affections or attractions. She hid her face in her hands.

'Are you all right?' said Maan uncertainly, as if feeling his way to something in the past. 'I am to blame for all that has happened.'

'You don't love me – don't tell me you do – I can see it –' she wept.

'Love –' said Maan. 'Love?' Suddenly he sounded furious.

'And even the shawl that my mother gave me –' said Saeeda Bai.

She was making no sense to him at all.

'Don't let them do anything to you –' she said, refusing to look up, unwilling for once that he should see her tears. Maan looked away.

ON the 29th of February, Maan was brought up before the same magistrate as before. The police had reconsidered their position based on the evidence. Maan had not intended to kill Firoz, but the police now believed that he had intended to cause 'such bodily injury as was sufficient in the ordinary course of nature to cause death'. This was enough to bring him under the hazard of the section dealing with attempted murder. The magistrate was satisfied with the result of the investigation and framed the charges.

I, Suresh Mathur, Magistrate of the First Class at Brahmpur, hereby charge you, Maan Kapoor, as follows:
That you, on or about the 4th day of January, 1952, at Brahmpur, did an act, to wit, that you did stab with a knife one Nawabzada Firoz Ali Khan of Baitar with such knowledge and under such circumstances, that if by that act you had caused the death of Nawabzada Firoz Ali Khan of Baitar, you would have been guilty of murder and that you caused hurt to the said Nawabzada Firoz Ali Khan of Baitar by the said act, and thereby committed an offence punishable under Section 307 of the Indian Penal Code, and within the cognizance of the Court of Session.
And I hereby direct that you be tried by the said Court on the said charge.

The magistrate also charged Maan with grievous hurt with a deadly weapon. Both these offences carried a possible sentence of imprisonment for life. Neither was bailable, and the magistrate therefore withdrew bail. Maan was recommitted to jail to await trial.

18.25

ALSO on the 29th of February, Pran's selection as reader in the Department of English at Brahmpur University was confirmed by the Academic Council. But he, and his family, and his father, were sunk in such gloom that this news did not lighten it at all.

Pran, his thoughts dwelling much on death these days, wondered once again about the remark made by Ramjap Baba to his mother at the Pul Mela. If his readership was indeed due to a death, whose death had the Baba meant? Certainly, his mother had died; but just as certainly this could not have influenced the selection committee. Or had Professor Mishra been serious when he had claimed that he had watched out for Pran's interests out of sympathy for his family?

I too am becoming superstitious, said Pran. It will be my father next. But his father, luckily for his state of mind, had something to occupy him over the next few days other than trying to organize Maan's defence.

18.26

AT the beginning of March, Mahesh Kapoor, though defeated in the elections, was asked once again to perform his duties as an MLA. The Legislative Assembly of Purva Pradesh had been elected, but the indirect elections for the Upper House, the Legislative Council, had not yet taken place. The legislature was therefore not complete. Under the Constitution, six months could not be allowed to elapse between sessions of the legislative body, and the old legislature was therefore forced into brief session. Besides, it was budget time; and though propriety demanded that the budget be passed by the new legislature, the financial wheels had to be kept turning somehow. This would be done through a 'vote on account' for the months of April to July, 1952, the first third of the coming financial year. This vote on account had to be passed by the old, soon-to-be-defunct legislature of which Mahesh Kapoor was a part.

In early March, the two Houses of the legislature met in joint session to hear the Governor's address. The discussion following the vote of thanks to the Governor turned into a noisy and angry debate on the Congress government itself: both its policies and the manner in which it had conducted the elections. Many of those who were most vocal were those who had been defeated and whose voice would be heard in this vast round chamber no more – or at least not for the next five years. As the Governor was the constitutional (and largely ceremonial) head of the state, his address had for the most part been written by the Chief Minister S.S. Sharma.

The Governor's address touched briefly on recent events, the achievements of the government, and its future plans. The Congress Party had won three-quarters of the seats in the Lower House, and (because of the system of indirect election) was bound to win a large majority in the Upper House as well. Discussing the elections, the Governor said in passing: 'I am sure that it will be a cause of gratification to you, as it is to me, that almost all my Ministers have been returned to the new Assembly.' At this point many of those in the House turned to look at Mahesh Kapoor.

The Governor also mentioned a 'matter of regret': that the enforcement of the Purva Pradesh Zamindari and Land Reform Act 'is being delayed for reasons which are beyond the control of my government.' This referred to the fact that the constitutionality of the act was still to be decided by the Supreme Court. 'But,' he added, 'I need hardly assure you that no time will be lost in implementing it as soon as it legally becomes possible to do so.'

In the subsequent debate, Begum Abida Khan brought up both these matters. She mentioned in one fiery breath that it was well-known that the Government had used unfair methods – including the use of official cars for ministerial travel – to win the elections; and that, despite this abuse, the Minister who was most closely associated in the public mind with robbing the zamindars of their land had very deservedly lost his seat. Begum Abida Khan had won her own seat, but most of the other members of her party had lost, and she was furious.

Her remarks created pandemonium. The Congress

benches were indignant at her attempt to rake up the embers of completed legislation. And even L.N. Agarwal, who was secretly pleased that Mahesh Kapoor had not won his election, condemned the means deployed not by the Congress but by 'rank communalists' in that particular race. At this, Begum Abida Khan began talking about attempted murder and 'a heinous plot to extirpate the minority community from the soil of our common province.' And finally the Speaker had to stop her from continuing in this vein by telling her, first, that the case he presumed she was referring to was sub judice, and secondly, that the entire issue was irrelevant to the question of whether the House should vote to thank the Governor for his address.

Mahesh Kapoor sat through all this with head bowed, silent and unresponsive. He had attended because it was his duty to do so. He would rather have been almost anywhere else. Begum Abida Khan, thinking of her nephew lying on what could well have been his deathbed, appealed loudly from the Speaker to God for justice, so that condign punishment would be meted out to the butcher responsible for his grievous injury. Dramatically she pointed a finger at Mahesh Kapoor, and then raised it heavenwards. Mahesh Kapoor closed his eyes and saw the image of Maan in jail; he knew too well that if he had ever had the power or the influence to save his son, he did not have it now.

The vote of thanks passed as overwhelmingly as expected. Various other bits of legislative business were also taken up – such as the announcement of the President's or the Governor's assent to various bills, the resignation of various MLAs who had also been elected as MPs, and the tabling of various ordinances that it had become necessary to promulgate when the legislature had not been in session. The session then broke off for a few days for Holi before going on to the vote on account, which it passed after brief debate.

HOLI was not celebrated at Prem Nivas at all this year, nor
at Pran's house. Maan and Imtiaz, high on bhang, helping
Professor Mishra into a large tub of pink water; Savita,
drenched in colour, laughing and crying and promising
revenge; Mrs Mahesh Kapoor making sure that her grand-
nieces and grandnephews from Rudhia all got their favourite sweets; the bejewelled Saeeda Bai singing ghazals before
a charmed audience of men while their wives looked down
from the balcony in fascinated disapproval: these must
have appeared as scenes of an unreal fantasy to anyone
who remembered them.

Pran took some dry pink and green powder and smeared
a little on his daughter's forehead, but that was all. It was
her first Holi, and he blessed her for her unawareness of
all the darkness and sadness that existed in the world.

Lata tried to study, but she was unable to. Her heart
was full, as much with Maan and the deep sorrow of his
family as with her own forthcoming marriage. Mrs Rupa
Mehra, when she heard of Lata's unilateral action in
writing to Haresh, was both furious and delighted. Lata
had passed on Haresh's message of love for her mother
and his words of regret before she had broken the real
news. Torn between hugging her daughter to her bosom
and giving her at least one tight slap for not having
consulted her, Mrs Rupa Mehra burst into tears.

Needless to say, there was no question of the wedding
taking place in Prem Nivas. Given Arun's views on Haresh,
Lata had refused to get married from Sunny Park either.
The Chatterji house at Ballygunge was impossible for
several reasons. That only left Dr Kishen Chand Seth's
house.

Had Dr Kishen Chand Seth been in Mrs Rupa Mehra's
position, he would certainly have slapped Lata. After all,
he had slapped Mrs Rupa Mehra when Arun was a year
old because he thought she wasn't controlling the baby
properly. He had never had any truck with incompetence
or insubordination. He now bluntly refused to counte-

nance, let alone assist, the marriage of a granddaughter in which he had not been consulted from the beginning. He told Mrs Rupa Mehra that his house was not a hotel or a dharamshala, and that she would have to look elsewhere.

'And that is that,' he added.

Mrs Rupa Mehra threatened to kill herself.

'Yes, yes, do so,' said her father impatiently. He knew that she loved life too much, especially when she could be justifiably miserable.

'And I will never see you again,' she added. 'Never in all my life. Say goodbye to me,' she sobbed, 'for this is the last time you will see your daughter.' With that she flung herself weeping into his arms.

Dr Kishen Chand Seth staggered back and nearly dropped his stick. Carried away by her emotion and by the greater realism of this threat, he too started sobbing violently, and pounded his stick several times on the floor to give vent to his feelings. Very soon it was all settled.

'I hope Parvati does not mind,' gasped Mrs Rupa Mehra. 'She is so good – so good –'

'If she does, I will get rid of her,' cried Dr Kishen Chand Seth. 'A wife one can divorce – but one's children – never!' These words – which it seemed to him he had heard somewhere before – sent him into a renewed paroxysm of weeping.

When Parvati came back from shopping a few minutes later, holding out a pair of pink high-heeled shoes and saying, 'Kishy darling, look at what I've bought from Lovely,' her husband grinned weakly, terrified to break the news of the inconvenience he had just taken on.

18.28

THE NAWAB SAHIB had heard about Mahesh Kapoor's question to Waris about Firoz's health. He also knew that when the count was over, Mahesh Kapoor had refused a recount. Later he heard from his munshi that he had even refused to lodge an election petition.

'But why would he wish to lodge an election petition? And against whom?' said the Nawab Sahib.

'Against Waris,' said the munshi, and handed him a couple of the fatal pink fliers.

The Nawab Sahib read through one and his face grew pale with anger. The poster had made such shameless and impious use of death that he wondered that God's anger had not fallen on Waris, or on him, or on Firoz, the innocent agency of this outrage. As if he had not sunk deeply enough in the world's opinion, what must Mahesh Kapoor think of him now?

Firoz – whatever he might think of his father – was, by the grace of God, out of danger at last. And Mahesh Kapoor's son was lying in jail in danger of losing his liberty for many years. How strangely the tables had turned, thought the Nawab Sahib, and what small satisfaction Maan's jeopardy and Mahesh Kapoor's grief – both of which in bitterness he had once prayed for – now gave him after all.

That he had not attended Mrs Mahesh Kapoor's chautha made him feel ashamed. Firoz had had an infection at the time and had been in serious danger – but now the Nawab Sahib asked himself whether his son had been in such immediate hazard that he could not have spared half an hour and braved the glances of the world to at least show his face at the service? Poor woman, she had surely died fearing that neither her son nor his might live until the summer, and knowing that Maan at least could not even come to her deathbed. How painful such knowledge must have been; and how little her goodness and generosity had deserved it.

Sometimes he sat in his library and went to sleep from tiredness. Ghulam Rusool would wake him up for lunch or dinner whenever it was necessary to do so. It was becoming warm as well. The coppersmith had begun to sound its short continual call from a fig tree outside. Here in the library, lost in religion or philosophy or the speculations of astronomy, even worlds might seem small, not to speak of personal estates and ambitions, griefs and guilt. Or, lost in his projected edition of Mast's poems, he might have forgotten the uproar of the world around. But the Nawab Sahib discovered that he could read nothing with any concentration. He found himself staring at a page, wondering where he had been for the last hour.

One morning he read in the *Brahmpur Chronicle* about Abida Khan's derisive ad hominem remarks in the House, and how Mahesh Kapoor had not stood up to say a word by way of defence or explanation. He was seized with pain on his friend's behalf. He rang up his sister-in-law.

'Abida, what was the necessity for saying these things I've been reading about?'

Abida laughed. Her brother-in-law was weak and over-scrupulous, and would never make much of a fighter. 'Why, it was my last chance to attack that man face to face,' she said. 'If it wasn't for him, do you think your inheritance and that of your sons would be in such danger? And why talk of inheritance, how about your son's life?'

'Abida, there is a limit to things.'

'Well, when I reach it, I will stop. And if I don't, I will fall over the edge. That is my concern.'

'Abida, have pity –'

'Pity? What pity did that man's son have on Firoz? Or on that helpless woman –' Abida suddenly stopped. Perhaps she felt that she had reached the limit. There was a long pause. Finally she broke it by saying: 'All right, I will accept your advice on this. But I hope that that butcher rots in jail.' She thought of the Nawab Sahib's wife, the only light of her years in the zenana, and she added: 'For many years to come.'

The Nawab Sahib knew that Maan had come to visit Firoz twice at Baitar House before he had again been committed to jail. Murtaza Ali had told him so, and had also told him that Firoz had asked him to come. Now the Nawab Sahib asked himself the question: if Firoz had chosen to forgive his friend, what was the law that it should insist on destroying his life?

That night he was dining alone with Firoz. This was usually very painful: they tried to talk to each other without really speaking of anything. But tonight he turned to his son and said: 'Firoz, what is the evidence against that boy?'

'Evidence, Abba?'

'I mean, from the point of view of the court.'

'He has confessed to the police.'

'Has he confessed before a magistrate?'

Firoz was a little surprised that this legalistic thought should have come to his father rather than to him. 'You're right, Abba,' he said. 'But there's all the other evidence – his flight, his identification, all our statements – mine, and those of the others who were there.' He looked at his father carefully, thinking how hard it must be for him to approach even indirectly the subject of his injury or the other matter behind it. He said after a while: 'When I made my statement, I was very ill; my mind could have been confused, of course. Perhaps it's still confused – I should have thought of all this, not you.'

Neither said anything for a minute. Then Firoz went on: 'If I fell on the knife – stumbled, say – and it was in his hand, he might, since he was drunk, have thought that he had done it – and so might – so might –'

'The others.'

'Yes – the others. That would explain their statements – and his disappearance,' continued Firoz, as if the entire scene was passing once again before his eyes, very clearly, very slowly. But a few seconds of the scene that had been clear before had now begun to blur.

'Enough has happened in Prem Nivas already,' said his father. 'And the same set of facts is open to many interpretations.'

This last remark conjured up different thoughts for each of them.

'Yes, Abba,' said Firoz quietly and gratefully, and with something of a renewal in his heart of his old respect.

MAAN'S trial came up in a fortnight before the District and Sessions Judge. Both the Nawab Sahib and Mahesh Kapoor were present in the small courtroom. Firoz was one of the first witnesses. The prosecution lawyer, leading him with quiet confidence through the phrases of the statement he had given to the police, was startled when Firoz said:

'And then I stumbled and fell onto the knife.'

'I am sorry,' said the lawyer. 'What was that you said?'

'I said, I stumbled, and fell onto the knife that he was holding in his hand.'

The government advocate was utterly taken aback. Try as he might, he could not shake Firoz's evidence. He complained to the court that the witness had turned hostile to the state and requested permission to cross-examine him. He put it to Firoz that his evidence was inconsistent with his statement to the police. Firoz replied that he had been ill at the time of his statement, and that his memory had been blurred. It was only after his recovery that it had sharpened and clarified. The prosecutor reminded Firoz that he himself was a lawyer and that he was on oath. Firoz, who was still looking pale, replied with a smile that he was well aware of it, but that even lawyers did not have perfect memories. He had relived the scene many times and he was certain now that he had stumbled against something – he thought it might have been a bolster – and had fallen onto the knife that Maan had just wrested from Saeeda Bai. 'He just stood there. I think he thought he had done it,' added Firoz helpfully, though he was fully aware of the limitations of evidence based on hearsay or the interpretation of the mental state of others.

Maan sat in the dock, staring at his friend, hardly comprehending at first what was happening. A look of disturbed amazement spread slowly across his face.

Saeeda Bai was examined next. She stood in the witness box, her face unseen behind the burqa she was wearing, and spoke in a low voice. She was happy to accept the contention of the defence lawyer that what she had seen was consistent with this interpretation of events. So was Bibbo. The other evidence – Firoz's blood on the shawl, Maan's identification by the railway clerk, the memory of the watchman, and so on – threw no light on the question of what had happened during those two or three vital, almost fatal, seconds. And if Maan had not even stabbed Firoz, if Firoz had simply fallen on the knife held in his hand, the very question of his intention to inflict 'such bodily injury as was sufficient in the ordinary course of nature to cause death' was irrelevant.

The judge saw no reason why a man who had been so badly injured would go out of his way to protect someone who had deliberately inflicted such an injury on him. There was no evidence of collusion among the witnesses, no attempt by the defence to suborn anyone. He was led to the inescapable conclusion that Maan was not guilty.

He acquitted Maan of both charges and ordered him released immediately.

Mahesh Kapoor embraced his son. He too was dumb-founded. He turned towards the courtroom, which was now in uproar, and saw the Nawab Sahib talking to Firoz. Their eyes met for an instant. Mahesh Kapoor's were full of perplexity and gratitude.

The Nawab Sahib shook his head slightly, as if to disown responsibility, and turned again to talk to his son.

18.30

PRAN had not been correct in imagining that his father would become superstitious. Mahesh Kapoor did, however, take an unsteady step towards countenancing superstition. In late March, a few days before Ramnavami, he acquiesced in Veena's and old Mrs Tandon's request to hold a reading of the Ramcharitmanas at Prem Nivas for the family and a few friends.

Why he agreed was unclear even to himself. His wife had asked for the reading the previous year and he associ-ated the request with her. She had even asked for a section of the Ramcharitmanas – the section involving Hanuman in Lanka – to be read to her on her deathbed. Perhaps Mahesh Kapoor felt sorry that he had refused her in the past – or perhaps he was simply too exhausted to refuse anyone anything any longer. Or perhaps – though it is unlikely that he would ever have accepted such a reason – perhaps he wished to give thanks to something beneficent and mysterious outside himself that had kept his son safe when he had seemed logically to be doomed and had restored his hope of friendship with the Nawab Sahib when it had appeared to be beyond repair.

Old Mrs Tandon was the only one of the group of three samdhins who attended. Mrs Rupa Mehra was in Calcutta, frantically making wedding purchases. And Mrs Mahesh Kapoor's small brass bell no longer rang in the tiny alcove where she used to perform her puja.

One morning, while the recitation was going on, a white owl walked into the room where the listeners were sitting. It stayed for a few minutes, then slowly walked out again. Everyone was alarmed by the presence of this inauspicious bird in the daytime, and took it as a bad sign. But Veena disagreed. She said that the white owl, being the vehicle of Lakshmi, was a symbol of good luck in Bengal. It might well be an emissary sent from the other world to bring them good fortune and to take back good news.

18.31

WHEN Maan was in jail, his mind had often turned to Rasheed's tormented madness and delusion. They were both outcastes, even if his own delusion had been temporary. The difference between them, Maan had felt, was that he, despite his physical incarceration, had at least preserved the love of his family.

He had asked Pran to send Rasheed some money, not out of a sense of expiation, but because he thought it might be practically useful. He remembered how gaunt and wasted he had looked that day in Curzon Park, and wondered if what his uncle managed to send him together with what Rasheed himself was earning sufficed for rent and food. Maan feared that sooner or later the tuitions too were bound to stop.

When he was out on bail, he did not visit, but sent some more money, again anonymously, by mail. He felt that for him, a man with a violent crime hanging over his head, to visit Rasheed in person might lead to unforeseeable constructions and consequences. In any case, it would not help Rasheed's balance of mind.

When Maan was found innocent and finally set free, his thoughts turned once more to his old teacher and erstwhile friend. But again he was not certain if seeing him was a good idea, so he wrote a letter first. He received no reply.

When a second letter was neither replied to nor returned, Maan decided that at least he had not met with a refusal. He went to Rasheed's address, but Rasheed was not there any longer. He spoke to the landlord and his wife, and told them he was a friend. He sensed that they were not very pleased. He asked them what Rasheed's new address was, and they told him they did not know. When he said that he had written two letters to Rasheed recently and asked them where they were, the man looked at his wife, appeared to come to a decision, fetched them from inside and gave both of them to Maan. They were unopened.

Maan had no idea whether Rasheed had got the money he had sent. He asked the landlord when exactly it was that Rasheed had left, and whether any earlier letters had been received. They replied that he had left some time ago, but he could not get them to be more specific than that. They appeared to be annoyed, but whether at Rasheed or at him, he did not know.

Maan, worried, now asked Pran to trace Rasheed through either the History Department or the Registrar's Office. Neither knew his whereabouts. A clerk in the Registrar's Office mentioned that Rasheed had withdrawn from the university; he had said that he refused to attend lectures when he was needed to campaign for the sake of the country.

Maan next wrote in his rather blunt Urdu script to Baba and Rasheed's father, asking for news and for Rasheed's latest address. Perhaps, Maan suggested, the Bear might know where he was. He got a short and not unsympathetic reply. Baba said that everyone at Debaria was very pleased with his acquittal and sent their respects to his father as well. In addition, the Bear and the guppi had both requested him to send Maan their regards. The guppi had been so impressed by reports of the dramatic scene in court that he was thinking of retiring from his life's vocation in Maan's favour.

As for news of Rasheed, they had none, nor did they have any address. The last they had seen of him was during the campaign, when he had antagonized people still further and harmed his own party with his wild accusations and insults. His wife had been very upset, and now that he had disappeared she was distraught. Meher was fine, except – and here Baba grew a little indignant – her maternal grandfather was trying to claim that she should come and live with her mother and baby sister in his village.

If Maan had any news of Rasheed, Baba said, he should inform them as soon as he could. They would be very grateful. For the moment, sadly, even the Bear had none.

18.32

SAEEDA BAI had left the court after her brief appearance, but she knew within half an hour of the verdict that Maan was safe. She gave thanks to God for preserving him. That he was lost to her she had the wisdom or experience to realize, but that his youth would not be spent in imprisonment and misery was a stifling weight off her heart. She saw Maan with all his faults, but could not cut him off from her love.

Perhaps this was the first time in her life that Saeeda Bai herself had loved unrequitedly. Again and again she saw

Maan as she had first seen him: the eager Dagh Sahib of that first evening at Prem Nivas, full of liveliness and charm and energy and affection.

Sometimes her mind turned to the Nawab Sahib – and to her mother – and to her own younger self, a mother at fifteen. 'Do not let the bee enter the garden' – she murmured the famous line – 'that the moth may not be unjustly killed.' And yet the strange and tenuous links of causation could act beneficently as well. For out of the shame and violation of her youth her beloved Tasneem had been born.

Bibbo rebuked Saeeda Bai for spending so much time these days looking into space. 'At least sing something!' she said. 'Even the parakeet's becoming dumb by example.'

'Do be quiet, Bibbo!' said Saeeda Bai impatiently. And Bibbo, glad to have elicited for once at least some reaction from her mistress, kept up the attack.

'Give thanks for Bilgrami Sahib,' said Bibbo. 'Without him where would all of us be?'

Saeeda Bai clicked her tongue and made a gesture of dismissal.

'Give thanks also to your mightiest admirer, who has spared us his attentions of late,' continued Bibbo.

Saeeda Bai glared. The Raja of Marh had been apparently dormant only because he had been busy with his plans to consecrate his temple with the installation of the ancient Shiva-linga.

'Poor Miya Mitthu,' murmured Bibbo sadly. 'He will forget how to squawk, "Whisky!"'

One day, to stop Bibbo's inane prattling, which was more painful than she intended, Saeeda Bai told her to fetch her harmonium, and let her fingers move up and down the mother-of-pearl keys. But she could not control her thoughts any more than she could in her bedroom, where the framed picture from Maan's book looked down at her from the wall. She called for that book now, and placed it on the harmonium, turning its pages one by one, pausing less at the poems than at the illustrations. She came across the picture of the grief-stricken woman in the cemetery.

I have not visited my mother's grave now for a month, she thought. In my new idiocy as a rejected lover I am neglecting my duties as a daughter. But the more she tried to avoid thinking of herself and the hopelessness of her love for Maan, the more it oppressed her.

And what of Tasneem? she thought. It was worse for her, Saeeda Bai reflected, than for herself. Poor girl, she had become more silent than that godforsaken parakeet. Ishaq, Rasheed, Firoz — three men had come into her life, each more impossible than the last, and in each case she had let her affection grow in silence, and had suffered their sudden absence in silence. She had seen Firoz wounded, her sister almost strangled; she had probably heard, though her strange silence gave no indication of it, of the rumours surrounding herself. What did she think of men now? Or of Saeeda Bai herself if she believed what she heard?

What can I do to help her? thought Saeeda Bai. But there was nothing to be done. To talk to Tasneem about anything that mattered was not within the bounds of possibility.

Though it was evening, and the first few stars had begun to appear in the sky, Saeeda Bai began to hum to herself the lines of Minai's poem announcing the arrival of dawn. It reminded her of the garden in Prem Nivas that carefree evening, and all the grief and pain that had intervened. Tears were in her voice, but not in her eyes. Bibbo came and listened, and Tasneem too walked quietly up from her room to hear what had become so rare. She herself knew the poem by heart, but, entranced by her sister's voice, she did not even murmur the words under her breath:

> The meeting has dispersed; the moths
> Bid farewell to the candle-light.
> Departure's hour is on the sky.
> Only a few stars mark the night.

What has remained will not remain:
     They too will quickly disappear.
This is the world's way, although we,
     Lost to the world, lie sleeping here.

18.33

RASHEED walked along the parapet of the Barsaat Mahal, his thoughts blurred with hunger and confusion.

Darkness, and the river, and the cool marble wall.
Somewhere where there is nowhere.
It gnaws. They are all around me, the elders of Sagal.
No father, no mother, no child, no wife,
Like a jewel above the water. The parapet, the garden under which a river flows.
No Satan, no God, no Iblis, no Gabriel.
Endless, endless, endless, endless, the waters of the Ganga.
The stars above, below.

     . . . and some were seized by the Cry, and some
     We made the earth to swallow, and some We
     drowned; God would never wrong them, but
          they wronged themselves.

Peace. No prayers. No more prayers.
To sleep is better than to pray.
O my creature, you gave your life too soon. I have made your entry into Paradise unlawful.
A spring in Paradise.
O God, O God.

18.34

FURTHER down the Ganga, with pomp and practicality, other preparations were proceeding.

The great Shiva-linga was about the size that the priest's

mantras had said it would be, and in about the same position under the Ganga. But layers of sand and silt covered it. It was some days before it was finally exposed below the murky water, and some days more before it was hoisted up by winches to the first broad step of the cremation ghat above water-level. There it lay beside the Ganga in which it had rested for centuries, at first merely caked with clay and grit, then washed with water and milk and ghee till its black granitic mass glistened in the sun.

People came from far to gaze and to gape, to admire and to worship it. Old women came to do puja: to sing and to recite and to offer flowers and to smear the head of the hereditary pujari with sandalwood paste. It was a propitious combination: the linga of Shiva, and the river that had emerged from his hair.

The Raja of Marh had summoned historians and engineers and astrologers and priests, for preparations now had to be made for the journey of the linga up the grand steps of the cremation ghat, through the dense alleys of Old Brahmpur, into the open space of Chowk, and thence to its place of final, triumphal, re-consecrated rest: the sanctum of the completed temple.

The historians attempted to obtain information about the logistics of other, similar enterprises, such as, for example, the transfer of Ashoka's pillar from near Ambala to Delhi by Firoz Shah – a Buddhist pillar moved by a Muslim king, reflected the Raja of Marh with bifurcated contempt. The engineers worked out that the cylinder of stone, twenty-five feet long, two feet in diameter, and weighing more than six tons, would require two hundred men to haul it safely up the steep steps of the ghat. (The Raja had forbidden the use of winches or pulleys for the unique and dramatic ceremony.) The astrologers calculated an auspicious time, and informed the Raja that if it was not done in a week, he would have to wait for another four months. And the newly appointed priests of the new Chandrachur Temple made plans for auspicious rituals along the route and a vast, festive reception at its destina-

tion, so close to where it had stood in the time of
Aurangzeb.

The Muslims had tried through the Alamgiri Masjid
Hifaazat Committee to obtain an injunction against the
installation of the profane monolith behind the western
wall, but to no avail. The Raja's title to the land on which
the temple stood, now transferred to a trust run by the
Linga Rakshak Samiti and dominated by him, was legally
clear.

Even among the Hindus, however, there were some who
felt that the linga should be left near the cremation ghat –
for that was where ten generations of pujaris had prayed
to it in sorrow and destitution, and where it would remind
worshippers not only of the generative force of Shiva
Mahadeva but of his destructive power as well. The hereditary pujari, having prayed to the visible linga in a kind of
ecstasy, now claimed that it had already found its proper
home. It should be fixed on the low, broad step where it
had chanced to rest, and where it had once again been seen
and worshipped by the people – and as the Ganga rose or
fell with the seasons, it too should appear to sink or rise.

But the Raja of Marh and the Linga Rakshak Samiti
would not have it. The pujari had fulfilled his function as
an informant. The linga had been found; it had been
raised; it would be raised further still. It was not for one
ragged, ecstatic pujari to obstruct enterprises of such great
moment.

Rounded logs were brought to the site by barge and
hauled up the steps of the ghat to form a track of four
parallel rollers, ten feet across. A hundred and fifty feet
above, where the track turned right from the broad steps
into a narrower lane, logs were interlaid to create a gentle
guiding curve. From here on, the linga would have to be
carried diagonally, and it was necessary to work out an
exact and elaborate drill to shift its position.

Long before birdsong on the appointed day, conches
began to sound their pompous, plaintive, enchanted calls.
The linga was bathed once more, and wrapped first in silk-
cotton and then in jute matting. Over the thick brown jute

huge ropes were attached, from which branched lesser ropes of varying length. Tens of thousands of marigold flowers were strewn on or stuck into the matting, and it was covered with rose-petals. The small drum, the damaru of Shiva, began to sound its high, mesmerizing beat, and the priests kept up a continuous chant that rose for hours through a loudspeaker above the undulating clamour of the crowd.

At noon, in the great heat of the day, the period of greatest austerities, two hundred barefooted, barebacked young initiates of a great Shaivite akhara, five each on either side of the rollers on each of twenty steps, straining forwards with the ropes biting into their shoulders, began to move the great linga. The logs creaked, the linga rolled slowly, uncomplainingly upwards, and from the chanting, singing, praying, chattering crowd rose a great gasp of awe.

The doms left their work at the cremation ghat to gaze with wonder at the linga moving slowly away, and the corpses burned on, unattended.

Only the dispossessed pujari and a small group of devotees cried out in distress.

Step by step the linga rolled upwards, pulled in controlled jerks from above. It was even pushed from below by a few men with crowbars. Every so often they inserted wedges beneath it so that the men hauling the linga could rest for a while.

The steep, irregular steps of the ghat burned the soles of their feet, the sun burned down on them from above, and they gasped with effort and from thirst. But their rhythm remained steady, and after an hour the linga had risen seventy feet above the Ganga.

The Raja of Marh, high on the steps, looked downwards with satisfaction and broke out into loud, joyous cries, almost roars, of 'Har har Mahadeva!' He was dressed in full white silken court dress despite the heat, his bulk was thickly beaded with pearls and sweat, and he carried a great golden trident in his right hand.

The young Rajkumar of Marh, an arrogant sneer on his

face resembling that of his father, shouted 'Faster! faster!' in a kind of possession. He thumped the young novitiates on their backs, excited beyond measure by the blood on their shoulders that had begun to ooze out from under the ropes.

The men tried to move faster. Their movement became more ragged.

The ropes on their shoulders, slippery with sweat and blood, had begun to lose some of their purchase.

At the curve where the steps narrowed into a lane, the linga had to be turned sideways. From here on, the Ganga would be seen no more.

On the outer side of the bend, a rope snapped, and a man staggered. The jerk caused a ripple of unequal stresses, and the linga shifted a little. Another rope ripped, and another, and the linga began to jolt. And now a wave of panic smashed through the formation.

'Insert the wedges – insert the wedges!'
'Don't let go –'
'Stay there – wait – don't kill us –'
'Get out – get out – we can't hold it –'
'Stand down – stand down a step – slacken the tension –'
'Pull the rope –'
'Release the ropes – you'll be dragged down –'
'Har har Mahadeva –'
'Run – run for your lives –'
'The wedges – the wedges –'

Another rope snapped, and another, as the linga shifted downwards very slightly, first this way, then that. The cries of the men in front as their bodies were snapped backwards onto the steps were interspersed with the quieter but still more dreadful sounds of the shifting and sliding of the monolith, and the creaking of the rollers beneath. The men below scrambled out of the way. The men above dropped their ropes in a bloodstained tangle, pulled their shocked and injured fellows to one side, and stared down at the orange linga, into the matting of which the marigold flowers had by now been completely crushed. The drum-beat halted. The crowd scattered, screaming in terror. The steps of the ghat below the linga were suddenly deserted, and, far below, the doms too fled from the ghat – as well as the relatives of the burning dead.

The linga protested against the hastily inserted wedges. But for half a minute, if it moved at all, the movement was infinitesimal.

Then it shifted. A wedge gave way. It shifted again and the other wedges slipped and it began slowly to roll down the way it had come.

Down the rollers rolled the great linga, past the next step, and the next, and the next, gathering speed as it rolled. The tree-trunks cracked under the impact of its weight, it veered to left and right, but it kept rolling on, down, down, swifter and swifter towards the Ganga, crushing the pujari who now stood in its downward path with his arms upraised, smashing into the burning pyres of the cremation ghat, and sinking into the water of the Ganga at last, down its submerged stone steps, and onto its muddy bed.

The Shiva-linga rested on the bed of the Ganga once more, the turbid waters passing over it, its bloodstains slowly washed away.

Part Nineteen

19.1

DEAREST Kalpana,

This is written in haste because Varun is coming to Delhi at the end of February or so to attend the IAS interview, and we hope you and your father can put him up for a few days. It is like a dream come true, though only one out of five boys interviewed for the civil service is taken in. We can only hope and pray, such things are entirely in his hands. But Varun has squeezed through the first hurdle, since thousands of boys sit the written exams for the IAS and IFS and so few are asked to go to Delhi.

When the letter came intimating Varun of the interview, Arun refused to believe this, and used some strong language at the breakfast table, with Aparna there and the servants, who, I believe, understand every word. He said there must be some mistake, but it was true all right. I was not there, being in Brahmpur around the time of Lata and Haresh's joyful news, but when Varun sent me a letter, I went to the expense of even booking a trunk call through to Calcutta from Pran's house to congratulate my darling boy, and I made Varun tell me all the details and reactions, which he could because Arun and Meenakshi were not at home, they had gone out to a party as is quite usual. He sounded quite surprised, but I told him that in life one only gets what one deserves. Now D.V. he will surprise us in the interview once again. It is all up to you, dearest Kalpana, to make sure that he eats well, and is not nervous and is on his best behaviour and dressed to the nines. Also that he avoids bad company and alcohol, which I am sorry to say he is a little susceptible to. I know you will take care of him, he is so much in need of boosting up.

I am not writing any more news because I am in haste and also have given you the joyous news of Lata and Haresh in the previous letter to which I have yet had no answer or congratulations, but you must be busy, I know, with your father's hip operation. I hope he is now fully recovered. It must be hard for him, he is so impatient with illness, and now he is himself experiencing it. And you must also take care of yourself. Health is truly the most precious possession.

With fondest love to you both,

Yours,
Ma
(Mrs. Rupa Mehra)

P.S. Please send me a telegram after the interview is over, otherwise I will not be able to sleep.

*

Varun looked nervously around at his fellow passengers as the cold, dry, flat countryside around Delhi hurtled past the windows of the train. No one appeared to realize how momentous this journey was for him. Having read the Delhi edition of the *Times of India* from the first page to the last and back again – for who knew what the predatory interviewers might decide to ask him about current affairs? – he stealthily glanced at an advertisement that seemed to leap out at him:

Dr Dugle. Highly honoured and patronised for his social services (Inland and Overseas) by many eminent persons, Rajas, Maharajas, and chiefs. Dr Dugle. India's leading specialist with international fame in chronic diseases such as nervous debility, premature old age, run down conditions, lack of vigour and vitality, and similar acute diseases. Consultations in complete confidence.

Varun fell gloomily to pondering his innumerable social, intellectual and other inadequacies. Then another ad attracted his attention.

Dress your hair with the creamed oils of Brylcreem. Why creamed oils? Brylcreem is a *creamed* mixture of tonic oils. It is easier to apply, cleaner to use and its *creaminess* gives the right amount of all Brylcreem ingre-

dients each time. Brylcreem gives that smooth soft lustre
to the hair which so many women admire.
    Buy Brylcreem today.

Varun felt suddenly miserable. He doubted that even Brylcreem would help women to admire him. He knew he was
going to make a fool of himself in the interview, just as in
everything else.

*

'The servants will be coming in half an hour,' whispered
Kalpana Gaur tenderly, pushing Varun gently out of her
bed.
    'Oh.'
    'And you'd better sleep in your own bed for half an
hour, so that they don't wonder.'
    Varun looked at her, amazed. She smiled at him in a
motherly sort of way, the pale green quilt up around her
neck.
    'And then you'd better get ready for breakfast and the
interview. Today's your big day.'
    'Ah.' Varun seemed speechless.
    'Now, Varun, don't be tongue-tied, it won't do – at least
not today. You have to impress them and charm them. I
promised your mother I'd make sure you were well taken
care of and that I'd boost your confidence. Do you feel
boosted?'
    Varun blushed, then smiled weakly. 'Heh, heh,' he
laughed anxiously, wondering how he was going to get
out of bed without embarrassment. And it was so cold
in Delhi compared to Calcutta. The mornings were
freezing.
    'It's so cold,' he mumbled.
    'Do you know,' said Kalpana Gaur, 'I often feel hot
spots on my feet which trouble me throughout the night,
but last night I didn't feel any at all. You were marvellous,
Varun. Now remember, if at any time during the interview
you begin to feel anxious, think of last night, and tell
yourself: "I am the Iron Frame of India."'

Varun still looked dazed, though not unhappy.

'Use my dressing-gown,' suggested Kalpana Gaur.

Varun gave her a grateful and puzzled glance.

A couple of hours later, after breakfast, she examined his appearance critically, patted his pockets, adjusted his striped tie, wiped off the excessive Brylcreem in his hair, and combed it again.

'But –' protested Varun.

'Now I'll make sure you get to the right place at the right time.'

'That's not necessary,' said Varun, not wanting to cause trouble.

'It's on my way to the hospital.'

'Er, give my best to your father when you get there.'

'Of course.'

'Kalpana?'

'Yes, Varun?'

'What happened to that mysterious illness of yours that Ma kept telling us about? It was more than just hot spots, according to her.'

'Oh, that?' Kalpana looked thoughtful. 'It sorted itself out the moment my father had to go to hospital. It made no sense for both of us to be ill.'

The Union Public Service Commission was holding its interviews in a temporary structure in Connaught Place, one which had been set up during the War and had not yet been dismantled. Kalpana Gaur squeezed Varun's hand in the taxi. 'Don't look so dazed,' she said. 'And remember, never say, "I don't know"; always say, "I'm afraid I haven't any idea." You look very presentable, Varun. Much more handsome than your brother.'

Varun glanced at her with a mixture of bewilderment and tenderness, and got out.

In the waiting room, he noticed a couple of candidates who looked like south Indians. They were shivering. They had been even less prepared for the Delhi weather than himself, and it was a particularly cold day. One of them was saying to the other: 'And they say that the Chairman of the UPSC can read you like a book. He can assess you as soon as you enter the door. Every weakness of your personality is laid bare within seconds.'

Varun felt his knees tremble. He went to the bathroom, got out a small bottle that he had managed to secrete on his person, and took two quick swigs. His knees settled down, and he began to think he would conduct himself superbly after all.

'I'm afraid I really have no idea,' he repeated to himself.

'About what?' asked one of his fellow-candidates after a pause.

'I don't know,' said Varun. 'I mean, I'm afraid I really couldn't tell you.'

*

'And then I said "Good morning", and they all nodded, but the Chairman, a sort of bulldog man said, "Namasté" instead. I was quite shocked for a second, but somehow I got over it.'

'And then?' asked Kalpana eagerly.

'And then he asked me to sit down. It was a roundish table, and I was at one end and the bulldog man was at the other end, he looked at me as if he could read every thought of mine before I had even thought it. Mr Chatterji – no, Mr Bannerji, they called him. And there was a Vice-Chancellor and someone from the Ministry of External Affairs, and –'

'But how did it go?' asked Kalpana. 'Do you think it went well?'

'I don't know. They asked me a question about Prohibition, you see, and I'd just been drinking, so naturally I was nervous –'

'You had just been what?'

'Oh,' said Varun guiltily. 'One or two gulps. Then someone asked me if I liked the odd social drink, and I said, yes. But I could feel my throat become dry, and the bulldog man just kept looking at me and he sniffed slightly and noted something down on a pad. And then he said, Mr Mehra, what if you were posted to a state like Bombay or a district like Kanpur where there was Prohibition, would you feel obliged to refrain from the odd social drink? So I said of course I would. Then someone else on my right said, what if you were visiting friends in Calcutta, and were offered a drink, would you refuse it – as a representative of a dry area? And I could see them staring at me, ten pairs of eyes, and then suddenly I thought, I am the Iron Frame, who are all these people anyway, and I said, No, I saw no reason to, in fact I would drink it with a pleasure enhanced by my previous abstinence – that's what I said. "Enhanced by my previous abstinence."'

Kalpana laughed.

'Yes,' said Varun dubiously. 'It seemed to go down well with them too. I don't think it was I who was answering all those questions, you know. It seemed to be a sort of Arun person who had taken possession of me. Perhaps because I was wearing his tie.'

'What else did they ask?'

'Something about what three books I would take with me to a desert island, and did I know what the initials M.I.T. stood for, and did I think there would be war with Pakistan – and I really can't remember anything, Kalpana, except that the bulldog man had two watches, one on the inside of his wrist and one on the outside. It was all I could do to avoid staring at him. Thank God it's over,' he added morosely. 'It lasted forty-five minutes and it took a year off my life.'

'Did you say forty-five minutes?' said Kalpana Gaur excitedly.

'Yes.'

'I must send a telegram to your mother at once. And I have decided that you must stay in Delhi for another two days. Your being here is very good for me.'

'Really?' said Varun, reddening.

He wondered if it might have been the Brylcreem that had done it.

*

VARUN BOOSTED INTERVIEW CONCLUDED FINGERS CROSSED FATHER MENDING LOVE KALPANA.

Kalpana can always be trusted to do the needful, said Mrs Rupa Mehra happily to herself.

19.2

IN Calcutta Mrs Rupa Mehra went around like a whirlwind, buying saris, herding her family into conferences, visiting her son-in-law-to-be twice a week, requisitioning cars (including the Chatterjis' big white Humber) for her shopping and for visits to friends, writing long letters to all her relatives, designing the invitation card, monopolizing the phone in a Kakoli-like manner, and weeping alternately with joy at the prospect of her daughter's marriage, concern for her daughter on her wedding night, and sorrow that the late Raghubir Mehra would not be present.

She looked at a copy of Van de Velde's *Ideal Marriage* in a bookshop on Park Street – and, though the contents made her blush, determinedly bought it. 'It's for my daughter,' she informed the sales clerk, who yawned and nodded.

Arun stopped her from adding the design of a rose to the wedding invitation. 'Don't be ridiculous, Ma,' he said. 'What do you think people will think of all that ghich-pich when they receive it? I'll never live it down. Keep the design plain.' He was very aggrieved that Lata, after receiving his egregious letter, had refused to be married from his house, and he was trying to compensate for his loss of authority by a commissarial attempt to take over all the practical arrangements for the wedding – at least those that could be managed at the Calcutta end. But he was up against the powerful personalities of his mother and his grandfather, both of whom had their own ideas about what was required.

Meanwhile, though his view of Haresh had not changed, he bowed – or at least nodded – to the inevitable, and attempted to be gracious. He had lunch once more among the Czechs, and balanced this with a return invitation to Sunny Park.

When Mrs Rupa Mehra asked Haresh about the date for the wedding, he said, beaming with cheerfulness: 'The earlier the better.' But in view of Lata's exams and the fact that his own foster-parents were reluctant to agree to a wedding in the inauspicious last month of the Hindu calendar, the date was set for late, rather than early, April.

Haresh's parents also requested Lata's horoscope in order to ensure that her stars and planets matched those of her husband. They were particularly concerned that Lata should not happen to be a Manglik – a 'Martian' under certain astronomical definitions – because then, for a non-Manglik like Haresh to marry her would certainly result in his early death.

When Haresh passed on this request, Mrs Rupa Mehra got cross. 'If there was any truth in all these horoscopes, there would be no young widows,' she said.

'I agree with you,' said Haresh. 'Well, I'll tell them that no one has ever made a horoscope for Lata.'

But this resulted in a request for Lata's date and time and place of birth. Haresh's parents were going to get her horoscope made themselves.

Haresh went to an astrologer in Calcutta with Lata's place and date of birth, and asked him for a safe time of birth that would ensure that her stars matched his. The astrologer gave him two or three times, one of which Haresh sent on to his parents. Luckily, their astrologer worked on the same principles and calculations as his. Their anxieties were allayed.

Amit, needless to say, was disappointed, but not as much as he might have been. His novel, now that he was free from the worry of handling the Chatterji fortunes, was going well, and many more momentous events were taking place on his pages than in his life. He sank deeper into the novel, and – a little disgusted with himself for doing so – used his disappointment and sadness to portray that of a character who happened to be conveniently on hand.

He wrote a brief note, not in verse, to congratulate Lata, and tried to behave in a sportsmanlike manner. Mrs Rupa Mehra, in any case, did not allow him to behave in any other way. The Chatterji children, like the Chatterji car, were pulled into her orbit. Amit, Kuku, Dipankar and even Tapan (when he had a moment to spare from his homework at St Xavier's) were each assigned various tasks: the making of guest-lists, the selection of gifts, the collecting of items that had been ordered from the shops. Perhaps Lata had known that of the three men courting her, the only one who could be rejected without the loss of his friendship was Amit.

19.3

WHEN Mrs Rupa Mehra told Meenakshi one afternoon to come with her to the jewellers to help her buy, or at least select, a wedding band for Haresh, Meenakshi stretched her neck lazily and said:

'Oh, but Ma, I'm going somewhere this afternoon.'

'But your canasta is tomorrow.'

'Well,' said Meenakshi with a slow and rather feline smile, 'life is not all canasta and rummy.'

'Where are you going?' demanded her mother-in-law.

'Oh, I'm going here and there,' said Meenakshi, adding to Aparna: 'Darling, please release my hair.'

Mrs Rupa Mehra, unaware that she had just been treated to a Kakoli-couplet, became annoyed.

'But these are the jewellers you recommended. I will get much better service if you come with me. If you don't come with me, I'll have to go to Lokkhi Babu's.'

'Oh, no, Ma, you really shouldn't. Go to Jauhri's; they're the ones who made my little gold pears.' Meenakshi stroked her neck just below her ear with the scarlet nail of her middle finger.

This last remark infuriated Mrs Rupa Mehra. 'All right,' she said, 'if that's how much you care about your sister-in-law's wedding, go gallivanting around town. My Varun will come with me.'

When they got to the shop, Mrs Rupa Mehra did not in the event find it difficult to charm Mr Jauhri. Within two minutes he knew all about Bentsen Pryce and the IAS and Haresh's testimonials. When he had reassured her that he could make anything she wished and have it ready for collection in three weeks, she ordered a gold champakali necklace ('It is so pretty with its hollow buds and not too heavy for Lata') and a Jaipur kundan set – a necklace and earrings in glass and gold and enamel.

As Mrs Rupa Mehra chattered on happily about her daughter, Mr Jauhri, who was a sociable man, added his comments and congratulations. When she mentioned her own late husband, who had been in the railways, Mr Jauhri lamented the decline in service. After a while, when everything had been settled satisfactorily, she said that she had to be going. She got out her Mont Blanc pen and wrote down her name and address and telephone number.

Mr Jauhri looked startled.

'Ah,' he said, recognizing the surname and address.

'Yes,' said Mrs Rupa Mehra, 'my daughter-in-law has been here before.'

'Mrs Mehra – was it your husband's medal she gave me to have made into her chain and earrings? Beautiful – just like little pears?'

'Yes,' said Mrs Rupa Mehra, fighting to keep back her tears. 'I will come back in three weeks. Please treat the order as urgent.'

Mr Jauhri said: 'Madam, let me check with my calendar and orders. Maybe I can give them to you in two-and-a-half weeks.' He disappeared into the back of the shop. When he returned he placed a small red box on the counter and opened it.

Inside, sitting on a cushion of white silk, was Raghubir Mehra's gold medal for Engineering.

19.4

TWICE that month did Mrs Rupa Mehra shuttle between Calcutta and Brahmpur.

She was so delighted to have the medal restored to her

('The fact is, Madam, I could not bear to melt it down.')
that she bought it back instantly, drawing out whatever
was necessary from her savings, and trying to economize
slightly more on the necessary wedding expenses. She was
– for a few days at least – entirely reconciled to Meenakshi
and her ways. For if Meenakshi had not given Mr Jauhri
this medal, it would have been stolen from the house in
Sunny Park with the rest of the jewellery, and, like the
Physics medal, would have vanished for good. Meenakshi
too, when she got back from wherever it was she had been,
looked happy and satisfied and was quite pleasant to her
mother-in-law and Varun. When she heard about the medal
she was not slow in claiming a perverse credit for events –
and her mother-in-law did not object.

When Mrs Rupa Mehra got to Brahmpur she brought
the medal with her and showed it triumphantly to everyone
in the family, and everyone was delighted with her good
fortune.

'You must study hard, Lata, there are so few days left' –
Mrs Rupa Mehra cautioned her daughter – 'or you will
never have your Daddy's academic success. You should
not let your wedding and other things distract you.' And
with that she put *Ideal Marriage*, carefully wrapped in the
bridal colours of red and gold, into her hands.

'This book will teach you everything – about Men,' she
said, lowering her voice for some reason. 'Even our Sita
and Savitri had to have these experiences.'

'Thank you, Ma,' said Lata, a little apprehensively.

Mrs Rupa Mehra was suddenly embarrassed, and disappeared into the next room with the excuse that she had to
phone her father.

Lata promptly unwrapped the package and, forgetting
her studies, began to look through the Dutch sexologist's
advice. She was as much repelled as fascinated by what he
had to offer.

There were numerous graphs describing the man's and
the woman's degrees of excitement under different circumstances, for example, coitus interruptus and what the
author called 'Ideal Communion'. There were multicol-

oured, copiously labelled, not very appealing cross-sections of various organs. 'Marriage is a science. (H. de Balzac)' read the epigraph of the book, and Dr Van de Velde evidently took this aphorism seriously not only in his illustrations but also in his taxonomy. He divided what he shyly called his 'Synousiology' into converse and averse types, and further divided these into the habitual or medial attitude, the first attitude of extension, the second attitude of extension (suspensory), the attitudes of flexion (favoured, according to him, by the Chinese), the attitude of equitation (in which Martial described Hector and Andromache), the sedentary attitude, the anterior-lateral attitude, the ventral attitude, the posterior-lateral attitude, the attitude of averse flexion, and the posterior-sedentary attitude. Lata was amazed by the possibilities: she had only thought of one. (Indeed, even Malati had only ever mentioned one.) She wondered what the nuns at St Sophia's would think of a book like this.

A footnote read as follows:

Arrangements have now been made for the manufacture of Dr Van de Velde's Jellies ('Eugam'): Lubricant, Contraceptive and Proconceptive. They are made by Messrs. Harman Freese, 32 Great Dover Street, London, S.E.1, who are also the makers of the author's other preparations and pessaries ('Gamophile') referred to in 'Fertility and Sterility in Marriage'.

From time to time Dr Van de Velde quoted approvingly the Dutch poet Cats, whose folk wisdom did not emerge well in translation:

> Listen my friend, and know the reason why:
> All beauty lies in the beholder's eye.

But for all that, Lata was glad that her mother had cared enough for her to overcome her own embarrassment and put this book in her hands. She still had a few weeks to prepare herself for Life.

Lata looked thoughtful through most of dinner, glancing at Pran and Savita and wondering whether Savita too had received an *Ideal Marriage* before her wedding. There was jelly for pudding, and to Mrs Rupa Mehra's puzzlement – and everyone else's – Lata began to laugh and would not explain why.

19.5

LATA took her final exams as if in a trance: sometimes she got the impression that she was someone other than herself. She felt she had done well, but this was combined with a curious, dislocated feeling – not like the panic of the previous year, but a sense that she was floating above her physical self and looking down on it from a height. Once, after a paper was over, she wandered down from the examination hall and sat on the bench beneath the gulmohur tree. Again the dark orange flowers lay thick below her feet. Had it only been a year since she had met him?

If you love him so much, can you be happy to leave him miserable?

Where was he? Even if his exams were being held in the same building, he did not stand on the steps afterwards. He did not pass by the bench.

Just after the last paper, there was a concert by Ustad Majeed Khan, to which she went with Malati. Kabir was nowhere to be seen.

Amit had written her a brief note of congratulation, but – after their few moments in the bookshop and the coffee house – Kabir had as good as disappeared.

Whose life am I living? Lata wondered. Was my acceptance just a reaction?

Despite Haresh's encouraging letters and her own cheerful replies, Lata began to feel both uncertain and very lonely.

Sometimes she sat on the banyan root and looked out over the Ganga, recollecting what it was pointless to recollect. Would she have been happy with him? Or he with her? He was so jealous now, so intense, so violent, so unlike the casual cricketer whom she had seen laughing and practising at the nets a year ago. How different he was now from the knight who had rescued her from the gulmohur bench and from Mr Nowrojee's.

And I? she asked herself. How would I have acted in his place? With a jovial attempt at good fellowship? Even now I almost feel it's he who's left me – and I can't bear it.

Two weeks more, she thought, and I will be the Bride of Goodyear Welted.

Oh, Kabir, Kabir – she wept.

I should run away, she thought.

I should run away, she thought, far from Haresh, far from Kabir, far from Arun and Varun and Ma and the whole Chatterji clan, far from Pran and Maan and Hindus and Muslims and passionate love and passionate hatred and all loud noises – just me and Malati and Savita and the baby.

We'll sit on the sand on the other side of the Ganga and go to sleep for a year or two.

19.6

THE wedding arrangements proceeded with great verve and much conflict. Mrs Rupa Mehra, Malati, Dr Kishen Chand Seth and Arun each tried to act as major-domo.

Dr Kishen Chand Seth insisted on asking Saeeda Bai to sing at the wedding. 'Who else can one ask,' he said, 'when Saeeda Bai is in Brahmpur? Her throttling has opened her throat, they say.'

It was only when he realized that the entire Prem Nivas contingent would boycott the wedding that he relented. But by then he was off onto something else: the length of the list of invitees. It was too long, he claimed: his garden would be destroyed, his pockets emptied.

Everyone reassured him that they would be careful not to expand their own invitation list, and everyone went ahead and invited everyone they met. As for Dr Kishen

Chand Seth, he was the worst offender of all: half the Subzipore Club and half the doctors of Brahmpur were invited, and almost anyone who had ever played bridge with him. 'A wedding is always a time for settling scores,' he explained cryptically.

Arun arrived a few days early and tried to take over the management of events from his grandfather. But Parvati, who apparently realized how good it was for her husband to exhaust himself with excitement, put paid to his attempts at usurpation. She even shouted at Arun in front of the servants, and he retreated before 'that harridan'.

The arrival from Delhi of the baraat — the groom's party — brought its own excitement and complications. Haresh's foster-parents had been satisfied on the score of astrology; his mother, however, insisted on various precautions being taken about the preparation of her food. She would have been horrified to know that at Pran's house, where she ate one day, the cook was a Muslim. His name was therefore converted from Mateen to Matadeen for the duration.

Two of Haresh's foster-brothers and their wives came with the baraat, as did the doubting Umesh Uncle. Their English was terrible and their sense of punctuality so lax as to be almost nonexistent, and in general they confirmed Arun's worst fears. Mrs Rupa Mehra, however, gave the women saris and talked to them endlessly.

They approved of Lata.

Haresh was not allowed to meet Lata. He stayed with Sunil Patwardhan, and the St Stephen's contingent gathered around him in the evenings to tease him and enact Scenes from Married Life. The vast Sunil was usually the shrinking bride.

Haresh visited Kedarnath's house in Misri Mandi. He told Veena how sorry he was to hear of Mrs Mahesh Kapoor's death and all the anxieties that the family had had to undergo. Old Mrs Tandon and Bhaskar were happy that he had visited. And Haresh was delighted to be able to mention to Kedarnath that the order for brogues from Prahapore would be coming through within the week, together with a short-term loan for the purchase of materials.

19.7

HARESH also visited Ravidaspur one morning. He took with him some bananas for Jagat Ram's children, the good news about the Praha order, and an invitation to his wedding.

The fruit was a luxury; there were no fruit-sellers in Ravidaspur. The barefooted sons of the shoemaker accepted the bananas with suspicious reluctance and ate them with relish, dropping the skins into the drain that ran alongside the house.

The news about the Praha order was met with satisfaction, and the fact that a loan for the purchase of raw materials was to accompany it was greeted with intense relief. Jagat Ram was looking rather subdued, thought Haresh. He had expected elation.

Jagat Ram reacted to Haresh's wedding invitation with visible shock, not so much because Haresh was getting married, and in Brahmpur at that, but because he should have thought of inviting him.

Moved as he was, he had to refuse. The two worlds did not mix. He knew it; it was a fact of life. That a jatav from Ravidaspur should be present as a guest at a wedding at the house of Dr Kishen Chand Seth would cause social distress that he did not wish to be the centre of. It would injure his dignity. Apart from the practical problems of what to wear and what to give, he knew that he would feel no joy and only intense awkwardness at being present on the occasion.

Haresh, reading his mind only partially, said, with brusque tact: 'You're not to bring a gift. I've never been a believer in gifts at weddings. But you must come. We are colleagues. I won't hear of your not coming. And the invitation is also for your wife if you want her to come.'

It was only with the greatest of reluctance that Jagat

Ram agreed. The red-and-gold invitation, meanwhile, was being passed by the boys from hand to hand.

'Haven't they left anything for your daughter?' asked Haresh, as the last of the bananas disappeared.

'Oh, her dust has been washed away,' said Jagat Ram quietly.

'What?' said Haresh, shocked.

Jagat Ram shook his head. 'What I mean to say –' he began, and his voice was choked.

'What happened, for heaven's sake?'

'She got an infection. My wife said it was serious, but I thought, children get high fever so quickly, and it comes down just as quickly. And so I delayed. It was the money too; and the doctors here are, well, high-handed with us.'

'Your poor wife –'

'My wife said nothing, she said nothing against me. What she thinks, I don't know.' After a pause he quoted two lines:

'Don't break the thread of love, Raheem has said.
What breaks won't join; if joined, it knots the thread.'

When Haresh commiserated, Jagat Ram merely sucked in his breath through his teeth and shook his head again.

19.8

WHEN Haresh returned to Sunil's, he found his father waiting for him impatiently.

'Where have you been?' he asked Haresh, crinkling his nose. It's almost ten. The Registrar will be at Dr Seth's house in a few minutes.'

'Oh!' said Haresh, looking surprised. 'I'd better take a quick shower.'

He had forgotten about the time of the civil ceremony, which Mrs Rupa Mehra had insisted on having on the day before the wedding proper. She felt that she had to protect her daughter from the injustices of the traditional Hindu

Law; marriages solemnized before a Registrar were governed by laws that were much fairer to women.

The civil ceremony, however, was such a brief and dry affair that almost no one attached any significance to it, although from the moment it was over, Haresh and Lata were legally man and wife. Only a dozen or so people attended, and Haresh was reproved by his mother for being late.

Lata had alternated between serene optimism and terrifying attacks of uncertainty for the last week. After the civil ceremony was over, she felt calm and almost happy, and fonder of Haresh than before. From time to time he had smiled at her as if he knew exactly when she had most needed reassurance.

19.9

AMIT, Kakoli, Dipankar, Meenakshi, Tapan, Aparna, Varun and even Hans had arrived together from Calcutta early that morning and had been present at the civil ceremony. Pran's house was bursting at the seams. Dr Kishen Chand Seth's house too, was entirely overrun. Only Prem Nivas, lacking its mistress, remained almost empty.

All manner of known and unknown people wandered in and out of Dr Kishen Chand's house. Since he had decided to operate on the unusually pacific assumption that anyone whom he didn't recognize must have been asked by someone else, or else must be involved with the lighting or the catering arrangements, he threatened very few people with his stick. Parvati kept an eye on him and made sure that no one came to grief.

It was a hot day. A few birds – mynas, babblers, sparrows, bulbuls and barbets – were disturbed in their nesting by this constant throng of noisy, busy humans. The beds in the garden had gone to seed; except for a few tobacco flowers, nothing on the ground was in bloom. But the trees – champa, jacaranda, and Sita ashok – were full

of white or mauve or red blossom, and bougainvillaea –
orange, red, pink and magenta – fell in great masses over
the walls of the house and down the trunks of trees. From
time to time, amid the continuous racket of the barbets,
the `call of a distant brainfever bird sounded high and
insistent and clear.

Lata sat in an inner room with the other women for the
singing and henna ceremonies. Kuku and Meenakshi,
Malati and Savita, Mrs Rupa Mehra, Veena, Hema and
her Taiji, all kept themselves entertained and Lata distracted by singing wedding songs, some innocent, some
risqué, and dancing to the beat of a dholak while an old
woman fitted them all with glass bangles of their choice –
from Firozabad, she claimed – and another squeezed bold
but delicate patterns of henna on their hands and feet. Lata
looked at her hands, covered now with the moist, beautiful
tracery, and began to weep.

She wondered how long it would take to set. Savita took
out a handkerchief and wiped her tears for her.

Veena quickly began a song about her delicate hands
and how she couldn't draw water at the public well. She
was her father-in-law's favourite; he had felt sorry for her
and had had a well made for her in the garden of the
house. She was the favourite of her husband's elder
brother; he had given her a gold vessel for the water. She
was the favourite of her husband's younger brother; he
had given her a silken rope for the bucket. She was the
beloved of her husband, and he had hired two water-
carriers for her. But her husband's sister and mother were
jealous of her, and had secretly gone and covered up the
well.

In another song the jealous mother-in-law slept next to
the newly-married bride so that her husband couldn't visit
her at night. Mrs Rupa Mehra enjoyed these songs as
much as she always did, probably because it was impossible
for her to imagine herself in any such role.

Malati – together with her mother, who had suddenly
appeared in Brahmpur – sang, 'You grind the spices, fat
one, and we will eat!'

531

Kakoli clapped loudly while her henna was still green and moist – and smudged it completely. Her musical contribution was a variant of 'Roly Poly Mr Kohli', which, in the absence of her mother, she sang to the tune of a Tagore song:

> 'Roly poly Mr Kohli
> Walking slowly up the stairs.
> Holy souly Mrs Kohli
> Comes and takes him unawares.

> Mr Kohli, base and lowly,
> Stares at choli, dreams of lust,
> As the holy Mrs Kohli
> With her pallu hides her bust.'

19.10

BEFORE dusk the next day the guests began to gather on the lawn to the sound of the shehnai.

The men of the family stood by the gate and received them. Arun and Varun were dressed in fine, starched, white kurta-pyjamas embroidered with chikan work. Pran was dressed in the white sharkskin sherwani he had worn at his own wedding – though it had been winter then.

Mrs Rupa Mehra's brother had come from Madras as usual, but had arrived too late for the bangle ceremony, which he had been expected to help perform. He knew almost none of the people he was greeting, and only a few of them looked familiar to him, perhaps from the time of Savita's wedding. He greeted everyone decorously as they passed into the garden. Dr Kishen Chand Seth, on the other hand, overheated in the straitjacket of an extremely tight black achkan, got impatient after a while with this endless meeting and greeting, shouted at his son, whom he had not seen for more than a year, loosened a few buttons, and wandered off to supervise something. He had refused to stand in for his late son-in-law in the ceremonies on the grounds that sitting still and listening to priests would destroy both his circulation and his serenity.

Mrs Rupa Mehra was wearing a beige chiffon sari with a beautiful gold border – a gift from her daughter-in-law that had made her entirely forget the incident of the lacquer box. She knew that He wouldn't have wanted her to dress too much like a widow on their younger daughter's wedding day.

The groom's party was fifteen minutes late already. Mrs Rupa Mehra was starving: she was not meant to eat until she had given her daughter away, and she was glad that the astrologers had set the actual time of the wedding for eight o'clock, and not, say, eleven.

'Where are they?' she demanded of Maan, who happened to be standing nearby and was gazing in the direction of the gate.

'I'm sorry, Ma,' said Maan. 'Who do you mean?' He had been looking out for Firoz.

'The baraat, of course.'

'Oh, yes, the baraat – well, they should be coming at any minute. Shouldn't they be here already?'

'Yes,' said Mrs Rupa Mehra, as impatient and anxious as the Boy standing on the Burning Deck. 'Yes, of course they should.'

The baraat was at last sighted, and everyone crowded towards the gate. A large, maroon, flower-adorned Chevrolet drove up. It narrowly avoided scratching Dr Kishen Chand Seth's grey Buick, which was parked somewhat obstructively near the entrance. Haresh stepped out. He was accompanied by his parents and his brothers and was followed by, among others, a motley crowd of his college friends. Arun and Varun escorted him to the verandah. Lata emerged from inside the house, dressed in a red-and-gold sari, and with her eyes lowered, as befitted a bride. They exchanged garlands. Sunil Patwardhan broke into loud cheers, and the photographer clicked away.

They walked across the lawn to the wedding platform, decorated with roses and tuberoses, and sat down facing the young priest from the local Arya Samaj temple. He lit the fire and began the ceremony. Haresh's foster-parents sat near Haresh, Mrs Rupa Mehra sat near Lata, and Arun and Varun sat behind her.

'Sit up straight,' said Arun to Varun.

'I am sitting straight!' retorted Varun Mehra, IAS, angrily. He noticed that Lata's garland had slipped off her left shoulder. He helped rearrange it and glared at his brother.

The guests, unusually for a wedding, were quiet and attentive as the priest went through the rites. Mrs Rupa Mehra was sobbing through her Sanskrit, and Savita was sobbing too, and soon Lata was crying as well. When her mother took her hand, filled it with rose-petals and pronounced the words, 'O bridegroom, accept this well-adorned bride called Lata,' Haresh, prompted by the priest, took her hand firmly in his own and repeated the words: 'I thank you, and accept her willingly.'

'Cheer up,' he added in English, 'I hope you won't have to go through this again.' And Lata, whether at that thought or at his tone of voice, did indeed cheer up.

Everything went well. Her brothers poured puffed rice onto her hands and into the fire each time she and Haresh circled it. The knot between their scarves was tied, and bright red sindoor was applied to the parting of Lata's hair with the gold ring that Haresh was to give her. This ring ceremony puzzled the priest (it didn't fit in with his idea of Arya Samaji rituals), but because Mrs Rupa Mehra insisted on it, he went along with it.

One or two children squabbled tearfully over the possession of some rose-petals; and an insistent old woman tried without success to get the priest to mention Babé Lalu, the clan deity of the Khannas, in the course of his liturgy; other than that, everything went harmoniously.

But when the people who were gathered together recited the Gayatri Mantra three times before the witnessing fire, Pran, glancing at Maan, noticed that his head was bowed and his lips trembling as he mumbled the words. Like his elder brother, he could not forget the last time that the ancient words had been recited in his presence, and before a different fire.

19.11

IT was a warm evening, and there was less silk and more fine cotton than at Savita's wedding. But the jewellery glittered just as gloriously. Meenakshi's little pear-earrings, Veena's navratan and Malati's emeralds glinted across the garden, whispering to each other the stories of their owners.

The younger Chatterjis were out in full force, but there were very few politicians, and no children from Rudhia running wildly around. A couple of executives from the small Praha factory in Brahmpur were present, however, as were some of the middlemen from the Brahmpur Shoe Mart.

Jagat Ram too had come, but not his wife. He stood by himself for a while until Kedarnath noticed him and beckoned him to join them.

When he was introduced to old Mrs Tandon, she was unable to stifle her discomfiture. She looked at him as if he smelt, and gave him a weak namasté.

Jagat Ram said to Kedarnath: 'I have to go now. Would you give this to Haresh Sahib and his bride?' He handed him what looked like a small shoe-box covered in brown paper.

'But aren't you going to congratulate him?'

'Well, there's a long line,' said Jagat Ram, tugging a little at his moustache. 'Please congratulate him for me.'

Old Mrs Tandon had turned to Haresh's parents, and was talking to them about Neel Darvaza, which she had visited as a child. She congratulated them and, in the course of the conversation, contrived to mention that Lata was rather too fond of music.

'Oh, good,' said Haresh's foster-father. 'We too are very fond of music.'

Old Mrs Tandon was displeased, and decided to say nothing more.

Malati, meanwhile, was talking to the musicians them-selves, a shehnai player who had been known to her own musician-friend, and the tabla player Motu Chand.

Motu, who remembered Malati from the day he had stood in at the Haridas College of Music, asked her about Ustad Majeed Khan and his famous disciple Ishaq, whom, sadly, he very rarely met these days. Malati told him about the concert she had very recently attended, praised Ishaq's musicianship, and mentioned that she had been struck by the indulgence which the arrogant maestro granted to him: he rarely, for instance, broke in with a dominating improvi-sation of his own when Ishaq was singing. In a world of professional jealousy and rivalry even between teacher and student, they performed with a sense of complementarity that was wonderful to see.

It had begun to be said of Ishaq — and that too within a year of his first strumming the tanpura before his Ustad — that he had the makings of one of the great singers of his time.

'Well,' said Motu Chand, 'things are not the same with-out him where I work.' He sighed, then, noticing Malati look a bit blank, said: 'Were you not at Prem Nivas at Holi last year?'

'No,' said Malati, realizing from his question that Motu must be Saeeda Bai's tabla player. 'And this year, of course. . . .'

'Of course,' said Motu sadly. 'Terrible, terrible . . . and now with that fellow Rasheed's suicide. . . . He taught Saeeda Bai's, well, sister, you know . . . but he caused so much trouble that they had to get the watchman to beat him up . . . and then we heard later. . . . Well, there's nothing but trouble in the world, nothing but trouble —' He began to hammer at the little wooden cylinders around his tabla to tighten the straps and adjust the pitch. The shehnai player nodded at him.

'This Rasheed you're talking about —' asked Malati, suddenly quite troubled herself. 'He's not the socialist, is he? — the history student —'

'Yes, I think so,' said Motu, flexing his well-padded fingers; and the tabla and shehnai began to play again.

MAAN, dressed in a kurta-pyjama, as suited the weather, was standing a little distance away and heard nothing of this conversation. He looked sad, almost unsociable.

For a moment he wondered where the harsingar tree was, before he realized that he was in a different garden altogether. Firoz came up to him, and they stood there, silent, for a while. A rose-petal or two floated down from somewhere. Neither bothered to brush it off. Imtiaz joined them after a while, then the Nawab Sahib and Mahesh Kapoor.

'It's all for the best, on the whole,' said Mahesh Kapoor. 'If I had been an MLA, Agarwal would have had to ask me to join his Cabinet, and I would not have been able to stand it.'

'Well,' said the Nawab Sahib, 'whether things are for the best or not, that's how they are.'

There was a pause. Everyone was friendly enough, but no one knew what to talk about. Every topic seemed closed for one reason or another. There was no mention of law or laws, of doctors or hospitals, of gardens or music, of future plans or past recollections, of politics or religion, of bees or lotuses.

The judges of the Supreme Court had agreed that the Zamindari Acts were constitutional; they were in the process of writing their judgment, which would be announced to the world at large in a few days.

S.S. Sharma had been called to Delhi. The Congress MLAs of Purva Pradesh had elected L.N. Agarwal as Chief Minister. Astoundingly enough, one of his first acts in office had been to send a firm note to the Raja of Marh refusing government or police protection for any further attempts to salvage the linga.

The Banaras people had decided that Maan was no longer a suitable boy; they had informed Mahesh Kapoor of their decision.

All these subjects, and many others, were on everyone's mind – and no one's tongue.

Meenakshi and Kakoli, noticing the notorious Maan, swept up in a shimmer of chiffon, and even Mahesh Kapoor was not unhappy at the diversion they provided. Before they got there, however, Maan – who had just noticed Professor Mishra prowling vastly in the vicinity – had made good his disappearance.

When they heard that Firoz and Imtiaz were twins, Meenakshi and Kakoli were delighted.

'If I have twins,' said Kuku, 'I shall call them Prabodhini and Shayani. Then one can sleep while the other is awake.'

'How very silly, Kuku,' said Meenakshi. 'You'll never get any sleep yourself that way. And they won't ever get to know each other. Tell me, which of you is the elder?'

'I am,' said Imtiaz.

'No, you're not,' said Meenakshi.

'I assure you, Mrs Mehra, I am. Ask my father here.'

'He wouldn't know,' said Meenakshi. 'A very nice man, who gave me a lovely little lacquer box, once told me that, according to the Japanese, the baby who comes out second is the elder, because he proves his courtesy and maturity by allowing his younger brother to emerge first.'

'Mrs Mehra,' said Firoz, laughing, 'I can never thank you enough.'

'Oh, do call me Meenakshi. Charming idea, isn't it? Now if I have twins I shall call them Etah and Etawah! Or Kumbh and Karan. Or Bentsen and Pryce. Or something quite unforgettable. Etawah Mehra – how exquisitely exotic. Where has Aparna got to? And tell me, who are those two foreigners there, talking to Arun and Hans?' She stretched her long neck lazily and pointed with the red-nail-polished finger of a delicately hennaed hand.

'They are from the local Praha factory,' said Mahesh Kapoor.

'Oh, how dreadful!' exclaimed Kuku. 'They're probably discussing the German invasion of Czechoslovakia. Or is it the communists? I must separate them at once. Or at least listen to what they're saying. I'm so desperately bored. Nothing ever happens in Brahmpur. Come, Meenakshi. And we haven't yet given Ma and Luts our heart-deep congratulations. Not that they deserve them. How stupid of her not to marry Amit. Now he'll never marry anyone, I'm sure, and he'll become as grouchy as Cuddles. But of course, they could always have a torrid affair,' she added hopefully.

And in a flash of flesh the Chatterjis of the backless cholis were gone.

19.13

'SHE's married the wrong man,' said Malati to her mother. 'And it's breaking my heart.'

'Malati,' said her mother, 'everyone must make their own mistakes. Why are you sure it is a mistake?'

'It is, it is, I know it!' said Malati passionately. 'And she'll find out soon enough.' She was determined to get Lata to at least write a letter to Kabir. Surely Haresh, with the simpering Simran in his shady background, would have to accept that as reasonable.

'Malati,' said her mother calmly, 'don't make mischief in someone else's marriage. Get married yourself. What happened to the five boys whose father you met in Nainital?'

But Malati was looking across the crowd at Varun, who was smiling rather weakly and adoringly at Kalpana Gaur.

'Would you like me to marry an IAS officer?' she asked her mother. 'The most sweet and weak-willed and idiotic one I've ever met?'

'I want you to marry someone with character,' said her mother. 'Someone like your father. Someone whom you cannot push around. And that's what you want as well.'

Mrs Rupa Mehra too was staring at Kalpana Gaur and Varun in amazement. Surely not! – surely not! – she thought. Kalpana, who was like a daughter to her: how could she have battened onto her poor son? Could I be imagining things, she wondered? But Varun was so guileless – or, rather, so ineffectual even when he tried to be guileful – that the symptoms of his infatuation were unmistakable.

How and when could this have happened?

'Yes, yes, thank you, thank you,' said Mrs Rupa Mehra impatiently to someone who was congratulating her.

What could be done to prevent such a disaster? Kalpana was years older than Varun, and – even if she was like a daughter to her – Mrs Rupa Mehra had no intention of having her as a daughter-in-law.

But now Malati ('that girl who makes nothing but mischief') had gone up to Varun, and was looking deeply, deeply with her peerless green eyes into his own. Varun's jaw had dropped slightly and he appeared to be stammering.

Leaving Lata and Haresh to fend for themselves, Mrs Rupa Mehra marched up to Varun.

'Hello, Ma,' said Kalpana Gaur. 'Many congratulations. What a lovely wedding. And I can't help feeling responsible for it, in a way.'

'Yes,' said Mrs Rupa Mehra shortly.

'Hello, Ma,' said Malati. 'Yes, congratulations are in order from me as well.' Receiving no immediate response, she added, without thinking: 'These gulab-jamuns are delicious. You must try one.'

This reference to forbidden sweets annoyed Mrs Rupa Mehra further. She glared at the offending objects for a second or two.

'What is the matter, Malati?' she asked with some asperity. 'You still look a little under the weather – you've been running around so much, I'm not surprised – and, Kalpana, standing in the centre of the crowd is not good for your hot spots; go and sit on that bench there at once, it is much cooler. Now I must have a word with Varun, who is not doing his duties as a host.'

And she took him aside.

'You too will marry a girl I choose,' said Mrs Rupa Mehra firmly to her younger son.

'But – but, Ma –' Varun shifted from foot to foot.

'A suitable girl, that is what I want for you,' said Mrs Rupa Mehra in an admonitory voice. 'That is what your Daddy would have wanted. A suitable girl, and no exceptions.'

While Varun was trying to figure out the implications of that last phrase, Arun joined them, together with Aparna, who held her father's hand in one hand and an ice-cream cone in another.

'Not pistachio, Daadi,' she announced, disappointedly.

'Don't worry, sweetheart,' said Mrs Rupa Mehra, 'we'll get you lots of pistachio ice-cream tomorrow.'

'At the zoo.'

'Yes, at the zoo,' said Mrs Rupa Mehra absently. She frowned. 'Sweetheart, it's too hot to go to the zoo.'

'But you promised,' Aparna pointed out.

'Did I, sweetheart? When?'

'Just now! Just now!'

'Your Daddy will take you,' said Mrs Rupa Mehra.

'Your Varun Chacha will take you,' said Arun.

'And Kalpana Aunty will come with us,' said Varun.

'No,' said Mrs Rupa Mehra, 'I will be talking with her tomorrow about old times and other matters.'

'Why can't Lata Bua come with us?' asked Aparna.

'Because she'll be going to Calcutta tomorrow, with Haresh Phupha,' said Varun.

'Because they're married?'

'Because they're married.'

'Oh. And Bhaskar can come with us, and Tapan Dada.'

'They certainly can. But Tapan says that all he wants to do is to read comics and sleep.'

'And the Lady Baby.'

'Uma's too small to enjoy the zoo,' Varun pointed out. 'And the snakes will frighten her. They might even gobble her up.' He laughed sinisterly, to Aparna's delight, and rubbed his stomach.

Uma was at the moment herself the object of enjoyment and admiration. Savita's aunts were cooing over her; they were extremely pleased that, despite their predictions, she had not turned out to be 'as black as her father'. This they said in full hearing of Pran, who laughed. For the colour of Haresh's skin they had nothing but praise; it would cancel out the flaw of Lata's complexion.

With matters of such Mendelian moment did the aunts from Lucknow and Kanpur and Banaras and Madras occupy themselves.

'Lata's baby is bound to be born black,' suggested Pran. 'Things balance out within a family.'

'Chhi, chhi, how can you say such things?' said Mrs Kakkar.

'Pran has babies on the brain,' said Savita.

Pran grinned – rather boyishly, Savita thought.

On the 1st of April this year, he had received a phone call that had sent him beaming back to the breakfast table. Parvati, it appeared, was pregnant. Mrs Rupa Mehra had reacted with horror.

Even when she had recalled the date, she had remained annoyed with Pran. 'How can you joke this year when things are so sad?' she demanded. But in Pran's view one might as well try to be cheerful, however sad the core of things might be. And besides, he felt, it would not be such a terrible thing if Parvati and Kishy had a baby. At present they each dominated the other. A baby would redirect the equation.

'What's wrong with having babies on the brain?' said Pran to the assembly of aunts. 'Veena's expecting, and Bhaskar and Kedarnath seem to be quite happy about it. That's some good news in a sad year. And Uma too will need a brother and a sister sooner or later. Things won't be quite so tight on my new salary.'

'Quite right,' the aunts agreed. 'You can't call it a family unless there are at least three children.'

'Contract and tort permitting, of course,' said Savita. Unhardened by the law, she was looking as lovely and soft as ever in a blue and silver sari.

'Yes, darling,' said Pran. 'Contract and tort permitting.'

'Our congratulations, Dr Kapoor,' said a strikingly inaudible voice behind him.

Pran found himself pulled into the middle of a little

pride of literary lions: Mr Barua, Mr Nowrojee, and Sunil Patwardhan.

'Oh, thank you,' said Pran, 'but I've been married a year-and-a-half now.'

Mr Nowrojee's face registered a fleeting and wintry smile.

'I meant, of course, congratulations on your recent elevation, so' – he smiled sadly – 'so very richly deserved. And I have been meaning to tell you for many months now how very much I enjoyed your *Twelfth Night*. But you disappeared so early from Chatterji's reading. I notice he is here this evening – I sent him a sheaf of villanelles a month ago, but have had no response so far; do you think I should trouble him with a reminder?'

'It was Mr Barua who was the producer this year, Mr Nowrojee,' replied Pran. 'Mine was *Julius Caesar*, the year before.'

'Oh, of course, of course, though one often wonders with Shakespeare – as I said to E.M. Forster in – was it – 1913? –'

'So, you bastard, you've managed to get Joyce on the syllabus after all,' broke in Sunil Patwardhan. 'An awful decision, an awful decision. I was just talking to Professor Mishra. He sounded stricken.'

'Stick to mathematics, Sunil.'

'I plan to,' said Sunil. 'Have you read Joyce on the sound of cricket bats?' he asked, turning to Mr Barua and Mr Nowrojee: "Pick, pack, pock, puck: like drops of water in a fountain falling softly in the brimming bowl." And that was early Joyce! Shall I do an imitation of Finnegan waking?'

'No,' said Pran. 'Spare us the joy.'

19.14

FOOD was served at the far end of the garden and the guests roamed around, meeting each other, replenishing their plates, and congratulating the bride and groom and their families. Gifts and envelopes of money piled up near the decorated swing where the two of them were now sitting. One by one Lata met those whom she had not met before.

Kalpana Gaur said: 'I don't know who I am – I don't know if I'm part of the groom's party or the bride's.'

'Yes,' said Haresh, 'it's a problem. A serious problem. The first problem of our married life.'

While Haresh laughed and joked with all his friends, and accepted their boisterous humour and congratulations, Lata said very little.

When Mr Sahgal, her uncle from Lucknow, approached them with a repellent smile, she held Haresh's hand tightly.

'What's the matter?' asked Haresh.

'Nothing,' said Lata.

'But there must be –'

Mr Sahgal was holding out his hand to congratulate Haresh. 'I must congratulate you,' he said. 'I saw from the very beginning that you two would get married – it was meant to be so – it is a match that Lata's father would have approved of. She is a very, very good girl.' Lata had closed her eyes. He looked at her face, at the lipstick on her lips, with a slight sneer, before moving away.

Elsewhere, Dr Durrani, eating kulfi with an absorbed air, was talking to Pran, Kedarnath, Veena and Bhaskar. 'So, er, interesting, as I was saying to your son, this insistence on the number seven ... seven, um, steps, and seven, er, seven, circles round the fire. Seven er, notes to the scale, speaking in terms of a modulus, of course, and seven days to the, er, week.' He suddenly remembered something and frowned, inching his bushy eyebrows upwards. 'I must apologize, it's Thursday, you see, so my son, my, er, elder son, could not be present. He has to be, er, er, elsewhere –'

The Durrani invitation had been a dreadful mistake in Mrs Rupa Mehra's eyes – and, once extended, was unretractable. 'Do come along – and, of course, bring your family,' Dr Kishen Chand Seth had told him over bridge, but Dr Seth was disappointed that the mad wife and villainous son had not turned up. Dr Durrani himself was so inoffensively vague that he was incapable of locating the groom at his own wedding.

Amit, meanwhile, had been set upon by two elderly women, one of whom was wearing a glorious ruby pendant, like a radiating star, on her breast.

She said: 'That man told us that you're the son of Mr Justice Chatterji.'

'I am,' said Amit with a smile.

'We knew your father very well from our Darjeeling days. He would come up every year for the Puja holidays.'

'He still tries to.'

'Yes, but we're not there any longer. You must remember us to him. Now, tell me, are you the clever one?'

'Yes,' said Amit resignedly. 'I'm the clever one.'

This delighted the dazzling lady.

'I knew you when you were that high,' she exclaimed. 'You were very clever, even then, so I'm not surprised you've written all those books.'

'Oh?' said Amit.

Not to be outdone, the other lady asserted that she had known him since he was a bulge.

'But a brainy bulge, no doubt,' said Amit.

'Now, now,' said the lady.

There was a commotion at the gate. A group of five hermaphrodites, hearing that there was a wedding in progress, had turned up, and were singing and dancing and demanding money. So shameless were their gestures that the nearby guests were turning away in shock, but Sunil Patwardhan rushed over with his friends to enjoy the fun. Dr Kishen Chand Seth, brandishing his stick, was trying to drive them off, but they were making lewd remarks about both it and him. They would have to be paid to go away. He offered them twenty rupees, and their leader told him that he wouldn't even service him for that amount. Dr Kishen Chand Seth hopped around in fury, but he could do nothing. They demanded fifty, and they got it.

'It's blackmail,' said Dr Kishen Chand Seth furiously.

'Sheer blackmail.' He had had enough of hosting this wedding. He went inside to lie down and cool his head, and soon fell asleep.

Mrs Rupa Mehra, though she had broken her fast, had not done so with her usual gusto because she had to at the same time accept congratulations, introduce people to each other, watch over Haresh and Lata, keep a wary eye on Varun, and supervise the catering. But she was tearfully happy, and as she looked around her she felt even happier to see Pran talking to Professor Mishra, the Nawab Sahib talking to Mahesh Kapoor, and Maan and Firoz laughing together.

Sunil Patwardhan came up to her.

'Many, many congratulations, Mrs Mehra.'

'Thank you so much, Sunil. I'm so glad you're here. You haven't seen my father anywhere, have you?'

'I'm afraid not – not after that altercation at the gate ... Mrs Mehra, I have a small problem.... Haresh left his cuff-links at my house, and he told me to put them in the room where he'll be staying tonight.' Sunil fished a pair of cuff-links out of his trouser pockets. 'If you would tell me where I should take them –'

But Mrs Rupa Mehra would not be gulled so easily. She had been warned about Sunil Patwardhan's pranks and practical jokes, and she was not going to allow him to disturb her daughter's night of Ideal Marriage.

'Give them to me,' she said firmly, taking them from him. 'I'll make sure he gets them.' And as a result, Haresh was the richer and Sunil the poorer by one pair of black onyx cuff-links.

19.15

KABIR had not been able to bring himself to come to the wedding. But though it was Thursday night, he had not gone to visit his mother either. Instead he took a walk by the Ganga: up-river past the banyan tree, along the dhobi-ghat, past the Pul Mela sands underneath the Fort, along the waterfront of the old town, following the black water for miles until he came to the Barsaat Mahal.

In the shadow of a wall, he sat down on the sand for an hour, his head in his hands.

Then he got up to walk again, up the tall stairs, across the parapet and to the other side.

After a short while he came to a factory, the walls of which came down to the Ganga and prevented him from going further. But he was too tired anyway. He pressed his head against the wall.

The ceremonies will be over by now, he thought.

He hailed a boatman, and took a boat down-river back to the university and his father's house.

19.16

THE morning after the wedding, Haresh suddenly decided over breakfast that since he happened to be in Brahmpur, he should look in on the local Praha factory.

'But you can't just leave me like this,' said Lata, putting down her teacup in astonishment. They were sitting at a small table in the bridal bedroom in her grandfather's house.

'No,' said Haresh. 'I can't. Why don't you come too? You might enjoy it.'

'I think I'll go over to Savita's,' said Lata, and picked up her cup again.

'What's that shoe-box?' asked Haresh, and opened it.

Inside was a small, carved wooden cat with a knowing smile on its face.

Lata picked it up and examined it with pleasure.

'It's from a cobbler I have to meet later today,' said Haresh.

'I like it,' said Lata.

Haresh kissed her and went off.

Lata walked over to the window after a while and looked out at the bougainvillaea, a little puzzled. This was a strange way to begin her married life. But then she thought about it and decided that it was just as well that Haresh had not spent the day with her wandering around Brahmpur – going to the university, the ghats, the Barsaat Mahal. Since they were going to begin a new life, it was best to begin it elsewhere.

Haresh's family left for Delhi that day, and Arun and Varun and the rest left for Calcutta. And the next day Lata and Haresh were themselves seated in a train bound for Calcutta. Haresh could not take a honeymoon immediately because of the pressure of work, but he promised to take one soon. He was even more considerate to her now than he had been on the journey from Kanpur to Lucknow. Lata smiled and told him to stop fussing over her, but she liked it.

Her mother came to see them off at the railway station, together with Savita and Pran. It was hot and noisy. Mrs Rupa Mehra dabbed first at her forehead and then at her eyes with her cologne-scented handkerchief. Standing on the platform between her two daughters and their husbands, she did not know how she could bear to be without either of them. She was suddenly tempted to go along with Lata and Haresh, but fortunately desisted.

Instead, she made sure that they had enough food for the journey; she had brought extra provisions, just in case they hadn't thought of it themselves, including a large cardboard box marked *Shiv Market: Superb Sweetmeats* and a thermos flask filled with cold coffee.

She hugged Haresh, and clung to Lata as if she would never be seeing her again. In fact she planned to return to Calcutta on the 20th of June – the birthday of a dear friend – and would visit Prahapore the very day of her arrival. She was delighted by the fact that she had yet another home to travel to.

Lata waved from the window as the train pulled out of Brahmpur Junction. Haresh appeared relaxed and happy, and that, she found, made her happy too. Tears came to her eyes at the thought of leaving her mother. She looked at Haresh for a second, and then turned to the view. In a few minutes they would pass into the countryside.

An hour or so later, during a halt at one of the smaller railway stations, she saw a small crowd of monkeys. They became aware of her looking out at them and, anticipating a sympathetic soul, approached her window. She glanced at Haresh: he was taking a nap. It amazed her how he was able to go to sleep for ten or twenty minutes at a time whenever or wherever he wanted to.

She threw them a few biscuits: they gathered around, chattering and insistent. She looked for a moment or two at her hennaed hands, took out a musammi, peeled the thick green skin with care, and began to distribute the segments. The monkeys gobbled them down instantly. The whistle had blown when Lata noticed a rather old monkey, sitting alone almost at the end of the platform.

He was contemplating her carefully and undemandingly.

As the train began to move, Lata quickly reached down into the bag of fruit for another musammi, and threw it in his direction. He moved towards it, but the others, seeing it roll along, began running towards it too; and before she could see what had become of it, the train had steamed out of the station.

Also available in paperback

A SUITABLE BOY
Volume 1

ISBN 0–316–78153–3
Price $7.99

A SUITABLE BOY
Volume 2

ISBN 0–316–78152–5
Price $7.99